$ 2⁰⁰

5

# Liberating Troy

# Liberating Troy

## A NOVEL

PAUL ELLEDGE

Charleston, SC
www.PalmettoPublishing.com

*Liberating Troy*

First Edition

Paperback ISBN: 979-8-8229-1578-7
eBook ISBN: 979-8-8229-1579-4

# Author's Note

*The following narrative continues a story begun in **Siege of Troy** (Palmetto, 2021) but stands independently of it.*

*Like its predecessor, this novel is largely fiction. The narrator's character and schooling may occasionally resemble the author's, but no representations are from life. Nor is the mild satire of institutions and practices intended to disrespect them or to discredit the value of their formative influence on the author, who honors them still.*

~PAUL ELLEDGE

# DEDICATION

*To all who taught me to read,*
*And to want to write,*
*And how to try.*

PAUL ELLEDGE

*"We were together. I forget the rest."*

-A popular paraphrase of lines from
Walt Whitman's "Once I Pass'd
Through A Populous City"

*LEAVES OF GRASS*

# Part One

---

## Orientations

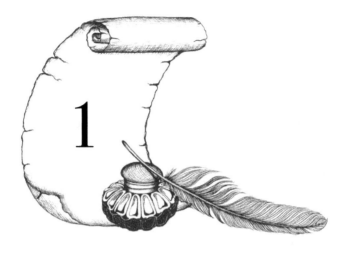

1

The New Orleans Union Passenger Terminal, opened in 1954, still showed new three years later when we spilled into it on a steamy, late-August afternoon after traveling for two-and-a-half days, with stops and transfers, from Santa Fe across leagues of featureless desert and then through the fetid, brackish swamplands of western Louisiana toward the pagan Babylon, as my Baptist parents reckoned it, where we would separate, Corky and I, after our summer of work and play at a conservative church camp to begin our sophomore years — he at Tulane, I at Lecompte Christian College (LCC) south of Alexandria — after Corky headed home by train up to Vicksburg, and I by bus to mine in Madison, east of Baton Rouge. Rumpled and grubby, greasy and sluggish from hot dogs and donuts and peanut butter crackers and candy bars off the porters' trolleys, we were pretty much talked out from non-stop probing of the adventures and personalities of our summer, figuring out how to extend the pleasures of some and erase the pains of others, and trying to dodge reflection on how we'd manage missing each other through the days ahead. That prospect sobered. We'd discussed "separation" a little, and the psychology of it, on our next-to-last day at Jubilee, the thousand-acre assembly for denominational lectures and seminars and workshops sponsored by and for the Baptist faithful, but the irksome subject got shoved aside by hustle-bustling enactments of it and kept there until our intermittent silences aboard the train opened space for it to emerge as a portentous shadow, tainting our temperaments, swelling disquiet.

What paradoxically subdued it, though, while also augmenting it, were what Corky called "flesh phases," for, sprawled as we were in adjoining seats, our hands and arms and legs and haunches touched, grazed, brushed against each other, skins rubbed, fingers stroked. When the lights dimmed for sleeping, we held hands under our thighs. Corky tucked his head into the cup of my shoulder, lightly kissed my neck, and dozed there. I let him. I even once, just east of Port Arthur, pecked his cheek good night. Understand, please, that flesh phases were new to us, and experimental, at least for me. Both of us admittedly still virgins at eighteen, Corky had realized he was queer at age twelve and was known to be so by his parents and around his Vicksburg school. But he'd had to remain completely closeted at Jubilee: revelation or discovery of his sexual preferences there would instantly have expelled him. By an adroit subterfuge he'd let me know because he craved my friendship, and, it turned out, suspected like preferences in myself, as, indeed, I secretly did too. Corky had obligingly explained to me how one might, if doubtful, ascertain his true orientation, and I became his interested if contingent pupil. But that's as far as we'd come. Flesh phases aroused us both. So that while they somewhat eased the anxiety around imminent separation, they also excited desire for more intimate and lasting contact. When and how remained perplexing riddles.

"This is so sad," Corky murmured, turning toward the window. "I'm already missing you. I may cry."

"I'm right here," I said, resting my hand on his thigh. "And we've said we'll visit. Try not to cry, or I might too. It's already soaking out there."

Why the angry storm should check our impulses to weep, I couldn't have explained. It just felt like collusion in a monstrous enterprise to overwhelm, inundate, and drown. For, from this side of Houma, heavy, wind-whipped rain had thrashed against the windows, swept the highways and streets in sheets, torn almost horizontally through the oak, cedar, and cypress branches and palmetto fronds, ripped fiercely at the towering magnolias. Lightning streaked and thunder boomed above and around our churning, clattering wheels and bogies.

"Is it an omen?" Corky asked. "Cajuns believe in omens. Is somebody sending us a message?"

"Naaah. It's just your regular old Louisiana summer thunderstorm. You don't really believe that crap about omens, do you?"

"I live in New Orleans, Troy. New Orleans believes."

"What would the message be, do you think?"

He waggled his eyebrows, ran the tip of his tongue across his lips. "W-e-l-l," he said, "may...be...?" He looked at my hand on his thigh.

"Oh, stop," I said, removing my hand and giggling. "I like storms, don't you? This is a good un."

"That wind may be whipping Pontchartrain over its banks and into neighborhoods. I know people who live out there."

"An omen for them, then. If it keeps blowing and pouring like this, my Madison bus could be in trouble. Your train should be okay. Wait. I just thought of something. What does a train have to do with Lake Pontchar*train*? Do you know?"

"Well, 'pont' is French for 'bridge.' And 'char' refers to the city Chartres, in France. But I doubt the lake's name has anything to do with the bridge. The lake had to be there first."

"Gosh, Corky, that's really interesting! Is that what they taught you at Tulane?"

"Smart-ass!" He poked me. "Tulane *did* teach me how to pronounce it, though. It's 'pahn-chuh-trayn.'"

"What I said. So...about omens: do you believe?"

"I don't think I actually *dis*believe. If I think I've seen one, I'm kind of...watchful...for a few days after."

"Did you just see one…laying right there on your thigh?"

We moved unencumbered into the aisle and toward the platform doors, for we'd fled Jubilee so abruptly, so impulsively, that we'd brought no luggage and had only the suits and dress shirts on our backs, although we'd need to fetch Corky's bike from the baggage car where a small cash bribe allowed us to stash it.

"You can't ride that that thing through the lobby," a sour-faced conductor warned us as we lifted it down and Corky checked its tires.

"Why not?" he asked. "I could."

"No, no," I cautioned. "Just walk it."

"Okay," he agreed, "but I'd sure like to ride it. Get the kinks out of my calves."

"I don't hear them moo-ing," I said.

He jingled the little bell on his handlebars, a punctuation mark on my lame joke.

"We might have to sit out the storm for a while in there," I guessed.

"Fine with me," Corky said; "do they have beds?"

Maybe it was innocent; but Corky hardly ever passed on an opportunity for doubtful innuendos. As we were already playing close to the flame, I favored some distance. "Better," I said, "to ask about food? This is New Orleans. They must have food. You're the food guy. You live here. Where's the kitchen?"

"We should check the timetable first," he sensibly said. "There may be delays."

And sure enough, his northbound train to Vicksburg was running 90 minutes late. A soft, plump granny at the Information Desk kindly rang the bus station for me, and learned that my coach was expected on time.

"Blast!" I said. "That means I have to leave first. I wanted it to happen the other way around."

"What difference does it make?" Corky sighed.

"I didn't want to leave first. Now I have to leave you."

"Don't be stupid. We're both leaving. About the same time. What's the difference?"

"I guess there's not any, really. It just doesn't feel right…leaving you. Like I'm leaving you behind or something."

"Well, in these circumstances, one of us has to leave the other. What're you thinking? I don't understand. Why're you getting upset?"

"I'm upset 'cause we're leaving. I'm leaving you behind. Like it's my fault or something…my initiative. I'm leaving you…before, well, before we hardly even got started…you know…. Before we had a chance…."

"Oh we had the chance, all right. Chances. We just didn't take them."

"This whole thing just feels so…so incomplete. Not just unfinished; broken. Like: by leaving, I'm breaking it."

"Listen here, Troy: nothing's breaking. We've said we'll visit. We'll write. C'mon, now. You're over-reacting."

"We left Jubilee together. Nobody left anybody behind. No, wait. We left Monte behind. But you and me, we left together. Fused and fastened together. Holding hands. You held me in your arms on the bike! It meant everything that we left together." My voice broke on the bike line. "I liked it that way."

"So did I," Corky said. "You know I did. But now we have to go home. It hurts me too, to…leave. But we'll fix this…make it right. And we'll…finish…what we've started. If we both want to. This is just a shitty little bump. We'll get back together soon. All right?"

I nodded. He swabbed his cheek.

"Can we hug?" I asked.

He glanced around. "Better not," he said. "This idn' the Quarter. But how about we hustle up some vittles? I'm hog-hungry, ain't you?"

"Vittles" is a funny word, and together with the porcine adjective and the hick contraction boosted the mood.

"Lead me to the slop trough," I said, and we stepped into the foot-traffic flow, Corky clasping the bike to his hip.

Following his gourmet's nose or his connoisseur's instincts, within minutes he'd found a neighborhood branch of The Camellia Grill installed right there off the terminal lobby.

"The original's a diner," he explained, "and famous. Real close to Tulane, where St. Charles turns into South Carrollton. Their menu's got everything: it's all native New Orleans and terrific. They even serve a Cannibal Special, which is raw hamburger with white onions and herbs and spices. The red beans and rice are fantastic. The best in town. That's what I'm having."

We tucked into the oversized platters brimming with hot thick bean juice like gravy for the rice, and recovered ourselves in no time.

"We *did* leave Monte behind, didn't we?" he said, not looking at me. It was half-affirmation, half-question.

Of course I'd named him first, and so first broken our silence about Monte — Charles Montgomery Trevalyn the Third — my Jubilee roommate, best friend, mentor, idol, and self-appointed manager of my lukewarm participation in a speech competition that I'd lost, thanks largely to his misguided orchestration of it, and then won, according to Corky's ingenious interpretation of it. Appalled and embarrassed by Monte's self-serving interference in the whole affair, and his dedicated alignment with the objectives of the camp's fundamentalist agenda, Corky and I had defied strenuous efforts to reorient ourselves and escaped Jubilee without so much as the salute of a middle finger to Monte and his devoted fans. I felt some regret over the brusque manner of our flight, but there was no forgiving Monte for his betrayal of my best interests in the promotion of his own. And Corky's matched mine. And yet…and yet: just as plainly, I had adored my former roommate, and I am not convinced that my worship was foolish.

"I think we did," I said. "I *think* we left Monte back there. But we *might* still be trailing sticky clouds of him. We don't need to talk about him. I don't know what I'd say about him."

"I have a lot to say about him," Corky said, "sometime. But it can wait. It had better wait. You've got a bus to catch."

As I never carried much cash — never *having* much cash — Corky'd offered to cover my ticket with his American Express card, heretofore activated but unused, and forked over bills to cover our trolley food en route. But now I needed bus fare.

"You'll want a cab to get to the Greyhound," he said. "Forty should cover the taxi and the ticket to Madison. Tip generously, in this weather. Your folks are meeting you, right?" He handed over two twenties.

"Does this leave you enough?" I asked with some apprehension. What if it didn't?

"I have the card," he said, showing the empty bill pocket of his wallet. He flourished the green plastic to pay for our beans.

Through the light foot-traffic, then, toward the glass doors to the rain-lashed street, Corky again clutching and balancing the bike on his left.

"Wow," he said, "look at that! The Keeper of the Omens is working overtime tonight. It's a typhoon out there! Let's light up some sage!"

"What?"

"Sage. Sage smoke purifies."

"You *do* believe!"

"Kidding!" he said.

Across the top tube of his bike, to my right, I glimpsed, in the gap opened by the loose top button of his shirt, the glisten of the chain suspending the medal

given all of us student employees by Jubilee management as souvenir mementos of our summer. I'd lost mine
straightaway but Corky had replaced it, attached to a
handsome chain, with my name and the date etched on
the reverse, just as he'd had his own medal similarly inscribed and dated.

"Corky," I said, stopping. "Hold on a second. Let's
do something." My heart raced. I released my shirt's top
button and reached for the chain around my neck, lifting it over my head. "You too," I said, facing him over
the bike bar. We both grinned as he caught my drift.
He dipped his head for my loop, then removed his medal, hung it from my neck, patted it in place. We both
giggled.

"Now we hug," he said, and we did, the bike clamped
between our waists.

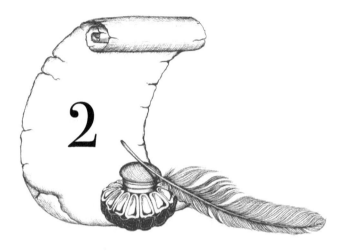

Lecompte Christian College replicated, after a fashion, Jubilee on a slightly smaller scale with annual
enrollments of about 1200 students, a similar curriculum, similar syllabi and courses and lectures and guest
speakers, similar musical and athletic programs (and no
mandatory phys. ed. classes), similar social opportunities and activities, similar guiding purposes and objectives, all colored vivid Baptist and designed to graduate
gospel-driven, denominationally dedicated believers so
profoundly grateful and beholden to alma mater that the
Development Office coffers would never want. Where
LCC most obviously differed from Jubilee was in its relative scarcity of moral monitors — "wardens," I'd named
them at the assembly — vigilant guardians and nurtur-
ers of the virtues and values that had paved our paths to
these holy grounds. It wasn't that our congenital guilt had

miraculously evaporated. Rather, it had receded, settled: in combination with our expanding secular awareness, our growing consciousness of ethical ambiguities and uncertainties, our *need* of narrow, supervisory curbs and constraints had melted away. The guilt implicit in our professed faith, and in the very self-discipline that both fueled and chastened it, had become so naturally and essentially fundamental to us, so foundational, that it no longer required external stimulation. We had become our own proctors, internalizing and selectively exercising the diligence that kept us more or less on the straight and narrow road, as Matthew tells it. But at the same time, that internalization inspired its own negation: for as our guilt seasoned and matured, necessarily revised itself in the light of reason and discrimination and good sense, it excited more complex, enigmatic, equivocal, and even scandalous agencies to nourish and justify itself. That is, measly little offenses like lying or cheating or speeding past the limit no longer triggered the guilt dynamic: now, to count, trespasses needed to involve — preferably — sex, or at least theft or abuse or drugs or blasphemy or public disrespect of the institution. As a consequence, LCC was pretty much a crime-free campus.

Which isn't to say it was guilt-free. Every one of us, even the internationals, brought whole reservoirs of guilt for expert exploitation by the guest speakers, usually preachers, imported for the thrice-weekly Chapel services, student attendance compulsory. These weren't for me as onerous as you might imagine, for even as a freshman I'd been accepted into the LCC chorus that usually performed at Chapel. And from sophomore year I was back-up pianist for the group. These engagements blunted the clout of the guilt, and granted me some welcome exposure.

Shortly before high-school graduation, I gave a senior piano recital at my father's church (Bach, Scarlatti, Beethoven, Chopin, MacDowell, Godowsky), the price I paid for discontinuing the private lessons I'd had once a week year round since my fifth. The best piano teacher around Madison, my parents learned, lived in Bunkie, about fifteen miles down Highway 71 from us, and one or the other of them drove me there and back every Tuesday afternoon after school for an hour's lesson with Mrs. Madeleine Thibodeaux, whose Juilliard performance degrees impressed us mightily, as did her gorgeously furnished home with two baby-grand Steinways side by side in her "parlor," she called it, where my lessons and our bi-annual recitals took place, I always going last in the lineups as her most advanced student. I never learned what these lessons and the travel cost my folks, not to mention the used Wurlitzer they bought for me when it began to look like I might take seriously to the instrument, but all of that instruction must have taxed our modest family budget. And the inconvenience of that boring drive surely wore them out. A first cousin of mine, a handsome guy but peerlessly sissy, had starred in piano at Juilliard, and I figured Mother and Father sort of wanted me to follow his track, at least at the keyboard. But I realistically understood the limits of my gift and of my commitment. Other interests had developed.

I gratefully acknowledged my folks' sacrifices and support, bid Mrs. Thibodeaux a fond adieu, and headed off to college.

Primary among those interests was law. Perry Mason had captured my imagination that fall with the premiere of the TV show, but even earlier I'd dabbled in high school politics (senior class pres, student body v-p), and won elective office at Louisiana Boy's State and again in Madison's "Mayor for a Day" annual handoff of city hall to high school seniors. Glamorous law was in my long-term picture. And with that prospect in mind, I signed up for an intro poli sci course in my first college semester. Before the six-week exam, though, I saw that the subject was more science than politics, at least at the entry level, and realized I had little taste for it. Late last year, I found that even pre-law undergraduates had to declare majors. With straight A's (and plaudits) through four years of high school English, and test credit for the required freshman course at LCC, I didn't dither over the declaration.

Dr. Park Royal, Assistant Professor of English and by some years the youngest member of the Department faculty, straightaway spotted me and two classmates as likely candidates for sophomore admission to the English Honors Program, which he chaired, and cultivated us — courted us, more like — from the start, because, learning that we'd tested out of the freshman English requirement, he'd researched our scores, and in light of them set about recruitment: reviewed and revised our course selections, directed our interests to belletristic opportunities, encouraged our creative writing endeavors, circulated among ourselves the literary periodicals subscribed to by the Department. He also foolishly risked arousing suspicions of favoritism by occasionally inviting us singly to lunch on sandwiches and sodas in his private office. Such attentions made it almost impossible, certainly unwise, for us to ask anyone else to be our official "advisor" on all LCC English affairs. Under his sponsorship, then, we shortly and prospectively became three of the dozen members of the Thomas Chatterton Honors Literary Society, named for the very young eighteenth-century British poet — younger even than ourselves — of doubtful repute whose stature Dr. Park, as he asked us to call him, was committed to restoring to the pantheon of Romantic art where his *oeuvre* "indubitably proved" him to belong, and a copy of whose famous deathbed portrait took up most of one wall in the professor's office. Our prof nearly always referred to Chatterton as "Tommy."

For several reasons Dr. Royal enjoyed some fame around the campus, for not only was he the youngest English teacher — probably fewer than ten years older than we (the other six profs, though able, were relics) — but also a lively, dynamic, exciting, and amusing one, and thus popular for his instruction as well as his ready availability for counseling and even some light recreation with us between classes (ping-pong, billiards, cards). But Park was *most* notable as the professor who referred to his students — all his students, boys and girls, in class and out, privately and publicly, individually and collectively

— he referred to each of us as *"darling"*! Or, often, *"dar-lin'."* We'd all heard that, initially, the endearment had earned Park an urgent summons to the Dean's office, but that he'd argued and begged his way, no doubt with invocations of his father's name and largesse, and possibly of free speech rights, into permission to continue using it until and unless anyone, boy or girl, formally complained; and as students normally side with favorite faculty against administration, nobody *did* complain, and after a while, and because he used the term with *all* his students and never appeared to intend anything unusually or unacceptably affectionate by it, hearing it became tolerable, almost routine, and in due course hardly noticeable, although always likely to produce a smile in the recipient of the compliment. And some of us, when we did notice it, came to think of it as sort of sweet, approving and supportive. Of course, new arrivals had to be warned and enlightened; and once in a while some sourpuss would complain, but by then objections looked so petty and cranky that the grapevine and a campus newspaper editorial and a little social ostracism pretty soon set everything to rights again, and Park could safely resume his sweet talk.

But he was interesting, and perhaps slightly at risk, for another reason. Campus gossip claimed that Dr. Park Royal hailed from central Texas where his father owned thousands of ranch-land acres that accommodated as many heads of cattle. Park spent his memorably distinguished undergraduate years at Baylor but then headed north for his British Lit Ph.D at Columbia in New York, and upon his graduation there the wealthy father, folks said, offered Baylor a most handsome endowment to be used at its discretion on the condition that it hired the doctorate son in a tenured professorial position. But Baylor balked, did not bargain, so the Royals allegedly approached the next nearest respectable Baptist institution with a similar deal, and in fact the LCC chapel we now sing in bears the Royal name. And Dr. Park was hired without tenure, which means that his LCC employment is subject to periodic reviews and the renewal of his contract depends upon the Department's recommendation and the Dean's approval. He could be fired for unsatisfactory teaching and scholarship. Of course he would know all of this, and so did we: at least the three of us recruits knew, and we sometimes worried over it and talked of what could happen and what it might mean for us, if anything, if it did. But *he*, Dr. Park, never appeared to think a thing about his LCC future or what he should be doing to guarantee it, or how he should be behaving so as not to jeopardize it. He seemed always boyishly carefree — even, some of us including me thought, too daring in some other unorthodox departures from standard protocol like the "darling" endearments. I mean, for example, on weekdays he wore the professorial uniform of a sport coat and slacks and a club tie — or, often, a flashy ascot instead — and dress loafers with socks for teaching, but then without warning or obvious reason he'd show up for class as though straight off the ranch in tight jeans and boots and a plaid shirt with snap pearl buttons and a bolo tie or a bright knotted handkerchief around the neck and a big brown Stetson hanging by a leather cord, without a single word of explanation. Tall and lean, he looked good in this outfit, and he'd repeat the cowboy costume for a week or so and then revert to traditional dress, offering not a syllable to fill us in or invite our guesses. I found it all too obviously defiant, too hazardous, too patently a middle finger in the eye of his superiors. As much as I admired and appreciated rebellion, this seemed to me reckless and unnecessarily risky: immature and purposeless and faintly embarrassing. And what did it all *mean*, if anything? Consensus held that if Park didn't himself verbally notice the act, we shouldn't either, and that he'd eventually, for that reason, give it up, which he did, every time. I went along with the more or less silent amusement everybody seemed to feel, but the whole shtick unsettled me.

And then there was his hair. Obviously dyed to a glossy russet hue, reddish-brown, slightly darker than weathered terra-cotta flower pots, moderately curly, it dressed the high forehead, piled in disorder on top, draped his neck, and then fell onto the shoulders like an overlong collapsed page-boy. Once you'd viewed the office wall-poster, you knew the hair-color's source, and you could deduce the provenance of the persona that Dr. Royal sometimes affected and that seemed to rule his professional thinking when he wasn't playing cowboy. But what you mostly remembered was the color: unnatural, definitely, and outlandish, theatrical, but luxuriously beautiful.

Anyhow, we three favorites of his were: Benjamin Arthur Moore, future Poet Laureate of British Columbia, Canada; Jonathan Jackson Latimer, who'd won a National Rotary essay contest as a high-school senior and already practiced what we would learn to call "literary scholarship" in term papers (although he'd eventually eschew it for fiction…until grad school got ahold of him); and me, who scribbled stories that embarrassed their author the next morning after I'd typed them out the night before. Ben and Jack knew each other from having shared a dorm freshman year.

I first clapped eyes on Jon Jack Latimer from backstage, where I dawdled while our freshmen cast rehearsed the little playlet we were required to compose and stage as the climactic event in our six-week "hazing" initiation to campus life, a long-standing tradition not yet challenged by reforming zealots. Obliged to wear vivid green "beanies" all day every day during this period, even at meals, we saluted upper classmen by name ("Mr./Miss Surname"), opened doors for them and stood aside, carried their books, if asked, and between 12 and 1 on weekdays, if asked, performed minor chores for them. It wasn't arduous; merely a little demeaning and at times inconvenient. Then, marking our release from this vassalage, came the festive, campus-wide party on the last Saturday night where, among other entertainments, we acted out our play depicting "LCC Life As We Know It…After Six Weeks." Lampoon, caricature, mockery, and spoof were our objectives in this folly, and we worked very hard to make our version witty, edgy, and irreverent. I mostly did behind-the-scenes scut work for the Production Assistant, and from back there watched Jack become our star.

Our skit featured him as a blundering, gauche, clownish wannabe Lothario whose signature shtick was his hopeless ignorance of and forgetfulness around contraceptives. Seamus ("Shaymus") Stud, we named Jack, and set him up in six encounters with females of various stripes where his coital obliviousness, absent-mindedness, and calamitously floundering incompetence in sexual affairs brought down the house. It fell to me to round up the bananas, cucumbers and carrots for the coarsest gags. Our emphasis focused upon Seamus's fractured memory, his befuddled failure to remember the condoms stashed in his pockets, pouches, cuffs, socks, and caps, and then his bewilderment over what to do with them. It was all slapstick silliness, of course. Jack took to it brilliantly, and hammed it up into an absolute triumph of hilarity, his success in part attributable to his Ichabod Crane physique, carriage, and manner that made him such an unlikely predatory rake — about which more shortly. He was so good, in fact, that the three classes behind us petitioned to re-use him in their adaptation of our skit; but the administration had taken alarm at our indelicacy and borderline lewdness, and demanded such sanitation of our script that most of the fun vanished too. Nevertheless, for three years Jack by presence and reputation became a sort of comic campus simulacrum for sexual stupor and discombobulation. He never brought the persona into the cafeteria or canteen or classroom, much less mentioned it; but students good-naturedly elbowed each other and grinned when he passed.

I didn't actually meet Jack until a couple of weeks later in Introduction to Drama 101. We'd both, after testing out of freshman English, selected Drama to satisfy one-third of the College humanities requirement. Most kids chose the Bible option to meet it and I probably should've, given my training, but as I'd pretty much owned my high school stage and entertained hopes of commanding LCC's, I figured enrollment in Drama 101 might give me an edge at auditions. Little did I know that Dr. DeWitt (DeWithout, some said) narrowed Drama to mean mostly Film, so that movie titles on his syllabus outnumbered plays by about three to one. At home, I'd been allowed to see only Disney through my twelfth year and hadn't begun to catch up on movies since then. I may have put myself in peril by dodging the snap biblical curriculum for this one.

When DeWitt called his name from the roll on the first day, Jon Jack Latimer actually stood in response to it and answered with an authoritative "Present," as though announcing it or already voice-auditioning for a part, his height accenting the oddity of his stance. I recognized him from our skit rehearsals. Several classmates tittered. But Jack ignored them, nodded to the prof, and resumed his seat two rows in front of me, unruffled, smoothing the backsides of his trousers the way girls do their skirts when sitting down. They were light chinos, snug in the legs but loose around his skinny ass, brown-belted, with creases from recent packaging. The white shirt tucked neatly into his thin waistline, the sleeves correctly rolled three times to his bony elbows. White wasn't the smartest color against Jack's pale skin, but the starched collar rose with stern dignity up the back of his neck where casually trailed the light, thin, brown, wispy hair. The fashionable button-down front framed a prominent Adam's Apple that bobbed slightly when he turned to declare his presence. The head seemed disproportionately small above the wide but narrow shoulders, the arms long, the hands slender and shapely.

*Ichabod Crane*, I thought again. Not the cartoon version, though. Or if a little bit the cartoon version, only so that I could revise it, correct it, sympathetically cleanse it of caricaturistic features. I know there's no definitive portrait of Irving's schoolmaster but Jon Jack Latimer's frame and proportions and loose-jointedness, his contours and couplings, again brought the character forcefully into my mind, and excited a charitable impulse to refine it without fundamentally changing its appeal: smooth its edges, retain the essence but polish away the impurities: purge any physical properties that might provoke giggles or sneers. Because behind the Cranian structure I caught the hint of a substance I instantly took to. Only perceptible intuitively, clairvoyantly as an air about him, a warm, even enticing, aura — a delicate mood or soft, yielding tenor innocently beguiling. If I keep fumbling like this to describe it, I'm certain to spoil it, so let me stop in the hope that it'll emerge on its own with time spent in his neighborhood. Suffice it for now to say that *something* spread a portion of itself from Jonathan Jackson Latimer to me, and in the instant I claimed it.

"Your first assignment," Professor DeWitt declared a couple of weeks later, "is to write an original theme of 500 words, due Monday, typed, about the new film, 'The Seventh Seal.'" I could handle the typing part but hadn't a clue to what a "theme" was, other than a repeated melodic line in a musical score. And DeWitt didn't elaborate.

So, upon our dismissal, I hustled to the back of the room to wait for Jack, my heart thumping. Lanky, gangly, loose-limbed, he sauntered up the aisle, saw me staring, slowed even more.

"Mr. Latimer," I said, stepping out, both hands pocketed, shoulders hunched, tight as a drum-head. "I'm Troy Tyler, sir. In this class" — as though elsewhere I was somebody else —: "May I ask you something?"

He grinned, shifted his notebooks to the left hand and extended his long fingers. "Sure," he said. "I'm Jack. You worked on our play, right? And you're in the Chapel choir, aren't you?" We shook hands.

"And in this class," I stupidly repeated. "Oh, sorry. I said that. That I was in this class. Sorry."

Still smiling, he took back his hand, let me sweat for a second, then reached out and gripped my left shoulder, gentled it. "There now," he said softly. "You okay? How can I help you?"

"Well," I said, breathing, "I've got a question... about the paper assignment. What's a 'theme'?"

It was too blunt, too forward and hurried. I flushed. "I don't know what...." I stopped, suddenly hot. "Oh well never mind. I should just ask Dr. DeWitt. I don't mean to bother you. Sorry."

"Come now," he said, the grin fading a little. "Do you want help or not? I can explain 'theme,' if that's what you need. And I know what DeWitt wants."

"You sure you have time? I wouldn't want to...."

"Stick with me, pal," he said amiably, shifting the notebooks back, "and you'll find I'm nearly always ready to talk 'themes,' if anybody else is. How about we discuss it over coffee?" He stepped aside, inviting me into the aisle alongside him. "I've seen you around," he said, the grin broad again.

He *had*? I was one of five baritones in the choir and hadn't yet soloed, and our initiation as Chattertons hadn't yet happened, and he couldn't possibly live in my dorm or I'd have seen him there, and I wasn't exactly, not yet, a BMOC or even visible among the popular sets as he was. And he *was*, and not merely as Seamus. I'd noticed him here and there on our small campus, most often at a cafeteria or soda shop table casually playing cards (Hearts) with classmates — usually girls — obviously so familiar with the game that it didn't require focused attention. He yakked and joked and laughed and looked like a desirable companion. He did seem to run mostly with girls. Not that he was sissified, no; but there hovered something faintly feminine about his manner, how he touched his face, stroked his forearms, tilted his head one way and another when a remark piqued his curiosity: something gentle and yielding when he leaned toward you across the table. But *how* had he seen me around? What seen to notice and remember? I wasn't a prospective card jock. I knew even less about cards than about film, for card games were forbidden at home — all but Old Maid, and nobody over ten ever found *that* one entertaining — as the final perilous step toward gambling addiction. And yet, notwithstanding the occasional frown from strict Baptist partisans, Hearts seemed to me *the* favorite pastime on campus, and Jack a devoted player. I couldn't see a future for us in that line. But wait: why was I envisioning any future at all? I had no clue what he'd seen to notice in me. And I'd have to wait to find out. He spied an empty cafeteria table and led me to it, waving at friends as we passed. "Leave your stuff here and grab some caffeine," he directed.

He drank his black. Still fairly new to coffee, I spooned in sugar on top of the milk. He tapped out a Viceroy for himself, offered another. I shook my head.

"You don't smoke?" he asked. "You will."

"Sometimes," I said. "I know how to inhale."

(Geez! How nerdy was that?! As though inhaling were an achievement!)

"There're great for relaxing. You ever relax, Troy?" he said, coyness in the eyes and tone.

"Can't even spell it," I said, and we both laughed. "You noticed?"

"With eyes closed," he grinned. "If you need help with that," he said, "I might could. You ever had a massage?"

"Maybe I'll take that cigarette now," I said, "if you're still offering."

"There's this parlor over in Alexandria," Jack said, laying the pack and his bic on the table between us. "In kind of a seedy neighborhood but their massages are sublime. And healthy. Good for your heart. Only two bucks plus tip. I could take you. I have wheels."

I faked a nonchalance I didn't feel in lighting-up — buying time — for the offer seemed coarse, even un-couth, and put me on edge. Or did my own arguably crude inspection of his person discolor my temper? Was he merely alerting me to the attractions of the metropolis next door or recommending joint patronage of a sala-cious salon? I searched his face for a grin or a smirk but found nothing except patient, biding interest.

"Or not," he finally said, sipping his coffee. "Maybe later. But you think about the health benefits of re-lax-a-tion! Never mind how it's spelled." He chuckled, pursed his lips. "Now then," he said; "about themes.

"'Theme' is just a college word for 'essay.' You've written one a hundred times. You wrote one to get in here. You wrote at least one for college boards. You wrote five in every English class you ever took."

Thus did he launch. In paragraphs. He explained systematically, methodically, comprehensively, precisely, with illustrations from music, literature, the visual arts, finally and pointedly from film.

"Sometimes the assignment asks for 'explica-tion,' which is analysis — fine-toothed detection — of how a central idea in a text gets developed, how it's

amplified and…you know, embellished. It's not my favorite way of writing, but it's required. Sometimes they
want 'exegesis…'"

This one I knew, and so interrupted: "Analysis of a
biblical text. I've done that. I know how."

"Not always biblical," Jack said, frowning a little at
my interruption or my mistake. "You can exegete texts
other than biblical ones. But if you can do that, if you've
done that, you almost know all there is to know about
writing themes: you just do it for longer around one
main idea, to *prove* your notion of what one principal
point the author or creator is *making* with his work and
wants you to take away from it: what *his* theme is and so
also yours. And *BAM!* There's your theme!" He spread
wide his eyes and arms.

And continued. It was big-time overkill, dilation
way past my needs for writing the paper, but now less
informing than continuing to assure me that I already
knew in my bones and fibers what "theme" meant and
had sufficient experience composing in the genre, only
not about film, to take it on successfully at the college
level for the fanatical Dr. DeWitt. Silently, I watched
and listened and soaked it up. And after a while he
moved on.

He came from Ruston — about an hour east of
Shreveport — and had graduated from University School
there, a respected private prep affiliated with Louisiana
Tech where both of Jack's parents held professorships,
Mom in Psychology, Dad in Mechanical Engineering.
Class valedictorian Jack finished with High Honors

in English, Honors in Latin, and won "Most Likely to Succeed" on the Senior Ballot (as had I: "Most Likely" was the consolation prize for losing "Smartest Boy") but had already actually *won* the big national Rotary essay award, which counted for more than all the rest put together. His Dad, associate dean of the E-School, had invented several patented devices; but Jack said he was prouder of having seen in person every home LSU football game since The War of Northern Aggression, and wanted Jack to go there even though Jack could have attended La. Tech scot free (one parent professor got you half fare). Besides teaching, his Mom raised Maine coon cats — *over-achieving* Maine coons, Jack said — and cultivated exotic plants that regularly won Garden Club prizes. Older brother Slade had a free ride on a fat Engineering scholarship at Duke's grad school. Jack had been so desperate to get away from the hearth at home that he accepted a generous scholarship offer from LCC partly because it didn't field a football team. His father hated schools that didn't. And as his parents were Baptist, he figured he knew his way around that territory, though drifting toward desertion.

Neither handsome nor pretty, Jack's face was sort of flat, plain but for a spatter of freckles over and around the straight nose with small nostrils and across the cheeks. The longish forehead reclined below a receding hairline, and already showed faint furrows. Rumpled straight hair down the sides of his head merged with lingering sideburns and partly screened undersized ears that angled out at about thirty degrees, and two distinct cow-licks disturbed the crown and the front edge of the part, so that the frisky follicles there, though oiled, never looked quite fast. He frequently fingered both patches. His lips were thin and pale, the teeth not perfectly straight and lightly tobacco-stained. His brows and lashes faded to an almost invisible beige, the blue-grey eyes under them vivid yet soft, serene. The cheeks tended toward hollow under high, defined bones, with dimples notching both sides, and the chin gently rounded. The only visible beard was blondish fuzz. But despite the plainness, the aura persisted. The tenor held. He stayed fetching.

While I gazed and studied, he'd shifted to talk of the assigned movie, Ingmar Bergman's recently released "The Seventh Seal," which, with Disney in my head, I assumed treated zoos or arctic regions, but the title did tinkle a faint biblical bell when Jack named it.

"Title's from 'The Revelation to John,' New Testament," he explained. "I've already seen it once, at the art movie house in Alexandria, but I'll need to go again. It's pretty dark, and...obscure; brings in the Bible with lots of allegory and symbolism. This character, Death, plays chess all through it. But I've got an idea for my theme."

"Don't tell me!" I exclaimed, afraid he might give away something I could use. Not that I mightn't have profited from help. But I knew from fresh experience at Jubilee how slippery, how tricky help can be. And we'd been so often warned about the risks of receiving it, at orientation last year and since, I'd become leery of offers, and figured I was maybe already over the line here for asking Jack about themes. Allegory I'd heard of around John Bunyan — required reading at home — and English teachers were forever yapping about symbols, so I had a clue, if a cloudy one. Better, I may have had a little ace up my long-sleeved polo: if the film rips off scripture, I reckoned I could swot that up and in my theme passably make do.

But Jack was saying, "You want to come with me, when I screen it again?"

"You mean like a *date*?"

My best Jubilee chum Corky Carlisle had tutored me on the signs to look for in guys suspected of having sugar in their boots, as some folks said of sissies, and to beware of revealing anything in my own manner, but here I had just flat-out handed Jack a darn near infallible indication of where my mind was already trending with regard to himself! What was I *thinking*? What was *he*? Had he, like me, given my reckless blurt the raciest possible reading? Mortified with embarrassment, I considered immolation by lighter. The remark had just thoughtlessly slipped out, of course, but there was no conceivable way of reeling it in or explaining it away. It sat there, almost palpable, a fat, lumpy question mark, on the table between us, as I writhed inside.

"Well," Jack said, the grin open and wide, "Why not." Stating, not asking. "Why not. Do I have to buy you popcorn?"

His eyes encouraged me to take it as a quip.

"And a coke," I said.

And just like that, we were off!

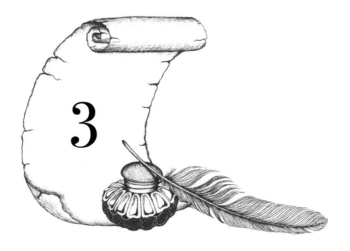

**3**

Or not quite just like that. There was, after all, Corky, down at Tulane, sort of first in line. For me. And right behind him, possibly, came Monte, at Baylor, my Jubilee roommate and for a while my idol, from whom a letter had just been forwarded inviting himself to visit me in Lecompte on any weekend of three in order to return the Levis and tees and sheet music I'd left in our flight, Corky's and mine, from the assembly at the midnight hour. But the paper assignment was due Monday. I postponed everything else as Jack and I decided on the movie for Thursday afternoon.

Meanwhile, I grabbed the daily bus, free to students, to Alexandria Public Library and there looked up magazine reviews and newspaper articles about "Seventh Seal," and discovered among other curious tidbits that Bergman was also a p.k. — preacher's kid — who'd also defied the strict paternal dogma and dribbled evidence of his rebellion here and there in the movie, if you looked hard enough for it. This seemed an unlikely providential gift. I could connect, and use my own mutinous experience, or invent some, to parallel and illuminate Bergman's as divulged or hinted in the film, and link it to whatever presiding "point," Jack had said, I'd found compelling. Easy-peasy.

He drove a big, boxy, green '53 Dodge Dependable handed down from his Dad and older brother with room for eight, it felt like, and whitewalls, a/c, and a am/fm radio, conferring on us a sense of swank as we sped up to Aleck, the largest metropolis between Baton Rouge and Monroe. I'd been to Alexandria many times, but never without a parent, for piano competitions and master classes, for concerts (once for the visiting Boston Pops), for movies ("The Robe," "Ben Hur"), for big-tent religious services, once for a circus (of a different kind), but mostly for the city swimming pool, an Olympic-sized job with three diving boards, two slides — one corkscrewed — a giant teak sun-deck, and some very deep water. Once in a while when Father had church business in Aleck, he encouraged me to round up friends — Eugene and Billy Clyde and Purvis and Neil and all them — for day-long Saturday frolics involving the only competitive sport I truly loved and showed any skill in performing. Back in the city with Jack, I kind of hankered to drive by the pool for old time's sake but he said he'd never learned to swim and didn't see the point of staying wet all day with towels at hand, so I dropped it.

He bought my ticket, popcorn and coke — *was* it, after all, a date? — and we settled studiously to view the film.

I thought it so self-consciously arty, so deliberately opaque, that I took little away from it but bewilderment. Jack, on the other hand, started talking of it as soon as the lights came up, and continued talking until we'd cleared downtown and reached the two-lane back to Lecompte. It came out right away that he played chess and would probably use the game featured in the movie as the focus of his paper, but I again stopped him from explaining lest he influence me and mine. Nothing in the cinematic game much advanced my search for autobiographical clues, although those bishops on the board *should* have proved consequential for me. Nevertheless, I found rebellion; I found heterodoxy and heresy and resistance and subversion enough to suggest a pattern with possibly autobiographical roots that I could experientially validate with details and arguments; but I wouldn't feel certain of its coherence until writing it down. So I kept quiet.

Unprompted, Jack eventually ran down, switched on the radio, and tuned up KALB, 96.9, with its fixed menu of classic rock. Back at Jubilee, we'd missed some of the summer releases but knew that Elvis still dominated the charts and airwaves with "Heartbreak" and "Hound Dog" and especially "All Shook Up," and for a change of pace there were "Love Me Tender" and "Wayward Wind" and the "Picnic" theme, the last of which I so liked that I learned and played it. What came up, though, when Jack roused the radio was Tab Hunter's version of "Young Love," which I preferred over Sonny James's screechier rendition, possibly because pretty-boy Tab was at the mike. I had to stop myself from humming along. We both listened, and when it ended, Jack lowered the volume.

"So," he asked, "d'you have a girlfriend?"

"Not really," I answered. "I went steady, with Allison, all through high school, but we broke up after I graduated. D'you?"

"Not just one," he said, but not like a brag. "I have some female *friends*. More like chums. We mess around sometimes."

"How 'mess around'?"

"Not much like that. We run together. Study together. Play cards and stuff."

"I've seen you. Hearts, idn' it?"

"You play cards, then?"

I'd walked right into it and now had to walk right back out again. Goofball!

"Well, no," I admitted. "I don't actually know how. We weren't allowed cards at home. But we've got cousins down in Houma, and sometimes, when we visited, they'd bring out a deck and we'd play *at* playing cards. I never learned much about it."

"Would you care to?"

"Well, what I actually *liked* was the shuffling. That shuffle where they curl and fan the cards. I liked the finger-work with shuffles and chips."

"Yeah," he grinned; "that can get pretty. You want to learn how?"

"I don't know if I could. It looks hard."

"I'll teach you," he offered, pulling into the drive of my dorm. "Wait," he then added; "you play the piano, right? You already *do* finger-work. Here," he said, "let's have a look at your fingers," reaching into my lap for them.

* * *

Ben Moore, the third of Dr. Royal's favorites among his students, already wrote poetry, a lot of it, regularly, and let himself be seen writing it, in dorm lounges, on the lawns, in the library, in the cafeteria, and especially at the Kalliope Koffee Klatch in downtown Lecompte, what there was of it, where he owned the same rear table nearly every night and, his cup of Morocco mint tea ever at hand, scribbled verse into black-backed note-books with white Roman numerals on the covers indicating volume numbers. You might say Ben was LCC's token Beat Generation representative, certainly its earliest spokesperson. He'd ridden his Harley down from Monroe, where he'd grown up in the Louisiana Baptist Children's Home (for orphans) before adoption by an owner of paper mills in Bastrop, and finished high school there (successfully avoiding, he told us, for five years a draft onto the football squad), and then won the single full-tuition, four-year scholarship from the Louisiana State Baptist Convention for LCC enrollment — rode his bike right onto the campus with only his saddlebags for luggage and found it instantly forbidden access to the college grounds until his sophomore year. Ben knew all about Jack Kerouac and Allen Ginsberg, had read *On the Road* and "*Howl*" and even without request would quote (or chant) long lines from the poem, and could hardly wait, he repeatedly told us, for the highly anticipated and already announced appearance of Lawrence Ferlinghetti's "A Coney Island Of The Mind"; but he loved to argue with anybody that Larry *wasn't* a Beat poet and in his verse a disciple of T. S. Eliot, whom he (Larry and Ben) championed. Ben admitted to influence by Ginsberg; Jack and I both thought his verse by turns imitated Allen's and Lawrence's, and complimented him by saying so, but I didn't much like it and found most of what he showed me impenetrable and often, well, dirty. For some reason, though, Ben became my fan. He was in my Romantics class with Dr. Royal.

Like Jack taller than I, he was burlier, too, big-chested, bi-ceped, rather broad of face, with abundant black hair hiding ears and the back of his neck and frizzling down his arms. Under dark brows and through heavy, black-rimmed glasses, his black, serious eyes sparkled, drilled, and unnerved you by rarely blinking. The Ginsberg beard covered the upper lip and lower chin, and framed the wide mouth and very red lips that opened upon even white teeth when he laughed, as he often did, a big, booming belly-laugh that invited participation. He wore black tees and jeans and boots, but the arresting, even forbidding attire yielded in effect to the gregarious, winning demeanor that earned him popularity without much diminishing the awesomeness we all brought to our regard of him. Ben kept ever current on literary affairs, especially in the hyped-up California scene; and although I figured he may have fabricated some of what he reported about it, the authority of his telling made you believe — or anyhow hope — he spoke truth, so we mostly forgave him. I think he took to me — liked me — because I so plainly admired his scholarly and literary smarts, and so obviously always craved his favor. Early on, I figured he saw me as an aspiring acolyte, not fawning, not even deferential, but approving, appreciative, eager to imitate and follow and learn to achieve, perhaps even similarly achieve, by his example as a creatively imaginative, accomplished, and cultivated man.

Ben tolerated dorm life for the one required year, then moved off campus to a rented room nearby and right away began riding onto campus with a girl on the pillion of his bike, a different girl from yesterday's and last week's. Some were classmates, and some were not, but the townies — "auditors," Ben called them — violated some rule by accompanying Ben to classes, and so had to be formally removed back to wherever he'd found them. But that development didn't appear to discourage the female campus population who continued flirtations with him at full throttle. No girls were ever spied at his downtown writing table.

Downtown Alexandria's Broadway Baptist Church dominated two city blocks — three, if you counted its parking lot — and had replaced First Baptist New Orleans as the flagship congregation of the Louisiana Baptist Convention when the relatively new Yankee pastor of the latter launched a campaign against "the wicked, dissolute, ungodly, and sinfully excessive gourmandizing" of his flock — so the newspaper stories quoted him — and thus just about turned the entire New Orleans economy against himself and his people, many of whom abandoned the assembly insulted and outraged by the man's misbegotten intolerance and benighted repudiation of the city's history and tradition, and his atrocious misreading of the Apostle Paul on food. Aleck is three and a half hours north of New Orleans, so Broadway Baptist didn't immediately benefit in membership from defections in New Orleans, but in reputation and prestige it did; and in light of the nay-saying of First Baptist's preacher, Broadway's early adoption and promotion of what would become the "prosperity gospel" agenda — its affirming message — excited local interest, especially among the disaffected unchurched, and increased its appeal and eventually its size.

Reflecting on it now, I understand that Jubilee was a sort of aberration in my new normal at LCC, a temporary throwback re-enacting an earlier religious selfhood nevertheless transitioning into a not-dissimilar world yet one observed with different eyes, eyes opened to new ways of seeing old traditions and habits and beliefs and ideas, eyes attracted by *possibilities*, opportunities, invitations; for my matriculation at LCC effectively liberated me from the obligatory church attendance twice on Sunday and once on Wednesday night (for "Prayer Meeting" and choir practice) that defined and determined every week of my eighteen years to date. It wasn't that I disrespected the religious focus of my training; I'd just had a surfeit of it, grew fed up with it, and agitated against its constraints. LCC's mandatory Chapel attendance more than adequately filled any gaps I might feel. And I took the precaution of familiarizing myself with Broadway's location and schedules and programs against the possible parental visits when we'd have to check out "my" church; but otherwise I kept away from Sunday services and quite enjoyed the freedom. So I was completely confounded when Jack said, out of the blue, a couple of days after our movie, "We should try Broadway Church some Sunday."

"But why would we?" I asked sourly. "I'm up to here with that scene."

"They run a bus to campus twice every Sunday, and a lot of kids go and like it. I went along a couple of times last year, and at least the rides there and back were fun. And the evening class was actually interesting."

"I doubt I'd find it interesting. I've done all that."

"The teacher was this high school principal and pretty liberal."

"Not likely," I grumbled. "I never heard 'liberal' in a Baptist church."

"He took us through the creation myth. Or myths. The two Bible stories of creation."

"There's just the one, Jack. I should know. The one in Genesis."

"There're two. Both in Genesis. That's the point. Chapters one and two; and they're different. They contradict each other."

I knew better, and found this banter dumb and aggravating. "I don't know what you're driving at," I said, "but it's flat wrong. I know this stuff. I've been around this stuff for…."

"All your life. Yeah, you've said. But that's partly why it's interesting. It was new to me, too. I think you *might* find the class interesting."

"I don't," I said, sullenly. "Could we just move on?"

We did, but I didn't. I went straight back to my room, found a Bible, and looked up the chapters.

This was all screwy. I liked Jack, but our nascent friendship seemed suddenly to have taken a hard left turn onto a one-way road headed the other way, back toward somewhere I'd left behind, or meant to. What happened to dates and playing cards and massages and fondled fingers, and all the fantasies they conjured? And to be thus mortified on my home turf by ignorance of the second Genesis chapter! That was cruel. I brooded and pouted for a day or so, and then DeWitt returned our drama essays and Jack's had earned an A-minus, mine a B-minus, and both an extended commentary, mine doubting the pertinence of my autobiographical experience to the movie but complimenting the collection of film data on heresy and rebellion, and praising my clean and coherent prose. Jack didn't share Dewitt's paragraph on his essay, and only observed: "He doesn't say what the minus is for." I'd also landed a speaking role at tryouts for the opening show of the LCC theater season, a small-fry, three-act, slap-sticky comedy that I figured functioned as a collective audition for the big-time, heavyweight dramas, including a Shakespeare, coming later in the year. My part was as the sassy, teen-aged son of a pompous strait-laced father and might have been thought type-casting, but it gave me exposure in the reflected light of the parental star. That I'd scored the role, along with a passing grade from DeWitt, lightened a little my heavy heart after Jack's invitation to church-school so markedly changed the tone of our fellowship. Not merely baffling, it disoriented, scrambled directional signals.

And further muddling matters, a second letter from Monte Trevalyn alarmed me by the urgency with which he announced plans to visit LCC next weekend. "We need to talk," he wrote: "There's something between us that needs clearing up, the sooner the better. Steph mentioned it before I left Jubilee, and I've now discussed it with my mom and our pastor, which leaves you. What if I fly in next Friday night? Can we be roommates for the weekend? How can I reach you? Call me? WAco 2-5836."

*Whatever can this mean? What* "something between us...needs clearing up"? Or rather, how many somethings do? So you know, Steph was our Jubilee boss and supervisor of the kitchen dishwashing crew that Monte and Corky and I worked on all last summer. Monte had been employed at the Assembly the previous summer too and knew Steph from there, but well enough to discuss "something between us" with her seemed both unlikely and undesirable. And then further to discuss it with his mother looked reckless, and yet further with his pastor, of *all* people, showed really rotten judgment. What had he revealed of our association as roommates and confidantes that compelled the inspection and possibly the advice of these authorities? "Something between us" sounded intimate; Monte deemed it too risky to name in a letter, and yet it had been considered by a boss, a parent, and a preacher, with Monte, before he laid it bare to me! Only it wasn't bare. It was hidden, held back. And what does "clearing up" signify? Was there — is there? — misunderstanding? Has misinformation created this "something," misleading produced it? "...something between us" isn't necessarily suspect. His judgment — his "needs clearing up" — makes it negative, or at least questionable. What if the "something" is desirable, to me and for me? His statement was so devilishly multifarious in its suggestive reach, so resonant with ambivalence, my efforts at understanding were baffled at every turn. Doubtful that a phone call would succeed, I nevertheless had to try it, for a visit by Monte right now would incontestably discompose and arguably derail me.

The phone call succeeded only in arranging his visit. He was adamant and I proved feeble. He'd catch the campus bus from the airport and meet me at the LCC front gate as close to 8:15 p.m. on Friday as we both could manage. He'd bring his sleeping bag, and my Levis, tees, and musical scores.

* * *

"It doesn't look good," Jack said, as we strolled toward the cafeteria for supper. "Ben says it's disrespectful. Rude."

"You told him?! Why'd you tell him I can't come?"

"Well, he'll know when you don't! He thinks you should."

He referred to the first fall meeting of The Chattertons on Friday night at 7 where we initiates were to meet members, learn about our induction at the October session, hear Dr. Park talk about Tommy, and socialize over punch and cookies to prove our creds as correct, cultivated candidates for acceptance.

"Can't be helped," I said. "You and Ben can tell me what happens."

"And who's this guy, anyway, and why's he have to come now? Couldn't he come later? Or you could bring him along?"

"No, that would't work. He's a poli-sci, French, and history triple major, and Air Force ROTC. He wouldn't fit. No, you and Ben'll have to fill me in."

Jack waited a couple of beats. "You know, Troy, it looks like you're hiding something. Hiding him. What're you hiding?"

This struck, because so close to a probable truth. I *might* be hiding something, only I didn't know what it was, or which "something" it was.

"Not hiding nothing," I said. "Look, this is someone I worked with all summer, roomed with, ran with. He's a pal. I can't not meet him when he gets here. *That* would be rude."

"Did you tell Park?"

"I wrote him a nice note."

"Chicken!" he said, punching my bicep. "Your grammar says you're hiding something. I'll remember that. And I'll miss you."

In his full AF-ROTC uniform and Garrison envelope cap, Monte looked supremely smart, smashing, in fact, as though striding off a recruiting poster rather than the ratty old yellow school bus LCC leased for airport runs. He'd trimmed his curls — leaving sufficient handfuls of ringlets to charm — into the neat, military style so that the ears stood out a little below the jauntily perched cap and gave him a slighter younger, almost boyish look. In the light from the shelter, the wide smile gleamed, the bright dark eyes shimmered with the charged intensity I well remembered as riveting and sometimes intimidating. The dark navy buttoned jacket, tapered to the waist, fitted snugly, the angular lapels framing the white, stiff collar and darker blue tie. The trousers, fuller than jeans and sharply creased despite travel fatigue, fell without a break to the glossy black shoes. He shrugged off the bedroll, dropped the backpack.

"Hey," he said. "Troy. Troj," he said.

"Should I salute?" I asked, grinning.

I didn't decide: it was instinctive. I moved forward, arms open, and he stepped into my hug.

We held for a beat or two before he moved back.

"Your stuff's in here," he said, shouldering the backpack. I took up the bedroll and we set out along the campus path.

"Thanks for bringing it," I said. "You didn't have to."

"I wanted to. It's yours."

"Well, thanks."

It felt awkward, getting started again. I couldn't very well just up and ask, "What's this 'something between us,'" like that, and didn't want to, although that very something had to be right at the very front of both our minds, which is why for a moment we couldn't, either one, think of anything to say.

And then he did say, if blandly: "So this is LCC," which jogged my memory.

"Oh," I said; "I forgot. Are you hungry? The cafe's open till 9, so you can still get supper if you like."

"No, they fed us on the plane. Not strawberries and shortcake, but good enough." He was recalling a Christmas-in-July party at Jubilee where I'd overstuffed on dessert and spectacularly suffered for it. It got us started. I introduced him to campus highlights, such as they were, we exchanged happy, safe reminiscences of the summer, he updated me on his early fall term at Baylor and asked about mine here, and by then, casually yakking all the way, we were back to my dorm room with a six-pack I'd stashed in the lounge fridge in case we needed beer to warm up the conversation. He sat on my bed, I at my desk, facing him at an angle.

"Here's to us!" he said, lifting the can. "They let you drink in the dorm?"

"No," I said, sipping, and waited.

He slapped at his pockets, dipped into the right one, came up empty. At Jubilee he always carried and often — vexingly — used lip balm. I knew he was searching for the tube. He grinned, sheepishly. "I forgot," he said. "I quit. Bad habit. Sorry."

He hunched over, elbows on his knees, both hands circling the can, eyes on it. Then he drew a long breath and sat back, glanced around.

"I like it here," he said; "I like being here with you. I've missed you. This is cool, doncha think, being here together again?"

"Sure," I said; "but why're you here?"

"Well, I've missed you. We lived together a whole summer, and I got used to you…to having you around. I mean, we had a great time, didn't we?"

"Monte," I said; "don't. Why are you here?"

He caught my eyes and held them for a while. Searching? Then he dropped his head, wagged it slowly back and forth, reached for a curl behind his ear.

"I've rehearsed this a hundred times," he said quietly, "and still don't know how to do it. I want to get it right. I don't want to hurt you or mess with your head."

"My hair's too short for messing up," I said, but he was closed to jokes. "I'm sorry," I said. "What?"

"No," Monte said. "*I'm* sorry. I'm the one who's sorry. Who's so very, very sorry." The tremor in his voice startled me. Monte never apologized. He didn't tremble either.

"You don't have to tell me," I said; "if you don't want to talk, we don't have to."

"I don't know what we'd do instead," he murmured, almost inaudibly. "But no, that's just it. I *do have* to tell you. I have to get this out and over with," sounding almost angry now. "I have to tell you how sorry I am. And not just for what I did. I *am* sorry. As a person, I mean. I'm a sorry person. And I'm sorry for that too." He took a long pull on his beer, then said: "Maybe…if you had a cigarette?"

"I don't. I'm sorry I don't." I could have used one too. "There's a machine downstairs. Should I?"

He emptied a handful of change into my hand. "If you don't mind…while I use the can?"

I have a basin and a mirror, but the toilets are down the hall.

"To the right," I said as we left together.

He'd resumed the hunched-over posture on the bed, nursing the beer, when I returned with king Kents and matches. I splashed water into a tooth-brush glass for the ashes, set it on the floor between us. We lit up.

"Where were we?" he asked.

"Why you're here."

"I'm here…I'm here, Troy…I'm here to ask you…to forgive me. Please." His voice broke on "forgive." It was almost a sob.

"What?" I asked, shaken by the surprise of it. "What?! Whatever do you think you've done that needs forgiving?! What're you talking about? Are you all right, Monte?"

"No, Troy; I'll never be all right until and unless you forgive me. I mean it."

"But for *what*? You're kidding, right? This is a joke? I've no idea what you mean."

"I thought you might know. I think you do have an idea. Actually, I know that you know. Maybe you don't know that you know. But you have to know. And I have to tell you anyway, and ask for your forgiveness."

My astonishment began fading into impatience. Monte had been given to making big deals at Jubilee, and this was starting to look like the foundation for another one.

"Okay, wait," I said. "Let's back up. Can you find a beginning here? Give me something to grab hold of? What do you think you did that I need to forgive?"

"Everything," he said, shuddering. He took another long swallow, a deep drag. "Everything I did. All summer. Every damn thing. Only I never, ever saw that any part of it…was wrong. I never understood how bad it was…for you. How completely wrong it was…for you!" He shook his head, kind of choked. "I was too damned blind to see the wrong of it, until you and Corky left like you did, right in the middle of the Commitment Night service, when I was trying to do the best thing I knew to help you, to encourage you, to give you another chance to prove how good you were, how promising…and you grabbed Corky by the hand, you ran with Corky right past me, holding Corky's hand, for Christ's sake, you ran down the aisle and out the door without even a wave…."

He took a minute to smoke, to drink, to wipe his eyes.

"You're still wearing that medal, aren't you," he said. "I can see the chain."

"Oh," I said, pulling my collar tighter. "Yeah, I guess."

"Can I see it?"

"You've seen it. You had one just like it."

"Not like that one. Not with your name on the back."

"How'd you know about…?"

"Travis told me. Travis said Corky asked him to cut your name on the back. Then he gave it to you, to replace the one you lost. Can I see it?"

"No," I said, holding my collar together. "There's no point."

It was, of course, Corky's medal I traded mine for that day at the terminal. No way could I show Monte.

"I just want to see the name, what it looks like on the medal."

"It looks like my name. C'mon, Monte: Jubilee's over. We don't need to go back there now."

"No, *that's* wrong! We've damn well for sure got to go back there to straighten all this out. *That's* why I'm *here!* To figure out this shit…and to get your forgiveness. Okay, I don't need to see the medal. But I need to finish. I want to finish…what I was saying. Could I get another brew?"

I cracked another two. He wiped his eyes, swiped his nose on the jacket sleeve, streaking it.

"I couldn't understand for the longest time what you did or why, but I kept working at it, thinking about it, until it finally dawned on me that what you and Corky did was like a kind of statement…to me, and maybe a declaration to everybody else, that everything I'd done all summer was, well, just shit for *you*. I finally figured that's what you *told* me by running off like that with

Corky: that I'd disregarded you, disrespected you, misdirected you…didn't let you be yourself, all summer long. I'd dishonored our friendship, I'd betrayed it, even, by trying to force you…to…well…*realize*…well, your*self* and all your obvious potential…when you already *had,* only I was blind to that. And I hurt you. I know I did, and I'm so sorry, and I hope you can and will forgive me and help me make it up to you for ruining your summer."

This wasn't performance. This was suffering. I'd misted up too by now and couldn't talk yet, not that I knew what to say. I drowned my cigarette butt in the glass and just sat there for a minute, looking down, while Monte, silent now, caught his breath. The thing was, I almost knew he was right, dead-on right in just about everything he said; but the whole monologue was so overstated, so exaggerated and melodramatic, that saying out loud — telling him — he was right would buy into it; and granting him forgiveness would affirm the offense as hurtful. I didn't quite feel, now, offended, and maybe not even back then. More like bruised and angry. Not hurt. What I finally said was:

"You did *not* ruin my summer, Monte. You just about *made* my summer. It was prob'ly the best summer of my life…a lot *because* of you. Truly. Don't ever say or think you ruined it."

"I can't see how I *didn't* ruin it. When you ran out like that with Corky, you left me for him. You bought whatever he was selling instead of what I was, never mind that I'd been trying to *give* it to you all summer in how I helped you with the speech (that you'd never admit was a crackerjack sermon!) that proved to everybody how perfect you were for ministry. Only not to you. You didn't accept that, and ran off, and by God *that* hurt like hell. I deserved it, though, for not seeing it was all wrong for you. You tried and tried to tell me it was, and I wouldn't let you. I was so certain you had a calling, a vocational calling to ministry, like I did, and I so wanted you to heed it and come with me to seminary. I so firmly believed you should publicly commit to ministry right there at that Commitment Service that I couldn't *hear* all your arguments for *not* doing it. I loved you so much I couldn't *not* tell you what I thought was best for you and lead you to it. Hell yes I loved you, man, I might still love you, and it *was* love, like Christian brotherly love, that made me want you to do the right thing, to heed the call, only you said it was the wrong thing for you. When you left me and took Corky's hand and ran out with him, I saw you were telling me it all was shit for you. That *I* was all wrong for you."

"But you took *my* hand, Monte, don't you remember? By the lake that night. You took my hand…in yours, and played with it."

He looked down, studied the floor.

"Steph asked me what I knew about Corky." He let it sink in. "After yawl left, I went to talk to Steph. I thought maybe I'd actually run you off, scared you away with all my commotion around the speech thing, and I wondered whether Steph thought I'd, like, overdone my…meddling. She said 'maybe,' and then asked me again whether I knew anything about Corky. Obviously, she did know something, or thought she did, but she never said what, and I, well, I let it go…until you guys left… holding each other's hands like that, in public and everything…my own roommate holding another guy's hand."

We went deathly still. I felt faintly nauseous.

"And you talked about all this with your mother?" I asked. "And the preacher?"

"I talked with Mom about the meddling part. I went over most of it with our pastor, especially the part about what I thought was your vocational calling."

"I don't have one. How many times must I say that?"

"I know. But I was so sure that you did. I'm not sure you don't. But I'm not going there anymore."

"Thank you."

After another little while I raised my eyes and found his looking directly into mine, holding them.

He said: "Did I hurt you so much that you had to betray me like that, with Corky?"

I suddenly imagined myself prostrate on the floor, crawling to his knees, sobbing, begging him to forgive *me* for leaving him for Corky, and the image was so absurd, so preposterous, I almost giggled. It momentarily relieved my tension but Monte looked like he awaited an answer.

"No, Monte," I said, "I reject 'betrayal.' What I did — what we did — had nothing to do with you. It wasn't about you. What I did was *affirm*. Corky said I 'claimed myself.' I'm sorry you took it personally. I did not, definitely did not, intend to hurt you."

"But what did you 'affirm,' Troy?"

It was a better question than I expected at that point. I thought for a second or two. "I think what I affirmed was independence. My independence of several things. Possibly of you."

No, no, this was too harsh. He was too tenderly vulnerable.

"Wait," I said; "I take that back. I didn't mean that last. I don't know that I even want to be entirely independent of you. No, I don't want that."

"Then maybe," he said, drawing in a long breath and releasing it, shakily, "maybe you can help me with something else, something maybe related but a little different?"

"Okay," I said. "Try me."

"Do you remember Laura McIntyre?"

"Sure. Your girlfriend. At UT-Austin. Why?"

"We broke up. I'd hardly unpacked at home before she called it quits with me. *Over the phone*! Said her mom's country-club friend had a son starting third year Yale Law who they met on a two-week cruise to Europe, and they were practically engaged by the time their ship docked at Le Harve. Crazy. But she dumped me."

"I'm sorry. Are you sad?"

"Not much. We've been kind of dead for a while. I'll have to find a date for frat dinners and parties...but this also gives me sort of an opening, you know, for...well... you know...like exploring other options."

He paused, watched me mentally stumble over what he'd said, whatever he'd meant. I waited.

"I'm so kind of mixed up about all this stuff through here, I don't hardly know where I am, except at Baylor and in the Air Force, and you leaving me like you did, that made me kind of uncertain, about everything and all, about what I'd done to you, and why, and about… well, you know…about you and Laura and Corky and all that. Maybe I'd never actually *thought* much about all that, but I guess…maybe…I've had feelings? Around all that. In…well…another direction? That I've sort of ignored, you know what I mean? Kind of not wanted to think about. But then…well, you showed up at Jubilee, and, I don't know, I focused on you, and I thought we had, you know, a really special brotherhood or something, like I told you that day at Seraphim, and we talked about plans…for, like, the future? But then you left with Corky. Just disappeared. Until I found you again. And you hugged me. You hugged me a little while ago, back down there, and I…well…I responded. My body responded. You know what I mean. And I don't know what to do, Troy, I just don't," he said, sobbing his sorrow and despair.

It was almost unendurably sweet, his strenuous fumbling. For all my astonishment, I was also a tiny bit amused, but deeply, painfully moved. Too moved to speak. I just looked at him, at his intense black eyes and their raw, wild, pleading bewilderment.

"That," I said softly, after a moment, "that, my dear Monte, is a powerful lot to process, and I don't think I'm up to starting on it tonight. If you don't mind, could we postpone until tomorrow?"

"If you promise to tell me then what to do. And to forgive me for what I already did. I really need you to tell me what to do."

"I've already forgiven you for whatever you think you did. But understand that you didn't hurt me or ruin my summer. Can you accept that?"

"I can try. Thank you."

"So let's call it a night. You can use the bathroom first."

"Troy," he said, as I stood. "Would you please hold me again?"

"No, Monte," I said; "I doubt that's a good idea. I don't think we should risk it."

Already showered and shaved and dressed — in a pale lavender Polo and jeans — when the college chimes woke me at 7 the next morning, Monte sat at my desk, legs propped on it and crossed at the ankles, my Jubilee yearbook in his lap. I could see that he'd neatly arranged my Levis and tees and musical scores on the dresser-top.

"You're keeping Jubilee hours," I said, remembering how we'd crawled out at 5:30 there for breakfast duty.

"Some pretty fine pictures of you, of us, in there," he said, closing the book and setting it aside. "Good memories!"

"I guess," I said, sitting up, stretching. "You sleep okay?"

"Well enough," he said, resting his elbows on my desk, and leaning across it toward me. "Troy," he went on after a pause, "I've decided to go back to Baylor this morning. Okay?"

"What? But why? You just got here! I've planned a whole weekend."

"Well, I think I've got a lot of what I came for. I mean, you've given me what I wanted from you. Generously given it. There's no point in staying. I'm sure you've got things to do, and you know I'm pretty busy at Baylor."

"Wait up here. Are you sure we've finished talking? I kind of cut us off last night."

"Troy, I doubt you and I could ever finish talking. We talk a lot. Maybe we talk instead of doing. To keep from doing. But I'm wondering whether more talking is going to help right now. Last night was kind of confusing. I don't know if I know *how* to talk to you through here…though here I am doing it all over again!"

"But what if I *want* to?"

"I don't think you do."

"See? You do that all the time! You tell me what I think. You think you know my mind better than I do."

This, I saw, was surly and rude and terribly timed. But he gave me no chance to retract it.

"You're right," he said. "I do that. I apologize. But it sort of makes my point. I don't see that more conversation, right now, is quite the right path forward for us… if there is an us."

This felt uncomfortably like a dead end, so I maneuvered.

"All right. Let's grab breakfast…and, um, process. Give me ten minutes."

"No, Troy," he said, standing up. "I don't think so. I'd better go now. I'll catch the bus. You've got my number."

"This doesn't feel right, Monte. Really. I don't like…."

"Well, pal, it didn't feel right when you and Corky left either."

But he grinned, put out his hand, firmly shook mine, hoisted his bags, and strode out my door, leaving me, just as I'd predicted, discomposed, half-naked in my jockeys.

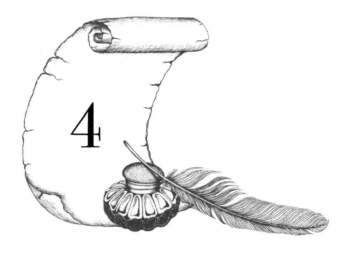

4

Not many patrons of the cafeteria ever showed up on Saturday morning before it closed at 9, but — wouldn't you know? — among them on this one was Dr. Park Royal, my teacher and advisor, and faculty sponsor of The Chatterton Honors Literary Society who, last evening, had chaired the first fall meeting of the club when candidates for membership, including me, were to be introduced and scrutinized for literary savvy and social grace. Bright in his yellow smock over a black shirt, dark gray slacks and weejuns sans socks, he sat alone at a window table, a newspaper spread across it. The tumbled hair glinted in the morning light. With my tray, I quick-stepped toward the rear wall, opposite the windows, but his shrill yelp — "You! Troy!"— stopped and turned me to behold the beckoning wave, his wrist flapping.

"Sit," he snapped.

"Thank you, sir. Good morning, sir!" I noticed the absence of his customary if always disconcerting "Darlin'." He silently folded the LCC *Witness* news sheets (whose name I thought an imperative as well as a title), patted his lips with a napkin, folded his arms across his chest.

"Who is he?" he asked.

"Excuse me, sir. I told you. In my note. He's a friend from last summer. I was his host for an LCC weekend."

"There is no 'LCC weekend.' Only one event was scheduled for last night. There were no official conflicts. You'll find that I'm supremely careful about such things. You intentionally skipped the inaugural meeting of The Chattertons to 'host' a friend who's not even a student prospect."

"I wanted to be hospitable, sir."

"Piffle!" he sniffed. "You were particularly invited as a special guest to attend the inaugural session of The Chatterton Honors Literary Society, and you chose instead to spend the night playing with a 'friend from last summer.' It's insulting, Troy. It's ill-bred and impudent. I am deeply disappointed in you, and ashamed for you."

"But sir. I wrote you. I explained."

"You *announced*, you *proclaimed*, your planned absence. You did not ask my permission to skip the meeting. The invitation did not include an RSVP. Your attendance was not optional. You were expected. And you flouted us. Your absence created unexpected difficulties. Rearrangements. It was an *exasperating nuisance and inconvenience."* He spit out the words in about sixteen sibilant syllables.

"I'm very sorry, sir. I apologize. I didn't realize…."

"The importance of our meeting? It was essential!" The spit flew again. "Especially for aspirants" (and again). "The interview is a prerequisite for admission. How do you propose to make up for your absence?" (Spit flying everywhere).

"Sir, I asked Jack and Ben to take notes and fill me in."

"*I* will fill you in. Please make two one-hour appointments with me with the Department secretary for next week. *I* will introduce you to Tommy Chatterton and his *oeuvre. I* will interview you. *I* will inform you of how to prepare for your formal initiation next month, conditional upon a satisfactory interview. Am I clear?"

"Yes sir. Thank you, sir."

"And darlin'," he said, standing and drawing himself up, "you really *must* learn some *gentility!*"

My breakfast had gone cold, and I had no appetite for it anyway, after Park's rant. Geez, was *that* genteel? Was he seriously pissed, or just showing off? I'd make the appointments, of course, but it all seemed much ado, and frightfully prissy…and wet. What I wanted at the moment, though, was some quiet, some private time in The Grove to process all the confusion and perplexity Monte had brought with him and unloaded onto me. The Grove was a sizable plot of naturally forested land spared through decades of college expansion and ultimately incorporated into the campus as a retreat from its noisy rush and hurly-burly (more or less on the order and with the purpose of Jubilee's Prayer Gardens, only much more spacious), populated mostly by oak and pine but also some crabapple and elm and an occasional Japanese maple, its floor softly carpeted in leaves and needles, all of it especially inviting now with mellow autumnal colors. Lanterned lampposts on automatic timers stood sentinel throughout the park. Reflectively, I passed into its amber shades:

What Monte mostly brought was a warped version of the guilt that powered Jubilee, a guilt bred by his recklessly zealous adoption and espousal of the Assembly's mission to identify male youths suitable for ministerial training in Baptist seminaries, and to convince them of God's "calling" of themselves to that vocation. Monte interpreted my success in the denominationally-sponsored, months-long speaking competition as a sign of my fitness for such training, and, against my stout and stubborn objections, organized a dubiously ethical campaign to secure my win at the national finals of the competition held at Jubilee near the end of the summer session. To my vast relief, I lost, but Monte, groundlessly suspecting a "fixed" judgment, persisted in his hope that I might join him in due course at a seminary.

But now he begged my forgiveness for his massive investment in trying to orchestrate my win, when winning and its consequences, he now believes, would have been "bad" for me, or "wrong" for me. This is true, or almost certainly true. But I've never understood the consuming energy of his effort: it was as though he owned a larger stake in me than I valued in myself, that he stood to lose more than I would lose were I defeated. And what had *he* to gain if I won? Where was the reward, the payback, for him? Was I somehow merely the *occasion* for the exercise and exhibition of his giant ego? And now he was equally dogged in repudiating the earlier effort because its success would have harmed me. I'd long ago worked out how ministry would ruin *him* — suppress his intensity, depress his charisma — but he'd forthrightly dismissed my arguments to that effect. *Why* had he now concluded that ministry was "bad" for me? Did he imagine that what Corky and I did that night might somehow disqualify me for the profession, so that he needed to be forgiven for urging me to accept a call I didn't feel? Or were these two elaborate melodramas — the persuasion, the cancellation — were they merely opposite sides of the same performative coin...or con? Were they meticulously designed schemes for showcasing himself and his directorial gifts?

They almost peaked at that Committal Service, where Monte cheer-led a congregational demand — a thunderous chant of my name — that I recite a portion of my competition speech to demonstrate and prove my sermonic skills, which incited my flight with Corky, right past Monte without acknowledgment. Such manifest scorn of him and his plan no doubt embarrassed and disappointed and angered him, and so inspired his wish to renounce it.

Then there was his strange fixation on our hands, Corky's and mine, as we fled him and the Assembly's agenda. They had possibly reminded him of a night-shrouded Jubilee occasion when a flock of us were gathered into a lakeside circle and urged by an unseen counsellor's voice to squeeze the hands we held in both of ours to signal our acceptance of a divine summons into "lifelong full-time Christian service." My room-mate's familiar cologne told me, despite the darkness, that Monte held one of my hands and toyed with it, stroked my fingers and tickled my palm and feathered my wrist, until I, feeling profaned, flung loose and split. I'm pretty certain that embarrassed him too. And now I wonder whether the repeated "hands" motif in last night's conversation registered resentment that Corky's hand and mine remained locked as we escaped.

At the Christmas-in-July dinner, Jubilee manage-ment had distributed to all staff a little faux bronze medal inscribed "Jubilee 1957," suitable for wearing as a pin or necklace or on a wristband. Corky asked our resident art-ist Travis to etch our names on the backs of ours, and bought matching chains for them. I'd been very careful never, around Monte, to wear my medal outside the shirt.

The remaining, and weightiest, mystery in last night's talk was everything about Monte's break-up with Laura and the opportunities it opened for his explora-tions of "other options." His skittishness and indirection were suggestive, but what, really, was he saying, and what meaning by it, or was it all only another ruse or trick or joke? All of it had vanished by morning, and maybe that meant we were both supposed to ignore and forget it. I think I'd like to. Representations of sexuality at Jubilee, beyond fitful flirtations, were almost invisible: I'd only once heard him jerk-off in his bed after lights-out, and once he'd complimented me on my "James Dean lips" and blonde crewcut and bone structure; and although he did push-ups now and then, he appeared less body-conscious than I was. What his talk hinted last night, *if* it hinted at all, I don't know, for certain. Which is why I completely ignored his repeated requests for my "help" in figuring out how he's to unriddle his bewilderment, or act in light of it. I didn't know about that either, or even whether I'd correctly interpreted his despair as such, not to mention his abrupt departure, or any intended meaning in his appeal for another hug. I believe the intention of my denial is clear enough, but its resolve is uncertain. For my body also "responded" to the welcoming hug.

\* \* \*

September 28, 1957
Corky Carlisle, Esq.
8 Irby House
31 McAlister Drive
Tulane University
New Orleans, Louisiana

Hey there, Corky!  What's shakin' down there in alligator land? I hope you're getting good grub. How's the roommate? Do you like your courses? What's your major, anyway? Home-Ec?! Do they let you bike on campus? Are you going to the clubs? *Those* clubs, I mean. In the

Quarter? Does your fake I.D. still work? Any brushes with voodoo? Tell me *everything*!

I'm taking:

Pre-Romantic and Romantic Lit (Dr. Park Royal, also my advisor and a screwball but I like him).

Soph Survey of Eng. Lit (req. for majors)

Physical Science (full year req.; six-week samples of six lab sciences. Ugh.)

Trig (req. math, double ugh!)

Intro to Drama (mostly film, it looks like)

Lots of homework. I got a B- on my first Drama essay.

I've met two guys who're probably going to be friends, both English majors. Jack's smart and plays cards and will teach me to shuffle. Ben is big and black-bearded and writes poetry and quotes Allen Ginsberg and rides a motorcycle.

I wanted to tell you that Monte just visited me. His girlfriend dumped him and he's unhappy. Kind of mixed up. He wanted to talk, and then he didn't. I think he's a little jealous of you. Of you and me. Are you jealous of him? Don't be. I still wear my medal, do you wear yours? No, wait: *I* wear yours!

Are you dancing with other guys at the clubs?

Don't leave my letters lying around open in your room.

I miss you.
Love, Troy

                 \* \* \*

"He didn't even mention you," Jack said.

I'd met Ben after Romantics — he and Park had argued about Blake on Wednesday — and then invited him to join Jack and me Monday afternoon to report on the Chatterton Society meeting. That morning I'd made my appointments with Dr. Royal through Thelma Burke, Mother Superior and English Department Executive Assistant, and checked out a Library collection of Chatterton's verse. We sprawled on the grass around the Crisswell Fountain.

"Not quite right," Ben said. "He didn't speak your name but he said we were one short. If you make it in, we'll be fifteen total."

"So what happened?"

"I don't know about this," Ben went on skeptically, scratching his beard. "This talk about the meeting: it's bound to give you an unfair advantage in your interview."

"How's that?" I asked, a little prickly. I looked at Jack. He glanced at Ben.

"He's kidding," Jack said, and Ben boomed a laugh.

"It's a piece o' cake," Ben added; "hardly an 'interview' at all."

"But it might be in private," Jack offered. "We had kind of a group interview. Nobody felt on the spot. We just said who we are and where from and what our favorite books are and what we write, if we write. No pressure. But in private he might get more personal and specific, especially if he's still pissed at you for not showing up."

"How 'more personal'? About what? And how would I prepare for that?"

"I wouldn't," Ben said. "Wing it. Or just think through your literary tastes beforehand, and name a favorite author and say what you write, in what genre. But don't fake anything and trap yourself. He's pretty shrewd. And don't get all spooked and antsy about it. He'll think you're over-prepared and not spontaneous."

"Did he ask about literary terms? Like sonnet rhyme-schemes or onomatopoeia or what an oxymoron is?"

"Naaah," Jack said, "no exam questions. And unless he asks you something, let him talk. He likes to."

"What'd he say about the initiation?"

"That's all hush-hush," Ben said, a finger on his lips. "But when he said the word, nobody giggled or grinned or winked, so I doubt there's much to it, nothing scary or worrisome, like frat hazing. I expect small-scale pomp and circumstance. He did say to dress."

"Should I bone up on Chatterton? I've got a library book."

"He's *writing* the book," Jack said. "He'll probably tell you that. You might want to place Chatterton historically, know some contemporaries, titles, kings and queens. Like that. But keep in mind Park likes to talk… about his guy."

"What about the others, the members?"

"Well, they won't be there," Ben said, "not at your interview. Can't tell much yet. About even, boys and girls. Nobody dominated. Nobody sucked-up. Nobody farted."

"But what's *his* story?" I asked. "Doesn't he seem… well…kind of wacky?"

"Unconventional," Ben corrected. "And unconventional is where it's at! Or hadn't you heard? Look, boys," gathering his things, "I've got a date. You get everything you want, Troy? Keep a record and let us know how it goes. If you freak out before, I've got weed. I didn't say that."

"Hey thanks, Ben," I said; "that was really helpful."

Jack and I stayed put. It was a lovely afternoon: 70's, low humidity, light breeze, no mosquitos.

"Once more now," Jack said: "Why weren't you there?"

"As I said, a surprise visitor. Well, no; not exactly unexpected. Short notice. I didn't know to expect till he was on the way."

"Someone special?"

I paused, shifted up onto my elbows and looked down into his curious, steady eyes. "I don't quite now know," I murmured. "At one time, he was special, very special. Now I'm not sure what he is."

"You broke up? I knew you were hiding something."

"No, not like you mean. We never were like that. He was my roommate last summer, like I told you."

"As you told me. What if you'd just said, 'He roomed with me last summer,' or 'I roomed with him last summer'? What would the difference be?"

"Sorry, I don't know what you mean."

"Sure you do: 'He was my roommate last summer' is more intimate than 'He roomed with me last summer.' Can't you hear it? It's more affectionate. Warmer. Listen to the ownership. Which do you mean?"

"I meant what I said, okay? What're you getting at?"

"Oh, nothing really. Not important. How'd the visit go?"

"Not well. His girlfriend dumped him. He left early Saturday morning."

"Why'd he come?"

"He gave me a reason but I didn't understand it, not really."

"Did you make out?"

"NO! I *told* you we…." But he was laughing.

"Didn't you *want* to?" he giggled.

I slapped him lightly on the shoulder. "Stop it," I chortled. "Shame on you!"

We laid back.

"He was the one in the blue uniform, wasn't he," Jack said.

"What?! How do you know…?"

"I was up early Saturday. He was at the bus shelter."

He turned his head toward me, grinning. "I might've wanted to make out," he said.

"So," I smiled, "might I."

\* \* \*

By the time I met Jack at 9 on Wednesday night at Calliope, I'd had my "interview" with Professor Royal, more classes on pre-Romanticism with him, and three hours with my library book on Chatterton, and was primed to float my recently hatched plan to the guy I hoped would help me implement it over the next months. We waved to Ben, scribbling his poetry at the rear table, and moved to an empty one away from the traffic flow. Jack smoothed the backs of his khakis as he sat.

"The interview was just what yawl told me to expect," I said, after we'd ordered tea and Jack had lit up, "only more so. He was already rarin' to go on about Chatterton after lecturing on him in class, and I let him run like you said I should. He did the routine drill on who-where-when-what-and-how and didn't say a thing about my absence Friday night. Oh, and he told me to dress up for the initiation, to bring my best manners.

And he said he expected you and Ben and me to become his Three Wise Men!"

"Does that make him Jesus?" Jack smirked and blew smoke.

"It makes us three kings," I said. "Maybe he was punning on Royal or something.

"So anyway, I've been reading my Chatterton book and working on this idea I'd like to run by you and see whether you'd want to join up and maybe work on it with me?"

Just going that far made me nervous. "Could I bum a cigarette?"

He passed over his Viceroys and the bic.

"Okay, here goes: What if you and I collaborated on writing a play about Chatterton? And cast it with members of the Honors Society? We'd ask Park if we could count it as the two term papers we have to write for Romanticism."

"But I'm not taking it."

"I know. I thought of that. You'd drop calculus, which you hate, and add Romantics next term. And we'd also get DeWitt to count our play as the term paper we have to write for Drama. We'd have to be up front about the double-counting, but I'm pretty sure I can make a good case for it, since learning about both subjects would be required to write and produce the play."

"What do you mean, 'produce' it?"

"Put it on. Stage it. Late next spring. Look: We write it this fall. We present it to the club at the end of the term, dedicate it to Park, cast it with club members in the early spring, rehearse and polish through the term, and stage it around graduation weekend in late May. And pick up six credit hours each semester! That's practically a full semester."

"You're serious?" He stared.

"Completely. Want to try it?"

"I don't know squat about writing plays."

"I don't either, but how hard can it be? And I *do* know a lot about them. I've acted in seven of them, mostly as the lead, through high school and in the summers, except the most recent one. I know about stagecraft. And *you* know everything about film. Films are just plays, aren't they, on celluloid? You know more than you think you know about plays. You just got an A-minus on your essay. And you won that national prize."

"Not for a play."

"It was writing. You can write."

"How come you thought of all this? Where'd you get it?"

"I'm still working it out. I'm hating this stupid farce I've got a role in, and I'm probably going to quit it; but I'd still want to be involved in something…well…dramatic. And I'm thinking this Chatterton kid — this 'marvelous boy,' Wordsworth called him — this Chatterton kid is 24-carat drama. There's not a whole lot of life to make a play *of,* but it's *all* high drama. If the Club's the cast, and they help out backstage, we can prob'ly get them academic credit too. As for Park, he's already such a show-off, he'll eat up the chance to do it in costume on stage. And you know what, Jack? I'm keen *mostly* to work with you…to write with you. Ben could write lyrical verse like Chatt's, and dialogue. We'll need a musician for some jigs and tavern songs and like that — I might be able to help. And by damn, this whole freaking project might stir up the campus better'n Chapel and bullshit sports."

"Well," he said pensively, "I sure would like to drop calculus."

"You could, and add Romantics, if we hurry. I want to bring it up to Park on Friday at our second interview… *instead* of our second interview, if you approve and are aboard. I'll say it's both our idea. Both our ideas. Our joint idea."

"I don't know anything about acting, Troy."

"Sure you do. You just acted out for me that you didn't know who Monte was, when you did know it, all the time. Besides, I can teach you what you don't know. I'd love to do that."

"Wouldn't Park want to play his hero?"

"Yeah. But I'm Chatterton. If Park wants it, we'll rehearse it with both of us…each of us…on alternating days. We'll rehearse it with each of us. Eventually, I guess I'll have to decide."

"Whoa!' Jack said. "You really want that job? I can't see Park under-studying you!"

"Wait. Let's think: We'll want to perform it at least two nights. Why not let me and Park play Chatt on alternating nights? That way, he and I would *keep on* competing, improving our performances by taking the best from each other… and so on. And audiences would *debate* who's better, and stir up interest; buy repeat tickets.

Hey, I like this. We'll double-cast the lead! I'll float it to Park on Friday. Can he *deny* the part to one of his Wise Men? And he'll take seriously the challenge to out-perform me."

"Better gear down, Troy; you're about to lift off."

"So you're on board? I can tell Park?"

"You honestly think we can…that we can bring this off? It's big, Troy."

"Damn right it is! And hey, we're *sophomores!* We can make this work. You and me on this, man? It's sure-fire!"

# 5

Ben Moore so roughly braked his "hog" at the curb, swerving sharply away from it, I jumped aside to escape him. "What the hell?" I exclaimed. "Watch where you're going!"

"Pardon," he said, sounding chagrined. I figured he'd scared himself. "You lookin' for me? Jack said you were. My place okay? Hop on."

My pulse pounded, but what choice had I? I was seeing Royal tomorrow morning.

"Grab a-holt around my waist," he instructed, as he eased into traffic and moved us tactfully into the oak-shrouded suburbs of two- and three-storied frame and brick homes and long, raked lawns with deftly trimmed hedges between the lots. His motor growled through the quiet.

"There've been some complaints," he said, "but my landlady's dealt. C'mon, I'm upstairs."

An imposing structure, the house soared upward, white with dark blue shutters, a spreading screened porch with two swings to the left, a wide veranda to the right and a white pebbled driveway running past it to a double garage behind. Four windowed gables topped the roof.

"My room," Ben waved vaguely at them. "Three flights up. I get to use the front door," he added, jangling a keyring.

The dark brown glossy door — mahogany? — with polished gold hardware opened upon an eerily silent entrance hall leading to the longest, widest, carpeted staircase I'd ever seen apart from the grand one gracing the Vanderbilt mansion near Asheville that the family had toured. Comparatively, the next stairwell up here was modest and the next after it of midget proportions, steep and narrowly enclosed by more dark wood definitely not mahogany. Ben stopped at the door and fished out the keyring.

He occupied the entire space. The finished attic, high-ceilinged, naturally lighted by the big gable windows looking down upon a massive roll-top desk facing the far left wall, an unmade double-bed against the right wall and next to it an extended floral-patterned screen trying to hide the corner "facilities," Ben said they were, although the protruding plumbing above betrayed the functions it accommodated. A tall, wide, spilling bookcase, flanked by two padded, old-fashioned parlor chairs and pole floor lamps, braced the left wall. Books, magazines, journals, folders littered the floor, and, scattered among them, Ben's signature black notebooks with the white Roman numerals. A full-sized refrigerator lurked behind the door we'd entered by; and across that entrance stood an even larger chifforobe with an open door revealing Ben's mostly black wardrobe. The opposite wall facing me was just about papered with newsprint clippings, snipped headlines, LP album covers, photographs — Ginsberg's frequent among them — and *Playboy* centerfold bunnies. A set of tv trays leaned against a wooden stool beneath them. Heavy glass ashtrays, each holding cinders and a brightly-colored pot spoon pipe, rested on crates near the chairs. Next to a Smith-Corona portable typewriter, a bong presided over the desk surface, under a boxy Motorola radio perched atop the roller case.

"Hope you don't mind the mess," Ben said, reaching out two Schlitz cans from the fridge. "Doris comes tomorrow to pick up. Let's take the chairs."

He flung himself into one, hiked a leg over its arm, and popped the top.

"These are *some* digs," I said, in true admiration. "Really cool! But how'd you fix them up so fast?"

"The former tenant left in June. Mrs. Harrison let me move in then. She's the widow of Samuel Robert Harrison, whose name's on the quad where you live. He chaired the LCC Board for about a century and developed a lot of real estate in Alexandria. He built this house. After he died, Mrs. H. opened the attic for rent to students so she'd have company in an empty house, not that I'm all that much company for her. She has a butler, too, to help out: Rodney; you'll meet him. She's a big Baptist, of course, but she likes her cocktail toddy every afternoon, and sometimes invites me to make it for her, and to join her on the veranda with one for myself. Sometimes she asks me to read my poetry to her."

"Really? A fan! You should dedicate a book to her."

"I plan to. She's kind, and gave me a deal on the rent. Sometimes she makes me supper. So what can I do for you today?"

"And maybe the day after and the one after that?"

Preliminaries obviously concluded, I sipped some suds and described the interview and began on the plan, but Ben already knew who Chatterton was and possibly more about the poet than I yet did, so I skipped that part and went straight to the play collaboration and the casting and the academic credit and the production and Royal's role, and how we were hoping he, Ben, would contribute verse dialogue and lyrics and help out anywhere else he could toward making ourselves major English majors and Park's Wisest Men Ever and maybe Somebodies around campus. He appeared to listen attentively, occasionally bending an elbow, and not interrupting even once.

"So that's it," I finished, slightly breathless. "Whadaya think? Want to join?"

He straightened up, set down his Schlitz. "I might just," he said. "Where would you say you most need my help?"

"Don't know yet. It's prob'ly too early to say. Where do you think you'd be most helpful?"

"Shit, we're just circling. Let's go at it another way. Are you aware that I volunteer with The Darkhorse Limelight Repertory Theater Company over in Alexandria?"

I almost chortled at the ponderous density of the name but saw that Ben's question showed interest.

"Um, no. I've not heard of it. What do you volunteer to do?"

"Whatever needs doing. I worked with them all last year. We staged five plays."

"Whoa! No kidding? You acted?"

"No, no acting. Not my thing. But I did just about everything else: built sets, worked props, rewrote scripts, helped make and assemble costumes, worked lights and sound, recorded stuff, took photos, ushered, sold tickets, organized cast parties…supplied weed!" The big laugh boomed. My jaw prob'ly dropped.

"Wow, Ben!? Really? This is fantastic! You've got EXPERIENCE! In THEATRE! Holy shit, can we count you in on this? Wait'll I tell Jack. Does he know this about you?"

"Dunno. It's not a secret. Nothing in the theater is ever secret. It started back in the Monroe orphanage. We did little plays all along, for the staff and each other, and I liked it. And then in high school I guess it was my favorite extra-curricular. But last year the opportunities seemed better over at Darkhorse than here, so I signed up to volunteer. Incidentally, I also had the intro to drama course you're now taking with Dewitt, only with Greg Sanders, Dr. Sanders, who teaches *drama*, not film. We actually looked at the guts of drama, not just the ruffles."

"Well, you might better replace me as leader in this Chatterton thing. You're a lot more experienced. Can I tell Royal tomorrow you're interested? That you're this experienced?"

"You can tell him you've approached me. But we'll have to decide what I'll do if I sign on. I'll need to know my assignment first."

"Well, I'm officially inviting you to join in and help us plan. Jack and me. Here's what I'm thinking...provisionally thinking: what if I ask Dr. Royal to recommend three top-notch books about Chatterton, one for each of us: introductions to the life, the poetry, the career, the relationships, the controversies, the reputation and so on, and then in a couple of weeks we get back together and share what we've learned and toss around some ideas on how to make a dramatic narrative out of it? I figure we should all three co-author the play but we'll need a framework, or a map to make assignments with: what happens and when and to whom and so forth. Maybe we could work that out first, and then get on with writing it? Should I maybe suggest to Park tomorrow that way of proceeding?"

"Wait," Ben said; "is he going to oversee everything? Censure us?"

"He should be an 'advisor' to the project. He's got to have a role in it, since we're asking for academic credit.

I don't see him telling us what to do, but we need his knowledge of Chatterton, at least to get started. I mean, in some sense he's kind of given me — us — the idea. It's going nowhere without his input and support."

"I don't want him whitewashing me," Ben said.

"We might need to whitewash Chatterton," I offered. "He procured whores, you know."

"Who gave him clap."

"I was thinking of giving him a boyfriend, too," I said.

Ben whooped. "Now *there's* a super idea," he laughed. "Let's run with that!"

"But are you okay with reading around first and coming back together to float ideas for a *plot*? A Chatterton *story, based* on historical info — dates, places, persons, publications, events — but spinning a completely new set of encounters and circumstances and consequences, all contributing to the suicide? Of course it has to end with the arsenic poisoning, that scene in the painting. Getting there is our new tale."

"You reckon there might be room in the play for some of my poetry? I could probably learn to do medieval, like Chatterton did. I've got some Latin and French."

"I've thought we should include music. You know, lute tunes or something? We'd need lyrics. You could compose lyrics. And tavern songs. We'll need a coupla tavern scenes, with fiddles. For jigs. Like English hoedowns."

"That's oxymoronic, buddy," Ben said, and after a pause continued: "It may have potential. Yessir, I think it just might. But it's going to be a mountain of work. Do we have time for it? Imagination ain't in doubt, but time and energy might be? I admire you for thinking it up, Troy, and I'm prob'ly interested. But I need to think. Just tell Park you've talked to me and I'm thinking, okay? How're you and Jack getting on?"

"Good! I like him. He got an A- from DeWitt, and helped me on my paper. He's going to teach me how to whiffle-shuffle cards. Says I've got the fingers for it. From piano and typing. He may join us in Romantics, and drop calculus."

"Well, that would be convenient. You got my phone number? Give me yours. And get one of those Chatterton books for me. We can meet here, if you and Jack want to."

"Sure," I said. "He has wheels."

\* \* \*

Twelve minutes late for our appointment, Professor Royal whipped around the far corner and came rushing toward his office — coattails flying, tie flapping, hair streaming — where I fidgeted with stress.

"I *loathe* being late!" he bawled, still several yards off, shifting his armload of notebooks and folders from one hip to the other. "I am punctual. I am punctilious. I am *never* late. I apologize, darlin'," he groused, fumbling with keys; "I'm so sorry to have kept you." He waved me inside, pointing to the French Provincial upholstered armchair abutting his orderly desk. "It just proves again what happens when people disregard etiquette. It's the very point I tried to make to you over your unexcused absence from our meeting. You defied decorum. You disdained civility. You *inconvenienced* ourselves. Like Dr. Rogers just did me, disrespecting my schedule. Keeping me past my appointment time. He's Department Chair, you know, and he can't even observe common courtesies. It's shameful, but here's a shining example of how serious and far-reaching transgressions of etiquette can be. How disruptive and upsetting. Learn from this!"

He sighed exasperation, arranged himself in the high-backed swivel chair, fingered a short, wooden wand off the desk, like a conductor's baton.

"Now...you're here to...?"

"To learn more about the meeting, sir, the meeting I missed."

"Oh, fiddle," he pouted dismissively. "Didn't I explain all that to you last Friday? Haven't Jack and Ben filled you in? What's the point of having Three Wise Men if two of them don't...oh, never mind. Just show up on time, darlin', at the initiation, in a suit and tie. We'll send a reminder. Everything's all arranged for a little ceremony, and you'll be directed. Suckled, actually." He giggled. "Not to fret, child. Just show up this time on time. I'm really sorry I didn't. You probably know I'm coming up for tenure this year, and Dr. Rogers wanted to advise *me* on how to prepare for *that* trial, and of course I needed to find out, and we ran over. It was rude of him to make me late for you. Please forgive him. Do you even know what tenure is?"

"Not for sure, sir. It's like a job guarantee? For life?"

"Not like. It absolutely *is*. A job guarantee for life. And you have to earn it with slave labor for seven years like Jacob did for Rachel and then got Leah instead, with no guarantee of Rachel even after seven more years of slaving either. How'd you like *them* apples?" He tapped the wand lightly on his palm.

"It sounds very hard, sir."

"Well," he said resignedly, "I chose it. We'll see how it plays out. But *you,* darlin', anything else on your mind today? You want to know about that beautiful painting on my wall there? I showed yawl in class, remember?"

He meant his poster of the Henry Wallis deathbed portrait of Chatterton.

"Why, yessir, I do. I remember and I do want to know. In fact, I was hoping to talk to you today...about Chatterton."

"You *were*? Well, that tickles my ribs. What would you like to know? I know a good deal."

"Yes sir. I know you do. Which is why we want you involved."

His eyes squinted a little, but the lips quivered toward smiling.

"Let's hear it," he said.

So I rolled it all out, the whole plan, however tentative every scrap of it still was. He listened, or seemed to, occasionally tapping the wand against his palm, his eyes flicking from mine to the big painting behind me, facing him. He didn't frown or shake his head or curl his lip. He nodded now and then. He didn't swivel or squeak.

"That's about it, sir. Jack and Ben are all in, Jack to help me write and Ben at least with song lyrics. We really hope you'll let us try it, sir, and help us out. We're ready to start on any books you recommend. I'm already into the one I found."

"It's hugely ambitious, Troy," he said, sounding hugely adult, "but I'm sure you recognize that. You'd only need my official help for authorization of the credit, but I might be willing to advise along the way if you *need* me and if — big if — I can find the time with this tenure thing and all. I can't predict the amount of time that's going to eat up. And I'm teaching, of course, and trying to finish *my* book. The bigger problem is, we don't *know* a whole lot about Tommy Chatterton, you see, and a lot of what we think we know is controversial, and his whole story is, well, definitively *incomplete*."

"Yessir, we know that, sir." I'd prepared for this one. "We'd take the historical and biographical 'facts' more or less agreed on out there, build a narrative framework out of them, and then fill in with *fictional* people and events, and make up details about his writing and relationships and stuff. We'll announce that we're writing plausible fiction about a real poet, and everything we write will *respect* and *honor* everything we know about the man, and we'll create a believable whole and beautiful person, a full *life* including what's already known to be true about him and his time and his art. That would be our goal, sir."

"What kind of input would you want from me? Did you say something about songs?"

"Yes sir. Ben writes and publishes poetry, you know. We think he might imitate some Chatterton lyrics — our own version of 'forgeries'?! — and we'd get them set to music for the play."

"Are you aware that I am a trained flautist?"

"Flutist? You play the flute?"

"Flautist. And the piccolo. I was Pied Piper in an eighth-grade show and piped all the boys into that big black cave! My mother made me a gorgeous green three-piece suit and a feathered cap for the part."

"It was all the children, wasn't it, sir, not just the boys?"

"Just the boys. Into the cave, piping all the way."

"No, sir. We were not aware. Wow!"

"And in high school band, I memorized that piccolo obbligato in 'Stars and Stripes Forever' and got featured every time we played it."

"Yes sir, that's very impressive, sir."

"And in the 'Donna Diana' overture. Resnicek."

"Sergeant Preston of the Yukon."

"Resnicek."

"Well, this is just terrific, sir. If you'd like, we could prob'ly find a place for you and your instrument in the play. I'm thinking about tavern songs…maybe a street scene with people dancing to a flute tune — or *you* dancing a jig to your own music?"

"I might oblige. What else?"

"Well, we've wondered whether you'd like to play Chatterton."

The world bumped on its axis. Park's eyes opened very widely. His face flushed. He glanced up at the poster.

"You've got the perfect hair for it, sir," I ventured.

"I do, don't I?" he said, touching it.

"Actually," I went on, "we're thinking about double-casting the role, you as Chatterton one night, me on the other."

He dropped the wand. I stood to retrieve it and returned it carefully to the desk.

"Thank you," he said, placing his fingertips together and thumbing his chin. "Might I also have a hand in writing the dialogue?"

"That's negotiable, sir," I dared to say, recognizing the risk. "We would certainly consider it, sir."

He looked hard at me, point-blank directly into my eyes, leaned toward me: "You, Mr. Troy Tyler, you are one fucking bodacious brassy little operator, ain't you, buster? You got Trojan blood in them skinny little veins? I'll grant you the guts! And what's more, I like the fucking *hell* out of your audacious little plan! I'm thinkin' I can *use* it. But that's for later. Here," he took out a pad, "here're three titles for you guys to read. Come back to me when you've got the framework. We'll go from there."

"Excuse me, sir. Hold on. I respect your initiative, sir, and I welcome your enthusiasm, but it's our project. We're in the saddle, and we hold the reins. I'll be grateful if you crack the whip when we need it, and you'll get to rate the rodeo, but we own the roundup and we run the livestock. Are we clear? Sir?"

He looked up from the pad, startled, and then burst out laughing. "Metaphorically speaking," he said, "that's an A-plus! Yup, I get it. I'm a meek little lamb. Sorry for presuming. It's a habit. We're clear."

"You're actually approving it, sir? We can do this, with your permission, for credit?"

"As far as I'm concerned, you may try. I'll try too. We'll negotiate."

"And I can tell them it's a go?"

"Ask again and it's off. Geez Louise, Troy. It's gonna be gone in a jiff if you keep calling the question!"

6

October 9, 1957
Mr. Troy Tyler
Box 1819 - B
LCC
Lecompte, La.


Hi, Troy, great to hear from you. Thanks for writing me.

Tulane's about the same as last year but I'm used to it and comfortable. My roommate's straight and doesn't mind I'm not but we don't bring dates to the room, not that I've had any yet. With chemistry and French and calculus, I don't have much time for running around. Audubon Park is right across St. Charles from campus and I'm over there a lot with the bike on really good paths. There's also a great zoo where the seals and I are friends. The waiters at Camellia Grille know me and tell me about other great N.O. diners. Tulane food is passable but dull.

I haven't been to church yet, have you?

The streetcar takes me right to the edge of the Quarter but I've only been to a bar once. Dick's and Daisy's (aka: Dicks and Daisies) on Decatur Street. I didn't much like it. Too loud and crowded and old. No other kids. I guess it's nice to be hit on by guys but it kind of turned me off.

Maybe I wanted them to be you. Anyhow, no flesh phases around here yet.

Monte spent the night with you? I don't mean it that way unless he did. That sounds like I <u>am</u> jealous of him, doesn't it? I probly am. I'd rather he didn't sleep with you. There I said it.

I wear your medal all the time. I kiss it good night every night.

I miss you so much, Troy.

Love,
Corky

p.s. (I'm changing over to Kaiden, my other name. Time to grow up from Corky.)

October 12, 1957

Dear Kaiden,

Monte did not sleep with me. He brought his own bedroll and slept on the floor.

Jack and Ben and I have started a big project with our English professor, for credit. We think it's going to be fun.

I haven't had any dates either.

We should fix that. How can we?

I just wanted to be sure you know that Monte and I didn't....

More later.

Love,
Troy

p.s. I like 'Kaiden' a lot! The name and the guy.

* * *

"I can use it," our teacher had said. The pronoun had no antecedent, but what other could it refer to than the plan I'd just spelled out for our project? Park didn't linger on it, and might have seemed eager to leave it when postponing deliberation until "later." But what exactly did he mean — "use" — and how "use"? It feels purposeful, aimed at accomplishment, and at an exclusive, not a shared fruition. But of what sort? A personal achievement or a professional one? Maybe both? Both sounds more Royalist. Is it conceivable that Dr. Royal imagines participation in our little project might be of some advantage to his professional advancement via this tenure routing, and also might enhance his social status and consequence? That looks like a stretch to me, but maybe we're talking about any port here. Could his job actually be on the line? That also appears doubtful to me, every bit as doubtful as the likelihood that any involvement in our play would lift him in collegiate and community prestige, but what do I know? Other agencies and resources than our pathetic ones would have to be found. Isn't it more likely that we bomb and he's blamed? We might feel disappointment and embarrassment for a day or two, but he would be reproached as responsible for any failure. I suddenly saw peril in every direction for everybody, personal and professional peril, with little to gain at considerable risk, and I could hardly not wonder if we should pull the plug now.

But my focus had fuzzed. The issue was *use*. Minimally, the word served as an alert, possibly an inadvertent one, and all the weightier for that. It signaled an evolving intent to manipulate — or to consider manipulating — our little project in ways unbeknownst to ourselves, to secure leverage for his ascendancy, for his purchase of power and control. It might even predict imminent theft, not that we yet had aught to steal. Maybe his "later" looked ahead to when we did. I needed to run all this by my fellow Wise Guys.

Or, first, just by Jack, because there remained this other thing I should go back over with him, namely: What did I intend, and what did he understand, when I allowed as how I "might" want to make out with Monte? I think "might" is honestly precise. I'm not dead certain I actually wanted to, not right then, anyway, not after all our talk the night before. But it probably sounded to Jack like I *did* want to. And how did or would he take that? As my admission to membership in a brotherhood he himself may have also pledged? There were signs — or I thought there were pretty unmistakable signs — that Monte's looks may have tempted Jack. He'd almost said they did. But what did or would my confession of sympathy with his view of these matters — what would that mean for my friendship with Jack? Could two queer boys be *just* friends, without bedding, or wanting to? I did not absolutely know whether or not I wished to sleep with Jack, but I knew that I wanted to keep thinking about it: I wanted to hold onto him as a possible prospect, just as I more intensely wanted to hold onto Corky in something of the same way and for the same reason although I plainly saw the impractical foolishness of that fantasy, and arguably its dishonesty and dishonor. Whether I wanted Jack to tell me what *he* wanted, I couldn't determine either. So how was I to clarify what I'd said to Jack about Monte without opening wider the door I'd cracked? But the holding pattern we'd assumed was already unacceptable, frustrating, and disabling for the future. Undecided about what I wanted to come out of it, I figured we had to talk over our expressed shared interest in making out with Monte, as absurd as it sounded, put like that.

So I didn't put it like that to Jack when he showed up after supper in The Grove, at my invitation, in khakis and a white dress shirt with correctly rolled sleeves, sock-less in weejuns, and carrying a small notebook. He stretched out — smoothing his pants — on the light blanket I'd brought to spread across the crisp leaves and soft needles. Light was fading but the lamps hadn't yet ticked on. The twilight felt soft too.

"You want to smoke?" he asked, fingering his pack.

"Not yet," I said; "depends."

He raised his knees, crossed his arms over the skinny chest.

"I thought I'd report what Park said about our plan. You ready to hear it?"

"Of course," he said, a hint of irritation edging his tone, as though I'd wasted time asking.

"He's in. He loves it. He's checking the credit angle. He recommended books for our research. He'll consider acting Chatterton. And he thinks we can pull it off."

"Well, okay, that's good," Jack said, picking at a thread on his cuff. "That's all good. Congratulations and kudos and such. Only, Troy, I'm not so sure about it anymore. Oh, you've done great getting it this far…but it seems like it's going to take up a whole lot of time over a whole year. I mean, do we really know enough and care enough to sustain energy and interest over a whole year? It's a huge, big-time commitment."

"Bad pun," I said; "also redundant. And you sound tired. Are you already tired of it?"

"Well, I might just be," he said, looking at me. "I don't want to disappoint you, but it's such a big commitment…and we know so little to start with — like, nothing, really — I'm just not sure we're up to it."

This sudden doubt, this slimy, whiney equivocation, on top of the misgivings I had myself so recently entertained about Park's unexpected "use," well, it stung and soured me, roused my bristles: "Now look here, Jack: I went to Park, I went to Ben, with your assurance of interest, your agreement to be part of this plan, and they climbed aboard expecting your participation. I'm pretty sure their agreement's conditioned on yours. So is mine. You wimp out now and everything falls apart. Prospects have only gotten brighter with everybody's consent and excitement. What terms have changed since you agreed? Why're you trying to chicken out now?"

"I said I might be. I'm being realistic, Troy. We're bright and creative, sure, but we've got no foundation, no platform of knowledge to build on, no *grounding* in Chatterton or eighteenth-century lit or even theater. Looked at objectively, the plan's kind of barmy, idn' it? Mad? It's, like, an air-castle. There's no solid base."

"We've got Park. What more 'grounding' do we need? He's base enough." We both grinned.

"Basis," I corrected.

Two boys approached, by appearance aimlessly chatting. One pointed at us. Jack turned his face away. I lifted a hand in an indifferent wave.

"A *picnic*!" the other one hollered. "But where's the food?"

"And the *girls*?" the first added. "Where *are* the *girls*, boys?" They both shrieked giggles and poked each other.

"Scram, jerks!" I yelled. They minced on.

"Park," Jack said, turning back, "Park has a full-time job. He's also writing a book. He's also trying to earn tenure. We're not going to be his priority. He gets crunched, we and the plan will crash. Inevitably."

"I know all about Park's other obligations. From him. He listed them to me. And he says he can work with us. He should know. It's not relevant."

"And *we're* busy too. We're full-time English majors…forced to take math! We're headed to grad school. We've got work."

"No, Jack, that's wrong. We're not busy. We've got homework, yeah, but not much else. Extra-curricular freaks we're not. We don't do sports. You play cards. I do choir. Our social life isn't exactly ripping. We're not busy. We've got time for this."

"I write. Ben's not the only one who writes."

"You'll still be writing. You'll help write the play. With Park and me."

"I dunno, Troy. From his antics in Romantics, I'd say Park is about half daft. What if it's contagious?"

Laughter slightly relaxed the tension.

"At least he's unstable, maybe manic," Jack persisted. "Quixotic. What if he folds under the pressure? Where would we be then?"

"We'll have to see that he doesn't."

"I didn't sign on for baby-sitting. But we're losing the point here. I'm talking about *our* preparation, *our* training, or lack of it, for *realizing* your...your dream. I don't see evidence you've thought through the nitty-gritty of putting this show together. For public performance."

"Of course I haven't. I've conceptualized an end, and assembled a team to accomplish it."

"An inept, inexperienced, unqualified team."

"Boy, Jack, you are so wildly wrong about that! You've discounted a whole third of our team! You've forgotten *Ben*! Ben, who's actually been doing theater just about since the cradle, and worked all last year at a theater over in Aleck, where he learned stagecraft. Ben has hands-on experience: designing and building sets, lights, sounds, costumes, all the nuts and bolts of producing a show. He's got that covered. And don't forget we've got the club, The Chattertons. The whole membership will work the project, Park can see to that. There's no telling how much more experience we'll turn up once we get rolling. Don't underestimate that potential."

"You hadn't told me about Ben. Yeah, that's an asset."

"Asset! Ben's a bloody gold mine! He prob'ly should direct. But his poetry comes first. He's going to write some ballads, or maybe saloon music. Maybe involve Park's flute."

"And who's going to write the rest of it?"

"Like I just said...."

"As I said."

"As I said, you and me and maybe Park will write the script. He's mentioned he'd like to help with dialogue."

"I don't know, Troy; you really think you and I could write...*with* Dr. Royal? *With* our professor? *About* his...Tommy?"

"It gets better. I'm thinking about giving Chatterton a boyfriend. You might could play the boyfriend?"

"What? Wait! There's no evidence...*is* there?"

"No. Well, I don't actually know. But remember: we're writing fiction...based on a real person. Yes, we'll have to be careful about Park and LCC. Maybe reserve the boyfriend scenes for when I play Chatterton, and rehearse it secretly; maybe perform it only once, at the final staging. Keep Park away from *it*! Or just hint the boyfriend? But think of the scandal! The publicity! The truth is, I think the boyfriend suits the real guy perfectly: Chatt's a sensualist. He breaks rules. He lies. He experiments. He's already a revolutionary. He's *bad*! He runs with whores. Why not also with boys? It's logical. He'll welcome a boyfriend…wouldn't you?"

Jack grinned at me, his eyes bright: "What're you doing here, Troy? What's all this really about?"

"Think what you like, my boy," I said; "just don't quit."

"I never said I would."

"I'll have that cigarette now."

Lightening-bugs flecked the dusk, answering the pulses of our Viceroys. Jack snared one, cradled it in his palm. We watched its knob throb, tinting the palm pink.

"It's code," Jack said softly. "Break it for me! What's he saying?"

"'Let me go'?" I ventured. "SOS? 'This little light of mine. I'm gonna let it shine…,'" I sang the church-school strain.

He shook the bug into flight. "We used to collect them in Mason jars. I'd put one on my side table and go to sleep watching them play. They're magic."

"Magical. I bet that blinking light is about mating."

"I'll show you mine, if you…!"

We both guffawed. He leaned over to crush his cigarette butt in the grass, sat up. "Do you remember saying the other day that you'd like to do a 'project' with me? I guess this play is it. I felt the same way, though, about collaboration…with you, but I was thinking about something different. Maybe, if I help you with the play, you'd help me with something else? It's not a bribe. Maybe a trade-off?"

"I don't know if we've got time for another project, but go on, tell me."

"Okay," he said, grinning again, scrunching himself up on the blanket, pulling his crossed ankles up tight toward the crotch like a meditating monk, only he squirmed with relish. "I know you've pretty much left the church and all that, but I think you should re-consider coming with me to the Sunday night Youth Group at Broadway Baptist. I went back last Sunday."

"You did? You didn't tell me. How was it?"

"Which part? The bus ride over and back was fun: we joked, we sang, goofed off, played games. On the way home, we stopped at the Diary Queen. Two couples in the back made out."

"And…?"

"The class was great. We talked about Cain and Able. Dr. Hale asked us to explain why God favored Able, or Able's offering, over Cain's. And whether Able's resentment wasn't justified."

"You mean Cain's. Why Cain's resentment…."

"Oh, right. I never can keep them straight. You see? That's why you need to come! To keep me in line.

"Anyway: we talked about the favoritism, and how it was or wasn't fair to…Cain, and whether Cain *was* his brother's keeper, and why God made Cain *capable* of murder anyway. We debated, and it got pretty lively. You'd like it."

"I told you; I've done it. I'm tired of it." This wasn't quite true. I knew the Cain and Able story backwards and forwards, but what the Deity's "favoritism" *meant* it'd never occurred to me to ask. Or what "keeping" my brother meant either. And the question about *capability* was already a stumbler.

"Well," Jack said, "it might not be what you're tired of. It might surprise you, what we do."

"I'm pretty sure I'd recognize it. That drill hasn't changed since the Flood."

"Hmmm. It surprised you with the Genesis story, the two Genesis stories, right?"

This was regrettably true. Undeniably true.

"And I reckon, Troy, I reckon that in your secret heart of hearts that surprise gave you pleasure. Satisfaction, anyhow. Oh, you didn't show it, and you're going to deny it now: but I believe you liked it that somebody found a hole in Holy Writ!"

"I didn't. It upset me. I don't think there's any contradiction in Genesis."

"Oh, shoot, that's just pride talking. You're upset 'cause you hadn't seen it yourself. You're embarrassed 'cause you got suckered. Idn' that so?"

"It's not just me. A whole lot of other folks believe exactly what...."

"And more and more other folks don't. And some of them're in the youth group. Here's what I'm getting at: you've told me so much about Jubilee I figure you weren't as with the program as they expected, as Monte wanted you to be. You're naturally skeptical. You want to doubt; you can't *not* doubt; you're too bright not to doubt. But your heart wants you to be loyal to a belief you distrust. You got mad at me because I tempted you to doubt…and half of you DID doubt, only you didn't trust yourself to doubt. *That* upset you. And a little piece of you found your doubt satisfying. It proved something you already at least half-suspected. It pleased you, right? Are you following?"

"Not sure. I'm kind of doubting what you're doing. Where you're going."

"Of course you are. That's the plan. Where I'm wanting to go is right back to the Sunday night Youth Group, you with me. You took fire when the Bible betrayed you: not like angry; you got upset 'cause stuff had been kept from you, and you hated that. You hate deception. But mostly you got *interested*. You got *engaged*. And you'll *be* interesting *about* it if you let yourself. The group lets itself doubt. Dr. Hale — the school principal, the teacher — may encourage thoughtful doubt. He asks tough questions. You and I're probably better *readers* than anybody in the class, including Teach. We actually know how to close-read a text. We can, you know, *a-na-to-mize* a piece of writing. I'm proposing we do it together, as a team, in a group that needs a little shaking up. Dr. Hale leans to the left, yes, but the *group* is so homogenized, so rote and predictable in the way it reads scripture, it can't see the possibilities for *other* interpretations — radically overturning interpretations. It misses contradictions, ironies, paradoxes, all the little subtleties *we're* trained to find and sort. Think about it: the possibilities for revolution are endless here! You said just now that Chatterton is a revolutionary. You've proposed a revolutionary interpretation of his sexual preferences.

Guess what: we've got a chance here to stir up a little revolution of our own in the unlikeliest of places! We're just adding a little depth to the shallows Dr. Hale is already searching. And we'll do it with his permission! I think we'd have one hell of a good time, the two of us, leading this charge."

"What makes you think I'm so hot to doubt? I didn't actually *like* finding that second Genesis story."

"You did and you didn't. You didn't like being fooled. But a little voice in your head whispered, 'I knew it all along!' It *confirmed* everything you DIDN'T like about Jubilee! Every reason you're not going to church now. You've been bucking the harness for a real long time, Troy; I'm just...um...spurring you along a little here."

"Supposing that's true. What's the point of going back to church if I'm trying to leave it?"

"What if it's to take the church with you? To bring the others along? Don't you see? We'll be *teaching*! It's our first teaching jobs...as Hale's teaching assistants! Don't you feel a little *frisson* in your belly at the very idea of teaching doubt?"

"I think Matthew calls this 'temptation.'"

"You mighty right, Troy Tyler. Spot on."

He stood, smoothed his trousers. "I brought this for you," he said, "in case you don't know it." He slipped a single folded sheet out of his notebook and handed it to me. "I'm going now." He rubbed his palm across my crewcut. "You think about it...in there," he said, stroking the back of my head.

All of that...and I still hadn't mentioned making out with Monte.

October 14, 1957

Dear Monte,

I've never written your name before, or seen it, except that time you wrote it on water and the letters drowned. I don't know whether it ends with an e or a y. I prefer the e. Does it need an accent mark?

Thank you for visiting me. It was great to see you again. But I don't think you ever did anything at Jubilee that needs my forgiving, except maybe forcing me to get a manicure. Because everything you did around the speech contest was to help me win it. You honestly thought that winning was right and best for me, so what you did wasn't wrong and doesn't need forgiving. But if it makes you feel better, I forgive you.

It seems like Corky and I shocked you, and maybe hurt you? I'm very sorry, if we did. But our leaving like that wasn't a message to you especially. I guess it was sort of a message to everybody, that I had to send. That's about as much about it as I understand. But it wasn't personal.

I didn't hug you at the end because I didn't want to. I think I wanted to. But the wanting kind of scared me. I figure you know why. I figure you were maybe a little scared too, which is why you asked to. This is maybe something we need to work on.

My new friend Jack saw you at the bus shelter. He liked your uniform.

I hope you're going to be all right, Monte, about the Laura thing and all.

Your old roommate,

Troy

p.s. That sentence up there beginning "I didn't hug you" is all balled up. I think what I meant is "I didn't NOT want to hug you." Sometimes I hate English.

\* \* \*

October 15, 1957

Dear Kaiden,

Are you going home to Vicksburg for Thanksgiving? What if we both get heavy homework and have to work on it and can't go home? If your roommate is gone, what if I took the bus to New Orleans to see you for Thanksgiving? Could you maybe put me up and show me around? I've never been to New Orleans. I think I'm asking you for a date for that whole weekend.

Love,

Troy

\* \* \*

October 18, 1957

Dear Troy,

Yes.

Love,
K.

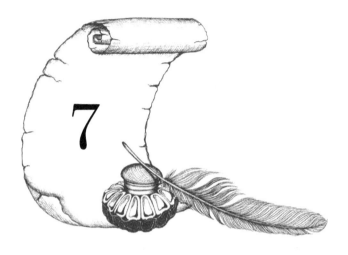

**7**

Our initiation into The Chatterton Honors Literary Society took place without much fanfare: we newbies were nine, which increased the Club membership to twenty-four — eleven guys (three of us Wise), thirteen girls — all English or Humanities majors pretty even-ly spread over sophomore, junior, and senior years, all on time and smartly dressed. In a navy blazer and gray slacks, a blue button-down hugging a startling pink as-cot, Park presided, introduced us (Jack again standing!), quoted from the charter about our purpose ("...to cul-tivate and promote the literary arts..."), read lines from Emily Dickinson and Walt Whitman and then asked Ben to deliver a (clean) section from Ginsberg's "Howl," which Ben ably did (with a little drama), and encour-aged us to write and to submit manuscripts to "Quill and Scroll," LCC's semi-annual journal of student creative work. Eventually, he said, we'd receive little gold lapel pins — shaped like the quill-and-scroll insignia — dangling from a tiny chain the last two digits of our graduation year. No sworn oaths; no sacred pledges; nothing about fees; no mortifying stunts, which I'd more or less expected even while knowing first- hand how Park prized decorum. Finished, he flung back the white tablecloth draping a huge crystal bowl of bright red punch ringed by plates of chocolate cookies with local pecans, courtesy of the Royal kitchen, which we now officially fledged Chattertons made short, noisy work of.

With mid-term tests, themes, and other deadlines approaching before the Thanksgiving break, I'd back-burnered Chatterton research but now needed to check-out with Ben my ideas for developing a plot for our play so he might begin imagining set designs to accommodate and complement them. Jack and I hadn't exchanged word one about the story we'd tell, and I didn't want Park to get the first one lest he thus capture the balance and the sway. I did want to float by Ben the few notions I had for dramatic situations wanting sets, and for sets wanting dramatic situations, based on my early research, but Ben had missed Romantics today and wasn't obvious in the Library or the student lounge. Boarding the bus for his neighborhood, I took a chance on finding him home.

The motorcycle wasn't parked on the Harrison drive but I knocked on the front door anyway. It opened upon quite a large black man in black formal wear, his collar and cuffs and starched shirt-front a gleaming contrast against all the black. "Yes?" he said in a deep, rising baritone.

"Good afternoon, sir," I smiled. "I'm Troy Tyler, from the College. I'm looking for my friend Ben Moore. I believe he lives here."

"You don't see his motor, he isn't to home."

"Excuse me, sir, but are you sure? He doesn't seem to be at school either."

"Mr. Moore wouldn't be here if his motor isn't. But you're welcome to check his suite, if you wish."

"Well, thanks. Yes, I'd at least like to knock. May I?"

"Of course," he said, stepping back, out of the entrance. "I'll accompany you."

We headed toward the wide staircase, him leading. But halfway down it stood a regal figure, her fingers trailing the handrail, her right hand gripping an ivory-handled cane.

"Who is that, Rodney?" she asked in a silver, fluty tone.

"A Mr. Tyler, ma'am, from the College, inquiring after Mr. Moore."

"A student!" she exclaimed, smiling and stepping gracefully down. "How heavenly! And just in time for cocktails! I'm Arabella Harrison, my dear."

"Yes'm. I live in your husband's quad. I mean, the quad named for your husband."

"My regrettably deceased husband. You may call me Belle. Everybody does, except Rodney. I adore students. Especially boy students. Do step into the drawing room, won't you, and join me for spirits? You're legal, of course?"

"Madam," Rodney said; "he's inquiring after Mr. Moore. We're just heading up…"

"He's away, Rodney. I heard him leave a while back. But Mr. Tyler mustn't be allowed to waste his trip. Please clear Mr. Billy's chair. And now, young man, you will join me, won't you, for a shocking New Orleans Sazarac?"

"Thank you, ma'am, but I prob'ly should be going, if Ben isn't here."

"Nonsense. You may take his place, if you'll confess your Christian name. I never take strong drink with anyone whose Christian name is kept from me. Please, what's yours?"

"I'm Troy, ma'am. Troy Tyler."

"That's pagan, isn't it, Rodney?" she fluted. "Are you pagan, Troy Tyler? You don't *look* in the least pagan."

"I hope not, ma'am. But I really think I should be going now, if Ben isn't…."

"Don't insult me child, and stop saying that! What's wrong with *me*? Won't *I* do for company?"

"Oh yes, ma'am, you'll certainly do…oh, rats, I don't mean it like that, sorry…."

She laughed, a big-voiced hearty peal, her eyes crinkling up and her lenses glinting in the light.

"Come, come, lad," she said gently, patting the seat Rodney had cleared. "You sit down here now, and compose yourself. I've frightened you, I see. Please forgive me. Any friend of Ben's…and so on. Prepare the spirits,

Rodney, light on the cognac for Mr. T. You just settle back there now, Troy dear, and tell me truly what I may do for you today."

"Really, ma'am, I'm fine. I just got a little flustered there. I'm so sorry. I apologize."

"Accepted. Now. How do you know Ben, and, if I may ask, why you came calling?"

And I told her, unwrapped the whole harebrained, cockamamie story of our unplanned plans for the play, feeling more foolish with every word, with every word more certain that she had zero interest in my raw project and regretted her hospitality. How could this matron of the regional *beau monde* and privileged daughter of the LCC peerage possibly afford the leisure and curiosity about me and my puny little scheme to produce a play about a moody, hot-headed and inconsequential eighteenth-century wannabe poet and proven thief and criminal forger who couldn't hold a job and ran with riffraff and patronized diseased whores and failed at everything he tried and finally poisoned his poor depressed self of seventeen years? What right had I to invade her home and tax her patience with boring yak about my half-baked notion to rally classmates I barely knew and other students I didn't to a doubtful cause I'd dimly imagined based on controversial facts and fishy speculations I'd lightly browsed? Yet here we were, I over my head, she surely dazed, sipping iced cocktails, I suddenly noticed, approximately the same copper color as Park Royal's hair.

We occupied two red-leathered, button-tufted throne-chairs facing the television set in the spacious living room with floor-to-ceiling, heavily draped windows across the front and along the side toward the drive, lighted by a massive and elaborately festooned chandelier behind ourselves. A dusky maroon rug stretched to the shoe-moldings on all sides. Oil and watercolor art in ruggedly sculpted gold-leaf frames hung the walls. A concert grand piano, its lid raised, swarmed the rear of the room. Clubs, wingbacks, armchairs and two matching Chesterfield sofas, all richly upholstered and cushioned by puffy pillows, joined tasteful tables of polished dark wood to fill out the space. An imposing silver tea service stood to the left of my hostess's chair.

She reigned. All she needed was a scepter, and her cane would almost serve the purpose, propped as it was, upright, in a stately posture against her chair-back, her high, coiled, luminous white hair glowing like a crown. The slightly blue tint of the hair matched the eyes, bright and sparkling with alertness and possibly mischief, the lips poised to smile. She showed large though not fat: big-boned, fleshed: matronly. She sat straight, feet in low-heels flat on the floor, both limbs resting on the chair arms, the drink glass cupped in her right hand, her left fingers jeweled in silver. The chin almost disappeared into the fleshy folds under it and the snug lace collar under them. She was maybe four degrees shy of majestic, but not at all monarchic: the demeanor was warm, kindly, even benevolent. Receptive. She let me ramble, occasionally nodding, after every sip touching to her lips a lace handkerchief then tucked back into her sleeve.

The cognac — my first, ever — had right away loosened my tongue, and the second Sazarac near 'bout unhitched it. I'd prattled far too long, laboriously, drably.

"So that's pretty much our idea, ma'am, Ben's and Jack's and mine, and Dr. Royal is giving us credit, and wants to help. That's why I wanted to see Ben, to catch him up on where we are…and aren't."

"And you aren't very far, correct? Had I known you were calling, I'd have kept him home. Sometimes he just disappears. I fancy with a girl. For a girl. I forbid them on the premises."

"Yes'm. Ben likes girls."

Another misstep. It begs a smart-ass reply: *Don't you?*

"I'm familiar with the Royal family, you know," she said, smiling at her own double entendre. "I've known Park practically from his nativity."

"Wait! You know our professor?" I almost fumbled my glass.

"You'll find Lecompte a very small, very southern town, my lad. My dearly beloved and sadly departed husband Billy chaired the LCC Board of Trustees for longer than he lived, and Papa Royal was on it for a while; but we knew the Royals mainly through the church and saw them every two years at the big Southern Baptist Conventions, often in Dallas, where Billy always had meetings and Papa Royal did ranch business and I'd baby-sit Park until Etienne arrived, three years after

Park. Billy helped him get the job here. You probably know to be cautious around Park?"

My mind was cloudy but I caught something in her voice, maybe the question mark.

"Well, he can be sort of...unpredictable?"

"He means well," she backtracked. "He tries hard. He'll offer aid and comfort to all yawl. But tell me more about this play. Who's heading the tech crew?"

"Wait, please. Who's Etienne?" I gave it the French pronunciation, as she had.

"Etienne Fontenot Harrison. Our son. I debuted as a Fontenot. Etienne died at thirteen of polio two years before the vaccine got here. That's part of the reason, you see, I like to have boys in the house."

"I'm so sorry ma'm, I had no idea. I'm so sorry to have asked."

"Yes. It is a great and everlasting sorrow. But we endure." She cleared her throat. "So. About the tech crew for the play?"

"Are you sure...ma'am...?

"Do you even *have* one...?"

"Well, Ben's got experience from working at The Dark Horse over in Aleck last year. He might be in charge of the tech stuff."

"Are you yet familiar with the name 'Gladiola Peytonberry'?"

"No, ma'am. I don't think I know her."

"Regrettable. You should. She's rather famous around New Orleans."

"Unfortunately, I haven't yet been to New Orleans. Except to pass through. I'm going, though, at Thanksgiving. To see a friend."

"Yes. Good. It is essential for all young men to visit New Orleans, once they're legal. But don't tell my pastor I said that." She sipped and patted, and went on.

"Did you check your horoscope this morning, Mr. Tyler? This just might become a most auspicious day for you! As it happens, not long ago Belle Fontenot majored in English and Drama at Sophie Newcomb College right next door to Tulane, which has always had a distinguished theater program. Tulane Theater got its women from Newcomb. I was already a little bit heavy for romantic leads, so I usually ended up on the tech crew headed up by Dr. Gladiola Peytonberry, Ph.D. in costume design from the Carnegie School of Drama. Dr. Glad's still the Edith Head of New Orleans theater. She taught me, and then I worked for her a couple of years after graduation."

"No kidding? You worked in theater? Wow! That's so cool!"

"Not in New Orleans, it isn't. It's very hot! Always hot. Anyhow, Gladiola and I keep in touch. She's retired from Newcomb but stays active behind the scenes in N.O. theater. I've brought her to LCC Drama for a couple of lectures."

She rattled the ice loudly and in a moment Rodney was there. I shook my head no. "Probably best," she said. "A half please, Rodney.

"But that's beside the point. I meant to say something else...about why it may be your auspicious day! You see, Troy, I've got this whole gaggle of widow ladies in Lecompte and Aleck who gather twice a month at somebody's home, sometimes here, for canapés and coffee and tittle-tattle, and we exchange patterns and compare piecework and join up on bigger needle-and-thread handiwork, and not just quilts either, we're past quilts. We just might be pining to tackle a prodigious project like costumes for your dramatis personae! What might you boys think of that?"

"I'm sorry, Mrs. Harrison, but I'm not quite sure what you're asking. Or offering. Would you care to explain...?"

"Is it really that unclear, Troy? Or are you playing hard to get? What if I turned my old girls loose to make costumes for your cast? You're certain to need a lot more help in that line than Park Royal can offer. You and Ben and was it Jack? will have to tell us the play plot, and in due course we'll measure and tailor and fit — I'll bet you've never seen how a real costume shop works? — and we'll have everybody dressed up to beat the band by opening night!"

"Yes'm, but, ma'am, we don't have a budget for... well...for anything, really, or any fund-raising plans. So we couldn't afford.... We wouldn't want to put you to the trouble...."

"Tell me not what I am capable of. You have no idea. I'm of a mind to give you help. And I can turn other minds."

"But we don't have, like, costume stock, or scraps or leftovers from other productions, like property or materials to start with…."

"Fiddlesticks! My girls and I have stuffed closets and packed trunks and jammed lockers running over with raiment from a hundred years just waiting and hoping for rescue and renewal! Just like *us*! And we'll have nothing better to do than stitch if also given a chance to relive happy college days. Why, dear boy, we'll *donate* the materials and the time. We'll turn my parlor into the Newcomb sewing room and become schoolgirls all over again! Stretch your mind and imagine the thrill it'll give us all to play at drama with youth a fourth our age! The fun we'll have decking yawl out!"

Right about here it flashed on me like a revelation that another strong personality mere weeks ago had taken the traces of Troy's project between his determined teeth and dragged it into directions and shapes undreamt of in my philosophy. Was I so pathetically needy, so worthlessly inept, that I was already on the verge of allowing my new project to risk similar distortion, similar deformity, through well-intentioned collaboration?

"It's a grand and generous offer, Mrs. Harrison, ma'am, and I'm most grateful for it. But we don't even have specific characters in mind yet, not more than two or three, so it would be premature to start thinking about costumes now."

"Dear boy, costumes look for characters to clothe! Costumes create the characters they cloak. You may trust me on that. Why, I've seen.... But no matter. You've heard, I expect, how God works in mysterious ways?"

"Well, sure, I've heard that said. But I don't see...."

"Maybe God called Ben away this afternoon so you and I could stumble onto each other and drink and talk. About theater. About costumes. Maybe this is supposed to happen? Don't you want it to?"

"Mrs. Harrison, that would be amazing. I'm very grateful. Of course I am. But I'll need to run it all by Jack and Ben."

"And Park. You should talk to Park."

"Yes'm. Also to Dr. Park."

"Pitch it to Park; get *him* to pitch Chatter-box to my widows since he knows all about the boy, and you need to be writing. Give us a chance here and we'll be singing at our treadles within a month, I guarantee it."

"I'll try to get back to you asap. Would that be okay?"

"That would be expected. Don't take long. I might cool off. And once my old girls know, there won't be any holding them back. And call me Belle. Everybody does, except Rodney."

"Nome, we won't take long. And now I should be getting home. Thank you so much for the drinks and the really interesting conversation."

"How did you arrive?"

"On the city bus, ma'am. It stopped only a couple of blocks away."

"The Lecompte system closes at 6." She pressed a small button I hadn't noticed on the arm of her chair. I heard a faint buzz.

"Rodney," she said as he appeared in the doorway, "the car. Please return Mr. Tyler to the College. To the Harrison Quadrangle. It's been a true and capital pleasure, Troy, to meet you," she said, extending her hand as though from queen to subject, for a kiss. I shook it. "You come back now, hear?" she said, turning. "I'll tell Ben all about it."

"Um, no, ma'am. I'd best do that."

"He's such a loser," Ben growled.

We three Wise Guys had fallen into step upon leaving Park's Romantics class where he'd lectured ably on the leech-gatherer in Wordsworth's "Resolution and Independence," scoring good points when spelling out the ambiguities of "resolution" as both *decision* and *solution* but then none at all when applying both meanings to his "boy" Tommy, and then straying, at line 43, into unrelated musings about his precious academic specialization:

> I thought of Chatterton, the marvelous Boy,
> The sleepless soul that perished in his pride…

Had he forgotten that at least three of us knew at least a little about Chatterton, too? But now I wasn't sure who Ben referenced with "loser."

"Who is?" I asked. "Wordsworth or Park or Chatt?"

"That boy!" Ben scoffed.

We got coffee and settled at a Snack Bar table. Jack lit up.

"I read that book you got Park to recommend," Ben continued, glaring at me, "and that Tommy boy is a complete deadbeat. He's not just a fraud. He's a cipher. There's nothing to him. Nobody knows who he is, or cares, or reads him, or ever did. Nobody talks or reads medieval, even in the eighteenth century. I dunno why we're making a play about him, or should want to."

"Nobody reads Blake either," I said, resenting the tirade, and alarmed. "But he's still in textbooks. On the syllabus."

"Wrong!" Ben barked. "Ginsberg reads Blake. Ginsberg *sings* Blake. Performs Blake. For audiences. There's no comparison."

"So what're you saying?" Jack asked. "Why're you so steamed?"

"Because this Chatterton freak is a first-class loser. He's nobody. I wasted my time reading that book, and we're wasting ours even talking about him. So is Park. The kid's the absolute definition of dead-end."

"Just hold up here," I said, "and keep your voice down. And how about cooling it on the name-calling? I don't know what's got into you, Ben, but I don't like it, and you need to get over it. We're all on the same project here, and I'm not letting it fall apart because you don't happen to like a book a qualified professor of English recommended as a valuable resource."

"Assistant Professor," Jack corrected.

"I like and respect you, Troy," Ben continued, "but I can't hardly believe you've let Park hoodwink you into idolizing this quack as a reputable poet. I bet you haven't even read whatever book Park recommended. You haven't if you still want to celebrate him with his own so-called play."

"Have you?" Jack asked me. "Have you read your book? Because I haven't read mine."

"No, I haven't finished mine either," I admitted. "But I've read around a lot. I know the story. And he's *famous*, Ben. He's *known*."

"Oh, c'mon, Troy. Stop pretending. Jack: say something."

"Well," Jack said, squirming, "I guess I have my doubts. More about us, though, than the project. I already told Troy I don't think we've got the background — the know-how — to make it work. We're short on basics: about Chatt, for sure, and also about the century, about playwriting and dramaturgy — I barely know the word — about Bristol and publishing back then, and law. About cultural context. Reading three books isn't gonna fill all those gaps."

"Park can do 'cultural context' for us. And maybe," I said, conceding a little to gain a little, "maybe Chatt wasn't such hot stuff *alive*, but after he died he got really popular. People got interested. Admiring. Even Dr. Johnson called him a genius. Everybody wanted a piece of him."

"And then they didn't," Ben said. "He got discredited. Discarded. He doesn't *matter* now. Nobody but Park thinks he does."

"That's not true. There's a whole library shelf of scholarly books about him."

"Has anybody ever checked them out? Look, Troy, if you *do* know the story 'generally,' and I don't doubt you do, you also know the guy is a creep and a con from the wrong side of Bristol and wrote shit. He's a freaking imposter, and he wouldn't even own the shit he published, but shoved it off on a made-up medieval monk."

"Like Walpole," Jack said. "Walpole did that, with *Otranto*."

"And then betrayed the kid when he asked for help. A bad lot, all of them. It's all hooey, boys. Why-ever would we want to make it respectable, give it fame by starring him in a big college drama we earn academic credit for putting together? I bet there's an honor code violation somewhere in that plan. It feels dishonorable to me, holding up this fake as a paradigm of Romantic art or something when he's first to last a freaking fraud. And it rubs off on us. How are we not fools for favorably spotlighting this…humbug?"

"You understand, Ben," I ventured, "that when you slam Chatt like that you're also slamming Park? You're saying Park's been suckered. And is suckering us. You're trashing our professor's competence and judgment."

"Well, about Park," Ben said, scratching his beard, "assistant professor. Park's a big part of the problem I'm having here: I know this thing is Troy's original idea but it feels like the whole project is sort of Park's baby, and we're his three little minions sent off to do the dirty work of putting together a public celebration of his boy. It's like the twerp in that big painting on his office wall has stood up and walked straight into our laps and said, 'Write me!' And we're supposed to do it because Park wants us to. To please Park."

This scored. I mentally calculated: do I tell them now? Do I tell them at all? Telling them could only hurt my case. What would telling them mean for the project? What would it mean for me re them? Would telling them mean I'd better also tell them about Mrs. Harrison's warning I should "be careful" around Park?

"There's something you should probably know," I said, not calculating very well at all. "When I laid out our plans to Park, the first thing he said was, 'I can use it.' Or maybe he said, 'I might could use it.' But the word 'use' was in what he said. I don't know what he meant."

"I could prob'ly guess," Ben said, after moment. "The guy's an opportunist. Maybe he didn't mean anything specific. Maybe he just stated an intention to watch it develop and stay alert. But I'll tell you what he *did* do, damn him: he claimed ownership. He made the project his own, right there. And he tagged us his little lackeys to make it happen."

We went very quiet. He let it soak. And then went on:

"You know, I feel kind of sorry for Park. He's staked his entire future on this shabby monkeyshine of a boy-poet. And sooner or later that's gonna expose him as a phony scholar with zero odds for career success, none with that albatross dragging him down. (Yeah, I've read the bird ballad.) And can you even imagine the LCC ruckus when word leaks he's sponsoring a show starring a high school dope-fiend con-artist with VD who killed himself? And if Troy gives Chatt a boyfriend, that'll rain down fire and brimstone like fucking Sodom itself!"

"We'd keep that quiet," I almost whispered.

"We'd never," Jack said.

"No," Ben said. "I don't trust Park to keep anything quiet. I don't trust him at all."

"So how," I asked, my dander up, "do you get off being so charitable and high-minded to feel sorry for Park when you're smearing him with every other word? You're cutting him no slack at all. He's not that bad. He's been pretty sweet to me."

Poor timing for that phrase.

"Not when he reamed you out for being absent," Jack said.

"My granny always said, 'You lie down with dogs…,'" from Ben.

"Oh please," from me. "Park's not contaminated. He's not poison. I don't see we're at any risk here."

"But he *is* contaminated," Ben insisted. "By Chatterton's poison. He's leagued with a scoundrel. And we *are* at risk. Our reputations are on the line here, as serious students of Brit lit headed to grad school and jobs as professors. Our future as published poets and authors is at stake. LCC people are gonna write rec letters for us in less than two years. Do we want them remembering us as Park's protégés? We get linked now with him in folks' minds, we'll always be."

"But," I said, "we'll want his rec, won't we? What'll he write if we drop him now, after getting this far with him aboard?"

"We're not that far," Jack said.

"Why would we ask him?" Ben said. "All of our teachers are more reputable than Park. And he mayn't even *be* here in two years. This isn't a worry."

"But what if," I asked, grasping, "what if the suicide exonerates Chatterton? What if guilt killed him? Couldn't we write the play to say that? Wouldn't that be redeeming?"

"That is such total bullshit, Troy," Ben said, "and you know it. There's no way suicide washes him clean. He's still and always the lying, swindling, cheating… blackguard…he ever was."

"Troy?" Jack said.

In the silence, I reached for his Viceroys and lighter, took a deep drag.

"Give me till Monday to talk to Park," I said. "I need to confer. Don't anybody say anything. Not even to Mrs. Harrison, Ben. But I may have a word with her. Okay?"

"Not unless I'm there when you do," Ben said.

"So we can just pause here through the weekend? Think it over? I'll see you in class on Monday?"

"No, no," Jack said; "we'll see each other Sunday night, remember, Troy? We're going to the Church Youth Group. I invited Ben, too. You're coming, Ben? The bus leaves from The Gate at 6:30."

"I'm considering," Ben said. "But if I come, it'll be on my bike. At 7?"

"At 7. Do come, Ben. I think you'll like it. Troy?"

"I said I would."

"I've got a date, boys," Ben said. "Better run. Ciao."

"See ya!" Jack said, scooting his chair nearer the table and folding his hands on it. "You *are* coming, right, Troy? On Sunday night?"

"I guess. I looked up the assigned Bible passage. It's got promise."

"See? I knew you'd think so, if you looked at it in the right way."

"You mean the wrong way. You want me and Ben to look at it...suspiciously. Unconventionally. Like it doesn't say what everybody has always said it says."

"Ben and me. And yes. That's what I hope you'll do. You want to try it out on me now?"

"No. I'm hungry. How about lunch? Let's get out of here. Go downtown. Sizz's?"

"Perfect," Jack breathed, jiggling his keys.

The Sizzle Griddle was an institution in Aleck, surely its oldest and most popular drive-in and dine-in restaurant for young and old alike, with girls to serve the cars, table-top juke boxes with current and oldies hits, rare steak burgers drooling grease, the biggest, crustiest fried onion rings ever, and thick, chocolate frosties you ate with a spoon.

The booth didn't let Jack smooth his khakis before sitting.

"They should hire boys to serve the cars too, doncha think?" he grinned.

"Or replace the girls with them," I wisecracked before thinking about it.

"Amen to that," Jack said.

I flipped through the box selections for some Elvis.

"Let's not," Jack said. "How 'bout we talk instead?"

"We just did," I said, sort of wanting a break from the intensity. "Or rather, Ben and I just did. You weren't a lot of help back there," diving right back into the intensity.

"No, you're right," Jack agreed. "I wasn't. Sorry. But I didn't know what to say. Ben was pretty overwhelming."

"He'd prepared. He'd decided to quit and didn't want to get talked out of it."

"Will you try?"

"Of course I will. And I will succeed. Once we get rolling, he'll come back. We'll ask him for some ballad lyrics, get Park to set them, to the flute or maybe a guitar. Ben'll volunteer set designs. He's invested. He just doesn't know he is."

"I dunno, Troy. He sounded pretty firm."

"Don't you be doubting me here, Jack. I need you with me. I'm not giving up on this just because…well, I'm not. There's certain potential here. We owe it to ourselves…."

We ordered "the works" and fell silent. He lit up, offered.

"You wanted to talk?" I asked, exhaling.

"Yeah," Jack said, his throat froggy. He cleared it. "I've been wondering…whether you ever looked at

Auden's poem. You haven't mentioned it." His blue-gray eyes searched my face, almost pleaded.

He referred to the folded sheet he'd handed me, at the end of our conversation in The Grove, bearing his carefully hand-written copy of W. H. Auden's "Lullaby." I'd never read the poem, or heard of it, but I liked it right away for its haunting, melancholy loneliness. On the other hand, some lines baffled and confused me: I couldn't quite make out the *point* of it, its *theme* or argument. So I researched it and found little except the fascinating fact that Auden was queer and the hypothesis that the poem was addressed to an unknown, young, also queer hustler: "trade," said one dictionary. Which raised the most interesting question of all: Why did Jack give it to me? What was the *message* of the gift?

"You know," he said, then quoted the opening lines of the poem:

"Lay your sleeping head, my love,
Human on my faithless arm…."

I understood, all right, that Auden, and through him Jack, was telling me that I'm safe while blissfully sleeping on the lover's arm, but not so much when I wake up. How is that "soothing," which is how dictionaries describe "lullaby"?

Jack went on:

"Time and fevers burn away
Individual beauty from

Thoughtless children, and the grave
Proves the child ephemeral:
But in my arms till break of day
Let the living creature lie,
Mortal, guilty, but to me
The entirely beautiful."

"Yes," I said, "but I didn't know it before. I kind of liked it, but I didn't understand all of it. Do you?"

"Maybe not all of it. Most of it. I think it's almost unbearably sad."

"Well, it's lonely. Is that what you're trying to say?"

"You know, I hate when teachers ask that. And they ask it all the time. We never know what anyone is *trying* to say. We only ever know what they *do* say. And poets nearly always say it very well. They *succeed* at trying."

"Oops. Did I touch a nerve there?" I asked.

"It's just such a dumb question, what they ask. It's always the wrong question. And we always let it pass and answer the other one, the right one, the one they never ask: What has the poet written? What does the writing say, in and beyond itself?"

"All right. So what has Auden written? What's he saying?"

Jack reached into his back pocket. "I brought a copy, in case," he said. I felt my heart kick.

He unfolded the sheet, pressed on the wrinkles, pushed it across to me.

"I've got most of it by heart," he said.

"Well," I said, "why don't you recite the first...paragraph? This time to me."

Our food arrived, and we busied ourselves with napkins and cutlery and shakers and bottles. Nibbled, bit, slurped the frosties off our spoons.

"You said 'paragraphs,'" Jack said; "I don't know whether they're stanzas or verse-paragraphs, but you may be right. They're all the same length; they all have the same number of feet per line. But they aren't rhymed. Is there a ten-line stanza in English verse?"

"Yes," I said. "And you know it. You've read it forever. We'll read it again later in Romantics."

"No, I don't know."

"Keats's 'Urn.' 'Ode on a Grecian Urn.' 10-line stanzas. Rhymed."

"Hot damn, Troy! How'd you know that?"

"Now you know it too! Actually, we did six weeks on genres in Junior High English. Teacher was a genre freak. I guess some of it stuck."

"Well, it's not Auden's stanza. But I think you're right. These must be verse-paragraphs."

"Okay. You're gonna recite the first one. I'd like you to recite it to me."

He wiped grease from his fingers and lips, moved the sheet to the side, dropped his hands into his lap, and recited the first paragraph again, with feeling.

"It sounds good aloud, doesn't it?" I said. "Musical."

"Well, it's a 'lullaby.'"

"Only it isn't." I took a loud bite out of an onion ring. "Not the way you think of lullabies. It's not what you'd sing to a baby. And anyway they're waking up. I think it's an aubade, speaking of genres. It's a dawn-song. Morning music. After a night of....whatever."

"But it's tonally dark. It's not bright, like morning. Look at that 'faithless arm.'" He brought the sheet back under his eyes. "And passing time and fevers burning... and the grave of lost children. And that guilty mortal. And yet it's all somehow still 'entirely beautiful'? That's what I mean about sad."

"And what I mean about 'confusing.' Don't you think it's confused? Contradictory?"

"No. Auden's a great poet. Everybody says so. And this is a very famous poem. We read it in high school."

"You *did*? Woah! That surprises me."

"Why?"

"Well, because it's...it's...so.... No, wait. Wait. Back up. I don't want to do it this way. Let's start over." I sat back, looked off. Fiddled the fork.

"What's wrong, Troy? What's happened? Why're you flustered?"

"There's another question. A prior question. I want to start with it."

I scooted my hands down the napkin along my thighs.

"Well," he said. "What question?"

"Why you gave me the poem?"

"I liked it. I thought you might like it too."

"No. Why, *really*? What were you *saying* to me with the gift? What were you *telling* me by *giving* it to me?"

He turned his head away but was almost grinning. "Oh, come on," he said, looking back at me. "Why't you take a wild, wild guess?"

"All right, then. But you asked! I think…I think… you're using this poem, and sort of copying it…by getting *us* to use it to start talking about something not this poem but maybe in it. Something we can't seem to get direct about. *And,* something Auden can't or won't get direct about either. How close am I?"

"To what? To talking about it?"

"Depends. I'm kind of scared of going on…without, you know, a signal from you it's okay to. Are we, like, on the same page here?"

"Auden's page?" Jack asked. "I'd say we're dancing around on Auden's page where he's also dancing around something. Maybe it's a fire. Maybe he's dancing around a fire but getting closer and closer to burning all the time? Is that what you mean?"

"Yes, Jack, I think that's pretty much what I mean. If it's what you mean. Can we just say that we mean it and move on… into it?"

"So what is Auden not saying? And why is he not?"

"Because he can't. Just like we thought we couldn't either. Only he *is* saying it…obliquely. Just as we've been half-saying it, sort of saying it, coyly saying it, right along, clumsily. Are you following me?"

"I don't know about 'following.' I gave you the poem."

"Okay. Cutting to the chase: you gave me the poem so we could talk about two guys waking up in bed together and how one of them feels about what happened. And what what happened means. How it affects *everything*! Experience, world-view, morals, memory, emotions, having sex, all that shit. All about how last night *matters*, but then again possibly doesn't?"

Jack picked up his burger and took a big bite, chewed slowly, looking at me. "Well. That's over. The poem worked. We're almost talking. How cool is that?"

"Half-cool. There's three more...paragraphs...in the poem."

"There *are*," Jack said; "there *are* three more."

8

Jack told me to "look nice" for the Youth Group meeting, so I'd brought out my freshly laundered and starched blue dress shirt, my suit trousers, my favorite blue-and-grey striped bow-tie and matching socks, my polished lace-ups, and figured to show passably chic for the event…except for my hair, still mostly blond but shading toward honey. On our train-ride to New Orleans, Corky/Kaiden and I had studied a magazine feature on men's hairstyles, and he, pointing to several labeled "Ivy League," suggested I should "mature" out of the crew-cut I'd sported since junior high and try the Ivy look: "it's still clean-cut," he said, "still classic," above the ears and short on the side, with a defined part, and the top combed over from the part and a low pompadour in the front. "Disciplined preppy," I said, and decided on the spot to go for it. No haircut since. So I'd grown shaggy, and conspicuously unruly, because while the crewcut had kept my three ridiculous cowlicks under control, the growing length delivered them, and only liberal applications of Brylcreem could at least briefly restrain them. He, sockless in brown weejuns and a white button-down and plain brown knit tie tucked neatly into his khakis, waited for me at The Gate shelter with several other LCC'ers he already knew.

"This is my friend Troy," he said, waving me to them; "he's giving us a try tonight."

Murmurs, nods, a wave, a smile or two; and then a short, heavy, round girl with bouffant hair and turquoise-rimmed, cat-eyed glasses detached herself from the group and stepped toward me.

"Hi-yah," she said, offering a plump hand with rings. "I'm Sheila Barnes," smiling around large teeth. "I know you from Choir. I'm contralto. Glad to have you. Great hair!"

"Oh, thanks," I stammered, fingering my sprigs. "I'm growing it out. It's kind of a mess."

"I might have something could help." She actually winked, and giggled. "This is Jeff," she said, tugging up a skinny, pale guy with a slight limp, "and that's Shirley and Eloise and Casey Mullins. Shirley's my roomie. You'll meet the rest on the bus. You want to share a seat with me?"

I didn't. I'd looked forward to sharing one with Jack, going and coming, again remembering having shared one with Corky on the long ride to New Orleans and what happened (and didn't) there. No graceful way, though, of dodging Sheila here, and Jack had fled.

"Sure," I said, as the muddy, grubby old yellow school bus rolled up and squealed to a stop.

"That's a D-flat," Sheila laughed.

She took the window and talked most of the way, around smacking Dentyne gum, its flavor steeping our air: about Choir, her hometown Biloxi, her Siamese Merlin, her voice teacher: "I'm a music ed major," she said; "what's your bag?"

"I'm an English major," I said. "I read a story where a student says that to his teacher, and the teacher says, 'Indeed. What regiment?'" But Sheila didn't get it.

"My worst subject," she said; "I never figured out diagramming sentences, did you?"

"Well, I got where I could do it, sometimes. I never saw the point, though."

She was staring at my head.

"Is it standing up?" I asked, feeling gingerly around my skull.

She sucked on two fingers and reached into my hair, pulled at some strands, pressed them into place. "There," she said. "Maybe that'll hold...."

Ben was leaning against his bike when we scraped the curb. I excused myself and joined him to wait for Jack, who'd sat with three guys at the back of the bus.

"Screen me while I smoke," he said, reaching for his pack.

But the three guys walked up to scope Ben's bike.

"Cool, man!" one said. "Okay if I touch it?"

"Naaw," Ben said, but grinning. "I just waxed her. She's allergic to fingerprints."

"Well," another drawled, "she's a true beauty. Where'd you get her?"

"Stole her!" Ben bragged. "Off a cop!" But when nobody laughed, he switched off, shrugged, said: "Naaw, I bought her second-hand in Monroe, where I'm from, fixed her up. She loves me, especially the beard!"

"She's really cool," the first one repeated, practically licking his lips. "I've always wanted one."

"Hey, Jack," the third one said to my hovering pal, still fiddling with his pack and lighter; "no smoking on church property. Besides, we better get inside. It's past time."

"Jake, David, Nathan," Jack said, skipping by the three and touching their heads: "Sounds like books of the Bible, dudn' it?"

"Are you with us?" Nathan asked.

"Let's find out," from Ben.

Dr. Luther Hale, Senior High Principal at The Rutledge Gentlemen's Academy — the nearest thing to a finishing school Louisiana boys had — greeted us at the door as we filed in, about fifteen of us, and took seats on the folding metal chairs facing a table and swivel chair, themselves sitting before a clean green chalk board. On the walls hung maps and framed sayings — Bible verses, pithy quotations, short poems — and children's crayon drawings and staged group photos of stiff, smiling adults. The thermostat was set so low that Jack and I both rolled our sleeves back down and buttoned our cuffs. Ben wore his usual black, including the leather jacket. Though we were quiet, our leader rapped loudly with knuckles.

"I'm Dr. Hale," he said, "And you are...?" He pointed at Sheila, in the first chair to his left, and we did the routine self-introductory drill around the ring, saying our names and hometowns and schools, the only curiosities for me two senior boys from Rutledge and two other guys from the Baptist seminary on the southern outskirts of Aleck. Then Dr. Hale prayed blessings on the meeting to follow.

"For first-timers," he said, "we usually begin by reciting the 23rd Psalm. If you need a copy, find a Bible under your chairs. The Book of Psalms is about halfway along."

Nobody reached for a Bible. I didn't check whether anybody's lips weren't moving but we sounded pretty unanimous.

Dr. Hale, probably mid-50's, was large and imposing: bald, thick-necked and tightly-collared, broad-shouldered and chesty in a buttoned dark suit and vest, his face ruddy, brows heavy over dark eyes behind gold, wire-rimmed antique frames like my grandfather wore, his mouth a thin, tight line. The beefy white hands played with the flaps on his coat pockets. His speech was measured, deliberate, maybe guarded. He lifted a large, gold watch from his vest pocket, opened its case, and placed it gently on the table, coiling the gold chain precisely around its face.

"Now the assigned passage for tonight's discussion...," he intoned. But Jack was waving his hand.

"Yes, Jack?" A trace of impatience. I sat up.

"Well, sir," Jack began, "before we get going, may I ask something about the psalm?"

"Briefly."

"Yes sir. It's just that I've always wondered why the writer personifies us as sheep? Why does he turn people into sheep?"

"It's a convention. A tradition. Goes way back."

"Yes sir, but why? I know another verse says 'All we like sheep have gone astray,' but *how* like? What about humans is *like* sheep? I don't see it. How is the analogy apt?"

I understood that Jack was wasting no time in rolling out a challenge to orthodoxy, and I liked the gutsiness of it. I also saw that with "personify" and "analogy" he was showing off, and I admired that too. Was it too soon for a newbie to help out? I thought about it.

But another hand went up. "I think I know what Jack means…."

"It's customary," Dr. Hale interrupted, "it's customary for us to await my acknowledgment before speaking. Do I know you, sir?"

"I apologize, sir. I'm Zeke. From the seminary."

"Zeke. Please continue. Briefly."

"Thank you, sir. I believe I know what Jack means. I've been lucky enough to go to England and Scotland and to work part-time around sheep over there, and I know sheep are about the dumbest, stupidest animals on the farm! Way dumber than chickens. And also the dirtiest. Sheep are absolutely filthy beasts. They don't do personal hygiene. They're always snowy white in pictures but they're brown. Dirt brown. I agree with Jack."

"You're missing the point," a girl across from me said. "The writer doesn't say a word about brains or baths, and neither did Jack. You're not discussing the analogy, or the question."

Two more hands were up.

"I welcome the interest, boys and girls," Dr. Hale said, "but we're off topic. We need to take up the assignment. I'll accept one more comment before moving on. Yes, Shirley."

"Thank you, sir. I think the psalmist is comparing us to the weakness of lambs, how frail we are, and dirty with sin, and all the time so needy. And sometimes we're dumb too."

"That's very good, Shirley. Excellent! Now, if we could take up tonight's lesson…."

"It isn't about lambs," Ben said. "The psalm says 'sheep-herd. And sheep are not weak…or frail. Try wrestling one. William Blake knows everything about lambs. Read Blake about lambs. Psalms is about sheep. Big, burly sheep, who get *comforted* by rods and staffs. Who eat big dinners."

Another girl piped up: "But Blake says they're 'meek and mild.'"

"No, he doesn't," from Ben. "He says their *namesake* is meek and mild. Not the sheep. The Great Lord Jesus is meek and mild."

Hands reached for Bibles.

The other seminary guy opened up, looking down at his: "These sheep aren't tame. They have to be managed...shep-herded, with rods and staffs, like he said. It takes *both*? They must be wild. Rowdy. What's the difference, by the way, between a rod and a staff? A crook? Which one has the crook? And how can a rod be 'comforting'"?

Another voice: "Good question! And what's so special about 'still waters'? Still waters are stagnant, aren't they? Scummy. With algae. Like swamp water. Why'd you want to walk by swamps?"

"Actually," said a small girl with pigtails and braces, "actually, I've always wondered why any hostess would set the table when 'enemies'" — she traced quotation marks in the air — "were in the dining room? Why would you feed a foe?"

A so-far silent, red-haired boy, with freckles and mischief all over his face, spoke up: "Cups running over need saucers. Somebody hand that guy a saucer! And who needs 'ointment' on his head when we've got Brylcreem?" (I glanced at Sheila.)

This was getting ridiculous. "Seriously, though," the first seminary guy said, "why would you want 'goodness and mercy' following you? Wouldn't you want them right up there with you, *beside* you? Not trailing behind? What good would they do you back there?"

I wasn't about to be left out of this little row — or rather, I *was*, if I didn't get into it pronto. I raised my hand and said: "What's all this about God 'making' me lie down in green pastures? Stretching out in the clover?

Why would He have to make me? Wouldn't I want to? It sounds forced. Not like 'allow.' More like 'compel.' Why wouldn't I just lie down on my own...unless cow-pies were laying around?"

"Correct!" Jack whispered.

Then, suddenly, everything went very, very quiet. As though we'd spent — emptied — ourselves, expelled something urgent and pressing, and turned as meek and mild as Blake's little lambs. Dr. Hale, vividly red of face and ears, who at some point had rested his substantial rump on the tabletop, now stared fixedly over us at the back wall, slowly stood, straightened his head, threw back his shoulders, and quietly asked:

"Anyone else?"

He gathered up the watch and chain, tucked them into his vest.

"Very well," he continued calmly. "You have thoroughly disgraced yourselves with this appalling pre-emption of the class. You have impiously highjacked it. You have insulted and abused me. I am now going to walk out that door and leave you to whatever wickedness and blasphemy and deviltry's left in you. But I shall return one month from tonight to complete the lesson that you have so contemptuously disrupted tonight if, *IF*, in the meantime I receive personal letters of apology from every one of you addressed to me at The Rutledge Gentlemen's Academy. Whoever was ringleader here tonight is responsible for getting that done. You'll know, if I'm not here in November, that my condition was not met. Shame upon you all."

And off he strode.

He was barely out the door when Jack stood, bent to smooth his khakis, and faced us. "Jack Latimer," he announced, "LCC sophomore. I guess maybe I started that. I'm probably the putative 'ringleader,' so I accept part of the blame. But if I may, I'd like to propose that we discuss, right now, all of us, how we want to respond to that demand, if we want to respond at all. Unless somebody else would like to, I'll emcee. What does everybody think? Starting with....Sheila," whose hand was up.

"That was terrible," she said. "Just awful. We were awful to him. Terrible."

"How about we start," I said, half to myself, "by finding synonyms for 'terrible' and 'awful'?"

"That's not funny," a girl's voice said.

"Zeke again," Zeke said. "Before we start 'responding,' I'd like to say that that little exchange was the liveliest, most exciting and stimulating conversation — and the most promising one — this group has had since I joined up last year. I'm not sure how it happened but I'd like to finish it and have more like it. Just my opinion."

Several nods. Some downcast eyes.

Then a very pretty girl with short blonde hair and red lips and small hoop earrings in a white, sleeveless shirt and dark skirt and heels — *heels*! — who hadn't yet spoken raised her hand and did: "I'm Leslie, LCC senior, pre-law poli sci. With all due respect: it must be obvious to everyone that Jack and his team planned a coup, and the takeover was not only exciting but also successful. At least it woke us all up. We've gone stale, and we can use new blood. But whether THIS is the new blood we need isn't clear. Let's say that Dr. Hale has handed us a ready-made blood test. Let's make our response to Dr. Hale's demand the test of our new blood and our old, and how well they mix. We're too big for a committee. So I propose that two of Jack's team and three from the rest of us form a group to consider how we — corporately — and most profitably can respond to Dr. Hale's demand...based on the discussion we'll have right now. And I'll end by saying that in my opinion, the very first article of our response must be a sincere apology for our rudeness, our bad manners this evening."

I believe I know leadership when I see it, and I saw it, plain as day, in Leslie. I saw a lot more than just leadership, too, but for now that was the important thing. Before I quite knew it, I was on my feet, saying: "I'm Troy and a newbie, but I think that's a fine idea. And I suggest we ask Leslie to chair the small group she's proposed."

As emcee, Jack needed to choose from the several hands now in the air. Maybe to compensate for my nastiness, and to show his impartiality, he chose Sheila.

"But Dr. Hale said he wanted personal letters of apology. From each one of us."

I looked to Leslie, and deferred. "I would hope to find that's negotiable," she said. "We would all benefit from one unified response, first apologizing and then perhaps offering ideas for how to refresh our meetings with variants of our routines?"

"Exactly," I said.

Number 2 seminary guy's hand was up. Jack pointed.

"I don't mind an apology," he said, "so long as we don't overdo it. What happened here tonight was really good, really promising. Let's not lose sight of that in any apologizing. As for variants in the routine: I'd say we stumbled on a pretty good one tonight."

"No," a girl said; "that was a free-for-all. I'm not comin' back for another one of those."

"We could and should be less unruly," Jack said.

Ben said: "I'd like to clarify: I wasn't part of any coup. Maybe I shouldn't have jumped in as a first-timer, but nobody encouraged me to be rude. I just wanted to correct the record about Blake. For what it's worth, though: I liked the discussion. And I like Leslie's ideas."

Uh-oh. I figured I knew exactly what Ben liked about Leslie.

"Do we actually *have* any new ideas…for variants?" This from the red-haired boy with the mischievous face, the high school senior. "What happened tonight was pretty much *all* variant…wadn' it?"

"I'm against too much structure," I said. "I favor the spontaneity of what happened. But we might need some format…to start."

"Didn't Troy make a motion?" Zeke asked.

"No," I said; "but I will. I move that Leslie chair… and appoint…a committee…a representative committee from those present to…prepare a response to…what Dr.…."

"Hale," Jack said.

"…Dr. Hale…wants us to do, told us to do. That's kind of a rough way of saying it," I added, "but does it get at what folks want?"

Number 2 seminary guy: "They should consider whether we actually need a leader. I mean, our so-called leader called us 'boys and girls' tonight. We're adults. Two of us have seminary training and are getting more of it. We've all been around church forever. We know this stuff…and we've shown we've got, well, inquiring minds about it. We can pick stories to discuss. Do we really need a nanny?"

"I could referee," Zeke said, laughing.

"Well," Jack said, "we have a motion. That Leslie…. Well, you know. Is there a second?"

"What does 'representative' mean?" Shirley asked. "Troy said 'representative' committee.'"

Leslie crossed her legs. I noticed nylons. "If this passes," she said, "I wouldn't want to be bound to a certain number of members. I'd want all views represented."

"Second!" somebody said.

"Question," somebody else said.

"Wait!" Sheila said; "don't we get some say on committee members?"

"Volunteer or recommend," Leslie said, briskly.

"In favor?" Jack asked, "raise a hand."

I kept my eyes down for the count but could tell from the rustle that it passed.

"You didn't ask for 'opposed,'" Sheila said.

"Thank you," Leslie said, when Jack didn't respond. "I'd be pleased to hear from anyone wishing to serve on the committee. Jack, could we get everybody's contact information, and send copies to everybody? The whole group should meet again next week, same time. For business only. Nobody write Dr. Hale before we meet again. Would somebody be sure the space is available?"

Zeke volunteered, and we began to break up, we three wise men drifting toward each other.

"Anyone need a ride?" Leslie asked. "I drove."

"I guess we better go back the way we came," Jack said, "but we're probably stopping at the Dairy Queen. Want to meet us there?"

She smiled. So did we.

"*I'll* meet you there," Ben said, "unless *you*" — pointing to Leslie — "want to ride the bike with me. I'll bring you back to your car."

Headed to the Dairy Queen, the bus buzzed with chatter about what had happened. Sheila, probably pissed at me, disappeared into the rear, so Jack and I took adjoining seats.

"I thought you said he 'leaned left,'" I began. "He's too stiff to lean anywhichway."

"We didn't give him a chance. I meant politically left. Biblically left...toward liberal. I've never seen him like that."

"How many times have you seen him at all?"

"Three. Something ticked him off tonight?"

I laughed. "You think? Isn't what happened just what you wanted to happen?"

"I didn't plan a coup, Troy."

"Of course you did. Maybe by a different name, or no name at all, but a coup is what you hoped would happen and what did, once you started it with 'personify.'"

"I didn't plan the rest of it."

"You didn't discourage it either."

"Neither did you! You pitched right in…with clover and cow-pies!." He giggled. "That was pretty funny. So why're you complaining?"

"I'm thinking about next time."

"That's Leslie's job. You angling for a berth on her committee?"

"I'm not. She's bound to ask you, though, and you'll accept. No, I'm thinking about what meetings will look like now. You can't go back to what you said they were: strait-laced conservative mainline boring Sunday school 'interpretations' of Bible stories. Tonight broke that model, doncha think? And that's also why Dr. Hale has to stay gone. There needn't even be a decision about that. Just so nobody apologizes. He's fired himself and he's through. But the group can't keep meeting just to trash scripture. That game was already starting to unravel tonight, into low comedy. That's gonna get tiresome fast, and just as 'stale' as Leslie said yawl already were. So what's the group going to be *about* from here on? Nobody *answered* those questions we made up tonight. Hale just walked out. I doubt the other side's strong enough to turn yawl into a debating society. I don't see any reason to come back, just for more of tonight."

Jack had turned his head toward me about halfway through that rant, and now looked hard at my face. And then he grinned: "Fella," he said, "you just talked your way onto Leslie's committee."

Leslie and Ben were already huddled at a table in the Dairy Queen courtyard when we pulled in. Both waved but didn't signal us over. We ordered chocolate dipped cones and took adjacent swings on the kiddie's playground.

"Don't recommend me for the committee, Jack," I said. "I'm not interested. I'd just as soon you didn't serve either. I need you to help write the play."

"But you'll come to the next meeting, right? The one next week. We'll need you there."

"Why? You've got Leslie and now prob'ly Ben and those two seminary guys. I guess I did sort of like messing with that psalm tonight but I'm starting to burn out on that kind of...well...pranking. I've been doing it, more or less, since sixth grade, being silly and irreverent about the Bible, and it's too easy now, and it doesn't go anywhere, or mean anything or make any difference. You know what I mean?"

"Not really, no. I see it as an intellectual exercise. We're probing the verses. There's no end to the questions any important verse asks, and every answer raises new questions. No interpretation is ever final. We're not discrediting other readings; we're opening them up, extending them, adding to what's known about that text. What we did tonight is what we did with Auden the other day. It's also what we're going to be doing every day for the rest of our natural lives to earn grocery money...and making a difference every time we do it. You understand that, surely."

"You're turning the group into a lit-crit class."

"And why not? What's better?"

He wiped his fingers and mouth, tossed the napkins into a bin.

"Hold on now," he grinned, grabbing the chains of my swing, "'cause I'm about to hurl you over that moon!"

9

We left the bus at the shelter and headed into the campus, toward our separate dorms.

"Want to come up?" Jack asked. "See my room? It's still early."

But just then we spotted a figure hurtling toward us down the dimly lit walk, elbows out, arms paddling, wrists flapping, a cowboy hat bouncing off the shoulders.

"Whatever *is* that?" I asked, almost knowing.

"Wait!" Jack said, and stopped. "I think...it looks like...Park!"

"It *is*!" I agreed. "What's he doing?"

"Coming this way. He'll see us in a minute."

He wore his full cowboy outfit, the boots turning his rush into clownish lurches. He was nearly upon us before staggering to a standstill.

"Professor Royal!" Jack exclaimed. "Are you crying?"

He was, his eyes wide and wet and red, little whimpers leaking from his lips.

"What's happened, sir?" I managed; "can we help?"

"No, no," he said, sobs catching in his throat, one hand adjusting the hat onto the heavy hair, the other waving a white envelope. "I don't think anybody can help. I've had a blow."

"A blow, sir?" Jack asked. "Are you hurt, sir?"

"I am," he said. "Deeply hurt and dismayed," fumbling with the free hand at the knotted scarf around his throat. He snatched at it, blotted his eyes, sniffed.

"Would you like to sit down, sir?" I asked. "There's a bench in the shelter down there. We could help you...?"

"No, not the...*bus* shelter." He shook his head, blew his nose. "Maybe The Grove. Is The Grove nearby?"

"Don't you know where you are, sir?" Jack said. "Are you...confused...?"

"Of course I know where I am. I'm not lost. I am only...wounded."

"But where, sir?" I asked. "Where are you wounded? What happened?"

"Would it *were* that kind of 'wound'...but it's equally painful," he said. "More painful. I am broken in soul. If I might rest...in The Grove, if it's nearby?"

"Not far," Jack said.

"Then come next to me, lads. Get under my arms here. Like that. Now walk me to The Grove. Slowly."

I was suddenly conscious of touching a teacher's body, of touching a teacher's body not his hands in a greeting, of embracing his back and cupping his shoulder with my hands. I may have shuddered at the awareness. It wasn't a sensation. Merely a thought. But unnerving.

"I'm lucky to have found you, darlings, in my distressing hour. Providential, one might say, our meeting. Can you let me down gently on that bench? And bide with me while I recover? Sit just there, on the earth."

"Could I get a nurse for you, sir?" Jack said. "Some water maybe? Troy can stay while I do."

"No nurse can heal my wounds. But you might bide a while. While I gather myself." He took a deep breath, shakily let it out. We arranged ourselves at his feet.

"Now darlings," he said, "you mustn't say that I wept. Especially not in my cowboy dress. It's so unbecoming...weeping. Especially in cowboys! But I *do* hurt. I *am* suffering."

"We know, sir," I said. "Would you care to tell us who hurt you and how?"

"Look up at me, boys. I would. I believe I should. You may be...implicated."

"Oh no, sir," Jack objected; "we've been off campus. We're just getting back."

"Calm yourself, Wise Man," Park said, gentling Jack's shoulder. "I mean, in the long run. In any fallout. No, you have no responsibility. This" — he held the white envelope against his chin — "*This* bears all the responsibility...all the blame."

He told us that after being away since Friday he'd returned to campus to collect mail and found the letter he carried, from The University of South Carolina

Press, declining interest in seeing the "prospectus" for his book-in-progress on Tommy Chatterton. "Not even my *prospectus!*" he wailed. His father, Professor Royal said, had business in the state, and possibly leverage at the University, and Park himself had once met the Press Director at a convention and mentioned the work-in-progress to him. "'It doesn't appear to be a good fit for our list,' is what they wrote. Imagine! Without even reading my outline! I don't know what I'm going to do."

"Well," I offered, "aren't there other presses? Doesn't LSU have one?"

"Oh, I suppose so," he said, "but I don't have a whole lot of time. And I still have to finish my prospectus. And with teaching and all, I don't know how…. I'll probably have to tell Dr. Rogers about this…unreasonable refusal…and that will be soooo *embarrassing.*"

"But it's not even Thanksgiving yet, sir," Jack said. "Do you have a deadline or something?"

"Thanksgiving. The Department wants my complete file by Thanksgiving."

"Couldn't you ask for an extension?" I wondered.

"That would look so *pathetic.* Like I wasn't prepared. It wouldn't set well."

"Sit well, sir," Jack just couldn't help himself.

"But how does it all work, sir?" I asked. "I mean, what happens? Who does what to whom?"

"*I* is to whom." I winced and looked at Jack but he shrugged. "This three-person committee of tenured English professors reads my file and recommends my promotion, or not, to the tenured faculty of the

Department; then that group votes whether to recommend me to the Dean, who's supposed to study the file and recommend or not to the President and the BOT. This is my fifth year, so I get one more on my second contract; but if I'm not promoted I have to leave after next year. There's no appeal."

"What's in the file?" I persisted.

"Everything: teaching evals, copies of my...writings; rec letters; service to the community; extra-curricular stuff."

"Testimonials, like, from your students?" I suggested.

"Sweet, Troy. I guess so. Nobody's ever said."

"Do they interview you," I asked, thinking of scholarship competitions.

"I don't think so. But I guess they could. No, wait; Dr. Rogers has already talked to me, about how to prepare the file."

"Do they get into personal stuff?" Jack asked.

"Well, not officially, I don't think. But of course they all know me. It probably matters some, when they vote."

"What matters most?" from Jack.

"They expect a book. A scholarly book, or monograph. Or at least a book contract from a respectable publisher. They told me that, up front, when they hired me. I don't think it's fair but I accepted it. And I'm working on a book, as you know. I'm a little behind schedule."

"Well, they'll read what you've got, right?" from me.

"It's not a lot." He paused. "Look, darlings, maybe we've talked long enough about all this. You can't be interested. I'm so sorry to have been such a trouble to you but I'm really and truly glad you were *here* to help me in my hour of trial. I guess I panicked, it was such a *shock*! When I saw the letter…. Oh, bother: let's not linger longer. *You* need to swot up Byron for tomorrow's class. But listen now, my darlings, this, all of this, has to be between us. Stay between us." (I looked at Jack; he shook his head 'no.'). "I can't be known for blubbering around students. Or talking department politics to them. So this never happened. We didn't see each other tonight. Scout's honor. So, okay then. Help me up. I don't remember where I parked, do you?"

He hobbled off, the boots still bothering his steps.

By mid-morning, everybody seemed to know, not about the tears but about the letter, though Jack and I hadn't leaked a syllable. And we couldn't correct the rumors without revealing our involvement.

"Is he fired?" Ben asked us.

"Not that we know of," I said. "Did you read Byron?"

"Oh, yeah!" Ben said; "I've read him before but I did again. He's cool. I really like 'Mazeppa.'"

"You should hear Liszt's symphonic poem of the same name," I said, showing off. "How's Leslie?"

Professor Royal, still in his cowboy garb only a different shirt and scarf, gave our class some pretty interesting biographical background on Byron, especially about his Cambridge years and his boyfriends there and his London years and all the women chasing him around town, and then he read, beautifully, the last lyric Byron ever wrote, "On This Day I Complete My Thirty-Sixth

Year," dedicated, Park said, to his young Greek page Loukas Chalandritsonos, whose name I memorized and liked to repeat in whispers to myself when I felt stressed or glum. Dr. Royal waved Jack and me to the lectern as the class adjourned. "None of it happened," he said grimly, and turned away.

Flesh phases on our minds, Kaiden hugged me hard and long at the New Orleans Greyhound Terminal, and we held hands in the rear seat of the taxi all the way back to Irby House, his dorm, on the Tulane campus. There, he produced a key to his housemother's apartment, which well-appointed space she'd allowed him to use over the holiday for the refrigeration of store-food he meant to prepare on her range, since nothing was safe from plundering in the dorm fridge — even though nearly everyone but the internationals had left campus for Thanksgiving — and the dorm kitchen had no oven. He removed a yellow bowl from the fridge, peeled off the plastic wrap with a flourish, and lifted down a package of pita bread from an overhead cabinet.

"Creamy Cajun Crab Dip," he announced, "a la Kaiden Carlisle! You want white wine?"

I dropped my backpack and checked my watch. "It's a little early, idn' it?"

"This here is Nu Awh-leans, my man," he said, toying with a corkscrew.

"Okay, then. Would it be all right if I used her bathroom?"

"Through there," he said, nodding. "Hang the towel back. Flush."

I peed, flushed, splashed my face, pressed my cowlicks down, smeared some Ipana on my teeth and tongue, swished, and spit. And flushed again.

He placed pretty glasses of wine on the table between two easy chairs, sat in one, pointed me to the other. "Toasting us," he said, lifting a glass. "Troy and Kaiden."

"Kaiden and Troy," I echoed, lifting and sipping. "Corky," I added after a moment, "may I just look at you?"

The red rose to his cheeks. His eyes didn't know where to rest. He shifted. "I wasn't expecting that," he said.

"May I? Just for a minute. It's been so long."

"Okay," he said, and stilled.

He was beautiful. He'd slimmed and lengthened into svelte, into a kind of uninterrupted flow top to toe, moving toward lean and lithe, close to being there. The similarity to Tony Dow (Wally on "Beaver") I'd noticed at Jubilee had dimmed, the slight stoutness thinned, the rich, soft brown curls less snug against the skull, looser and longer, now tossed rather than groomed, and falling toward the front and over the ears and neck. The hint of puffiness had drained from the face, the bones easing into definition. The sweet single dimple had slackened, evened with the skin, and taken with it some of the dawdling stripling charm. The plump lower lip remained but the mouth had relaxed, somehow widened, so that the slightly rabbity front teeth appeared less pronounced, and the smile shed pure light. His dark, kind eyes still glimmered under lengthened lashes. Back at Jubileee I'd named Corky the perfect incarnation of American boyhood, but the boyishness had slipped into glowing, urgent youth. Everything had smoothed out, as though polished. He shone.

"You're a beautiful man, Kaiden, can I say that?"

"You just did," he said, reddening again. "I don't know about that, but thank you. I like the new hair, yours, I mean. I like where it's...um, headed. Not quite Ivy yet but on the way." He swiped a pita through the dip. "What're you using?"

"Oh, just Brylcreem."

"Try butch wax. You must have some left."

Of course. Why hadn't I thought of that?

"Some girl spit on it. To make it lie flat."

"You're kidding. What'd you do?"

"Shampooed. Ditched her. Kaiden, this dip is fantastic!"

"Thanks. It's pretty standard down here. Mine has extra horseradish. If you'd rather have crackers...."

"No, this is great. What's the wine?"

"Gewurztraminer. Like it?"

"Say it again?"

"German. Gewurztraminer. Perfect with shellfish."

"How do you know these things? Are you showing off?"

"A little. I'm learning."

After a pause, he said: "We're volleying."

"I know."

We both grinned. Sipped.

"You want to move over here onto my lap?" He patted it.

"Yes, but not yet," I said. "Not here. You want to smoke? I brought fags."

"Not really. Troy: what's wrong? Is something wrong?"

"I don't know. No. Nothing. I'm not sure. I'm nervous. I'm sorry, but I am. Maybe we could take a walk or something. You want to show me the campus?"

"You really want to see the campus?"

"Actually I do, sometime. If we start something here now, we might never get to."

He laughed. "*Actually*, a walk sounds good. Let's dump your backpack, see our room, and head out for a tour. Swallow your wine."

Mrs. Logan's door opened onto an ample railed balcony running all the way around the dormitory; each of the four floors had one. Kaiden's and Shelby's second-floor corner room featured two plate-glass windows, one overlooking the fading green lawn of the quadrangle, the other facing down onto McAlister Drive, the main drag through this part of the campus. Straight ahead inside across the room was the large bath shared with the suite opposite theirs. In between, the single beds, now pushed together and made up as one, met the wall at right angles, half-blocking the lane to the bath. Two tables with chairs but no drawers faced the long window to the left of the door, the far one affording a view out the second window. Two cushioned easy chairs with floor lamps filled the space between the desks and the closets. Matching blue vases with yellow buds blossomed on both neat desktops.

"Drop your backpack anywhere," he said, closing and locking the door, "and come to me."

He took me by the biceps, looked straight at me with brimming eyes, and said, "Welcome to my home, Troy Tyler." And kissed me softly on the mouth...for quite a while, our lips moving, exploring, but our tongues behaving. When we broke, we touched foreheads for a while longer, grinning. His dark eyes glistened.

"Your eyes are *so* blue," he said. "Blue blazes burning."

I gently kissed his lids. "Thank you," I whispered.

"Stay tuned," he winked, and stepped back, adjusted his crotch.

I adjusted mine. "You want a cigarette now?" I asked, remembering something. "I once saw this magazine cartoon. A guy and his girl in a rumpled bed; she's holding a lit cigarette. The guy says, 'Do you always smoke after sex?' And she says, 'I don't know. I never looked.'"

We cracked up. "We should look," Kaiden said. "Bring your smokes!"

To my eyes, the Uptown Tulane campus, as it's called, is impressive but not beautiful. I don't mean it's ugly. Just not exactly pretty. Stately is what it is, august. With long, level stretches of strictly trimmed glass and magnificent spreading oak and magnolia trees and huge stone structures looking more like sculptures than schoolrooms.

"Which one's English?" I asked him.

"Gibson Hall," Kaiden answered, "the biggest one, beyond that column, straight ahead. Looks onto St. Charles as the awesome face of the institution. It's also the Administration Building. Deans' hangout. The Pres may live there too. English is on one."

I stopped to take it in, tried to see myself climbing the long steps up toward the towering arch over the central door, or even entering the smaller one to the right onto the ground floor. Both looked daunting, firmly locked. Did one knock before entering? Would it sound timid to ask Kaiden? Did he even remember that I might apply to Tulane English for grad school, if he stayed in New Orleans after graduation?

Two-lane Freret Street cut like a belt across the middle of the campus, separating the student-life part from the teaching part that stretched on the other side to the busy St. Charles Avenue with very old red and dark green electric trolleys clanging down its center, and beyond it to the many acres of Audubon Park with graceful paths and gardens and water features and the exciting zoo we would tour on Kaiden's bike on Saturday. Farther up the Avenue came the intersection with Broadway, a street with shops and cafes and clubs and cheap student housing — there's no zoning in New Orleans, Kaiden explained: a kind of bohemian sector starkly contrasting with the majesty and elegance and dignity of St. Charles.

"You know," Kaiden said, "I'd planned to fix supper for us tonight but it'll keep, and as long as we're near, we might as well eat at the *real* Camellia Grill. Remember the other one at the station?"

"The red beans and rice, sure!"

"So let's cut down Broadway and come up on Sophie Newcomb from this side and have a look around and circle back to the Grille for supper? All right with you?"

"Lead on," I said.

The brick classroom and office buildings of the famous former all-girls college with the famous pottery collections seemed less imposing, less austere and monumental than Tulane's, the lawns less precisely groomed and of slightly darker hues. The whole place felt layered in softer textures. Maybe it was the light, though: the afternoon had moved along; the overhanging limbs were heavier, denser, gave darker shade. Distant thunder growled, and a breeze had kicked up. Leaves romped, whirled. I pressed my hair.

"It's more comfortable over here," I mused.

"You think? I haven't noticed. But I'm not much here. All my classes are back there, except one. Nutrition. And it meets just twice a week."

"You like it?"

"Prob'ly better than the others. I'm learning useful stuff."

"Have you picked a major yet?"

"No, and I was going to ask you about that. I've looked through the catalogue and can't find a major matching my…cooking interests. There may not be enough courses either. I mean, enough to make a major out of. What if there're not? I've thought about dropping out…."

"What? Don't be ridiculous. You can't drop out."

"…and applying for an internship…at Commander's Palace. We're eating there Saturday night. They're the finest…."

"But you have to finish college first. Then intern."

"Majoring in what, though? I have to have a speciality."

"Wait. Aren't there other colleges around? Maybe you could get transfer credit?"

"For a major? I doubt it. But yes," Kaiden said, "Loyola's right next door. And I'll bet those Jesuits know how to cook."

"And the University of New Orleans started up just this fall. Out on the lakefront. But now you mention it, transfer credit for a major prob'ly wouldn't pass."

"And I have to have a speciality."

"Are you sure? Maybe there's a General Education degree, where you don't."

"Never heard of it."

"Me neither. So pick anything, any subject that's easy. If there's nothing about cooking or chef-ing, sign up for any major that's easy…or come on over to English! I could help. Just to get the diploma. You can't enter the work force without a diploma. You said 'interestS' be-fore. What're your others?"

"Sex? Could I major in sex? Or boys. How 'bout boys? I could bone up on boys!"

I laughed with him but wasn't sure I wanted to. Something dark hung around the joke.

"No, seriously," I said. "Health? There must be health courses. Couldn't you cobble together a major in, say, Health Affairs? Nutrition and Health?"

"Sounds like pre-med."

"Wait a minute. I met this girl who's majoring in 'something something Human Development.' I don't get the sense it means anything much, but you could hook the words to 'Health,' say, and get 'Health and Human Development'...or 'Nutritious Health and Human Development'?" Get Health course descriptions and reason out relations among them, and...Eureka, a *major*...and a chef-career at the end of it! Isn't that how Independent Majors happen?"

"I don't know, Troy. Are you making this up?"

"Yeah, but doesn't it sound reasonable? Listen, talk to your Nutrition prof. Tell her what you want to be and ask how to major in Chef. If you like her and what she says, ask her to be your major advisor in Food or some-thing. Take her some brownies you've made."

"'Audition,' you mean. And you sound like Monte."

"And some course names, to prove you've thought about taking them."

"Would you help?"

"Now, Corky. You know I know nothing about food except how to destroy it, but of course I'll help if you get the materials, like catalogues and reading lists."

"Cool. Aren't you *getting* hungry after all this? It's kind of a hike to the Grill from here."

The breeze had stiffened, cooled; smelled of damp. The light had dimmed another degree or two. You couldn't see through the oak and magnolia branches, but I figured the routine late afternoon thunderheads had built across the west and were lumbering our way.

"It feels like rain," I said.

"It feels like Thanksgiving...Eve," Kaiden said. "I wouldn't mind walking in the rain with you. We could huddle."

My arm stretched around his shoulder, clenched, withdrew.

"The wine's worn off," he said. "Let's stop for another. I know this bar, up ahead. Delphine's. They've got a piano."

Delphine's was a ramshackle old frame house squatting under a huge purple flashing neon sign, its extended front porch littered with rockers and benches, and at one end hung a ratty old hammock. Half a dozen white people with cigs and beer and bellies slouched around it, all nodding and grinning as we came in. Plinking piano jazz welcomed us.

"A player piano!" I exclaimed, spotting the instrument with nobody on the stool. "Oh wow! My granny had one. I hate the sound but that contraption is a hoot to watch!"

"What's wrong with the sound?" Kaiden asked.

"It's a machine," I answered, "and sounds like one. You think they'd turn it down?"

He waved at the bar, touched his ear, and the jangling ebbed. We took a window table and ordered, a gin and tonic for Kaiden, more white wine for me, for I fretted about mixing.

"So," he said, sitting forward, toward me. "How's Monte?"

"That's kind of a non-sequitur," I dodged, fingering the Delphine matches.

"Well, you don't have to tell me. I'm naturally curious, though, after he visited you and all."

"What 'all'? I told you we didn't sleep in the same bed."

"And I believed you. Don't get defensive. But in fact that isn't what you told me. It's okay, though. I got your message."

"He broke up with his girl. Or she dumped him. He's kind of messed up over that. Or over something. He's quitting stuff."

"What?" He stopped, reached for the Kents. I waited for him, lit the tip. "Quitting what?" he exhaled.

"Activities. Glee Club. Swimming." I lit up too.

"Truly?" Kaiden asked. "That doesn't sound right. I don't like the sound of it. Is he taking up something else instead?"

"He hasn't said. Why?"

"I can't see Monte not busy. Is he depressed?"

"I don't know. He hasn't said."

"Well, he wouldn't, would he?"

"He might. To me. I'm thinking he almost did, on the visit."

"What? What'd he say?"

"Oh, not really much, I guess. He's prob'ly just missing the girl. It's prob'ly just late teen angst. That's what Jack says."

"Who's Jack?"

"Oh, my other LCC friend."

"Other? Who's the first? Just how many boys have you got stashed away up there?"

Kaiden wasn't smiling. Not quite frowning either. But staring. Waiting.

"Jack's in a coupla my classes. Really smart. We're doing a project for Romantics."

"For what? Romance?! What 'romance'?"

"A Romantics class. It's a historical period in English Literature. I think Jack might have taken a shine to Monte."

"How'd he meet Monte?"

"He didn't. He saw him. He liked the look."

"If Monte's in love with Jack, maybe that's why he's depressed."

"Well, if you want to write and ask him, I've got the address."

"Oh, stop. Just stop. Why're we even talking about Monte?! Didn't we say on the train, didn't we agree on the train, we'd left Monte behind?"

"You brought him up."

"Well, let's put him down. He doesn't belong here. I'm sorry. Don't let's mess this up. Please."

"No. Let's not. Monte is…herewith…flushed. Okay?"

I finished my wine in a gulp, stood, and moved behind his chair. "Allow me to assist you, Mr. Carlisle," I said, tugging on his chair. He pushed back into my crotch.

"Ooof. You'll be sorry if you damage the goods," I said.

We walked, huddled, through the misty rain, toward the Camellia Grill.

His: Grilled Reuben Special (corned beef with melted Swiss, sauerkraut, Thousand Island dressing) on rye, chocolate pecan pie with vanilla on top, Dr. Pepper.

Mine: Mardi Gras (turkey, bacon, lettuce, corned beef, Thousand Island dressing) on rye, pecan pie, red creme soda.

I don't know whether it was the little almost-spat we had back there, the long hike, the rain, the nervous anticipation, or maybe that we'd almost talked ourselves out, but we kept pretty quiet over the amazing food. Kaiden analyzed it, of course, listing its successes and (many fewer) shortcomings, and I invited info on the neighborhood and his courses and his new friend and straight roommate Shelby while we dried out and my cowlicks lifted into comical twists. "Butch wax," he reminded me. He drew out the green American Express card.

"My treat," he said; "the whole weekend. Maybe a Thanksgiving gift for everybody. My father knows you're here, said he wanted you to 'enjoy the full benefits of New Orleans to the max'. On the card. So don't hold back."

I owned my own card now, "for emergencies," my folks said. But as I had no income but the monthly scholarship funds, I was trying to learn a little economy. I burbled my sincere, fumbling thanks.

Back inside the dorm, he passed me a hand-towel and toothpaste. Returning, I found him in his T-shirt and Jockeys.

"My boy Troy," he said, opening his arms. "Come, help me be good for you."

Later, I wrote about it, kept copies:

We explored and discovered, exclaimed, and caught-on.
We hugged and we snuggled, kissed, tongue-ing, and clung.
We touched and we tasted, we teased and we traced;
We tickled and tumbled, we petted and pawed;
We nipped and we nibbled; we rocked and we rolled;
We stroked and we fondled, and fumbled and grasped.
We wrestled and grappled and tussled and thrashed;
We ached and we shivered; we trembled, we swore.
Spoke endearments, our names, sweet nothings, and more:
"Don't be afraid of touching me there."

"Where have you dreamed of me touching you,
how?"
We sighed and we whispered; we purred, and cried
out:
Gasped, clutched hard; we shuddered and moaned:
And wept in our pleasure and joy.

~TT

We had sex three more times before I left, and although
I don't have anything to compare it with, I thought we
got better at it, or anyhow more comfortable about having it, with the practice. And I want to say, right away,
that every bit of it felt completely natural. Not that I
expected it not to. But it's important to say that it did.
We didn't talk much about it, though. I mean, we didn't
*analyze* it: we didn't discuss how to improve it or change
what we did, which I guess means we were both satisfied
with how it went. But I think we both also felt a little
*shyer* afterward than even before it happened. I don't
mean guilty. I know all about guilt, and it wasn't guilt.
It was more like a kind of contingent embarrassment;
like *everything* had been exposed, nothing held back: utter nakedness of body and soul. Nothing to regret, no;
but some surprise and even awe that someone other had
climbed into our skins and our heads, and was looking
around at the layout.

On the bus back to Aleck, I didn't want to think
more about it lest I work myself up again right there in
public, so I mentally switched over to LCC and what

had happened there and might happen next. Park's letter didn't implicate us but surely carried implications *for* us. Whether we could expect — much less ask— him to stay aboard the play project wasn't clear. Whether we could move forward without him wasn't either. Ben had his doubts. Jack was wavering. Everybody appeared to know about Park's letter and showed curiosity, not alarm; but his behavior around it, his pretense with us that none of it happened, his *disorientation* by it, had shaken me. For all his Chatterton expertise, was he who we wanted to pilot the play? Moreover, I needed to get to the bottom of Ben's objections: why, after early enthusiasm, was he now so angrily against? Nor was I sure where I stood with the Youth Group: whether to serve with Leslie Anne Symington, or cut bait with the whole scene? Jack's keen on the group. What happens to *us* if I leave it? But such considerations as that brought me right back to the dirty deed I was trying not to remember, and stirred up bother between my legs. I drifted off, and slept.

*  *  *

December 3rd 1957
Mr. Holt Carlisle
444 Wisteria Drive
Vicksburg, Miss.

Dear Mr. Carlisle, Sir,

I am Troy Tyler, Kaiden's friend, and I wanted to thank you so much for treating us to good times in New Orleans. We saw the campuses and rode his bike around the Park. We also went to the zoo. Thank you for the really great meals. Commander's Palace serves amazing food (aka cuisine. Kaiden taught me the word). He wants to intern there. After graduation of course. You and your wife should try Commander's sometime.

Anyway, thank you again. Kaiden says hey.

Sincerely yours,
Troy Tyler

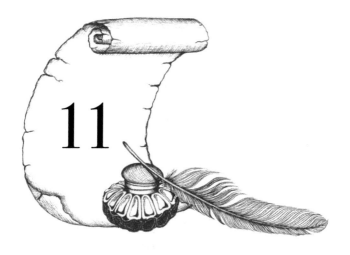

11

After Romantics on Monday, I waylaid Ben.

"If you finish writing by 9 tonight, want to stop by my room? I'll have beer."

"Sure," he said; "what's up?"

"I'd like to talk. That's all."

He stared for a moment. "Secrets! All right. Where are you?"

"210 Buckley."

"So how'd it go, New Orleans?"

"Great! Just great! What'd you do?"

"Homework. Ate, slept, read. Not much. I'm glad to be back. What'd you do?"

"The same, except no homework."

"The French Quarter?"

"Never got there."

"What? You never got to the Quarter? Why the hell not? The Quarter's the main thing!"

"Well, we were…you might say…hard pressed. Had our hands full!"

"Yeah," he laughed, "I figured. Say more!" The grin was downright wicked.

"I'm not talking," I talked.

"You don't have to. I knew it all along."

"Not talking to you," I said, walking away, blushing ferociously.

Ben arrived promptly at 9. We cracked the Millers, and got right to it.

"You know about Park's letter, right?" I asked. "He may be in trouble over tenure. So we need to talk about the play. I know you're not gung-ho. I want to understand why."

"The guy's a fucking fraud."

"You mean Chatterton, correct? Not Park?"

"Well, now you mention it…."

"Ben. Please. I'm kind of serious here."

"Seriously, Chatt's a fucking fraud."

"I understand you think that. What I don't get is the anger part. Why you're so mad over it. What's all the emotion about?"

He paused, turned the can in his fingers, studied it.

"I've thought about that too," he said, carefully. "I don't figure it's any of your business, but then again it may be…if you have to deal with it as…what?…leader of the project? The honest truth is, Troy, I don't myself completely understand all the emotion that gets me so riled up over that guy. It's ridiculous, I know, but it's so...*real*. I mean, I can't help feeling it...toward that jerk. I just kind of swell up...with, like, *heat* when you talk about... honoring him with a play about what he did."

"Can you say exactly what ticks you off?"

"Maybe. He didn't *earn* anything, any honor or celebration. He's phony. It gets under my skin."

"Have you ever known anybody like that? Does he remind you of someone?"

He took a long swallow, sat back in the chair, studied the can again.

"I'm pretty sure it goes way back. You got all night?"

He grimaced, then drowned it in another long pull.

"Yes," I said softly; "I've got all night," feeling the weight of the moment in my belly and bones.

"I didn't go anywhere for Thanksgiving, you know. Didn't have anywhere to go. I couldn't go back to the orphanage like last year. That was a big mistake."

"I'm so sorry, Ben. I should have realized...."

"No, no, don't. I can take care of myself. I've taken care of my self.... No, wait. Let's don't go there."

"I wish we would, Ben. I'd like to. Take me there."

"That's good play dialogue. Remember it." He almost grinned. Drank, looked hard at me for a beat or two. "All right. Maybe a little bit." Deep breath.

"I've more or less taken care of myself since I got adopted at 12," he began. "Before that, I'd been in the orphanage since infancy. I don't remember either of my parents but I know who they were and something about them from the Super at the orphanage who thought I should before leaving it with my adoptive parents. My father was a low-life and my mother a tramp. He worked as a Mississippi Riverboat gambler until he got fired for cheating customers *and* the house, and spent a coupla years in jail where he met Jesus and commenced preaching. When he got out, he took his rackets and his gospel on the road, the Super said, and made a pile with loaded dice and marked cards, and ripped off country churches with phony revivals, but drank and gambled it all away, had huge debts, and finally blew his brains out, dead drunk, with a stolen pistol in an alley in Natchez at about 37 years old. Between jail and suicide he sired me but left my mother before I landed, and *then* married her, so I've never known, for sure, whether I'm legit. He left her after six months or so and, the Super told me, never came back but did more jail time for swindling."

Ben drank several swallows. Crushed the can.

"Another?" I asked. He nodded.

"You want more?" he asked.

"If you want to tell me. Ben, are you really okay telling me? It's so raw…."

"It's raw, for sure. I can't tell it…cooked." He grimaced, and slurped from the can. "If you want the rest, it might help you figure out whatever you're trying to figure out here."

"Why you're angry, Ben."

"Yeah, but you understand all this crap is strictly between us. All of it."

"I do. Absolutely."

He took another swig. "My mother is supposed to have worked at the Morgan and Lindsey ten-cent store, me on her hip, after my father decamped. But before I was a year old, the Super guesses, *she* left with another guy, passing through, and disappeared forever. I'm the child left on the orphanage stoop. How's that for a tired cliché? You don't know how I *hate* being a fucking cliché." He chugged.

"There weren't any grandparents? Uncles or aunts?"

"The Super said no one came forward."

"How'd they know…who you were? Your name?"

"The note left on me had one word: 'Benjamin.' The story was that whoever picked me up off the steps brought me in and said, "More'! Meaning, 'another,' I guess; 'one more.' And I became Moore. Benjamin Moore, cliché. My mother was Molly Edmunds. My father, Theo Boswell. After he died, the authorities traced him back to Miss Edmunds, and folks remembered that she'd had a baby before running off with that stranger. By then I was in school as Ben Moore."

He handed me the empty can. I fetched another two while he peed.

"You should write it, Ben," I said. "It's an incredible story. Amazing! And look at you, where you are, after such a start as that!"

"Not incredible. It happened. But it's not verse material. And I'm never going public with it. You're not either."

"Got it," I said. "How about drama? Do you write plays?"

I *did* get it in another sense too. I began to get a little bit why he was angry, and at whom…besides Chatterton…and why at Chatterton too. It looked almost obvious now: about harm and hurt and taint from misrepresentation; unearned recognition; fakery. And Ben must have seen it as well, a long time before now, and figured why I should know the roots of his objections to the whole play project. I didn't have to press him for more history. Or? Had he set me up? Was he encouraging my sympathy — tugging my heart-strings — to make me cancel a plan too painful for his participation? No, that didn't fit. But dicey as it might be, I still needed to sound him out on the future of our play.

"So, Ben, can we still count on you for, say, lyrics… ballads…tech help? Or would you rather write dialogue?"

He made me wait. Then: "I hope those aren't my only options. I'd like to help *you*, Troy. I know this means something to you. But I'm not sure this is the right project for me. It's not just Chatt. It's also Park. His part. He'll have to decide about his time. But we — *you* — should decide about his *use*, and his reliability. He's flighty, Troy; he's so…unsteady. He's like a stage flat about to tip over. That's sort of what I meant about not trusting him. He's not dependable. And now with this news about his book…."

"But he knows everything about Chatterton. That's why we need him."

"For what, exactly? What's his expertise *for*? To check us historically? Factually? We don't need that.

That would handicap us. We're writing *fiction*! Tell me what, *practically*, Park brings to the project."

"But we couldn't dump him *now*."

"Ignore him. Leave him out. Ten-to-one he won't even notice. He's gonna be so tangled up in his own affairs all year, he'd be worthless to us anyway. And have you even considered that helping you with the play would slow down work on his book? I mean, what's in it for *him*? How does work on your play help him get tenure? Hasn't that got to be his priority?"

This stopped me. I *hadn't* thought of that. What *was* in it for Park?

"Well, he wants to play Chatterton."

"*We're* supposed to be earning academic credit for this thing. We can't have faculty starring. *You're* Chatterton. Or Jack. Just announce it. Done!"

"He's offered to play his flute. You know, flute tunes, maybe for dancing."

"Phooey on the flute! Too sissy. Look, Tommy Chatt's already a little suspect, doncha think, never mind the whores. Any drama around him's got to be tough. Robust."

"You're the only robust guy working on this one!"

He laughed. "Not working. Not yet anyway."

"You're talking like you are," I said.

"I'm advising. I dunno, maybe I want to be convinced. Right now things look mighty fragile. Like a risky investment. What's Jack say?"

"Ask him. What he says to me is what he's always said: that we don't know enough. About anything. I

figured Park could help fill in those gaps. But now...
now I don't know."

We went quiet for a few seconds. "I don't want to
pry or anything," Ben said, "but are you and Jack...
well...you know...involved?"

My heart bumped. But his little grin was kind.

"Not yet," I replied, truthfully. "Why?"

"Testing my instincts. It's fine with me, of course,
if you are. Not *for* me, but I think it's kind of cool. You
know: Ginsberg and Kerouac and Auden and Baldwin
and all them."

"Who's Baldwin?"

"James. *Giovanni's Room*. It's just out. Great read!"

"So. Where are you, Ben? With the play?"

"Sidelined. Suspended. Tell you what: you find me
an assignment — a related assignment — that'll be decisive for me. Something that'll whet my appetite for
Chatt. I'll work on the mad thing. I might could cool
down. But you need to excite me. Stir up my robust
blood!"

"Okay. I'll think of something."

"Oh, and Mrs. Harrison's wondering what's happened to you. She's lining up her girls for costume design
and wants to know where things stand."

"Yeah, I need to get back to her. If we're going
ahead...or not. How's Leslie?"

"Leslie Anne Symington! That name just sings,
doesn't it? She postponed the next meeting. Too many
kids gone for Thanksgiving. You'll probably hear something soon. Jack may know."

"Thanks a lot, Ben," I said, "for coming by. And for telling me your story. I'm sorry...for all you went through...and...impressed how well you...survived. It helps to know all that. Please don't regret sharing, okay? It's all totally safe."

"So's *your* secret, mate!" He slapped me gently on the back, and sauntered out.

\* \* \*

I awaited Jack after Romantics on Wednesday. "You doin' anything this afternoon?"

"Botany lab at 2, why?"

"Want to cut it? This may be the last good afternoon before winter. I've had an idea."

"Oh?" His tone and eyebrows lifted suggestively. "It's about time!"

We tittered. "No, I'm wondering if you've ever been over to the Alexandria Zoological Park. Wanta take a tour? We saw a zoo in New Orleans, and I liked it."

"Maybe, but that's not your reason, to view the varmints."

"Okay. I want to run something past your...inquiring mind."

"We can't do it here? Over lunch?"

"Boring. Better over there. How about driving?"

I knew he hated botany lab, and I was antsy. Besides, it *was* a gorgeous afternoon — mild, clear, bright, calm — and I *had* liked the Audubon zoo.

We grabbed burgers and fries and shakes at this new pit-stop named McDonald's on the outskirts.

"Park was pretty good, didn't you think, on 'Childe Harold…'?" I offered. "He likes Byron. I may have to memorize those lines on Napoleon. Especially stanza 42 — and then, later on: 'I have not loved the world, nor the world me…,' and so on. Pretty fine verse!"

"And at the end of Canto IV," Jack said; "the address to the Ocean.

> And I have loved thee, Ocean! and my joy
> Of youthful sports was on thy breast…
> To wanton with the breakers….

Who knew 'wanton' was a verb? 'To wanton' on your breast! Gotta love that."

"But it was an awful long assignment. Two whole cantos!"

"Awfully."

"It can be an adjective, 'awful.'"

"Not there. It would mean 'terribly bad' there."

"One of these days, Jack, I'm going to tell you to stop doing that."

We walked the wide path into the park, under shading palms and palmettos, and beside planted and potted ferns and clean wooden benches.

"Can we sit here?" I asked. "I need your full attention. Before the monkeys grab it."

"What *can* you be up to?"

We sat. He reached out his Viceroys, offered.

"No thanks. Now listen, Jack. I've had a different idea for the play."

"You've dragged me all the way over here to talk about that non-existent play?"

"No, not that one. Maybe one more likely to get born…if you'll let me. Okay? Here goes:

"What if we contemporize? Modernize everything? Forget Bristol. Forget Rowley and Redcliffe. Forget all that eighteenth-century shit. Instead, we bring everything forward to contemporary San Francisco. People do this all the time: dress up old films and plays in contemporary garb, update settings, cars, hairdos. *Our* Tommy Chatterton is twenty, a dropout from Berkeley, but still an aspiring poet. Are you with me? He's placed a few lyrics in 'little magazines,' they're called, but nothing big-time, and he's desperate to. He lives in a slum with his ailing, widowed, welfare mom, and works oddjobs — message-boy, mail-boy, delivery-boy. He rides a second-hand beat-up old Honda Super Cub motorbike. He hangs out at the City Lights Bookstore and loves that scene. He's asthmatic and bi-sexual. He sleeps around. He smokes weed and does psychedelics when he can get them. He's never forged anything, and wouldn't."

Jack fumbled his Viceroy onto the ground, kicked it away.

"Are you following?" I asked, a little trembly.

"I'm listening."

"He doesn't forge. But he's written what he calls his 'epic.' Hold on, now: his 'epic' is a modern, vernacular version of the combined narratives of Matthew, Mark, Luke, and John of the New Testament, only written in regular blank verse — unrhymed iambic blank verse: virgin birth, baptism, miracles, last supper, crucifixion, resurrection: the lot. He's peddled it around town as a counter-counter-cultural work for a counter-cultural population, including the gang at Ferlinghetti's shop, but hasn't had any takers yet. He believes he will, and keeps re-writing and adding and pushing. He finds encouragement and loses it. He has affairs with girls and boys. He falls in love. But then he gets the pox, comes down with pneumonia, and despairs. You know how the story ends. In this case, with an accidental overdose. When he's about our age."

I sat back, took a breath. Waited. "I'd be obliged for that cigarette now."

Jack took one, lit it, reached it across to my lips. "Be my guest," he purred.

"It's got grit, Troy," he said. "I'll give it that. And originality and imagination. And color and spunk. But it's not Chatterton."

"It's our Chatterton. That's the point. It's ours. We've got a new story 'loosely based' on Chatterton. We can be selective. We don't have to mention forgery. We're not obliged to any more than we have to say...well, how his father died, or where his boy got baptized. We'll *say* we're 'loosely based.' We'll give Park credit. But we lose Park with this version, since we don't need his history or his cultural background info. We lose your objection that we don't know squat. We *do* know it now. We gain LCC support with the gospel stories. We tidy up Chatt's act so Ben can abide it. And best of all, we secure Ben, and add a whole lot of pizzazz, by putting Chatt in the San Fran beat scene. Where's the problem?"

"'It's not Chatterton,' Jack said, quibbling, "but it's got something else. Life, I'd say. Energy. Pluck. Juice. I'll need to hear it again, maybe read a write-up and think about it, but I'm pretty sure I like it. Yessir, I think I do. I sure as hell like it a lot better than what it's replacing. Which is nothing. This at least looks like a plan. We flesh it out?"

"Exactly. We invent a plot. Characters. You and I and Ben build on this or something like it for the story. Write it to attract other kids to join up. We'll have to talk Park into sticking with the credit hours guarantee, and get LCC to sign off on the sex and drugs, but that's later. I'm also thinking the Youth Group might want to pitch in: there's room here for some 'revolutionary' thinking about scripture."

"Yeah," Jack agreed; "I can see that."

"This all got going," I said, "when Ben asked for an assignment to kick-start his interest in Chatt again. You think this might do it?"

He grinned broadly. "I think it just might…you freakin' little genius! The motorbike alone should do that much! Wanta go watch the monkeys jerk?"

The monkeys proved more interested in each other than in their own privates.

"It's so *unnatural*," Jack quipped. "Those guys don't know what they're missing!"

"And so promiscuous!" I added. "Trading partners like that! So…*rude*. So *random*!"

"Well," he said, as we moved along. "It reminds me we never finished thinking about Auden's 'Lullaby.' You know, the other three stanzas. Verse-paragraphs."

"We didn't. We should. But I don't remember it by heart well enough…."

"I thought it might come up," Jack said, reaching into his back pocket and bringing out neatly folded papers.

"You *planned* this?" I asked. "Why?"

"I was a Scout. I come prepared. Here's your copy. So: what's Auden 'saying' in that first part?"

I refreshed. "He's saying that what he's watching is 'entirely beautiful.'"

"'Faithless' is beautiful? 'Ephemeral' is beautiful? 'Mortal' and 'guilty' are beautiful? The answer is yes. *Human* is especially and entirely beautiful *because* it's faithless and ephemeral and living and mortal, and guilty because it's promiscuous and faithless. You following?"

I'd stopped to re-read and think. He was interesting me.

"Look next," he went on: "Venus's slope is 'tolerant'; these lovers' experience is 'ordinary' and the goddess is sympathetic because what's happening is about to stop happening, and always will be…about to stop. It's special because it isn't…for long. And look: 'certainty, fidelity' pass: they lose themselves…in trying to stick. Fidelity's faithless. Knowledge is fantasy. Bad raps nuke it. And 'knowing' all of that swells its value, hugely: the precious value of every whisper and thought and kiss tonight. Get it?"

"About the value of every whisper and kiss? Or what you're saying Auden says? I'm not sure. It's pretty radical, idn' it? If I'm understanding you."

"The last paragraph is more of the same, affirming it. The joy of the nighttime gives way to the dawn that deserves blessing *because* it will pass back into joyful nighttime again. The voices of the night that insult how you spend yours don't cool down your pleasure because you're protected and embraced...and...and... even *nurtured* by *every human love*, because it's always temporary...and provisional. 'Find the mortal world enough' sums it all up...exquisitely...as a command, as, like, instruction: find total satisfaction and completeness and joy in what you're *moving through* right now even while you're losing it *because* you're losing it. It's not just enough. It's absolutely *everything*, for this moment. What more could you possibly want than that?"

"It's an argument for one-night stands?" I asked.

"Crudely put, yes."

"No, not crudely. Because beautiful. Entirely beautiful. Isn't that what you just said Auden says?"

I tried not to think about monkeys.

**12**

December 6, 1957

Dear Troy, how are you?

I went home for Thanksgiving to see my folks,
what did you do?

My exciting news is the USAF is short on pilots
and trying to recruit college guys. By paying for
flight training. If you sign up for Air Force 101
and 102 to show you're interested you can apply
to this new program. If you get in, the AF will
pay for flight training. No kidding. No military obligation either. And you pick your own
school. I already had those 2 courses freshman
year. So I should be a shoe in.

I quit swimming but I stayed in Glee club. I get to solo in a Bach Christmas Cantata. I'm skipping the KA formal.

Do you hear from Corky? Tell him hay.

Your friend forever,
Monte

ps  My next stop — the wild blue yonder!

*  *  *

Saturday afternoon was the only time Leslie could find for the Church Youth Group committee meeting back in the basement of Broadway Baptist. To my surprise and disappointment, Jack wasn't invited, and as I didn't cotton to riding behind Ben all the way over from school, I hitched a lift from Leslie, who was already bringing a couple of others, including the smart-ass red-headed high school senior who'd wise-cracked about cups and saucers and hair oil, for Leslie wanted a "representative" group and he was probably the youngest. "Gavin Mallory," she said, as he piled in, looking especially smart in a navy V-neck over a white button-down and dark gray chinos, rolled sleeves pushed up to his elbows above toned forearms lightly dusted with reddish hair.

"Party-time!" he clowned. "Where's the suds?"

"I'm Troy," I said, offering a hand; "glad you're aboard." He couldn't be legal.

"I know you," he said, grinning through the freckles. "You smacked Sheila."

"No!" said Leslie from the wheel. "That was unkind. Don't do that again, Troy."

"Yes'm," I said, winking at Gavin. "Nome, I won't."

"I haven't apologized," he said; "has anybody?"

"Not that we know of," Leslie answered. "I hope not. We need to hold against that."

"Holding on," Gavin laughed; "holding in, holding up, holding out, holding off...but never, *ever* holding back," he added, twinkling with bright, brassy mirth.

We were: Zeke, the seminarian; Shirley — Shelia's roommate; Julia, absent that Sunday but a founding member and Leslie's pre-law friend; Leslie; Gavin, Ben, and me. At seven, too many, but aptly uneven and possibly balanced in a way Leslie thought important. After the others unloaded, Leslie said: "I'm sorry about Jack, Troy, but including the ringleader might have looked prejudicial. You'll represent Jack's views. Will he mind?"

"Being left out, for sure. My relaying his views, prob'ly not. But he'll have some. May I know why you asked Ben?" What I really wanted to know was why she asked *me*, but maybe that would slip out sometime.

"He's precise," she said. "Ben distinguished between sheep and lambs. He apologized for rudeness. The only one who did. And — not least — he said he liked my ideas. I'm no more immune to flattery than anyone else!" She smiled hugely.

"I've drafted a statement," she announced, handing copies around as we settled in, "to send to Dr. Hale. I'll read it in a second, and we'll all revise it as required. I'll do a final copy and get one to everybody who was there and to anyone else who ever was that you can remember. We'll allow a week for responses and then collate them and decide, as a committee, whether to send the statement to Dr. Hale."

She read: "'Dr. Hale: On behalf and with the permission and endorsement of the Sunday Night Youth Group at Broadway Baptist Church, I write to apologize sincerely for our discourtesies to you at a recent meeting, and gratefully and respectfully to accept your withdrawal from the leadership of our Group. After prayerful consideration and discussion, we believe ourselves capable of pursuing our Biblical inquiries independently of a director. Thank you for your long and generous supervision. With all best wishes…my name…for the Group.' Comments?"

"Maybe we'd better pray," Gavin said, "so it's truthful."

"Volunteers?" Leslie asked.

"Silently, then," she said; and we dutifully bowed our heads.

"Amen," she said, after a pause. "So…?"

"I don't think we should send copies to anybody not present at the…event," Judith said, "like me. I wouldn't know what to make of it."

"Point taken," Leslie agreed. "We'll send just to attendees."

"Otherwise," I said, "I think it's perfect. Don't change a word."

"What kind of responses do we expect?" Zeke asked, "and what'll we do with them?"

"Honestly," said Leslie, "I don't know. I just thought we should be open to them, in case. Let what they are determine what we do with them?"

"But what if somebody wants to keep Dr. Hale?" Shirley asked. "Shouldn't we decide whether he goes or stays before we take all this trouble...?"

"I think we're empowered to act on the Group's account," Leslie said. "But I see the risk of inviting responses. We could save time if we didn't. We'd need formally to decide...."

"Leslie's statement is decisive," Ben said. "Inviting responses risks a leak. Blunts impact. Risks counteraction. I recommend we assume we've got the power to act, and tell the group we have it by circulating the statement. I'll deliver the original by hand to the doctor at his school."

"Could we do that?" Leslie asked her pre-law friend Judith.

"I wasn't here," Julia said, "but it sounds like he fired himself."

"No, he didn't," Shirley said. "He promised to come back."

"On a condition," Zeke said. "We don't meet the condition, he's fired."

The daring of it felt kind of empowering. The momentum bred on itself. We silently gave Leslie a few seconds to consider.

"Okay," she said. "Without objection, we'll ask Ben to deliver the letter to Dr. Hale at the same time we inform the Group what we've done. Is everybody all right with that? And none of us apologizes, beyond the one in my statement."

"We can't control that," Ben said.

"Could I see a show of hands?" Leslie asked.

Everybody's went up but Shirley's. "I'm going to abstain," she said. "I can't vote to kick him out."

"He kicked himself….," Gavin began, but Leslie cut him off. "It's decided," she said.

"Moving on," she continued, "to next steps. Here's what I'm thinking about format for future meetings: I'm betting that every one of us has at least one Biblical moment that's always kind of bothered us for one reason or another, or maybe no reason at all. Some incident or saying or story that's never had a completely satisfactory explanation. One of mine, for example, is in Genesis. We talked about it a while back in this class, but I'm still bothered by it: why Cain's offering wasn't just as good as Abel's. There really should be an answer to that one, and there isn't, not that I know of. So it nags. Or, for another example, all those questions we raised about the 23rd Psalm that started all this."

"Yeah," Gavin said. "Those were great!"

"So I'm imagining that everybody has at least one passage he or she'd like to work on. You could write it down and give it to me, with the source reference, and I could schedule it for group examination. You'd lead. It's not like homework. You'd just raise some questions and we'd get to work on the passage. I don't mean like how did Jesus do the miracles, or anything blasphemous. Something unanswered or incomplete or bewildering. Maybe how it's relevant now."

"We have to answer the questions?" Shirley asked.

"No," Julia said. "We might stumble on some answers but hypotheticals are more interesting than determinations, which by definition are dead-ends."

"Pardon my French," Ben said, "but what we're basically talking about is bullshitting. Bullshitting around scripture. I don't have any objection; in fact, I'm pretty sure we'd all get a kick out of it. I'm just calling it by its name."

"Not that name here, Ben," Leslie said, her face flushing. "This is still church. So what do others think?"

"Would we research our topics?" Shirley worried.

"So long as you acknowledge it," Leslie said; "but it's not expected. Just talk about what you think of it, why it's nagged at you. It's a *group* discussion."

"We should give it a try," Zeke said. "We know how. We're just not conscious we do. I mean, we do it all the time in classes. What's to lose?"

Such out-loud reflection continued for a while longer with folks chiming in with favorite Bible puzzlements and refinements of Leslie's general plan for future meetings. She'd edit the questions and schedule and let us know.

"Just remember," Leslie said. "Write *questions*. Not necessarily irreverent, but a little respectful irreverence is acceptable if it cuts to the heart. Questions is where we'll start."

And for the time being, that's where we officially ended, only everybody sort of hung around, meeting and milling and mixing, casually relaxed, trading Bible discombobulations and threatening hellfire if somebody stole theirs, joking, teasing, laughing. What struck me was how light-hearted we all were, even jolly, as though we'd accidentally come on, by ourselves, how to have a really good time in church. Ben huddled with Leslie, I with Gavin, who'd after all predicted a party.

\* \* \*

"Benjamin," I said, when he picked up his private line at Mrs. Harrison's the next morning, "are you on campus today?"

"This aft," he said; "I have a game at 2. What's happening?"

Ben volunteered as a student coach for the girls' softball team; and although everybody understood what cable jumped his battery, word got around that he passed well enough as a coach too, popular with the girls and compatible with the staff. I figured a rule forbade hanky-panky with the team but maybe not with the all-female coaching crew, which might have been his prime target anyway. They practiced and played year round, Sundays too, weather permitting.

"Well," I said, "you asked for an assignment. I may have one for you."

"What assignment? I don't remember asking…."

"For the project. You said maybe a different Chatterton assignment might get you interested again."

"Oh, right." He paused. "But I didn't…."

"How about lunch at 1? In the cafeteria? You good with that?"

"Well…okay, then. How about a hint?"

"Sure. Our next assignment is to modernize everything! We move to San Fran. We dump forgery. Chatt's a beatnik, a Berkeley dropout druggie. An unpublished poet with an epic to place. How's that grab you?"

"Whoa!" he exclaimed. "How'd *that* happen? What's *that* boy smokin'?"

"Details at 1!" I said.

Not openly as an invitation to sleep-in on Sundays — since LCC openly expected everyone to attend Sunday school and church — our cafeteria nevertheless accommodated delinquency by serving breakfast till mid-afternoon, so Ben and I heaped on the pancakes, forked up extra linked sausages, and poured on enough syrup to soak the stack right through, with sugared coffee on the side.

"You haven't done this — made these changes — for me, have you?" he asked.

"In the sense of 'for your benefit,' no; in order to *get* you, to secure you for the project, arguably yes. But you in any sense are only part of my reasoning. May I explain?"

"I wish you would."

"The general idea is to familiarize by contemporizing. We make Chatterton recognizable. We 'loosely base' our play on what's known about him, but we don't hesitate to be selective and creative. You've heard of artistic license. We're using some, in the interests of better drama. Our Chatt is twenty, lives in The Tenderloin with his widowed mom and a red long-haired dachshund Noodle who goes with him everywhere. They're all three very close. Chatt works odd jobs part-time — office boy, message boy, mail-room boy— and writes poetry full-time. Mom wants him to find a regular job but encourages his ambition. Some conflict there. He's finished an 'epic' in blank verse retelling the gospel narratives of the New Testament but can't find a publisher. Discouragement there. He hangs out at the City Lights bookstore, meets Ferlinghetti and Burroughs and Ginsberg, all of whom take an interest, Allen a sort of paternal one. Ginsberg becomes a mentor for our guy. Thinks he's got something. Chatt's a sensitive, good-looking boy; a bit delicate — asthmatic — moody, stubborn about his art. He likes boys *and* girls, sleeps around with both. Of course he falls in love, maybe with a boy and a girl who leave him for each other. To be decided. He boozes and smokes and does drugs. But he lives for poetry and means to succeed at making it. That's the basic story: how he lives and works that passion. Eventually he gets the pox, then pneumonia. Dies of an accidental overdose, maybe of medicine? The funeral's at City Lights. In an Epilogue, Ginsberg announces the epic has a publisher, then recites an elegy in tribute to the boy, written by himself."

Ben was looking very hard at me, straight into my eyes, his own dark, burning, and unblinking, his fist at his mouth. Slowly, he moved the fingers aside to speak. "Fucking A," he said matter-of-factly, and then, grinning, again so loudly that it alarmed neighboring tables: "Fucking A-plus, you wunderkind dickhead! That's a fucking grand slam!"

"Maybe in the making?" I said, though mightily pleased. "You and Jack and I'll need to flesh out a plot. Build drama. It's a little short on conflict and tension."

"I don't act, though. I told you that. I'm behind the scenes."

"Writing's behind the scenes. And you'll have to act Ginsberg. That's firm."

"I can't act queer. And that's firmer."

"Oh, Ben. Don't do this. There's nobody else. You *are* Ginsberg. You're already Ginsberg, all the time!"

"I can't act queer Ginsberg."

"Okay. Let's not get stuck here now. Say we don't *write* queer for Ginsberg. You be 'normal' straight Ginsberg. We'll figure it out. But that's got to be your role. You know you'd hate anybody else doing it."

"What's Park's part?"

"I don't see one for him. I guess he might could still advise, but we're pretty much outside his time-frame here. And he's going to be so distracted.... And, really, there's nothing in it for him...now."

"Jester? Fool?"

"*Ben!*"

"We're still getting course credit, right?"

"I'll have to work on that…with Park. We may have a little leverage.  Oh, and  LCC will need to sign off on the sex and drugs."

"Is Mrs. Harrison still in the picture?"

"Yes, and would you please speak to her for me, Ben? Tell her I'll ring in a day or two.  She and her girls can still do costume design, though it'll be easier.  Maybe more fun. The Beats *do* have a defined look, don't they?"

"They think so. Maybe we do? And Troy: you do know that Mrs. H. has a theater friend in New Orleans?"

"I'd actually forgotten. Thanks.  Now Ben: We *can* count on you being back, and fully aboard, correct?"

"It's not a ship, sailor. But yeah, pipe me aboard."

"Just one more thing: that anger under control?"

"'I was angry with my friend; / I told my wrath, my wrath did end.' William Blake. Balls and strikes now. Gotta run."

Two steps off, he turned back: "Still, Troy," he said; "nothing changes the fact of his fraudulence."

"No," I said; "but we write him a respectable life."

"You write," he said; "you and Jack. I write verse."


After Romantics on Monday, I made an appointment with the Department secretary to see Professor Royal and explain the revised project to him. I believed we Three Wise Guys ought to defend it together, but chicken-livered Ben and Jack argued that since the revision was mine, I should solo its pitch to Park. He'd strutted his way though the morning's lecture on Canto

1 of Byron's *Don Juan*, so I hoped his high spirits would carry over into our meeting at 1.

"Come in, darlin', do come in," he said cheerfully, "and please take your appointed chair. I've not had the pleasure of seeing you privately for some days. I trust you are well-disposed?"

"Yes sir, thank you, sir. I am well. And yourself, sir?"

"As well as may be expected under the dire circumstances, yes, thank you. Now what brings you so punctually under my tutelage this fine afternoon?"

"It's about our play, sir, the Chatterton play," I signaled with my thumb at the large death-bed poster on the wall behind me, "the project Ben Moore and Jack Latimer and I are writing, for course credit, this term, you may recall."

"I well remember. You're here to report progress?"

"Yes, sir. And a revision of our plans."

His eyes narrowed. "It's early December, I believe. Possibly somewhat behindhand for amendments of *plans*?"

"We trust not, sir. You see, we've found it necessary, for the good of the project, to *contemporize* everything. We're very grateful for your advice, sir, and we read those books you recommended, but we've decided to move our story from 18th century Bristol into 20th century San Francisco where Chatterton is a Beat Generation poet associated with the City Lights Bookstore people. And we've cleaned up his act."

"Wait...wait...," Park sat forward, fluttered his hands. "What? You've moved...? Say that again."

So I did. And he let me. I had his attention. I rolled out details, rapidly, to head off interruptions. His brows had lifted at "San Fran" and stayed up. I may have added a little spice around sex and drugs, but otherwise kept pretty much to The Wise Guys' blueprint. Winding up, I said: "And we're scrapping the hoax part. We don't mention fraud."

"Well, that part's always been problematic anyway." He stared at the poster, swiveled his chair slowly. "He publishes his epic?"

"Ginsberg gets it published, yes."

"He doesn't kill himself?"

"Not deliberately, sir."

"Is he buried from St. Paul's? You see the Cathedral there, through his window."

"Um, it's San Francisco, sir, not London."

"Oh. Well, Grace Cathedral, then. But Tommy *should* be buried in The Poet's Corner at Westminster." He actually crossed himself.

"I don't believe we can make that happen, sir."

"Maybe they have a columbarium at Grace. You should check."

Not knowing the word, I let this pass.

"So that's it, then?" he asked, after a pause. "The Marvelous Boy by Three Wise Men. *Au courant.*"

"Well, sir, that's the plan."

"Sweet Jesus," he sighed, wagging his head. "Please pardon me while I calm my knocking heart." He fanned his face with both hands.

Then he rocked back, stiffened, turned his whole body to face me.

"Where'd you get all this, Troy? How'd you come up with it? No kidding, now."

"I just thought of it, sir. Ben's told us about the Beat scene; you've mentioned it. We've read. It just seemed like a natural fit for Chatt...Chatterton, sir. Like he'd... well...want to live there...with those...types. Those poets."

"So what're you asking me? What do you want from me?"

"Permission, sir. To proceed with the idea. For course credit."

"As an *idea*, it is *in-can-des-cent*! Absolutely *phe-nom-e-nal*! If I may so put it. An exquisite vehicle, I might say, for showcasing his gifts. Someone should ring Hollywood. You are to be commended: for imagination and daring. For *balls*! The burning question is, are you boys up to finishing the job?"

"We want to try, sir."

"With my help?"

"Yes, sir. We hope for your support. Will we earn credit for...for...making...the play?"

"Hmmm. Let us ponder together the meaning of 'making.' Composing? Producing? Staging?"

We wise men had not been wise enough to antici-pate these reasonable questions, so I had to wing it from here.

"We believe," I said, "that we can give you a com-plete draft of the play by the end of this term. We would, the three of us, hope to earn three credit hours each for this work. As credit for the Romantics course. Without other papers or tests. If you agree, we'd sign up for three hours of Independent Study next semester, and put on a stage version of the play at the end of that term, next June, for three more credit hours, each."

"And if you don't finish?"

"We'd get Incompletes until we did. And then a grade."

"Back to 'support.' What manner of support is expected from me?"

"We're aware, sir, of how busy you've…become… and the pressure you're under…."

"Never you mind about that!"

"…how…overloaded you are…and out of respect for that we'd expect only advice from you about the play. We'd like to know we can come to you at any time, if we get stuck, knowing that you'd…. But we'd try not to be…nuisances. Sir."

"Don't truckle, darling. It's unbecoming. But what I meant…I meant…would you want me…involved…in, say, performances?"

"With respect, probably not, sir. Maybe, though, with your flute, for music? We haven't thought about a score yet, sir."

"Could you stop with the 'sirs'? I welcome your respect but all the 'sirs' are fatiguing."

"Yes s…. We can think about the music next term."

"Who's cast as Chatterton?"

"We haven't definitely decided."

"I might want some input on that."

"Yes, sir. What about the credit…sir?"

He pushed back, turned away, toyed with the baton. Went quiet for a few beats.

"For credit," he said: "each of you will write a precis for me, a full narrative summary of the plot; also a characterization of each principal, including motives, functions, conflicts, relationships, contributions to the overall dramatic effect intended by the script; also an analytical description of the *theme* your play will enact: the driving *idea* you want your audience to come away talking about. That is, your *purpose* in undertaking the project. Write that up and give it to me by the end of this semester's exam period. But you still have to take the Romantics final. You'll learn nothing about Romanticism by writing this play."

"Sir, would you please repeat the assignment? If I could borrow a sheet of paper to write…?"

"No," he said.  Then: "Oh, all right. I'll write it up. Collect it from the secretary in a day or two. Are we copacetic?"

"It's not fair," Ben said. "How're we supposed to prepare for the exam if we're writing this paper at the same time?  Didn't you point that out, Troy?"

"Well, he laid this thing out so…suddenly, I didn't think to. Besides, everybody else in the class'll be writing *their* term papers at the same time. And he said we wouldn't learn anything about Romanticism by writing the play."

"No," Ben said; "that's not right. The guys in San Fran are all over the Romantics. Ginsberg *performs* Blake. Greg Corso idolized Shelley, and even thought well of Chatterton."

"Well, you can appeal Park's ruling," I groused.

"I bet you didn't mention DeWitt's class either, and *that* paper," Jack said. "Weren't we going to use the play to count for the drama paper too? You blew it, Troy."

"*You* should have come with me. Both of you. I wanted you there. If you've got a problem with the results, take it up with Park."

"Well," Ben said, "we should agree on the precis. The three precis should match. We'd better meet and crank out one right away. Why don't we each think of a plot line — a story — and meet to talk them through? Then one of us — you or Jack — can draft it. And from there we refine. Actually, we'll have to collaborate on the other parts too, or we're off the rails from the start and looking at a train wreck for a play."

"I can't just sit down and spin out a plot because you and Park say to," I whined.

"Fuck that! " Jack said. "You already did. That's what started this shit. All that 'revision' stuff you told us and then Park. Just 'flesh it out,' you said. So *flesh*!"

I left this meeting sour and crabby for having disappointed my friends, and increasingly doubtful that we could team-write the play. Whatever *was* I thinking when proposing that we do? We three novices actually knew precious little about writing anything. But what we did for certain know from experience and reports was that writing is nearly always a solitary and lonely affair and that the isolation and the lonesomeness are part of its romance. But romantic or not, how would a collectively produced script from diverse minds ever achieve any consistency or even coherence? Collaboration wasn't a sport, with co-operating, choreographed players performing programed moves. Writing was a painstaking, time-consuming, trial-and-error, blood-sweat-and-tears grind. A sweaty, grueling slog. I couldn't see us, as us, succeeding at it.

Besides, the relationship among ourselves was suddenly stressed. Jack was right that I let everybody down with Professor DeWitt (but they should have helped me out with Park). Ben was right to step up with plans when I didn't, but I felt at least temporarily displaced as leader. I lost control with Park when allowing him, without challenge, to impose an unfair assignment, and the boys saw that and had a right to resent it. I felt put out, maybe depressed, a little lost. I thought of Corky, of seeking comfort there.

But that's another thing: "Kaiden" wasn't working for me. It's partly the name, but not just that. Where's the cocky boy in "Kaiden"? It's too adult, too insistently mature. He always said he'd lose "Corky" when he outgrew it, but I hardly knew what that meant or that he meant it. "Kaiden" couldn't be everybody's All American Boy (excepting for the moment the queer and cooking parts). I needed him to be Corky (not excepting the queer and cooking parts). The change wrought by "Kaiden" was hard to pinpoint, exactly, but I needed to try to. I didn't and don't think it's about the sex. I mentioned the expanded exposure by the sex but I'm okay with that. I kind of like that. It was rather the vague sense during our visit that I was being "managed" or something. Yes, he was my host; he was supposed to lead me, show me what's what. But he kind of *directed* me. Those two times right before intimacy he'd said, "Come to me," and while it was stirring and enticing and even sexy, it sounded and felt more like an instruction than an invitation. And it sounded experienced. But here's an example of the opposite: when we were sitting in Mrs. Logan's living room and he patted his lap and invited me onto it, that felt almost more thrilling than the later hugs. There wasn't any directing in it. And even better: when we were obviously dallying and delaying, and he said "We're volleying" and I said "I know": that tiny moment of held back want and agreement — of agreement *in* desire to hold back — felt and still feels more intimate and even loving than all our clasping and clutching later on. In that sweet second he was Corky, whose comfort I wanted. Not the kidder who joked about majoring in boys, plural.

As for Jack, well, what *of* Jack? I usually envied and competed with people I knew to be smarter than me, as Jack is. (So is Ben, and way more experienced.) I admired Jack. He wasn't handsome but his longish, slender frame attracted me, his direct, forthright manner drew me; his beautiful hands and the graceful ways he used them, especially with cigarettes, turned me on. I imagined them on me. I knew that Jack wanted me to want him, and sometimes I did. But Jack seemed also to want everybody else as well, including Monte in his uniform (only, I guess, out of it). I'm sure I was supposed to believe Jack sexually experienced, and I guess my assumption that he *was* is a reason I withheld my sexual favors, such as they may have been, or because I'm scared of being one of many. It was not a subject I was willing to bring up with him, no matter how many Auden poems he wooed me with. But sex as a subject between us might hinder amiable alliance over the play. I would especially need to confirm Professor DeWitt's willingness to give credit for the play and relieve Jack and me of the final paper assignment, although he'd be no more likely than Park to waive the exam. Meanwhile, Jack continued keen on the Church Youth Group and on my continued involvement. The truth is, I was more likely to stay for Jack than for Biblical inquiry. But staying for Jack could get complicated: young Gavin Mallory had entered my fantasy realm, and I figured he was romping around Jack's too.

Ben had set the date and offered his apartment for our meeting to "plot the precis," he said, and suggested that I see Mrs. Harrison beforehand to bring her up to speed. He'd ferried me from campus and disappeared upstairs. We expected Jack to arrive in a half-hour or so.

"Rodney," she said, after he'd escorted us in, "please bring Mr. Tyler a beer."

"Oh no, ma'am," I said, "thank you but I'd better not."

"Tut, tut, young man," she replied, waving me to the chair. "Don't think I'm unaware the first thing ya'll do up there is crack a brewski."

We laughed. "Nome. I mustn't. I'll need a clear head. Thanks, anyway."

"Very well, Rodney," she said dismissively. "Nothing for me either, as I never imbibe alone." If this was meant to change my mind — and she paused long enough to let me — I wasn't biting. "So," she continued, "Ben tells me you've…revised?"

"Yes'm. And it should greatly simplify costuming, if you and your ladies and your New Orleans friend are still able and willing to assist us."

"I cannot promise Dr. Gladiola Peytonberry but my widows are impatiently waiting, on pins and needles I might say, for their assignments. You have them?"

"Yes, ma'am, but the Beat uniform — you understand the term 'Beat'? — the 'uniform' is very simple. I'm not even sure we need…."

"I read the newspapers, child, and my contacts keep me informed. I believe the basic costume is the red-tag Levi jean and the white crew-neck short-sleeved T-shirt, am I right? Sometimes called 'the muscle-shirt,' and borderline vulgar?"

"Yes'm, you're mostly right, but we won't use muscle-shirts. We want sleeves. Short sleeves on the T's. And — I'm sorry about this — they're not clean. The shirts and jeans should be at least a little soiled. And maybe saggy and wrinkled. Well-worn but not threadbare. Not ragged. They could be torn."

"And everybody wears them? Even the girls?"

"No, ma'am. There won't be many girls but they should be in bulky, oversized dark sweaters and skin-tight black jeans, or looser pants ending just below the knees or mid-calf. And sandals. The boys get sandals too. The girls needn't look as shabby as the boys."

"I've seen photos of the females in pencil skirts."

"If that's tight and narrow, skinny? Yeah. Sometimes with bright, blousy — loose — like, silky, shirts? I doubt heels. I don't know about stockings. But sandals. Nothing formal, ever. Oh, and if it's cold, maybe sheep-skin jackets, for both sexes. And motorcycle jackets for the guys."

"Jewelry?"

"I'm not sure. I'd guess not. What do you think? A guy might have a heavy ring. Oh, wait, let's give Chatterton a small metal crucifix on a chain. He'll always wear it. Even during sex. Oh, sorry ma'am, I didn't mean to say that."

"We'll ignore that...but I rather favor the idea." Whether she liked the idea of the cross itself or its display during sex, I really wanted to ask but didn't dare.

"Anything else special about your hero's dress?"

"Well, ma'am, he should dress...distinctively. So you know he's the one to keep your eye on. His hair...his hair is about the color of...well...a Sazarac, only darker. 'Russet,' I think it's called, so maybe a T-shirt in a color that'll go with...dark orange, and make him stand out. And worn Levis. Faded...."

I paused, an idea forming. Whoa! Why hadn't I thought of it before?

"Just a minute, please, Mrs. Harrison," I said, scrambling for my backpack. "I almost forgot. I brought you something to look at." I pulled out the large book and opened it to the marked place where a reproduction of the Wallis death-portrait spread across two pages.

"You see," I handed it to her, "you see he wears long sleeves. It's a white shirt, all right, with almost no collar, but long sleeves with lace at the sort of scallop-shell cuff...and I've just decided, ma'am, that we want him in that exact shirt for the whole play! If one of your widows could copy that exact shirt, with a whole lot of creamy chest and stomach showing, why, we'll keep Chatt clothed just like that in every scene."

She studied the page. "Oh, yes; Clementine can certainly cut out a blouse on that pattern and sew it up to a fare-thee-well! Are you aware that he's wearing Capri pants? Would you want us to copy those too?"

I moved to look over her shoulder at the image, and I saw the body as I never had seen it. I saw Jack, and almost gasped.

"What is it, child?" Mrs. Harrison turned sharply toward me, nearly bumping my face. "Are you faint? You look pale...!"

"No, I'm fine, ma'am. A little spell of the fantods there," I said, recalling a word from my granny's store. "I'm good. I just realized.... Well, ma'am, yes; we'd very much like you to copy those...pants, too. Everything he's wearing. That right there has got to be his costume for the entire play. That'll make him...distinctive. Recognizable. And that pale chest will just glow, with the cross always showing."

And as though my fancy had summoned him, at that moment Jack rang the door chime.

Upstairs, in Ben's disordered room, we decided:

The time: 1957.

The place: Three settings:

(a) The shabby kitchen and parlor of Chatterton's walk-up in the Tenderloin district of contemporary San Francisco where he — age 20 and a Berkeley drop-out — and his ailing, fortyish, widowed mother discuss their situation and prospects, his dynamic father (now dead), his own fierce literary ambitions, his part-time jobs, his associations. C's beloved red, long-haired dachshund Noodle lives with them and accompanies the boy everywhere as his popular side-kick. The relationships are tight.

(b) The City Lights Bookstore, 261 Columbus Avenue, SF, where C holds a part-time job sorting and stocking books and assisting customers. The owner, Lawrence Ferlinghetti, has furnished a stockroom corner with a small desk, a chair, and a cot for C's use. Noodle enjoys the run of the shop and is a great customer favorite.

Allen Ginsberg, frequently in the store, mentors C, "parents" him, critiques his poems, promotes him with customers, presses Ferlinghetti and influential patrons to market his verses. C meets and fancies customers Cheryl Ryan and Craig Briscoe, both aspiring actors at Berkeley roughly his age, and dates both. The store hosts a large 21st birthday disco dance celebration for C — a sort of store mascot — to which poets, publishers, and the press are invited, and where C is touted as a "coming artist." A raucous, colorful, high-energy dance concludes Act 2.

(c) C's garret in the Tenderloin, furnished as in the Wallis portrait, with the addition of a small desk, a chair, and a crammed bookcase. Here C writes, heats meager meals, smokes weed, does drugs when he can afford them, entertains an occasional whore, sleeps separately with Cheryl and Craig, and always with Noodle. Here C also completes and obsessively revises his epic narrative retelling in blank verse the narratives of Matthew, Mark, Luke, and John. Grace Cathedral appears though the garret window. C twice hosts the major SF publisher, Joseph R. Murray, a deeply religious man with philanthropic interests who wants to support C's artistic endeavors but expects personal favors from C in return. The failure of negotiations on this point bitterly disappoints C, but he cannot oblige.

C is treated, with marginal results, for venereal disease, loses the affection of Cheryl and Craig in a blowup, following which they "find" each other. C becomes despondent but continues to compose and revise, curtailing his involvement at City Lights. We last see him bent at his desk, exhausted, weak, writing by candle-light, as the spotlight fades to darkness.

On a bare, dimly-lit stage, Ginsberg delivers an Epilogue in prose — Noodle in his arms —recounting the death by drug over-dose, possibly accidental, and recites a tribute to the boy, concluding with the announcement that Ferlinghetti will shortly publish the epic.

To these details of a precis — of a plot — we remarkably agreed after a long and intense but generally affable conversation. Since the outline was mine, I volunteered to draft copies for them to use as models for their own precis for submission to Park, disguised enough to forestall charges of plagiarism but similar enough to confirm our unanimity on the general plot and to assure that we all got credit. I also thought I should proceed, through consultations with Jack, to sketch out action and dialogue to carry forward the narrative from the skeletal precis. Eventually, I'd submit that draft to Jack, who'd revise and refine it into final dramatic form for each of us to sign off on. It had grown very late, but we were pumped, shamelessly pleased with ourselves, and seemed a little reluctant to break up.

"Thanks, guys," I said, grinning. "We did it!"

"We did something," Ben said, also grinning. "I dunno what it'll look like in the morning. But revision is fun."

"Who said it needs revising?" Jack asked, laughing. "It looks like Wise Men's gold to me!"

"Well," I said, "we ain't leavin' it lying around the stable for the donkeys to pee on."

"Laying," Jack said.

He gave me a ride back to campus. The streets were deserted, the neighborhoods quiet. He left the radio off. But the car's air buzzed.

After a while he said, "We were pretty good back there, wouldn't you say? I always said we should do a project together."

"We've still got a lot to do. Most everything, really."

"Together," he said, and went quiet, letting it sink in. I waited.

"Troy," he said, his voice a little strained, husky. "Why don't you scoot over here next to me? Wouldn't you like to?"

I didn't think about it. I moved over.

"Next to me," he prompted. "Not over there in the center. Next to me where I can feel you."

I shifted. Our shoulders touched, our thighs. "I don't want to get in your way," I said.

"You can put your hand on my leg, if you want to." His dropped off the wheel and onto my thigh, and stayed there, a finger stroking.

"What're we doing here, Jack?" I asked quietly.

"I guess we're starting what looks mighty like a make-out session," he grinned. "What's your guess?"

I tucked my head into his shoulder and brought my right arm over and around his neck, lifted my lips to his cheek and kissed it. I sat back, not touching him, and turned sideways on the seat to face him.

"Like that?" I said.

"Are you asking about similarities, or whether I enjoyed the kiss?"

"You're red-penciling me for ambiguity! Don't you ever stop *grading* people, Jack?"

"I'm not aware of it. Does it bother you?"

"Of course you're aware of it. You do it on purpose. To embarrass people. Even Park."

"Maybe especially Park. Okay, I do it. Sometimes unconsciously. Automatically. If it bothers you, I'll stop."

"Well, I guess I learn something when you do it. Like that time with 'awful.' I guess I don't really mind… that much."

"So come back over here, why doncha? I liked your head up here."

But I slid away, toward the window.

"What's wrong, Troy? Don't be mad. Are you mad?"

"I'm not. I'm just…well…kind of confused. I mean, we were good tonight, back there at Ben's. That was actually fun. Working through it with you, getting something done, and a lot planned. And then…touching you was also nice. Really nice…and…sweet. But then you… well…you *graded* me. You judged me. And as always I came up short. I don't know if I disappointed you, or if I just disappointed *me*...in your eyes. But I feel like a disappointment. You make me feel like a disappointment. And you always make me feel like we must be looking for different things."

"You mean different from what most guys are looking for, or different for you, from what you think I'm looking for?"

"See what I mean? Case closed," I said.

"What is it you think I'm looking for?" he asked, looking hard at me and away from the road for longer than he should've. "I don't know what *you're* looking for. But you're kind of exaggerating, aren't you? Over-reading? Or is that also grading? Have I actually hurt your feelings? God, Troy, I didn't mean to. Lord, no, you don't disappoint me, never! That little smooch was sweet, and a very nice surprise! So...come on back over here. Put you head back up here. Please."

"No, I can't. Not now. Just take me home."

"I was hoping you'd come up. See my room."

"Maybe some other time. But there's one more thing. I was going to save it, to tell you later. But maybe this is a good time. You know when I was visiting Mrs. Harrison, before you came, to plan costumes?"

"Yeah, what?"

"Well, I had this moment, when we were looking at the Wallis portrait of Chatterton...in a book. It was sort of spooky, kind of like a vision or something. I was looking down at Chatterton, stretched out on that bed in those clothes, and I saw...Jack! I saw you, Jack, as Chatterton. I don't mean you were dead or anything, but he was you. I want you to be our Chatterton, Jack. You're perfect. You'll do it? There's nobody else."

He stopped at my dorm and turned off the motor, stared ahead.

"Park wants the role," he said. "He expects to get it. He can force us to give it to him."

"Ben won't stand for that. Ben doesn't trust him. I don't think I do either. And I want you as my Chatterton."

"That is so sweet to hear, Troy," he said. "I'm flattered."

"You're complimented," I corrected. "Flattery's always a lie. You meant to say 'complimented.'"

And we both cracked up.

# 13

December something

Dear Troy

The great news is I got accepted to the AF-ROTC flight-training program at Nellis AFB in New Mexico. It's close to Vegas. They'll fly me out during Christmas break and show me around. And look me over. And then next semester they'll bring me back weekends for two more training days all through the semester. And for three months next summer. No more Jubilee for me. I'll soon be solo-flying jets. You never said what you did Thanksgiving. Or about Corky. The Bach cantata is next week.

You owe me a visit to Baylor. I guess you'll go home Christmas.

Your friend forever. I think about you all the time.
Monte

* * *

December 1957

Dear Monte,

Congratulations on your acceptance into the AF-ROTC flight training! That's very exciting. Will you actually start piloting jets soon? Flying this way?!

For T'giving I bused down to New Orleans, to check out Tulane for possible English grad school. Corky showed me around and said to tell you hello.

Good luck on your Bach solo.

I'm busy with assignments. Several of us are planning to put on a play next term. For credit. We have a loony professor.

I won't be taking any trips soon. Maybe for spring break? Yes, I go to Madison for Christmas.

Would you actually visit Vegas? Do you remember, at Jubilee, promising to teach me to gamble? And shuffle cards. You never did.

Your friend anyway,
Troy

\* \* \*

One month and one week after the ruckus with Dr. Hale, Leslie Anne Symington called us to order in the Alexandria Broadway Baptist basement and announced that Ben's delivery of our "statement" to the Doctor had produced no response — to her, anyway — so we'd proceed on our own according to the format she'd suggested. Present were the seven committee members plus Jack and Shirley and four others from the regular group, including Zeke's seminary pal Jeff and the three guys I'd met my first time. Leslie had followed through with her favorite Bible puzzle by assigning the Cain and Abel story for studying at our first session without Hale, probably unaware that three of us had the possible benefit of Professor Park Royal's lectures on Lord Byron's drama *Cain: A Mystery* in three Romantics classes the week before. Ben might have tipped her off, of course, if they were still seeing each other, but he might just as well have kept quiet about what he'd learned and where in order to improve his chances of impressing Leslie with it at our meeting. For his protection, Jack and I needed to be aware of that possibility.

"My question is," she began, "why does God prefer Abel's offering to Cain's?"

"There's already a problem," Zeke said. "The King James Version says God 'respects' Abel and his offering. The New Revised Standard says he has 'regard' for Abel but not for Cain. I've got both versions right here. I hear a difference. 'Respect's' more valuable than 'regard'. Warmer. Preferable. The KJV favors Abel and disfavors Cain in its very language, doesn't it?"

"Maybe," Jeff said, "but more important is that the Bible and Hebrew culture always privilege the first-born. Cain's the first-born. The first born *ever*! Why doesn't God automatically prefer him over his brother? And besides, how is it fair or even possible for God to have any preference at all? We're all equally lovable in God's eyes."

"He makes the rules," Gavin said.

"I notice Cain acts first," Julia said. "Cain sets the example of honoring God with gifts. He's the first human ever to pay homage to the Deity with a gift. That ought to earn him a little favor with God. Abel's just copying his older brother's model."

"But look back at Chapter 3," David said, "verse 17. God says to Adam: 'cursed is the ground because of you....' God condemns Adam to 'eat of the plants of the field...all the days of your life' (3:17-18). Cain tills the ground that's already polluted by his mother's sin. Maybe his gifts from that same earth are defiled and so unacceptable to God?"

"It sounds logical," Jack said; "and in 3:19 the earth gets another bad rap. But it's the same ground, isn't it, that grows the perfect garden that includes the Two Magical Trees? And why should some flaw in the earth make Abel's sheep — 'firstlings,' notice: first-born — the better gift? After all, it fed them."

"I don't really like saying this," Shirley said anyway, "but let's don't forget that Abel kills. Abel is the first killer in history. He slaughters lambs. And those killings look ahead to and link up with the fratricide, and connect the brothers by blood and by deed as killers. You could even say Cain imitates *Abel's* previous murder. And that shows God's inconsistency and self-contradiction in respecting Abel's act and condemning Cain's. God looks bloodthirsty and hypocritical both!"

"The picture in my Bible," Jake said — "I guess it's of a painting — shows Abel standing outdoors by a stone altar sending up smoke, like he's made a burning sacrifice of his lambs. Where do they get that?"

"Not in Genesis," Gavin said.

"It seems to me," Jake continued, "the Lord doesn't distinguish between the giver and the gift, between human and object. He values and devalues both equally. And then Abel doesn't just kill his lambs; he dismembers and mutilates them, evidently to get the fat which — not to be irreverent — which makes lamb such a great stew! But does he keep back the fat for himself? Does he hold onto the best part of his gift and so cheat God out of it? If he doesn't, what's the point in mentioning the fat? Do only firstlings have it? I really don't understand what's happening here, or how it matters in God's responses to the gifts."

My turn, was it? "I figure God's put out 'cause Cain's scowling. Verse 5 says Cain's 'countenance fell.' If God slights your gift, scorns it, wouldn't you scowl too? And then for Him to ask *why* you're sulking after He's scorned your present when He knows why…well, that just adds insult to injury. Rubs it in!"

"What follows," Leslie said, "is a conditional and a leading question. 'If you do well, will you not be accepted?' For all Cain knows, he *did* do well, and is *not* accepted; he's forced to assume he didn't do well. But *how* has he done *ill*? What ill? Maybe he's frowning in bewilderment. We know he's angry. What else can he be angry about except that God dislikes his gift? He just doesn't know *why* he and his gift are disliked."

"May I point out," Ben at last asked, "that in verse 7 God brings sin back into it? He says to Cain, 'If thou dost not well' — as apparently Abel *has* done — 'sin lieth at the door' — 'lurking' at the door in the NRSV: sin is laying for you at your front door, possibly with the apple in hand, and 'its desire is for you.' Sin targets you: 'unto thee shall be his desire.'"

"Yeah," I chimed: "that masculine possessive pronoun practically names the serpent who temped Eve."

"Both translations," Ben went on, "say Cain'll 'master' this sin, but neither one says what the sin *is*. The only sin we've got so far is Mom's and Dad's disobedience. Nobody's sinned since Cain and Abel arrived. Is Cain's gift itself a sin? The future tense verbs in God's warning *anticipate* Cain's sin. His 'mastering' lies ahead, if he can bring it off. I don't see what God's disciplining Cain *for*.

Some future act He foreknows? So Cain gets no chance to master that sin. In that case, Cain's sin happens when he *invites* Abel into the field for a chat. Cain is pre-meditating murder."

The sudden silence felt edgy, apprehensive.

"I tried to kill *my* younger brother," Nathan said.

Everybody stared.

"What?" Leslie asked. "You tried to kill...?"

"My younger brother Gary."

"Are you serious?!" from Jack, gaping.

"That's what the judge said."

"Well, it happens," Jake said. "Romulus killed Remus his twin. Absalom killed Amnon. Claudius killed King Hamlet. Didn't Medea kill her brother to help Jason escape? It can happen."

"Well, I didn't succeed," Nathan said. "And I got off. But I'm pretty sure I tried. The judge *was* sure."

What Jack said then surprised me almost as much as Nathan's confession.

"Okay, so does that help you understand what Cain did to Abel?"

"Kind of. Maybe he wasn't *sure* he was trying to kill his brother. But he killed him anyway, and had to live with that: the doubt around it: that uncertainty. Maybe that's what the curse of wandering is. Means. God would understand the doubt. God understands everything, even when we don't. Especially when we don't."

I took to the sweet child-likeness of Nathan's words. They struck the same note as Jake's about the picture in his Bible.

After a time, Leslie said, "I believe all we've had so far is questions. *Are* questions."

"Is," Jack of course said.

"I realize," Leslie said, "that questions is…are… what I asked for. But maybe we should try now for some answers."

"It might be easier," Ben offered, "to frame some why-questions about the main event coming up, the fratricide. Why does Cain slaughter his brother?"

Murmurs rippled around the room: "Jealousy." "Envy." "Anger." "Original sin." "Frustration and disappointment." "Resentment." "Sibling rivalry." "Blind hate." "To inherit the flock of sheep?"— inevitably from Gavin.

Zeke stood, addressed the room: "I don't see how the motive can be anything but envy. God's played favorites, for no good reason we know of, and it's pissed Cain off. Who can blame him?"

"God," Gavin said.

Ben stood. "In the interest of full disclosure," he began, pausing and waiting for our full attention. Nobody competed for it. "In the interest of full disclosure," he repeated, "Jack and Troy and I are in an LCC literature class where we've been reading a play by the poet Lord Byron titled *Cain: A Mystery,* a three-act drama based on this Genesis story but adding a lot to it. Our professor has lectured three days on the play, and I may owe him for some of what's coming here, this first part for sure: he told us about a letter Byron wrote to his publisher that set down his — the poet's — understanding of Cain's motive for the murder. I looked it up and made a note of it if you're interested."

I remembered this reference only vaguely, and Jack looked as if he didn't recall it either, so we joined in hums of assent.

"Here's Byron," Ben continued. "Quote: 'The object of the Demon' — that is, the tempting Snake of Eden — 'is to *depress* Cain still further in his own estimation…by showing him infinite things and his own abasement, till he falls into the frame of mind that leads to the Catastrophe, from mere *internal* irritation, *not* premeditation, or envy of *Abel* (which would have made him contemptible), but from the rage and fury against the inadequacy of his state to his conceptions, and which discharges itself rather against Life, and the Author of Life, than the mere living.'

"Of course Byron is describing his play, not the Biblical story; but we might consider whether what he says could apply to Genesis. Notice he eliminates envy as a motive."

"Byron says he's depressed," Jack offered, "and irritated. And then rages in a fury…?"

"But not against Abel," I said, remembering a phrase I'd liked: "he rages against an 'inadequacy.' Or *the* inadequacy…of his state to his conceptions,' right, Ben?"

"What's he talking about?" Gavin asked.

"His mortality," Ben said. "The Demon takes Cain on an act-long flight through space and time, through 'myriads upon myriads' of stars, past planets, across and beyond galaxies into gloomy phantom realms, through stretches of space so vast that Earth behind them seems the merest pea, and humankind a speck."

Ben had thus launched himself on a parallel rhetorical flight and swept us up along with himself, abandoned to imagination. He must have had a script in his head but it didn't *seem* like he did, or even could've. It all looked — felt — entirely spontaneous, improvised. He took a breath, brought himself back and down. "Sorry. It's Byron's unleashed imagination showing Cain how cramped and restricted — how...well...how *finite* he is: how stifled his *state* compared to the *conceptions* imaged in the flight. They fly into infinity, beyond opposition, where possibility is absolute and aspiration unchecked. So he acts out his fury against the Author of that 'inadequacy' represented by Abel. With the murder, Cain as he says 'looks the Omnipotent tyrant in His everlasting face and tells him that his evil is not good.'"

"Whoa!" Gavin breathed.

"That," Ben added, "is how Cain defies a god who amuses himself by 'flattering dust with glimpses of Eden and immortality only to resolve it back to dust again.' Yeah, I memorized it."

His voice and hands trembled as he finished and sat down. In the quiet, I glanced at Jack, who only stared back, looking as dumbfounded as I felt. I didn't remember any of this from Park's lectures, or from reading the play, but I was pretty damned impressed by what I'd heard. By what I'd just seen and heard Ben *act out*. He was absolutely and deliberately *performing*. And he not only *knew* he was. He *loved doing* it!

"Thank you, Ben," Leslie said softly, ending the hush. "We have a motive. Offhand, I don't see evidence of it — direct evidence — in Genesis, but maybe I'm missing...."

"I don't see anything to rule it out," Jack said, "except the flight. But even the flight doesn't necessarily rule it out. Cain still has his imagination. It's still functioning, with its blessings and curses."

"Maybe," Jeff offered, "maybe somebody who hasn't read Byron should say. I haven't; and it makes sense to me that Cain blames God for banning Eden after creating it for Adam and Eve and giving it to them for their playground and home. And what other way does Cain have for being angry?"

"In the play," Ben said, "he disputes the logic by which God 'plants' the Garden and then 'prohibits' it."

"Well, who wouldn't?" Gavin asked. "Abel?"

Others voiced cautious observations and pussyfooted questions for a while — little hesitant hunches and guesses about Genesis — but the zip had split; the very air had flattened. Had Ben's show sapped our energy and drained off whatever curiosity and nerve and zeal we'd brought to the session, to the story? No, that didn't feel to me like a sound explanation for whatever had lowered the broody mood settling over us. Dissatisfaction, was it? Disquiet? Fret? My mind strayed, drifted back to "inadequacy." Had *that* kicked in the discontent? Eventually, Leslie tired of pumping.

"All right," she said, "maybe that's enough for tonight. I'll set a January date, and accept written suggestions for topics. And if you have follow-up thoughts or questions about tonight, please share with me. May I be the first to wish everyone a Merry Christmas?"

"And auld lang syne!" Gavin cried.

It occurred to me to ask how he was getting home, but as Jack was driving me, there seemed no point.

"What happened back there?" I said as we both lit up and headed out. I was now carrying my own king Kents. "How come we petered out like that?"

"We were mostly just talking to ourselves anyway," Jack offered. "Nobody listening much. Nobody answering. Maybe we exhausted the text. It happens. There wadn' that much of it."

"There's a lot *to* it, though. Didn't anybody answer a question?"

"Zeke tried, there at the end," Jack said. "But I wadn' keeping track. Prob'ly not."

"See? That's what I said before. Those little games never *lead* anywhere. They don't accomplish a damn thing. We play at irreverence, and giggle, and get nowhere. Sometimes it's interesting but it never settles anything. I mean, people have been asking for a zillion years why Cain did it, and nobody still knows. I mean, still nobody knows. It's such a waste of time and mind to keep poking at it. I'm sick of it."

"You want to quit?"

"I might."

"You didn't learn anything from Ben tonight?"

"I sure as hell *did*! About Byron, though. A lot mor'n I learned from Park. Didn't you?"

"Ben was downright *perspicacious*! Made me want to re-read *Cain*."

"Maybe we should switch our play to *Cain*."

"Don't think I didn't think of that! Except for the spaceflight, we might could!"

"Have you yet read the draft I gave you?"

"I haven't finished it. I didn't want to say anything until I had. The truth is, I got so excited about it I stopped reading…to write. It's wonderful, Troy. It's really very good. I hope my follow-up can be as fine!! I might get done with mine over the holiday break."

"Well, let's don't overlook Park's deadline. You know, tonight's talk might have hinted at a theme for our play: the main idea of it that Park said our audience should walk home thinking about: our 'point.' The three of us should probably name the same theme, more or less. Wouldn't that help our case?"

"Undoubtedly it would, if we differed enough so he didn't think we copied. Would you care to share your main idea?"

"Well, I guess it's actually Ben's," I said. "Maybe I'm already copying him. It's what Ben said Byron said in that letter: how Cain's 'state' wasn't 'adequate to his conceptions.' How he imagined more than he ever was, or could be. And I thought maybe that was Chatterton's problem too?"

Jack studied the road, worked his lips: took a last drag and flipped the butt through the window. He looked over at me, his eyes narrowing almost to a squint, then turned back to the road, scratched his temple.

"You know what, Troy?" he said, a husky pleasure in his throat; "that just might be fucking breakthrough brilliant. 'Inadequacy of state to conceptions.' You realize it's not just Chatterton's problem. Think about it. What if it describes the whole wretched Romantic dilemma? What if it's what drove Blake crazy? What if it's why Billy Wordsworth couldn't finish the damn *Prelude* for fifty years? What if it's why Coleridge ate opium? And for all I know why the other three all died early, from the sheer aggravation of it? Oh, I know I'm exaggerating now, but holy shit, Troy, I think you're onto something. I think *we're* onto something here, if we make that idea the center of our play, don't you?"

He pressed on the horn and held it.

* * *

The remainder of the semester passed as a blur. I had finals in every course but term papers only in Romantics and Drama, and our Chatterton project might substitute for one or both of them. I had solid B's going into exams in Soph Survey and Physical Science, but Trig was borderline C; and I had no backup paper topic for Drama if DeWitt balked on credit for Chatterton. Corky wanted us to visit over Christmas; Ben needed a next Chatterton assignment; Jack wanted conferences almost every day about the Chatt script; and all three Wise Men scrambled to meet Park's demands for the project. At least Mrs. Harrison required no immediate help with costumes.

Professor DeWitt seemed rattled and distracted when without an appointment I showed up at his office to plead for project credit, and vague on what prior agreement we'd reached on the credit question. He recalled a conversation with Professor Royal about our plan but not whether he'd promised term paper credit. I too felt uncertain on exactly what if anything had been agreed to, but I resisted the temptation to take advantage of the addled professor on that point. He looked up my record, saw that I'd improved to a B+ on my second paper (a nasty pan of the conclusion of "The Bad Seed," a film I'd admired until it disgraced itself with a stupidly absurd ending), and finally agreed to accept and grade the same package of materials Park had assigned us for Romantic credit, including the play script, provided that Jack and I truly collaborated on it. But he wouldn't waive the final exam.

I'd finished in good time my precis of the play and passed on copies for the boys to use as we'd agreed, drafted my "characterization of the principals" (subject to revision in light of Ben's sketches of Ginsberg and Ferlinghetti), and in a revised version of the draft play (now in Jack's hands) bore down on the "theme" question, interpreting the mismatch between Chatterton's situation/character and his imaginative conceptions and aspirations. I figured it too risky to extend my speculation to the other Romantic authors, but my interest in the idea survived my application of it to Chatterton. I had a whole next semester of Romantics to ponder the relevance beyond Chatt.

Corky proposed to bus over to Madison from Vicksburg after Christmas. I went along until second thoughts called time-out. This guy comes from Vicksburg and lives in New Orleans. About as rinky-dink and deadbeat a town as ever blemished any Louisiana landscape, Madison boasted one pool hall, two barber shops and two movie theaters, three domino tables on the Courthouse Square, four cotton gins, five car dealerships, six stop lights, seven cafes and drive-ins (no restaurants), eight churches, and a dozen or so tacky, nondescript stores selling everything from gumdrops and nails to seed corn and snuff. Whatever of any possible interest or amusement in the middle of winter could Madison offer a guy who had electric trolleys at the ready to bear him cheaply to countless Babylonian entertainments all over the parish, not to mention a hometown of tremendous historical importance and color? True, though, that my mother's kitchen could out-perform everybody's except her own Mom's, and Corky might get a kick out of clattering the crockery in there with her. Father could spin some pretty fair yarns about growing up poor among Tennessee hillbillies, and again and again proved himself master of the chess board with his deacons and their kids while completely failing to interest me in the game.

Even so, he was still a preacher and ran a preacher's house, with prayers before meals and Bible readings and devotionals and certain expectations that might get under the skins of less spiritually-minded guests. Corky grew up Baptist, of course, and would probably remember all the drills, but whether he'd still be cozy with them, as I wasn't, I wasn't sure. And how would we talk to my parents...without giving anything away? Slips could be dicey if not lethal! And how would we sleep...in a parsonage...belonging to the church? The house had only three bedrooms: theirs, brother Mark's, and mine, all with double-beds, all right next door to each other. I supposed Mother could make up the sofa for Corky or me or Mark, but none of us would like that, and it would look weird, like they were on guard and taking steps, preventive steps. And giving up sex for the visit would defeat the whole point, wouldn't it?

There was also this other thing: I kept thinking I should invite *Ben* home for Christmas, after he'd said he had no place to go at Thanksgiving. I'd felt terrible about that, and wanted to ask him for Christmas, but hadn't, sure he wouldn't want me to feel sorry for him. But I did. I figured Mrs. Harrison would give him Christmas dinner, but he'd prob'ly end up eating it with Rodney in the kitchen. Still: consider bringing a big burly bearded beer-swilling bawdy-mouthed Beat poet into the hallowed home of a fundie Baptist preacher to observe the anniversary of the Christ-child's birth! It sounded like a brazen dare to myself! But Ben *was* mighty savvy at the chess board.

The LCC girls' softball coaching staff traditionally hosted a Christmas social event for the team to remind everybody when spring training began, to announce the season's schedule, and to be sure last year's standouts were returning in good shape. This year's event was a wiener and marshmallow bonfire roast. I'd asked Ben to stop by my room when it finished. Perspiring and red-faced around the beard, he arrived riding high after milling with all those babes.

"That was a ball!" he said. "You shoulda come. I told you you could."

"And I told you I couldn't," I laughed. "Girls' ball's not my sport."

"You got one?" he joked, sprawling into a chair.

"Yeah," I said; "I make plays."

"Good one!" he grinned. "And so *quick*!"

"You'd better be too. That's why I asked you by. Are you writing yet?"

"I've done my 'characterizations' of Allen and Ferlinghetti, like you wanted. Still thinking about Chatt."

"Don't think too long. Your mood under control?"

"You'd know if it weren't."

"Good. I'm about the same place with the assignment. Except I've started on the 'theme' part — the thematic point of our play."

I paused for him to pick up and run with it, but he only crossed his legs, ankle to knee, and waited, the foot jiggling.

"I'm pretty sure," I went on, "that you actually framed a possible theme the other night at Group when you talked about *Cain*. You were incredibly...smart there."

"If I was 'incredible,' you'd better not believe me."

"Don't sound like Jack. You know what I mean. Take the compliment. You were very...perceptive."

"Sorry to sound like Gavin, but what're you talking about?"

"What you said Byron said about *Cain*. About 'inadequacy.' The discrepancy between 'state' and 'conception.'"

"Oh, that. Well, I thought it explained Cain pretty well, didn't you? But I've thought since that it's sort of unusual, idn' it, for an author to explain himself, to tell what he means or wants his work to say?"

"It might sort of limit interpretation?"

"Ha! It might forestall a lot of crackpot analyses! Shut down some journals!"

"And crimp our livelihoods!" We laughed. "But listen: why shouldn't an author *want* readers to know what he means…what he actually says in the work? To prevent misinterpretation?"

"Is that what you brought me over here to find out?"

"Well, no. But don't you think it's a kind of interesting question?"

"Maybe for another time. What *did* you want to talk about."

"The note you read from Byron to his publisher: the *motive* he gave for the killing: 'the inadequacy of Cain's state to his conceptions.' Jack and I think that might be Chatterton's problem too. Sums up what drives him and maybe kills him."

I almost held my breath. I heard my heartbeat. Ben looked away, his eyes darting. He moved his tongue around inside his lips, poked his pinkie into his ear, wriggled it.

"You're saying Chatterton worries about theology? I doubt it."

"No. We're wondering whether Byron and Chatterton don't worry about why they can't be and do what they imagine, as *much* as they imagine: why they can't *achieve* what they *conceive*. Because of the 'state' their creation traps them in. Jack thinks Blake and the other Romantics might also be…handicapped…by an awareness of that same disparity. By that *incongruity* between condition and conception."

Ben didn't respond right away, but now he stared hard at me, the eyes drilling, the foot and the finger very still. I waited. He scratched his beard and wiped his mouth.

"Blake's imagination," he said slowly, "was probably the wildest of them all, and he wrote it more vividly and graphically than anybody ever did. But I don't know that he *felt* the kind of threat or hassle you're talking about."

"Of course I don't know Blake as well as you, but maybe he wrote that vividly and graphically because and while reaching for a still higher level of vividness and graphic representation because that was as close as he could get to it — always beyond grasping but not imagining? Maybe that drove him nuts?"

"Blake wasn't crazy. He was visionary. Not delusional."

"Okay. Fine. That's not my point. We're not right now concerned with Blake anyway. What I'm saying is that Jack and I think we three could make that anxiety over 'inadequacy' the main theme of our play, and, immediately, also the theme of the essays we're writing for Park *on* the theme of our play. That frustrating, maddening disconnect between situation and concept. I do it in my draft of the actual play."

He pondered. Then: "We'd need evidence. Lines from Chatt's poetry…or letters, like Byron's letter. Something from his own pen to back us up."

"Of course. And we'll look for it. But remember: the plot we're writing — I'm writing and Jack's refining — is fiction. Based on fact, selective fact. If we can't find evidence, we'll make it up. We can show Chatt speaking it or writing it. But I figure we can find some too."

"What if Park spots it as fake? In our essays? And if we manufacture the evidence to prove Chatt's dissatisfaction, aren't we repeating the fraud he's suspected of?"

"We'll claim 'artistic license,'" I said, grinning. "But it's a fair point. Let's run it by Jack. See if he's got ideas from reading me for writing up some 'evidence' of Chatt's... discontent. Meanwhile, we assume in our essays Chatterton's...what?...let's call it his 'Romantic compatibility' with the Cain-ian complaint...as Byron wrote it. Frankly, I doubt Park's going to pay enough attention to us to pick up a little slip in that direction. His involvement's gonna shrink by the hour."

"All right," Ben said, "but I think I'll re-read some of the poetry with 'inadequacy' in mind. I might turn up evidence. That would lock in an A on the essay. You might do the same thing."

"Good thinking," I said. "I'll talk to Jack."

Ben made to leave. "No, wait," I said. "There's two more things. There *are* two more things. At Group the other night, Ben, when you talked about Cain, whether you knew it or not you *performed* Cain: you *acted out* Cain's frustration and dissatisfaction. Are you listening? When you described that space-flight you took us along *with* you and Cain and the Demon. You *acted* it: we *felt* Cain's...well...his misery and anger. Your passion showed it. You once told me your place in the theater was backstage. But you also told me that you did plays back at the orphanage and all through grade school and high school, and then all last year over at The Dark Horse in Aleck. And you were *on* stage the other night at Group. Where you were completely convincing. And when you got to the bit about 'the Omnipotent tyrant' and 'His everlasting face' — the part you memorized — you memorized it because you liked the sound of it from your own mouth: you *liked* saying it, performing it! Even Gavin was knocked out. You can and did act; you're actually an experienced actor. So I need you to sign on, definitely, to be Ginsberg in our play."

"You're not kidding?" he asked after a pause. "I acted? Not consciously."

"All the better. It came naturally to you. You were completely authentic. Nothing artificial or faked. Convincing as spokesperson for Cain's suffering."

"But I told you. I can't play queer Ginsberg."

"Well, you could. But I'm not asking you to. You won't act queer. Ginsberg will *mentor* Chatt. He's a substitute dad. He's not after the boy for sex. He wants to bring him along as a poet. That's his only interest, but it's a consuming one. And you, Ben, know exactly what that's all about and how it works; you've been bringing yourself along as a poet for as long as I've known you and longer. That's how we'll write it. Ginsberg will tutor Chatt in composing verse."

"I dunno, Troy. I don't know if I can actually get on stage...."

"I cannot believe I'm witnessing a failure of confidence in Benjamin Moore!"

"It's not that..."

"It's exactly that. Look, how many times have you read your own poetry to an audience? In bars and classrooms and lecture halls? You were completely comfortable addressing the Group. You speak up in class all the time. How's this different?"

"Well, it *is* different. Don't pretend it isn't."

"Ben," I said, with as much resolution as I could summon, "Do this. The part is you. We need you to be Allen."

"You think I can?"

"I think you are."

He smiled.

"There's one last thing: I also need you to come home with me for Christmas."

# 15

December 18, 1957

Dear Mother and Father,

I'll be there shortly but I wanted to ask you as soon as I decided if I could bring home two friends for Christmas. Not together. Ben Moore could come for Christmas and stay a couple more days. Kaiden Carlisle (Corky) might come over from Vicksburg after that. Ben grew up in the Monroe orphanage and doesn't have another home. I knew Kaiden at Jubilee. He's at Tulane. Ben and I are working on a school project. Could you call me if it's okay to invite them? Ben will probably come on his motorcycle.

I look forward to seeing everybody and enjoying some great meals. Corky's into food.

Love, T.

\* \* \*

December 18, 1957

Hey, Corky,

Would you like to come over to Madison 3 or 4 days after Christmas for a visit? I don't know what all we'll do, or how we'll manage to do *THAT,* but we'll figure something out. I get home on Saturday 21st. The Madison phone is 318-279-5001. Let me know. I'm excited to see you.

Love,
Troy

\* \* \*

"Professor Royal?" I rapped lightly on the doorframe of his office, through which I saw him bent over his desk, his head resting on folded arms, his heavy hair draping them. He jerked up, looked back, ruffled his hair, adjusted his jacket.

"Oh, darlin' Troy, I've been thinking of you lately. Do step in."

"Am I disturbing you, sir? Are you all right?"

"I am indeed very busy these days, my dear, so I am delighted to be disturbed. I was only resting my eyes, from their busy work. May I be of service, Mr. Tyler?"

"You said you'd been thinking of me. Did you wish to see me, sir?"

"As a matter of hard fact, yes, I do so wish, and here you are, with astonishing promptitude! I congratulate you!" He actually shook my hand. "I have been updating and preparing my personal file for departmental and administrative review. You may be aware that LCC evaluates every class every term. On the final day of our Romantics class in January, you'll be asked to complete a form that grades me on the success of the class. The results are tabulated and added to my file. But in addition, I am allowed to include testimonials from students and other associates in witness to my qualifications for promotion and tenure. Do you understand me?"

"Perfectly, sir. I believe you're asking me...."

"I am inviting you, if you wish, to write a letter on my behalf elaborating whatever you've reported on the official form, and adding your views on other outstanding competencies you have observed in me, qualifying me for advancement in the ranks. If you accept my invitation, you need only post your confidential letter to the College Dean by January 15th of next year."

"I'd be honored to accept your kind invitation, sir. Thank you for asking me."

"Inviting you. You're welcome."

"May I ask, sir, whether three letters might be better than one?"

"A dozen would be better than one. A score better yet. What have you in mind?"

"Obviously, sir, your Three Wise Men. Would you like me to ask Ben and Jack to write as well? I expect they'd be willing. And also honored."

"Can we be confident...?"

"Well, they're aware of how helpfully you've advised us on our play...."

"Yes, and I sponsored all three of you for The Chatterton Honors Society. By the way, I've simply not had the time to schedule meetings of The Society this term. You understand that. But second term is more important anyway, when everybody's writing for the spring competitions and publications. So we'll gear up then."

"Yes, sir. Would you want me to...?"

"I should probably ask them myself. But I'm just so hard pressed through here, so hectic and frazzled... if you don't mind, then yes, just pass the word that favorable and heartfelt testimonials would benefit a good cause. To the Dean. By January 15th."

We paused. "Was there anything else," he asked.

"Yes, sir. I wanted to let you know...."

"Oh my yes of course," fluttering. "You came to *me*! How may I be of service?"

"I wanted to let you know that Professor DeWitt has agreed to award Drama credit for the same materials, on Chatterton, you're accepting, also for credit, in English. In case you all wanted to confer...?"

"You might want to get that in writing," he said, pointedly.

"What?" I asked, startled. "Why would I?"

"Well, there's been a development."

"What development? I don't know what you mean, sir."

"No, of course you don't. You wouldn't. But you will."

"From you, sir? How about now?" I tried to swallow my alarm and choked on it, coughed. "Why should I need Professor DeWitt's assurances in writing? Is there a problem?"

"Dear boy, there are always myriads of multitudinous and multiplying problems. I devoutly hope you are spared them all. You might want to protect yourself from one by getting Professor DeWitt's promise in writing."

"But I can hardly ask him now without appearing to doubt his word. Why would I distrust it? Do I need to get *your* agreement in writing?"

"No, darlin', my word is rock solid. But Benedict DeWitt — that dick Benedict — is leaving LCC for a Film Studies Professorship at LSU at the end of this month. Just like that, he's gone."

"You can't be serious! He's *leaving*? At mid-year?"

"He evidently cooked up some sweet deal between LSU and LCC that cuts him loose from here and sets him up for life eternal there. LSU had a death or something, and were...was...desperate, and DeWitt's been trying to leave us ever since he got here, and he talked them into establishing a whole unit in Film Studies for him to run. He got a big salary boost plus a leave from teaching to get the thing organized next term, and somebody's said LSU bought out his contract here. He's supposed to grade his papers and exams, and clear out...for the big time."

"Wow!" I breathed. "That's something! Does everybody know?"

"I hear it'll be all over the last *Witness* of the term. Our secretary found out from his."

"Well, I guess 'papers and exams' includes ours; but maybe I'd better stop by and ask, to be sure." And then, I had a thought:

"Will you apply for his job, sir?"

"What? What was that?" He looked nails at me. "I have a job," he said.

"Yes, sir; I know. But...but...in light of...you know...?"

"Maybe not for long, you're thinking. But maybe for the rest of my long sweet life. We don't know yet. And besides: I'm Romantic. Not Drama."

"But you teach drama, sir. You just finished teaching us *Manfred* and *Cain*. Dramas, both of them. And you're...um...helping...to direct our play. And anyway, sir, you are...well, you're Drama Personified! If I may say so. Everybody here knows that, and respects that. You are the most dramatic...well, anyway, you know drama and can teach it. You do teach it. DeWitt doesn't... didn't...teach it...often. He taught film."

He was smiling. "I guess I...am...what you said. Drama personified...around here." He giggled. "I am...

am I not?" But then he picked up his little wand and pushed back in his chair, swiveled slowly back and forth, obviously thinking. "Jesus," he whispered; "there'll be a faculty vacancy. In Drama. I hadn't registered that. I need to call my father."

"Have you graded our precis yet?" I asked.

"No, I've just been so very busy, you see. Not yet."

"I'll speak to Jack and Ben about the recommendation letters."

"You do that. Only let's call them 'personal testimonials.'"

"You know, sir...if I could add: we might bring a little more passion and conviction to them if we knew you'd reconsider waiving the Romantics exam for us... in light of the magnitude of your assignment."

"It isn't the assignment that freights the magnitude, Mr. Tyler; it's your essay that requires it. And now I'd be obliged if you removed your impertinent self and your threat from my presence. I have an important call to make."

I hoofed it right over to the Theater and asked to see Professor DeWitt. "He's already left campus for the holiday," the secretary said, "and he can't be reached. We don't know when or if he'll return."

The *Witness* made it official the next morning. Professor Benedict DeWitt had resigned his LCC position effective January 15, 1958, to accept a Professorship in Film Studies at Louisiana State University, Baton Rouge, the first such professorship in the United States. LCC had begun its search for a replacement in Drama.

* * *

For the third time that afternoon, I rapped on a door —
was I lonely? — this one to Jack's dorm room, this time
with a six-pack in hand.

"I thought I'd finally take a look at your room," I
said, grinning a tease and handing him a Pabst. He wore
a blue sweat shirt, belt-less jeans, and bright, patterned
socks as slippers. He grinned too.

"It's kind of a mess," he said; "I'm packing to go
home tomorrow."

"I should be too, but I wanted to see you before. You
got time?"

"Just throw something on the floor," he waved, "and
take a seat somewhere." He closed and locked the door.
The wind whistled through cracks around the windows,
rattled the blinds. He looked for his smokes amid the
clutter.

"Dunno what I did with them," he grumbled, rum-
maging through piles, tossing stuff aside. He closed the
suitcase and slid it under the bed. "Let's sit here. You got
a Kent?"

I handed him my pack and matches. The bed sat
against the exposed brick wall running between the closet at one end of the room and the wood panel screening the desk at the other. He smoothed his khakis and
stretched out, his head propped on a pillow squashed
against the closet wall. I took the foot and hooked one
leg onto the bed, inches from his feet. He set the ashtray
between us. We both sipped, and lit up.

"I wanted a word before we left. Park just told me DeWitt's resigned. He's moving to LSU to do Film Studies. But he's agreed to give us course credit for the play. I mean, if we pass! He'll grade the same package of essays we'll give Park...only without Ben's part. But we still have to take the Drama final exam."

"Well hot damn, Troy! That's great news! That's a nice little Christmas gift from you, thank you very much!" His toes rubbed my knee. "When's he leaving?"

"He's already gone. Officially in January. After turning in grades. I don't know about January classes. We'll give our work to the secretary. I asked Park if he'd apply for DeWitt's job."

"Now there's a thought. What'd he say?"

"That he'd call his Dad."

A hard gust slapped at the windows. Lightening flashed.

"I bet he did too, and Dad'll make some calls. DeWitt's a loss, though. Not to Drama. But Film's the next thing. Smart move to switch."

"I doubt it much affects our plans."

We went silent. The lights flickered.

"Jack, I invited Ben to come home with me for Christmas. He's going to."

"Sounds nice. Good of your parents."

"He doesn't have anywhere. Prob'ly just for Christmas dinner...and the next day. We should get him a couple of presents."

"Oh, that's a great idea! I'll help with that."

"No, no, Jack…I didn't mean us two. I meant my folks. You don't need…."

"Stop. I want to. Here," he passed me a twenty from his wallet. "Buy him something from me…or just add that to what you're spending. I'll be his secret Santa!" He giggled.

"Are you sure, Jack? It's very nice, really, but you don't need…."

"You're doing me a favor. I wouldn't know what to get Ben."

"Neither do I. Gas? Goggles? Leslie?" We laughed.

"I figured maybe she'd ask him home with her."

"I'd have asked you, too, Jack, and I thought about it. But we're kind of a small house…for a lot of guests."

"Don't give it a thought. My family's going to Asheville for a week, thanks anyway. What'll yawl do… the day after Christmas?"

"I dunno. Maybe work on the project?"

"Probably not."

"How's your writing coming along?"

"Well enough? It's hard, though. I've got zero confidence about what I've done. I'll need input soon."

Silence again. He lit another Kent.

"Jack, I'm thinking I might quit The Group next semester. It's boring me. I'm boring it. It's juvenile. And it's, like, dead-end, idn' it?"

"Might it be better with Hale back?"

"Hale, no! Would you stay?"

He paused. "Would it matter to you if I did?"

"Well, you said way back you'd like to do a project with me, so I went to Group with you. I should let you know if I'm dropping out…of the project…we developed there. It's sort of died on us. That's all I'm saying."

We sipped. He thought. "No, I'm not sure I'll stay if you go. No, not even for Gavin!" He winked and grinned. "I agree about 'juvenile.' And we do still have a collaborative project."

"It might be easier to quit it if you did too. Kind of a joint statement, of principle?"

A sharp crack of lightening. A huge crash of thunder.

"Was that God approving or disapproving?" I asked, and we laughed, and again went quiet.

"I was kidding about Gavin," he said, wiggling his toes against my knee again.

"Jack, I also invited Kaiden home. After Christmas. You remember: my Tulane friend. Corky."

"I remember," he said quietly. He moved his foot back. "How'm I supposed to respond to that news…that surprising news?"

"I thought you should know. I didn't want to look like I was hiding something."

"You *did* hide something. Over Thanksgiving. Or tried to. Only I figured it out."

He took up the ashtray, stubbed out his cigarette, and then kept stubbing it, moving it around the tray among the ashes, watching his fingers work.

"I don't know about 'should'; but I'm kind of glad you told me…even though it doesn't make me happy. You know I'm jealous of him…of your time with him."

"Oh, Jack. You don't have any reason to be."

"Don't I? Why shouldn't I be?"

"Well," I said, hardly knowing what I said: "I'm here. On your bed."

"Let's watch the storm," he said.

We moved to the windows, stood side by side, not touching, watched the trees toss, the rain sweep and slash, the lightening streak and shimmer. He slowly drew the blinds, and, bringing his hands to my shoulders, turned me gently to himself.

"Troy," he breathed, "I'm going to kiss you now."

And he did, slowly, softly, caressing my lips with his lips, pressing lightly, his fingers moving to fondle my ears, stroke up and down my neck, his tongue sliding across my teeth, seeking mine, his palms light against my cheeks. Our breaths quickened, our hearts thumped. He ran his hands lightly, ever so lightly up and down my back, all the while holding his mouth lightly against mine, whispering my name into me over and over. I shuddered, pressed my body head to toe against his.

He took a small step back, slid his hands onto my chest, trailed his fingers across my nipples and down my ribs and back up to my throat, slipping one between my teeth, onto my tongue. Gently he wrapped the other hand in mine and led me back to the bed, knelt into it, stretched out against the bricks. I followed, sank into his enfolding arms.

We lay quietly like that, breathing, settled, for some while. Then he sat slowly up and rested his open hand on my stomach.

"You're a sweet boy, Troy," he said gently. "I like you. And I want you. And I like wanting you so much that I'm going to keep on wanting you right through Christmas rather than taking your gift of yourself to me now, as beautiful and tempting as your offer of it is. I don't know whether you know whether you want me, but you might know after Christmas. Let's see then whether I'll unwrap you and make you my own sweet man."

I may have swooned.

16

Benjamin Arthur Moore surprised us by roaring up onto our Madison lawn on Christmas Eve afternoon in a Santa suit with a tumbling fake white beard masking his own black one and the red tasseled jester's cap hugging his head. By the time we'd rushed to the front porch, neighbors had begun to gather on theirs to learn what all the racket was after Ben gunned the engine several times to announce his arrival. Mother looked non-plussed — maybe more by the noise than the timing — while Father kept calm, glancing down at our lawn-grass, and appeared to defer to me for the formalities, while brother Mark, just turned fifteen, practically danced with excitement. Grinning pleasure, Ben wrapped me in a big bear-hug — I don't remember us ever before touching — pounded my back, and boomed, "Is it okay if Santa's early?"

"Of course it is," Mother said, stepping forward; "you just come right on in. We're so glad to see you!"

Father maintained his usual reserve but shook hands graciously: "We're pleased to welcome you to our home, Ben. Troy's told us so much…." He signaled Ben inside ahead of us, Mark skipping alongside burbling questions about the cycle.

Mother busied herself brushing cushions, fluffing pillows, gathering up magazines. "You make yourself right to home here, Ben. The bathroom's down the hall there…if you want to…. Show him, Troy. I'll be right back with treats," excusing herself to the kitchen.

"What a super surprise!" I said, probably beaming. "The suit's groovy! And you *act* Santa so *good*!"

He got it, and laughed, handing me the cap, mussing his hair.

It came out that Mrs. Harrison, his landlady, had directed Rodney to search attic trunks for the Santa costume her late and sadly departed husband always wore to the College Board of Trust Christmas parties; she'd then tacked and tucked and torn and re-sewn parts of it to fit Ben. He already owned the black boots, of course, and she found one of *her* wide black belts of stretchable fabric to circle Ben's girth, the glitter on it ably suiting the season. He said he'd gotten her to photograph him in the outfit.

"Did highway traffic part for you?" Father quipped, the Red Sea allusion lost on none of us.

"Lots of waves," Ben said, waving. "I'll wash up." I pointed where.

"He's cool," Mark said.

Mother reappeared with a tray of chocolate-chip-and-pecan cookies and small glasses of cold sweet milk, and when Ben returned we settled comfortably down for easy chatter about his drive, what he'd seen of our town, what we might do.

"Can I look at the motorcycle?" Mark asked, "sometime?"

"May you?" Ben said, whether consciously copying and mocking Jack at Mark's expense I couldn't tell; but nobody else seemed to notice the correction. "How 'bout helping me unload it," he went on, "after Santa's had his cookies?" He lifted the fake beard away from his face and set it down. "Whew! Hot!" he said.

"Sure," Mark said. "I always wanted to sack Santa's sack!"

"Whoa!" Ben exclaimed. "That'll write! Good one, guy!"

Mark flushed.

"Are there plans for church…tonight and tomorrow?" Ben asked. This also surprised me but I instantly saw how shrewd it was. For one thing, it respectfully invited Father back into the conversation. Moreover, Ben knew from his Baptist orphanage days that church was always on the Christmas menu in every Christian home, and he wanted Father to know that he knew and would honor that tradition while visiting us. And by introducing the subject himself, he might gain some control over its discussion: might be suggestive rather than instructed. Of course Father had pastoral responsibilities on Christmas Eve and Day, but to what extent our houseguest was expected to participate in them wasn't yet certain.

"Yes," Father said. "We have services tonight and tomorrow morning. Tonight's the more popular one, with lots of special music and candles and flowers and The Lord's Supper at the end. The family will probably dine around 5:30 — Prissy? [meaning my Mother] — and church starts at 7. You're very welcome to join us for both, Ben."

"Please do," Mother said, "and bring Troy along to church!"

"What shall I wear?" Ben said, grinning.

"Not that!" we chorused, laughing.

"I'd like to come, and thank you," he said. "Want to unload now, Mark? Your brother can help!"

He'd roped his backpack and another package onto the pillion and now set about carefully removing them, at the same time pointing to and explaining the functions of various parts of the bike to the riveted Mark, instructing him not to handle them. "She's allergic to fingers, and breaks out," he said, wiping his own prints off the polished metal with a chamois cloth handily tucked under the seat. Working over a knot, I decided the church arrangements had fallen into place agreeably enough: I'd have to attend at least one service; and tonight's with Ben would probably excuse us from tomorrow's if I asked nicely enough, and might even give us boys the run of the house during it, unless Mother stayed home to finish preparations for her Christmas feast, ever her favorite occasion for showcasing her cooking genius.

"These aren't all *gifts*, are they, Ben?" I asked, patting the box, before hearing the presumption in my question.

"It's Santa's sleigh!" he said; "what else would it pack?"

"Has it got a horn?" Mark asked.

Ben touched the handlebars. "It's in there, but we don't use it much. The engine always says we're here… wherever we are. Nobody argues that! Let's get this stuff inside."

Inside, the parents sat conversing on the sofa. Father stood.

"Gifts!" Ben cried, dropping his backpack with a thud that made Mother jump. "Gather round, people, and prepare to receive," he added, taking the box from Mark.

"Hold your horses," Mother said, and stepping over to the hallway closet brought out a shopping bag with string handles. "All right," she said softly.

I half-wanted to echo her exclamation about waiting-up. What was Ben's rush? He was barely in the door, and already handing out presents, almost as though paying his way in.

Playing Santa, he distributed. "For the Reverend!" A rectangular box in wrinkled, grocery-bag paper, Scotch-taped. "Please wait for everybody to get theirs!

"For the Mrs.!" A longer, softer package loosely wrapped in white tissue.

"A special one for Mark!" Also soft, the brown paper wrapping torn in places, revealing dark cloth.

"And for Troy!" Long, narrow, hard-surfaced box, in store-wrapped green seasonal foil.

"Now!" Ben said, sitting back on the sofa, his face, around the beard, bright and expectant.

Father held up a hexagonal, prismatic heavy glass paperweight enclosing a small parchment scroll inscribed with the verse from Isaiah he solemnly read out: "'Here am I. Send me.' How perfectly apt, Ben," he murmured, "and tasteful. I'm touched. It'll go on my office desk… and stay there. I'm very grateful."

Mother gushed and golly-ed over her set of three blue and white tea towels with floral embroidery.

Mark actually gawked and squealed upon discovering an LCC baseball warm-up jacket with the gold college letters on a navy background and "**Baseball**" stitched in capitals across the back. Ben later told me he'd found it abandoned in the men's locker room and after nobody claimed it he took it to donate somewhere, and then when I invited him…. Mark hugged and cuddled it for a while before trying it on, and then didn't take it off. It was slightly long in the arms and loose in the body but we all said he'd soon grow into a snug fit. He kept saying, with every opening, "I really *love* it, Ben!"

"Troy," Ben said; "your turn." Mine was a lustrous black Sheaffer fountain pen nestled in dark red velvet, and a 2-ounce bottle of Skrip Deluxe blue ink in the distinctive yellow box. "For the writer," Ben said softly.

I choked up, it was so sleek and professional, so perfectly chosen…to honor effort, I imagined, and to encourage ambition. Mark was watching me closely, letting me recover before speaking his word: "So cool," he said.

"There's more," Ben whispered; "for later."

"You so surprised us today," Mother said, "I didn't have time to properly wrap these little...tokens, so I'll have to give them raw, you might say, and hope you won't mind. From the four of us, although Mark actually picked out two of them. You know he's always messing around at Sperry's Antiques, just down at the corner there, and that's where he found this little...toy...." She pulled out, very slowly and carefully, a greatly detailed and brightly painted miniature sculpture — plastic or ceramic? — of a motorcycle with a helmeted rider, and handed it gently to Ben. Mark's eyes grew very wide, his face frozen in anxious anticipation. Ben accepted it tenderly onto his open palm, weighed it, wagged his head in wonder.

"It's heavy," he breathed; "and...and...so *beautiful*. And *delicate*. So...counter-intuitive! It's a little masterpiece of arrested motion, isn't it? It must be extremely valuable. I can't accept such a precious...."

"Of course you can and you must," Mother said. "It's just a thing. We want you to enjoy it. And Mark also found these at Spiller's, and his father and I want you to have and use them if you can." She drew up from the bag a vintage pair of airman's goggles, the lens tinted dusty orange, the frames chipped black, the strap slightly raveled but the buckle intact. "Oh wow," Ben sighed. "Wow! I can't believe you found these...Mark found these! WW One? Two?" He tugged them on. Posed.

"Completely special! I'm so glad to have them! But you really shouldn't have. Thank you so much!"

Mother handed me the sack. "Hmmmmm," I mused. "There seems to be something else left in there. Whatever…?" I reached in and withdrew…black leather driving gloves. He gasped. Stroked them. "You know I don't have any," he said, looking at me. "I know," I said; "now you do." He slipped them on, made two fists, flexed his fingers. Modeled. Smiled hugely. "Thanks, Troy. They're great. Wow!"

I shook the bag. It rattled. "Would you believe…?"

"This last," I said, "this last, Ben, is from Jack. Jack, people, is our LCC pal on the project. We're sometimes known on campus as The Three Wise…Guys, though we're not."

"Speak for yourself," Ben said.

"And Jack asked me to give you his Christmas present." I brought out a brown cow-hide leather journal notebook with a strap lock and custom embossing of his initials in the lower right corner. "Replaceable lined pages," I added.

"I can't hardly talk," Ben said; "I'm truly overwhelmed by all this. Really," his voice shaking.

"Isn't everybody trembling?" Mark asked. "I am."

"Amen," the Reverend said, quietly.

"We have two baths, Ben, but only one shower," he continued after a pause, "and only three bedrooms, so Prissy'll make up the sofa, and my boys will flip for it. You may have the loser's room."

"No," Mark said, firmly: "Ben can have my room. I'm the best fit for the sofa."

On my way past Mark's door to mine, Ben beckoned me inside. "Here's the 'more' I promised," he said, scrabbling in his backpack. He handed me a thin, softcover book, not wrapped. The title read:

*Lawrence Ferlinghetti*
*A Coney Island of the Mind*

and under it rose the park's fully lit-up Tower of Light with endless strings of bulbs and other illuminations in every direction just about singeing the cover.

"Ben! What? How'd you get it?"

"Advance copy. I got three. That's yours."

"Whoa, man. No, you can't. I can't...."

"It's done, Troy. Look at the title page."

I read: "For Troy Tyler, from his great friend Ben Moore, by way of the author, Lawrence Ferlinghetti, on December 15, 1957. Ciao, [signed]...."

"Holy shit, Ben. I may freak out! This is unbelievable! Are you sure?"

"With that inscription, it's no good to anybody else. City Lights made it happen. It'll be on their shelves in a while. You prob'ly better not show it to your father."

"No. Maybe to Mark."

"I wouldn't. He's a sweet kid. He'll discover it when he's ready to."

"However can I thank you, Ben?"

"You already have. Or maybe I'll figure out a way. Now get going!"

Supper was thick, steaming cream of tomato soup and fat egg salad and/or chicken salad sandwiches on Sunbeam white bread: nothing fancy but filling and delicious, and a lot less trouble for Mother than the feast she'd been stewing over for weeks. Ben asked Father to explain "how the Psalms are poetry," which started a long and technical conversation about Hebraic metrics and Psalmic structure and translations that left us three in the dust, although Mother, having had some seminary training, chipped in what Ben said were several helpful comments. Mark wore his jacket all through dinner, frequently pushing its cuffs away from the soup bowl. Mother handled the soup tureen with her new tea towels.

Ben borrowed one of my regular ties for church, and I knotted a dynamite red bow and Brylcreemed my attractively lengthening hair. The congregational turnout was respectable, Father thought, and he obliged it and us by preaching fewer than ten minutes without an invitation hymn to finish; and his presiding at The Lord's Supper (Holy Eucharist, with the bread and grape juice) struck me as particularly dignified and graceful, even a little dramatic. We all partook.

Back in the olden days when I still lived at home, our post-service routine on Sunday night included popcorn and sweet milk in front of the TV, but as we returned home from church Father said, "Ben, how about chess? You up for a match?" Together they set up the game on the dining-room table while Mother prepared another plate of cookies. Mark, still in his jacket, took an Archie comic and a *Sports Illustrated* to the sofa, stretched out, and probably remained there till morning, Mother no doubt providing a pillow and a blanket after she finished with the stockings.

"Folks," I said, "if it's okay I'll excuse myself to read in my room. See yawl in the a.m. Happy Christmas to all, and to all a good night!" I knew Mother would shortly settle with her sewing in her chair under the lamp and wait everybody out before bringing in the stockings, stuffing them with fruit and gum and candy and trinkets and trifles she'd collected all year for the purpose, and lay them out for our discovery in the morning. I also knew she'd find and fill a stocking for Ben.

I figured he'd have been completely happy with his haul from yesterday, but the helmet along with the stocking just about sent him over the moon. He already *had* a helmet, of course, but not so flashy as the new one with the red lightening streaks our parents had somewhere found at the last minute. Mark and I both got the 35mm cameras we'd wanted for taking slides — his a Kodak, mine a Canon — already loaded with film, so we frolicked around snapping in our p.j.'s and underwear, Mark in his jacket and Jockeys, until, tiring of the silliness, we withdrew to clean up for breakfast.

Our Christmas breakfast was always a highlight, possibly our favorite hour of the holiday. Because Mother owned the New Orleans French Market recipe for beignets and cooked them to perfection every time! We never had them except on Christmas, so we ate for the full year that morning. Mother cut the little squares of dough with a metal tool, and we all watched them puff up sizzling in the very hot, bubbling cottonseed oil. By the time she'd rolled them around in the powdered sugar until coated, they'd cooled enough to eat. Mark didn't yet like coffee, but the rest of us dunked our beignets and sucked and smacked that sweet swollen fried bread as it just kept coming and coming off the stove. For her trouble, Mother always got to have the final one, and she teased us by lingering with it, licking and nibbling and making it last. Before we finished, powdered sugar sprinkled the whole kitchen, dusted our sticky selves.

Father cleaned up and made off for his 10 a.m. service without inviting any of us to join him, and Mother shoo-ed us boys out of her kitchen in order to pick up prep for the mid-afternoon feast. Mark had been clamoring for a motorcycle ride since Ben's arrival, but I thought it still a little early to rev the engine in our neighborhood, especially in light of the service next door, so I suggested we take the eight-block walk down to the bayou where we'd drop a line for anything biting. Mark left to get different shoes from his closet while Ben and I headed to the garage for poles and the tackle box; we'd meet Mark by the row of catalpa trees separating the parsonage from the church and use the poles to joggle off the broad leaves those plump worms that made the best fish-bait ever. December had been unusually warm thus far, so I hoped enough leaves had survived to feed enough worms to give us a full can. Mark detested the worms and wouldn't help collect them, much less spear them onto hooks where the slimy yellow and green goo spilled all over your fingers. As it was still Christmas, we wouldn't rib him for his squeamishness. He'd brought along his Daisy Red Ryder BB gun.

"What's that for?" Ben asked.

"Oh," Mark said, holding it out proudly. "Birds. Blue-jays. Maybe a squirrel or rabbit. Scare off a snake. I'd rather hunt than fish."

"I wish you wouldn't," Ben said, frowning.

"What?" from me. "Why not?"

"I'm not comfortable around weapons."

"It's not a weapon, Ben," I said, not quite sneering. "It's a BB rifle."

"A rifle's a weapon, I believe."

"It's completely harmless, Ben," I said, my voice rising. "Mark's had it since 10 or something. I had one. All boys start with one. I don't understand."

"I didn't. I'd rather not come if Mark's bringing it."

"I'll be really careful," Mark said. "I know how to use it. It's not dangerous."

"It's a gun," Ben said. "It's dangerous. Look," he continued after a pause. "I can just stay here. Yawl go ahead. I'll see you later, for Mark's ride."

"Now wait," I said, my temper rising. "This is ridiculous. We're going fishing. Mark's gonna look for some birds or critters for a little target practice. There's not a chance in hell of any danger. And besides, a little BB under the skin's no problem. It's a *toy*, Ben! What's the big deal?"

"I don't do weapons," he said.

"I just told you. It's a toy."

"It shoots."

"BB's! Tiny little BB's. This is crazy, Ben. What *is* your *problem?*"

"You'd know if you thought about it," Ben almost whispered.

We went quiet, looked at each other. I thought about it.

"Wait," I said. "You mean...? You're thinking about...?"

"Hush up" Ben said, nodding toward Mark. "Don't say any of it!"

"I'll just go on ahead," Mark said, and turned away.

"Wouldn't that be okay, Ben, if Mark just... separates...?"

"If he leaves the weapon here."

"But where? He can't just drop it anywhere..."

"Wherever he got it."

I didn't like it. He was stupidly spoiling a promising ramble. It was wacky and selfish and mean. But I couldn't think what else to do.

"Okay, Mark. Maybe you'll be a prince and take the gun back. To your closet. Wait, no. Put it in the garage...out of the house. And meet us under the bridge at the bayou. Is everybody okay with that?"

Mark nodded and slouched off. Ben just stood, looking at me.

"Let's get some worms," I said.

Pole in hand, I attacked the remaining leaves with some vigor, and they yielded enough worms to fill half the can. Ben dumped in four or five more.

"Was that about your father?" I asked after a while.

"You know I don't talk about it," he said.

"Well, maybe you *should* talk about it...with a professional."

"Troy, please. I'm sorry. I can't just *like* guns because you tell me to. I can't just suddenly be comfortable around weapons."

"Yeah, you make that clear. And you hurt some feelings."

"I'm sorry. I'll make it up to Mark. I'll give him a good bike ride later."

"He may not want to go."

"Well, talk him back into it."

"I may not want to."

"Oh, come on, Troy. Don't sulk. It's over. Let's catch some fish."

"Doesn't that motorcycle sound like gunfire to you?"

Mark had shed his jacket for a sweater and added a creel to his outfit, and brought his casting rod and reel as well. But the squabble had cast a pall, no doubt about it, over a really beautiful, clear, crisp morning. Notwithstanding my sour mood, I felt obliged as host to try to salvage at least a little of the day while we sought to ruin it for some fish.

"We could whistle a merry tune," I ventured, conscious of my inanity. "Or sing the chorus of 'Joy To The World.'"

Mark made a dour face. "We'd scare the fish," he said, casting a plug into midstream.

"That would be whistling in the dark," Ben said.

Well, it was a start. Okay, giving Ben a reason for remembering his suicidal father on Christmas morning was a rotten thing to do. But who knew a BB gun would trigger the funk? How would I have checked Mark's impulse to bring the gun without dragging Ben's unhappy history into the light of Christmas Day? And wasn't he being just a little bit unreasonable and hypersensitive and stubborn and inconsiderate himself toward the family that had...no, wait, that's unfair. I won't say that. But what if "family" itself is offensive and hurtful to Ben? Maybe that's why he rushed through the gift-giving yesterday, to get past family joy he'd never known. And what if the gun was a weapon after all, aimed at his loss?

But then the fish woke up. Mark thought a bass had slammed his lure. Our corks began to bob and dip, and before long we had three blue-gill and two crappie in the creel, and I'd snagged a mud-catfish off the bottom. Mark hadn't yet landed anything but had loved playing two — bass, he figured — till they threw the hooks. We ran out of worms too soon.

Father fished the swamps to our south when he could, with sportsmen from the congregation, but claimed never to have known our local bayou to produce such fine specimens as we caught, my mud-cat excepted.

"We're having something else for dinner, though," he laughed. "We'll need to clean these and freeze them for later."

As Mother never ever cleaned a fish, or even allowed them into her sink, I volunteered for the job, maybe to make myself feel better and to make it up to Ben. Father surprised me by saying he'd help. Mark changed back into his jacket, and Mother left the kitchen long enough to walk us out to the cycle.

"You hold on now real tight," she said; "and Ben, don't you speed. There's a limit. And don't go near the railroad tracks. Sometimes the coming trains are hard to hear."

Grinning now, Ben brought Mark's arms around his stomach. "Lock your fingers, yeah, like that. And flatten your chest against my back, your face against my shoulders. All set?" He lowered his goggles, wriggled his helmet on, strapped it. Admired his gloves on the handlebars. Saluted us. "Here we go!"

On the back steps, Father and I spread the newspapers and set about cleaning the fish, scraping the scales back with tablespoons, slicing the bellies open from the anus and sliding out the slippery entrails with a finger. I loved the satiny feel of clean fish skin.

"We don't know much, son, about this 'project' you've mentioned," Father said.

"It's a historically based drama," I began, calculating what it was safe to say, "about a misunderstood poet. Ben and I and our friend Jack are collaborating. For credit."

"And what is its point?" he asked, scratching hard at scales.

Had he been talking to Park? "Well, we hope to restore his reputation."

This was already misleading if not downright falsifying. But would Father understand or care about any disparity between situation and conception? Wait, though: he'd know about Cain, wouldn't he? He must have preached Genesis. Why hadn't I thought to ask him?

"What had he done to damage it?" he sensibly asked.

This headed toward danger. I dodged.

"He made a couple of mistakes in publishing that got exaggerated, but it turned out okay. We just want to set the record straight."

Mealy-mouthing, I was.

"Would I recognize his name?"

"Probably not. Thomas Chatterton. Minor, really."

"Ben's from the Monroe orphanage, you said. So he's Christian?" He sliced the head off his bluegill.

"I guess so. He must've been raised Baptist. At the home."

"You should ask. Does he attend church?"

"We both belong to a Youth Group at Broadway Baptist in Alexandria. So does Jack." I split a belly.

"Well now, son, that's very good! You hadn't told us! I'm delighted to hear it. What sort of group?"

"Inquirers, you might call us," I said, rather proud I'd come up with that word on the fly. "We ask about scripture."

"Ben seemed very interested in Psalms, curious about it as poetry."

"Yes sir. Ben writes poetry, did he say? He's very gifted."

"Is your group mixed?"

"Yes sir. Boys and girls. Leslie's our leader."

"Your teacher."

"Sort of. She's an LCC senior."

"Who teaches you?" He set down his crappie, looked at me.

"Well, sir, we sort of teach ourselves, I guess. We're not bad at it either. We don't have an adult…at the moment."

"You might want to find one. Somebody trained. I'm not crazy about the idea of college sophomores teaching themselves…anything." But he almost grinned.

"Your studies going okay?"

"Oh, yes. I've got a solid B average. With a shot at an A or two. If I'm lucky."

"Don't trust luck. Luck is the Devil's temptation. This fellow who's visiting us next week: you knew him at Jubilee, right? He's the roommate that's headed to seminary?"

"No, sir. That's Monte. This is Corky. Kaiden Carlisle. He's at Tulane."

"Did we know he's in New Orleans?"

"Maybe not. We were really great friends at the camp. Monte's at Baylor."

"Oh yes. I remember now. Wonderful school, Baylor. Well, Troy, overall it sounds like you're doing pretty well as a college man. We're proud of you. Just keep up at Broadway Baptist. Who's the pastor there now, by the way? I probably know him."

"I can't think of the name right now, sir. Sorry."

"Cliff Dalton, perhaps?"

"Oh, right! That's it! Reverend Dalton!"

"Cliff Dalton was my ninth grade civics teacher, Troy. Do try to learn and remember your pastor's name."

The boys returned as we cleared out our gore and wrapped the cleaned fish in Saran for storing in the new Frigidaire chest freezer Father had bought on the installment plan for the half-cow of beefsteak Mr. Spraddle his head deacon had given us for Christmas, all butchered into meal-sized portions and neatly bound in white paper and labeled. His was so pleasing and imaginative not to mention generous a variation on the usual congregational Christmas gifts for the preacher's family that Mother talked Father into the extravagance of the freezer as a long-term economizing measure. (All during my high-school years, the standard go-to congregational Christmas present for us was a Brock or Beatrice Barrett box of chocolate-covered maraschino cherries in sticky, sugary white syrup: they piled up like old scrapyard bricks under our tree, mocking our expectations with their monotonous predictability, insulting banality, and cheapo tabs. I don't mean to sound ungrateful, but *really*! They might as well have been fruitcakes, which we got a lot of too. I reckoned we'd freeze them all now.)

Anyhow, Mark wanted to call on his pal Tracy and his crush Karen to show off his jacket and the motorcycle and Ben, and they'd driven out to the lake too and cruised around town and all told spent about an hour away. Mother had taken advantage to grab a nap.

The big golden-brown burnished turkey just about glowed at the head of the table, of course, but the main feature always of our holiday meal, for me, was Mother's cornbread dressing. She baked the buttermilk cornbread in the old cast-iron black skillet inherited from her mother and wrapped up the loaf in a towel a couple of days before mixing the batter. Crumbling it up fine, she added six or eight chipped green onions, two chopped hard-boiled eggs, three cups of chopped celery, salt and pepper, garlic powder, oregano, and…and…*especially* sage, her choice ingredient: "When you think you've used enough," she'd say, "add another tablespoon," and poured in enough of the re-heated water from boiling the giblets to moisten everything, and baked it for an hour in a 350 oven. Father and I would gladly have made a meal of that dressing. The squash and green bean casseroles and sweet-potato pudding and mashed potatoes under giblet gravy were special too, and all the little frills like black olives and dill pickles and carrot sticks and Mother's favorite cold spiced peaches with cloves, but nothing ever beat or rivaled the dressing. Not even the standard dessert, which knocked me over every time. Snowballs, she called them: heavy cold sugared whipped cream with shredded coconut layered between four thin chocolate wafers stacked and topped with more of the sweet creamy mix. I preferred them after two days of refrigeration so the wafers could relax into a soft, soggy texture.

Super-high from all the sweet tea and dessert, we helped Mother clear the table so Father and Ben could set up the chessboard again. The TV ran football in the living room. She washed, I dried. Mark read his Kodak instruction manual and snapped photos of us at work and play. Father said we should all gather at seven for the Mormon Tabernacle Choir Holiday Concert Special on TV. Cold turkey sandwiches on white bread with mayo and lettuce would accompany. And sweet milk.

"Let's walk," I said to Ben.

A cool, quiet, crepuscular interval (the Romantics favored the adjective, meaning twilight), before Christmas fireworks blasted it. Ben would leave in the morning. I wanted a wrap-up.

"You and Mark okay, Ben?"

"I think he'd say we're cool. He's a good kid. Smart. Nice."

"He likes you. Thank you for being good to him. And thank you again for the book. I'm diggin' it."

"Well, you and your folks have been great hosts. I'll write that, but I want to say it too. I'm very grateful for your invitation and all the gifts. This has been an unforgettable Christmas for me."

"We didn't get much done on the play, though. Jack said we wouldn't."

He laughed. "I haven't once thought about it. Back to work on it now, I guess."

"Yeah, but the term papers first."

"Park's essays are due the last day of exams. We've got to have a script for him by then."

"Maybe Jack'll have a draft when we get back. No, wait: they're spending the break in Asheville."

"May I ask how you and Jack are doing?"

"We're still parked in idle. I don't think we're sure what we want from each other. No, that's not right. Desire's there. Passion."

"And this other friend is coming here? Tomorrow?"

"Saturday. Corky. I knew him last summer."

"Competition for Jack?"

I paused. "A while ago, I'd have said Jack was competition for Corky. Now I don't honestly know. Maybe that's why Corky and I need to visit. You know I visited him in New Orleans over Thanksgiving."

"Yeah. Jack thinks yawl slept together."

"Yes. My first time. But don't confirm it to Jack."

"Will you sleep together Saturday?"

"Well, I think I've figured out how we could manage it…but I don't actually know whether I want to, whether we should. I'm pretty mixed up, I guess."

"If you're unsure, don't. It'd be a pretty big risk anyway."

"How're you and Leslie?"

"We're drifting too. She's preoccupied with law school applications. We don't study well together. She doesn't much like my poetry. I doubt she really wants a steady boyfriend."

"Are yawl sleeping together? I know it's not my business...."

"No. Is that what people think?"

"Well, people think you're a stud."

"A lot of that's...bravado. But don't spread that around! Maybe I am. I guess I'd like to be."

"Do you want a steady?"

"Possibly not. But I want *something*. I'm restless for *something*." He paused. "You know, I've felt kind of...content, though, these last forty-eight. That's interesting."

"How...interesting?"

"Not sure. Just a thought."

"Ben, I'm thinking I may quit The Group. Would you mind?"

"Not if you took me with you!"

"I wouldn't want you to leave on my account."

"No, I wouldn't do that. But I kind of embarrassed myself at that last meeting. I got pretty carried away. I think I misrepresented the degree of my interest in the subject."

"Ah-HA! Isn't that exactly what I said? You acted! You acted a part!"

He stopped, looked hard at me. "Guilty!" he laughed. "Touché!"

"I don't think I'm really that interested either. I've told Jack. It feels dead-end. We're going nowhere. But I actually like some members, don't you?"

"I do. And I respect Zeke and a coupla others. We'd need direction, though. It's kind of like a class that's lost its way in the weeds and is choking on them."

"That sounds like we need a scythe."

"Wha'd you think's gonna happen to Park?"

"I don't quite know what I want to happen to him, do you?" I asked.

"Prob'ly not," Ben said. "I doubt he's going to make tenure but he's not a bad person. And he's actually a pretty good teacher. And I'll write the letter. I wouldn't like him to lose his job."

"He might apply for DeWitt's old one. You know it's vacant."

"I heard. But would they hire him back after firing him?"

"Don't you think they might? Because Park's not really a *failure*. He's a successful teacher. He might be an even better one teaching drama. I mean, he's drama personified! He should be allowed to teach. No, not *allowed*. He should be *hired* to teach. *Tenured* to teach. I could write that in my letter."

"I agree he's not a failure. But he's a certifiable flake…as lots of professors are. *We* might be!"

"Want to head back?" I asked.

"Okay. Your mom's meal was great but I'm already hungry again."

"Ben, we're all right, aren't we? Our friendship, I mean. We're…stable?"

He stopped again. "I'm not queer, you know, but c'mere. Gimme a hug."

We embraced. "Oh, what the hell," he said, and kissed my brow.

After he left the next morning, Mother found on the dresser the little ceramic sculpture of the motorbike and rider, with a note:

> For Mark. Enjoy it till you get the big one.
>                     Your friend,
>                         Ben

Vicksburg is only about three hours from Alexandria but with stops and layovers and the additional leg to Madison, it took the Greyhound nearly five to deliver Corky to me around three on Saturday afternoon. That morning, Father, with a full day ahead of sermon preparation in his church office next door, had handed me the keys to the Plymouth to run errands for Mother. Swiftly done with them, I headed out to Neil Grady's place, my favorite farm-boy friend among the several I grew up and messed around with on junior-high Sunday afternoons after we'd ridden horseback for a while through their fathers' fields and forests. Some folks said Neil and I favored each other — as in looked alike, not privileged, though we might've in that sense too: same height and weight, same blue eyes and blonde crew-cuts, same winning smiles and affable manners; but he was a year older

and a junior in mechanical engineering and animal husbandry at Northwestern State in Natchitoches (Nack-
a-tish), just over the way in the next parish, and aways
seemed more mature and confident and settled than I
ever felt. Back in earlier grades, I imagined I might be a
little in love with Neil, long before I had a clue what that
could mean. I'd looked up to him, admired him…and
his father's horses. He waved me into another cane chair
on their front porch.

"You're lookin' great, Troy," he said amiably.
"Everythin' goin' good at LaCollege?"

"Good enough. How 'bout at Knick-Knack U?"
Both nicknames, long familiar now, were more harmless
jokes than derisions.

He brought me up to date on our old buddies still
in the area, asked after my folks (he and his belonged to
"our" church), pointed to his new old vehicle — a flam-
ing red '52 Ford pickup parked out by their barn awaiting his repairs — and inquired about girlfriends.

"Nope. Not yet," I said. "Too busy with school."

"Hmmm. You always had plenty of time for Allison!"

"And she never enough for me!"

"You remember Linda McGuire? In your class?"

"Sure. Linda Faye. Linda Tits! Cute. Flirty."

"That's her. She's still got 'em. She's also at Northeast.
We might get engaged next Christmas."

"What? Engaged? No kidding? Wow, that's some
news! No wait: you don't *have* to, do you?"

"No. Next Christmas might be a little late, in that case! No, we're just mentioning it," he went on after a giggle. "I just think I'm about ready."

"Really? But how do you know?" I asked, truly interested.

"Well," he said, "I'm almost done with school. I know what I'll do after. I want my own family, kids. Why not marry, is how I look at it."

"Seriously, Neil? You know what you'll *do*? Forever?"

"Don't *you*? You still want to teach, right?"

"Well, yeah, I guess. But I can't exactly *see* it yet. I mean, it's so far off. And marrying...! I've never even thought...."

"Think back: you remember I like tinkering with machines. Motors. And I really like farm animals, working with them. I'll prob'ly come right back here after graduation and help Dad with the farm...as his employee. We're adding acreage all the time, and stock, too. So a wife just seems like part of that picture, you know? And I prob'ly love Linda, or will. Everything just kind of falls into place like that...when I think about it."

"Okay, I guess I can see that. It just feels like... well...so *soon*."

"Linda's already a sophomore."

"So am I, Neil,"

"But I'm not marrying you." We laughed.

"I meant, as a sophomore myself, it seems soon to me."

"Well, we're not shopping for rings. The wedding's a ways off. I haven't asked her yet. I'm just sharing a little dream of mine with you."

This touched a nerve. I swallowed. "It's very sweet, Neil. Thanks for telling me your...dream. You look... pleased."

"I'll look more pleased on my honeymoon!"

We readjusted. "Yawl still have the horses?" I asked. "That's what I wanted to ask about."

"Oh yeah. I've still got Scout, and you remember Rebel. You used to prefer Rebel. And Arizona and Thunder. And a new one, Caesar, a fine five-year-old you might want to try sometime. He's still a little frisky and skittish but you could handle him."

"How about Monday? I've got this friend coming to visit later today, and I thought maybe your father would let us ride for a while like we used to with you and maybe your brother and Mark...if you'd like that?"

"Who is he?"

"Kaiden Carlisle. Corky. I knew him last summer at camp. He's a sophomore at Tulane. From Vicksburg."

"Does he ride?"

"Oh yes. We spent a day last summer horseback touring this big Indian park in New Mexico. He handled his horse as well as I did, maybe better. He's a good guy."

"Well, sure. You mean just around the fields? My brother's not much into horses — prob'ly 'cause I am — but I'll ask Dad. He may want to see...your friend... ride a little first. He'll be glad to see you again. Monday afternoon? Around two, say. Would Caesar be okay for you?"

"Julius? Augustus? You decide. Not Caligula, though!"

"Show-off," he said. "You always were."

So that was pretty much set. Corky *had* ably enough managed his mount at Bandelier Park on our one day there away from Jubilee; and since the plain, straight turn-rows across the Grady's land weren't exactly challenges for man or beast, Corky should be easy with my idea…although it's true that the Park's horses were trained for tourists and as docile as horses ever come. Corky always naturally made a good first impression, and would on Mr. Grady. But I'd been thrown, so to speak, completely thrown off by Neil's rollout of his plans. Whatever did he *mean*, already talking about marriage and family? Here I was blindly bluffing and slogging my way through weeks and weeks of useless math and science courses while sweating my ass off trying to scratch out a dopey play about a deadbeat, lame-brain poet that nobody — except a half-looney unstable assistant professor of English at a jerkwater school — cares a shit about and never will; and also loitering around a damp, chill church basement nitpicking Bible verses with a bunch of other wise-ass peacocks…while Neil's talking about marrying a hot co-ed and making a passel of little bitty babies! How'd he get so far ahead of me? He's out yachting on the mighty main while I'm still back here paddling in the shallows with my sissy little boyfriends! Was Neil actually already *dreaming* about full-time farming and fixing motors and minding a bunch of squalling brats all the livelong day? Lurking somewhere in these blurry speculative shadows was a really weighty question about growing-up or rounding-out or settling down…or something. I needed to process. But how could I process the future without having the maturity to process my own maturity, such as it was?

\* \* \*

Corky looked supremely attractive — smashing, really! — when he stepped off the Greyhound at Madison's dilapidated excuse for a station: navy blazer, gold buttons, spread collar blue dress shirt, navy-yellow-white striped bow-tie, charcoal-gray chinos, black loafers, naked ankles. Glinting on his right wrist hung a new, thin gold-link I.D. bracelet. He'd slimmed even more, seemed taller, straighter, his stride longer. He shrugged off the backpack, opened his arms.

"It's not New Orleans," I said, but returned his embrace anyway. "You look *amazing*! I *love* the tie!"

"Thought you might," he laughed. "*You* look straight from the barn! But the hair is *excellent*! Just the Ivy look we're after! Can I mess it up?"

"Not yet!" I said. "And I *am* straight from the barnyard," glancing down at my dirty jeans and ratty shirt. "Been visiting a friend. You'll meet Neil on Monday. They feed you?"

"I had a Hershey's almond. Remember? Babs's favorite? I can wait for supper."

Caroline Babcock beat me at Jubilee's auditions for official Camp pianist.

"Here," I handed him a Cloves stick of gum, peeled one for myself. "Let's find the Plymouth."

"Mother'll appreciate you dressing up to meet them."

"It's actually for you." He cut his blue eyes my way. "You're blushing."

I pushed his shoulder gently. "Stop it."

"Ben left Thursday," I said.

"Who's Ben?"

"You know. At LCC. I told you. We're doing a project."

"He was here? Visiting?"

"Didn't I say?"

"Nope. I'd have remembered *that*."

"Sorry."

"What'd yawl do?"

"Ate, mostly."

"Did you not tell me on purpose?"

"No. I thought I *did* tell you."

"Well, you didn't." He stopped. "Look," he said, "we'd better clear this up right now or we're in serious trouble. Who's this...Ben...that you spent Christmas with and didn't tell me?"

"He didn't spend.... Wait. Slow down, Corky. Everything's cool. Ben Moore is my classmate. He's an orphan. Doesn't have a family. We invited him for Christmas dinner...so he'd have some place to go. He's gone back to Lecompte. Nothing's happened to worry about."

"Why didn't you tell me?"

"Honestly, I thought I did. It was a last minute thing. I didn't have time to write…."

"It's *my* fault for living somewhere else…that you didn't tell me?"

"Oh, for Christ's sake, Corky…."

"I just think it's a little strange…."

"Don't you keep a few secrets from me?"

"You just said it *wasn't* a secret."

"Well, shit. It wasn't. Could we…could you just get *over* Ben? He's gone. You're here."

"And who's next? After *I'm* gone?" But he was grinning. "I've never seen you drive. You've got your permit?!" He slammed the door and scooted over next to me. "Can we cuddle? Are flesh phases in my future?"

"I'm driving, Corky. But you can put you hand there on my thigh."

"How far up?"

"Not that far…yet. Nothing like a little dalliance to clear the air," I said.

"What 'dalliance'?" he asked, tickling my leg. "I'm flirting."

"'Dalliance' is sophisticated flirting. You'd better stop now."

He softened down. "I'm really glad, I'm happy, to see you, Troy."

"Me, too. It seems like forever."

"It was."

"The lake's out that way. Wanta take a look?"

"We might get delayed," he teased.

"Better not then. They're expecting us home. My brother Mark's really excited to meet you. He's fifteen. He loved Ben."

"Don't do that, Troy. I really don't want to compete with this Ben."

"You won't. Ben's not like that, or us. But I take your point. And I'm sorry. I won't make that mistake again, I promise. Mark's gonna love you too. You dress way better'n Ben."

"We'll go to church with your folks tomorrow, right?"

"We'll go with them tomorrow morning for church, not Sunday school. I haven't cleared this with them yet but that's the plan. If I don't make a fuss over attending church, they may not insist on Sunday school. So we take church in stride."

"Fine with me, either way."

"Now listen up. About tomorrow night. Sunday night. They'll all three go to 'Training Union,' which you remember is the equivalent of Sunday school, only at night, before evening worship. I'm going to get us out of going to *anything* tomorrow night. So we'll have two to two-and-a-half hours, 150 minutes, of the house to ourselves. If you're following me."

"I'll be following you —'Wherever he leads' — tomorrow night!"

"We'll have to be careful, of course. Keep everything clean and neat, to look exactly how it looked when they left. And we'll lock the doors, just in case."

I heard myself going a little bit breathless as I laid out the plan.

"Are you sure, Troy? I want to, of course, but it's a pretty big risk, idn' it?"

"I don't think so. These things never vary. The routine's locked in. We'll have at least 150 minutes alone. Plenty of time."

"We'll be watching the clock, though. Listening...."

"Not the first hour, when we're safest."

"What if they catch us? They'll make me leave."

"I'll go with you. We'll head back to school. The dorms stay open for the internationals."

"You've thought this out."

"So you needn't. It's for us. It's our time."

"Yes," he said. "It'll all be our very own special time." We pulled into the drive. I beeped.

Everybody exclaimed over how "dapper" (Father) and "becoming" (Mother) and "sharp" (Mark) and "handsome" (me) he looked, and Father seemed especially warm in his handshake and Mother's eyes widened and lit up and Mark grinned at me, discreetly nodding approval, and I picked up his backpack and started toward Mark's room before remembering I hadn't mentioned sleeping arrangements. *Were* there any? Was that what Mark meant by his nod? I couldn't count on it. Father understood, and began his explanation of our predicament.

"Excuse me, sir," Corky said. "I actually prefer sofas, sir, over beds. Sofa arms suit my neck. Pillows put a crimp in it. I'm absolutely fine sleeping on a sofa with a blanket and a pillow. If that wouldn't be an inconvenience."

"You can have my room," Mark said, not at all reluctantly. I should have said the same thing, first, but something — some hesitation, some propriety — checked my impulse to offer my bed to my…boyfriend. It didn't feel quite right either to keep it all to myself with him on the sofa, but I couldn't very well offer to share it with him.

"Really," Mark said; "I'm used to the sofa now. C'mon, Corky. I'll get my stuff."

"Just a sec," Corky said, unzipping his pack. "I brought a little present for Mrs. Tyler, the famous chef, from another one, maybe on the way to fame!" He held up a slender copy of *The Creole Cookbook: 201 Celebrated New Orleans Creole Recipes*. "By Melanie De Proft," he said, "Director of the Culinary Arts Institute. With illustrations. Copyright 1955!" The gaudy cover foregrounded a round table loaded with recognizable Creole dishes, and a couple, the male in a purple cape and cap leering at the maid and the spread. "Mardi Gras colors," Corky said; "and that's the famous St. Louis Cathedral there in the background! It's not the fattest cookbook around, but it's got the best local food recipes."

Mother gushed: "How charming, Corky! You're so sweet and kind. How generous of you to honor me and my kitchen!"

He colored, grinned. "Check out the Bread Pudding Soufflé on p. 62," he said, omitting the remainder of the recipe name, "with whiskey sauce," which I saw later, leafing through the book.

He changed into a soft pink button-down and a pale blue crewneck sweater — his "pastels," he'd called them at Jubilee — and joined Mother in the kitchen to help prepare our supper, or at least to look over her recipe collection. Her pot roast from the freezer simmered through the afternoon and filled the house with stirring aromas that it didn't seem possible could come from a cow.

I resumed acquaintance with my old chum the Wurlitzer spinet — Mozart, Chopin, Beethoven, show tunes, hymns — in the living room, ahead of my treacherous betrayal planned for tomorrow. "We love to hear you play those hymns!" Father sang out, over them. "And the Chopin nocturnes!" Mother added.

Corky commanded the supper conversation. When I'd returned home from Jubilee late last August, I'd shared little of the summer's experience with the family. This was partly because I sensed that it had disappointed them on two counts: (1) I'd lost the speech competition; and (2) I'd not made a decision, like my roommate Monte and dozens of other staff members, to head for seminary after college for ministerial training. In our home church, the precedent for public reporting on summer religious occupation had been set a couple of years earlier by one Butler McDonald, an attractive young man who'd spent three months performing missionary work in Hawaii, and described it to an enchanted congregation one Sunday night with fabulous colored slides and hilarious anecdotes. That glamorous presentation had inspired my application for an identical appointment with the Baptist Foreign Mission Board, but I was rejected and settled for Jubilee instead. I wasn't about to compete with Butler's sensational report by giving my own, and besides I didn't have any spiritual experiences to lift my summer up to the expected hallowed rank. So I'd kind of dodged and pouted whenever folks, including my own, had inquired about my Jubilee months. Also, Corky had sworn all of us who knew about it never to reveal his clever argument that I'd actually *won* the speaking contest and *then* been disqualified for using "unauthorized special effects" to do it, when my roommate Monte was completely responsible for every one of them.

Wait, that's not quite right: Monte thought up the special effects. I performed them, successfully enough even in the judges' view to win the thing, only the same judges then determined that "special effects" was cheating and so disqualified me. Corky opened up about Jubilee over supper, from how we met to where we worked to how we played and with whom, and how Monte'd orchestrated my part in the competition, and how I got to be official Camp pianist, and all about the Cinco de Mayo party except the beer, and the picnics and the games and the campfires, and his and my great day on horseback at Bandelier National Park but not the electrifying conversation about sex we had there that helped get us where we were today. I got anxious through this last part but he kept it discreet and them clueless. The parents and brother ate it all up; and I felt grateful to him for making me look a lot better out there than I was. I believe he re-set the Jubilee episode in their minds.

The Sunday morning church service was arguably memorable for the figures we struck, Corky and I, in our nearly identical dress — only the colors of the striped bow-ties differed — and carriage and manner both to congregants and to each other. We were so elegant and appealing, so obviously together and happy in the attachment, and so plainly pleased with ourselves, even these innocents flocking around us might have guessed, except that I was still the preacher's kid and, as here returned after an absence, sort of a novelty, and Corky such a cordial gentleman and personally interested in everyone he met, that we seemed to pass, triumphantly pass, without arousing suspicion. It helped a good deal that the parents appeared to be approving and proud of us both. Mark looked to be too, and just about strutted along with us. If I thought about it, that appearance troubled my plan for the evening.

And it mildly bothered the afternoon. Corky and I felt and probably looked restless, antsy. For dinner, we'd polished off the remains of the pot roast — the better for an overnight's rest in its juices — with mashed potatoes from the leftover little golden ones for supper and fresh asparagus and more cornbread stuffing with sausage and collard greens; but I'd not scheduled anything for the afternoon except the conversation with Father about skipping evening church, and I'd put it off about as long as I dared. I didn't have much of a strategy for it, other than including Corky in it, since Father might find it harder to say no if he knew our guest preferred to skip too. I hoped and believed our compliance and cooperation and good will that morning would boost our chances.

"We'd just like a little private time," I pled. "We haven't had any since...well, since Jubilee, really, and we'd enjoy catching up. We wouldn't go anywhere."

"People would wonder where you are, though," Father said. "They saw you this morning. They'll expect to see you tonight. And you were such obvious hits!"

"Why tempt fate?" I ventured. "We'd be...less... *vivid*, second time around!"

He laughed. "What d'you need private time *for*?"

"To unwind. We've been kind of 'up,' you know? The whole time, like on stage, for inspection or something. We'd just like to relax...renew. And catch up with each other. We haven't, not really, had a chance to *talk*, since Jubilee."

"What shall I say to explain?"

"Say we're worn out. We're resting for school. We've got papers and finals coming up. All that's true. We're behind on homework. That's true too."

"It is, sir," Corky finally said. "I brought textbooks."

We were sounding lamer and lamer. I was losing fast.

But Father smiled again. "I won't make you prove it. I guess it won't harm anything. Just stay out of trouble for two hours. Don't leave the house or call anybody over. Have your private talk and then rejoin the family. We'll be back by 9 or so for a snack."

Corky and I very carefully did not lock eyes. "Thank you, sir," we mumbled.

"We'll wait ten minutes," I said, as soon as they'd left, "in case they forgot something and come back. Then we lock the doors. We can't start anything until then."

"What do we do until?" he asked, obviously feeling as uncomfortable as I.

"Anticipate," I said, winking.

"Your room or…Mark's?" he said.

"Mine. You don't have any idea how many times I've wanted you in my bed in my room. Now you will be." I shivered at the prospect.

"That's awfully sweet, Troy. But I've had another idea."

"BUT…? What BUT? It's almost time to go there."

"What if we…what if, in the interest of *stealth*…"— he whispered the word, hissed it — "what if we change sites…the scene of the crime?"

"What're you talking about? Where would we go? You heard what Father said…."

"How'd you feel about taking a shower together?" The brow furrowed. The grin curled.

I stared. "You mean like…under a garden hose?"

"Sort of. Only we'd be naked."

"You mean…have sex…while showering?"

"I dunno how much showering would happen. I mean have sex in the shower. Under it."

"You ever done that? I haven't."

"No, not with anybody else. I've done it with myself by myself often enough, and so have you. Why not together?"

"The clean-up would be a lot easier, wouldn't it? Little or no evidence left behind. Is that what you're thinking?"

"Not primarily."

"There'd only be wet towels."

"You have a hamper. I've seen it. If your Mother finds wet towels, we've showered. Which would be true."

"There'll be room?"

"For what I'm thinking, the less room the better."

"It's been ten minutes. I'll get the back door."

We moved through it with unusual haste, finishing quickly and with twin yelps, shuddering in the after-spasm, slowing only then to stand chest to chest, loin to loin, quivering against each other's flesh, caressing, nuzzling, nibbling, brushing lips everywhere reachable, skin tingling under the fizz of the scalding water, its steam fogging the doors and sealing us in delicious seclusion. I held him, pressed him hard. He shut off the tap behind me, cupped my cheeks, my thumbs gently swabbing his lids until they opened upon those blue, blue eyes. I touched his brow with my own.

"Mine," I breathed.

"Yours," he whispered.

We slipped into robes, hampered the towels under soiled clothes already there, replaced them with an identical set; rinsed the shower, neatened the room.

"Isn't that better than changing the bed?" he asked.

"Look around," I cautioned; "is everything just as it was?"

"That soap bar looks skinnier," he laughed.

"Let's leave the doors locked," I said, taking him by the hand and leading him to the living room sofa.

"A cigarette would be wonderful," I said, for I'd sneaked a couple of packs of king Kents into the house. "But Mother has a bloodhound's nose."

We cuddled, he into my shoulder, my feet crossed on the coffee table.

"What's next for us, Cork," I asked, without thought clipping the name to one syllable.

"Spring break?" he said.

"I mean longer term. Where're we going? Anywhere?" Of course I was thinking of Neil.

"Aren't you still coming to Tulane for grad school?"

"I hope. They might not take me. And I should prob'ly shop around anyway...for a better deal." This was new! I didn't remember ever thinking of it. What did I even mean? I diverted.

"You have a major yet?" I asked him.

He sighed. "Could I talk about that when you talk about what you mean by 'shopping around'? You never mentioned that. Besides, there's something else. I've waited for the right moment to tell you. Stay right there."

He returned momentarily, fingering a small, prettily wrapped package. "It's 8:25. We've got a while yet. Here, Santa left this for you...in my stocking."

"Oh, Cork," I said, "I can't. I didn't get anything for you...."

"Oh hush up. Santa, I said. We don't re-pay Santa."

I opened the black lid upon a shimmering, delicate, gold-link I.D. bracelet like the one gracing his wrist at the station but not since. He lifted that one from the pocket of the robe and laid it gently on my lap alongside the new one.

"Choose one," he said, "and put it on me," holding out his wrist.

"Aren't they identical?" the slow-witted sod muttered. "They look the same."

"Of course. That's the point. I'll put the other one on you."

I chose the warm one for him, and we slotted them on. I teared up. We kissed softly.

"Now take it off," he said, removing his. "We can't wear them here."

"No," I agreed. "But I want to. How do we tell them apart, without names?"

"Well, I left the plates blank...so we could each decide...which of our names we wanted on the ones we wear."

I was again slow catching on. "You mean...?"

"I might wear the one with your name...," he said, shyly.

I melted. Swallowed hard. "God, Corky, that's so... beautiful! But they're...well...aren't they *I.D.* bracelets...identification bracelets?"

"Of course they are. Maybe I'd like to be identified with you. As yours."

"I'm sorry to cry, Cork. That's just the sweetest thing to say. You're the dearest man…boy…youth…boyfriend! What the hell *are* you?! I don't even *know* anymore… what I want you to be." I sniggered and sniffed.

"Let's go with boyfriend. That's what I want to be. You were saying…."

"Oh, right. Sorry. I meant… would you do that? Would you wear the bracelet with my name on it? Would you want me to…?"

"I'll tell you what: why don't we both think it over. Leave off any names for now. Wear yours blank, if you like, after I leave. That should be safe. You can say where you got it, maybe not I have one like it? I'll wear this one blank, too. When we decide which names we'll wear, we'll get 'em engraved. It's just an idea."

"I love the idea, Cork. And the bracelet. It's fantastic! Thank you. I'll figure out a gift for you…next time we're together. Your Christmas present."

"Don't you dare," he said. "Just wear that one. What say we get dressed now? We should be watching TV when they get back. From separate chairs."

"That shower… our shower…was…*transcendent*, Cork! And this *bracelet*!"

\* \* \*

En route to his usual Monday afternoon pastoral calls on the halt, the lame, the blind, and other shut-ins, Father dropped off Corky and me at Neil's, Mark having opted to meet Tracy "for some hoops" around the basket in his backyard. Mr. Grady proved as boisterously welcoming as I remembered him being, glad-handing and slapping backs and scattering rambunctious good will all over the place.

"They been askin' 'bout yawl," he said, gesturing toward the fenced corral where the horses stood eyeing us, already fitted-out in full riding gear: Scout, Neil's smoky black long-time favorite prancer with the darker mane and tail; Arizona, a smaller, ginger mare with soulful buff eyes; and presumably Caesar, a studly, strutty fellow with a blaze and a rich chestnut coat in a shade reminiscent of Park's hair and the widow Harrison's Sazarac.

"All mixed breed quarter horses," Mr. Grady bragged. "Caesar's our latest and almost five now, a bit high-strung and skittish but Neil says you can handle 'im, Troy, just be patient. Arizona'd be a pussycat, Corky, if she wadn' a horse and the out-and-out sweetheart of the entire herd: quick of mind and kind of heart. You'll wanna kiss 'er at th' end o' th' day. Come on over, boys, and meet 'em, you too Neil."

He tugged a little brown sack from his bomber jacket pocket. "Ease up on 'em, boys, slow like, no sudden moves. No loud talkin'. Come up to 'em frontwise, your hand out like this, for smellin' and lickin'. Here, grab a sugar cube or half a apple."

Gosh, Mr. Grady, I thought: This is mighty nice and all but we're not exactly tenderfoots here. We know a thing or two about horses.

Caesar shied a little as I approached, side-stepped. "Say his name," Mr. Grady prompted, "soft-like. "Don't look 'im square in th' eye. Slant-like."

I offered the half-apple on my palm. Caesar nudged it, wrapped his lips over it, chomped, raking the rough lips back across my fingers.

"Tickles," I chuckled.

"No loud laughin'," Mr. G. said, "till he's used to your voice. Go ahead, slow now, and mount up." I watched Corky do it with surprising ease and grace. Neil boosted me up.

"You forgot to fix the stirrup's length," Mr. Grady said to me. "Do it for 'im, Neil. Easy, Caesar."

Geez, I thought: how many Sunday afternoons for how many years had I ridden how many of his horses up and down these very turn-rows through his fields with nary a slip-up or screwup or goof, or even a risk of one I could remember. Why was he on such high alert? Was all this for Corky's benefit? These instructions were pre-school. He was embarrassing me in front of my friends.

"Dad," Neil finally spoke up: "they sort of know how to ride."

"'Sort of' ain't good enough. I'm just makin' sure," he said.

"Relax," he said to me. "You're tight, and you're makin' him tense too. Take some deep breaths, Troy. Caesar…," he said softly, stroking his flank. "Now sit up straight, Tyler; don't slouch. Reins loose. Don't pull his mouth. Now press in your heels, *just a touch*. Yawl walk 'em around the barn and back, single file."

I couldn't hardly relax with Mr. Grady correcting my every move like that. Now it was irritating, and Caesar picked up my mood. Shook his head. Did a quick little two-step. "Whoa, Caesar," I said quietly, patting his neck. He seemed to calm. Neil turned us around.

"Okay, now," Mr. Grady said. "Walk 'em out to that grove yonder: you lead, Neil, and you two fall in behind, single file. Relax your shoulders, Troy. And Corky, don't clutch the horn for balance. Let your body balance with the horse's back and steps. Move with his muscles."

Whatever that means, I thought. Caesar wanted to push up toward Scout but I ticked the reins and he fell back. I could do this.

"That's swell, boys," Mr. Grady said. "Now: you know walkin's best. Neil can set a pace for walkin', and these other two'll match it. If Neil wants to *try* a jog or trot after yawl've warmed up, you could but I'd rather you don't. No gallopin' or canterin', though. Don't forget to talk to your horse an' to each other. But don't say nothin' secret. They're listenin' an' might tell!" He laughed. "Any questions? Don't be out longer'n two hours. Maybe 90 minutes. Ride good!"

*Now* we relaxed, and so did the horses, we could tell. After about ten minutes, we pulled abreast and got comfortable. Like old times for Neil and me. "You good, Cork?" I asked.

"This is great," he grinned.

It was a beautiful afternoon: clear, blue, about 75, the air dry and faintly scented with...what? Earth? Weeds? That "outdoor" aroma of fresh and clean and quiet and...well...contentment. What was Park's word: copacetic? Nice.

We ambled along: Neil talked about Northeast and his husbandry training and Linda and the family's farm. He and I reminisced about high school and church socials and our old gang and how Madison didn't seem to have changed one bit over all the time we'd lived here, and probably never would. Corky told us about New Orleans and the Quarter and the parks and how terrible Tulane was at football. We mused about these Christmas holidays and wondered whether we'd ever do this again, like next year?

"Linda might want to come along," Neil said. We agreed she couldn't.

At the bayou, coursing lazily through the dense patch of trees and bushes, we let the horses drink, stretched ourselves, and sprawled on the bank, drifted. Turtles sunned on half-sunken branches. Birds skittered and twittered. The horses dozed, flicking tails occasionally against the bugs. Dragonflies darted. The odd fish jumped to snatch a midgie. Squirrels rustled. An owl hooted.

"Idn' that supposed to mean something?" Corky said, drowsily.

"Prob'ly," I said; "doesn't everything?"

"I won't have to think like that much longer," Neil said. "I'm about done with that."

"What *will* you think about then?" Corky asked.

"Yeah, Neil," I said, teasing: "What?"

"He wants me to say 'kids,'" Neil said.

"And so you did!" I said.

"Meaning what?" Corky asked, laughing.

"Stop," I said.

"Yawl ready to head back?" Neil asked.

Caesar actually nuzzled my chest when I walked up to untie the reins from the branch. Or maybe he just pushed me back. Anyhow, he stood still for my awkward mounting.

"Yawl want to try a little jog?" Neil said, as we jostled.

"Naaah," I said, edging Caesar forward. "I'll race you home!" I cried, lightly nudging my heels against his flanks. In a flash, we were flying!

Well, maybe I should've known, as everybody else on the planet *did* apparently know, that you never, *ever* race a horse toward home: the horse, I now know, always knows where the home barn is and will lickety-split hell-for-leather always make for it if you don't hold him back or re-direct his head, no matter where you're starting from. But wouldn't you have thought Mr. Grady would've included that little piece of important information among all the advice he'd earlier laid on us? Anyway, here we were, Caesar and I, ripping — galloping! — full speed down that road, me ecstatic in the haughty thrill of it...until reminding myself that the turn-row intersected, way out there in the blurry distance, with State Highway 71 running south from Alexandria straight through Madison to Baton Rouge and beyond, always thick with cars and pick-ups and thundering semi-trailer rigs. Choking back the acrid panic, the reins in my hands hopeless as brakes, I figured my only chance was to turn the surging Caesar into the adjacent field, so I jerked and tugged him into a hard right. Without slowing, he leapt the shallow ditch and landed, smashed me into a telephone pole, scraping me off his back and free of the stirrups, my left arm out to cushion my thudding slam to earth.

Dazed, I wildly wondered whether I'd broken my neck, and raised up to feel the back of it; reassured, I lay back, and may have lost consciousness for some seconds. It turned out that Mr. Grady was watching all this commotion from his back porch, and concluded the worst from my moves.

I opened my eyes to see Corky right up in my face, his lips moving but making no sounds I could hear. Neil stayed in his saddle, staring at me, his father just stepping down behind him from the pick-up. Caesar stood some way off in the field between us and the house, his head down, warily observing us. My knee throbbed. My shoulder hurt. "Take Arizona," Mr. Grady said to Neil, "and round up Caesar there, and get them back to the barn. Call Troy's folks. Tell 'em I'm takin' 'im to the hospital. Corky, you come with me."

I stopped Corky from standing. "Tell him it wasn't Neil's fault. I started it."

Mother and Father met us at the Bunkie hospital, the nearest clinic to Madison, where Mr. Grady had brought me in the bed of the pick-up, under a blanket, Corky by my side the whole way, giving me gentle little pats here and there. Two doctors, a nurse, and an x-ray technician hovered and prodded and murmured. My knee pulsed, my shoulder ached, and my arm lay weirdly skewed on the sheet. They peered into my eyes with little pen lights.

"There might be a mild concussion," someone said.

They processed me pretty quickly through Admissions and the E-Room and then X-rays and got me into a regular hospital room where, alone, I drifted off into a light doze...awaking to see Father tall and stiff at the foot of the bed, his hands on the frame, Mother on the edge of the only chair, Corky looking lost and forlorn over by the sink. Seeing I'd awakened, he gave me the tiniest little wave.

One doctor from the E-room stepped briskly in.

"Awake, Troy?" he asked, kindly. "Have a good nap? I'm Dr. Prescott. How're you feeling?"

"Sore," I said. "Not like moving much."

"No," he said, "you needn't. If you're up to listening, though, I'd like to explain what's happened and how we're going to fix it. Understand?"

"Yes, sir. Thank you."

"And then you can ask me anything you'd like. Okay? The radius in your left arm is broken close to your wrist. You probably tried to break your fall and cracked the bone when you landed on your side. That forearm fracture will require a plastic cast from your hand to your elbow for about six weeks while it mends. There shouldn't be any permanent damage...and you'll have lots of signatures as mementos!" He smiled a fetching grin. "You also sustained a clavicle fracture," he patted his left shoulder, "from the electrical pole you hit. You'll need to wear under your shirt what we call a figure-eight bandage to protect the clavicle for six to eight weeks. It won't hurt but it'll feel a little tight and awkward. I'll check it tomorrow before you go home. Your left knee is badly bruised and may balloon up big as a basketball" — he grinned again — "but luckily you didn't break anything down there. It'll go technicolor before returning to its normal shape and shade. You're not likely to have any permanent damage or scarring from the accident. You took a very hard hit, Troy; but in a way you were lucky. Your head was spared, except for the fall. You'll have a bump from that, not for long. But we don't see any signs of shock. We're going to keep you overnight, though, to be safe. You need some rest. Take it easy for a few days. No more riding for a while, okay? You'll have some pain. Aspirin will help. No more than six a day, though, Mrs. Tyler? Now, ready to get those bones set?"

"How's Caesar?" I asked. "The horse?"

"Right outside the door," the doctor said, "waiting for you to wake up. He wants to share the purse with you!"

Everybody laughed.

"What about Neil? And his father? I need to talk to Mr. Grady. It wasn't Neil's fault."

"Don't you worry about any of that," Mother said. "We'll take care of that later."

"Where's Mark?"

"Your brother's still at Tracy's," Father said. "We'll pick him up on the way home."

"Could I talk to Corky? In private, please?"

"Do you have any other questions for me," Dr. Prescott asked. "Reverend Tyler? Mrs. Tyler?"

"I don't think so, sir," I said. "Will I see you later?"

"Right away, for the settings. I'll be back in the morning."

"We'll step outside too," Father said, nodding at Mother. "We may have another question or two for the doctor. And of course we'll wait for Corky. He'll have your room tonight at home."

Mother bent over to kiss my cheek. "We're so glad you're going to be all right, Troy. God was looking out for you this afternoon."

"I know," I said, not at all sure that He wasn't.

Corky stepped up to the bed.

"What were you mumbling to me back there in the field," I asked, "when I first came to? I couldn't hear what you were saying."

"Well," he said, reddening a little; "I was actually praying. Just not out loud."

"Really? You were? How...thoughtful of you! Thanks."

"I can't believe I'm getting to sleep in your bed tonight," he said, the red deepening.

"Don't change the sheets!"

"Before or after?"

"Neither one!"

"And...," I added: "about this afternoon: I *won*!"

"Well whoopitty-doo-dah and joy to the world!" he said sourly. "God, Troy! You beat us home but I'd say you lost."

\* \* \*

It was already New Year's Eve day when I returned home at mid-afternoon all bandaged and casted, and of mixed mind about resuming relations and routines, insofar as I could, on a turf almost certain to feel at least a little foreign or different in light of circumstances intervening since I'd left it. I'd not slept well the night before at the hospital, partly from discomfort, of course, but also because I was troubled by Corky's parting shot and by his hours since then alone with my parents when private information about ourselves might inadvertently have slipped out. Moreover, I still had to face Neil and his father with admissions of my sole responsibility for the mishap, and apologies for abusing the privilege of riding the Grady horses. Surely I also owed Corky something for so miserably screwing-up his holiday, to say nothing of my own, and now having to rearrange plans for finishing term papers and taking exams and picking up the project and maybe quitting Group and pacifying Jack, not to mention Park. It's a good thing my *right* arm wasn't in the cast.

I felt capable of moving around the house but Mother insisted on continuing bed rest and propped me up with pillows and blankets and my Romantics text and a pad and orange juice, and allowed Corky in for a visit.

"Now be quiet," she counseled, "but call me, son, if you need anything. Don't excite him, Corky," she added, closing the door.

"So," I said to him, "excite me already!"

He grinned, and took a chair out of reach of the bed. A little static still crackled between us. We went quiet, waited on each other.

After the pause, he said: "They put me in your bed last night. Right there."

"They did? Right here? Well," I teased, "how'd you like it, hmmmm?"

"I'm too embarrassed to say," he giggled. "Do you hurt?" The tension eased.

"Some, I guess. You want to see my knee?"

"I don't think so. I can tell it's swollen."

"You want to sign my cast?"

"Sure!"

"You'll be the first," I said, scrabbling in the bedside drawer for the new fountain pen Ben had brought me."

"Fancy!" he said. "Where'd you get it?"

"Christmas."

"What name should I use?" he asked.

"Whadaya mean?"

"Well, you've been saying 'Cork.' What name should I use… on the cast…on the bracelet, when we engrave? Shouldn't we settle on one? There's another choice: my middle name? Do you even know it?"

I didn't. I'd never thought about it. "What is it?"

"Craig. I'm Kaiden Craig Carlisle."

"Hey!" I exclaimed. "I like *that*! Craig Carlisle! Rugged! Movie-star tough! Cool alliteration! Why'nt you use it?"

"I like 'Kaiden.' I know you don't."

"I don't *dislike* it. I dunno why I said 'Cork' those coupla times. Except I kind of like the one-syllable punch to it."

"'Cork's' blunt. Like 'plug', which it means, or 'bung.' And are you conscious of how close 'Cork' sounds to 'Qwork'?"

"Qwork" was the name Corky invented back at Jubilee to substitute for 'queer' when I couldn't bring myself to *say* 'queer' or even *think* it much less imagine its application to me.

"No, I wasn't," I admitted, "but now you point it out…. Except nobody but us knows 'qwork.' Nobody'd make that connection."

"We would. Every time. D'you know what 'Kaiden' means?"

"No. How would I?"

"You might've asked. Me."

The tone accused. The same tone of his rebuke yesterday over my winning the race home. For an instant we both carried back to there.

"All right. I'm asking now. What does 'Kaiden' mean?"

"Scottish derivation," he explained, now sounding official, almost boastful. "But way back it lost that vibe. It can be a girl's name too. And spelled lots of ways… beginning with C…without the i. Nowadays it *means* 'warrior' or 'fighter.' And it also, and equally, means 'a loving companion.' Also: 'exciting'!"

"Ha!" I said. "What Mother just told you not to be for me! Exciting!"

After another pause I added, soberly: "A loving companion fighter is pretty much what you were for me at Jubilee."

"Do you know what 'Troy' means?"

"Why, no. Does it mean something? No, wait: Monte told me…Monte said it meant…well, Trojan."

"He's sort of right. I looked it up. It means 'soldier.' 'Foot-soldier.' And therefore also 'fighter' and 'warrior.' Our names have the same meaning. How cool is that?"

"Very. But yours also means 'a loving companion…a fighter.' It's kind of a paradox, idn' it, when you put 'em together. Are you a paradox, Cor…Kaiden? Are we?"

It's odd, maybe, that we'd never, either of us, used the momentous word — starting with 'l' — to each other in any of its forms, although he must've been tempted to, in some unguarded moment, as had I. My reluctance was deliberate, calculated. I'd never used it with Allison either, though she had, first paving the way by whispering "darling" into my thrilled ear one night in the back seat of Jerry Graham's Buick Skylark, and then "sweetheart" when we exchanged the ring and the lavaliere formally to attach ourselves in a "steady" relationship, and then the very word itself to assure me of her continuing affection despite refusing me access to intimacy. But I didn't say it, and not just because I didn't feel it. I didn't want to cheapen or exhaust it on misdirected investment. Mother and Father never used it either, to each other, within my hearing anyway, although Mother sometimes explained to Mark and me how much she loved our Father. And both of them used it all the time

— recklessly, I thought — about God and Jesus. But I was reserving it. I might could allow how Corky was a loving companion to me because that shifted the loving to him. I'd gladly commit to the companionship, but I held back on the loving part. On the other hand, I couldn't have told you either why I *didn't* love Corky, or even *that* I didn't. I just didn't feel up to saying it yet, not even to myself. Everything had to line up right first, and it hadn't yet. Obviously not for him either.

"So which name should I sign?" Corky asked.

"Kaiden," I said decisively.

And he did, in bold, blue ink, holding what he could grasp of my left hand in his own while with his right he signed a big, swirling, flamboyant "Kaiden" across the bottom edge of the cast, inches above my wrist.

"Date it," I said: "December 31, 1957."

He didn't move back to the chair.

"Are we celebrating tonight?" he asked.

"We might swing a quick New Year's smooch," I said. "Mother and Father'll be back in church for what they call the 'Watch Night Service.' From nine to midnight. I won't feel up to it, and you'll be excused to nurse me. Mark's old enough to go now but I figure he'll want to hang out with us, and they'll likely let him. But he's good at entertaining himself, and'll prob'ly fall asleep at the TV by ten. Obviously, we won't shower; we'll just ad lib…carefully."

Someone tapped lightly at the door. Mother opened it.

Luckily, Kaiden still held my pen.

"Look, Mother," I said, "Kaiden just signed my cast!"

"Very…stylish," she said; "the first one! What an example to follow! Look, Troy, Mr. Grady's here, with Neil, wanting to see you. Are you up for more visitors?"

Kaiden backed over to the window. I smoothed the blankets, punched the pillows. "Sure, bring 'em in!"

I wasn't keen, but we might as well get it over with.

Neither Mr. Grady nor Neil showed the slightest hint of temper or ill humor, both grinning hugely and talking over each other with loud, happy noise.

"See what he's brought you?" Mother said, opening the white box Neil handed her. "Your favorite: coconut cream cake!"

"Mom made it this morning," Neil said. "Says it has healing properties!"

"Let's have a look at that knee," Mr. Grady said. He flung back the covers, exposing me and my Jockeys and my knees. "Damnation, Troy, that's a good 'un! He popped you, all right! Look-a them colors!"

Kaiden gawped too.

"Does it hurt?" Neil asked.

"Not much," I said. "Hey, this cake is a great gift! Will everybody have a slice?"

"Naw, naw," said Mr. Grady, "all that's for yawl and your folks. We done had ours. You comin' along good with th' repairs, Troy?"

"Yessir, and I want to thank you again for letting us…letting us ride your mounts, sir. And I need you to know, sir…I need to say…that it was all my fault. The accident, I mean. Not Neil's. I didn't know. About not racing...."

"Well, you did," he said, now sober-faced but not scowling, "I told you not to gallop. But never you mind about that now. You don't get damaged like that and not learn somethin'. You're two wounds smarter now! And you're man enough to own your mistakes. That there's mor'n good enough for me. Ain't it for you too, Neil?" He grabbed my hand again and shook it.

I winced but smiled anyway. "Thank you, sir."

"Dad said you're welcome to ride again," Neil said; "didn't you, Dad?"

"I sure did, son. You and your friend come back any time. Caesar owes you one!"

"I thank you too, sir," Kaiden said from the window. "I really liked Arizona."

"You kiss 'er then?" Mr. Grady said, booming laughter. Kaiden blushed.

"We'll be movin' along now," he continued; "just wanted to stop in and check. Happy New Year, all yawl! Troy, you might wanta slap a mustard plaster on that knee."

Carrying the cake, Mother led them out, leaving the door wide open.

"Well now," Kaiden said, returning to his chair; "that went just fine."

"Couldna gone better."

"You know," he went on, "you're supposed to get right back on any horse that throws you."

"Already too late! Mother," I yelled, "could we get some cake and milk?"

She readily obliged, coming back in with slices, wiping white icing off her chin.

"Lord a-mercy," I moaned through a mouthful; "isn't that divine? Ambrosial! Can you make this, Kaiden?"

"It *is* heavenly! Yeah, I could. Piece o' cake."

Audible groans.

"So, Kaiden. *Do y*ou have a major yet?"

"I talked like you said to my nutrition prof, and did some research, came up with some info. I'm thinking I might major in sociology. Some folks say it's about human relations, which means I might've been pretty close when I said I'd major in sex! Or wanted to. Relationships and human behavior generally, and stuff like race and class and culture. And I found this one article said people in the *hospitality* profession sometimes majored in socsh. That sounded kinda like me. I signed up for the intro course next semester."

"No kidding? Wow! That's super! You found your slot?! I'm truly glad for you…after all that angst! Put 'er there!" I held out my good hand.

"It's not final. I haven't declared. But the only other choice looks like Economics, and I'll quit college before I go there. Would *you* ever be an accountant? They wear ten pens in their shirt pockets! No econ major was ever queer!"

We cracked up.

"I'm supposed to leave tomorrow," he said, suddenly sober; "the first, but maybe I could stick around one more day, to be sure you're all right? We haven't finished talking yet. Should I ask your mom?"

"Why don't I ask Father?" This was duplicitous. Father might be a harder sell. But I wasn't sure I welcomed a longer visit. We were already getting relaxed, and relaxed, careless. Mother opening the bedroom door on Kaiden practically sitting in my lap was a warning. And keeping him around even another day or two in the close quarters of our home without the freedom to touch his sweet face with a hand much less a lip might tempt the gods, after we already had. And I was starting to panic a little about homework and exam prep. It *had* occurred to me to wonder whether I could finagle postponements of deadlines and exams on account of my injuries, but that would only pile up everything on top of beginning the next term. Probably better to tough it out now.

"If he vetoes," Kaiden was saying, hiking his right foot onto the cushion, "what would you think about coming home with me through next weekend?"

"Are you actually comfortable in that pose, Kaiden? Or just being provocative?"

"*Am* I provocative, Troy?" he grinned, glancing down.

"Stop it," I laughed. "Close your legs."

"If you say yes…to my invitation."

"Which one?" I giggled.

"No, seriously," he said. "You could come to Vicksburg. Meet my folks, who'd love to have you, tour the sights, stay with us. They're real liberal, you know."

*"That* liberal?"

"Maybe not. But they'd give us a car, let us loose…."

"It's very kind, Kaiden, and tempting, but I doubt my folks…the accident and all. And I've got all this homework. You must too."

"We could study some. And I'd make you some great meals."

"I'd have to come back here…before school."

"Or you could train back to New Orleans with me for the weekend there! And I'd help you board the Sunday bus back to Alexandria and Lecompte. What's wrong with that? We could finally get to the French Quarter together!" He resumed his provocative pose. Laughed.

Now he *was* tempting me. School pressures waned.

"I guess it couldn't hurt to ask. We could leave tomorrow? The bus wouldn't be crowded on New Year's."

But my mother said they'd be tearing me — still sick — away from tender loving care at home, and Father audibly wondered whether we might be planning to head past Vicksburg to another tempting destination someplace further south, distaste in his tone.

So that was that. I wasn't much disappointed but pretended to be for Kaiden's sake and to play for concessions. Everybody agreed Kaiden should stay through New Year's and would help Mother with the meal. Father would ask his Youth Director to take Sunday's evening service so they could drive me to school that afternoon and, Mark helping, unload baggage, books and me back into my dorm room. Mark's pal Tracy and his parents were hosting a non-alcoholic Eve party in their basement while the adults sipped and swilled upstairs, and after a consult with Tracy's dad, Father gave his permission for Mark to go if a sober chaperone swore to get him home by eleven. That gave the house to Kaiden and me from nine. It would have to do.

New Year's food was a no-brainer in our home: shrimp gumbo with rice on the Eve, black-eyed peas with ham on the Day. Mother had stocked the shrimp, crab, crawfish and sausage, and Kaiden patiently stirred the roux, and Mark chopped the onions and peppers and celery, and Father de-veined and tailed the shrimp while I washed and dried as used tools collected, and before long the mixed aromas teased our imaginations. Mother was already soaking (overnight) the black-eyed peas for tomorrow's meal, and had baked the cornbread and towel-wrapped it. The cooked ham cooled in the fridge, and the cabbage and onion and cheddar and cream of chicken soup and Ritz crackers for the casserole spread out on the counter awaiting cooks' assembly on the morrow. Amiably, like one contented family, we murmured and hummed along in comfortable anticipation.

The house quiet, the doors again secured, Kaiden and I settled on the sofa, holiday celebrations around the world flickering on the muted TV.

"We can nuzzle?" he asked.

"Horses nuzzle. We cuddle."

"Can we? Without hurting you?"

"I think so. I just feel awkward, though, my right arm around you. I'm used to having you on my left."

"You can't rest your leg on the table this way."

"It's fine."

"Is the color fading…on the knee?"

"Not yet. You said we weren't done talking."

"Right. What'd you mean, 'shop around'? For grad schools?"

"Well, I don't exactly know. I hadn't thought of it before. It kind of came out of nowhere. But why should Tulane be my only choice? I mean, we applied to more'n one college. Why not other grad schools? I only said Tulane 'cause you'd be there."

"Which made me wonder whether I would be. Maybe I should shop around too. New Orleans doesn't have a single culinary school."

"But apprenticeships? Weren't you thinking of Commander's Palace or…was it Brennan's?"

"Sure, but there's no guarantee. What would you shop *for*?"

"There's no guaranteed grad school admission either. But I don't really know how it all works. And I don't yet have a favorite literary period or person to focus on. I wouldn't know how to pick a department or school. Or how to look for scholarships. Park would have to help with all that."

"I don't know whether culinary schools even have scholarships. Who's Park again?"

"My Romantics professor. Advisor on our project. Of course he might't be around."

"Where's he going?"

"It's complicated. And not very interesting. Did you notice how many times we just said we don't know....? Maybe we're getting ahead of ourselves here. [Was Neil getting ahead of *him*self?] Don't we have time to figure out how all this stuff works...in literature and cooking? I'm not shopping yet."

"Good," he snuggled. "I like to think about figuring it out together." He raised his face to mine and we lightly kissed.

"Do you want kids, Kaiden?"

"What? Children?" He sat forward, looked back at me. "Wouldn't I need a wife?"

"Sure. Would you want one of those?"

"No. Would you?"

"I guess not. Now. But I don't think I even wanted one when Allison and I went steady. You know, though, I used to look at Sunday newspaper ads from jewelry stores and price engagement and wedding rings. Isn't that weird?"

"You were thinking of buying one?"

"I don't think so. I wasn't thinking about marrying, God no. When Neil said *he* was, it about knocked me over. Maybe it was something about the *glamor* of the rings...not that I could've afforded one. Of course I didn't know I was...queer, then."

"Not even a little bit? You didn't even *suspect*?"

I paused. "Maybe? Doesn't every guy? A little?"

"I dunno. I sure did. Not suspect. I *knew*."

"I actually sort of envy you that, Kaiden. Knowing. And you never doubt?"

"Never. Do you?"

This approached quicksand.

"Well, I don't want kids," I said. "I know that much. Wait: I might't mind *siring* them. I'd mind a lot being a father. Performing fatherhood."

He moved a hand gently onto my lap, lifted his lips for another kiss.

"We better handn't," I said, moving his hand, and feeling frightfully like Allison denying me. "We'd better not...just because I'd like to so much. I'm still kind of sore."

We kissed anyway.

"It's a good thing you don't want kids," he said; "I'm pretty talented, but I couldn't give you one of them."

18

Mail stacked up in my LCC box:

1) A glossy black package from Jack holding a polished chrome Zippo with the three T's of my initials in swirling, intertwined capitals (just in time for the one-handed wonder);

2) A sweet thank-you note from Ben;

3) Professor Royal's announcement that The Thomas Chatterton Honors Literary Society would meet in mid-February;

4) A Christmas card from Mrs. Harrison asking for Jack's measurements;

5) A note from Jack asking me to stop by his room asap;

6) Leslie's announcement that the Youth Group would meet on Saturday, 25 January, at 7 to consider why nobody in the Bible ever apologizes: nobody ever says "I'm sorry" in a book packed with human errors, mistakes, regrets, remorse, and redemptions;

7) A holiday card from Monte exclaiming over his first ride in a fighter jet;

8) A reminder from Professor Royal to write my "personal testimonial" about his exceptional qualifications for promotion and tenure;

9) A typed, undated, unsigned note, sealed in an envelope marked "Confidential" in large, stiff capitals, as follows:

> *"I can't excuse you from the exam, but you might benefit from reflection upon how the itinerary of the Pilgrim in Childe Harold 3 & 4 captures certain Romantic themes, and upon the function of the marriage frame in The Ancient Mariner."*

I re-read. And again. It took some seconds to register. I must've gawped; prob'ly gasped. Imagine my shock! I wasn't just jolted; I was astounded, aghast…and verily frightened. I tasted bile, and thought I might hurl. On impulse, I crumpled the paper (in my good hand) and shoved it into my jeans.

Rattled and confounded, I retreated to my room with the mail but, too anxious to sit, I pocketed the Zippo, hunted out the Kents, and set off to walk, digest, process. The Grove offered.

How dare he? If the he was the he I was 95% certain he was, how *dare* he set me up with this worthless bribe threatening big-time trouble for everybody? And all for a few lame letter-lines from me that couldn't possibly make a dime's worth of difference one way or the other in his recommendation package. Or maybe he was trying to guarantee the absence of negatives, making sure I wasn't ripping him up?

But the *audacity* of it! He knows I'm not likely to turn him in — and in any case I don't see how I could absolutely *prove* him the author of the note — because whatever comes out, I'll look complicit with him, now and always. He'll have trapped me in collusion. I can't even ask Jack and Ben if they got similar letters, because they'll then know for certain I did; and in the end, we'd all be convicted of honor code violations and sent home. Because the one thing I was dead certain of even at this point is that everything *would* eventually come out. Even if the other Wise Guys *hadn't* gotten the same letter, my reporting mine to them would oblige them to report its contents...or violate the code. And am I not honor bound to share with them the two exam questions leaked to me? And what if they find out that I haven't? They'll drop me. Exposure of one tiny detail of his offer would start the thread unravelling unstoppably. Nor could I take my letter to Dr. Rogers or the Dean, because their first question upon reading it would be: What about Troy made the author think I'd be receptive to his offer? Was there something about *me*...and I instantly saw that there *was*. Was I afraid of *that* coming out? Of course I was. To my shame.

But all of this was so manifestly cheating...on so many levels and in every respect cheating, I couldn't abide it. Nothing obliged me to respond to the letter... except the code, I guessed, but I'd have to check it to be sure. If I knew of an *effort* to cheat, must I say so? Possibly only if it's a *student*. Nobody expects a professor to cheat, and professors might not be covered by the code.

What is lost, I wondered, by doing nothing? How is indifference and inaction risky? I won't destroy the letter — it *might* come in handy if things got *really* bad — but I could safely hide it, say nothing to my boys, nothing to the professor — maintain all these relationships exactly as they were yesterday, and wait. I am an experienced actor. I can fake normalcy. But I hate it that I can't talk to anybody.

No, wait, that's not quite right. There's still my rec letter to write. I can't not write it, since I promised. And it can't be a bad one, since he wouldn't have asked me unless he was pretty sure I'd write positively. To write otherwise would betray his trust in me, never mind that he's betrayed mine in him. But if it's a good letter, I'd be helping to keep him around LCC, maybe for life, when he's just handed me the best possible reason for canning him. But I'd just argued with somebody that's he's a good teacher. I have to tell that truth. Even to tell it without enthusiasm would be a sort of lie.

As for the exam questions: well, we don't absolutely *know* they're on the exam. If they don't show up on it, then he'll again have betrayed my trust in him, even in a crooked cause, but I'll not have cheated. But if they *are* on the exam, won't I have betrayed my boys by not sharing them? In any case, there's no way I cannot now *think* about them: I can't not know that they might be on the exam. Knowing that they might be, I cannot not prepare answers to them. I don't like that it's still cheating, but what else can I reasonably do?

But no, absolutely no: I do not forgive this person for laying on me a weighty burden I will think and fret and wonder about every hour of every day between now and the end of exams. He has been mean and selfish and conniving and corrupt and horribly inconsiderate not only of me but of his other students as well, and of the whole institution that gives him honorable work. He has disrespected the whole lot of us. I don't honestly know whether I'm a good enough actor not to show how disappointed and angry I am over it. How can I not despise him?

After chewing all this up into slushy muddled pulp, here's what I decided to do: I'd type an unsigned note to the suspected author of the offer saying that if either question turned up on the final exam, I would report the bribe to authorities; if neither did, I'd bury the whole affair without a word. In the event, neither did. I got my B in Romantics, Ben and Jack their A's.

\* \* \*

"You rang?" I asked.

"Troy!" Jack exclaimed, stepping back. "What the *hell*?! What *happened*? Are you okay?"

"Almost," I said, handing him a glossy black package with white ribbons, courtesy of nice granny types at the LCC Bookstore counter where leftover holiday gifts were marked down. With some of the Christmas money the parents gave me, I'd bought him a small bottle of Chanel Pour Monsieur, and one for Kaiden.

Whatever plans for unwrapping me and making me his own sweet man Jon Jack Latimer may have had for my return to campus took instant flight upon his response to my rapping on his dorm door. "I got whomped by a stallion!" I said, grinning, and stepping inside. The quip quickly became the accepted campus explanation of my casts and braces, and, moreover, of any other suspect scrapes and bruises — in fact, of nearly *all* other blemishes, blotches, and hickeys of doubtful origins on the pearly pink necks of LCC co-eds. For a time, "Oh, she got whomped by a stallion!" became a byword for the giveaway zits under heavy caked makeup on Monday mornings around campus.

Politely, even respectfully, Jack allowed me the privilege of a melodramatic summary of my accident, but through it I could detect a mild impatience, even a little antsiness, to move on to whatever had urged his note to drop by asap.

"That's about it," I wrapped up. "What's cookin' around here?"

"You ready?" he grinned slyly, and slid a black folder from under a stack on his desk. "My draft," he said, his hands slightly trembling.

I read the title: "Muse's Matchless Boy."

My jaw dropped. "You finished it?! A complete draft?! It's *done*! Holy crap, Jack, I can't hardly believe you finished it! An entire draft?! Oh, wow! I can't wait...."

"Well, it's a version. That's your copy, to read and critique. Ben has his. The title's from Thomas Dermody, a contemporary of Chatt who died at 27; wrote that line about Chatterton at twelve! It might't be our best title, but I thought we could discuss it and whether to present parts of the draft to the Chatterton Club meeting Park announced in his note. If you and Ben think it's fit for public view. Maybe I should mention my major revisions...of your draft?"

"Sure, if you like."

"Well, I've brought Mrs. Chatterton forward, more prominently. She's still fiercely ambitious for her boy and his literary aspirations; but she has a street reputation, let's say, that may or may not compromise them with some of the heavy hitters who could be helpful. Anyhow, she's known — doubtfully known — around the Tenderloin.

"Second: we need music. Something more and other than Ginsberg's finger cymbals and Park's silly flute. Let's give Chatt a Best Pal — call him Bud — maybe sixteen or so; sort of an Artful Dodger type — who teaches him the street and also the basics of the recorder, which he plays well for spare change. Together, Bud and Chatt try to teach Noodle to dance to their little tunes. Of course they won't succeed, but showing them trying will earn some coins and offer bits of extempore comic relief amidst all the grime and grit of the District.

"Third: the blow-out 21st birthday bash for Chatt that finishes Act Two now ends with a big police drug raid on City Lights Bookstore where nearly everybody gets arrested and booked and packed off to jail...only Ferlinghetti spirits Chatt off to an attic closet, and then pulls strings and cuts deals and calls in favors until everybody's released free and clear, and dawn breaks over Columbus Street where Chatt and Noodle quietly dance to Bud's slow recorder notes of 'Happy Birthday to You' as the curtain drops."

"We might," Jack added after a pause, "we might also need to patch in a little drama at the very end, so Chatt crosses himself and kisses his Crucifix just before falling asleep over his manuscript. To ratchet up the poignance factor?"

"Yes," I said quietly, impressed, reaching out my cast carefully to hug his neck. "They're genius, Jack, the revisions! Masterful. The raid's exactly the triumphant touch! This is flat-out *great*, man! Really great! It's all in this copy? We've got a complete working draft now? What's Ben say?"

"Haven't heard back yet. He may want changes."

"We'll hear him out, of course, and then pull everything together for a final draft. But how it can get better? We've nailed it! Let's smoke to celebrate." I fingered my new lighter. "Talk about the perfect gift!"

He touched his fingertip to the open scent bottle, and stroked it softly down my lobes.

Ben, having broken his own leg at fifteen in a motorcycle smash-up, cut me no slack in touting my whomping by the stallion. Indeed, he made fun of it, challenging me to arm wrestle at our McDonald's table and drawing a very funny cartoon on my cast of a big horse-face affectionately sucking my neck. Happily, it turned out that Ben also *loved* Jack's revisions. He'd practically flipped out over Jack's notion to feature Noodle as a dancing dog and climax the birthday party with a police drug raid. Such success among ourselves thrilled and emboldened us, and we naturally grew reckless, incautious... and talked, leaked beyond our tight little circle, which not only spawned complimentary feedback but aroused general curiosity and inquiry. Unmistakably, pride was the prime mover here, and eventually — too late! — we recognized our folly. Meanwhile, we yakked, and practically begged to be entreated.

"So," I asked, thinking to formalize what was already beginning to transpire, "why don't we advance the next meeting of the Chatterton Club to a week from now, way ahead of Park's schedule, and open up about the project, now we've got it pretty much finished?"

Why hold back? As a sensible, practical next step, why not share our complete plan for producing the play: casting it with Clubbers, appointing designers and construction crews and stage hands, rolling out the whole project for everybody to help develop and stage? That way we'd publicly claim it as *ours, our Club's* — our concept, our scheme, our methods. Wasn't that the original idea? We wouldn't inform Park yet of the new meeting time. We knew he wasn't really interested in any of it except as a possible medium for showcasing his dramatic flair. In other words, we'd take control, publicly make it exclusively ours: a Wise Guy production, for the whole campus, sponsored by the Chatterton Honors Literary Society.

I also made it official over dinner that I was withdrawing from Leslie's Broadway Church Group, although I hesitated because seriously interested in the topic she'd scheduled for discussion at the next meeting: why nobody in the Bible ever apologizes for *anything*! Now there's a topic for thoughtful investigation: in a heavy tome thronged with mistakes, errors, regrets, remorse, rebellions, punishments, and repentances, why does nobody ever say "I'm sorry" or any even remote equivalent? Did the expression, the apologetic impulse, not even exist in the culture of the day? If I hadn't been so burnt-out on dead-end inquiries mostly valuable for their impertinent irreverence, I might have stuck for that one. But as it turned out, other matters intervened.

Torrentially:

The *Witness* carried a page-three below-the-fold paragraph announcing that Professor Park Royal had not been recommended for promotion to tenured rank by his department faculty. I asked Leslie and other upperclassmen, and insofar as I could learn the campus news organ had never before carried faculty personnel stories or decisions in its pages. That it had now done so was obviously extraordinary and betokened something remarkable. Details were scant. Professor Royal's scholarly achievements had not been deemed "sufficiently meritorious of professional distinction," so he would be granted a one-year extension of his employment contract.

None of us insiders was actually surprised, but the bold, black headline conveyed a sting. Even I felt a wave of sympathy, and I had better reasons than most for believing Park unworthy of retention. Still, to read that one's teacher had been fired was a shock. Something beyond incompetence was signified. *Was* incompetence signified? Park was not an incompetent teacher. Substance of wider import was at stake here.

Professor Royal taught Shelley as though nothing unusual had happened but left the room immediately afterward. We three drifted by his office where the door blinds were tightly closed.

And then at mid-afternoon, Ben, Jack, and I all at the same time received identical typed hand-delivered letters from the office of Dr. Jarrett Wilson, Arts and Science Dean, ordering us to appear at his office tomorrow at 3 p.m. "on a matter of extreme urgency."

I was so thunderstruck, so deeply shaken and bewildered, I hardly remember a reaction except a wild and frenetic retreat to my room behind a locked door under a darkening cloud of ominous apprehension having something to do with Chatterton and the play: I later thought we *must* have known, or at least suspected, but in the first fraught moments I wanted only to hide, to crawl into my covers, calm my knocking heart, weigh my nightmare fantasies, imagine flight. I shuddered and writhed and sobbed, and eventually settled enough to smoke and try to piece together a sensible version of whatever must have brought the summons from the Dean and what it signified for my suddenly uncertain college career. Somewhere about 2 a.m. someone knocked lightly on my door but I ignored it and kept isolated until nearly three the next afternoon, when I dressed in my blazer and bow and pressed gray slacks.

The first person I saw when led into Dean Wilson's inner office was Dr. Luther Hale, Senior High Principal of The Rutledge Gentlemen's Academy, formerly adult leader of the Broadway Youth Group, darkly suited and vested and standing grimly to the side of Dean Wilson's desk like a Doberman sentry.

"Good afternoon, boys," the Dean greeted us affably enough. "Thank you for your promptness. I believe you know Dr. Hale. He's a long-time friend and supporter of the College, and has led our investigative team in the matter at hand." Dr. Hale did not acknowledge us or we him.

"I'll be obliged," Dean Wilson continued, "if you boys remained standing, as a sign of respect, while I address you. I'm told you've been a little short of respect here lately. Some practice might be in order." He opened a file, glanced down at it.

"Now, boys," he said, "it's our understanding that you have conspired and collaborated on a dramatic project deliberately designed to bring shame and disgrace upon this Christian campus. We understand that you intend with this pornographic production to honor a disreputable scalawag historically recognized and universally renounced as a reprobate, a forger, and a fraud; a sexual deviant, a whoremonger, a blasphemer, and a notorious pothead. We've learned that you plan to 'contemporize' this thoroughly discredited scoundrel and humbug of a poetaster by associating him with the reprehensible riffraff of the so-called 'beat generation' of degenerates currently corrupting the youth of this blessed land, and celebrating his profane, godless retelling of sacred Gospel texts in the vulgarities of the gutter. These and other unspeakable indecencies you have plotted to depict — to *represent* — for the wicked atheistical entertainment of the sacred lambs under my protective charge on this hallowed campus. Do you *dare* to deny these several charges, boys?"

"Sir," I began, "I believe you have misunderstood...."

"We have understood only too clearly. We have a copy of your filthy script" — he slid a file from under the pile — "and we know exactly what you intend to do with it. You will as of this moment cease and desist all so-called 'work' on or associated with this despicable foulness, and never mention it again within my hearing or any other faculty or student with official connections to this college. And this, mind you, upon pain of your instant expulsion!"

"Sir," I began again. "I don't believe…."

"Troy," Jack whispered a warning.

"You'd best heed your friend," the Dean snarled. "Upon pain of your instant expulsion! Am I understood?"

There was nothing else to do.

"Yes, sir." I said.

"All of you," Dr. Hale said.

"Yes, sir," we chorused.

"Now," the Dean turned the pages of his file. "Your parents and guardians have been informed of our findings. Their discipline is up to them. The only questions remaining for us involve punishment. You cannot be allowed to trample with impunity upon the honored Christian values and traditions of this institution. Unfortunately, you have already been awarded course credit for some first term 'work' — graded 'work' — on this wretched play. I would invalidate it if I could, but it's faculty-authorized and officially in the record. But you have all three signed up for one or more Independent Study courses in this current term, for which you propose to earn credit for 'work' associated with this cursed play. You will immediately drop these Independent Study courses, and for them substitute regular college catalogue courses, which you will 'take' through this term for regular credit. You will select these courses forthwith and submit them for my approval. Should you fail one or more of them, you will retake them until earning a passing grade.

"Finally: by graduation day this spring, you will submit to my office a detailed, minimally 2500-word autobiographical account of your individual and collective participation in the dramatic project for which you are being punished, together with an equally detailed statement of repentance and apology for your manifold offenses against God and the institution by collaboration on this unspeakable mockery of Himself and of this holy ground. Your essays will be evaluated by Dr. Hale and myself for their introspective and conscientious integrity, their heart-searching sincerity and candor, and their evidence of authentic repentance. If your essays are unsatisfactory, you will rewrite them. They must have my approval before you are allowed to re-enroll next fall.

"The Charter for the Chatterton Honors Society is herewith revoked and its campus status officially ruled probationary until further notice.

"Boys, you have gravely offended your God, your college, your faculty, and your fellow Christian comrades. I hope you learn from these punitive measures. I will pray for your repentance and redemption. That will be all."

He eyed the trashcan but shoved the files into a drawer.

"It could have been worse," I said, as we cleared the outer office.

"At least we're shut of that damnable play," Ben said, "although I'm going to miss the gamboling Noodle!"

"No, I'm not giving up on it," Jack said, through gritted teeth. "There's value in that script, serious dramatic potential. We might shelve it, let it season, consider rehab in a year. It really isn't that bad. It only looks bad now because the Dean banned it. For God's sake, the *Dean's* judgment can't be final...on the *play*."

"Actually, " I said, "that's a point."

"So don't cancel Noodle yet, then," Ben laughed. "You know, the Dark Horse theater over in Alexandria where I worked employed a pet-trainer who I bet could teach Noodle...? Well, stand by, everyone. Who knows what any of this will look like in a year. At least we don't have it hanging over us and mucking up everything now."

"We have the satisfaction of knowing the Dean's wrong," I offered, "but his ruling is kind of relieving, wouldn't you say?"

"I wouldn't," Jack said.

"So what new substitute courses will you take?" Jack asked. "Instead of the independent studies crams?"

"Well, we'll have to scope the options," I said, "but I'm pretty sure I'll sign up for Music Theory. I've never had a scrap of it, and I barely know what it even *is*, but I'm pretty sure its absence has handicapped me, musically, and this looks like a great chance to fill a gap."

"And the other one?" Jack asked.

"Don't laugh. But I might think about the new one, the one that's supposed to show how current and 'with it' the college is: Home Economics for Men! It's supposed to be a snap but my Tulane pal has had it down there and thought it great fun. Wouldn't it be lark if we all signed up?!"

"Dean-ass wouldn't permit that," Ben said, "and I'm not wearing an apron. I figure Accelerated French for me this term. I'll need French for grad school, and if I start it now, I'll have three terms through first semester senior year, which is when they give the GRE language exams. Should be enough to get me through. And for the other one, maybe Mechanical Drawing." It sounded kind of lame to me but Ben did enjoy tinkering with machines and spun a pretty swift pen on cartoons. So maybe the rigor of the French would excuse the flimsiness of the sketching option.

"Non-fiction prose for me," Jack said, "and Intro to Journalism. Kind of automatic, I guess, for an English major. But when you think about it, the essay the Dean wants from us is basically a memoir; and I might as well get some professional help writing it. And besides, 'memoir' as a genre's gonna get hot one of these days; I could learn how to write steamy now! What with all my experience…! Who knows, I make mine racy enough, somebody might buy it!"

Ben guffawed. I blushed.

We let these conjectures settle against more serious searching and thinking for later on, but I for one kind of liked the way they were lining up. So apparently did Jack: "How long," he asked reflectively, "how long do you figure it'll take the Dean to figure out he gave us a pretty sweet deal? Anybody else feel like a brew?"

We headed out in what might have passed for a jaunty mood.

But not for long. Dean Wilson's revelation that "your parents have been informed" focused my mind as nothing else might've over the next thirty-six hours. The open-endedness of that statement wracked and haunted my very soul. Of *what* had my folks been informed, and with what reaction? Thus ignorant, what could I or should I do? What step take toward what end? I weltered in uncertainty. My phone jangled: I answered and hung up, promised to call back, and didn't. What utterance served, to whom and why? I won't say I panicked, but panic threatened. I sickened and puked, pounded my walls against imagined entrapment. Weighed equally insupportable options. Stared wild-eyed and sleepless, restless, torn.

I recognized Jack's rap-rap but he stepped in before I denied him, already tugging the white shirttail from his waistband, reaching toward my buttons with trembling fingers. He gently peeled the cotton fabric back from my shoulders and arms, at last freed of their bandages, and stroked the pale, tender flesh. I reached around him to snap the lock.

"Troy," he cried, "we cannot be alone through this. Please. *Please.* Be with me." He pressed into me, his cock thick and heavy against mine. "Please," he pled, into my lips, "please, Troy. Hold me."

I knew the timing was off, knew the moment was wrong for this long delayed union, knew that desperation would mark and maybe disfigure it. And yet I had so often denied him, with paltry excuses denied him, further denial now seemed cruel, callous, and — worse! — reasonless. We both required comfort, at least comfort, and comfort was at hand. I wrapped his slender frame in my arms and walked him to my bed, tumbled into it. It felt like salvation.

In our heartache, we clung, writhed, shuddered, gasped; wept; dozed, slumbered, and awoke to begin again, his lips brushing, his tongue probing creases no tongue had ever grazed, but slowly, gently, as if tasting, murmuring endearments, "darling Troy" among them. It startled me, but I heard comfort in it — felt the sweet, simple, warming solace of it — and knew it for tenderness. He fitted himself against me, slid against me, urging, hurrying now, raking his hands heavily down my torso and onto my groin, moving my hand onto his own pulsing dick, stroking until we came again, hard, shuddering and moaning and gripping our bones, spent.

I don't know how long we slept but I awoke at three p.m. with a clear head.

"Jack," I ran my fingers across his nipples, making him shiver. "I'm going home now. I have to go home and fix this. Now."

"Okay," he said. "You want me to come along?" He sounded sincere. "I will."

"No, but thanks. This is my game. Solo."

"What if I moved in here while you're gone?"

"What? Wait. Why?"

"I'd like to. Would you mind?" He was grinning all over his skinny face.

"All right, if you want to. It's kind of a mess."

"I'll clean it up."

I tossed the sheet and stood, in bright, blunt nakedness, and strode to the phone.

"Father?" I said into it: "I'll be on the 6:10 bus." And hung up.

En route, I thought I might work out a plan for explaining whatever had been reported to my folks, but how could I without knowing what that was? The only safe alternative I had, or so it appeared to my muddled mind, was to start with the truth, putting the best possible face on it, and see where that led.

"I don't know what you were told," I said to Father in the car, "by whatever school official reported the story, but I'm here to tell you the truth of exactly what happened. So you can understand. A while back, a few weeks into the term, a couple of classmates and I got interested in this sort of neglected eighteenth-century boy-poet we'd read a little about in class. He was very gifted, very prolific, but also kind of a rascal. The three of us hit upon the idea of writing a play about this kid for credit, possibly for the LCC stage. We updated his story to nowadays San Francisco, made him a Berkeley dropout, gave him an ambitious writing project, some colorful, influential friends, and set him loose to make his way in the literary world. We thought other students

might get a kick out of it, maybe even see themselves
or a part of themselves in him. Our professor helped us
research the guy and encouraged the project. We wanted
it marginally risqué, for student appeal, but kept it respectable: now and then hinting at bawdy, maybe, but
never lewd. Basically, we told the true and entertaining
story of the kid's extraordinary life…and mysterious
early death…and the really fascinating myths — sad,
shocking, peculiar, kinky tales — that grew up around
him as his fame spread. Details of some stories leaked,
of course, as they do, and the Dean got wind of exaggerated versions of a couple of the smuttier ones, and hit
the roof — just completely lost it, big time. He called us
in and raked us over the coals and rolled out penalties,
thinking we'd flouted LCC's moral codes and damaged
the school's reputation, or were planning to…when we
hadn't and weren't. My pals and our professor and I believe he's totally wrong — actually mistaken and unjust
— but we understand he's the boss and his views matter.
We're not disputing the penalties. And we're taking full
responsibility…for our actions. What we did. But that's
as far as we're going. We don't believe we've misbehaved.
We might have miscalculated reactions, but we don't see
how we owe anyone an apology. We're taking our medicine like good boys.  But we haven't hurt anyone, not
even one little bit. We haven't damaged: not the school,
not the students, not the dean, absolutely not anybody's
parents. No one is worse off for having read our story
or knowing about it. Why you were even 'informed' is
a puzzle to us. We agree that the Dean's lecture and the

essay we have to write should end consideration of the matter. His, yours, ours."

"Not so fast," Father said sharply. "I commend you on so neatly sanitized a version of what you say happened, and I'm actually impressed, Troy, by the maturity you show in accepting responsibility for your part in offenses against LCC. But you conveniently forget to mention your responsibility to us, your reputation in your family, in your church, in your community, and to your God, and how your behavior reflects back on all of us. This…this…taint of yours, this blot, is more widespread than you may realize."

"With respect, sir, I don't see that. And I don't accept 'taint' or 'blot.' How have I tainted anybody, and with what? I'm a college man now, really, with new allegiances, shifted obligations. I owe an explanation, I may owe repentance, to the College. And as I've said, I'm prepared to pay what's owed."

"Rubbish. You're still my son. I'm still in charge of you."

"Pardon me, sir, but you're not. I am an LCC undergraduate now in charge of myself. And I am here to take charge of this entire situation — of my making — and to sort through it with you to a satisfactory resolution. In your language, sir, I have sinned, I have repented of my sin, and I am prepared to accept your forgiveness of my sin, if in fact I have offended against you. What else is left to do?"

"Were I not driving, I'd slap you for that impertinence. How do you imagine your mother feels about what you've done, the shame you've brought to our house and our community? How is she, how am I, to face our…constituencies…with this disgrace on your record? You have dishonored us, son, by betraying us and your heritage. By publicly consorting with riffraff and disseminating filth, by creating a character who writes a blasphemous revision of Holy Scripture! You are seriously out of line here, Troy, and you know it. Do you remember what the Prodigal Son says to his father upon returning home from living with pigs? 'I am not worthy to be called your son,' is what he says. You might want to think about that."

"But the father forgives him. He takes him back. Where is forgiveness in your picture?"

"Don't be insolent! You're missing the point. You behaved unworthily. Now listen here: you are welcome into our home, and always will be; but you will not disgrace it by shaming the guardians of it. You will honor your father and your mother all the days of your life, in all that you do, if you expect to dwell in the house of the Lord forever. I cannot tell you how ashamed of you I am."

"But, Father: what have I actually *done*? I intended harm to no one. Who's been hurt? And how?"

"*Me*! Your mother! You have hurt us with your contemptuous rebellion. You have hurt us with your scorn of everything we've taught you from the cradle, everything we stand for as holy and decent and godly." He pulled into our driveway, braked. "How can you even bear to face Mark now, who adores you and the ground you walk on? Your dear brother who was so proud to show you his new driver's license? How can you look him in the eye after what you've done?"

"How would he know? Did you say something?"

"Everyone will know. That's what you seem not to understand. You have disrespected everyone who knows you and admires you and loves you and expects only the best out of you. You have alienated yourself from a beloved community by affiliating with depraved degenerates engaged in unspeakable indecencies unworthy even to be named, and you have *written* about them! And you ask me where is the harm in your behavior?! You know, you know too well where it is, Troy; and all the greater is your shame for pretending not to." He paused, took a breath. "Look: I am going to give you two days to come up with a fitting punishment for what you've done. It has to be commensurate with the offense. It has to hurt and trouble you! You come up with a plan to settle this account: you figure out a discipline severe enough to give you pain and cost you effort. Your conscience is going to suffer from this...this heretical transgression...for a very long time but I also want prompt amends to show remorse and contrition. I want them to sting. You start right now figuring out how to square with us the...the wreckage...you've made of our family and reputation. I want a plan in two days. Now get inside and apologize to your Mother."

I'd have sooner accepted the pitiless flogging of a studded belt across my bare back than that sorry excuse for a punishment assigned my misdeeds. Could anything be feebler, less substantial, less manly? Anything less decisive and resolute? It was so hopelessly unimaginative and wimpy, it insulted the offense it meant to discipline. It felt decrepit and puny, weak-kneed and pigeon-hearted. It admitted ignorance of a fitting penalty. And it embarrassed and angered me by its frailty and obtuse irresponsibility. I knew in the moment that I'd ignore it. To comply would emasculate my blunder.

In his blessing over our meal later that evening, Father asked God to forgive me for all the harm I had wrought. Mother whispered a seconding "Amen."

"I don't feel harmed," brother Mark said to me, lightly massaging my shoulder as we brushed our teeth at the lavatory. "I feel sad for you."

"Thank you," I said, tearing up. We hugged hard, smearing toothpaste everywhere.

Mother tiptoed into my room on her way to bed. "You've made your father cry, Troy," she said. "You must apologize in the morning at breakfast."

"I can't, Mother. I'm due back at school and I'm leaving on the 6:30 bus. I'll walk to the station. Tell him goodbye."

Fully intending to ignore Father's demand for a punishment of my own designing, I realized on the bus that he wasn't bound by his demand; he might well change his mind, and in that event would almost certainly conceive a stiffer discipline than any I would impose upon myself. I therefore decided to write for him the essay ordered by the Dean describing my participation in the

Chatterton project, demonstrating its harmlessness, accepting such responsibility as was mine, and repenting of it. But not apologizing. Double-dipping, I suppose, but to serviceable ends. Much as it galled me to write as punishment, I gave way, and actually enjoyed setting down a permanent historical record of our adventure. And I had in hand an essay if the Dean actually demanded one.

**19**

Back on campus and at least reasonably conscious of being there — (Jack's conspicuous pride in having tidied my room was unfounded: it remained a hodgepodge of litter and disorder) — I could not but notice the extent of Professor Royal's efforts to insert himself into the spaces once occupied by Dr. DeWitt of campus dramatic renown, or anyhow to situate himself so prominently everywhere that nobody, observing him, could avoid remembering his candidacy for the open faculty slot. He resumed the cowboy outfit two or three days a week for no obvious reason other than to draw attention (still without comment), and swashed around the canteen with a breezy aspect almost contemptuously careless of professional heft. More to the point, he rearranged our Romantics syllabus. Park told us that the English Romantic poets were infamous for writing deplorable drama; their disposition for solitary reflection, he held, was unsuitable for dramatic expression. But most of them wrote dramas anyway, and in his self-promoting hustle to succeed DeWitt, Park excavated a dusty old unread-able dud by the early Wordsworth titled *The Borderers,* and then no fewer than *four* historical dramas by Byron (one featuring the decadent, dissipated mythological Assyrian King Sardanapalus whose lifestyle pleasingly titillated us all), and added two of Shelley's plays to his already overlong syllabus. One of them, *Prometheus Unbound,* is a wildly abstract, heavily symbolic, daunt-ingly erudite drama way beyond the reach of innocent sophomores and juniors like ourselves, but we were not immune — were hugely susceptible! — to our profes-sor's in-class *renderings* of extended dramatic sections of this and other plays: his gaudy enactments of quarrels and combats and courtships and intrigues and betray-als and even suggestive love scenes right there in our classroom! The whole point, of course, was to display his *performance* skills, sometimes even with period cos-tumes: to get us excited and talking about how compel-ling an *entertainer* he was, never mind the half-baked, wild-haired philosophical humbug that Ben said Park probably picked up from all the plot-summaries and study-guides suddenly flooding the student market at about this time. We understood that Park's sole purpose was — to use the fancy word kicked around by some wise-asses — "exhibitionistic," not truly educational: we may have learned a few sensational tidbits about Shelley and the others but mostly we learned how captivating a performer Park was, and how passionately committed he was to getting that word out. Always suckers for amusement, we fell for it, and talked him up. Never less so than around the climactic Shelley potboiler *The Cenci,* which plumb knocked us out. This was old-fashioned theater more or less in the Shakespearean mold, only darker, bloodier, more depraved, and said to be historically factual. We took warmly to it, possibly even lasciviously, and lingered over its pages right along with our pruriently absorbed professor. Tittle-tattle about Park's latest spectacle became a campus craze.

His showmanship through these largely unknown dramatic obscurities was of course outrageously overstated and embellished, inflated and exaggerated, like this sentence, driven as it was by his single-minded objective to clinch his entitlement to the Dewitt vacancy. But it was also distinctive for another reason. Through it all, day after day, Park systematically ignored Jack, Ben, and me — in class and out, in the hallways and on the lawns — no matter the doggedness of our demands to be recognized and admitted to the generally lively class discussions. It was obviously a plotted, sustained snub on his part, possibly payback for our exclusion of himself from late planning sessions on the play, although the Dean's blowup over "Muse's Matchless Boy" had effectively sidelined it in campus consciousness for the time being. Scheduled meetings of The Chattertons had also vanished from the calendars with its loss of charter status. Romantics classmates were mildly amused by Park's (also performed) indifference to our demands

for recognition, but after a while they bored even ourselves and we gave up on interruptions after Ben tried a
couple and got shot down for cheeky impudence. Park
was firm. We were inadmissible. He'd gotten his complimentary letters out of us; for the present he needed
nothing more; and he seemed determined to register
his distaste for the formerly favored Wise Men at every
opening for disdain. Whether any of this scorn reflected
his and my ugly little secret about the proffered bribe, I
hadn't a guess. But meanwhile Park continued to parade
across the sawdusted boards of our classrooms the most
daring and arresting diversions ever mounted on College
grounds. Everybody buzzed about them.

\* \* \*

Jack caught up with me after choir rehearsal several days
later. I hadn't seen him since reclaiming my room and
had wondered if all was well. "You got time for a brew?"
he asked, gently touching my shoulder. "There's a little
something I wanted to discuss."

"Your housekeeping fees?" I asked, laughing.

"Well, actually," he said, almost frowning; "it's sort
of about that. I need to be sure we understand...each
other. It's kind of crude."

"Beer's good lubricant. What's going on?"

"It's about what happened, Troy. I didn't want you
to think I was moving in or anything, or assuming you
wanted me to. I think you saw I was...well, kind of desperate...for company. I couldn't be alone, with all we
were worrying about...and I wanted to be with you. The

sex was a plus. I didn't exactly plan it, but when it looked available, I grabbed it. So did you."

He lit up, took a long drag, watched my eyes.

"And it was great!" he went on. "But I didn't want you to believe…I didn't want you to…well…exaggerate…what it meant. Or could have meant. Or what I meant by inviting myself to…move in with you. I was thinking I wanted to repay you…for…sharing yourself with me…when I needed…."

"It's fine, Jack. I don't think I misunderstood. I was very happy…very relieved by your company. I liked what happened.  Surely you saw that."

We sipped. Studied each other. He sat back, took a deep breath.

"You know, Troy, I liked you from that time you asked me, in DeWitt's class, to explain 'theme' to you. I was attracted to you right then. Turned on, actually. And I tried like the devil to get you into my room just about every day after that until a coupla days ago when I practically broke down your door. But you'd prob'ly already heard around campus that…that I'm kind of… well…always randy. You know, stirred up. Free-spirited? Not terribly discriminating. I play around. Always have. Yes, with both sexes. I figured you knew that."

"Yes. I'd heard that. I'd wondered some about it. But I didn't fix on it. It's your business."

"Well, so long as you didn't expect…expect anything different…I mean…from what happened. I didn't want to mislead you."

"How 'mislead'?" I drank, lit up. "Where're you going with this, Jack?"

"Think about it," he said quietly. "You prob'ly already know."

"You mean, you're not a faithful lover?" I asked, remembering the Auden poem. "We didn't exchange rings, Jack, or plight troth."

I wondered whether we might be more or less on the same page here — highly unusual as such loose, even wanton behavior was in my experience thought to be — but I began to find his maneuvering slightly vexing, vaguely rude.

"I think I get it. We enjoyed each other, but it might have been a one-time fling? Maybe I disappointed you? Let you down...sexually? Is that what you're saying?"

"No, not at all. Good Lord, I certainly wasn't disappointed! I loved our...fling...our, um, closeness."

"'Closeness'? Is that what you call it? How about 'intimacy'? You know about 'intimacy'?"

"Surely you could tell I enjoyed our intimacy. How much I enjoyed it. I just didn't want to...you know... arouse any, well, special expectations."

"Okay. You didn't. To be honest, I was kind of uneasy myself, afterward, when you offered to clean up. We don't know each other *real* well, yet, certainly not well enough to start packing the trunks. So I'm not assuming anything...."

"The crude term," he said, emboldened now, "for what I'm talking about is 'fuck buddies.' You've heard it? It's boyfriends who...sometimes...fuck. Not routinely;

when they're, you know, hot. Amorous. When they're horny and have to get off…and are convenient to each other. Maybe that's what I was thinking about, for you and me. It doesn't mean we might not fall in love or like that, down the line, but for now we're…well…casual about it, without promises or pledges, or even assumptions about, um, availability…and need. D'you think you could you be more or less comfortable around an understanding such as that?"

Oddly, I thought of Corky, and of Monte, wondering whether either of them would ever offer such a proposition as that one. It was actually sort of endearing, though, Jack's fumbling and stumbling, his edgily impolite and disparaging manner: his proposal of an arrangement that might suit us both amiably enough, only so coarsely and even grossly stated as to embarrass us a little in the explaining of it. I'd never heard the phrase, but it did appear to allow the kind of casual, random, even fashionably cool and low-demand trysts nevertheless satisfying enough to keep one from climbing the walls with raging sexual lust every third hour of the livelong day. Jack's love-making — if that's an apt term for it in this context — left nothing to want in the way of pleasure, but the expressed limit on obligation, on indebtedness and recurrence and frequency, brought a new dimension to sexual congress in my thinking; and however scandalous to my religious training, it found a little nest of comforting approval in my esteem, at least in this moment of our entertaining it. The term itself struck an agreeable note of snug camaraderie free of fetter.

"I believe I might could get comfortable around that," I said, grinning. "If you are."

*  *  *

Sunday, June 5, 1958. From the final issue of *Witness* for the school year:

> "...LCC Chancellor and President Whitaker Blankenship announced at Friday's 1958 Graduation Ceremony that a generous gift from the Augustus and Susannah Royal family, of Houston, will enable construction to begin over the summer on the Lecompte Christian College Theater and Dramatic Arts Institute on the large meadow bordering The Grove on the main campus. The four-story brick and stone columned building will feature a one-thousand seat state-of-the-art amphitheater with the very latest in acoustical and lighting technology, two smaller rehearsal stages for ensemble musical and acting classes and performances, and a research library devoted to the history of Southern Theater, particularly musical theater, the only such research facility in the United States. The Institute will also support the development of a new undergraduate program in Theatrical Arts and Business Careers, for which recruitment of faculty will shortly begin. The new building will house classrooms, studios, practice rooms with instruments, conference rooms, a

cafeteria, faculty and student lounges, and faculty and staff offices. Chancellor Blankenship expressed his and the entire LCC community's sincere gratitude to the Royal family for their magnificent gift, which will bear the name *The Augustus and Susannah Royal Home of Theatrical Arts*. Its first staff member as Assistant Director of Theatrical History and Media Studies is Dr. Park Royal, formerly of the LCC English Department faculty."

"Dr. Royal Asshole" Ben scowled, scrunching the paper as though strangling it. "We all lied, you know. He wasn't a good teacher. All he ever taught was his asshole self. Anybody got a match?"

END OF PART ONE

# PART TWO

---

## OPPORTUNITIES

# 20

To no one's surprise, Jon Jack Latimer, Benjamin Moore, and Timothy Troy Tyler walked off the Lecompte Christian College baccalaureate stage on Friday, June 3, 1960, with most of the senior literary awards in hand, Ben having recited his hilarious and then stirring — gripping! — "Ode to Us" to the rapt throng, Jack and I bound for the Tulane University Graduate Program in English Literature, he on a Woodrow Wilson Scholarship, I on a one-year tuition-free ride to prove myself worthy of appointment at least to a grad student teaching assistantship, in charge of a freshman class-room, for the duration of my four-year Ph.D. program. Armed with pens and notebooks, Ben would move to The French Quarter seeking interim employment while sounding for inspiration among the literary ghosts who made it famous. Jack's Wilson award, usable anywhere that accepted him, also covered only the first year of graduate study, but carried such prestige that most recipients nearly always enjoyed three or more additional years of local institutional support, as TAs or research assistants. Jack's parents pushed hard for Harvard or Princeton for their son's advanced degrees, but he figured that the hotshot Ivies, already overstocked with Wilson winners, offered fewer chances for continuing aid, and he might find himself without it after a couple of years, given the competition. Much more important, though: Jack distrusted the academic programs touted by English disciplines at the blue-blood schools. He pored over the catalogue course descriptions and requirements with a skeptical eye and a doubtful heart, and ultimately concluded that every one of them betrayed a disqualifying bias: every one of them, he found, openly favored and urged the intense analytical inspection — the avid, squinting, anatomical, stupefying dissection — of literary texts over the creation of them. Where, he would ask in weary exasperation, where are the scholarships for creative writers? Where are the writing workshops, the seminars and symposia and forums and panels where students present drafts and famous novelists and poets critique them and recommend publishing outlets for them? Where are the summer writing conferences packed with renowned teachers of verse and narrative composition and their celebrated students who'd "made it" as writers and modeled what it took to do so? Instead, Jack found pages devoted to the reverence and illustration of "critical discourse": exemplary paragraphs tracking pursuits of irony and paradox, of imagery and conceit, of symbol and archetype, of synaesthesia and onomatopoeia, and of the multitudes of other literary "devices" that swarm honored texts and qualify them for meticulous autopsy and elucidation. "But to what point?" Jack complained. "Does anybody actually *care*?" After all, he'd won the LCC college-wide prize two years running for the best short story submitted to *Quill and Scroll*, our college journal. He doubted the utility and even meaning of such "critical" exercises, lamented the imaginative creations they stifled, and wanted nothing to do with any curricula they branded. And finally — of considerable weight — Jack also loathed cold temperatures, and especially the bulky, lumpy winter wear they mandated. "It ruins my slender lines," he whined. "And I can't write in mittens."

And then there was this other startling consideration, emerging slowly but unmistakably over the last two years: Jack and I had become close; tight; attached, you might say. We didn't fall in love, no; but by the time we began to talk seriously about graduate school, it's probably fair to say that we had begun to feel something strongly for and about each other. We never said so; but a bond had grown, call it a like-mindedness, a density of affectionate, co-dependent association between ourselves. A similarity of literary tastes partially accounted for it, to be sure: his artistic bent neatly paralleled without criss-crossing and paired with my more critical, scholarly turn, such a divergence perhaps witnessed by my winning the *Quill and Scroll* essay competitions over the years when he prevailed in fiction. Through long nights over coffee and cigarettes in campus hang-outs, we fancifully imagined a future with me as Coleridge to his Wordsworth, his Whitman to my Emerson, in our destined literary endeavors. I would champion his fictional achievements in my essays about them. We never got as far as formalizing anything, not even imagining official collaboration (we'd tried that!), but a mutual understanding or at least an unspoken assumption seemed to take ever more distinct shape in our heads and others' that Jack and I were somehow literary kin, linked in mind and spirit if not blood, and likely to remain so at least through school. It might have been wishful thinking. But we shared classes, meals, study spaces, walks, sympathies, activities, leisure, and always showed up together for guest lectures and poetry readings and plays. That we were so often seen together unavoidably spawned rumors that we were queer for each other, as the saying went then, though not after Bailey began tagging along; but nobody seemed much to care if we were, especially after we coyly shrugged off the suspicions without so much as a blush. And we were reasonably popular, too, with peers and profs. Strangely to me, no one ever *asked* about our relationship. I've wondered if I wanted them to, to force us to name and account for it. But to the credit of our mates, we became a "live and let live" item.

Now in light of our little unofficial "understanding" about sex — our "gentleman's agreement," you might say — this next will seem weird, I know. But after

several weeks of consciously observing its constraints
— of acknowledging availability but declining opportunity — it was as though our "deal" had diluted the
sexual attraction at its foundation: as if the opportune
potential for sexual play blunted or moderated its appeal. It wasn't exactly that familiarity bred contempt so
much as that ready access drained off any exotic allure.
The bait had evidently tarnished and dulled on both
sides. Where no seductive effort was required, no surprise entailed, and no conquest achieved, where was the
incentive? I'm not saying we lost interest in sex. Jack
eventually met Bailey, I fantasized Kaiden (and, increasingly, Monte) and discreetly cruised campus cuties and
still admired Jack's tight little butt so neatly sheathed in
the always smoothed khakis, and caught him now and
again checking my crotch for signs of telltale arousal,
but I figured these glances were mostly habitual and
not serious inquiries. At all events, not long after we'd
agreed on our "understanding," other interests began to
distract our minds and to challenge the command of
sex over our libidos.

The most memorable thing I can tell you about
Bailey is that she actually once mounted a stepladder
to access Jack's bed from the second-story balcony that
flanked it on two sides of the large, Audubon Place
antebellum home where he and I initially rented a spacious bedroom. Oh yes, from LCC days we'd imagined
ourselves blissful, compatible, productive Tulane roommates, but that arrangement went wobbly less than three
months after our move-in. Jack's a nocturnal creature

who kept his bed-lamp burning into the wee hours; I'm usually up at 6 and at the desk by 7. Early on, he showed himself a slob, I regret to say, leaving his bed unmade for days, wet towels and soiled socks on the floor, ashtrays overflowing, mirrors spotty, toothpaste uncapped and leaking, the toilet un-flushed and the seat always down, his desk piled in disarray. It wasn't exactly unsanitary; and his personal hygiene was exemplary; but the careless clutter of his trail actually offended me, and became an irritant that aggravated minor squabbles. For example: I thought that as graduate students in line for teaching assistantships and classroom responsibilities, we should frock fittingly, in dress shirts and ties, maybe blazers. Jack favored casual shirts, rolled sleeves, open collars, even when presenting in seminars, even for student cocktail parties. I found accompanying him a slight embarrassment, and we bickered. Worse, he liked fraternizing with undergrads, which I thought indecently unacceptable. As we shared a few Tulane classes with upperclassmen, Jack took to hanging out with them afterward, sharing cigs and coffee at the canteen, wandering off with them to lounge on the lawns under the oaks on fine afternoons. I probably was a little jealous — of the guys — but mostly the inappropriateness disturbed me, the indignity of the association. We were *graduate* students, in training for the professoriate, and set apart as a special class on the way to distinction. We demeaned ourselves by undergrad affiliation. I never said it but I felt it. And Jack and I quarreled — I guess childishly quarreled — over it. "You've no call to dress me," he said.

But Bailey's invasion proved the pivotal incident. Tulane's graduate student housing office had directed us to Mrs. Lucille Burkhart's grand mansion — reminiscent for us of Mrs. Harrison's, only grander — on Audubon Place, a private, guarded, gated avenue directly across St. Charles from the Park and technically part of the campus, only for decades restricted to imposing residences occupied by distinguished and exceedingly affluent University personalities, including the President, the Provost, and several deans. Mrs. Burkhart now lived in a retirement home elsewhere in the city, but she'd retained ownership of the property and still used it for entertaining Tulane muckety-mucks for Homecoming and BOT meetings and important sporting events but turned maintenance of it over to a management company and a resident Creole couple — currently, Camille and Christophe Trudeau — who lived in an apartment at the rear of the home: they kept the lights blazing and the furniture polished and the yard manicured and the white gravel raked for instant use should needs arise. The Housing Office interviewed applicants for the one-bedroom rental — to boys only (no girls allowed, as renters or guests; especially as overnight guests) — from the graduate ranks, and the Creoles likewise had to approve. The always well-supplied kitchen was ours for breakfast every morning…when Jack awoke for it. We considered ourselves extremely lucky to have been chosen for this select residence.

Quite large on the second floor facing the street and shaded by magnificent oaks and magnolias with glorious blue hydrangeas around the bases, it housed two side-by-side single beds, two smallish desks with chairs at the two floor-to-ceiling windows also overlooking Audubon Place, two large matching wardrobes with tall mirrors, two easy chairs fronting the second set of windows to the right and left of the beds looking onto the low fenced balcony — over the two-car garage — extending around from the front porch and balcony. The sizable bathroom, with a tub under the shower-head, sat opposite the beds at the far end of the room. All four windows had sheers half-covered with dark gray draperies, and a pale blue carpet overlay the hardwood floor. Desk-, bed-table, and floor-lamps lit the room. Jack's radio ran most of the time, but at least he preferred classical. I owned ear-plugs.

Bailey Edgerton, as I saw her, was a squatty, lump-ish little smart-mouthed pipsqueak of a girl from Southwestern in Memphis squarely in the tribe of fe-males who'd failed to land their man in undergraduate school and continued on, one assumed, guided by that intent, as the still then current cliché held, not without reason. Except that Bailey was crackerjack smart, as her class performance and other indicators almost daily demonstrated. And not only smart. Also savvy. Shrewd. "Designing," as I said to Jack, after she joined us, un-invited, on a stroll following the Anglo-Saxon class we shared near the beginning of the year. "You don't mind," she declared, actually linking her arm with Jack's and smiling pertly up into his astonished face, gaily brushing up her sleek brown hair with the free hand. "I'm Bailey," she continued, "from Memphis. You look smart: how 'bout we study Anglo-Saxon together?"

This was beyond bold, and Jack almost bolted. The gall irked me. She needed reining.

"How 'bout I read you 'The Lord's Prayer' in Anglo-Saxon?" I said, stepping up and in, for she'd tugged Jack slightly ahead of us. We'd had a couple of weeks of A-S in our LCC History of the English Language course last term. I reached into my bag for the current text.

"Naaaah," she almost jeered. "You'd have that memorized, both of you, if you're actually from LCC."

Jack stopped, stared down into her upturned face, at least half a foot below his shoulder. "How on earth would you know that?"

"Research," she stated archly. "Isn't that what we're all about here? You and me and your...friend?" The acknowledgement was belated and the pause saucy. I swallowed pique and skipped up a step to align with their increasing pace. "I'm Troy Tyler," I said, putting out my hand.

"Sorry, mine's engaged" she said, squeezing Jack's scrawny bicep with her free hand, "or I'd shake yours. I know who you are, too. Troy. If Jack doesn't work out as a study-buddy, you stand by. We'll compete for teaching assistantships next fall. And for A's in Anglo-Saxon."

"Are they in limited supply?" I asked.

"Not for some of us," she said. "Are they, Jack?"

He looked as flummoxed as I felt, and only mumbled a feeble "I don't know."

"I do," I said, determined to register my presence. "Dr. Haggerty," our professor in the course, "knows it's required for the Ph.D. He's reasonable, I've heard, even lenient, and generous with help, private tutorials sometimes. He's on our side."

"I doubt that," she stopped and turned back to me, frowning. "Professors aren't ever 'on our side.' It's never in their interest to be 'on our side.' It's in their interest to defeat us. We want their jobs."

"That's just horseshit, girl," I snapped, moving toward her. "With that crappy attitude...that twisted view of the whole grad school project, you're in for one helluva bumpy ride through here. This isn't a *competition,* for God's sake, with *teachers!*"

"And I'll win it, mister, going away, as I always do, without depending on 'leniency' or favoritism...except maybe a kind hand from study-buddy Jack along the way. And right now I'll thank you to show me some respect as your female colleague in competitive arms. C'mon, Jack, why're we hanging out with this cretin?"

"We have an appointment, Jack," I lied, "in ten minutes. We need to go."

He disengaged his arm but left it dangling within her reach.

"Let's talk after class on Wednesday," Bailey said, all sweetness and light again right up in his face. "Without your...friend." She patted his cheek and flicked her fingers across his butt, stepping away.

"I'm Troy," I said loudly, to her back.

"What was *that*?" he asked. But he was grinning.

"Oh for God's sake, Jack," I groaned; "don't you go getting flattered by that hussy! And wipe that grin! That's one nasty piece of work, that one: a cunning, conniving bitch of the worst order. She's already got you in her sights as a soft touch, and she'll be taking me out one way or the other within days. I dunno why she drew such hard lines there...other than to seal your doom. But she's set the trap for your sweet ass, and I'm warning you to look out."

I surprised myself with the vigor and nerve of my response, but she'd riled me with her aggressiveness and discourtesy and unprofessional attitude, and thoroughly irked me by her possessiveness of Jack. Of course he wasn't my property, but she'd assumed his vulnerability and begun a campaign to take advantage of it. It was bitchery — be-witchery — of lethal portent and potential, and I wasn't standing still for an outcome I foresaw as clear as day.

"Keep away from her, Jack," I said, more moderately. "She's poison. That's only a sip of the toxin she's brewing for you."

"Well, she is kind of...cute though, even through the sass and brass. Plump can be good. Cushy."

"The only cushy around there has pins."

Now, I know it's a stretch, but maybe the principal reason I could so confidently predict the "outcome" up ahead is because I've been vividly imagining it at least ever since Seamus Stud became for me a symbol of Jack's general unpreparedness in sexual affairs: the impersonation that registered himself in students' minds as wanton and impossibly klutzy. No, he wasn't even close to Seamus in most respects; but his dead-on representation of that bonehead's sexual benightedness in our freshman skit was so compelling that it began to transfer itself to *him* in one particular and thoroughly upsetting regard. I began to notice, with fret and foreboding, Jack's carelessness, even recklessness, his negligence in small affairs, and how easily it slid into irresponsibility in larger ones. I began to find him inherently improvised, and in that imprudent: sort of paradigmatically shortsighted and unready, intrinsically risky. He winged it a lot.

Here's what I'm trying to say: Jack's habitual unreckoning frightened me because it had everything to do with Bailey. Jack as Seamus impacted Bailey big time. Never once — and I'd looked, searched — through all the time we'd spent together, never once had I glimpsed a condom packet among Jack's belongings, never a contraceptive wrapper slung aside with his keys and loose change. I never spotted the bright foil corner of a pack poking out beyond the folds of his wallet. He never mentioned needing to buy or borrow a condom. I don't recall his ever cracking a joke about rubbers. It was almost as though the word found no use in his vocabulary, or its protective function any import in his awareness. Of course I 99.8% knew that he and Bailey were sleeping together, almost surely without caution. So I worried a lot about an accidental but virtually inescapable "outcome." That Bailey might be any source of protection ran squarely against her patent agenda.

(Why, well may you ask, didn't I just ask? But one didn't, then. For all the current ballyhoo about liberation and such, there remained some things a civilized person did not do. Some things were still private, intimate, and necessarily confidential. One didn't inquire.)

So I take no joy in saying I was right about Bailey's program, and that the road to Bailey's success — her personal success — was no less rocky than I imagined on the day of our first meeting. She proved relentless and ruthless, single-minded and tireless; she threw herself at him, publicly and privately, played his skin and bones like an instrument tuned to her fingers, captured his fancy with wit and ribaldry and innuendo, and disappeared with him into the Grove just when I thought I might have him to myself for a moment. Needless to say, our secret understanding — Jack's and mine — vanished into airy nothingness, less from neglect than displacement. *She* was ever "there" — intent, determined, steadfast — and he wasn't, or if he was, so outshone as to be a shadow of his self. And all this while, Bailey began to emerge as a rising star of our class. Intelligence was the least of it: she was lucid and fluent, intuitively anticipating questions and responding ahead of professors' queries. Alternately subtle and direct, roundabout and piercing, she could knock you over with a word and restore you with a wink. She could be blindingly quick and tiresomely deliberate, and throw you off balance with a quip. She could quote stanzas, rattle off dates, name laureates, identify monarchs, and fry a crackpot with a sizzling retort. She wasn't shy about flashing the

A's on her papers and the absence of red marks on their pages. Especially galling were the 100's on her Anglo-Saxon vocabulary quizzes, whereas Jack and I were lucky to break 80. I would almost certainly have admired her academic brilliance had I not been so eternally over-wrought by her absolute absorption of Jack — hapless in her hands — who blithely — eagerly! — permitted him-self to be suckered by her canny wiles. I knew the God's truth of how it would end — and I sometimes panicked, sickened, at the prospect. But Bailey — I have to give it to her — Bailey cleverly and tenaciously left me no room to manipulate his escape.

So I cannot claim stupefaction when, returning home on Tuesday from my 7 - 10 p.m. Shakespeare seminar in the Library, I stumbled upon them coiled together in his bed. She shrieked, snatched at clothes and scampered into the bathroom. Jack sat up, his hair pointy, eyes puffy, his bony ribs starkly bare and sallow in the light.

"What time is it?" he croaked.

"Damn near midnight," I cried. "What the fuck is going on?"

"Fucking," he said, scratching his head. "You've heard of it?"

"*In this room*?! This is *our* room? You know the rule about female guests! How did she…?"

"Tonight, the ladder," he said, nodding at the win-dow to the left of his bed. "I forgot my keys. Locked us out."

"What? What ladder? What're you saying…?

"She found it out back."

"What back? What was she doing back…? Hold on: she's been here before? You brought her…?"

"Well, we came together. We wanted some private…."

"And she *broke* into our *home*?! You helped her climb a ladder and break into our *room*? I'm not believing this shit! Get her the *hell out* of this house! Right now!"

"The windows weren't locked. We wanted in…"

Hugging a towel to her chest, she poked her tousled head around the bathroom door. "Cool those jets, boy. Everything's copacetic."

"It's completely fucked up, you mean! This is un-fucking believable. You need to get your slutty ass out of my room."

"You mean 'unbelievable,' but let it go," she said. "I'm not leaving till Jack tells me to. I'm his guest. It's partly his room. Get control of yourself."

"I find the two of you in *our room* doing *what all* in *that bed*…and you expect…*composure*…you expect *poise* out of me?! How long has this been going on?"

They looked at each other. She padded over to the bed, tucking the towel over her boobs, and cuddled against him.

"Don't *do* that," I said. "Take the chair, Bailey."

She moved. Jack slid under the sheet.

"How long…have you been…*violating*…this property? Breaking the rule?"

"A while," he said. "On Tuesdays. When you're away. Only when you're away. The ladder's new. I've had my keys before."

[*Loukas Chalandritsonos*, I murmured to myself; *Chalandritsonos. Chalandritsonos!*]

"Hold up. Let me get this straight: in this ritzy neighborhood, with that tart, when I'm in seminar, you sneak up here past the Creoles through the front door or off the roof.... Damn it, Jack! I can't believe you did this...behind my back! Without telling me. It's such... such an *insult*...to our...our...relationship."

"It helped ours," Bailey said. "And you weren't using the room."

"You shut the fuck up...tramp. You soiled this room...you... *blighted*... our bedroom. This place is contaminated. You need to leave."

"Troy," Jack wimped from the bed, "don't do this. It's not that big a deal. We can talk. We can get over this. Just slow down a minute, okay?"

"I want you both out of here."

Once spoken, the idea seemed unavoidable, and indubitably right. "Here," I said, jerking his suitcase from the wardrobe, flinging it open. "Pack."

"Whoa, man!" Jack said. "Where would I go? Where would we...?"

"I don't care. But you can't stay here. You've fouled everything. And you haven't even said you're sorry. Are you?"

"We're not," Bailey said. "This has been good, very good. It still can be, again. We can work this out...for the future."

"Je-sus!" I practically wailed. "I can't believe you people! You say to my very face it's good to do this to me?! To pull this shit...?"

"We've done nothing to you," Bailey said. "We did something for ourselves...in your absence. We used un-used space. We gave it purpose. You weren't affected. Get real here, Troy. How is this room spoiled?"

"Soiled. Yawl dirtied it, like I said."

"As I said," Jack corrected.

"'Unused space' is such horseshit. Get Bailey the fuck out, Jack. I won't have her in here. Or you.... You take the living room sofa tonight and find a new place tomorrow. And no, I don't want to talk. I can't think of a goddamn thing to say to you...about this...this... outrage. This unbelievable *insult* to me. And to our... our history. You can go straight to hell, why don't you?!" I kicked the case to his feet. "Now get going. I'm taking a walk."

"If I say I'm sorry too," Bailey said gently, "would you hold on and calm down and think this through for a minute, and just talk with us about it? It's not half as bad as you're making it. We *can* work something out."

I gave her the finger, headed out. "And get rid of that *fucking* ladder!"

It was a Park-worthy conniption, my eruption. A tantrum right out of the professor's playbook. And as soon as that thought dawned on me, a whole new light flooded our little set.

"Wait a minute," I said, stopping. "Wait just a second here." I could not suppress the grin. "Look around. Look around at what's happening here! What's going on here is a broken-down, shriveled up, burned-out fucking CLICHÉ! Christ a'mighty, it's a brain-dead, asinine, freaking French farce!"

",,,he said, alliteratively," Bailey tittered.

"...We're acting out the lowest, dumbest form of comedy ever written!" I went on. "Why the fuck aren't we laughing?!"

And then we were. Smirking at first, snickering, tentatively giggling, then outright laughing as the titters gave permission to.

"You're right!" Bailey said, guffawing. "It's cheap burlesque. Tawdry vaudeville fare. We're parodying a thousand shit-can movies. *That's* what we should be ashamed of. It's borderline grotesque, but it's also hilarious. And it's pretty damn shrewd of you to see that, Troy. Can you laugh at the absurdity of getting yourself all riled up?"

"I don't know," I mumbled, because I didn't: *was* my rage misplaced?

Disproportionate? It seemed a little early to bring out the white flag, although my supply of powder was running short and prob'ly damp: it looked premature to write all this off as harmless folly. They had seriously offended me. They had affronted and mocked me. They should pay...something.

But on the other hand:  Shit, could Bailey be right about harm? How *had* they actually harmed me? Hadn't I just debated my own harmlessness with Father? Since I almost knew for sure they were already sleeping together, why should it matter to me where, so long as it wasn't...well...here? (But in mentally framing the question I noticed, to my surprise, that it DID matter to me, at least some, not only where but that.) Still, it *was in* my room. Half my room. They took possession without my leave. No, I didn't actually own the room. Was I being unjustly proprietary? Inhospitable? Was she legitimately Jack's "guest"? He'd have admitted her, helped her inside. And they broke the rule. But they hadn't damaged. They'd hurt my feelings, yeah. But which feelings, and how hurt? What *exactly* was my complaint?  Why was I so steamed?

Well, this part *wasn't* complicated, was it? The answer self-evident. I was dissembling, and needed to get honest. This was raw jealousy. Not really of the sex. Of her possession. She owned Jack. She'd stolen Jack. Snatched him right from under my nose, me watching. I'd been outsmarted. Outclassed. My anger was born of loss, of grief, and of the loneliness already and to come.

"Yawl get some clothes on, will you?" I said. "We better talk."

This felt like concession because it was. But the temperamental dynamic in the room had shifted. Something had opened, a band of tension slackened.

They dressed silently. Jack smoothed his backside and propped himself against stacked bed pillows. I sat stiffly on the edge of my bed, facing him. Bailey folded herself cross-legged at the foot of his.

"Not there," I said; "pull that desk chair over here, between the beds."

She settled, picked at her cuticles. It felt like a moment for a Bailey wisecrack but she remained quiet.

"We need to decide what to do," I said.

"Why do we need to do anything?" Jack asked.

"I mean," I said, a little vexed by his sprightly tone, "how do we handle…this…what happened here tonight?"

"What do you mean, 'handle'?" Jack went on, in the same bright tone.

"I mean, it can't happen again. You and Bailey have to find another place…for your…trysts. I can't be dodging around you in my own room…never knowing whether I might bust in on you…."

"You're not here on Tuesday nights," Jack said.

"Technically you and Jack share the room," Bailey said; "but I get you don't want to be disturbed…by unexpected visitors. I live in the dorm, so I can't help with accommodations."

"Here and the Library are where I study and write. You and Jack should… visit each other somewhere else. I can't concentrate with you…visiting here. And I don't want to think about you being here, doing whatever, when I'm not."

"Did you say a while ago you might move…to somewhere else?" Jack said.

"That would be difficult, mid-term. Vacancies will be scarce now."

"You want we should set 'visiting hours' or something?" Bailey asked; "around your study schedule?"

"It might help. I'd welcome a little respect of my time and space."

"Well, what do you propose?"

"That's not my job. You're the ones with the problem. You find the solution."

"Well, if you move…," Jack said.

"I'd like where I am if you and Bailey would leave it to me."

"But where would I go?" he whined. "We had a deal. We agreed to be roommates."

"Yeah, well, we had another deal too, and you also broke that one. You broke faith with me, broke a rule, broke into my bedroom."

"Whole lot of breakin' goin' on 'round here," Jack said.

"We're stalemated," Bailey said. "Look, Jack," she sighed. "Drive me home, okay? You and Troy decide who sleeps where tonight — downstairs on the sofa or here."

"Take the sofa, Jack," I said. "Grab your keys and drive Bailey home, and don't come back up here tonight. There's an afghan and pillows on the sofa."

"Let's plan on lunch tomorrow," Bailey said, "to consider…next steps. Don't decide anything between now and then. Won't that work? How about the cafeteria at noon?"

"You could ask around about vacancies," I said. "And Jack, if you're staying here tonight, pick up after yourself. I don't want wet towels and smelly socks...."

"What?" Jack snapped, too loudly. "What's he mean?"

"I'll explain," Bailey said. "Never mind."

"There's one more thing," I said. "I dunno what all this is gonna look Iike after lunch tomorrow — who's going to be where — but I want one thing understood: there won't be any more lovemaking, any more sex, in this room, not as long as it's rented to Jack or me. It's ruined for that. No more love-making by anybody...on these beds."

"Nobody?" Jack said, his eyebrows raised, his grin sly. "Not anybody... ever?" Bailey didn't move.

A hairpin had dropped, but I covered. "Nobody. Not even after yawl break up...whenever. This room is officially off limits for sex. And oh," I added after a breath: "Bailey said she'd apologize for tonight. She hasn't."

"I will," she said firmly. "I'm sorry we shocked and upset you, Troy. That was inconsiderate. But it was also completely innocuous."

"And that's disingenuous," I growled.

"We fell asleep. And I repeat: the room wasn't in use. We borrowed it, harmlessly. Are we all clear on that now? Take me home, Jack. We'll be more careful from here on."

I almost bit my tongue. For with that thoughtless line Bailey had unknowingly evoked the one heavy-weight issue I hadn't gotten to in my litany of complaints, and could never get to as forbidden terrain. It grounded the very foundation of my distress and my alarm. Precisely that Jack and Bailey were NOT "careful" in their assignations — and might never be — anchored and infused the entirety of my apprehension over their relationship. The matter was by definition proscribed: it lay out of bounds, inarguably none of my affair. I knew, though, I fearfully knew as surely as I knew my name, that it would recur and amplify, be laid bare, grow ugly, explode, and wound. The dread of it haunted my heart.

# 21

August 18, 1961

Hey, Troy:

I got your New Orleans address from LCC's alumni office. I hope you don't mind. I need to ask you something and get your advice.

Do you remember that essay Dean Wilson told us to write about our parts in the Chatterton project? The 2500-word confession and repentance paper?

Did you write it? I started it, and then with exams and papers and graduation I completely forgot about it, until lately. Nobody from the

Dean's office ever said anything. Obviously, its absence didn't keep me from graduating.

But I've been thinking about all that and wondering if I actually OWE the Dean that essay, or the School. I mean, it's kind of an unfinished assignment, like homework, that we got graduation credit for finishing, when at least one of us didn't. If you wrote yours, and Jack wrote his, I'd feel like I should too, just to sort of close the book — the grade book — on the whole affair. I know it's dumb, but I sometimes feel like I should return my diploma until I submit that paper.

But if you didn't write yours, I wouldn't want to open up everything again and maybe get you and Jack in trouble. I won't do anything until I hear from you. You can write me here.

It's cool we're both in New Orleans. Maybe we could meet up. I work part-time in two motorcycle repair shops, on Carondolet and South Carrolton, and live above the second one. 504-322-2158. Or give me your number.

I'm also working p-t at Le Petit Theatre Vieux Carre in the Quarter, and loving it!

Your friend,
Ben Moore

p.s. Did you and Jack get full credit for the substitute classes we took when the Dean scratched
our independent studies? My French is practically fluent now!

p.p.s. Tell your brother Mark hey from me.

\* \* \*

Hi, Ben,

What a great surprise to hear from you!

I wrote and turned in a short paper. Piece of
shit, really, but never an apology: I took responsibility but admitted no guilt, no harm.

My Father ordered a similar confession, so I
wrote him a longer one along the same lines.
Nobody ever responded to either one, not even
an acknowledgment. I didn't see Jack's letter,
but I think it was about the same length as
mine, and to the same effect.

Since you've heard nothing, why stir the pot? I'd
just let it lie. They've forgotten us. Let's forget
them. Jack and I won't say squat.

Very cool that you're nearby. AND working at
La Petit! I always said your veins ran drama!

I'll be in touch.

Troy

\* \* \*

Following Kaiden's surprisingly eventful Christmas visit to Madison, our contact diminished in frequency and substance under the pressures of classwork and other local activities on our separate campuses, but with notes and occasional phone calls we kept abreast of what passed for significant developments in each other's lives over the next months. I learned, for example, that Kaiden hated dorm living, that he detested cafeteria food, that he abhorred the dominating, dictatorial influence of Greek societies on University life, that he scorned athletic ardors that wrecked campus weekends, that he found New Orleans itself less tolerant of "difference" than he'd imagined it would be. From me he learned too much about Chatterton, Park, Broadway Church, and Romantic literature. Much more critical for him, though, Kaiden soon found no match — no proximity of a match — between academic sociology and his own interests and objectives. Classes, textbooks, lectures, and labs bored and provoked him by their "irrelevance" to everything he thought vocationally compelling. Sociology's allegedly "scientific" methodologies baffled and angered him. At the same time, its loosey-goosey sentimentality pissed off even his sweet geniality. The obviously circular arguments, he said, made him dizzy. His general aggravation with the discipline ratcheted up as weeks passed, and took over our communications. I could read and hear his restlessness and impatience and ennui. Back at home during the summer after his sophomore year, his charm eaten away by ceaseless complaints of Tulane miseries, his father, he told me, threatened psychological counseling. By the fall, in notes and phone calls to me, he began to talk of dropping out.

The threatened withdrawal made me cross, and I wrote him accordingly. Having urged Kaiden's selection of a major when delay threatened penalties, I was emotionally invested in forwarding his formal education. I firmly believed he'd need a degree, no matter his profession. It's what one did. One earned a college degree. It wasn't debatable. And I also wanted him in New Orleans — fully credentialed, primed for respectable employment — when I arrived there. But while I was bothered by my friend's disquiet and agitation, his father became "apoplectic" (Kaiden's word). I don't think they much cared about his major, but the parents deeply believed in the indispensability of a college degree, at least for their boy, he said. "Those neurotic dissatisfactions," Kaiden said his father obsessively said, "really may require the attention of a psychiatrist...and don't think I won't call in one. There just might be another kind of institution in your future!" "He seriously thinks I'll starve without a degree," Kaiden said, "and mortify the family...through coming generations." Quintessentially, the father would not abide Kaiden's consideration of departure from Tulane. I was totally on his side, and didn't screen my bias from Kaiden in our decreasing exchanges.

So I wrote him, rather sternly and at length, counseling patience and industry and perseverance. For quite a long time, he didn't respond. In fact, he never exactly responded. And events intervened.

Mr. Holt Carlisle, the fuming father, a prominent real estate mogul in Mississippi with interests along the Gulf Coast and connections in New Orleans, ultimately proved open to negotiation. As Kaiden's dissatisfactions became ever more vocal and bitter, and domestically disturbing, Mr. Carlisle at last looking closely at them offered to move his son — on Kaiden's sworn oath to remain in school — out of the dormitory over the January semester break in his junior year, and into a chic, furnished, fashionable, ground-floor Magazine Street boarding facility for the remainder of his Tulane career. The suite's main attraction for Kaiden, he told me, was a large and fully supplied kitchen, available to the tenant; but on the phone to me he also approved the adjoining parlor with a piano, a long front porch with a swing and rockers, and an extensive back yard with trellises and vines. "The living space is so big," Kaiden gushed, "it almost echoes. The bath's bigger than my dorm room." I was less interested in his promised lodgings than in his commitment to remain for the diploma, but it was good to hear him sound content and even pleased with the offered arrangement.

And then in a stunning surprise, it was even more pleasing to see him — Kaiden! — just before I started grad school. On a for me economically hazardous shopping venture to Newt's in the Quarter (exclusive caterers

to extravagantly dolled-up gentlemen, if you get my
meaning), I suddenly glimpsed him, Kaiden — unmistakably him — casually pedaling down Royal Street on
an eye-catching, reconstructed bicycle. He'd fitted the
handlebars with a bright rainbow awning spanning the
front third of the bike, and attached to its rear fender a
two-wheeled wooden cart carrying samples of his own
Creole and Cajun cuisine specialities, available as tid-
bit handouts to passers-by and, if they fancied them, for
sale. (New Orleans always swarmed with street food:
trucks, wagons, extempore stands and racks, doorway
counters, spontaneous spreads on park lawns and court-
yards, community cook-outs, fish-fries, fried rattlesnake
and gator platters, barbecues: far too numerous for strict
city regulation, open to everybody.) The painted yellow signs on the cart's panels read "Kaiden's Cajun" and
"Kaiden's Creole," his old fondness for "k-clucks" still
in play. It was his hope, he'd long said, and his goal, to
attract the admiring attentions of French Quarter res-
tauranteurs open to hiring an intern like himself to learn
the business by doing it, from the kitchen up.

"Well, well," he grinned, stopping and steadying the
bike. "Where've *you* been?"

"Corky," I said cordially, in my pleasure forgetting
his preferred name. "I guess waiting for you, Kaiden.
Hey, there."

"Well, after those letters, I wasn't sure...."

"I'm sorry. It wasn't my call."

"Well," he said, gesturing at his gear, "the folks gave me nine months to find a job with a living wage," he said, offering me a colorful business card.

"Is it happening?" I asked.

"Maybe. I'm getting some attention." He flipped the lid on the basket behind him. "Here," he said; "have some gator."

I bit. It was tough but agreeably spicy. "Good," I said. "Thanks."

We paused, studied, then started to speak at the same moment, over each other, laughed.

He looked yummy. I inferred vigorous workouts were responsible. The core had continued to slim; the hair had lengthened, after current fashion, into glistening, tangled, tumbled curls: like Monte's. The thighs, packed into tight, faded cut-off Levis, attracted more stares than mine. The forearms showed veins; the calves, below the shorts, spoke husky. His delectable boyishness had seasoned toward virile self-possession. Flirtation felt feasible. But we had history. I checked my impulse.

"You graduated?" I asked, uneasily.

"It was a narrow squeak. I almost dropped out. That's what you wrote about."

"Those letters were prob'ly out of line."

"They prob'ly weren't. I heard you. I just didn't know how to write back. Things were touch and go for awhile, and I didn't know…."

"Understood. Do you know what turned you around?"

"My father's bribe. He let me leave the dorm. For an apartment."

"Yes. Well, congratulations on your diploma! I'm really glad for you."

"You're in grad school now?"

"Starting next week."

Another awkward pause.

"Let's sit," he said, kick-stading the bike and squatting on the low curb.

"It's been such a long time," I said. "Since we began…."

"I've missed you," he said quietly.

"And I you, Kaiden. Want to smoke?"

We lit up, exhaled, our smoke mixing in the still air.

"Why was it so long?"

"Well, the letters. I kind of thought you were pissed off."

"When I told you to stick it out."

"Yes, like my dad. You sounded like him."

"Well, you did the right thing."

"I don't know, really," he said. "I was kind of messed up. I hated school. I hated socsh. I hated my folks. I got depressed, smoked a lot of weed. Had a lousy hook-up."

"You did drugs?"

"No; grass though."

"What happened?"

"I got clean. Stayed clean. And I graduated!"

I slipped my arm around his shoulder and hugged. "This is the Quarter. We can hug and nobody cares! Do you still have that boyfriend?"

"Oh no. And he wasn't ever….."

"You don't have a boyfriend? How can you not have a boyfriend?! You're too beautiful not to have one!"

"Do you?" he asked, quietly. "Have a boyfriend?"

"I…I…don't think so. No, not really. Not what you'd call a boyfriend."

"We should get together," he said frankly. "Get re-acquainted."

"I'd like to. Got a pen?" I scribbled Mrs. Burkhart's number on receipt paper.

"Mine's on the card," he said, lifting a hand to rub his chin, lightly rattling a chain on his wrist.

"Oh my God," I exclaimed. "Is that the I.D. bracelet? Oh, shit, Kaiden; I forgot mine! Damn it, I've disappointed you again! I am so sorry!"

"We need to get them engraved. If you still want to." He paused. "Do you?"

"Well, sure. I mean, I don't know, I guess so. Why shouldn't we? That's what they're for. It's what we planned." I was babbling.

"I know a shop," he said, "where they engrave."

"Excellent," I said, standing.

"I guess I'd better try to sell some grub," he said, mounting the bike.

"Really great seeing you, Kaiden! Gimme a hug!"

We tried, but the top tube was in the way.

\* \* \*

The morning after the blow-up with Jack and Bailey I awoke tired and fuzzy-headed and furry-tongued, as though hungover, but I'd only had caffeine and Kents, and frequent memory-flashes all night on scraps of our squabble. Downstairs, the Creoles, apparently innocent of our spat, offered fresh coffee and pulpy orange juice, which I brought back up to linger with. I lingered too under the scalding shower, shampooed vigorously, shaved with painstaking care, snipped brow and ear and nose hair after digging at the canals, scraped and clipped toe and finger nails, scrubbed the teeth to a sparkling polish, brushed, lightly oiled, and styled my hair into the Ivy-sculpt Kaiden favored. The snug white T and trim boxers streamlined my trunk, and the freshly pressed dark chinos preserved the line right down to the gleaming black Weejuns with navy socks. The azure blue of a clear, dry October sky matching my eyes hued the button-down fitting my chest: I rolled the sleeves three times, snapped on the bracelet, and sat for a long time on the edge of my bed, gazing out across our balcony and into the trees, Jack's radio softly purling Schubert.

Precisely at 9, I dialed Kaiden's number. He picked up on the fourth ring and yawned a "Hello."

"It's Troy," I said. "So sorry to bother you."

"Hey, Troy," he said. "Wow! It's really you?"

"Do you have company?"

"Company? It's not even 9:15. Who's up?"

"Me. Now you. Listen, Kaiden, could I see you this morning?"

"I should be on the street by 11, and I've got to prepare nibbles. But, sure. You want to come over? You know Magazine?"

"Yeah. What numbers?"

He gave them. "Troy, is everything okay? You sound...funny. I mean...stressed."

"No, things aren't exactly okay. Nobody's hurt or sick or like that. I've just got a little situation."

"You're not in jail, are you?"

"See you soon! Thanks."

The majestic house commanded the block. Three sturdy stories in steely gray with black shutters flanking tall windows, it loomed. I shrank just looking up at it, cowed. The long railed porch extended across the front — a swing, rockers, large pots of greenery, and a glider strewed across it — and, fully screened, all the way down the right side of the house. All of the windows showed graceful, heavy, and varied treatments. Two brick chimneys and a stone one stood like stout sentinels on the gabled roof. Ornamental black trim marked the story divisions. Running between the sidewalk where I stood and the lower porch fretwork ran a strip of rich green, aromatic mint. Live oak, cypress, and magnolia trees crowded the house, the oaks towering over it. The polished brass door-knocker, big as a buckler, glared like an eye. An eight-note chime answered my touch of the button. Kaiden swung wide the door.

"'Will you walk into my parlor?'" he grinned. "Holy cow, you look fantastic! You always did dress up good!" He was casual in a yellow sweatshirt and jeans.

The inside spread matched the grandeur of the exterior: stretching behind him ran an extravagantly over-sized space — a stately stone fireplace to the right and ceilings rising heaven-high hung with glittering chandeliers — whose depth kept rolling backward as you scanned the long stretch of walls defining it. At the far end a row of windows looked onto a jumbled green space that might once have been a garden. I could make out another large swing, a multi-storied birdhouse and concrete baths, and some ivied trellises out there. French glass doors cut the room in half about two-thirds of the way down.

"That's the dining room on the other side of them," Kaiden said, "and the parlor's to the right," gesturing, "where the piano is, if you'd like to try it, and another bed."

"Maybe later. It's so *big*, Kaiden! What do you do with all this space?"

"Explore it! Stretch out in it! Bang around it! I could prob'ly play tennis in here! After the cramped dorm room for all that time...I actually just enjoy it. Sometimes I shift around from chair to chair, bed to sofa to stool...just because I can."

"*Two* sofas...?"

"They're both beds, too. Queenies. I've got them facing but off-centered, so when you pull them both out, side by side, you've got this incredibly wide single bed to spread yourself all over. To the left there is the guest bedroom, and a full bath. Come see the kitchen. You're not gonna believe the kitchen!"

It was opposite the parlor, off to the left, beyond the guest bath. And it was also huge, walls banked with cabinets and packed shelves; shiny pots and pans hung from the ceiling; the doors of the lower cabinets wouldn't quite close on the bulk behind them. The fridge was probably twice as big as our back porch freezer, and the natural gas range-top had eight burners, its oven like a trunk. A round butcher-block table with four drugstore metal chairs hugged a corner; the double-pantry doors occupied another. A big block of slotted wood on the counter housed about sixty knives. The double-sink must have been the size of Jubilee's, where I scoured all those grungy pots and pans.

"It ain't the Sweat Shop, is it, Corky, for us Scrub-Squad veterans?" (Those were our names for ourselves and where we worked out west.)

"It sure never was over the rainbow, was it, no matter how often Monte sang the song!"

"Would you believe an actual chef once lived here?" he went on. "Ran the original Brennan's kitchen. Died back there in his bathtub. There's a plaque in the yard. Some folks say his ghost still rattles the crockery in here!"

"You're a believer?"

"If I step on broken crockery…There're lots of ghosts in New Orleans."

"I'd get lost in all this," I said, pressed and weighted by the mass and stretch of the space.

"My bedroom's upstairs, above the parlor. The steps are back there, near the door, and in the parlor. My studio's on three. Sometimes I do get lost" he said, "on purpose, though: I like exploring. I've not found any secret panels or false doors, but there's always a chance…."

"You don't get a little…lonesome?"

"Oh no. I just roam. There's too much in here to get bored. The library's amazing...and those paintings.... And hi-fi and records in the parlor."

"You're a lucky guy, Kaiden; and your father's amazingly...generous...!"

"Oh, don't get fooled about that and feel sorry for my father's cost. He's prob'ly got some rich friend needs a sitter for an empty house. And anyhow he can afford the rent. Besides, I know exactly what he's doing. He's trying to show me what real chef success can look like. He's demonstrating what a true master in the kitchen can achieve, in personal rewards. And at the same time he's trying to shame and embarrass me with all this excess, which is kind of wasted on me. He wants me to regret costing him a pile. He's rubbing my nose in all this...glut... at the same time he's trying to motivate me to want it enough to earn it myself. That's his game. Don't you forget what it cost *me*...what I had to do to earn all this...splendor!"

"And you graduated!"

"But you've got a 'situation,' you said. Here I am showing off and you've got a situation. We better watch the time...," glancing at his watch. "Your bracelet's the finishing touch! Here, let me look again. Put yours up here against mine. We're matched!" He giggled. "We've gotta get 'em engraved."

He poured coffee into green and white Tulane mugs. "Let's sprawl in the living room."

He grabbed an empty ash tray. We settled into two large, puffy club chairs, a side table between us.

"So," he asked: "what happened?"

"My roommate and I had a row."

"Over *ME*?!" he cracked.

"Not *YET!*" I countered.

"You wanna move in here?"

I felt the blood drain from my face and a faintness daze my mind. Tired from little rest, still shook-up from last night's quarrel, I was unprepared for his throwaway joke-line, and the tears welled. His wisecrack was so innocently and accidentally attuned to the unformed, nascent, timid, barely conscious yearnings of my heart, I could not stay the leaking tears. I swallowed hard.

"No, no; I wouldn't want to impose. I can't foist myself.... No, I didn't come over here...not with anything like that in mind."

"Well, Troy, why not?" Kaiden asked, almost indignantly. "What's wrong with you that it *wasn't* in your mind? Why is it the first thing I thought of? It could be your perfect solution!"

I took a long breath, wiped my eyes. "It's really sweet, Kaiden, but I couldn't. I just thought that with your contacts you might could help me find a place. I think I need to leave where I am now."

"It's that bad? Who's this roommate?"

"Jack Latimer. Friend from LCC. He and his girl had sex in our room last night. Sneaked in while I was out. Not for the first time. I walked in on them."

"Whoa, man! That's rough! What happened?"

"I lost it. Got nasty. I think I told them both to get the hell out and not come back. I can't live with him any more, this was such a gross fucking outrage, so disrespectful, so indecent…and…and insulting."

"Yeah," he said; "I get that. It was kind of…thoughtless. Inconsiderate. What'll you do?"

"If he won't move — and I doubt he will — I'll have to. I know it sounds rash, but Kaiden, this was a big-time rupture. It hurt. We've known each other…well…for a long while. And he dishonored all that…all that…history. I can't *not* feel that…that wound."

"No. But Troy, let's be sure you're not over-reacting, leaving your room. Rushing to judgment? Are you telling me everything?"

This stopped me only a moment. "No," I said; "I'm not. Maybe I'd better. I'm…I guess I'm prob'ly a little jealous. But it's complicated. Jack and I've slept together. We're not lovers, but we've…experimented…once. He wants — or wanted — or said he wanted — us to be fuck-buddies, if you know what that is, but we've sort of left that behind now. I don't know what we are now, but it's not fuck-buddies…and it's not friends either and prob'ly not roommates. I can't go on living with him. Especially not with Bailey — that girl — hanging around his neck. And she's not leaving."

"Tell me about her."

"That's complicated too. She's our classmate. Extremely smart. Tough and sassy. Not refined. I don't get it but Jack's besotted with her. Basically, she stole him…but he went willingly. It's complicated because of where it's going. Jack never uses protection, so they're going to get pregnant. That's as certain as tomorrow.

And it's going to be catastrophic. I can't be around for that."

"You love Jack, Troy?"

"I've asked myself. And the answer is, I don't. I was attracted. I felt something.... Affection? Camaraderie? Warmth? Dependence? Eventually we kind of fell into bed...in...distressed circumstances...and then Bailey arrived and everything changed. Jack and I went through college together, sharing literary tastes and even ambitions, and we thought we were a good match for tackling grad school together. The linking up just sort of naturally happened along the way...and then this did. I don't even much like him any more. I can't."

"What if Bailey left the picture? Would your feelings toward Jack change?"

"I don't think so. He'd replace Bailey. He admits to promiscuity, brags about it, with both sexes. I hate that. I was raised to think sex special, not random. No, I think the foundation of whatever Jack and I had has cracked. Beyond repair."

"Will you tell him?"

"We three are supposed to lunch after while, today, and talk about 'next steps.' Bailey's words. I'm thinking about skipping it."

"And do what...?"

"Maybe check in at Tulane's Grad Student Housing office. See what's available."

"How about this instead? Now listen to me, Troy: How about I take the afternoon off and we pick up some clothes and toiletries and books from your room. You take my parlor back there — with its bathroom and shower — for free, for, say, a month, while you look for a new place. If at the end of a month you've found nothing suitable, and we're getting along, we reconsider my offer...to move in. You could pay whatever you're now paying. No strings attached."

He was grinning broadly. My jaw was prob'ly hanging.

"Kaiden...I don't know. I don't know...it's so sudden. Maybe we'd better think...."

"What's to think? As I said, it's the perfect solution. Where's the problem? Look: we practically roomed together at Jubilee. I wanted to. Only Monte got to you first. Here's my next chance!"

"I don't know.... It's...incredibly sweet and kind... and...hospitable. But are you *sure*? What if...?"

"No 'what if's' allowed. Let's just do it."

"But what about your father?"

"I'll take care of my father. I don't know of any restrictions on how I use my space. You're hardly a risk. You'll be my guest, for a month. A visitor in my home. We'll worry about laws if you lease."

"I should prob'ly show up for the lunch...to let them know."

"Tell them we're experimenting. You're not giving up your room today. You might return in a month. They can do whatever they like in the meantime — I mean, you'd have to lose temporary 'control' of your room — but you have the right to return in a month, to live there, and yawl can then decide who goes where. Meanwhile, they'll 'experiment' too."

"I guess we might could try that," I said doubtfully.

"Great," he said, putting out his hand. "Shake on it! Now, what shall I plan for our supper tonight?!"

So we bought time.

## 22

August 27, 1961

Hey, Ben!

You wrote that maybe we should meet up. I'd like to.

Do you remember that my Jubilee pal Kaiden Carlisle visited my home in Madison just after you did last Christmas? Keep your eyes peeled and you might see him someday when you're cruising the Quarter: he'll be hard to miss on a bicycle with a rainbow canopy, and a cart hitched to the rear, peddling Cajun food. It's really good! You should try some.

Kaiden and I are sharing an apartment on Magazine for a while. You said you work in a repair shop nearby. I thought it would be cool if you and Kaiden and I met some time. You can use the number below to reach me, if you'd like to meet and catch up.

Mark says tell you hey from him.

p.s. I reckon you didn't write that dumb essay for the Dean.

Your friend,

Troy  4318 Magazine.  504-298-4281

\* \* \*

27 August 61

Dear 2nd Lieutenant Monte Trevalyn!

Hey, Monte!  Congratulations on your rank! I know I'm way late with kudos but I wanted to see what the title looked like on you! I'd love to have a picture of you in full dress with the silver prop and wings!

I graduated too, of course, a year ago, and will begin teaching freshman English here at Tulane in a couple of weeks. It's exciting and scary. I'll get my Master's Degree in January, if I finish the thesis in time.

You remember Corky Carlisle from Jubilee? Corky now uses his real name Kaiden and is here in New Orleans, working in the food industry. We were visiting the other day, and talking about you made me want to write. I'd love to know what's been happening to you (and with whom!) and what's coming up. I'm sending this to General Delivery at Nellis AFB, pretty sure the generals will know where to find you!

You've never seen New Orleans, have you? It's a totally amazing city. May I show you? I've got plenty of room to put you up. We've got a little unfinished business from your visit to LCC, and it would be good to tie that up, doncha think? Don't you get breaks? Furloughs? If you go home to Houston, it's just a hop skip and a jump over here! Why don't we plan something?

I miss you a lot!

Your old roommate,
Troy.   4318 Magazine.  504-298-4281

\* \* \*

Kaiden and I settled pretty quickly into a makeshift but comfortable routine. I'd have my breakfast — and sometimes set up for his — make a sack lunch of cheese and fruit or a PBJ or BLT, leave by 8 for teaching or my private carrel at the Library, and prepare lessons and stay around in the afternoon in case students wanted help with papers or had complaints about grades. Kaiden would work the Quarter from 11 to 5 or 6. I'd set the table for dinner in the dining room — between the French doors and the garden entrance — while he prepared it for eating around 8, and we'd both clean the kitchen after. If we could find a decent movie or sit-com on the tele, we might watch in the living room for an hour or so and chat, or listen to the hi-fi in the parlor, or separately read, or I might write or grade. If the weather and bugs let us, we'd sometimes walk for half an hour around the District, admiring the lights. We weren't sleeping together, or talking about it. I can't account for what we might have been thinking in this regard.

Back in April, about ten of us in my graduate class received official letters appointing us to one-year Graduate Teaching Assistantships in English — conditional upon our continued satisfactory performance as students through the spring term — which meant that we'd instruct one or two classes each of about twenty freshmen in the fall. It also meant we had to enroll in the summer course required for new instructors on how to teach. None of us believed we needed it, for we'd closely observed teachers for nearly twenty years, culling through their tics and tricks and techniques and collecting those to imitate when our turn came, and had no doubts of our readiness. Moreover, our instructor was a dead-beat relic kept around only to teach how-to (because nobody else would) in the same way with the same tattered brown notes he'd used for decades. But he was a kindly-disposed old dear who knew his dwindling worth and the doubtful value of the course, and didn't press us too hard, except in demanding that we outline the textbook. Imagine! Outline the book! And then in the last two weeks, instead of a final, we had to teach a story or a poem of our choosing to the class for a grade. I chose Marvell's "To His Coy Mistress," researched it, dissected it, and taught the very hell out of it to the class — my audience fully aware of a less coy mistress in our midst — for my A. We understood these requirements as part of the drill to win us a lectern and a classroom, and didn't much complain. Besides, we paid no tuition for the course and were given a small stipend to carry us over the summer.

Our "office" was a giant room in the basement of Gibson Hall, the main administration building and home of English, where each of us was assigned an old wooden desk for conferencing with students and doing such work as we could between classes and at night, although the noise level of "the bull pen," as we called it, was often prohibitive. "Bull" wasn't intended as sexist. Ours was the first graduate English class at Tulane to admit women. Bailey had of course won her TA, as she predicted, and was given a desk among ourselves, but objected to our sobriquet and petitioned to have it dropped and the neutral "Graduate Associates" or "GA's" substituted. As we already *were* "TA's," and "GA's" reminded all the Baptists of "Girl's Auxiliary" in the church, "bull pen" survived against Bailey's pout. As a courtesy to Loyola next door, a nun or two were occasionally allowed unofficially to audit a class, but no additional women enrolled during my time there. Bailey sketched a little sign for her desk reading "Not A Bull."

Jack's desk sat next to mine, two down from hers, so it was impossible for us to avoid each other, but we did little more than nod and divert for some while. They bridled at my terms for a month's experimental housing on Audubon Place, Bailey arguing that all the options were mine and they the passive victims of my whims, but finally accepted the offer of the room for Jack's use while I made up my mind. I think we silently understood that nothing (except the rule) kept them from trysting there as long as Jack stayed and I kept away, but they also understood my preferences in that regard. It kept the tension fast. My "bull" colleagues noticed, of course, and instead of inquiring apparently concluded that the Jack-Bailey alliance explained the Jack-Troy division, and let both simmer. Jack assumed his casual wear to teach in — open collars, rolled sleeves, sweaters, khakis, no socks — and easy fraternization with the students, who were to call him "Jack," and who flocked to his desk during office hours and beyond, even in the evenings, for noisy chatter having nothing to do with their class. Sometimes he'd leave with them for what I suspected were brews at the nearby taverns. During his "conferences," Bailey would often perch on the end of his desk, against the wall, her crossed, podgy legs blocking drawers.

No doubt looking every bit as up-tight as I felt — in navy blazer with gold buttons, lighter blue button-down dress shirt, diagonally striped blue-red-yellow-black tie, gray slacks, black dress shoes and socks, and my bracelet — I approached my first class needlessly apprehensive (I'd as usual over-prepared) and yet deeply proud for having at last arrived here. For this was it! This what I desired and worked to become! I was at last to begin my life. I was a teacher.

"I'm your teacher," I said, "Troy Tyler. I'm not a professor. I'm a second-year teaching assistant. Please address me as Mr. Tyler. We're going to learn how to think and read and write. To begin, read Nathaniel Hawthorne's 'Young Goodman Brown' for next time."

They were twenty-three men, all around nineteen, a pale blur as I began to call roll but beginning to define themselves when responding to their names: high voice here, deep tan there, shaggy hair, thick lenses, big feet in flip-flops, slumpy posture, football thuggish, basketball skinny, tennis perfection.

"All right," I said. "Let's talk literature."

\* \* \*

3 September 61
Nellis AFB, Nev.

Dear Troy,

Wow! How great to get your letter! Thanks for the congrats! I'll see if I can find a photo, with all the trimmings. You should send one too.

I'm flying pretty regularly now — one variety or another of the F-105D Thunderchief — and our training has ramped up, they're not telling us why, but extending our flights and adding new and complicated stuff — like maneuvers and gadgets and commands and maps — and I'm eating it up but curious about what's behind it.

Funny you should mention furloughs. There's talk around here that we might get a longer holiday in the spring, maybe up to ten days. If that happens, I might come home for three and head your way for three or four more if you're on spring break or could take off. No, I've never visited New Orleans and would love to see the French Quarter and cruise the River and eat... maybe even some of Corky's treats. And see you! I'm not sure I understand what you mean about "unfinished business," but maybe I do. Private business. There's a Baylor grad here, Rex Lawtry, who rounded up five other Bears for a frat reunion stag party a while ago, where we got loaded and things got out of hand, and I'm thinking that what happened then might be connected with our unfinished business. Anyhow, I'll check dates, and you can let me know when you're on Spring Break. I'd really love to see you and your city.

And Corky! Yawl are actually rooming together? How'd he get my place! I always figured he wanted it. Ha! Tell him I said hello. And yawl stay out of trouble.

I'm still thinking about ministry after AF. Or staying in as a chaplain. I wrote for information to the New Orleans Baptist seminary a few weeks ago.

So how's teaching? Anything like preaching?!

I still miss you, old roomie guy! I hope we can visit sometime. Can't wait to take you up up and away!

Fondly,
Monte

\* \* \*

"You about ready to go?" Kaiden asked over his breakfast coffee.

He'd scheduled an appointment for us at Julien's Gems and Jewels, on the corner of Chartres and Bienville Streets in the Quarter, for Saturday at 11, to get our bracelets engraved.

I folded the *Picayune* (ours on his father's subscription) and set it aside. "We've got half the morning yet," I said. "What's your rush?"

"I might make a few sales on the way," he said. "You know: munchies for mid-day. You're welcome to come along."

"You'd want me eating," I said, "to boost sales. And it's kinda early in my day for gator."

"You want I should carry Twinkies?"

"Sure! Stuffed with cream of snake! Now tell me about this shop."

"Julien's isn't Adler's or Rau's," he said, "but Julien's a good guy and their rep is sterling — the store's always busy — and they know me and sometimes buy Creole. We can leave them the bracelets, and have lunch on the Square. They'll probably be ready in a coupla hours. Then I've got to shop for tonight. I'm fixing you a surprise supper."

"What? Why?"

"That's part of the surprise," he said, cocking his head in a tease. "You have to wait."

"Do we know what we're ordering…I mean, for the bracelets? Which names, and where, and so forth? We'll have to pick out a font."

"Whichever we pick, the fonts should match," he said.

I paused. "Well, I don't mind…but why…? Oh, all right, fine. The fonts can match. Will you want first and last names on them?"

"I think so. Won't you?"

"I suppose: they're ID tags! We have two names."

"Three, in fact. How about on the backside?"

"Well, you gave me the bracelet. D'you want your name on the back? Behind mine? Saying… 'to' and 'from…' or something?"

"I dunno. Do you? Isn't that your call?"

"Then they wouldn't match. I didn't give you…."

"Gosh, I never thought we'd have to make all these *decisions*!"

"Maybe we better leave the back blank," I said. "We might lose track of which is whose…if both names…. Okay, then, Christian name and surname name on the front. Blank back. That leaves the font."

"I kind of like swirls," he said, "spins and curls and twirls. Not stiff block print."

"Not sissy swirls, though. Not flamboyant."

"They'll show us samples, won't they?" he asked. "We'll have to agree. They should match. I mean, the styles should be identical."

"Hold on," I said. "What if we put the date on the back? Today's date. And 'New Orleans.' That locates us…in time and space. It's kind of part of our 'identification,' idn' it?"

"I reckon." Kaiden said. "I like it. But let's use different fonts, back and front. Swirls for the names; blocks for the date and place?"

"Shouldn't the writing style be consistent?" I asked.

"Well, you couldn't ever read both at the same time. I take it back: I believe I'd like the formality of the block print on the back. And the…contrast, against the swirl."

"Best make up your mind. Let's put the date first," I said: "the month — spelled out — day, comma, four-digit year. And then the city. No 'Louisiana' after it. That'll look classy. There's only one New Orleans. But we can always ask the clerk at the store? She'd prob'ly have an opinion on that."

"The print on the back should be smaller than the names," he said. "And centered."

"Well, the names have to be centered too. Look, Kaiden," I said: "we don't stop this, we're gonna nitpick ourselves into a quarrel. Let's just give it to the clerk to decide differences, okay? According to what most folks do?"

"We can talk about it. Now don't forget to *bring the bracelet*!"

"Right here," I said, patting my pocket.

"Why aren't you wearing it?"

"It's not finished yet. I can't wear a partial I.D.!"

Julien's saleslady Janet heard what we wanted, took a hard look at us and rather snidely suggested that her colleague Rafael might be better suited to assist us, and indeed he was, as attested by his mincing approach.

"Inscribed I.D. bracelets for each other, is it, boys? How sweet! Just lovely! This way, please," he simpered.

I glanced at Kaiden, shook my head no.

"Excuse me, sir," I said. "We have our bracelets; we want them engraved, and we'd like some help choosing the fonts. May we see samples?"

"But of course," he said; "I understand. And you'll surely want the Edwardian font, hardly a question about it. Here we are!" he went on, slipping a sheet from a soft gray folder and adjusting his wire-rimmed glasses. "Sublime elegance in ink, I always say, and when etched in GOLD, as you'll have, totally divine! Nothing can touch it for exquisite grace and symmetry, you see. Why, your delicate little wrists are the perfect abodes for this princely cursive. Search no farther, lads: wreath your limbs in this royal Edwardian embrace, and go forth to conquer hearts! (Oops. I forgot. You already have each other's!)"

"The swirls may be a bit rich," I ventured; "maybe something a little less...embellished? Not so gaudy?"

"Oh, but boys: You WANT flash and dash, don't you now? These ornaments are the crowning touch of your wardrobes! You want to be *arresting*. A *dazzling* script highlights the gold, and the gold consummates the dazzle! Here: look at it on this bracelet: at that magnificent sweep of line, the supple dip and flare of the flow. Ah, names are never so lovely as when choreographed in calligraphy, don't you agree? What are yours, may I ask?"

"Kaiden. He's Troy."

"Royalty! Well, Edwardian is king of scripts. Long enthroned. Long may he reign!"

"Whadaya think, Kaiden?"

"I dunno. It's pretty, all right. But awfully fancy."

"Think of all the flair as musical," Rafael offered. "Musical accompaniment to the names. The decoration makes the whole bracelet *sing!*"

"I don't think so," I said. "No, Edwardian is kind of…noisy. Let's do something…less…well, ornamental. Quieter."

"How about the 'classic,' then? 'Classic' is straightforward, no frills, standard, safe. Maybe a little dull, compared to Edwardian, but…let's see…direct, reserved. On the conservative side. Here."

"More masculine," I said.

"Less girly?" Rafael offered.

"I like it," Kaiden put in. "Edwardian's lovely, Rafael, but this is classic. Business-like. I think it suits us. Troy?"

"Let's go with it," I said. "And on the back, Rafael: in smaller lettering: a straight, square, frank, bold, simple line — no frills! — with today's date. And after it, 'New Orleans.' No state name or abbreviation. All right?"

"As you wish, sir. Now the names: K-a-d…."

"K-a-i-d-e-n," from him. "C-a-r-l-i-s-l-e."

"Troy T-y-l-e-r. And spell out the name of the month, please."

"Carlisle. Tyler!" said Rafael. "They rhyme!" his smile wide, his eyes bright. "Oh, you boys…!"

"I'm responsible," Kaiden said, handing over a credit card.

"Yes sir, Mr. Carlisle. These should be ready for you by 3 p.m. today."

"Would you please pack them in a single box, and wrap it as a gift? In white paper with black ribbon."

"What? I thought you…. Yes, sir. Good day, boys! It was my pleasure… Yawl come back now, hear? Thank you!"

Outside, I asked: "Are you really okay with that font, Kaiden?"

"I mostly wanted to get it over with. That guy's creepy. But yeah, I'm cool with the font."

"He's nice. He was sweet to us. But he's a complete *parody*. You reckon they let him out at night…onto the streets?!" We laughed. "We shouldn't laugh," I added.

"Nobody really looks at bracelet names, do they?" I went on. "I'm glad we got rid of the frills, though. But I sort of liked that clever thing he said about music. What's my half of the bill?"

"It's on me. It's the balance of your gift. You can't pay for your own gift!"

"Oh, Corky; please don't. This is too much, what with everything else. I can't…."

"It's Dad's card."

At Schwegmann's, he made me wait in the car while he shopped for dinner provisions.

"I remember you prefer white wine?" he asked, getting out.

"Not really," I said. "I like red too. What am I supposed to do while you…?"

But he was gone. We didn't normally drink evening cocktails, or wine with our meals, although he kept wines for cooking in the kitchen and a few bottles of good vintage on a rack in the pantry. So this planned dinner was something special. I'd no clue what he was up to, but his excitement had spread to me and sharpened my own anticipation. Did he have news of a job? An interview? Heard from his father? Surely nothing so banal as a new recipe for pancakes? Had he met someone?

Other concerns fretted my mind; a moment to reflect was welcome. The month's grace period on the Audubon room must be nearly expired, but I'd deliberately not kept track of the days, thinking I'd leave the monitoring to Jack while knowing he wouldn't either. But Bailey might have. I should check. Nor had I heard from Grad Student Housing on availabilities. I should check there too. And I really needed to write the conclusion to my thesis: I'd made my case for Whitman's "Lilacs" as a romantic narrative, after the necessary chapter on the inherited elegiac tradition, basing my meticulously developed argument, with his permission, on a formula that Professor Adams invented and applied to stories by Hawthorne and Melville in our American Romanticism class. I only needed to nail down a few loose ends and type it all up on the new electric Smith-Corona I'd bought with the grant money from the Grad School given me to pay a professional to do it. And I needed, without exactly wanting, to think about how Monte's proposed visit might impact my current situation re Corky and Jack — if I *had* a situation re Jack, who had expressed warm interest in Monte's person. I was also supposed to be teaching myself French this summer, for the required foreign language exams coming up in the fall. Thus — partly — my note to Ben Moore, who now *had* French and might help; but I also found myself interested in his activities at Le Petite Theater, where he appeared to be exploring those hidden theatrical gifts I thought I'd detected in him at the church group meeting last fall. And I wanted updating on his connections with San Francisco. I surprised myself a little by feeling keen to reconnect with Ben.

Kaiden had slipped an empty sack over his full one to cover its contents from my inquiring eyes. "Not yet!" he said, sliding under the wheel and handing me a third, smaller sack obviously holding two bottles.

"Red?" I guessed.

"Not sayin'."

"Did I ever tell you I used to work in a grocery store? A&P. All through high school. Friday night and all day Saturday, and full time in the summers. With my piano practice and all, I got very fast on the cash register. Customers complained — couldn't check my accuracy — and I got bounced back to bag boy."

"Any customers ever make a move on you?"

"Now what would make you ask that?"

"I thought everybody got a crush on their bag boy, at least once. I sure did."

"Well, yeah. There was this older guy, around forty, Hallmark artist, waited in my line every Friday night with his two cigarette cartons and seven cans of cat food. He asked me to spend the night at his house."

"Really? Just like that? What'd you do?"

"Ran! I ran! You laugh, but that's exactly what I did. I didn't know...."

"What would you do now, bag boy? Want to spend the night at *my* house?"

Trailing uselessly behind, I followed Kaiden into the kitchen where he rested both sacks on the counter, along with the skillfully wrapped and ribboned Julien box. "Now you vamoose," he said, "and I'll get started."

"Can't I help?" I almost pled.

"Maybe later. I'll call you when."

"Okay. I think I'll shower. Should we dress for dinner?"

He looked up, startled. "Now that's a great idea! Yes! Let's dress. Cool, dude!"

From where had that notion sprung? It surprised me as much as it evidently did him. We'd never dressed for dinner. Why would we? But his coy secrecy, all day, his air of itchy anticipation so plainly exclusive of me, had frayed my patience. He was up to something celebratory; he intended a revel that affected me but required furtive preparation. Maybe if I pressed him with my own supplements to his plan?

For the second time in twelve hours I showered and shampooed and shaved and brushed. Knotted my nattiest bow. Pulled on freshly pressed dark chinos and a narrow-point collared blue dress shirt, to pick up my eye-color. Whisked the navy blazer, dusted the weejuns. Checked and buffed the nails. Combed, re-combed just so. Adjusted the bow. Dabbed cologne. And then remembered…to dig back into my recently used bag for an oft-moved box.

"They took or locked up all the good china and crystal and silver," he called from the kitchen as I entered the dining room, "so just use the regular, everyday ware. Orange juice glasses for the wine." He'd laid a white cloth and found a few blue and yellow blooms out back for a clear glass vase centered at the left edge of the table. In its center stood a three-armed silver candelabra with white tapers, the Julien package nestling its base. I leaned my little wrapped box against it.

"Whoa!" he exclaimed, entering and spotting me. "Aren't *you* chic? Best not let Rafael near *you!* You *do* look extremely…desirable, Troy!"

"Thanks. I dressed for your surprise, whatever it is."

"Would you please set the table while I run up and dress? Don't mess with the kitchen, though. Everything in there's stable for a bit. Oh, and could you pull out both sofa-beds in the living room, and straighten up in there, for after dinner TV digesting or something? And put some music on the hi-fi in the parlor?"

I found white ironed napkins in a drawer, checked the cutlery and plates for spots, polished the juice glasses, washed and dried some utensils stacked in the sink, tidied the living room. Releasing the mattresses for folding-out was a challenge, and I couldn't find bed pillows, but Chopin piano music was plentiful and soothed my wait for Kaiden to return.

"It all looks great," he said, appearing classically glamorous in his dark navy suit, dazzling white shirt, and striped tie in deep pink, black and sky-blue, with a matching pink pocket square, his hair fluffed and glistening. "Pillows are on a high shelf in the hall closet. It won't take me long to finish up. Come on in the kitchen and pour us some burgundy."

Tiny, unpeeled, golden potatoes lightly boiled on a burner. Fresh chopped mushrooms bubbled in sauce on another. He reached out from the fridge a sizable bowl of cooked, chopped spinach, poured heavy cream into it, stirred in cream cheese, dumped a cup of yellow onion and a handful of chopped fresh garlic into the mix, and slid it carefully into the oven. "Four minutes," he said, setting the timer. "Eight ounces each," he grinned, lifting from the fridge two beautiful tenderloin filets on paper. He placed a skillet on another burner, turned it to HIGH, lightly salted and peppered the meat on both sides, and eased them into the skillet: "Forty-five seconds searing per side, time it, Troy," he ordered. And when they'd passed, he moved the skillet into a 300 oven. "For exactly twelve minutes," he said, "for medium rare." A tray of Pillsbury biscuits went into another oven five minutes later. Out came the steaming creamed spinach. Kaiden stirred the mushrooms, simmering while he'd dressed, with butter, yellow onion and garlic chips, fresh thyme, broth, whipping cream, and Merlot, and removed them from the stove. "Use your lighter on the candles, Troy," he said, "and bring the plates in here for serving."

"Should we say a blessing?" he asked when we'd settled.

"On this feast?!" I answered. "I believe we should!"

"Would you?" he said.

So I did, meaning every word of it, too.

"That was very nice, Troy," he said. "Now what's that other package?"

"You're not the only one with a little surprise," I said.

"What?" he asked.

"Not till we open the other one," I teased.

We tasted, exclaimed enthusiastically, congratulated, dug in.

"So what're we celebrating, Kaiden?" I asked. "You've been so secretive…!"

"Not yet," he said, again. "When we finish…."

I won't even attempt to write how good everything was. I called it perfection. I happen to adore creamed spinach, and I've never sampled better. I've also never before or since savored more tender, flavorful beef. Kaiden said the wine was "mellow and luscious." As I don't speak wine, I'll go with those descriptives.

"Before dessert," he said, scooting his chair around to the table's side and gesturing me to do the same, so that we sat at its middle, side by side. "Troy," he continued, "if you'd please open the Julien package." He moved it and the candelabra toward ourselves.

"First," I said, "you open the other one. It's way, way overdue for opening. When you gave me the bracelet at Christmas, I didn't have a gift for you. Now I do. It's been aging ever since then!"

He held up the bottle of Pour Monsieur cologne, grinning; screwed off the cap, tilted the bottle against his fingertip, dabbed behind both ears. Handed it to me. "Now you," he said softly.

I followed suit, returned the bottle to his waiting hand. It felt ceremonial.

I unwrapped and opened the Julien box. The polished bracelets lay longwise, side by side, on black velvet.

"Ohhhh," I breathed, sincerely impressed.

"Now, Troy," he said: "Here are two bracelets; and here are two wrists," laying his bare, and pointing at mine. "Choose one bracelet, and ring one wrist."

We locked eyes, and held.

"I can't, Kaiden," I whispered. "What would it mean?"

"Whatever we each want it to mean. We needn't say."

I studied the bracelets, stared back at him.

"But it feels so…weighty. So, I dunno, momentous."

"It could be. Or not. Depending," he said.

"Why don't you choose for me?"

"I don't think you really want that. And besides, I can't choose for you. I don't know which you want."

"But I don't know what choosing one means."

"I think you do. That's why you don't want to."

"But if you choose first…."

"That forfeits your choice. It relieves you of choosing. It makes me responsible for what happens next. Would you want that?"

"Is choosing final?"

"That's a fair question. No, I don't think choosing has to be final. Only death is final. But maybe this choosing is premature. I didn't think it would be so hard for you. Maybe that was wishful thinking. Possibly there's another way of choosing, or another choice." He gently lifted the bracelet inscribed with my name. "Give me your wrist," he said softly. He joined the links, snapped them fast, and covered my fist with his hand. "There. Your bracelet on your wrist."

"I'll do…here, let me do yours," I said, my fingers trembling as I did.

We leaned together and kissed. The gold winked in the candlelight.

Dessert was a Schwegmann's disk of frozen vanilla and crème de menthe ice cream studded with chocolate chips.

"Coffee?" Kaiden asked.

"None for me, no."

"Let's clear the table," he said. "And retire to the living room. Clean up tomorrow."

"I'll clear," I said. "You go ahead."

By the time I finished, he'd shed his jacket and shoes, loosened his tie, pulled out his shirttail, shut off the Chopin, and stretched on the bed, head and shoulders against two puffy pillows I'd brought from the closet. Muted, the tv flickered. Because we hadn't to my knowledge even opened the beds since my arrival, I didn't know quite what might be expected here, so I copied his relaxation but sat on the outer edge of the second bed.

"What're you doing over there in France?" he asked, smiling and patting the sheets at his side. "Over here's cozy."

I crawled to his side and stretched against him, on my back. His arm eased around my shoulder, his fingers straying inside my open collar to stroke my neck.

"This feels so good, Troy. You do. By me."

"Yes, it does." I shifted toward him, snuggled into his armpit, my hand on his chest.

"Are you ready for the rest of your surprise?" he whispered.

"There's more? How could there be more? There's already heaps!"

"I'm inviting you to move in here with me. I want you to live with me. I want us to live together."

I moved my hand from his chest up to his cheek, stroked it, traced his lips.

"Oh, Kaiden," I breathed; "I think maybe I want that too. But are you sure?"

"I don't want to talk about it tonight. I wanted to invite you tonight, and then we'll think for a while, experiment with what it means and how it feels...with the *prospect* in mind. And when either one of us has made up his mind either way, we'll talk. Do you think you could live with that, Troy?"

"I think I'd like to try, Kaiden."

"But for now, my dear Troy, I'm going to make sweet love to the best most beautiful boy in the whole wide world all the live long night!"

# 23

A week later on Sunday afternoon, with Kaiden pedaling and peddling hard in the Quarter, someone knocked
lightly on his — our — front door. From my desk in the
parlor, I barely heard it, and doubted it. We'd still had
no visitors, expected none, wanted none I could think of.
But I slipped my canvass sneakers back on and headed
out through the living room, yelled "Coming!"

His left arm stiffly braced against the doorpost,
socked ankles crossed, right hand dangling a cigarette
mid-thigh, Jon Jack Latimer posed, Ichabod Cranishly
gawky but groomed, spotless, pressed, combed. "Ah," he
said, "it is you. I wasn't sure.... Hey, Troy."

"What do you want, Jack? How'd you know where
I was? Am?"

"The Department said you left this address for emergencies. No phone number. You prob'ly ought to give them one."

"Don't advise me, Jack. It's not my number to give out. Why'd you come?"

"We need to talk. Can...may I come in?" He flipped the cigarette butt over the railing, into the mint bed.

"Pick that up on your way out. We can talk, if we have to, here on the porch.   For the third time, what is it you want?"

"C'mon, Troy. Be civil. Can we at least sit down?"

"Don't get comfortable," I said, but gestured toward the rockers, taking one.

"Thanks," he said. "How are you, Troy?"

"Busy."

"Me too." Long pause.   "Okay then. I'll cut to the chase, and then fill in. Look," he said, "I don't *have* to be here. I came voluntarily because you need to know what's happened. If you can't be civil long enough to hear me out, I'll leave... at your peril."

"My *peril*! Is that a threat?"

"Possibly; you'll have to decide." He reached for his Viceroys, I for my Kents and the Zippo, his holiday gift.

"Handsome!" he said, grinning. "May I borrow it? Are you enjoying it?"

"It's useful. Thank you."

"So, Troy," he said, exhaling: "a vacancy's opened up in your former room.   You should decide whether you want it back. If you don't, you should come pick up the stuff you left."

"What? You're moving?"

"Um, no. I hope not. It sort of depends on you."

"What the hell are you talking about?"

"Well, Bailey's leaving the room to go back to her dorm. Prob'ly already has."

"Wait up there, mister! Bailey doesn't have a room to leave. Does she? *Does* she, Jack?"

"She has to leave the one she's sometimes…borrowed, and she can't ever come back."

"She never could. That was the rule. Jesus, Jack, has she been *living* there? She's been living there, hasn't she?"

"Kind of, yeah. In and out. Time to time. It's been convenient…for both of us."

"I'll just bet. Christ, Jack, I can't believe you…. And somebody found out? And ratted."

"The Creoles. Camille and Christoph. After they'd seen Bailey split one morning by the dawn's early light. We tried to explain, but they feared for their jobs etcetera etcetera and tattled to Mrs. B. who freaked out and banned Bailey permanently."

"And you?"

"Well, that's a weird thing. Of course she's royally pissed at me for allowing it but she hasn't exactly said I have to go. She actually hinted I might could stay, *if* I swore to keep the rules etcetera etcetera…and had a roommate to, well, watchdog me and keep me…on the queer and narrow! She's basically against girls, you know, won't have 'em in the house except Camille, but she's crazy for us guys. I'm kind of on probation while she decides. So Bailey's back in the dorm....which is fine with me."

"What? Wait. Yawl broke up?"

"Not...decisively. But we're...we say we're 're-considering.'" He paused, dribbled spit on the half-smoked cigarette tip, pinched it between thumb and forefinger, held it up for my instruction. "Basically, though," he added, "I figure we're as finished as this fag."

"Just toss it, " I said, disgusted. "But yawl were so tight."

"That's how she made it look, all right. And I guess we were, for a while. But I've thought a lot about it lately, and as a couple we're not working. You know, Troy, I have to admit you got it right right away about Bailey that time just after we met her, when you warned me. You saw straightaway how overbearing she was; and designing and manipulative, and aggressive and consuming. And autonomous. She doesn't relate. She chews you up. She devours."

"None of that's headline news, Jack. I did warn you — I told you! — and you flicked me off. Now you've got her figured out...what? By the sound of it, you might be breaking up. Or want to."

"I reckon we might. It's not working."

"No surprise there. But I thought you wanted to talk about...housing. I'm not, you know, your romance therapist."

"I'm talking about housing. Housing's one of the things — maybe the main thing — that's not working. How about *being* my therapist for five minutes here, would you? I'd benefit from a little…unloading. Conversation."

"I doubt I'm the best person to counsel you on relationships, Jack. Ours is pretty ragged."

"We're going to talk about that too, in a minute. But can I just say a coupla more things about Bailey? Run 'em past you? You're kind of indirectly involved."

"Which disqualifies me as your adviser. I'm what they'd call an 'interested party.' I'll have no objectivity at all."

"That you're 'interested' is all to the good, idn' it? I need 'interested.'"

"You know what I mean and it's not that."

"But you know *me,* Troy. And that's what I need through here. You're my longest friend. My best friend. Like you said that night, we have *history.* A history together. Just give me ten minutes. Please, Troy. It's really important."

"It's making me uncomfortable, Jack. I wish you wouldn't…."

"The discomfort tells you it's important. Just two more things: Bailey and I also aren't working because we're forever *competing.* For grades and honors and recognitions and 'firsts' and 'favorites' and student popularity and all like that, and then pouting and sulking when we come in second. And we get jealous of each other, and crabby around that, and pick and nag at each other all the time. We're *rivals* in just about everything all day every day. It's juvenile and ugly, and it's tearing us apart."

"Welcome to the bloodsport of graduate school! You've been competing ever since first grade, Jack, and thriving on it. You can't pretend you didn't expect competition here."

"Maybe not in such close quarters, though. With people you think you might love? And I'm starting to believe that maybe one result of intense rivalries is stale sex. Sex gets routine and fizzles. Turns blah. She's ho-huming me to death, Troy. And she makes me feel like I'm boring her. *I am* flat-out bored with this woman."

"And I am *absolutely* not qualified to discuss the intimacies of your sex life, Jack, and you must stop exposing them. I am, or was, involved, and I have...I have feelings I can't be objective about. I cannot dig into this subject with you, so please drop it."

"No! Hold on. We're just getting to the heart...of everything here. You have to let me finish. Just listen for one more minute.

"You know I've fiddled and flitted around forever with bisexuality. I've tried — really hard — to believe, to convince myself it's a valid, legitimate orientation. I thought maybe I could, you know, divide my attentions equally between boys and girls, desiring both, favoring neither. The truth is, I doubt I can, and I'm worn out with trying. Being all the time with Bailey for these months, I've missed guys. Seriously missed them. I've missed *you,* hanging out with you. I'm bored with Bailey because she's not Boy. To be crude, I like cock. Hell, I adore cock. And that crazy little song-and-dance I did for you around 'fuck-buddies' was mainly to guarantee availability of the forbidden without obligation to respect the owner, and was terribly unfair to us both and shouldn't have worked any better than it did. I apologize for putting us through that. I honestly believe, Troy, that if either of us had been courageous enough, and daring enough, and *honest* enough to reach a hand across those two feet of space between our beds in those early weeks, and brush the bare thigh of the other, we'd have spared ourselves a trainload of emotional turmoil and practical inconvenience."

He took a long breath. Despite myself, I felt my throat constrict. Cleared it.

"We may have an opportunity to redeem those mistakes," he continued quietly. "Please come home and let me make you my own sweet man. I'm asking you, respectfully, to reclaim your room."

"I can't, Jack," I managed to say. "I live here now."

"Alone? It looks like there's plenty of room…."

"No. Not alone."

"A boyfriend?"

"Dare I say, 'God willing'?"

"The guy who helped you move?"

"Yes."

"You still have stuff there. You can leave it, if you want to, in case you change your mind."

We went very quiet for a moment.

"What will you do now, Jack?"

"I guess I'll stay on Audubon alone, for now. If I can afford the double rent. I doubt I can. But I don't know anybody else I'd care to share a room with."

"Will you see Bailey?"

"I'll have to…for a while. She's missed two periods."

Nearly tripping over the heels of the weighty conversation just concluded, Jack's long-expected, long-dreaded and fateful revelation felt to me like piling-on, and together with hunches aroused by our talk restrained any impulse to over-react, as was my custom. To be sure, I was stunned, even shaken by this fulfillment of my prediction, but I took no satisfaction in it. I rather inclined toward unworthy suspicions that the whole of our encounter here bore the marks of Jack's self-interested calculation: he was on a mission, working an agenda that involved my return to close association. Was I being set up?

It seemed so: Jack would shortly need either a new roommate or new lodging, and was sounding me out, and with all the gentlemanly behavior, the flattery, and the compliments buttering me up, shamelessly ingratiating himself in my regard. His total silence on the illicit use of our bedroom bespoke deceptive suppression meant to cover-up, discount, erase, or bury; at the least it avoided assigning any consequence to that eruption, and shifted to Mrs. Burkhart the entire responsibility for Bailey's eviction. He viciously and repeatedly trashed the woman he knew to be bearing his child. He decried her rivalry but silently coveted mine as her replacement in the ranks. He implausibly, lamely rejected bi-sex for homo-sex with me. His nasty metaphor degraded her but meant to cultivate my admiration. Too late he repented his reserve in the bed next to mine. And in his desperate coup de gras, he pathetically pled my help.

And yet. And yet…. He'd also invoked our 'history.' It was indeed long and rich; it recorded an abundantly rewarding friendship, and I should be mindfully appreciative of it. I was in manifold ways indebted to him. Inarguably, we had been well-matched through college. We'd depended upon each other. Once desperate, he'd sought me out for comfort. He'd anointed me with oil. If we hadn't quite entered the golden Canaan land of maturely ripened love, we'd expected to. Maybe the quarrel was only an erasable smudge on an otherwise unblemished page. Perhaps it merited no reference. And maybe, in light of yore, I was morally obliged to offer him help. The announcement disappointed me, of course, but what I mainly felt was a sort of bitter desolation, a mournful regret for loss.

And besides all of that: hadn't he just replayed — without realizing it, of course — my own recent, wily stratagem for securing alternative housing from Kaiden? How dare I begrudge Jack a similar tactic?

"Is there another….beau?" I asked.

"She says not, and I believe her."

"Are you making plans?"

"We're waiting…to be sure."

"How long?"

"She'll decide."

"Well, how are you feeling about it? What're you thinking."

"I can't be a father."

"But you are."

"I'm not. No. Not yet. And I won't be."

"Don't say that, Jack. How about a husband? A spouse?"

"I don't see how. I'm a student."

"Other students do it all the time."

"You're not being sympathetic, Troy."

"No, I'm probably not. I'm not sure sympathy's in order, Jack. What does Bailey want to do?"

"Oh, of course she wants the baby. Marriage and the baby."

"And you?"

"No, as I said. I can't do it. I *won't* do it. I just told you…I'm incurably queer."

"Does Bailey know that?"

"Not from me. And she'd better not from you. I think she suspects, though. How could she not suspect?"

"If Bailey suspected, she'd ask."

"Not if she believed I was. She wants marriage."

"So what do you…what will yawl do?"

"I guess we have to lose the baby."

"Oh no, Jack! That is not an acceptable way out. You cannot do that. You won't, will you?"

"You don't understand. We have to. There's no other way. And I'll have to ask you to help."

"What? Help? What does that even mean?"

"With the cost. We can't afford the expense."

"What? You've already…asked?! No! I won't help with that. It's too…horrible!"

"I have to ask."

"I won't. Never. I can't. I think you'd better leave now, Jack. You're kind of…making me sick. Please go."

"Okay, but let me know about the room."

\* \* \*

"Troy!" Kaiden yelled from the living room. "Get in here! Guess who's come to dinner!"

"In the kitchen," I called back. "We have a guest? Who's here?"

"Come see!"

And in a moment I clapped delighted eyes upon Benjamin Arthur Moore in all his bearded glory, in a torn black T and greasy black bib overalls and scrungy boots, gripping a Schlitz, and laughing.

"Ben!" I cried, tossing my towel and meeting his embrace with mine. "Holy crap, what a tremendous surprise! Oh, wow! C'mon, sit. Another beer? How'd this happen?"

"It's really great to see you, Troy. Kaiden said you wouldn't mind my just dropping by. But I really need to wash up. May I?"

"Right this way," Kaiden said, leading him off.

"Hurry back," I said. "Let's get started."

Returned, Kaiden asked, broadly grinning: "You don't mind?"

"Mind! I'm thrilled," I said. "How'd it happen?"

"Just like you said. I was cruising down St. Peter when he spotted the cart and came right up, bought sausage, and asked if I knew Troy! And here we are. He's good people. I like him."

"Have you planned dinner? Why don't we just order pizza in?"

"I've always planned dinner, Troy, but yeah, pizza sounds perfect. It's been a while. Shall I order two supremes?"

"Better make it three."

Ben hadn't exactly slimmed so much as smoothed some edges into contours, but he persisted as big, burly, and robust, his booming laugh still a fetching and distinctive feature. "You're sure this is no bother, dinner, I mean?" he asked. "We can go out."

"Pizza's on the way in," I said, "if that's okay. So how'd yawl get here?"

"Well, that's a story," Ben laughed. "We tried to side-saddle the cart onto my bike but it was too heavy and awkward for Kaiden to hold, and we looked so freakish anyway, this other food guy I know with a pickup had mercy upon us and loaded us on and drove us here. The cart's safely parked out back, and I can bike home in minutes. I live above the shop on Carondolet. Not far."

"Yeah," Kaiden said, "and thanks for the lift! Kaiden's Kwirky Kart of Kommendable Kuisine thanks you too!"

"How about Kompelling?" I offered.

"How about Kapital?" Ben said.

"Done!" Kaiden said. "Kapital it is! Wow, thanks, Ben. Great idea!"

"So you guys knew each other at LCC, right?" Kaiden asked, handing Ben a Pabst and sprawling onto one sofa.

"Yeah," he said, sipping, "we shared a coupla classes and a jerk of a teacher who called us and another guy his Three Wise Men, and collaborated on a play that got us censored and the teacher demoted. We might still do something with that script."

"Ben's a poet," I said. "You still are, right, Ben? You've published poetry, correct?"

"Some. In little magazines. I'm working on a volume."

"A book of your own poetry?" Kaiden said. "Now that is very cool."

"And you're still working two jobs!" I put in. "And something else," I said, impishly. "Tell us what you're also doing…in your spare time, Ben."

"Well," he said, not booming: "I fill in at Le Petit Theatre in the Quarter. As a volunteer. Just helping out here and there. Backstage and out front, as needed, and a few walk-ons and understudy roles. We usually work evenings, but I wasn't on call today."

"He said," Kaiden interrupted, "Ben said he might help me mechanize my bike. 'Motorize' it? Anyway, put a motor on it to cut down on leg wear. You really think you could do that, Ben?"

"I might have to get some help from the other shop guys, but yes, I think we could do that. Or if we can't, I can just about guarantee we can find you a second- or third-hand motorcycle for your work, and fit it out with a better and larger cart, with refrigeration and heat, and another awning."

"Wouldn't that be cool, Troy? I love my old bike, but I guess it's about ready for the museum. Do you also do taxidermy, Ben? No wait, that's something else. Preservation work, I mean. Like a conservator?"

"Let's get back to Le Petit for a second," I said. "You did some theater growing up, didn't you, Ben? Are you thinking you might get back into it, into acting, on a broader scale? You remember I've seen you…perform. I think you've got a gift."

"Well, thanks, Troy. I'm interested, and I've talked a little to Le Petit management, and told them I am. I don't have any serious professional training, though, and the field's so jammed. For the time being, I'm happy just hanging around down there doing odd jobs."

"There must be lots of beautiful girls to hang around with!" Kaiden said.

"There certainly are lots of beautiful girls, mostly focused on their careers, which I'm no help with. They're nice, though, and some are friendly. So you and Troy share this apartment?"

"We're roommates," Kaiden said.

"To be clear," I said, "we're boyfriends."

"What happened to Jack?" Ben asked. And for Kaiden's benefit: "Jack was the third Wise Man at LCC."

"He's also in grad school at Tulane," I said, "and involved with a girl."

"He's very smart," Ben said to Kaiden; "and Jack also writes: fiction…and…sometimes drama" (a glance at me). He appeared to wait for me to pick up. I passed.

"Troy does too," Ben said. "Has he showed you his own writing?"

"He hasn't," Kaiden yelped. "Why hasn't he, well might we ask? Why haven't you shown me your drafts, roommate?!"

"Actually, I've sent an article off to a professional journal. It's way early to be trying, but what the hell? I might as well get some editorial feedback along with the rejection slip."

"What's it about?" Ben asked.

"Whitman's 'Lilacs.'"

"Isn't that candy?" Kaiden asked.

"That could be why you haven't read his drafts," Ben said lightly. "I would," he added, seriously. "I love that poem. And that poet. So how're your folks, Troy? And my man Mark? Everything good in Madison."

"I've not been home for a while," I said. "But Mark's cinched second base on the high school team, no doubt warming up in your jacket at every workout!"

"Tell him Ben said to keep his spikes clean!"

"In a former life," I said, "Kaiden and I knew each other at a summer church camp. Did I ever tell you about that, Ben? Why don't you give him some high-lights, Kaiden?"

And he did, until the pizza arrived. Ben seemed interested. "Is that where you learned to ask all those irreverent questions about scripture at the Broadway Youth Group?! Do you go to church here?"

"No," Kaiden said; "Sunday's a great food day on the street. But I did in Vicksburg, where I'm from."

We made quick work of three pizza slices each and then settled in to leisurely nibbling of the remainders, chatting comfortably of this and that. Ben told us a lot more about his jobs at the two motorcycle repair shops but necessarily in a professional lingo foreign to me. One of his bosses had hinted that if as expected a full-time position might open up soon, Ben would be first in line for it.

"Would you take it?" I asked.

"It'd prob'ly depend on how much time it took away from Le Petit."

"Good man!" I said. "Have they announced next season's shows yet?"

Ben ducked his head, swallowed. "They've selected but not announced. It's still confidential."

"But you've seen the list, right?" I said. "C'mon, give us a hint."

"I'm not supposed to."

"You're whetting the appetites, Ben. Let's hear it. Just one title?"

"If you guess, you can't tell. Anyone."

He started to chuckle and couldn't stop. "You really cannot tell," he said, desperately wanting to.

"Okay," he said. "One little hint. 'Brick.'"

"'Brick'?" I said. "Oh. The cat on the roof."

Ben whooped. "They've asked me to read for Big Daddy,"

# 23

Dr. Leonidas Grant led the British Romantic constituency at Tulane and chaired the Department of English. He taught a one-semester graduate lecture course in the period and then specialized graduate seminars in the individual poets if enough students asked for them. I took the survey course my first term and earned an A but didn't differentiate myself to the professor, didn't individualize myself with suck-up conferences and appointments and slimy, brown-nosing requests to join him for coffee in the canteen. For I feared him: and I feared him because I worshipped him. He was a prominent name in the field, had published books on Shelley and Keats and Charles Lamb, and was writing another on the literary criticism of Coleridge. About 5' 8" and slim, maybe 45, black-haired but beginning to bald, he always spoke in a low growl, and laughed a gruff rumble, but you could tell from his twinkling eyes and amiable manner that he was a gentle-spirited, kindly-disposed man not prone to frighten or intimidate. But my respect weakened my knees around him. His teaching uniform was one of five light-weight cotton suits — navy, tan, brown, gray, and pin-striped charcoal — with solid, sober ties on white shirts. He lectured without notes, thoughtfully pacing back and forth before the lectern, and sometimes among ourselves, never inviting or tolerating interruptions until five minutes shy of dismissal, when he routinely did. He strolled four blocks home every day for lunch and a nap, walked back and worked until 6 in his office or the snack bar, and again trekked home for martinis and dinner. He'd never learned to drive a car. He enjoyed nothing more (after martinis) than a multi-faceted, well-turned pun, and he peppered his conversations with them, always watching to be sure you'd "got" them, and if you had, he'd join you in a big boisterous laugh. He was almost as fond of limericks, made them up and wrote them out in ink on napkins in the cafeteria, and had even published several in the *Norton Anthology of Modern American Literature*. I feared him because I so deeply respected his mind and his command of "the age of revolution," as he called the European Romantic phenomenon, and didn't wish to waste his time with my puerile and pedestrian queries. Not only had he read and remembered all the primary texts; he knew the associated art and music and science of the age, and carried the knowledge so lightly that a mere sentence or two would send you scurrying to the Library to learn more, not to impress him but to try to catch up with him, so to understand him. I'd long ago resolved to secure him as the director of my graduate program but shrank from actually requesting that huge and unwarranted favor.

"You smoke, I believe," Dr. Grant said, taking a Marlboro himself and offering the pack to me. "Your undergraduate professors thought very highly of you, Mr. Tyler. I've just reviewed your impressive file. They promised us you've got a future in literature."

"I hope I do, sir. In Romantic literature. That's sort of why I'm here."

"Wasting no time, I see. 'Thrift, thrift, Horatio!' as Hamlet quoth," he laughed. "Straight to business, is it?"

"If you please, sir. I'd like respectfully to ask you to direct my graduate program. I hope to specialize in Romanticism, take all the courses offered, and write my dissertation under your personal supervision, if you'd be so kind...and have the time."

"You were in our class last year, I recall, Troy. I've never known a Troy. May I call you Troy? I like it. It's a sturdy, strapping name."

"Thank you, sir. Some friends call me 'Trojan. Troj.'"

"Even better!" he laughed. "It's classical...but it has Romantic resonance, color, potency. Might I use it too?"

"As you wish, sir."

"You're nearing the end of your second year, right? You've another year of course work. You still lack a couple of required courses, and seminar hours. Have you yet begun to narrow your interests to a single Romantic phenomenon or genre or author or emphasis?"

"I think I'd like to focus on Lord Byron, sir."

"The least Romantic of them all, eh?"

"Pardon me, sir. Everybody always says that, but I think it's a...misunderstanding...a mis-perception. Byron's early and mid-career work may be the most 'Romantic' of them all."

"Have you read much of his later work?"

"No sir, not much."

"Might look into it, before you commit."

"Yes, sir," I said, nodding. "I shall."

"Other than his early romantic inclinations, what's attracted you to his Lordship?"

"Well, sir, I like the personality, the character... the defiance and rebellion. The revolutionary impulse. The...um...the tempestuousness! And also: nobody appears to be writing about him. Scholarship, I mean. I'm not finding much criticism of his verse in the library."

"You're smart to look...and you're right. His poetry appears to be the least written about in the Romantic canon. The life has overshadowed it from the start. Can you say what interests you in the poetry?"

"The imagery, sir, among other things. He's not Keats, but he's no slouch with imagery."

He laughed. "No, but nobody's Keats but Keats." He leaned back, watching me. "Let me be honest with you, Troy: I'm not a Byron scholar; I know him less well than I do the other Romantic poets. I don't greatly admire what I do know of his work...but I favor the satires. If we work together on Byron, you'd probably end up teaching me. And wouldn't that be a grand adventure!" He smiled expansively. "But we've got time — even if you're in a hurry — we've got time to think and plan before you'll need to declare any specialization. Meanwhile, we can explore. Would you have any interest, for example, were I to offer a graduate seminar next year in Lord Byron's poetry. It's probably past time I patched my Byron gap. I'm not promising, mind you; but perhaps we can both meditate on that possibility, and check back before we leave for the summer? In case we need to spend it with his Lordship?"

"Oh, sir, I'd sign up for the seminar today! Yes, sir, I would have interest. Thank you, sir."

"You might start with a late poem. See what you make of 'The Vision of Judgment.'

"And, for your initiation into formal Byron studies, I'm now going to dictate to you the first and second lines of The Great Unfinished Limerick. See if you can finish it before we next meet. Ready? Write it down:

> *The beautiful Countess of Guiccioli*
> *Slept with Lord Byron habitually….*

It's spelled G-u-i-c-c-i-o-l-i. Pronounced Gwich-o-lee. Emphasis on the first syllable. Have fun, but don't break your head on it!"

\* \* \*

September 2, 1961

Hey, Monte!

Tulane's spring break begins on Saturday, March 17, and continues through Sunday, March 25, 1962. Would you be able to visit me then? Kaiden Carlisle (formerly Corky) and I have lots of space and guest bedrooms, and would like to host you here.

Our "unfinished business" includes talking about personal stuff that needs to come out if we're to get back the relationship we enjoyed as "bunking" roommates at Jubilee. You hinted at it during your visit, and again in a recent letter (Rex Lawtry's party), as I did in saying Kaiden's my roommate. Please let me dare to go further, and maybe get us started.

Since our summer together, I've figured out why I've always preferred men's company over women's, and I've sometimes experimentally practiced that preference sexually and found it satisfying. Kaiden has helped me understand this preference but never pushed me to admit it. Since I don't like any of the names used about men with similar tastes, I say that Kaiden and I are boyfriends who share an apartment; but you should know that he and I sometimes sleep together. You should also know that I often day-dream and fantasize about you.

Whether this news makes any difference in plans to visit, I won't know unless you tell me. I sincerely hope I've not shocked, hurt, disappointed, or offended you. I think often and fondly of you and of our wonderful summer (which you did not ruin; you *made* it!), and I write now hoping to make everything finer with uplifting contact.

Looking forward,  Troy

\* \* \*

24 August 61. Nellis.

Hey Troy

No shock, no hurt, no offense, no chance of disappointment. Would you believe I've experimented too! (I'm laughing at that punctuation mark. I never noticed it before…in this way!!)

Thank you for the spring break dates. I'll work with them.

Tell Kaiden I've got dibs on you as my roomie.

I'm looking forward too.  We see pretty forward, uplifted at 40,000 feet! (There it is again!)

Monte

\* \* \*

"Hello, Troy?" my brother said into my ear; "it's Mark. You got a minute?"

"Hi, Mark! Nice surprise!" He'd never called me at school. "Has something happened?"

"We may have to move."

"What? Move? No. What?"

"It's true. We might have to move. Father's looking at a new job."

"At or for? Back up, Mark. Tell me what's happened."

"There's this committee, from some church in Lake Charles, coming here to poke around. Mother told me."

"Is she there, Mark. If she's there, put her on."

"They can't make me move my senior year, Troy. I won't do it. You don't want to move, do you?"

"Mark, stop. If Mother's there, please put her on."

"Troy," she said, "your Father was going to tell you. Nothing is definite, and won't be for some time. Mark overheard your father and me talking, and panicked. They're just beginning a search. No visit's been scheduled."

I knew, oh too well, I knew this miserable drill, from having gone through it twice before, when I was eight and thirteen, and I hated it. In the Southern

Baptist tradition, when a pulpit vacancy occurs, a committee of five or six congregants is chosen by the Board of Deacons to compile a list of possible pastors to fill it, collect credentials, get recommendation letters, and visit the candidate to check out his sermonic skills, his personality, his demeanor, and not least to inspect his family, if any, for its compatibility with the new environment and community. It was always a hugely disruptive and disquieting process for the family, and always crushing to unsuccessful candidates, who took risks at home by becoming candidates. And here was Mark already sounding off in protest, and I didn't blame him: the visiting committees not only attended one or more services, unavoidably revealing their purpose and inciting rumors of change that upset everything; they also crowded your table for Sunday dinner and picked at you about school and sports and pastimes, and tried to make nice against your sure and certain knowledge they were trying their damnedest to screw up your entire life big time. It put everybody on edge for weeks.

Mother's "they," I shortly learned, referred to the Bethany Baptist Church search committee from Lake Charles, about 200 miles west of New Orleans. "It's about twice the size of ours," she continued to me, her voice already strident with hope, "and prob'ly has a budget at least twice ours. Two of its former senior pastors were presidents of the whole Southern Baptist Convention. And two of your Father's seminary pals in Nashville Baptist headquarters recommended him. It's quite an honor to be included in the search. You should be proud of him. Of course, as I said, it's early. And we mustn't take anything for granted. Also, Troy, you'll remember from before: you can't talk to our members about this. If anybody asks, you don't know a thing!"

"Except I do. Why can't I just say I can't talk about it?"

"Refer them to your Father, then."

"It's all so completely unfair to me!" Mark yelled from the background. "It's so *inconsiderate!*"

"It would be a wonderful opportunity for the whole family," Mother said.

"Well," I said, "it wouldn't affect me, would it? I wouldn't be moving."

"I heard that," Mark said, on the extension line. "But they'd make *me* move," he said. "They'll make me go with them. And I won't. What about my team? What happens to my second base?"

The catch in his throat stirred me. Remembering again, I understood all over again. I'd loathed moving: not only becoming the new kid in class but also the "new preacher's kid" in school: a double whammy: a stigma to be lived with over weeks of differentiation, of whispered suspicions and pointed fingers, of proving oneself "regular" before a fraction of normality might be recovered. It would be painful and pitiable for Mark to begin his senior year knowing nobody and inspected by all.

"And what about college recommendation letters?" he went on. "I won't know any teachers? Who would write for me?"

"Listen, Mark," I said; "don't panic. I'll do what I can. I'll talk to them both. Mother says the search is just beginning. Nothing will be decided for a while."

"And then we'll move," he said. "It's so…it's so God damned *unfair!*"

"Mark!" Mother snapped. "Mouth!" And to me: "I have to go; your Father will call you."

He didn't before I went home for four days over Thanksgiving. But there he gave me an appointment to talk privately with him in his home office at 11 a.m. on Thanksgiving Day. In a vested suit and tie, he sat behind his desk, fingertips pressed together in inverted V's. I'd cleaned up for dinner but was casual in a sweater and jeans.

"Your Mother has told you about Bethany's interest in me, as a candidate for its senior pastorship. It's an attractive position. There are other candidates, I don't know how many or who they are. They're certain to be well-qualified. The Committee will visit us over the weekend after next. You'll be back at school then but if you wish to return home for their visit, you're welcome to."

"Thank you, sir, but I think I won't."

"I will explain that you're swamped with work for your Ph.D."

"Don't say 'swamped,' sir. It'll sound like I'm behind or can't keep up."

"Very well. You're busy with it. Are there any particular questions you want to ask me about this review process and how it might eventuate?"

"Well, sir, why are you a candidate? Are you unhappy here? Restless?"

"No. I wouldn't want that said about me. It's a great opportunity. To grow...spiritually. To preach and teach and reach more souls. To expand my ministry. Perhaps to refresh and renew myself in a new and stimulating environment."

"To increase your salary?"

"That might be a consideration."

"What's going to happen to Mark?"

He paused. Shifted and stiffened. "I'm sensitive to the difficulties a move could impose upon Mark at this time in his life, and I will try to keep them at a minimum. But he's young. He's adaptable."

"He's seventeen. He's vulnerable. I think he's feeling pretty fragile."

"No, he's strong. A little sulky right now but that will pass. He'll adjust. We'll all have to adjust...IF I'm offered the job."

"You'll take it then, if it's offered?"

"That's not yet decided."

"Well, yawl should keep an eye on Mark. He's pretty upset."

"Pray for him. If you talk to him, try to point out the advantages to him of the move. You're experienced: remember how well you worked through those other moves."

"But I didn't, sir. They were hard."

"Were they? You never said."

"You never asked."

He paused. Flushed. "You could be helpful with Mark, Troy. Just speak with him about advantages. Be encouraging."

"And what would you say are the advantages to Mark in moving? Just so I know? What's so encouraging about it?"

"I haven't had a chance yet to investigate the schools in Lake Charles, but I'm certain they're better than Madison's. There will be more of them. More opportunities."

"And reasons for encouragement...will turn up?"

"Undoubtedly. Also: remember that we mustn't talk about this possibility with the congregation. It needs to remain confidential within the family as long as possible, although once the committee visits, of course, word will leak…. And you might be contacted."

"What? By whom? What do you mean?"

"The Search Committee might want to meet you, and if you're not here…?"

"But why? I'm hardly involved. I wouldn't move."

"You're still my family. They like to meet the family. If they call or visit you, just be respectful. Answer their questions but don't volunteer...personal information. Just be businesslike; courteous and discreet."

Ah: *was* he thinking about the Chatterton project. I almost giggled. Was he truly worried that my contributions to an inconsequential aborted unpublished chickenshit stunt might turn a pulpit committee against him? It seemed preposterous.

"I'm just saying that if you're contacted, you should be on your best behavior for any interview, all right?"

"But of course I would be. I'd never do anything…."

"No. Is there anything else in this connection you want to ask or discuss?"

"It's really the prestige, isn't it, Father? You'd enjoy the esteem. I get it, but shouldn't we factor in the plus for your reputation?"

"I've always tried to keep humble, Troy. As an example for you boys."

\* \* \*

A couple of weeks after Jack's unexpected visit, he informed me — by a letter left in a cardboard box of my belongings on our porch — that Bailey had miscarried, noting by the way that one in every five pregnancies so terminated, and was recovering in her dorm. Mrs. Burkhart — after only a little haggling, he boasted — had allowed him to keep the Audubon room, on the conditions already named, at the single-occupant rate through the end of the academic year, although she'd instructed Christoph Creole to lock the ladder into the shed out back. I'd told him on campus I'd stay on Magazine Street but thanked him for the invitation to return. "It might not always be open," he said, grinning.

Gradually, he and I began to resume cordial relations in the bull-pen, as he and Bailey drifted farther apart: she actually moved to a far-corner desk and fell in with Rebecca Ward, a History TA from Mobile, whom we knew as a classmate in History of the Language.

Bailey cut me routinely, and I bled not a drop. Under my still but less disapproving glare, Jack continued to cultivate his students socially, especially, I noticed, two comely males who looked with favor upon each other; but I also didn't see any harm developing from it, and the rollicking good times they obviously enjoyed made me doubt my disfavor and envy their joy. I said nothing to anyone, including Jack, about Bailey's misfortune, if that's what it was. Of course I felt some relief, for Jack's sake, but I also wondered...I could not help but wonder...over the circumstantial convenience. Not yet, not yet could I fully trust my old friend; and yet I sometimes caught myself thinking thus of him.

Coincidentally on my October birthday I received notice from *The Walt Whitman Review* that my paper on "Lilacs" would appear in a forthcoming issue. My first scholarly publication! An essay in a minor journal, to be sure, and in the event only nine printed pages; but I, a mere student, was suddenly a published critic...with a (short) bibliography. Kaiden wanted to celebrate with a party including bull-pen mates, but I vetoed the idea, too well knowing how my good fortune would set in that quarter: oh, public plaudits would pass, but blood would curdle and teeth grind, and the bull-pen seethe for a time. I had unmistakably advanced one small step ahead of my cohort.

Jack Latimer seemed genuinely pleased when I showed him the acceptance letter. "You *did* it!" he cried. "Fantastic! Your inaugural entry into the lists of jousting journalistic competitions, and you won the fair lady's garter! Where is it, by the way? Why aren't you wearing it? Wow, Troy, I'm truly proud of you! Will you tell Grant?"

"Not yet. I'll give Adams an offprint when they come since I cite him, but I dunno about The Chair. It's not that great. It's terribly overwritten."

"It's *accepted*. You're *published!* Well-done, you!"

"Your turn," I said.

And only a day or two later, Kaiden's new signage — melodramatically larger and colorfully different under Ben's imaginative direction, although still dressing the bike not a cycle — attracted the attentions of a Broussard's representative with whom he now had a second appointment to discuss a deal. Among the more famous of Quarter restaurants, and only a block and a half from both Bourbon and Royal Streets on Conti, Broussard's had been popular and fashionable since the late '20's, particularly for its Creole cuisine, private dining rooms and stunning patio.

"It's upscale and famous," Kaiden continued, as we sipped celebratory cocktails in the so-called garden behind the house. "I didn't pitch much in that neighborhood because it's so hoity-toity, and I never imagined Broussard's would notice me. But Esteban — Esteban Chauvin, the sous-chef who came out to meet me — said they'd already sent out a couple of staff to sample my food. It was the Exec Chef's idea to hire a street-food person to help advertise the place, and there I already was! Nobody's said whether I gave him the idea.

Anyhow, I'm on the payroll for six weeks starting Friday. Can you believe it? I can't hardly!"

"It's really super, K, and I'm so proud of you! You do well enough, you may get your own franchise out of this!! But how does it work? Do you know details yet?"

"Not many. That's why I'm meeting with Esteban and maybe even the Exec Chef on Thursday afternoon, to talk about schedules and my menu and salary and such."

"But they've actually hired you? I mean, you're on board with a full-time job?"

"Not yet. Everything's provisional for now. Tentative. Depending on how I do during what I guess will be a sort of probation period. For now I'm a temporary employee. But after Thursday…."

"They must have said, though, what they're thinking about for you? I get your uncertainty, but surely they gave you some idea…?"

"Yes…I just don't want to raise expectations…or get ahead of myself. They're thinking about letting me sell — on the street outside — their own appetizers along with my Creole dishes to tempt patrons indoors for fine dining, where they'd find selections from my specialties added to Broussard's small-plate menu. We'd split the profits from sales of our respective snacks."

"Now that sounds like a really great idea! What if yours outsell theirs?"

"That won't happen. But here's the even better idea, except you mustn't breathe a word of it anywhere: they also might offer me a part-time internship in the kitchen under one or more of their famous chefs! I'd work after-noons in the neighborhood and for two hours five nights a week in the regular kitchen, for a salary. It would be fantastic for learning what happens in there."

"No kidding! Isn't that sort of what you hoped *would* happen from all this peddling around town? Did you propose this to them…or the other way round?!"

"A little of both, maybe?"

"Good God, Kaiden! You're *negotiating*! With Broussard's!"

"Don't sound so surprised, Troy, or I'll think you've underestimated me!"

"I may have! This is terrific, Kaiden! Can't we tell anybody? What if we round up a crowd and storm your cart Saturday afternoon…to prove what a hit you are?!"

"Now you're sounding like Monte!"

"And speaking of: he's coming to see us over Tulane's spring break."

\* \* \*

Meanwhile, I had schoolwork: last themes of the semes-ter to assign and grade for my freshmen; three term pa-pers to finish, one for my Shakespeare seminar, one each for the graduate lecture courses in 16th/17th century British Literature and 19th Century American Authors (Poe, Dickinson, Emerson, Thoreau). I'd also teach the Introduction to Poetry course for the first time in the spring term (required for majors), and, while excited by the prospect, I needed to read the textbook prescribed by the Department and prepare a syllabus. And it never hurt to get a little start on courses for the spring term: the second semester of the grad Shakespeare seminar (the tragedies!), Modern Poetry (with Grant), and Milton. Professor Royal talked a lot about Milton's influence on the Romantics; and I figured that my Biblical background would serve me well in studying this vitally significant poet. I would complete my required course work in the spring, and then a year from now sit the qualifying exam. Passing it would enable me to begin researching and writing the dissertation immediately, assuming approval of a prospectus by the director and a committee of graduate faculty. I'd passed my German language exam but still had to teach myself French. These two foreign language tests weren't taken with particular seriousness even by the Graduate School, which required them for the doctorate, and the Department requirements were downright lax: candidates chose two critical monographs from the library in the foreign language on an English literature subject or author, had them approved by the language department, brought them both to the exam where a monitoring professor selected a page or so from one to be translated, in writing, over the next hour. Notes were forbidden but dictionaries allowed. Of course most of us had already translated blocks of our chosen texts, and were generally familiar with their subjects and styles and critical orientations. A few candidates still somehow managed to fail but most of us got through with minimal linguistic skills. Next summer I would prepare for the early fall French exam and spend the rest of it swotting up for the big "prelim" exams in November. If you failed them, you got one more chance to pass. A second failure kicked you out of the program.

At the moment, Byron's "The Vision of Judgment" awaited my own. Judgment, I mean. On Professor Grant's recommendation, I read it, and about it, as an example of the poet's late satiric work, which he thought I should sample before casting my scholarly lot with the "romantic" Byron for the foreseeable future. The hard truth is, I liked the back-story of "Vision" better than the poem. The original "A Vision of Judgment" was Poet Laureate Robert Southey's smarmy elegy on the death of King George III. Notoriously, Byron thought it despicable verse, another fawning, suck-up celebration of a corrupt monarch, particularly blasphemous in its inclusion of the Almighty Himself among the heavenly throngs welcoming the King into glory; and Byron responded with his own corrective *"The* Vision of Judgment," a savage parody of Southey's elegy showing the King slipping furtively into Paradise past an angelic host in scattered flight from the Laureate's recitation of his poem. This concluding scene struck me as slapstick funny but tonally discontinuous and borderline tastelessly juvenile even for a parody. Yes, Southey's Preface to the poem viciously attacked Byron as head of the "Satanic school of poetry," and merited a rejoinder; but "The Vision" hardly refutes the charge, and might even stoke it. If I found the denouement amusing, I thought the body of the poem weighted down by a debate between the archangel Michael and the Devil over eternal ownership of the Royal Soul, and then by the testimony of a "cloud of witnesses" to the dead King's doubtful reign. The *ottava rima* stanza — requiring four rhymes — showcased Byron's dazzling ingenuity but I imagined that, repeated thousands of times in an epic the length of *Don Juan,* it might tire. Beyond and deeper than these reservations, I felt that something essential was missing in the verse, something perhaps inimical to the genre itself? I don't have a satisfactory name for it. Let's call it emotional warmth. Satire is by definition, I guess, acerbic, caustic, sometimes bitter. The *tone* of "Vision" did not engage me, even when it amused me. The cynical cast of mind behind this verse — the sneer, the unrelieved acidic scorn — chafed and rankled me. Even the humor felt laced with unforgiving regard. It sounds sentimental to say, but "Vision" didn't reach my heart or stir my spirit. But could I repeat that to Dr. Grant?

On the other hand, in the volume of Byron's collected works where I found "Vision," I also stumbled on those plays of his that Park Royal assigned in his performative frenzy back at LCC: *Marino Faliero; Sardanapalus; The Two Foscari.* Historical, character-driven dramas, with challenging moral dilemmas and complex relationships and engaging emotional turmoils and ethical questions like those asked in *Cain: A Tragedy,* which work I'd like to get back to sometime. The *human* element in those works stirred me like passages in, say, some of Byron's lyrics, in many stanzas of *Childe Harold's Pilgrimage,* even in *Manfred* and some of the oriental tales. It occurred to me to wonder whether human hurt and pain and sorrow and doubt and fear were apt subjects for satire? And love? But now I'm out of my depth. I might have to go there, though, to explain my dissatisfaction with Byron's "Vision" and my preference for his "romantic" art.

Brother Mark rang again on the Monday evening after the weekend visit by the Lake Charles committee.

"I still don't want to move," he said, "but this one guy on the committee coaches Little League baseball and talked sports to me for a while. I'm too old to play for him but he knows the high school baseball coach and says he's a great guy and would want to see me right off."

"So you're feeling better?"

"Not much, but these folks seemed pretty nice. Two women, two men. The women helped Mother in the kitchen, and Father showed the men all around the church property. They took me along. And after dinner I walked the guys down to the bayou and the school ball field and back. Just the three of us. They asked about you."

"And what'd you say?"

"Just that you're studying for your Ph.D. at Tulane and were very good on the piano and had worked at a church camp in New Mexico. And I said you were sorry to miss them."

"Did they say anything about...well, about Father's chances?"

"No. I asked whether they had other visits to make and they said yes but not where or when. Oh, and they asked how Father got along with young people in the church. I didn't know what they were getting at so I just said fine."

"That was the right answer."

"But he doesn't actually hang out with any, does he?"

"So why'd you call, Mark? I'm glad to know you're feeling better, but was there a reason you rang?"

"I thought you'd want to know about that visit, is all."

"I did. That was a thoughtful thing to do. Thank you. And by the way: I'm thinking about asking Ben Moore to come home with me again for Christmas. Would you like me to?"

"Oh, wow! Really? That would be great! How's Ben getting along?"

"He's good. I've got stories. I'll invite him. But let me ask the folks."

Christmas Eve was a very big night at Broussard's, and Christmas Day already fully booked, Kaiden said; and as now an official employee not to mention a brand spanking new one, he didn't think he should request any holiday time off. We planned to decorate the exterior of our house before the 25th and take up the interior when I returned from Madison three days after it, and mark our first Christmas together then. Traditionally in New Orleans, the official party season begins with Christmas and schlepps along through New Year's and then speeds up toward Mardi Gras festivity with increasing delirium no matter how many weeks down the line Lent begins. Kaiden thought we should somewhere in there host an open-house social event for school friends and Ben's clients and some of his own new pals from the restaurant, assuming his father permitted and helped with expenses. Meanwhile, Ben could drive me home and spend a couple of Christmas days with us…not on his bike (I still wasn't comfortable on the pillion for a long drive) but in the rattly old Ford pickup he'd re-fit for his shops to haul in damaged bikes and ferry their owners back and forth. I invited him to lunch to talk it over. He chose Chinese.

"I can't use chopsticks," I admitted, ashamed.

"They'll give you a fork but I can teach you chopsticks. With your digital dexterity," he laughed, "it'll be a snap."

It wasn't, of course, but I gamely struggled and Ben patiently taught and tolerated, even taking my right hand into his and guiding my fingers around the tools. I could manage the veggies but the confounded noodles slid away every time. "Okay, use the fork," he instructed.

"So, Ben," I asked, "would you drive me home if we feed you Christmas?"

"Will Mark be there?"

"Of course. And he's keen to see you."

"Well, sure, if it's okay with your folks. That would be very nice. Thank you. You can stand the truck?"

"If I don't have to drive it! But look: my folks say absolutely no gifts this time. No gold, frankincense or myrrh. Just you and your appetite."

"And my chess game? Your father'll still want to play, right?"

"Oh yeah, for sure. But Ben, they're serious about no gifts."

"Well, I'll bring Mark something. He'll expect it."

"The more reason not to. I doubt they'll let him accept anything, Ben. Best not."

"No, I won't come then. Something small. Just a token. I want to."

"I'll have to ask them."

"Then do."

I forked my noodles around. "You'll notice the house is a little tense right now, Ben. Something's happening I should tell you about."

Grinning, he reached across with his chopsticks, caught up a heap of noodles from my bowl, and balanced them before my mouth. "Open wide," he giggled.

"So what's going on there?" he asked.

"Those are really good!" I exclaimed. "A church in Lake Charles without a pastor is looking at Father for the job. He and Mother prob'ly want it. Mark is very worried they'll get it and move. It's his senior year."

"God!" he put down his sticks. "That's…sickening. That would break his heart. Or it would mine. What's he saying?"

"He's very upset. I expect he's depressed. He says he *won't* move, but I don't see he's got any choice, if it comes to that. Of course Father doesn't yet have the job. He and Mother are worrying about the competition. So things are a little wobbly around there."

"Maybe a little chess would distract your dad."

"I expect it would. He'd enjoy some matches."

"And look: why don't we bring my bike in the truck. That's its calling, after all, hauling around bikes. I could give Mark another couple rides on it. Didn't he like those before?"

"He did. A lot. That's a great idea, Ben. If it's no trouble."

He paused, fiddled with the sticks, thinking. "Is Mark talking to your father…about the possible move?"

"I don't know. Mark's called me twice…the only times he's ever called me at school. Father hasn't really talked much to me about it either, so I doubt he's saying much to Mark…or listening to him. Father thinks he'll get over his sulk soon. Says he's strong."

Ben looked hard at me. "I wouldn't have thought he would be, not about losing his senior year."

'No. I wasn't strong about our two earlier moves."

He went very quiet.

"What're you thinking, Ben?"

He picked up his sticks and forked another heap my way. "Well, I was just remembering. When my own father…died, the orphanage gave me a lot of counseling, over a couple of years, about him and what had happened and how I felt…and how my feelings changed and all that. At first I didn't want to talk at all, but when I started, I saw it made me feel better, sometimes, and then often. And then I looked forward…to talking more. We talked a lot about, well, about fathers and sons. I mean, I'm not a doctor or anything, but I learned stuff. Useful stuff that helped me get better."

"Yes," I said. "You seem fine. Except maybe around guns."

"There is that. I don't remember whether we ever talked about guns."

"But about fathers, you did, and sons. So…?"

"Maybe I could talk with Mark?"

I looked at him, into his unblinking eyes, eyes kind and soft and vaguely imploring, like the question mark at the end of his sentence.

"Of course," I said, "but informally. I mean, not by appointment or anything, just casually. Listening to what's on his mind…about this whole ugly business. I bet he'd go for it. And it would prob'ly help."

"I'll think about it," he said, leaning back. "Then we can play it by ear when we're there. Let it just happen, if it wants to. I can't promise to tell you anything he says."

"One more bite?" I said, leaning in.

* * *

We timed the trip to Madison so we'd arrive on Christmas Eve Sunday night after they'd left home for evening church, and then spend Monday, Tuesday, and Wednesday eating and catching up. Ben found in a New Orleans antique store a framed print of a 1930 *Saturday Evening Post* cover showing twelve rag-tag boys scattered around — including the baserunner, water-boy, and ball-boy — with game gear, all facing away from home plate, all watching an unseen baseball sail overhead toward an unseen fence, with the unnecessary title "Home Run" attached, for hanging on Mark's bed-room wall. My brother's guileless delight in it passed to the rest of us, and the general amusement silenced any objections to the gift. Ben also gave Mark two extended bike rides, played four chess matches with Father, winning two, dried dishes from five fantastic meals, and joined Mark on the school baseball field for a couple of hours of batting and fielding practice that ended with a long talk afterward about the possible move to Lake Charles. Ben didn't offer me details of their conversation, but I thought Mark seemed of lighter mood when they returned. Avoiding ticklish topics, my folks and I got on fine, although over these three days I felt rather like a visitor in my own home: it was almost as though they'd already moved. Anyhow, well-fed, somewhat refreshed by the change of scene, and satisfied that we'd *meant* well with attempted good deeds, we headed back on Thursday morning.

"How'd you find Mark?" I asked him.

"He's a great kid," Ben said, "just angry and confused about his dad's plans. We talked about a couple of ideas, and we're going to stay in touch."

"Well, I have his best interests at heart too, you know. He's my bro. You can confide."

"Better not. I think we should hold tight right now. IF your Father gets an offer and takes it, AND sill wants to move Mark, that's the time to roll with ideas. For now let's just keep in touch regularly with Mark."

"Should I call?"

"Every day. If he tells you to stop, don't. I'll call him too. Maybe every other day. And he has my number."

This both irked and scared me. It felt a little like Ben was taking over as Mark's brother. The frequent checking suggested a graver state of affairs than I'd imagined. But Ben's experience was after all what brought him into this affair, and I should trust it.

"He really liked your gift," I said.

"I hope so. By the way, what do you know of Jack? Didn't yawl room together….?"

"We did. That didn't work out so well, and then I found Corky…Kaiden, and as you saw that's working out fine. Jack had some girl trouble but that seems to be over. I see him in our TA office but not much otherwise. He seems okay. We're not as close as we were at LCC."

"Girl trouble? I thought Jack was…you know. Yawl were pretty tight at LCC."

"Yes. We were. It's kind of sad…that things didn't work out better here."

"And you're happy with Kaiden now?"

"Pretty much, yeah. He's got a great job, and we're in that terrific house, and we're about to make our first Christmas together. You might've noticed this bracelet. Kaiden wears an identical one. I'd say things are pretty good. Do you ever see Leslie?"

"No, but I think she may be in Loyola Law."

"Well, who do you see these days? You were such a stud at LCC!"

"Mostly girls from Le Petit, when I see anybody. Nobody steadily. I keep pretty busy."

"This doesn't sound right, Ben," I said. "It's not natural for you to be without a woman! What gives?"

"Not sure. Ask my poetry. I'm writing some about that."

"Publishing any?"

"A few short lyrics, in some VERY 'little magazines.' I'm actually thinking about a one-act play. As long as I'm working on drama at the theater."

"No kidding? That's cool. And you're understudying Big Daddy! How's that going?"

"Oh, we're not rehearsing yet.  The play's down for August, to run the month.  We won't begin rehearsing till summer."

"Tell me when tickets go on sale!"

"Happy New Year, Troy!"

# 24

He let me off at our house but declined to come in for a beer. It gleamed in the soft blue of lights strung densely along our porch railing, across the front and down the side. Kaiden had hung holly wreaths with red ribbons and single bulb candles in all our front windows, and quite a large matching one over the front door knocker. The aroma from the mint garden hung heavily in the humid air. I stood on the walk for a minute taking it all in, feeling pretty good about things.

Inside, a huge, thickly-decorated live Fraser fir stood regally in the front corner to the right of our entrance, its hundreds of colored lights blinking to a rhythm heard only by themselves. Red tapers in crystal holders with green leafy necklaces stood around the room, patiently awaiting a match. Another holly wreath hung above the glass doors to the parlor that reflected winks from the tree. A radio somewhere softly sounded seasonal notes. Silence from the kitchen told me Kaiden wasn't yet home from work.

I took another sweet moment to soak in the quiet restfulness of the room before heading to mine for a shower and a change of clothes. Maybe it was the restful word passing through my mind that inspired the idea, but I suddenly knew I'd dress in my white pajamas and navy robe to welcome Kaiden home. It would astound him, and maybe please him, and possibly draw him to join me in soothing wear for relaxation that might lead anywhere. I added black slippers and cologne, and gave the bracelet a quick polish.

Hearing his Nash door slam and his step on the porch, I flung open the door upon him setting down a stack of boxes named Broussard. His jaw dropped, his eyes popped, he said "Wow!" and swarmed all over me.

"The boxes are dinner," he said, when we'd recovered our breaths from the welcoming frenzy. "Would you please take them to the kitchen and plate the contents…while I change into something…kinky?!"

"Make it twisty," I laughed, and obliged.

"Bone-in pork chop," he recited, glowing in his blue pajamas and white robe, combed, perfumed, his bracelet jingling: "cornbread bread pudding, green tomato chili verde, bib lettuce salad. And in here," opening a last box, "orange ricotta cake, rosewater creme Anglaise, raspberries, and for the freezer, pistachio ice cream!"

He poured burgundy while I lit candles, and we settled to our feast at opposite ends of the dining table.

"Happy Christmas, boyfriend," he said, toasting. "Welcome home!"

"Thank you, swain Carlisle," I said, "cheers! You surprised me with the decorations! They're very beautiful! The tree, especially."

"They're compliments of the pater," he said. "He found the tree at a seasonal lot where they also decorate, and ordered a thousand lights! As compensation to us for the disappointment they cost."

"What's that? What disappointment?"

"He won't let us host a Mardi Gras party here. Says there's too much risk of damage to the property. And he's probably right: people go crazy for Mardi Gras. I'm sorry, though. I was hoping we could entertain."

"Maybe we'll be invited somewhere?"

"But then how'd we repay?"

"Reduce the scale. Surely we can entertain for dinner. He didn't object, did he, when Ben dined here?"

"I don't think he knew. But sure, we can invite for dinner. If I can get nights off."

"You're off weekends. Saturdays and Sundays."

"Oh, that's going to change. I forgot to tell you. They need me on weekends. They're already closed on Mondays, so I'll have Monday and Tuesdays off."

"Well, we'll entertain for dinner then. How about Mondays. Mad Mondays, we'll call them! Mad Martini Mondays?"

"Have you ever even *had* a martini?"

"High time I did, doncha think?"

"Right. We'll plan something. But we have to wait to hear back from him. He wants to '*borrow*' the house! Use it for his own corporate party. He gives two every year, one in Vicksburg, one here, for local employees. Sometime here during the Mardi Gras weeks."

"If we're not invited, where'd we go?"

"We'd either come back very late, after the party, or he'll put us up in a hotel for the night, our choice. His caterers will do everything: come in the afternoon, clean, decorate, bring the food and drink and prepare it, serve it, clean up after. He says we won't even know anybody's been here. But we have to leave for it."

"Shouldn't be a problem. We could catch a movie… and, hey, why don't we plan to hit a few bars in the Quarter after it? We've been talking forever about doing that. You know I've never been to a queer bar. You could show me!"

"You might not like it."

"And then again I might. Didn't you?"

"Well, some. It might feel better with you along. Sure, we can think about that. So I should tell my father we'll come home late?"

"I dunno. It might be more convenient just to slip into a hotel…near dawn. No worries about driving home after the bars."

"Good point. I'll see what Dad says."

"Let's clear the table," I said, "and bring dessert to the sofa-beds in the living room. Oh, and our gifts for each other. Time to open!"

We'd agreed a while back to give each other sweaters for Christmas. We probably loved them because New Orleans winters didn't often require them, and their relative rarity made them more desirable for our wardrobes, to say nothing of their beautiful designs and colors. We hadn't specified types or tints, so to guarantee some surprise. His was a lavender wool V-neck, a brilliant match for his dark hair and gold bracelet; mine, a 3-ply cashmere, sky-blue crew-neck, the shade of my eyes. Tucked inside it was a rose-pink, button-down dress shirt.

"That's cheating, Kaiden. You shouldn't have done that. But I love it. Thank you, boyfriend!"

"I have the same set," he said; "should we twin?"

"That would be incest," I said.

"I'm for that!" he giggled, and kissed me hard on the mouth. "I love the lavender," he added. "I don't have that color."

"I know," I said. "I researched your drawers."

"You may research my drawers any…," but we both cracked up before he finished the line.

I opened the beds, smoothed the covers, and grabbed pillows from the closet while he sliced the cake and dished up the ice cream and raspberries. I added kindling to the fire and poked it around. We were still figuring out the sex…or at least where to have it, and how. Of course the queen sofas offered the most spacious stretch for intimacy, but neither of us was quite comfortable canoodling in a formal living room; and although we both preferred sleeping alone, toddling off to separate beds after sex felt inconsiderate, fragmentary, and sad. The pajamas were experimental: we'd never before begun sex wearing them, and usually bedded in boxers and T's. Kaiden liked to keep his socks on; I preferred bare feet on both of us. I think we both liked *falling* asleep in a cuddle but not waking up in strangleholds. And both of us sometimes snored. The mechanics of the sex themselves, while completely satisfying, lingered in the amateur precincts. I don't think either of us actually knew what constituted sophisticated, experienced, mature sex between men, and may have still been a little afraid to find out. I might have been about ready to move on in that direction, but until we'd talked about it, I lacked the nerve to take the step. I wouldn't say we were novices in bed, but we weren't aces either. I wasn't unhappy with what we had and did. A move away might forfeit it.

"Raspberry?" he said, holding one against my lips.

We sat cross-legged against our pillows and nibbled the desserts.

"Everything okay with your folks?" he asked.

"They're obsessing about the possible move to Lake Charles. And Mark's miserable about it. Ben talked with him."

"Yeah, that would be cruel, moving him his senior year."

"Anything new at Broussard's?"

"Me! I'm the only new thing in that very old shop."

"Nothing like being the new kid in school, though."

"No. Listen, what's happening with you and Jack? Have yawl patched it up?"

"Sort of, I guess. Why?"

"Well, I was just wondering: I'm kind of curious about him, yawl were so close for so long. Would you like to have him over for dinner some night? Let us meet? We could have Ben too. They know, or knew, each other, right?"

"They did. What brought this on?"

"Well, two things, maybe: since we can't have a big Mardi Gras party, why not a small version dinner event? We're not using all this social space. And I'd love to plan and prepare a good meal for guests. And second, we should rehearse for entertaining the famous Monte! See if we can do it up right for him. What do you think?"

"You know what? I like it. But what about this? Let's do invite Jack and Ben…but for when Monte's *here*! Let's give Monte a dinner! Jack and Ben used to get on just fine, and I bet they'd enjoy reconnecting. And Monte needs to know everybody. Can you handle the dinner? Shall I look at dates?"

"Martini Mondays or Tippling Tuesdays." He gathered our bowls and set them on the side table. "Are you certain you want to share Monte with everyone?"

"I don't see why not. I'd bet he's already curious. And he'll be complimented. But I'll run it past him. You remember he'll be here during my spring break."

"Have you thought about what we'll do with Monte? Where we'll put him?"

"In either of the guest rooms, I guess. He'd expect that," I said, but a frisson ran down my spine as I did.

"Are you certain you know what Monte expects on that visit? And what about you? What do you expect on that visit?"

"What I expect now," I said, sliding down into the covers and turning to him, "is you. Let me taste the creamy on your tongue."

\* \* \*

Mr. Troy Tyler                    January 10, 1962
4318 Magazine Street
New Orleans, La.

Dear Mr. Tyler:

My name is Graham Hollister, and I am a member of the Bethany Baptist Church Search Committee in Lake Charles, Louisiana. You probably know that we are currently considering your father, the Reverend Ernest Tyler, as a candidate for the pastorship of our church. He has kindly provided me with your postal address.

My business — I'm a lawyer— takes me to New Orleans next week. I wonder if it would be convenient for you to meet briefly with me — for no more than half an hour — perhaps on Wednesday afternoon, January 17th, around 5 p.m. at your residence? If that doesn't work for you, please suggest an alternate time.

Please don't be alarmed. This won't be a cross-examination. I anticipate a cordial conversation about your father as a pastor and a parent, and will welcome any relevant observations you believe might be helpful to our Committee's considerations. I enjoyed meeting your parents and brother on our visit to Madison.

If you wish to confer before our meeting, please use the number below.

I look forward to seeing you on the 17th.

Sincerely yours,
Graham Hollister
337-456-1900

Hmmm. Why caution me against alarm unless imagining I might feel some? I also note the prioritizing of "pastor" over "parent," which would be in line with my father's thinking. Otherwise, everything here looks proper but gives away nothing as to what he really wants with me. Probably a good thing Kaiden will be at work, and not have to be explained. I should dress. Best not offer him a cocktail or a cigarette. Coffee? Cookies? I don't think I've ever been interviewed, except in competitions.

\* \* \*

Dr. Grant kept student office hours from 4 to 5 MWF. He looked up from his pad as I tapped on his open door at 4:01 p.m. Monday.

"Ah," he smiled broadly, "it's the man with the Guiccioli rhyme! Come in, Troy; rest from your labors and give me your word!" He gestured at the chair next to his desk.

"I have grievously failed, sir," I said, with mock pathos. "I have only one word, and it's not the right one. I apologize, sir."

"No one has the right one. That's why it's the Great Unfinished Limerick! But tell me what you've got, and let me be the judge. I am all anticipation!"

"Shall I recite it, sir? The full limerick?"

"I won't be content with even one word less than the completed limerick!"

"Yes, sir. Here goes:

The beautiful Countess of Guiccioli
Slept with Lord Byron habitually:
Said she with a wink —
— A lascivious blink:
'Pinch me hard, my Lord B., masochistically.'"

He burst into a guffaw so loud that I jumped. "Priceless!" he chortled. "I've heard dozens, but never that one! Splendid, Troy! Please write it out in your hand, sign it, and give me a copy, dated!"

"Yes sir. Feel free to substitute any other one-syllable verb for 'pinch.'"

Another guffaw followed. "Yeah, I hear it; but 'pinch' is just right. Byronically right. I believe we can mark this assignment complete, don't you? Well-done… Trojan!"

I felt myself blushing intensely.

A shadow crossed the open door. "Frank," Dr. Grant shouted. "Frank, come in here and close the door. Franklin Meyer, this is Troy Tyler, a second year grad and possibly my dissertation student. Troy, this is Professor Meyer, chair of Newcomb English, and a great fan of clever limericks. Frank, Troy has triumphantly finished the Great Unfinished one. Recite it, Troy!"

"Oh, why don't you, sir?" I said, handing him my copy.

And he did. More hilarity followed, and Professor Meyer shook my trembly hand before leaving.

"Woof!" Dr. Grant exhaled, still chuckling, wagging his head. Reaching for his cigarettes, he handed me the pack. I took one and we lit up.

"Sit," he said. "Have you now read some late Byron?"

"I have, sir. 'A Vision of Judgment,' and a good deal about it."

"And…?"

"Well, sir: I'm sorry to say this, understanding and respecting your admiration of Byron's mature work, but it's not much to my taste."

"And why is that?"

"Actually, sir, it's not so much the poem as the genre. I don't think satire suits my…temperament."

He looked hard at me, not smiling. "Your temperament?"

"Um, perhaps that's not quite the right term, sir."

"No. Try another one."

"I've tried several, sir. And I haven't found a better term. Satire strikes me as sort of the opposite of 'romantic.' It's so often, well, negative. Cynical. A lot of what I've read is bitter…and belittling. It lacks sympathy. It scorns…more than it loves, if it loves at all. Its laughter is harsh and unforgiving. I know I'm sounding sentimental, but satire doesn't… well, sir, it doesn't move my heart, or, really, touch it."

He was watching me very closely. I had his attention.

"You don't love satire, then," he said.

"Sir, I don't believe satire loves. A lot of what I've read hates. It encourages my…dislike. Sometimes it hurts."

"It has impact, then. It affects you."

"Well, yes sir. Not the way, say, Keats does…but yes."

"It has power for you, over you?"

"I wouldn't say that. It doesn't move me to act… except to close the book."

He sat back, folded his hands. Looked at his thumb-tips tapping each other. "Thank you," he said, faintly smiling. "That cannot have been easy for you to say to me. But it's very important that you said it. I welcome your candor." He paused, studied his hands, looked back at me. "You're an interesting young man, Troy, and thoughtful. I see that you've *reflected* on the satire you've read, and observed your reaction to it. It's not a sophisticated reaction but I believe it's an honest one, and at this point the honesty is more valuable than the sophistication. I don't believe you're ready — let's say temperamentally ready — to undertake disciplined study of satire. I've told you that I favor Byron's satiric works. We may not presently be a suitable match as director and student. What would you suggest we do?"

"I've actually thought about that, sir. And I have a proposal for you. What if I write an essay for you on Byron's play *Cain*, which is not a satire but it is fairly late, and written while he was also writing *Don Juan*? I have an idea about how imagery works in that play, sort of along the lines you follow in studying Keats's and Shelley's imagery in your book. My paper wouldn't be for credit or anything, but it would give you a chance to see how I think and write about Byron, and maybe tell whether you could...well...re-direct me...to better ends?"

"I know the play," he said, "or at least I've read the play, and although it's melodrama, I agree that the poetry is worthy. Shelley and Goethe thought so too. And it's little written about. I won't promise to critique your paper but I'd be pleased to read it, if your offer is serious, and chat with you about it. We're to regard this as a test of our compatibility over Byron, is that the intent of your proposal?"

"Yes sir. And I am serious, sir."

"Oh, and by the way, Troy: you might want to look at the first stanza of the epic, to learn how Byron pronounced — or wants us to pronounce — the Don's second name."

Imagine my mortification when I did! (It was that fool Park Royal's fault, for ignoring the masterpiece to perform the plays...*in class!*)

Frustrated with efforts to prepare for my interview with Lawyer Hollister, I invited Ben to stop by after work on the Tuesday before Hollister was due at our home the next day to conduct it. What baffled me was how to protect and benefit Mark while trying to promote Father's suitability for a job that might disadvantage my brother. Of course I didn't want to hurt Father's chances, but helping them disfavored Mark, at least as he imagined his future in a new environment. My puzzle was: what *were* Mark's best interests? *Did* getting his senior year at Madison really trump every other consideration? What if Lake Charles's schools were better? The city was larger; it might have finer schools; almost certainly, it offered wider choices. Its most attractive asset might be that it isn't Madison, and could hardly be more provincial, more insular and small-minded than our current home town. The almost guaranteed higher salary at Bethany would benefit us all. Ben would have information about Mark's thinking from those private talks they'd shared at home. Whether he'd confide any of it to me under pressure from my pending interview with Hollister was uncertain. But he agreed to meet for a beer at our home.

"So what should I say in the interview?" I asked him, opening a Pabst and handing it over.

"As little as possible," Ben said. "Let him ask. Answer vaguely. Volunteer nothing."

"It'll sound like I'm hiding something."

"You are. You're hiding everything except what he *has* to know — job-related — about your father. But don't lie about anything. And don't say everything you know about anything. Sometimes you overtalk, Troy. Don't."

"How can I help Mark in this interview? How can I explain how bad this move would be for Mark?"

"You can't, and you mustn't try. Surely you see how that would harm your father. This interview is not about Mark. It's about your father, and maybe a little bit about you. Decide beforehand what you're willing for this guy to know about you, and stick to that. Let's imagine that he asks you: 'What would you like to tell me about your father? Something we don't know from other sources?' Prepare an answer to that one, and look for an opening to use it. Say nothing else about your father unless directly asked. And nothing at all about Mark, even if directly asked. If directly asked, refer him to Mark."

"Okay. But for my information, Ben, I need to know what's so upsetting Mark. I don't want to go in blind about Mark with Hollister. I need to know, specifically, what's eating him up about moving."

"Remember when you moved twice. Those same things that ate you up then are eating him up now, plus a coupla more. You prob'ly do need to know them, though, for the full picture, and to help you deal with Mark. And he didn't tell me they were secret from you.

From your parents, though, absolutely, and the lawyer! Keep the focus on your dad.

"First, baseball: Mark's got second base locked up; most of this year's team is returning next, and Mark's coach is telling the boys they've got a shot at the district championship next season, if they hold together. Mark thinks he might be elected team captain. And he'd love that. He knows that one of the Committee's members coaches Little League in Lake Charles.

"Second: he's been class vice-president two years running, and wants to try for the senior class presidency. It may sound silly and meaningless, but it's really important to him to head up his senior class. Preside at graduation and all that ceremonial stuff. He figures his success at fundraising for uniforms and team trips will get him votes. (And while I'm thinking about it: he's probably right about teachers' recommendation letters for colleges: Lake Charles teachers won't know him well enough to write good letters, detailed, warm letters, and rec letters really are important in application packets.)

"And third: of course there's a girl in the picture."

"What? Mark has a girlfriend? Well, it's about time. Who is she?"

"I won't give you a name. But I'll tell you the issues: she's very young, an eighth grader this year. And she's Cajun. They don't yet date. They hang out together after school. Her parents are of course Catholic, and they're also divorced. She lives with her mom. Mark thinks he's in love. Your parents will of course find this liaison a first-class reason for moving him away from Madison. They cannot know about it. Okay?"

* * *

"Would you care for a cup of coffee, sir? I've brewed a fresh pot."

"I would," Graham Hollister said, easing into a chair and settling his thin, sleek black briefcase onto his lap. "With two sugars, please."

He was tall and slim, pale, with gray temples and black, neatly combed hair, black-framed glasses on his blade of a nose screening dark eyes. The gray suit looked tailored, its narrow lapels cradling a burgundy tie. The long fingers tapered into manicured nails; the unnaturally white hands, lightly veined, rested on the briefcase, then moved gracefully to accept the cup and saucer.

"Thank you for seeing me, Troy; I'm pleased to meet the rest of the family," he smiled. The voice was musical, the enunciation precise. "They spoke well of you."

"I hope so, sir."

He sipped the coffee, set it aside. "That's very good coffee, Troy. I congratulate you. You're not having any?"

"I prefer tea, sir. With lemon." This was untrue. Why was I already lying when Ben had told me not to?

He opened the case, took out a fresh yellow pad, uncapped a fountain pen.

"As you know, we're reviewing your father's qualifications for the senior pastorate at Bethany Baptist in Lake Charles. I'm here for a cordial conversation with you about your father as you've known him for, what, twenty-some years? May I take a few notes as we go along?"

"As you wish, sir."

"Thank you. Now, thinking about your father in his various capacities known to you, what would you say he's particularly good at? At what is he expert?"

"Other than preaching and pastoring, you mean? He's very good at those."

"Yes. Other than those."

"Chess, sir. The board game. He's an excellent chess player."

"With whom does he play? You?"

"No, I couldn't learn the oddball moves."

"Your mother then? Mark?"

"No, sir. Sometimes, when we have a guest."

"Not much practice then?"

"No sir. I guess not."

"Other hobbies? Pastimes? Golf? How does he relax?"

"Oh, he likes to fish, when he gets the chance."

"Does he take you fishing?"

"Sometimes. He usually goes with men from the congregation. They have boats and motors and gear. I've been along a few times."

"Do they take refreshments?"

"Cokes. Chips. Father doesn't drink beer, if that's what you're asking."

"And you?"

"I thought you wanted to talk about Father."

"We're also interested in the family."

"I know what beer tastes like."

He didn't take a note, but he looked at me, half-smiling.

"And at what is your father not so good? Anything particular come to mind?"

"He's no good at disentangling fishing lines. You know, when the line snags on the reel and balls up, or knots up around a tree limb. He has trouble getting it straightened out again."

"Anything else he can't quite manage? Does he get upset easily, when things go wrong or don't suit him?"

"No sir. Father is emotionally stable."

"Does he discipline you and Mark?"

"Of course. He and mother both."

"How?"

"They've both spanked us…when we were smaller. He once slapped me for sassing mother."

"Have you ever been arrested? Gotten a traffic ticket?"

"No."

"How does your father get along with young people in the congregation —youth around your own age, and younger?"

"Oh, just fine, sir. He drops in on our church socials. He can play the piano, you know: one song. It's a boogie-woogie tune he remembers from his piano lesson days, and he likes to play it for the kids. It always gets a big laugh. You know, the preacher doing boogie-woogie!"

"How do you parents get along with each other? Have you ever heard them quarrel, seen them fight?"

"Never, sir. They're very respectful toward each other."

"They must have the occasional argument. Have you never heard them argue?"

"Yes, sir. They argue every Thanksgiving over who gets the turkey's gizzard. They both like to chew the gristle of that piece. Oh, that doesn't sound very nice, does it? Can we scratch that? Let's see: they argue a little whether Father should wear a hat: he's bald, you know, and she always wants him to cover his head. He says his head needs to breathe."

"And church policy? Do they ever argue over church politics?"

"No, sir. They never talk about church business in front of us."

"But you know about your father's candidacy for our job. Have they talked to you and Mark about that?"

"They've talked a little *with* us about that, sir."

"And what do you think about it?"

"It's their decision, sir."

"Of course. But you must have an opinion."

"I don't believe I know enough about it to have an opinion, sir."

"And Mark?"

"I'm sorry, sir; but you must ask Mark about that."

"Are you and Mark close?"

"I'm not sure what you mean."

"Close. Do you run around with your brother? Confide in him, and vice versa?"

"There are four years difference in our ages. No, we don't often run around together. He calls me at school. We talk. I care a lot about him."

"But you don't know what he thinks about a possible move to Lake Charles?"

"Excuse me, sir: but you said this wouldn't be a cross-examination. It's starting to feel like one."

"I said I would interview you. I believe that's what I'm doing. But I don't want you to break any confidences…with your brother. Perhaps we'll talk to him again. How do you think your mother feels about moving?"

"I believe she'd like to. She doesn't seem unhappy here, but I think she's excited about…new opportunities…for the family."

"Are you?"

"I'm not affected. I don't live there any longer. I wouldn't be moving to Lake Charles, even if they do…."

"It smells a little like smoke in here. Do you smoke, and if so, what?"

"Kents, sometimes. Never around my folks. I wouldn't want them to know."

"Understood. Is there anything you'd like to add, Troy, anything else you'd like to say about your father and his ministry, your family, what we've discussed?"

"Yes. Can you tell me why you're interested in him? What you like about him or want out of him, expect from him?"

He stared at me, silently, looked away. "I'm afraid that's confidential," he said, putting away his pad, snapping his case shut, standing. "Thank you for your time. It's been good talking to you," extending his hand.

But at the door he turned back. "Does the name 'Thomas Chatterton' mean anything to you?"

[*Loukas Chalandritsonos* almost slipped out, but, seeing what was happening, I caught it back in time.]

This charade was so obviously planned and staged, I almost laughed. I also almost invented plans for the next hour to postpone any extension of the conversation, but then figured we'd best just get it over with.

"I recognize the name."

"Perhaps we should continue our talk, then. May I sit?"

He resumed his chair, retrieved his pad, and twiddled his pen.

"Who was he — this Chatterton person?"

"You must know, if you know to ask me about him: he was a gifted young English poet of the late eighteenth century, much neglected and abused."

"You wrote about him?"

"Two friends and I collaborated in college on a research and creative writing project for which we received academic credit that counted toward our graduation."

"And you were disciplined for doing so?"

"We were mildly chastened and penalized…for a harmless college prank. It didn't amount to a hill of beans."

"It amounted to enough to get you punished."

"We repented and took responsibility. It's all long ago over and done with."

"We'd like to see a copy of what you wrote."

"Why would you? I told you it was a harmless stunt. We hurt nobody."

"May we borrow your copy?"

"I've no idea where one might be, and I won't look for it. It's nothing you need to see. Whoever told you about it must have seen a copy. Ask them."

"The Dean's files don't seem to have one."

"I guess you'll have to do without one, then."

"Who were your collaborators?"

"I won't tell you. They're guilty of nothing that concerns you. Nor am I."

"We can ask your father."

"Ask him. He never had a copy. He never read it. It wasn't worth his time. Or yours. What is it you expect to learn from seeing a copy of that...ridiculous piece of shit? You're investigating my father. It never did have squat to do with him."

"It's an important record of your behavior. You are his son. We might hire him. We need to be sure...to be sure his family's...well, clean."

I stood. "Mr. Hollister, I don't want to hurt my father's chances with your committee. But you need to remember that I no longer live under my father's roof, nor am I beholden to him or accountable to him, or he to me. But he is an honest, hardworking, respectable, and deeply religious man who deserves a fair appraisal from your committee. Whatever I did or didn't do in the past is done, over, and paid for. Don't punish my father for a meaningless juvenile prank I stumbled into years ago.

My family is as clean as a whistle, and so now I must — respectfully — end this conversation...and tell you goodbye."

January 17, 1962

Dear Father,

Mr. Graham Hollister, a lawyer and member of the Bethany pulpit committee, just interviewed me here. They know about the Chatterton project. Or at least they know there was one. They don't have a copy of it. I said nothing about it but took responsibility for my part in it, and assured Mr. Hollister that we had all three paid our dues for our harmless, meaningless prank all that while ago. But then he got nasty and insulted our family (he actually said that the committee's job is to determine whether we're "clean"), and I asked him to leave. I practically begged him not to let my stupid mischief years ago influence their judgment of you. I'm sorry this has happened, but I thought you should know it did.

Love,
Troy

p.s. I refused to tell him my collaborators' names or give him a copy of our script, for I don't have one and don't know (for sure) anyone who does.

**25**

Classes moved along satisfactorily: in the Shakespeare seminar, I drew "Julius Caesar" as my assignment for a one-hour report to the class later on. Fortunately, I'd seen and liked the movie (Brando, Gielgud, James Mason, Garson, Kerr), and found the play itself riveting drama packed with issues ripe for analysis. Jack had joined the class at mid-year and drawn "Romeo and Juliet." It was our first class together since Anglo-Saxon. He sat by me at the table. The Milton class was your standard 3-hour grad lecture course, with Professor Schwartz, Belinda Schwartz, one of two female professors on the graduate faculty, recognized among Miltonists for her monograph on "Lycidas," of which I knew a little from my research on "Lilacs." She required a term paper, researched, on "Paradise Lost," stipulating, though, that it could not focus on Book IX (the temptation of Eve): "I cannot," she said, "I *cannot* bring myself to read one more syllable of analysis about that scene. I have myself written about it, and so has every other Miltonist, so enough already! There is no more to be said...except what I say in my lectures!" Dr. Grant thought modern poetry began with Hardy, and included Yeats, Eliot, Pound, Frost, Auden, Stevens and Cummings on his syllabus. Jack enrolled in this course too. I admired "Prufrock" but thought "Waste Land" more puzzle than poetry — grandstanding erudition! — and Cummings a lame and unfunny joke. As a subject for my term paper, I chose Yeats's "The Second Coming" and got my A on it, although it contained my most egregious interpretative error ever that made me a laughingstock in the bull pen when — because I too thought it hilarious — I confessed it there: I'd written that the beast's slow-moving thighs referred to sluggish sexual activity. Grant's wryly understated marginal comment: "The beast is walking."

Otherwise, I had the voluntary *Cain* paper to write as well to persuade Dr. Grant that Lord Byron and I were worthy investments of his scholarly expertise. I identified four imagistic motifs in the play that I thought collectively expressed and reinforced Byron's theme on "the inadequacy of man's state to his conceptions" as the protagonist experienced that condition — blood-fire; organic nature; light-darkness; clay-dust — and examined the poet's variations on the motifs and how they articulated and advanced his theme.

"I'm convinced," Jack said, after he'd read a draft. "I especially like the clay-dust part; 'organic nature' may be a little weak and too routine, but the rest is very good, and your climax is tremendous."

Dr. Grant's secretary called me the day after I'd left a copy of the essay for him. "He wants to see you about it," she said.

"It's that terrible?" I gasped, visions of another gaffe like "moving thighs" running through my mind; but I made my way to the office.

"It's superb," Grant said, smiling! "Surprisingly persuasive. Solid and well-written. I respect your wish to focus on the imagery, but you can't so completely ignore the theological implications of the play, which as you know have preoccupied earlier critics. You have to show familiarity with them, and good reasons for subordinating them in your own argument. You can do it in two paragraphs, with notes. It's an honored tradition in scholarship, and as a young man starting out, you can't afford to flout it. I've raised a couple of questions and tinkered a little with your style, but on the whole I believe that with these changes it's ready to go out."

"Out, sir?"

"For review. For publication. Have you thought about where to send it?"

"Um, no sir. Might you have any suggestions?"

"I'm on the board at *Keats-Shelley Journal*, which means I cannot review it for them, for I'm an interested party. But I know other board members and might put in a word. They can at least know you're my student."

"*Am* I your student, sir? Have I passed the test?"

"What say we give it a shot, Trojan? Your paper has encouraged me to take Byron's verse — his so-called 'romantic' verse — more seriously *as verse* than I've done. You've shown me the value of considering it as art, as consciously crafted. And for that I'm grateful. We'll need to negotiate other matters as they will, inevitably, arise. But yes, you've passed your test. We won't ponder too long the fact that you designed it!"

"And you think I should send this essay out...for review?"

"Don't get your hopes up too high. I'll hope for an evaluation, a reader's report that gives you suggestions on how to make the essay even better. How to bring it up to the standards of the journal. Don't be discouraged if they request revision and resubmission. That happens to a lot of us old hands, too. Such a request doesn't mean you failed. It only means you can get better. Do you know how to write a cover-letter?"

"I think so, sir. I've already had one success."

"You *have?*"

*  *  *

Monday, January 22, 1962

Dear Father,

I'm expecting any day now to learn that you've been invited to become pastor of the Bethany Baptist Church in Lake Charles, and that you've happily accepted this wonderful opportunity.

Please allow me to congratulate you and to wish you all the best in your new position.

But this brings us back to the question of what happens to Mark, now that you and Mother may soon be moving. I know you're aware of how disturbed Mark is over the prospect of losing his senior year at Madison High. Surely you can understand why. He has very interesting, very ambitious, even exciting plans for his final school year among long-time and very close friends. I'm sure you and Mother want him to move to Lake Charles with you, but I wonder if you truly believe that would be best for him. Does he really need or deserve to upset his life to that extent just when it's beginning to blossom? I'm certain that such a move right now would cost him severe emotional pain, and perhaps even impair his mental faculties.

So I want to propose an alternative, although he's not aware that I'm doing so. Please don't inform him of what follows until you've replied to me about it.

You know that Mark and Tracy Wright have been close friends forever, and that Mark happily spends Saturdays and sometimes weekends on their plantation. You also know that Tracy and his parents are good and faithful members of our church, and strong supporters of yourself and all aspects of your ministry. You'll remember trusting them with Mark a couple of New Years' Eves ago. You may not remember that Tracy's older sister Marcie is a sophomore at Millsaps, so that her room in the family home is vacant during the school year. What if you and Mother asked the Wrights to consider boarding Mark in Marcie's room during his senior year, after he's helped you move and spent the summer with you? He and Tracy would attend school together and perhaps help out with chores on the farm as they had time. You and Mother would of course pay a reasonable rent to the Wrights from your increased salary. The arrangement would end with Mark's graduation, and he would move to your home in Lake Charles before going off to college.

Assuming the Wrights' agreement, where are the flaws in this idea? I would be willing to speak with them about it, but surely it's your place to float the suggestion to them first. Would you think and pray about it, and please let me know your thoughts? I know Mother won't want to part from her baby boy, so we would have to depend upon you to convince her that the temporary separation is necessary and in his best interests. And besides, weekend visits both ways are entirely feasible.

Thank you sincerely for your sympathetic attention to this overlong letter. I look forward to your reply, either by phone or mail.

Your loving son,
Troy

\* \* \*

Mr. Carlisle's corporate party for his local business associates was scheduled to happen on our ground floor beginning at 6 p.m. on Tuesday, February 27th, exactly one week before Mardi Gras, although the balls and parades and soirees would have been intoxicating the city with Carnival juice since Christmas. Our holiday decorations had long since disappeared under the hands and machines of professional house-cleaners, and would soon be replaced by the Mardi Gras colors of purple, green and gold as arranged by Mr. Carlisle's caterers all over our living space. Nobody had thought to reserve a hotel room for us on the 27th — desirable French Quarter hotel rooms were usually booked years in advance — and of course the Monteleone Hotel suite permanently reserved by Mr. Carlisle's business was long ago assigned to Mardi Gras guests; so he gave us taxi fare, along with dinner cash, to get us to and from the Quarter for our night on the town. Kaiden chose Arnaud's at 7 p.m. for our meal (so we could get a peek at his father's guests on our way out the door), and used one of his Broussard connections to book a table for us at this always popular venue, since staff were ever eager to check out the competition. In jackets and ties but prepared to shed them for the bars — our bracelets freshly brushed and in place — we headed off for the St. Charles trolley, saving the travel funds for later.

Our menu selections (or Kaiden's; he ordered for us both): shrimp Arnaud; turtle soup; crab cakes; broccoli; Caesar salad; chocolate hazelnut pot de crème; Sauvignon Blanc. Kaiden declared the whole feast "ambrosial," and I reckon it was, but I found the setting — however elegant — too starchily formal for comfortable eating or easy conviviality, notwithstanding all the alcohol apparent on every table. Kaiden tried some light flirtation with our waiter to encourage familiarity, but he neither bent nor wrinkled. My roommate's knowledge of wine and cutlery and fine-dining protocol mightily impressed me, but the waiter — used to it? — didn't bat an eyelash.

"Your father's generosity is astounding," I said. "Please thank him most sincerely for me!"

"The price of getting us out of his way." He tucked three ten-dollar bills under the edge of his plate.

"Whoa!" I said. "Seriously?"

"It's expected. Look, it's still kind of early for the bars. Why don't we just stroll Bourbon for a while and take in the sights?"

No parades were underway but color swarmed the sidewalks and streets, bedecked the balconies overhanging Bourbon, flashed from shrill neon offering flesh and folly, billowed from the bunting stretched across the upper floors of bars and restaurants and shops and burly houses packed cheek by jowl in both directions down the blocks. Well-dressed patrons like ourselves caromed off each other through the teeming streets, those not carrying foaming plastic cups instead gripping signature Pat O'Brien ice-packed goblets to the brim with the potent red "hurricane" drink mix. More casually, women in lingerie and negligees and men in briefs and sprinkle-spangled jockey straps, and hunky males in heels and bikinis strutted about, posed for cameras, swirled and swilled, shrieked and shimmied to the deafening cacophony of rock, jazz, pop, swing, r & b, black, ragtime, dixieland, gypsy, and zydeco flooding through open doors. Small bands gathered and dissolved. Paired policemen on horseback threaded through the mass, their mounts indifferently spattering waste.

"Like the looks of that one?" Kaiden asked, poking me in the ribs as a young man in sailor togs strolled by, giving us both a meaningful look. Uniforms identified military personnel, police, athletes, carpenters and plumbers and mechanics (with tools), priests and nuns, chefs and waiters, ballet dancers, safari hunters (with weapons and whips), ships' captains, pirates and witches and Tarzans and astronauts. Ball gowns, bridal gowns, evening gowns, night and judicial and academic and clerical gowns spun and scattered motley street rubbish while beer empties piled four-deep in the gutters. Bright and dark, skimpy and voluminous, costumes featured cherubic and demonic wings, feathers fluffy or flat, blossoms, ivy, fruit, capes, masks, veils and trains, bells and finger cymbals, head-coverings of every variety: helmets squatted, tiaras sparkled, hardhats crouched, crowns glittered, derbies perched, sombreros fanned, cowboys fussed with the angles of their hats, and towering, pillared rainbow hair perilously teetered. The puckish sailor's tilted cap teased from heads of both genders. Fairies and elves and gnomes and imps pranced singly or in packs, like rodents, darted hither and yon among bunnies, kittens, chipmunks, and cats. Make-up caked almost every face. And beads, plastic beads, thousands and thousands upon myriads of multi-colored strands of multi-sized beads littered like sown shrapnel, spilled buckshot.

"Can we get out of here?" I shouted at Kaiden. "It's making me sick."

"Really?" he asked, concerned.

"No, but I'm not much liking it."

"Okay. Let's head down to Jean LaFitte's Blacksmith Shop. Right around the corner from LaFitte's in Exile. One or the other of them is the oldest queer bar in New Orleans, dating back to the 1700's. You've probably heard of them."

I had, from him. We showed our I.D.'s at the door of the Shop and stepped in. I thought the building itself, on the outside, almost attractive — stout, solid, and sturdy; but the ill-lit interior was also ill-kempt, the stucco walls soot-smeared, with exposed patches of board where paint had peeled; scattered frames held portraits too darkly smeared for identification; illegible black graffiti crawled the walls. The unshaded overhead bulbs cast a dull dun tint on rickety, unmatched chairs and tilty tables. Not at all sinister or threatening as I'd half-expected, the place reeked of dilapidation, of shabby, decrepit seediness; it felt not thoroughly clean, the smell of stale mixing with that of weed. Patrons slumped and huddled at the bar, or around an old-fashioned black stovepipe heater in a far corner, its low flame barely visible. Several wore sad, lackluster drag.

"You want a table?" Kaiden asked. "A drink?"

"I don't think so," I truthfully said, aware that I was probably disappointing him. "We've seen enough to say we have. Let's move on?"

"You haven't given us a chance!" a high voice rang out from the bar as we made for the door.

"Next time," Kaiden amiably waved back.

Lafitte's In Exile was louder, livelier, fresher, almost crowded, a lot of the well-buffed men shirtless. I was right away taken by a sign on the wall defining "Queer" as "Extraordinary." The coolest thing was a railed balcony on the second floor overlooking the first. We climbed up and took a table for two. Four guys at the next table smiled and nodded. One pantomimed removing a tie and jacket.

"Right!" I said, and tugged mine loose and away. The guy dragged an empty chair toward us for hanging our clothes.

"Thanks," Kaiden said. "We're Troy and Kaiden."

"Really?" the same guy asked. "Those sound like real names."

I looked at Kaiden, puzzled. The guy clarified:

"A lot of Tulane guys use fake names."

"No," Kaiden said; "we're real. Should we...use fakes? Pseudonyms? We didn't know."

"As long as they match the ones on your fake I.D.'s." We all laughed.

"I'm Carl...truly," the guy said. "Your first time?"

"Our first time in here," Kaiden said. "How'd you know we're...Tulane?"

"Oh, you guys all look exactly alike," from another of the group. "Your pal's just a little blonder than most of you."

I hoped it was too dim to see my blush. Did you thank a guy for coming on to you?

"I'll have white wine," Kaiden said to the hovering waiter. "Troy?"

"Juice," I said, without thinking. "Cider."

They snickered. "We just finished a bottle of wine over dinner," Kaiden said.

They'd shifted their chairs so that we all faced each other, more or less, kind of inviting us into their circle.

"So you're getting a head start on Carnival?" Carl asked.

"Actually, we're escaping Kaiden's father. He's borrowing our house."

"You own a house? I'm Stan."

Kaiden frowned my way and shook his head no.

"No, it's his. We rent from him."

"You're roommates, then?" Carl asked. "Lovers?"

"We're boyfriends," I said, sipping my cider.

"Looking for more?" Carl continued, grinning.

"Not consciously," Kaiden said.

"Then why're you out here on the happy hunting grounds?"

Kaiden tried to explain but everybody was laughing now, and nobody wanted an explanation anyway.

"That's why *we're* out here," Carl added, "and everybody else in sight. So if you change your mind….!" He shifted his chair back to their table. "Good meeting you, boyfriends!"

I found myself slightly disappointed. We'd actually been cruised. And showed ourselves rubes. It might have been nice to chat with these boys…a little older than us, more experienced in this world than us, probably able to tip us off to its rules and habits and expectations. I'd blown it.

"He liked us," Kaiden quietly said. "That was nice."

"Did he actually make a pass?"

"The other guy did; the one who liked your hair."

"Was I supposed to say something?"

"Did you want to?"

"No. But now I'm kind of…uncomfortable. Like we're being shunned. Over a faux-pas, or something."

We finished our drinks quickly, grabbed our jackets, waved to the gang, and headed for the door, drawing looks as we went.

"Don't be strangers!" somebody called. "Tra-la!"

"What're they looking at?" I asked. "Are our flies unzipped?"

"Don't check yours. They'll think it's a signal."

"Dixie's Music Bar, or Dicks and Daisies, or just Dixie's," Kaiden said, "is the centerpiece of queer life in New Orleans, at least during Carnival. It's just down there on the corner of Bourbon and St. Peter, with a huge marquee and a tuba over the door, and always a bunch of guys milling around outside. Miss Yvonne Dixie Fasnocht owns the place, and she sometimes shows up to entertain with her clarinet or sax. Pat O'Brien's is a few doors down St. Peter to the right; it's got two grand pianos on the stage and two big broads banging away on them all the time, and the drunken crowd sometimes sings along. Every queer who loves the Quarter stops by one or both bars on every trip. You can see Dixie's from here."

From here it appeared to occupy the entire block: a vast, barn-like structure, two-storied, with a chimneystack and at least four gables and an iron filigreed railing running completely around the second floor balcony, doors opening out along the entire length of it. You could hear the rhythmic thump of the music a block away. Inside, a throbbing sea of sweaty bodies swayed and heaved, pitched and surged, flung about heedlessly across the jam-packed dance floor slashed by blades of purple, green and violet light from overhead spots. Through a far door, we glimpsed the draped stage of a back room dedicated to scheduled drag shows, Kaiden said. A shifting mass in there apparently awaited the next one.

"Want to check it out?" Kaiden, asked.

"Let's dance," I said, and we merged into the roiling, steaming crush.

One hour and one beer each later, we sprawled into the chairs at the table we'd been lucky enough to snare, winded but invigorated by the exercise and the come-hither glances and batted eyes we'd fetched from other customers.

"But it's not really a cruising joint," Kaiden explained; "of course people do, but Miss Dixie's pretty strict about keeping hanky-panky to a minimum. You want another beer?"

"No, I'm ready to go. This racket…!"

We tucked our shirttails, gathered our jackets and moved toward the door where four well-dressed, well-groomed young men, mid-twenties, were just arriving. They paused, blocking our exit. The taller one, his eyes shining in the floodlight, looked directly at me, then at Kaiden, and back at me. He smiled.

"Well, well!" he said, "look who's here! It's, um… wait…give me a sec: it's Troy, isn't it? We know you, don't we, boys," looking to his companions, who looked doubtful. "Sure we do. It *is* Troy, isn't it? From Louisiana. At Tulane." He extended his hand. "I'm Kyle. We've been wondering when you'd show up down here."

I looked at Kaiden, who gawked.

"I'm sorry," I said; "I don't believe I know you…."

"Not yet," Kyle said; "but you will. This is William…Gordon…and Crew. Or at least that's who we are tonight."

"Sirs," a waiter interrupted. "You need to move away from the door."

Re-situated to the side, we shook hands all round, me muttering Kaiden's name, he staring dumbstruck.

"I'm sorry," I stumbled; "I'm afraid you've mistaken me for someone else. Unlikely as that seems, with my name."

"Your name," Kyle said, "and your reaction to my using it, is how I know I'm right. But not to worry. Let me welcome you to…our acquaintance. We'll be in touch. Tra-la!"

And they strode — or swished — into the crowd.

Outside, on the walk, Kaiden erupted: "What the *fuck*?! Who are those creeps, and how do you know them?"

"Easy, Kaiden; I *don't* know them. But don't make a scene out here. Let's walk."

A few steps along, obviously steaming but holding back, he continued: "You owe me here, Troy; let's hear it!"

"I'm as puzzled as you. I never saw them before. I don't know them. How they knew my name, or who they thought I was, I've no idea. Truly."

"But they also knew you're at Tulane and where you're from. How would they, if you've never met? And how do they know your contact info? They said they'd be in touch. Are they going to show up at our front door…?"

"It's a mistake, Kaiden. It has to be a mistake. I never saw them before. We'll probably never see them again. Can we forget that…mistaken encounter, and finish our evening?"

"I can't forget they know you!"

Napoleon House — so-called, Kaiden explained, because once reserved for the former Emperor after his exile who then died before he could claim occupancy — stood at the corner of Chartres and St. Louis Streets, and was normally a quieter bar, even sedate, Kaiden said, than it turned out to be one week before official Mardi Gras beset the Quarter. It consisted of two rooms with old, scarred round tables and wooden chairs, and long-legged, high-backed stools at the bar, its walls decked with historic pictures and photos and newsprint that related countless stories about the site and the state of Louisiana and the bar's owners and patrons through the 200 years of its existence.

"Somewhere up there," Kaiden said, waving at the walls, "somewhere in there is probably the story about Napoleon once saying his sale of Louisiana was the worst decision of his life."

"What if he saw it now?!"

In the front room, a sideboard held a box phonograph, and on the shelves behind it, almost to the ceiling, hundreds of classical records, which customers were invited to select for playing on the hi-fi box. Unspoken but faithfully observed rules kept human relations civil around the machine, and everyone understood that the music was background to, not competition against, the quiet conversations going on at the tables and bar.

"I can pick whatever I like?" I asked Kaiden.

"If there's nobody else around at the time."

Nothing was playing at the moment, so I made my way over and scanned the collection. It was pretty standard classical, and so mostly familiar to me.

"Pimm's Cup is the house drink here," Kaiden called over to me, around our waiter at the table.

"Just tonic for me, please."

I selected a recording of Beethoven's "Pathetique" sonata by Wilhelm Kempff. I'd played the first movement of the sonata on my senior recital but hadn't mastered the final rondo.

"Beethoven," I answered Kaiden's question. "A favorite."

"Nice," he said, sipping his Pimm's. "So's this. Want some?"

"No thanks; what is it?"

"Well, Pimms. A liqueur. Like gin, with fruit. Very British. More for summer than now. You feeling better."

"Sure. So why is drag such a big deal at Mardi Gras?"

"Well, one story is that way back the parade floats began featuring handsome young men from the best families dressed in women's clothes. But the guys always had to carry with them on their person one article of *men's* clothing, and get out of the women's dresses before sunset, because drag was illegal."

"You ever done drag, or wanted to?"

"Never in public. I used to sometimes dress up in my mother's things, just to see what I looked like. I kind of liked clumping around in high heels."

"Make-up?"

"I smeared on lipstick a coupla times. Mother said I messed up her tube. What about you?"

"Well, yeah. As a school assignment. You remember that hit 'Hernando's Hideaway,' from *Pajama Game*? In my high school speech course we had to lip-sync a record in front of the class — perform the lyrics — and because of the castanets and all on the recording, I dressed up in Spanish drag, with tortoise-shell combs and a knitted shawl and a big flowery skirt and heels, and a black-lace veil, and fish-net gloves up to my elbows! I was ugly as sin but they said I was very good, and the teacher was so impressed she cast me in the lead — a drag role — of *Charley's Aunt* in the next semester's play. Where I was also, they said, very good again!"

"No kidding? Wow! Right out there in public!"

"Photo and headline on page one of the school paper!"

"And did you actually *like* getting dressed up?"

"Well, that's the thing: I didn't much. I liked the attention. But it was awkward and uncomfortable, and it wasn't a good look — I mean, I was part of the play's big joke and didn't need to look good. But I never understood why it should be so funny, or what everybody was laughing at. And I don't at all understand why all these queers *like* dressing up as women...why they want to? What's the kick for them?"

"It's funny because we're gawky in women's wear. And we like to get laughs."

"On the street, yeah; but not on the drag stage. Drag show audiences aren't laughing, have you noticed?

They're open-mouthed awe-struck! Pop-eyed with wonder. Those eyes beam envy. They want to be those performers."

"Well, don't some queers feel more like girls than boys?" Kaiden asked.

"I don't. I doubt you do. Why do those others?"

"Lots of queers're sissies. Isn't sissy girly? Girlish?"

"Sure. But what're we missing in being queer if we're not girlish? Are we supposed to try to act girlish and skip rope and hop-scotch and…?"

"Cook?" he asked. "What're you saying, Troy?"

"I didn't mean you. You're not girlish. Here's what I'm trying to figure out: Is drag popular with queers because it lets them look and act like what they wish they were instead of boys? I never wished that, did you? And second: why are they coming on *as* girls to the guys they want to attract? They present these ugly caricatures of girls to the very boys they'd love to bed! I don't get the logic, do you?"

"No, I never wanted to be female."

"And I'm also asking this: what does it *say* about being queer that you want to look female? Where's the connection between queer and drag?"

"What do you think made you so good as a female in that play? Was it the queer thing in you that enjoyed looking girly?"

"No. I was good because I'm a good actor. I acted a role that required me to act girly. So I did. It had nothing to do with my…my sexual…preferences."

"Well, maybe it's *about* something sexual. What if there's something about queer sex…?" He broke off.

"What?"

"I dunno. I just thought: maybe drag says, 'This is what I am sexually. What I sexually *do*.' Maybe drag admits…announces 'I am, sexually, the vessel…the only way I know how to be!'"

We both went very quiet and still. This was not merely bold. It was unprecedented. This was, so to speak, virgin ground; we had hardly a clue how to tread it. Our eyes locked, and looked away.

"Not here or now," I finally breathed. "Let's get some air."

In the back seat of the taxi, we held hands and kept quiet. Could he be right? Was it that subtle? There was nothing subtle about drag. Was it that straightforward and plainspoken? Unlikely. It did appear to suggest the connection, or *a* connection, I'd said I sought, between queerness and drag, but it was so startling, even shocking, and so far-reaching, and so demanding of further investigation, I was almost sorry to have it. Kaiden's demeanor was impenetrable: did he anticipate ramifications of what he'd said, or did his silence signify boredom with the subject? My own disquiet wasn't without fear, but what was I frightened of? I squeezed his hand and brought it into my lap. He tucked his head into my neck.

It was well after midnight but Mr. Carlisle's party still rollicked on, its shadows flickering across our translucent living-room sheers. Chauffeurs dozed in several of the limos parked along Magazine.

"In the back," Kaiden said, leading me past the side veranda toward the so-called garden, where we picked our way carefully through the weeds and ornaments to a long bench near the rear wooden fence.

"Here," he said, "until they've gone."

He shed his jacket, folded it, tucked it against the warped arm-rest of the bench. "For your head," he said. I stretched out, my spine against the back of the bench, and he slid in against me, his own spine an inch from the edge. We snuggled up to await clearance of the house.

After a while I asked: "We're not like them, are we Kaiden?"

"All the queers, you mean?"

"Yes. Them. Are we like that?"

"I don't know how you mean."

"I just don't think we are. I think we're different. And what we have, with each other, is different. Don't you think queerdom itself is sort of coarse and crude, even vulgar? It's all noise and drink and cruising and hooking up...and...I don't know, hysterical! Frantic. Everything's always...overwrought. It sounds prissy to say, but it's so...unrefined! It has no class. I wonder sometimes where's the gentleness and tenderness, you know? Like this. This is queer too, idn' it, but it's sweet and soft...and gracious. Special. It's different... and special."

"I dunno, Troy. What we've got is special, all right, but I don't know how different. We're just not seeing the other side of what we saw tonight. They prob'ly get quiet and gentle too, doncha think?"

"It's hard to imagine, they're just so everlastingly… loud and…you know… hyperactive. It's hard to imagine that they *feel* the same as we do…like, now. Would they be *comfortable* with us out here now?"

"Well, were you 'comfortable' dancing with me earlier? With them?"

"I'm never comfortable dancing. I'm not a good enough dancer. Alison used to say we didn't dance; we just made-out standing up. But yes, I was comfortable dancing with you. I tuned 'them' out. I didn't much like being around them…surrounded by them."

"You didn't have a good time tonight?"

"I had a great time…a wonderful time with you, Corky…Kaiden. And I'm having a better one with you now. I guess maybe I just don't like the…well…the interference and distraction. It does, though, I guess, help define the difference, you know, between us and them."

"It's a difference in taste, not a difference in being. In queerness, there's no difference. We're all in this… queerness…together."

"No, I don't accept that. I don't believe that. I wish you didn't believe that. There's a difference in *essence*, somehow. I feel it keenly. Essentially, we're different from them. Like spiritually, or something. We have to be. Look, I *have* to hold onto the specialness we have, you and I. That specialness, and the difference it spells, makes this so fucking valuable! It's what makes it acceptable! Don't you get that?"

"Are you getting mad, Troy? Please don't. I said this is special. Okay?" He stroked my cheek, traced my lip.

"Okay?" he repeated, pulling up, looking down into my eyes.

"Thank you for this fantastic evening," I whispered. "Now kiss me. And make it special!"

26

March 5, 1962

Dear Troy,

I'd rather discuss these matters with you in person, but since a visit doesn't appear convenient right now, I'm writing instead, first with an apology for my delay in replying to your recent letters, and second with some news you may find interesting. You will understand that we've lately been very busy.

Thank you for the report on your interview with Mr. Hollister, and for your defense of our family's honor against his imputations. You overstepped in asking him to leave but I respect your impulse. I've heard nothing about the matter from the committee, so we may not need to concern ourselves with the interview at this time.

Meanwhile, I have received a cordial invitation from the Search Committee to join Bethany's clerical staff as its senior pastor, pending the satisfactory completion of on-going negotiations between ourselves. I have provisionally accepted the invitation.

Your mother and I very much appreciate your concern about your brother Mark and your thoughtful suggestions on how we together can meet new challenges. But we do not believe boarding him with our friends the Wrights through his next school year is the best thing for him. We agree, however, that removing him to a new environment at this juncture is not in his best interest. Here then is what we propose: I will move with my personal things and essential furnishings into the parsonage in Lake Charles as soon as it can be made ready, probably within three months. It's empty now, but we've asked for some renovations. Your mother will assist in the move but remain, with Mark, in our home here until it is required by my replacement. Adjustments will then be made for Mark's continuance in school until he graduates. He and your mother will then join me in the Lake Charles home. You would be welcome to visit any time.

Bethany will provide me with a car and a small travel allowance while your mother keeps the Plymouth for her use here. She and I will visit, here and there, as often as we conveniently can, but her primary residence will remain in Madison until Mark graduates. We hope that both of you boys will find these temporary arrangements satisfactory in the circumstances.

The situation is still to some degree fluid. No contract has yet been signed. I have not officially resigned my office here. But pending unexpected developments, it appears that our family will relocate to Lake Charles. I'm informing Mark later today. Your mother and I have prayed long and hard about this matter, and are persuaded that God is calling us to this new ministry. We hope that you will assist us in the transition as you are able, and that you will come to rejoice with us in new opportunities. Please visit when you can.

Your loving father,
(signed)

p.s. The Lake Charles parsonage has three bedrooms and a den. Your mother finds herself in need of an office, so we are thinking of giving her the third bedroom for such a purpose. If you anticipate needing space with us for an extended time, perhaps you should so indicate now. For your always welcome visits, you might use the den or negotiate with Mark.

\* \* \*

Dear Monte,

Kaiden (Corky) and I want to give you a small dinner party. Would it be okay if we invited our friends Jack and Ben to meet you here for dinner one night during your visit? Jack, who remembers seeing you at the bus stop on your earlier visit, is my grad school buddy, and Ben is an LCC college friend who knows Jack, writes, and works as a mechanic at two motorcycle repair shops here in N.O. Ben also volunteers at a community theater and thinks he might try acting sometime.

Would you also please give me your arrival and departure info? Are you flying or driving or bussing? I need you to be as specific as you can, since Kaiden works some afternoons and most evenings, so we'll have to arrange things around his schedule. We expect you to stay here with us. I'll be free to show you around. I'm thinking about an afternoon cruise down the Mississippi on one of the big old steamboats. You needn't bring dress clothes but of course we want to see you in your uniforms! It should be pretty comfortable outdoors while you're here. You'll be coming from Houston, right?

Thanks! I'm so excited to see you and catch up!

Your roomie,
Troy

*　*　*

"Jack," I nudged him as our Shakespeare seminar dismissed the next afternoon, "how about we stroll over to the Park for a while, if you've got time?"

"Good idea," he said, smiling and gathering his things. "Clean off some blood and guts." The class had been considering *Titus Andronicus*, arguably Shakespeare's most violent, bloodiest tragedy.

Outside, the breeze had warmed, the sky had cleared, and faint hints of spring sifted the air. Early daffodils nodded along the curb; pink buds peeked; birds trilled. Beyond the gate, Audubon Park turned green.

"Yeah," I agreed; "that's a nasty one. And not very good. How've you been, Jack? I've missed talking with you."

"Really?" he asked, amiably enough but sounding slightly surprised. "Well, come to that, I've missed you too. But hold on: I need a cigarette after all that *Titus*, don't you?"

"How're things at Mrs. Burkhart's place?" I asked. "The Creoles good?"

"Hardly ever see them. Mrs. B. dropped by last week to pick up some spring clothes and actually knocked on my door. Poked her head in, I guess checking for girls! First time she ever did that."

"Have you started on your "Romeo" report yet?"

"Barely. I may write about Tybalt. He's gone by Act III!"

We laughed. "And what about the paper for Dr. Grant? You've picked a poem?"

"Oh, yes. I knew right away what I wanted to work on there. You might be interested. Care to take a guess?"

"Lord, Jack, I wouldn't know where to begin, there're so many. What?"

"You're not thinking...or remembering. You could guess it."

I saw he teased, but I was blank.

"Well, Auden," he said.

"Ah. 'Lay Your Sleeping Head....'"! Of course."

"And Grant approved it. As my topic."

"Well, be sure and let me see it when you're done. Something you might publish, you think?"

"Who knows? I might try. I need to get something into print. Have you heard anything about your *Cain* essay?"

"*Keats-Shelley Journal* has it. It may take six months for any report. I'm probably going to do something on imagery for the seminar. But I don't have a poem yet for Grant. Maybe Hardy, whom I like a lot, don't you?"

"I do. Under-rated as a poet; everybody loves the novels so."

"You've read *Jude*?"

"Oh my yes. I'd love someday to get my analytical hands on Sue Bridehead!"

"Or around her throat!"

We laughed.

"Not to suggest any connection...but do you see Bailey?"

He sniggered. "It's a thought, a connection with Sue! No, I don't see Bailey, except once in a while around the bullpen, where she's not much either. I think she's running with the History TA's."

"Are you seeing anyone, socially?"

"Not really, no. A couple of my students once in a while, and I know you don't approve. One current, one former. And there's this small group of guys, former Tulanians, I have a drink with now and then. But no, not like you mean, I'm not seeing anybody."

"'As I mean,' I think you mean!"

"Okay," he said, and we laughed again.

"Are we okay about all that Bailey stuff, Jack? I want us to be."

"I guess so. Wouldn't you say?"

"I want you to know I'm sorry I was so awful about it. So mean and ugly and unfair. You do understand that I was just jealous. Insanely jealous. And hurt. But I needn't have made such a terrible mess of it."

"Well, we misbehaved. And maybe something else: I've wondered if I wanted to make you jealous. Had you thought of that?"

"No. I hadn't. Whoa."

"I don't know, now. But maybe we can agree we all pretty royally fucked things up."

"Yeah, we for sure did that," I admitted.

Jack leaned down and plucked a daffodil blossom. "Peace," he said, handing it to me.

"Peace," I repeated, taking it, and almost tearing up.

"You might want to know that I've bought a pack of condoms," he said, "just in case opportunity calls!" We both laughed.

"Well," I mused, "maybe something good did come out of all that…if you remember to use them!"

"How's Kaiden? Yawl getting along and all?"

I instinctively pulled a cuff over my bracelet.

"Oh yeah. Did I say he has a job? He's interning at Broussard's Restaurant in the Quarter. And hawking their appetizers and his own in the afternoons on the streets. He seems very happy with the arrangement, and says he's learning the business. Which reminds me….

"I wanted to invite you to dinner…at our place. On Tuesday the 20th. It's an occasion! Do you remember, back at LCC, when my old friend Monte Trevalyn visited me there? He was the Air Force Lieutenant you saw and admired at the bus stop the morning he left. You said at the time you'd like to make out with him! So… here's another chance! Monte's coming for another visit during our spring break. If you're in town, Kaiden and

I want you to dine with us and Ben Moore, whom you already well know. Kaiden's keen to prepare a meal for more than two people!"

"Well of course I'd love to come! Yes, I'll be in town. I've got to get on all these paper assignments and student themes. I would be honored to come. You recall you never let me in the door before!"

"Great. I'll tell Kaiden and ask Ben. We'll be casual. I'll let you know about times. Get it on your calendar."

We headed back across the trolley tracks.

"What'd you do for Mardi Gras, Jack?"

"Oh, those guys I mentioned? They rent a French Quarter apartment, above Royal, for a week every year at Mardi Gras, and invite friends to use it for a week leading up to the day. It's party-time 24-7 for that week. I popped in there a couple of times."

"C'mere, Jack," I said, stepping onto the grass of the campus. "Sit down. I have to ask you something."

"What?" he said, hesitating. "What're you doing?"

"Please," I said, sitting. "These guys….? Is one of them named 'Kyle'?"

"Well, yeah; but how'd you know?"

"Oh, shit!" I said. "Oh fucking shit! We met him. Kaiden and I met him. Four of him. At Dixie's. Just the other night! I can't hardly believe this."

"They like Dixie's, for certain," Jack said. "But how'd yawl meet?"

I started laughing, and could barely stop; probably in relief, partly at the coincidence. New Orleans is as small as Madison!

"No, no," I said. "You first. Tell me all about these boys of yours. "

"Well, it's sort of a club. A queer club. They're trying to get official Krewe status with the Mardi Gras people. Most went to Tulane. And they kind of recruit — very carefully and discreetly recruit — like-minded Tulane students, grad students and some undergrads. They cruise the bars, on the hunt, so to speak, and think they can tell college students by the looks of them, especially Tulanians. But they also cruise the college yearbooks, just to see what's out there. They've got a collection of annuals in that Royal Street apartment. That's where they meet. I guess it belongs to one of them. So how do you know Kyle?"

"This is unbelievable, Jack, but it's the truth: Kaiden and I ran into four of them, including this Kyle, when we were leaving Dixie's a week before Mardi Gras; and Kyle claimed to know me. Used my name. Placed me at Tulane and in Louisiana. Said they'd been looking for me...down there. It like to've scared the shit out of me, and I've worried about it ever since. But I did get my photo taken my first year at Tulane, and it came out in the small grad section of the yearbook that year. I've seen it. Maybe Kyle did. But how he remembered it, I can't imagine. This is all crazy, Jack. What does it mean? Should I be concerned?"

"You should be complimented. These are good guys, Troy. They're all smart, sophisticated, pretty well-off, good families, civic-minded, and queer. Some have political connections. They might ask you to join their little club. I don't know what fees are, but I'm pretty sure there are some. They're not dangerous. They're not going to report you as queer. They might come onto you, but that's just part of their shtick. They come on to everybody, especially Kyle, who knows he's hot. But they all are. Anyhow, that's who they — we — are. I don't belong, but they treat me well, and sort of like I do belong. They're probably still checking me out. They'll love it that we know each other!"

"But how...why'd Kyle remember my photo? Out of hundreds?"

"Kyle's phenomenal, in lots of ways."

"Geez, Jack! This is amazing. You're not making it up? Can I tell Kaiden? He should know too, just to be clear about who they are...and what happened. Wow, this is a story for the dinner table, with Monte!"

"So, Troy: You remember Mrs. Burkhart's home is a block and a half from where we're now sitting. Why don't you come up and have a look at my room now?"

"You know what, Jack? I'd like to. I really would. But you know I can't. I just can't."

"You can." He paused. Plucked at some grass. "But I guess I understand why you say you can't. It's okay. I expect there'll be another time...for us. Don't you?"

"Maybe. Thank you for inviting me. I'd better get the trolley home. I'm really, really glad we had this talk, Jack. It's meant a lot to me. And not just about the guys."

"Me too," he said, giving me a quick little hug.

"Get us on your calendar," I said. "Tuesday the 20th."

\* \* \*

Hey Troy,

In by air at 8:57 a.m. Saturday 17th from Houston. Out at 9:50 a.m. on Thursday 22nd. I'll grab a bus to your neighborhood. It's for more than three days. Do I smell bad already?

The dinner sounds great! Looking forward to seeing Corky and sampling his food. Of course I want to meet your other friends…especially anyone who admires my regalia!

Whatever you want to show me I'll be happy to see. Mostly I want to see as much of you as possible, take that however you want to. Except not as an offense! Thank you for inviting me to stay with you two. I gladly accept.

Can't wait!
Ciao. M.

\* \* \*

"D'you want to take the Nash and meet him?" Kaiden asked. "I could make a late breakfast for us and see him before going to work."

"Oh, Kaiden! Could I? I'd love to surprise him at the gate! But it might be a little late for breakfast. A snack, though? Tea?"

"Have you decided where you want to put him?"

"How about the blue guest room? It's not as sissy as the yellow one, and the blue will flatter his tan. He'll be tanned, of course, but his skin is naturally darker than mine."

"I'll check to be sure the bed has sheets. He can share your bathroom and shower, right? I mean, yawl were roommates. I'll put in fresh towels. What else do we need to think about? Maybe a bathrobe? D'you have a spare? No, wait. I do."

"He can borrow mine."

I'd asked Ben to meet me for lunch at The Maple Street Cafe, near Tulane — with the best roast beef sandwiches on heavily mayo-ed white bread in town or out of it — to invite him to dinner, but I first had more pressing news, which he anticipated by asking, as he sat down, "How's Mark?"

"Father's provisionally accepted an offer and Mark is fine! Hey, Ben!"

"Wow! Really? That's terrific news. But what happens to Mark?"

"You don't know, then." I filled him in.

"Well, how do you feel about it?"

We ordered the sandwiches with drafts. Ben wanted a side of dill pickles.

"So long as Mark gets to finish his school, I'm fine. I'm not really affected. Father pointed out that Mother gets the third bedroom for an office, so I'll have the den sofa for visits, but I don't think either of us expects there to be many of those."

"It sounds too easy, doesn't it, too good to be true? I'm sorry Mark had to go through all that…pain…and doubt."

"We both should probably call him. Father must have told him by now."

"And it's okay for me to know? And for him to know I know?"

"Well, since it's not official, and Father hasn't actually resigned, and his congregation only suspects, it's probably best not to spread the word to any Madison-ites or Baptists you know. And it might be fun for you to let Mark tell you. You could call him and open the door."

"I was thinking the same thing. I'll do it that way."

"*And*," I said, "I'm inviting you to dinner at our home, Kaiden's and mine. With Jack. Tuesday the 20th at 6. I'll remind you. You remember my great friend Monte Trevalyn…who made me miss the first Chatt Club meeting? He's now an Air Force Lieutenant and is coming to visit in a couple of weeks. He flies fighter jets out of Nellis AFB near Las Vegas. I thought maybe yawl could compare engines or something?"

"He might teach me to make mine louder," Ben laughed. "He's your age?"

"Almost exactly. Jack got a look at him when he visited LCC. He's a great guy, and I want all yawl to meet him. You'll come to dinner?"

"You and he were…um…*really* close friends…at the camp?"

"We were roommates. And yes, very close."

"Don't make me ask, Troy."

"Okay. The answer is, I don't know, for certain. I don't think Monte knows, for certain. He knows about Kaiden and me. He'll probably suspect Jack right off. He might be coming here to find out…about himself. I just don't know. Does it matter to you…all that much?"

"Well, I'd like to know where everybody stands, so to speak."

"Monte looks and acts as straight as anybody I've ever known. If he's inclined, you'd never guess it. I can guarantee you wouldn't be uncomfortable around him. He looks and acts every part the soldier, the airman."

"I'm not uncomfortable. Remember, I work in a *theater*. I just like to know. But I'm beginning to wonder about this church camp of yours! Monte would be number three that we know of! What'd they put in the water out there?"

I mock-kicked him under the table. "Be careful, or I'll sic Jack on you!"

Our food arrived. We dug in.

"There's one more thing, Ben. Would you consider favoring us by reciting one of your own poems for the group? I know Jack and I would really like that, and I'm pretty sure Kaiden and Monte would too. Kaiden knows you write, of course."

"I dunno, Troy; I may not have anything appropriate."

"I've no idea what that means. What 'inappropriate' do you write? Poetry for porn? Anything you like. You could say something about it."

"I wouldn't want to be a bore."

"How about something by a poet who influenced you? Ginsberg, maybe? They'd probably know who he is."

"I never heard anybody recite at a dinner table."

"Folks recite The Lord's Prayer there all the time. Or wait: you could recite something from a play you're rehearsing at the theater! You know, set up the situation, and let fly! Think about that, daddy-o!"

**27**

Monte skipped smartly down the stairs of the twelve-seater and headed across the tarmac, swinging his duffle, strutting a little in his dress blues and cap and AF shades, the silver wings glinting on his jacket. Striding through the gate and spotting me, he stopped, flung aside the bag, and ran straight into my arms, pressed his lips to my neck.

"Troy Tyler!" he said, "my guy! What're you doing here?!"

"Surprising you! Claiming you!" I grinned. "Somebody said you might show up!"

"You dog," he said; "I wasn't expecting you out here. Near 'bout took my breath away. Great to see you, man!"

"You too! So…dashing!" I reached to remove his shades, tugging my cuff over the bracelet.

"Oh, yeah; those." He took and folded them, slipped them inside his jacket. "There you are!" He touched my cheek gently with his palm, his eyes shimmering.

"You too! Let's go home. You got everything?"

"I dropped my bag back there. That's all there is. You're driving a car now? What?"

"Corky lent me his Nash. It'll get us home. Maybe not much farther."

"Nice of him. You can manage New Orleans okay without a car?"

"So far. You still have the little MG?"

"Oh yeah. My baby."

"Our friend Ben the motorcyclist will like to hear about that. Your folks okay?"

"Well enough. You know, it's kind of strange, though: we don't seem to have a lot to say to each other any more. It's kind of hard filling up the empty space at home."

"I've felt that too. Mother keeps on talking, and I half-listen, but we don't...you know...chat...back and forth. And Father never talks about anything but church, which I've kind of left."

"You don't go to church either? I sort of miss it sometimes, but the base chapel isn't really a church, so I don't much go. Jubilee knew how to do church, didn't it?"

"It did. But I don't miss that. My father has a new one, did I say?"

"One what? Church?"

"Yeah. They're moving. To Lake Charles...off there on the western horizon. It's kind of a big deal. Larger.

More pay. He says more opportunity. I figure more prestige."

"You'll move?"

"Not really, no. I've pretty much moved away from home for good. Unless, of course, I can't get a job after grad school. Always a possibility. But I wouldn't want to move home even in that case."

"This is a really ugly highway, Troy."

"Airline Highway. Yeah, it's pretty much Trashville all the way in. Don't judge New Orleans by these suburbs. Did you have breakfast? Kaiden's fixing eats."

"Cool. How're yawl doing?"

"I'm not sure what you're asking but I'll try to answer. We're getting along fine. Kaiden's so easy-going, so good-spirited all the time, it would be hard to stay cross with him even if he pissed you off. But he doesn't. And we're in this great house. We never know for how long, but for now it's choice. And he's got a job he loves: as an intern at a famous restaurant in the Quarter, and learning the business."

"But as roommates? It's working out?"

"I think so. We're…we're figuring it out…as we go. Tell me about your friends at Nellis."

"Well, I mentioned Rex Lawtry, formerly Baylor. We grab beers sometimes, and once drove to Vegas for a weekend, and there're a couple of other Baylor guys, and five of us play basketball now and then; oh, and Bob Mullins, from Topeka, is my work-out partner. Keeps me in shape."

"You work out regularly?"

"We try to get to the gym twice a week. But the drilling keeps us pretty fit even when we don't. Do you and Kaiden?"

"You know, we've never even talked about it! I do a lot of walking to and from campus, and of course he's forever on his bike — now a food cart — but that's not like working out at a gym."

"Well, you look in shape to me!" Monte said. "Almost buffed. You've put on about ten pounds since Jubilee, doncha think? How much do you weigh now?"

"Around 130, 135, I guess. You?"

"About the same. But you're taller. Everybody's taller. You remember I barely made the AF height requirement for enlistment."

"Does Rex date?"

"He talks about girls but I've never seen him with one. There're not a lot of them around the base."

"Are you dating anybody, Monte? Since Laura, I mean?"

"No, I never found a replacement, and haven't much looked recently. Not much time. And I have my car and my birds...my jets. You?"

"I sometimes look around at the girls in my graduate classes and wonder if I'm missing something, missing something I'd enjoy having. I enjoyed Allison a lot in high school. I'm sure I did. But now I hardly know what it was, or what exactly I'd be looking for in a girl if I dated one now. Maybe there has to be sexual attraction before you can appreciate...whatever the rest is? And the sexual attraction ain't much there right now!"

I pulled into the driveway and stopped. "We're home," I said. "Slide over here and tell me hey." He met my lips with his, moved into my embrace, and moaned.

We broke, but he stayed in my arms.

"What're we going to do. Troy?" he asked, staring out the windshield.

"Trust ourselves," I said. "But we have to wait a minute before getting out." He looked back at me, both of us grinning.

"Let's find Kaiden."

In a white bib apron, Kaiden stood over a large flat pan of heavily-iced sweet rolls awaiting oven heat.

"Hey-hey, fellas!" he cried, "come on in! Monte! How grand to see you! Watch out for the flour but give me a hug!"

"Kaiden!" he said, getting the name right. "You look funny without the bike!" They hugged warmly and stepped back, Monte brushing flour from his dress blues. I patted Kaiden's arm.

"These will take about ten minutes to bake," he said, sliding the sheet into the oven. "Meanwhile, Monte, what sort of tea would you like? English breakfast, spice, vanilla, green, herbal?"

"You choose," Monte said. "Chef knows best!" He removed his cap, and set it on Kaiden's head. Kaiden pirouetted, posed, adjusted the cap to a flirty angle. "Just call me Sergeant Mess!" he laughed.

We relaxed at the kitchen table over the tea and the warm, sweet cinnamon rolls stuffed with an almond paste that drew exclamations from two of us. They chatted about Monte's flight and the kitchen furnishings and Kaiden's job and then got on to reminiscences of Jubilee. I stayed mostly quiet, respecting Kaiden's need to leave soon for work, but also thinking of what Monte and I would do next, after Kaiden left and we had the whole house to ourselves. We could put away his things, of course, in his bedroom, but then what? I was his host; I should decide and lead. I had not thought how to fill these early, empty hours. Or possibly I had.

"I'll shave and change for work," Kaiden said, excusing himself. "Yawl make yourselves to home."

"Let's wash up," I said, stacking the plates and gathering the cups. I washed, he dried; I stored, he swept. We scrubbed the counters, wiped the oven, polished the plumbing of the sink.

"There now," I said; "neat as a pin. You want to unpack?"

Kaiden swung back through, looking neat in a red shirt and black chinos and sandals. "Come out and see the bike in its new clothes," he said, piling white boxes from the fridge onto the counter. It was actually a new bike too, larger and better proportioned to the awning and the cart, with better brakes and a louder bell, and two rear-view mirrors.

"Can we help with those?" Monte asked, stepping forward.

"My treats," Kaiden said; "fresh and for sale. Maybe I'll bring some home for cocktails?"

We loaded the cart and helped him move the rig through the thick grass and gravel of the neglected driveway. He pushed off, waving: "Yawl have a great day!"

Was it permission? We moved back toward the house. Inside, beyond the locked door, I hooked my little finger inside Monte's tight collar and led him, unprotesting, down the hallway toward the blue bedroom, where we'd stashed his duffle. Ripe with desire, I turned him to me and gently loosened the knot in his tie as he tugged up my shirttail and eased his hands across the bare skin of my chest, murmuring my name, faint moans from his throat urging us on.

Afterward, we lay wrapped for a time, breathing, fingers drifting across ticklish skin.

"Are you there, Monte? Okay?"

"Never better. You?"

"Never. What was that?"

He grinned. "It's called 'frottage.' Maybe not the most…refined sex ever, but pretty…satisfying, wouldn't you say, when everything…synchronizes…like that?"

"Monte," I said quietly: "It was…rapture! I never felt that before. Where'd you learn to do it?"

"From a book. You can sort of do it with your pillow or mattress…only of course it's not the same. I'd never done it with a real person either. Yeah, it was pretty great, wadn' it, matching like that. Did we just lose our virginity?"

We giggled. "Not technically. But in a manner of speaking, maybe we did. It was our first time…finally. And our first time, like that."

"So: technically, you're still a virgin?" he asked.

"Yes. You're not?"

"I am."

"So we have miles to go before we sleep…as technical virgins? What did you and Rex do?"

"We just made out. Then jerked each other off. Nothing memorable. What do you and Kaiden do?"

I hesitated. I didn't want to say. I wasn't exactly embarrassed. Or possibly I was. It just seemed so profoundly private. And yet he'd told me.

"Kaiden and I are still sort of finding our way, learning how to do sex…various sex. Looking for what's best for us. I guess we explore and experiment."

"You've tried everything?"

"We prob'ly don't know what everything is. So, no."

"Don't you want to?"

"Do you? And Monte: are you even sure this is… well…*you*? I mean, what about Laura…and other girls?"

"I don't think I know. Maybe I'm trying to figure that out? Queer was always such a forbidden thing, unthinkable, really; I wouldn't even let myself think about the possibility…. Until Laura left…which kind of opened a door and I *began* thinking about it. I mean, I always knew I noticed guys. I noticed you…from that first day…and I noticed Corky and some others…but I didn't let myself think about it much. And then you ran off with him. Back in Houston I actually went to a couple of queer bars after that…just to test…and I didn't much like them. And of course there was seminary in my future."

"Yeah. What about that?"

"I don't know. I'm not dealing with that. I can't let that determine who I am. I have to know who I am first."

"Kaiden says there's one sure-fire way to know whether you're queer. I dunno whether it's proof, but it's pretty interesting. He says, just ask yourself who you think about when you masturbate?"

He turned his head to look at me. "Really?" he asked. "God. I doubt it's that easy."

"But what'd you mean when you asked, twice, what we're going to do? You and I?"

He sat up and went quiet. Laced his fingers in his lap. Hung his head and studied them. Sighed.

"I didn't mean anything specific. I meant everything. You, me, queers...girls...church. And Kaiden. I meant all of it. What're we going to do...about all of it?"

"I'll have to tell him eventually," I said, "after you leave."

"But I mean...how does he figure...how do *I* figure...in all this now? Like I said in the car, what do we do now, Troy?"

"And as I said in the car, we trust ourselves. Come on back down here: straighten out next to me." I fluffed the pillow, tucked him in, bent down over his face and spoke softly: "Honestly, I don't know, Monte, what happens now. Look: I'm really glad we did what we did. That just *had* to happen. And it was terrific. But I don't know what it means...or what it doesn't mean. I don't know what it *can* mean...as long as you're living in Nevada and I'm here. I can't leave Kaiden now...not even for you. I'll have to tell him and hope he understands…how we had to do what we did. But over the longer term, who can say what will happen? I feel closer to you for what happened. But I don't feel less close to Kaiden. He's still my boyfriend. And so are you. You will always be my boyfriend…just as you have been ever since Jubilee. What we just did sealed that bond even tighter than it was before. But it doesn't change Kaiden and me. I know I'm going to want to have sex with you again, but I'll have to see how Kaiden handles this before we do it again. I don't want to hurt him if this does. Of course I don't want to hurt you either. But I don't necessarily think we've got an impossible situation. We three just have to figure out how to make it work. Am I being clear?"

"You sound annoyed," Monte said. "Have I made you mad?"

"I'm prob'ly a little annoyed at myself for not handling things better. No, Monte; please don't think I'm mad or annoyed with you. I might be in love with you. And love can be annoying, sometimes. Just give me a little time with this. Can you?"

"I'm pretty sure I'm in love with you, too, Troy."

"Oh, God, Monte. Come here. Hold me. Let me hold you. I wish we could just hold each other like this forever and ever." I felt the tears rising and tucked my head into his shoulder.

"So do I," he said, tears in his own voice.

"We're such messes," I said after a while. "We've got four more days together. Let's be happy. Let's clean this place up and get out of here. We've got a city to see."

That afternoon we toured the two campuses, bowled a few lanes at the alley in Tulane's University Center, changed into the swimsuits I'd remembered to bring and on my I.D. card swam laps and horsed around in the Olympic pool upstairs in the same building. We dined at the Camellia Grille and walked back through the Garden District where all the lights always blazed until midnight in the elegant homes for the tourists driving through and gawking. Kaiden was waiting for us at home, as tired as we were and showing no signs of suspicion, so we made an early night of it and retired to separate bedrooms.

For Sunday, I'd splurged and arranged a nine-hour excursion for Monte and me that included three plantation homes, a pontoon boat tour of a swamp, and, after a stop at the French Market for white coffee and a basketfull of the famous beignets, a paddle-wheeler steamboat cruise of the city's harbor with a stop in Algiers and a tenmile ride up the mighty Mississippi. We liked the houses well enough and all the huge, sprawling, stately oaks on their grounds, and heard glamorous tales about plantation life and sad ones about slave days; but the highlight was the lazy drift through the swamp with heavily mossed cypresses and a dozen or more alligators and countless turtles on half-sunken logs and raccoons and hogs and armadillos and a couple of creepy possums and the really nasty nutria and even a few moccasins plying the waters, and the weird, spooky stillness of the whole scene bathed in shadowed green light. One plantation gave us a mint-julep and another a praline, but we waited for the steamboat's stop in Algiers to grab a late lunch at the Landing Diner, a ramshackle wreck of a place with fantastic food, where we both ordered the sautéed soft-shell crabs. The afternoon cruise up the Mississippi invited relaxation in deck chairs with our feet on the railing, watching the green levees unroll along the bank, and, beyond the city, stretches and stretches of perfectly flat cotton and cane fields to the horizon, with occasional white plantation homes and dark crumbling shanties declaring the different lifestyles of the delta. We sipped iced tea and exchanged greetings with strolling tourists and checked out what we gleefully imagined were cabin boys for hire. Back on shore, we hailed a taxi for home, only Monte wanted to visit a New Orleans cemetery, so we got the cabbie to stop at the St. Louis Number 1 graveyard and then at the Lafayette Number 2 in the Garden District near our home, and tell us about these famous "cities of the dead," as Mark Twain named them. I knew snatches of stories about New Orleans aboveground burials but listened to our driver retail fuller versions. He dropped us off at Marchetti's afterward for muffulettas. Exhilarated but exhausted by our packed day, we staggered home where Kaiden had already fallen asleep on a sofa in his briefs and T.

Monday he was off and all ours, so we piled into the car and headed out for a drive along the shore of Lake Ponchartrain and around the nearby beautiful city park. It's not really a lake but an estuary with the longest continuous bridge in the world, appearing from this side to vanish into distance without connecting to any other side. It's also not very deep, and had to be dredged for ship channels. Then we were off through the Quarter for a daytime tour, first of the magnificent St. Louis Cathedral, the oldest cathedral in the country, and then around Jackson Square itself, formerly a parade ground, with the rousing equestrian statue of Major General Andrew, the surprising hero of New Orleans for preserving the city against British conquest. We visited the Cabildo and the Presbytere flanking the Cathedral — both now historic museums housing valuable documents — wondered at the cast iron galleries of the Pontalba Buildings — shops on the first floor, apartments above — and strolled over for a close-up view of the swirling, muddy River. In the alleys around the Square, fine artists dabbed at canvasses, cartoonists parodied tourist faces, fortune tellers laid out Tarot decks, card tricksters suckered sightseers, voodoo merchants fingered their greasy wares...and street food-enthusiasts like Kaiden pushed their samples our way: he greeted them amiably but passed on their offerings. The bars opened early in the Quarter, but apart from asking permission at the Monteleon Hotel to view the Carousel Bar and take a quick ride around on it, we kept mostly to the antique stores on Royal, which Monte pronounced exceptionally fine. Who knew? (I'd heard rumors that some of the larger antique stores manufactured their own antiquities out back, but I didn't credit them.) Anyway, lots of stores drew us in for looks around: they ranged from tawdry to high-end jewelry stores and galleries with museum-quality paintings and boutiques and astonishing craft shops featuring local and international artists. We found Preservation Hall, newly famous for extemporaneous jazz by random musicians more or less spontaneously gathering in the evenings. Ben's Le Petit Theater was in the same neighborhood. And while in the area, we peeked into Pat O'Brien's of the two-piano duo and the syrupy, red hurricane concoction but decided it was too early for us on an empty stomach.

"Everybody hungry?" I asked around 2 p.m.

"Can we afford Brennan's?" Kaiden asked.

We'd all heard of Brennan's and its celebrated day-long breakfasts, but two of us were at least mildly intimidated by the fame and by the probable expense. Kaiden, though, encouraged us to be daring, and to trust him.

A line backed up at the entrance. Kaiden spoke to the doorman, who disappeared inside while waiting customers glared darkly at us. The doorman returned and signaled us to follow him to the side of the building, saying audibly to Kaiden: "Knock on the second door down there. Tell whoever opens it that Sebastian is holding a table for three for you. He'll meet you at the door to the dining room."

"Don't worry," he whispered to us as we waited inside. "I can handle this. It's going to be fantastic!"

Monte and I may have paled, or flushed. We were both non plussed. But Kaiden confidently led us behind Sebastian and oversaw our disposal at the immaculately arranged table with very white china and dazzling silver and sparkling crystal. He murmured something to Sebastian who handed him a large, leather-bound menu and departed.

"Kaiden," I said, "it's not too late to leave. Shouldn't we?"

"Don't be absurd," he almost snarled. "This is Brennan's. Nobody ever leaves before dining. Plan on being here a while."

He ordered three Brennan's Bloody Marys for the table, three appetizers, and three entrées: to start, a baked apple (oatmeal pecan raisin crumble, brown sugar glaze, sweetened crème fraiche), a Tropical Trifle (passion fruit and tumeric curd, coconut chia pudding, banana sponge cake), and a steak tartare (beef tenderloin, herbed potato waffle, black garlic aioli, chicken egg bottarga); and as entrées: Eggs Hussarde (homemade English muffins, coffee-cured Canadian bacon, Marchand de vin sauce), Artisinal Eggs Benedict (homemade English muffins, coffee-cured Canadian bacon, hollandaise), and a Breton buckwheat crepe (sunny-side-up duck egg, Benton's coffee country ham, sweet potato agrodolce, mustard frill salad), with New Orleans coffee (details copied off Kaiden's menu).

"It's customary," Kaiden explained, "to drink several rounds of aperitifs before a Brennan's breakfast, and then champagne with the meal, but we'll be forgiven if we don't. And Sebastian won't mind if we share entrées."

All three of us got a little woozy and silly after sipping the spicy cocktails but the appetizers and the fresh, warm rolls with sweet butter set us to rights again. About halfway through the meal a middle-aged, distinguished-looking man in a suit and tie stopped at our table and introduced himself, smiling, but we all missed the name. He actually welcomed us, complimented Kaiden's menu choices, and said the coffee would be on the house. He signed and dated, illegibly, an unbound menu and handed it to Kaiden.

"Who is he?" I asked, after he moved on.

"I think he could be one of the Brennan brothers," Kaiden said. "That might be a 'B' at the start of the signature. Oh, and in honor of the gentleman back there on the rearing horse in the Square, you boys might want to kick in a twenty toward the cost of this fine meal!" We did. And although I figured I should pay Monte's share, I was still a grad student on limited income and needed to be careful of coins.

Monte and I had felt — and I expect showed that we felt — nervous, somewhat cowed, and dislocated in this posh dining room, and had probably eaten too fast, but even so it was nearly dark by the time we left the restaurant. The streets were just beginning to come alive with crowds and color, and as we were too juiced on the coffee to call it an early evening, we took up Kaiden's suggestion and circled back to Preservation Hall to see whether a band had yet gathered. It was settling in and tuning-up as we arrived. We took seats on the first row of rough, unfinished benches, like pews without backs, felt warmly welcomed by the black faces and big, broad grins up front, and nodded and tapped along through a half-hour jam session of traditional New Orleans jazz, including "Little Liza Jane," "Clarinet Marmalade," "Bourbon Street Parade," "St. James Infirmary," and others we didn't recognize or I've now forgotten. The seven musicians, probably fifty or older, in dark Sunday suits and ties and fedora hats, showed by their smiles and whole jolly manner how thrilled they were to be there. So were we: the jazz, the antiquated, rough-hewn, improvised milieu, so different from everything surrounding it, felt downright refreshing, uplifting.

Kaiden roused us the next morning around 8, and the smell of frying bacon got us stirring and to the kitchen for buttered biscuits (from cans) and white Karo syrup and freshly brewed coffee.

"Okay, boys," he said cheerfully, "I need for you to make your beds, pick up and put away your clothes, and take these items" — he gestured to the counter clustered with rags and cans and bottles and other assorted clearing materials — "to both bathrooms, and scrub up everything to a high polish. Change the towels, bring in extra t.p., mop the floors, empty any trash, and wipe down the mirrors. After that, tidy and dust the living and dining rooms. The vacuum's in the hall closet. And somebody should sweep the porch and the front walk. Work together or separately, as you like, but we need to get the place ready by noon. You're on your own for lunch. I'll be in here all day; yawl can spend the afternoon wherever, just not around here! Plan to be back and ready to receive our guests at 6. Okay?"

I felt like saluting but saw the sense of his plan. Monte sopped a biscuit in syrup and nodded at me: "Sure," he said, "glad to help out."

"How about we trolley down to Audubon Park this afternoon and visit the zoo?" I asked; "it's a pretty good one."

We separated to arrange our rooms. I figured that two hot guys in the close quarters of the bathrooms would find occasion to bump into each other, and who knew where *that* would lead? So we divided the cleaning stuff and got to work. It occurred to me to wonder whether Monte was reminded of latrine details from his training days, and hoped he wasn't.

We checked with Kaiden in the kitchen when we'd finished and offered to fetch him lunch, but he shooed us out, thanking us for the assistance but not inspecting our work, and said he'd make out with nibbles at hand.

"Are we dressing tonight" I remembered to ask.

"No," he said; "casual and comfy. It's not a formal dinner, but don't come barefoot!"

It was another gorgeous spring afternoon, bright, warmish, low humidity, inviting. We decided to walk down Magazine toward the Park and check out the home gardens visible from the sidewalks, Monte having already remarked on the neighborhood dwellings and eager to see more of them.

"How d'you know so much about antiques?" I asked, remembering his interest and information from yesterday's tour of the Royal Street shops.

"Oh, my aunt's a docent at the Bayou Bend Museum in Houston. She used to take me around on her tours and I picked up a little here and there. I don't know much."

"We should've looked into museums in the Quarter. There're quite a few. Kaiden's been to the one on voodoo history."

"Not for me. We did fine."

"You hungry? There's a kiosk right outside the park entrance. How does cotton candy sound to you?"

"Sticky. But I'd take a sno-cone."

"Probably too early yet. Listen, there's a po-boy sandwich shop just off Magazine down there. Lots of different varieties. Let's check the menu."

The menu offered about twenty different species. "We forgot to ask Kaiden what he's fixing for tonight, but the chances are good it's seafood. You might want to try something else on your sandwich."

"Not alligator," Monte said, making a face.

"No; I think I'll go for the veggie po-boy, with grilled asparagus and goat cheese, it says here."

"Following your lead," he said, "I'll have the fried green tomatoes sandwich, with avocado slices. And remoulade sauce is the preferred choice down here, right?"

"You learn fast."

"Shouldn't we pick up something for dinner? I mean, like wine or dessert...or flowers or chocolates? I need to get something for Kaiden, as my really great host."

"That would be very nice. On the way back."

"Will there be cocktails? If asked, what should I say?"

"I'll say white wine. That's probably what we'll have with the meal. Would white wine suit you beforehand?"

"Very well. Are any topics verboten at the table? Anything I shouldn't bring up?"

I looked at him, trying to read the eyes. Nothing. Then he winked, grinned.

"Sex?" I asked. "We're five hot guys: how is sex not already and always on the table? Or anyhow on our minds. I'd rather we didn't talk about who's slept with whom among ourselves, but we can hardly forbid the subject, or avoid it. Let's just try to be polite and discreet."

"Remind me of who everybody is, and what I'm supposed to know about them. Please let's not go around the table introducing ourselves! Tell me now."

Our sandwiches arrived, packed to overflowing.

"Well," I said, "I'm Troy, your first boyfriend." I watched to see how this went down. He blinked, and waited. Clearly, there was no way around saying what I — caving — then did say: "And you're mine." Not that I was looking for a way around saying it. He nodded and grinned.

"Kaiden you know. Ben Moore is my pal from college, also an English major who writes poetry and drama and drives a big loud motorcycle and will be interested, I imagine, in your jets. He's a cycle mechanic in two repair shops here. He volunteers, and more, at Le Petit Theater, which we saw yesterday in the Quarter. He may have an acting role there this coming summer. Jack might be the tricky case: another LCC buddy, he's the one who admired you in your uniform that day. Jack and

I roomed together for a while my second year, and were briefly intimate, broke up, and I moved in with Kaiden. He might still have a little crush on me. He's a really sweet man and I like and admire him a lot, and he's book-brilliant and a first-rate writer. But Ben is prob'ly my smartest friend."

"You've actually slept with three of the dinner guests tonight?" Monte asked.

"Well, now that you've counted, yes, I guess I have. Does that make me promiscuous?"

He went a little broody, then brightened: "Not necessarily," he said, "going forward."

We paid about as much attention to the animals as they did to us. Preoccupied, we showed them mostly indifference, might as well have been walking the streets as zoo paths. I mused on the pending dinner, on what topics I might lead discussion of and how to engage everybody in it. Tomorrow, Wednesday, Kaiden would return to work and Monte and I would have the house to ourselves unless I found more diverting entertainments than the zoo was turning out to be; and then he would leave the next morning and I'd have to face Kaiden. What occupied Monte's mind came out in hints and tips and cues all deriving from and expanding upon his earlier question — thrice repeated — "What are we going to do now, Troy?" It also occupied — dominated — mine, for I had no answer. Would there even *be* a "we" after Wednesday? Almost ashamed of the question, I recognized its weight. And what and whom did "now" encompass and imply, and on what prior circumstances depend?

"When will I see you again?" he asked, a little plaintively.

"I don't know. Will you come this way again at Christmas?"

"You should come to Nellis. Fly with me!"

"Oh, I don't know about that. Would they let us?"

"Just for a few loop-the-loops!"

"Not sure I'd go for that. I might throw up."

"Are you afraid of flying, Troy?"

"Would you believe I've never flown? I might be afraid."

"Five minutes in the air, you'd love it. No more fear!"

"Promise? Would you hold my hand?"

He laughed. "Might be a little awkward, the controls and all. I wish we could hold hands now. Walk the park holding hands. Wouldn't that be cool?"

"I've seen women do that, in the Quarter. People stare...even in the Quarter."

"What're you going to tell Kaiden...about us, I mean?"

"I don't yet know. Maybe nothing, unless he asks. The truth, if he asks."

"Are you in love with each other?"

"I believe Kaiden believes he loves me. Sometimes I believe I love him. In some moments I do love him. I don't think I want to lose him. But whether I want to be permanently in love with him above all others, I kind of doubt."

"Have you forgiven me for what I did to you at Jubilee? For taking over your life out there?"

"You know, you were such a maestro of a manager, such an amazing organizer and arranger at Jubilee, maybe we should give the job to you of figuring out what *we're* going to do! But I've told you. There is nothing to forgive. You brought out something good in me. In a sort of indirect and roundabout way, but you did, and I'm grateful for that."

"Do you ever think you might have a ministerial calling?"

"No, Monte, I don't. Please."

"I sometimes wonder about my own. If I'm queer, I mean. Why would God want me if I am?"

"IF? You doubt you're queer?"

"Don't you...about yourself, I mean?"

"Well, maybe. Kaiden and I have had this conversation. I'm pretty sure. All the signs line up. Nothing's to be gained by my doubting. I'm not unhappy to like boys. And I don't think it's wrong. God does not hate queers."

"He may not want them preaching, though. Would the seminary even let me in, if it knew?"

"I doubt they'd make you sign a disclaimer."

"Does Kaiden dislike me?"

"What? No, of course not. Whatever makes you think he might?"

"I think I might, if we traded places. If you and I were... lovers."

"What are we talking about here, Monte? Can you be a little plainer?"

He stopped; I turned and waited. He took a deep breath. "I came to see you to find out where I stand with you. I'm pretty sure I'm in love with you, Troy, fell for you at Jubilee and then messed everything up, and made you break my heart. But then we...we got close again, and you say you've forgiven me, and we've made love... but I still don't know where I stand with you, not with Kaiden and now Jack in the picture, not even today, much less tomorrow. I would like to know."

"We had sex, Monte; we had beautiful, loving, thrilling sex. I don't know that we made love."

"I know what it felt like, and I'm pretty sure you were totally with me in the feeling. But I need some direction here: I don't know what to expect, what to count on. Can't you see that?"

"Yes, Monte, my dear boyfriend, I can. But I don't know that I can give you, right now, what you want and seem to need. I don't *know* what we're going to do now. Except go on just as we are. I know that won't be the most comfortable thing for you, but it's as much as I can give you...right now. I'm pretty happy with that; I wish you could be happy with that. I'm loving you the best I can, and I'll be happy if you give me the best you can. And together we'll see what happens. I've made you cry, I see, and I'm about to cry myself. But damned if I can see why we're crying: we've just said we love each other. How great is that? What's better than that, or more than that? And now I'm going to hug you right here in front of God and everybody!"

He let me, and hugged me back, hard, and kissed my neck. "All right," he said, snuffling. "That's a gift. I'll bank that. And you, Troy," he added, grinning irresistibly, "you can always bank on me for my love."

This was my United States Air Force First Lieutenant saying that, right out loud, in the open air of a park, to my very face!

# 28

Jack looked like he was already waiting for Monte when we got to the kitchen after cleaning up and changing clothes.

"Here he is," I said to Jack, "the pilot you spied at the bus stop! Monte Trevalyn himself!"

They smiled and shook and got right to chatting.

Kaiden, already changed into dark Levis and a tight black shirt defining his pecs, stirred a huge steaming pot on the stove emitting a distinctive and alluring aroma.

"File powder," he said, "from ground-up sassafras leaves, the key ingredient in Cajun gumbo, with shrimp and chicken and sausage and a wagonload of veggies and spices. That hint of scorched popcorn tickling your noses is from the roux, and will shortly fade. The gumbo will also start to smell kind of earthy, like tea, but you won't taste that. Served with white rice, which we'll start cooking when everybody's here and had one glass of the dry Riesling. Troy, would you uncork and pour?"

The doorbell chimed and I went to admit Ben in his black jeans and boots and a dark purple Tee under the black leather jacket with silver studs. He handed in a bottle and gave me a light hug.

"Thanks, Ben," I said; "come in, come in. Great to see you! We're in the kitchen."

There, I introduced Monte, who said something about motorcycles that made Ben chuckle, and he greeted Jack and Kaiden. I busied myself with the wine.

"Florals are by Monte," Kaiden said, waving at the vase of red roses with greenery he'd arranged. "Troy, would you move those into the living room when everybody's got wine, and take some matches to the table for the candles?"

Jack sported a loose, blousy, pale-green long-sleeved shirt buttoned at the the cuffs and tucked casually into the brown-belted waistband of his unusually snug khakis. The top button of the shirt opened upon his white neck and hairless chest. His thin, ginger-brown hair was freshly cut and combed neatly flat against his head from the part on the right. Monte looked movie-star handsome, distinguished even, in a navy blazer over a blue button-down and light gray slacks, his dark skin glowing above the blue and below the glistening, tumbling black curls. I felt reasonably attractive, kind of collegiate, in my sky-blue cashmere crew-neck and pink dress shirt, generous Christmas gifts from Kaiden. Both of us wore our bracelets.

"I'll light the candles," Ben said.

Kaiden spooned hot white rice into the individual bowls resting in white plates, heaped on the gumbo, and invited us to take one and move to the table while he brought out the cast-iron skillet with freshly baked cornbread and sliced it into slabs. The tray with them in place, we settled — Monte opposite me at the far end, Jack and Ben to his right, Kaiden to my left. I pronounced a brief blessing, and lifted my glass:

"To our special guest," I toasted, "U.S. Air Force First Lieutenant Monte Trevalyn, of Texas and Nevada! Welcome!"

"Monte, please help yourself to the cornbread and pass it along," from Kaiden. We all noticed that he offered the tray to Jack before taking a slab himself.

"Now the butter," Kaiden added, taking some and handing it to Monte. "Slip the butter inside the slice, and let it melt. And drink up, people; we've got vats of wine back there!"

"Chow down, folks," I said, taking a bite of the smoking stew and a sip of the wine. "Kaiden! It's fantastic! Amazing!" Assenting exclamations followed, and when they subsided, I began, having warned Monte that I would:

"So, Monte, how about describing a typical day at your base...what you do?"

"Sure," he said; "but first: Kaiden, this is spectacular food! No kidding! This really is...well...luscious! I love the spicing! Wow! Nothin' on the base anywhere near this fine. It's outstanding!"

"Glad you like it," Kaiden said, blushing. "Thanks!"

"My day," Monte began, and told us how it routinely unfolded. It took maybe three minutes, during which we were riveted. He completely captured us when naming his plane, the F-105 Thunderchief, nicknamed "Thud" by its crews, a supersonic fighter-bomber with nuclear attack capability in service since 1958 with a top speed of 1400 mph, faster than the speed of sound, and at really high altitudes it could reach Mach 2. It was, he said, the biggest single-seat, single engine combat aircraft ever built, weighing fifty-thousand pounds. And it could also carry, he said, fourteen thousand pounds of bombs and missiles.

"Here," he said, reaching into his jacket pocket, "here're a couple of photos of the jet…and me, if you'd like to see what it looks like. These aren't secret, but we have to be careful about taking pictures of it. I wouldn't be allowed to snap the cockpit or control panel."

It was galvanizing, his account and the photos, and it had the instant effect of relocating the focus of interest from Kaiden's food to Monte's status as a fighter-bomber pilot in that distinctly phallic plane. Even Ben's mouth gaped at the stats. Monte went on for a bit about his barracks, his schedules, his training flights, his classes, his mates — all fascinating news to me too.

"What's the highest altitude you've flown?" Ben wanted to know.

"Its service ceiling is fifty-thousand feet," Monte said.

Kaiden asked whether he'd ever carried nuclear weapons.

"Sorry, Kaiden," Monte said, "I can't tell you that."

"I'll bet that means you have," Jack said, grinning at Monte but not pressing for an answer.

"How much runway do you need for take-off?" Ben asked.

"All of it," Monte laughed. "9000 feet is adequate. It takes a while."

"Have you ever parachuted?" I asked.

"We're trained to parachute and then we practice jumps. It's pretty simple, and actually kind of fun."

"What about ejection?" Ben asked.

"That would not be fun," Monte said. "We learn where the handles are and we know to hold on and expect a bumpy ride, but it's something nobody really wants to think about very much and we don't spend a lot of time on it."

"Did you have to go through boot camp, and was it as bad as its reputation?" Kaiden wanted to know.

"In two words, yes and yes. You probably don't want to hear the details; they might ruin your appetite! And maybe we've talked enough about me. I'd like to hear from Ben about motorcycles: how you got interested, Ben, and what keeps you interested in them?"

So we heard from Ben on mechanics, and from Kaiden on how to prepare food in kitchens on wheels and sell it on streets, and from Jack and me on research and writing and on teaching spoiled, privileged, preppy boys.

"But don't you fall in love with them all the time?" Ben asked.

"Not permitted," I said.

"Of course we do," Jack said; "what's not permitted is acting on our crushes."

Thus was the ice was broken on a subject closely touching four of us, by the one of us arguably least interested in it. Jack had looked hard at me when addressing it, and Monte had too; Kaiden examined his gumbo.

"You've never dated a student?" Ben continued.

"To be precise," Jack said, "you mean a male student and one of my own while he was my student?"

"Yes, have you?" Ben replied; "I'm not going to report you."

"Never," Jack and I chorused.

"To be precise," I said, "I may have wanted to, once, after he'd left my class, but I didn't."

"How unSocratic of you both!" Ben said.

"But would it be such a terrible thing," Monte asked, "for a student to know his teacher loved him? Didn't we all love one or another of our teachers as we came through the grades? I mean, couldn't we learn better, do better, if we knew a teacher loved us? Wouldn't we want to please her and make her love us even more?"

"If she were a he, a man?" Kaiden asked.

"It's wrong either way," I said. "There's a line. You can't cross it without asking for trouble."

"I agree with that," Jack said. "But we can be their friends. We should be their friends. We just can't be their lovers. Teaching requires distance."

"Well, that's manifestly false," I said. "Parents taught us. Where's the distance there?"

"And love was there," Monte said.

"But showing it is where trouble happens," Jack said. "They're in our custody. We abuse it if we try to show them love. They'd lose respect and take advantage. Discipline would evaporate. Teaching would degrade."

"Even student friendships are risky," I said. "I know this TA, not here, who became friends with a handsome, hunky male student who fell for him and wanted to sleep with him. The TA said no and no and no but the kid kept coming back and begging, until finally one day he showed up in the TA's office with this obvious gigantic hard-on, and pled with his teacher, 'Isn't there anything, anything in the world I can do, anything I can offer you, to persuade you to sleep with me?' The teacher thought a minute and said, 'You'd already done everything decent you could do, Mr. Cocque, to get into my pants. Indecency isn't going to work either.' Imagine the deflation that followed!"

The laughter was cautious. Then Jack said, "The TA should have stopped it on the first request. The kid had obviously crossed the line."

"What I was really asking, I guess," Ben said, "is how you deal with your attraction to a boy in your class?"

"You ignore it," I said.

"You jerk off and forget it," Jack said. "You withdraw your friendship. Yes, the kid'll be hurt. But in a year he'll love you for a lifetime for what you did. And you'll still have your job."

"So how can you encourage friendships with students?" I asked.

"I know how to control them," Jack replied, then added, with a grin, " I prob'ly jerk off a lot."

This time the laughter was general and loud.

"With that," Kaiden said, "it's time for refills. Troy, how about topping up the glasses? Everybody else, bring your bowls to the kitchen. Jack, would you bring Troy's bowl?"

We amiably milled and loitered while Kaiden reloaded the bowls and sliced more cornbread from a second loaf. Ben followed Monte in, asking more questions about the phallus he flew. "I can't talk about that either," I overheard Monte say.

"I was wondering," Monte said into the lull back at the table, "I was wondering if Ben would talk about his work at the theater. Le Petit, is it, Ben? What do you do there?"

"I volunteer," he said, smiling, obviously pleased to be asked. "For over a year now. I grew up in an orphanage where we did a lot of children's theater, and I kind of got the bug as a kid, and Le Petit gave me a chance to hang around and learn how-to at a professional theater. I do everything from scut work behind the scenes to sweeping the lobby to tending the box office. I was supposed to usher tonight, but we've got plenty of part-timers, so finding a sub was easy."

He paused. "And…?" I said. "And…? Hold on people, the best is yet to come. Ben?"

"Oh," he added, "I've done a few walk-ons, stand-in gigs...and I'm understudying a part for a play we're planning for the fall."

"And what part would that be, Mr. Ben?" I asked, teasing him.

"Well, it's Big Daddy in Tennessee Williams's *Cat on a Hot Tin Roof*."

The table actually buzzed: "Oh wow!" "Hot damn!" "Great movie!" "Burl Ives!"

"Paul Newman!" Jack said.

"Everybody's seen it?" I asked. All hands went up. "Let's talk about it," I continued. "Is it okay, Ben, if we do?"

"I guess so. Just don't say too much about my role. I'm trying to define what I want to do with it, and I don't want a lot of interference. I guess I mean, don't say too much about Ives's interpretation. Of course I saw the movie when it premiered but that was 1958 and I've forgotten a lot of it. I'd rather not remember Ives's version too...vividly."

"We'll be careful," I promised. "Okay, people: *Is* Brick or isn't he? Isn't that the great burning question of the play? Why don't you not weigh in on this one, Ben, until we have? I'd like to know what everybody thinks... before you tell the truth. You want to go first, Monte?"

"I say no, he isn't queer, but it's complicated."

"It's fucking complicated," Jack said. "That's my answer. It's complicated."

"Yes or no?" I said to Jack.

"Yes and no," Jack said.

"Kaiden says yes," he said.

"Troy says no," I said. "I've actually changed my mind. Yesterday I'd have said yes. Now, Ben."

"I don't think Williams could make up his mind," Ben said. "As Jack says, it's fucking complicated. You can make good arguments both ways. We haven't yet determined, at Le Petit, which way we're going to play it, if either, or just pump the ambiguity for all it's worth, and let each audience decide."

"I'm the only yes?" Monte asked. "I can change. I agreed it's complicated."

"I'll join you," Jack said. "I can so to speak swing both ways here! The thing is, in his heart of hearts Brick wants to be queer. He truly loves Skipper. He wants to screw Skipper. He may have. Big Daddy thinks he has. Brick can't admit to himself that he wants Skipper, but that doesn't mean he isn't queer. The very insistence of his denials is suspicious."

"Remember," I said, "Brick is the only one of the whole stinking lot who always tells the truth, at least in every other respect. If he's lying about Skipper, there's no truth-teller in the house. That's pretty dark."

"No," Kaiden said, "Maggie tells the truth. That's one of the things Brick despises about her. She tells him the truth about himself, and she suspects he and Skipper were lovers. She's slept with Skipper, so she knows he can't make it with a girl. She tells that truth too."

"But she lies at the end," Jack said. "Maggie wants the inheritance more than she wants Brick *or* a baby. She's always been poor and she wants to be rich and the quickest way to get rich is to get Big Daddy's property. So she promises him an heir."

"And immediately promises to make her lie about pregnancy become true by bedding Brick," I said. "But there's no guarantee that's going to happen. Brick doesn't seem inclined to cooperate."

"He'll have to," Monte said, "to get his liquor back. She's locked it all up. She says they'll celebrate with it when she's truly pregnant. But remember why he's a drunk. He drinks because he loves Skipper, loved and lost Skipper."

"Killed him," Ben said. "Big Daddy says Brick's rejection of Skipper's sexual overture to himself made Skipper kill himself. Big Daddy accuses Brick to his face of kicking Skipper into his grave. Brick was already drinking in part because he could't let himself have Skipper, in part because he's a washed-up former athlete and a failed sports announcer: in other words he's lost his manhood in those identities too. And the whole house is haunted by those two old bachelor queens — Peter Ochello and Jack Straw — who owned the house and fucked in that very bedroom their whole lives before Big Daddy bought it. Homosex is all over the place in this play, and Maggie and Big Daddy are the only ones who admit to seeing it."

"And the only ones who don't mind it, who don't bad-mouth it," Jack said. "Maggie even calls it noble, like the Greeks thought about it; she names it clean. And as a young man Big Daddy lived with it in hobo-jungles and tramp camps when he bummed around the country.

Brick *imagines* himself 'disgusted' with homosex because it differentiates you, isolates you; and he projects onto Big Daddy his own 'disgust' over sex between men when it's actually the disgust he shares with Big Daddy over all the lies in the house, while in fact BD and Maggie have no problem with men loving men…except in the latter case it keeps her from giving Big Daddy the heir he so desperately craves."

"And homosex is right there in our faces at the end, too," I said. "Maggie declares her eternal love for Brick as part of her strategy to get him between the sheets, and Brick says, in the final line of the play, 'Wouldn't it be funny if that was true?' In other words, it *isn't* true. He knows it isn't true, and he's not going to be suckered into bed by this last Maggie lie."

"She lies," Kaiden agreed, "but Maggie's the real life force in the play, isn't she? Isn't she forever talking about all the life in herself? But she's also a ball-buster: remember how she takes away Brick's crutch and tosses it off the balcony? Isn't that a symbol or something for all of her emasculating words and actions. Maggie takes away the only remaining thing that lets him stand up like a man."

"I think that's right," Ben said. "Go back to that last line. Just before Brick says it, Maggie asks him, 'What do you say?' and Brick says, 'I don't say anything.' He becomes not only immobile and inert but also mute, *like* a brick. Maggie takes it as a surrender. She tells him what he wants, like baby-talk, sort of makes him into the baby she hopes to have with him, promises to hand him his life, like mothers do. And declares her everlasting love. Which he then mocks with his final cynical line."

"And the last word of that last line," I said, "echoes its earlier use, by Brick, in two sentences that say almost the same thing. Please correct me, Ben, if I misquote them. Both of them happen in Brick's exchange with Maggie when he declares that his friendship with Skipper is 'the one great good thing which is true' in his experience. And then, repudiating 'love with you, Maggie,' he repeats, 'friendship with Skipper was that one great true thing....' He makes it special, different, an affection wholly unique in the world of relationships. And in the resonance of 'true' in that final word, Brick affirms the ringing truth that his friendship with Skipper was 'the one great good thing which is true' in his life, and that Maggie's just proclaimed 'love' is utterly false — nothing but another lie."

Everybody went quiet.

"Are we done?" I asked into the silence. "I guess we didn't solve anything, but that was fun. Maybe we should all plan to see the play together at Le Petit — you too, Monte — and see how close we got? For now, Kaiden, do we get dessert for our efforts?"

"We do," he said; "you want to refill the glasses again and help me in the kitchen?"

We brought out plates with slices of four-layered chocolate cake he'd brought home from Broussard's, with scoops of vanilla flecked with chocolate chips on the side.

"It's too late for coffee on a work-night," Kaiden said, "and hot chocolate would be overkill. If anyone wants milk or ice-water, please say so."

"I wouldn't mind milk," Monte said, and then nobody would.

As we spooned up the crumbs and cream and chips, I said: "Now there's one more surprise treat...I think: when I asked Ben to come tonight, I invited him to end our evening by reading or reciting one of his poems, or a speech he'd learned for one of his roles. Wouldn't we all enjoy that?" Genial smiles, hums and nods of assent, light patters of applause. "Ben?"

"If you're sure," he said, blushing, and reaching inside his jacket. "I thought I'd read a little narrative verse I wrote a while back that's now being considered for print by a small magazine nobody's ever heard of." He unfolded two sheets of paper. "It's titled 'A Christmas Gift,' and I hope you like it."

The poem described a young man's visit, on his motorcycle, to his college roommate's home for a Christmas holiday where he and his roommate's younger brother struck up an immediate friendship around sports. The visitor, an orphan, had no home of his own and was grateful for the invitation. The boy's family presented him with several seasonal gifts, among them, from the boy, a small, delicate ceramic sculpture he'd turned up at a local antique store of a man riding a motorcycle. The visitor took the boy for several tours around town on his bike, explained its various controls and functions, let him "ride" it in stationary mode and race its engine, let him refuel it, adjust the tire pressures. Early on the morning he left, the visitor returned the ceramic sculpture to the boy's dresser, with a note: "Keep this till the real one finds you, with love."

He folded the sheets and smiled, sweetly, at me. It was probably clear to others that something passed between us, but we didn't speak. Monte did:

"That was beautiful," he said. "Thank you, Ben." Others chimed in, softly.

* * *

Kaiden banged hard on my bedroom door, awakening me. "It's nine o'clock," he yelled. "You in there? I'm off on errands and to work. See yawl this evening." I heard the back door slam, and a minute later his cart wheels on the gravel. Taking two peppermints from the bed-table drawer, I made my way down the hall, still in my boxers and T, tapped lightly on the blue bedroom door, and moved quietly to sit on the side of the bed. "Rise and shine, pretty boy," I said as he stirred, "and pardon the pun on 'rise'!" I slipped a lifesaver between my teeth and touched one to his lips.

He giggled, taking it.

"Let's pee," I said; and we walked together into the bathroom, faced each other over the bowl, and let rip two liberal streams.

"You know what Jack said to me at the door last night?" Monte asked. "He said, 'If you ever leave Troy, call me.'"

"That dog. He's smitten. Well, you did look very smart, and you made yourself downright tempting over dinner, you and that phallic jet of yours!"

"I did not," he said sternly. "But I really liked your friends. I see why you do. I'm glad you asked them over."

I'd resolved, after our two conversations about next things, to make Monte feel good about ourselves in these few remaining hours before releasing him back into the arms of his beloved Air Force: to give him some parting satisfaction in 'us,' never mind that neither of us knew quite what that meant right now, or might come to mean. But accusing him of playing the phallic jet card was a rotten first step.

"I'm sorry," I said. "I didn't mean that, about the jet. It was a cagey move, showing those snaps, to illustrate. Everybody lit up. I'd never seen the plane either, you know. It's very cool."

"Well, I like her. Look, I want to clean my teeth."

"Me too. There's an extra brush in the cabinet."

We playfully bumped hips and elbows at the sink, swished and spat, and then I turned him to me, sliding my fingers into his swarming curls, feeling myself sink right into his dark, bright, very wide eyes: "I do know what to do now, Monte."

I tugged off his T, stretched him out on his stomach, and began my massage at his neck and shoulders, working his biceps and forearms and hands and even fingers, elbowing the back muscles along his spine, probing and kneading to his little grunts and moans, squeezing the quadriceps and hamstrings, rubbing the feet and bussing the toes, slowly working my way back up again, pressing and stroking and brushing my lips along his quivering skin, not neglecting the genitals with my gentlest tongue. I raised his waist slightly to signal the turnover I wanted, and began anew at his lips and lobes, his fluttering eyelids, tracking down his neck to the stiffening nipples, lifted to my lips, his torso beginning to rise and fall and shiver with heavier breaths, the moans themselves now aural shivers. I tongued the graceful recesses east and west of his navel, its own shallow folds, and pressed gently on the shudder my fondling coaxed. My teeth nipped gently at the dark line of hair trending south, the tip of my tongue licking salty traces off pearly skin. I fingered ever so lightly his throbbing, flexing dick, aware that his head rolled back and forth on the pillow, his lips breathing my name among syllables of oh and no and god and yes, and his rapid breaths rasping and his thighs and knees rising and collapsing back; and I took him fully into my mouth, my lips working, my eyes open and watching, my head bobbing, my fingers revolving his balls, his hips thrusting now, and again, and again, heaving, and his words tumbling "Ohmygodohmygod, Oh, oh Troy…!" And a long, inarticulate choking sound, wracking spasms, a shudder, then whimpering, soprano breaths. I held him in until he pulled slowly away, still panting; used my tongue to cleanse his loins, rested my head against them. He toyed with my hair. I watched, felt him relax. Heard him sniffle.

I didn't move but quietly asked, "Are you crying, Monte?"

"A little," he said. "I don't know why."

"Please don't," I said. "I want you happy."

"Oh, Troy. I am. I am happy. That may be why I'm crying. You're so good to me. So…so incredibly sweet… and giving."

"It was good for me, too, Monte. It was good for us."

We were quiet for a bit.

"Your turn now," he said, sitting up, reaching down for me.

"Oh, Monte, you don't have to do that. Truly. I'm fine."

"No, I want to. I really want to. Let me try."

"Seriously, Monte, you don't have…."

"Yes, I do. I want to do it…for you. For my love of you."

He was suddenly all over me, hands and face and mouth, tearing at my shorts and T, licking and biting, trickling his nails tremulously across and around, along and into; rooting and burrowing and nuzzling, slicking my skin with his avid tongue; and then with the softest of grips he lifted me into his mouth, his lips tingling my glans, opening in welcome to my shaft. It was unutterably thrilling, the blinding joy of it stifling any protests I might have voiced. Eager and vigorous, intently focused, he plunged and dipped, rubbed and stroked and sucked and guzzled, and I was soon lost, dizzied, in the ascent to frenzy, accompanied by his low, purring urges. "Yes," I rasped, "yes…oh my yes, please…" and thrust and bucked, groaned and pleaded, "Oh Monte…my boy Monte, my boy, my boy, please…yes…oh yes…oh

God...," my heart racing, my lungs panting, my whole body poised — held — at a precipitous edge, before pitching into bliss. That I finished so quickly, and so copiously, felt mildly embarrassing, but Monte seemed so pleased with his service that I didn't want to spoil the moment with editorials.

He bent over my loins, cooling them with his breath, then settled back, propped on his elbow, looking down into my wondering eyes.

"My Lord," he said, "that was fantastic. You were fantastic."

"Not sure what you mean? When?"

"Just then. You really got into it."

"Well, you brought me there. You did it."

"We did it. We did it twice. Is that how it's supposed to work?"

"I've never had lessons! It felt natural enough. For you?"

"I actually liked it. Did you?"

"I loved it. You were great."

"*We* were. That was us. Monte and Troy. My Troj."

We kissed — gently, tenderly — and snuggled together, back into the pillows.

For the afternoon, we devoted ourselves to clearing the evidence and tidying the house, so that by the time Kaiden returned from work it was clean and orderly — the kitchen in particular neat and bright — with an unneeded fire in the hearth and Schubert on the hi-fi in the parlor.

"Wow!" he said, "It looks great in here and smells even better. Thanks, guys, for cleaning up that mess."

"We couldn't stand it another minute," Monte joked. "It was our pleasure."

"I wouldn't go that far," I said. "You want a scotch, Kaiden? I'll fix it."

"You know," he said, "I don't think so. But I don't want to cook either. We could heat up the leftover gumbo…or order…pepperoni pizza. Let's do that."

So we settled down in the living room to await the delivery and to post-mortem the party.

Monte led off: "It was a huge success, didn't you think? The dinner was fantastic, Kaiden. Thank you so much for spending the day making it. And thank you, Troy, for managing the whole thing with such class. I loved meeting your very nice friends. Everybody welcomed me and made me feel like part of the group. I'm very grateful to you both for hosting such a wonderful evening. I'll never forget it!"

"It was our honor and privilege" I said; "now tell us what you really thought!"

We laughed. "I thought Ben was especially good," Kaiden said. "He knows a mighty lot about that play. And his sweet poem near 'bout made me cry."

"How'd *you* know so much about it, Troy? The play?" Monte asked.

"I cheated," I said. "Of course I loved the movie and saw it at least a couple of times. And when I decided to bring it up to talk about, I got a copy of the play from the library and read it. So it was fresh in my mind. How'd yawl think the discussion went?"

"It made me want to see the movie again," Monte said. "I can't decide whether Brick is or isn't."

"He's both," I said. "Is in his heart, isn't in his head. He knows that, can't live with the division, and so is killing himself with drink. He wouldn't say it, but subconsciously he wants to join Skipper."

"It's just too depressing," Kaiden said. "Can we talk about something else? What time's your flight, Monte?"

"That's also depressing," I said.

"Around ten. I can get a bus, maybe around seven-thirty?"

"No, no," Kaiden said, "Troy can have the car. Yawl should prob'ly leave by 8. You'll want breakfast…let's say, seven? May I make you sandwiches for lunch?"

"Thank you, but don't. I'll be back in Houston by lunch. Mother'll meet me."

"Unless…," Kaiden said, "unless you run away with your airline steward and live happily ever after. You'll be wearing your spiffy uniform, of course!"

This fell flat. I was stunned. Monte looked at me for a clue but I had none. Kaiden lowered his eyes and cleared his throat.

"Sorry," he said. "It was supposed to be a joke. But Monte does look mighty…um…fine in that uniform." This verged on making it worse but he caught himself in time.

"Thanks," Monte said. "They encourage us to wear one when we travel."

"You sure I can't make sandwiches for you?"

"No, but thanks for the offer. Can I get a Coke to have with the pizza?"

"I'll get it," Kaiden said, and bounced up.

"What'd he mean?" Monte asked.

"Honestly, I don't know. It prob'ly was a joke…a thoughtless joke. He said he was sorry. Let's try to forget it."

"It sounded kind of insulting."

"I'm sure he didn't mean to be."

The doorbell chimed. "I'll get it," Kaiden yelled again, from the kitchen.

Over supper Kaiden told us a couple of funny stories about encounters with customers on the streets and staff in the Broussard's kitchen, and mention of the kitchen led me to remember episodes from Jubilee's, and Monte perked up with very funny tales I'd never heard about our boss out there, Sergeant Stephanie, and how butch she was and tried to disguise her interest in some similarly large girls on the staff.

"You're making that up, " I said. "I never heard that."

"But it might be true," Monte said, laughing in a way I happily remembered from the camp.

"And now, boys," he continued. "We have an early morning ahead. If you'll excuse me, I'm going to turn in. Will somebody wake me by 6? Sleep well. See you in the dawning!"

"I'll be up," Kaiden said. "I'll do it."

More morning "thank-yous" and warm farewells behind us, Monte and I — he freshly shaved and dashing in his uniform — headed back out Airline Highway into a fresh, cloudless spring morning.

"Good day for flying," I said.

"I wish I weren't," he said. "I'd rather not leave."

"Well, I wish you didn't have to; it's been terrific having you here. You don't have to sit all the way over there, though. I'm over here!"

He grinned and scooted over, next to me, and laid his hand on my thigh.

"I've been thinking," he said after a pause. "I feel different. Like something has changed. Do you? Like we're different,"

"Not sure what you mean. How different?"

"I dunno, but it's like I feel a little more grown-up or something, maybe more self-confident…in light of what we did. It feels like we took a step, sort of reached a plateau?"

"Lost our virginity, you mean?"

We laughed. "No, not that. We know each other better, though, and that's part of it, but it's not just that. Things feel more stable or something, more definite, I guess I mean. I feel kind of, well, settled. I feel comfortable. Except I wish I weren't leaving. You."

"For sure we know each other better, and we certainly took a step. And I feel more relaxed with you too. But we're more than five years older than we were at Jubilee. We should feel different. We *are* more mature, and know ourselves better than we did then; and that helps us know each other better too. Is that what you mean?"

"I guess so. But I'm pretty sure the comfort — or maybe it's satisfaction? — has a lot to do with being with you. You give me something — your presence gives me something that makes me feel better, a little more sure of myself, maybe. It's like you kind of support me without doing anything obvious. I may like myself a little better for being around you."

"Well, I like being around you. I'm going to miss not being around you."

"I'm carrying a little bit of you back with me," he said, looking up at me and smiling. "And that's a comfort."

"And I some of you. And it is."

He stroked my thigh with a finger.

"Better not do that," I said; "I'm driving."

We went quiet for a mile or two. "Want some gum?" he asked, fishing into his pocket. "I wish we could stop and move to the back seat and make out for a while."

I smiled and dropped my hand onto his for a few seconds.

"You should think about visiting me at the base, Troy," he said. "I'd love to take you up for a ride. Not in the 105, though; it's a one-seater. But other fighter jets have two. Wouldn't that be great?"

"I'd probably barf all over you."

"How about at Christmas? You don't have to go home for Christmas, do you? Why not spend it with me? We could rent a house for a week."

"I don't know if I could afford that, and I wouldn't feel right about asking my folks to fund it. Would there be guest houses on the base?"

"I'll find out. So you'll think about it? That would be something to look forward to!"

"Yes, it would. But let's not count on it yet. I'm going to be really busy in the fall."

"We're talking about the Christmas vacation! Maybe Houston is more feasible. Maybe you could visit my home in Houston. It's time you met my folks."

"That sounds really serious!"

"I mean for it to be," he said, seriously.

"Troy," he said after more silence; "don't come inside with me at the airport. Just let me off at the entrance, okay?"

"I'd rather see you to the gate. I don't mind parking."

"Let's say bye here. I want to hold you and kiss you goodbye. If you come to the gate, I'll cry. I don't want to cry...until I cry I on the plane."

"Sure. We can park to unload. They'll let us stay there for a bit."

"What will you do the rest of the day?" he asked.

"I'm going straight to campus, to the Department, to see what's happened during the break. And then get to work. I'm really backed up. When're you flying back to Nellis?"

"Sunday. I'll have one day at home."

"I'm so very glad you came, Monte. Your visit has meant...has meant...just about everything to me. Please know that."

He gripped my thigh.

Arrived at the terminal we hugged and kissed, with maximum clumsiness, there in the front seat. He rolled down his window, stepped out, grabbed his duffle from the back, and leaned into the window, smiling: "The all grown-up First Lieutenant Monte Trevalyn loves you, Mr. Timothy Troy Tyler, and always will. You can bank on that!" His eyes glistened but the voice rang strong.

A mile down the highway, I pulled off onto the shoulder and sobbed.

**29**

My Department pigeonhole overflowed with textbook advertisements, announcements, memos, and several U.S. Postal, stamped, mailed envelopes, including a large brown one and a small, boutique-flavored, card-sized one with elegant black script on the front and a French Quarter address engraved on the reverse. The return address on the brown envelope was *Keats-Shelley Journal* at the Houghton Library of Harvard, at which my heart sank, for it must contain my rejected paper on *Cain*. I opened the small one first to find a hand-written invitation from "Kyle Mason" to Kaiden and me for cocktails at "our" apartment on Royal Street on Saturday, two weeks from tomorrow, at 6 p.m., business dress. "Please come," he'd added, above his swirly signature. I remembered Kyle, less from the encounter at Dixie's than from Jack's description of his "group" and their little club. I set aside the card and turned to the large envelope, my fingers atremble. Yes, my essay was in there, but behind a typed letter on letterhead stationery and a paper-clipped packet of pages. I looked away and took a breath. This could be something. I read: "Thank you for sending your essay, 'Imagery and Theme in Byron's *Cain*,' to *Keats-Shelley Journal*. We are pleased to accept it, provisionally, for publication, pending your review of and response to the enclosed comments from our editorial staff, and two reader's reports from distinguished Byronists, one of whom chooses to identify himself to you. Please return the marked essay to us with one copy of your revision of your work. After our staff reviews the revision and finds it satisfactorily responsive to the critiques, we will resubmit it to at least one of the first readers. When we receive his (their) responses and recommendations, we will inform you of our final decision on publication. Please let us know if you have any questions about the enclosed materials or the procedure here described. Thank you again for sending your work to us, and congratulations on the positive evaluations of our readers. With all best wishes...."

I re-read, my stomach jumping, heart pounding. This was something, all right. Not the gold medal, no, but something. The packet held a typed, four-page report from Professor William Marshall of the University of Pennsylvania, whose letter invited me to be in touch with him if I had questions about his critique. The second report was three, mostly complimentary paragraphs without recommendations for revisions.

I stepped inside the Departmental Office, surprisingly open on the holiday, and met the Chairman leaving his inner sanctum.

"Professor Grant!" I exclaimed. "How lucky I am to see you!"

"Hello, Troy. I'm on my way to a meeting, but can I help you?"

"Well, sir, I've just this minute heard from *Keats-Shelley Journal*, and they've *provisionally* accepted my *Cain* essay for publication! Pending my revisions, of course."

"Well that's outstanding, Troy," he said, holding out his hand and smiling broadly. "Congratulations! I'm so pleased for you! It's a significant achievement. Do you know who your readers were?"

"One was William Marshall. He included a long report. I haven't read it yet."

"Oh, Bill Marshall. Penn. A fine man and a coming Romanticist. Worth cultivating, if he's willing."

"Would you care to help me with revisions, sir?"

"It's better that you work with your readers' reports. They're tuned in to what the *Journal* wants."

"May I use the telephone here in the office, sir?"

"For a local call, of course. Just pull the door to when you leave. And enjoy a day of celebration! You've earned it! Congratulations again!"

Jack picked up. "Jack? Troy. You've got your own extension now? Cool. Look, I'm on campus. Could you meet me over here for lunch? Oh, right. Nothing's open.

How about at Maple Street? In half an hour? Thanks. See you there."

"Hey, again," he said, pulling up a chair and smoothing his khakis as he sat. "You sounded breathless. What's going on? No, wait. First: That was a really great party! Thanks again for inviting me. Kaiden's a fantastic cook. And Monte's a dreamboat!"

"Yeah. He told me what you said at the door."

"Was that okay? Is that what you're about to beat me up for saying?"

"No, it's all right. I kind of like you noticing what a stud he is. And he's out of your reach now! Although I wouldn't trust you not to chase him."

We ordered cheeseburgers and tea. And onion rings.

"What'd you do over break, Jack? You didn't leave town?"

"Nope. I worked the whole week…till now. I pretty much caught up. Nobody was around. You?"

"Not a lick of work. A few other licks, you might say." He smirked. "But I got great news today. May I share? *Keats-Shelley Journal* wants my *Cain*. The one you read. *Provisionally*, they want it. I've got to revise; and I haven't absorbed the long readers' reports yet, but I figure I can revise enough…. I'll want you to look it over again, if you would. That's the first thing I wanted to tell you."

"God, Troy, you are on the fast track! That's tremendous news! Bravo, fella! Well-done! Sure, I'll read your revision. Are you telling it around?"

"Just to you...and Kaiden. Until it's officially accepted. I ran into Grant on campus and told him."

"You're kind of his boy, aren't you? He likes you."

"Well, he's going to direct my dissertation. Maybe. I've asked him to. Is that what people say, that I'm his boy?"

"Just me," he grinned. "So what's the second thing you want to tell me?"

"You remember Kyle. Kyle Mason, I now know."

"Yup. Why?"

"He's invited me, by mail, me and Kaiden, to a cocktail party at an apartment on Royal two weeks from tomorrow. Did you get one?"

"Not yet. I told you, I'm not exactly one of his group."

"Well I'm sure not either. What will happen if we decline?"

"I don't know. He prob'ly won't ask you again. Why wouldn't you go?"

"I don't think I want to get mixed up with him...or them. I've got enough going on."

"No, really: why?"

"Well, I guess I'm a little scared. If it's a queer club, if queer is all they are and do — their raison d'être — I don't think I'm into it in that degree. I'm not interested in groupie fucks and daisy chains and all that. I don't want to accept an invitation that's expected to end with me in the sack with Kyle."

"Why not? There could be advantages."

"What?"

"Well, they're rich. They're connected. They have pull. Or so I'm told."

"The whole idea makes me nervous. Why would they want me...except, you know?"

"What does Kaiden say?"

"I haven't told him. I may not tell him. I think he'd want to go."

"You won't tell him? That doesn't sound right. You have to tell him. You're both invited, right?"

"I might not tell him. The more I think about it, the less I want to go."

"Well, Kaiden and I could go! How's that?"

"You're not taking this seriously, Jack. It's kind of a problem. If you knew more about...about what's going on....why they're asking me, us, I might could figure it out...and make a smarter call."

"Maybe they want to talk literature with you? Get you to teach them a story. A queer novel? *Giovanni's Room*?"

"That one keeps coming up. You've read it?"

"Yeah, and you should."

Our food arrived. We dug in, crunched the rings.

"Okay," I said. "Maybe I should talk it over with Kaiden. I've kept too much from him lately."

"What does that mean?"

"Oh, nothing."

"Oh. That. Monte, you mean."

"So, the third thing: I also want your help with this.

"Let's go back to 'Cat.' You were, by the way, very good

on the play over dinner. You made excellent arguments. I didn't know you'd studied Williams."

"I haven't. I've read the play and seen the movie."

"Well, you were good. But there's one mystery in it I didn't bring up...because I thought I should have figured it out. And I hadn't...haven't. Maybe you know. You remember how Brick is always talking about that 'click' in his head he's drinking in order to hear? If he drinks enough, he says, he'll hear that click and find peace forever after. And then near the end he takes three quick swallows of the whiskey and declares, 'There!' Like he hears it, that click. What's the click?"

"I remember. But I don't know. Aren't there any other clues in the script?"

"Not that I can find. But use your imagination. What clicks?"

"Light switches? Tongues? Dogs' toenails on tile? Locks? I dunno."

"I read somewhere somebody's idea that 'click' is the last thing a suicide hears before the gun explodes, and that would sort of fit with Brick's suicidal drinking, and maybe peace in death is what he's after...but wouldn't the last thing he heard be the explosion, not some mechanical click? Does a trigger click? Not if there's a bullet in the chamber. And anyway, none of that happens in the play."

"No, and I don't think he's suicidal."

"Well, I thought after lunch we could run over to the Library and look up the word in the OED and see if we can find a clue there. Want to do that?"

"Sure, I need to check out some books anyway."

"Look, Jack," I said, "at the very first definition: 'a short sharp sound, as produced by...operating a switch.' So Brick — or the alcohol — switches off anger and anxiety and restlessness, and switches on peace? And later on, this: 'a sudden moment of understanding, realization, or recognition.' And this example, from William James: 'This is a state of consent, and the passage from the former state to it...is...characterized by the mental "click" of resolve.' And this one, from *Boy's Life:* 'with a click of his brain, a scheme was born.' So the click enables mental passage from one troublesome, psychological condition to another, more desirable one? Doesn't that work for Brick?"

"Yeah, I guess. It's just not very poetic. And Williams is a poet. But if Brick's click opens a passage to peace — if it 'resolves' or settles an agitation or eases an anxiety — and isn't the pop of a cork or the twist of a cap — then it works, and possibly gives him hope. Maybe it's the click of a light bulb chain?"

Jack found his books to check out and we left the stacks to sprawl on the broad front steps for a smoke. "So, Troy: how'd things work out during Monte's visit? You and Kaiden survive it intact?"

"I think so. Something happened right at the end I'm a little worried about. But Kaiden gave us lots of room. And...and we...aw, fuck, Jack, I just don't know. I really don't know what to do about all this. It'a maybe a good thing Monte doesn't live here. I might...I might... have to choose, you know?"

"You want to talk about it?"

"No. Yeah. Do you think queers can love two boys equally?"

"How about three? Do I hear three?"

"Stop it. I'm serious."

"I doubt anybody can do that...equally. Any better than our minds can do two or more things equally well at the same time."

"Wait. What? Say that again."

He did.

"Is that really true?" from me. "We can't? We sure as hell try all the time. I bet Monte didn't learn that in flight school."

"But I don't think we can...not equally well."

"Well, I guess I've got a little problem here, you think?"

\* \* \*

"I feel like a martini," Kaiden said, dropping his jacket and heading toward the kitchen.

"You're early," I said. "Everything okay?"

"Not at Broussard's. Low turnout tonight. They said I could leave."

"We're having dinner together?"

"Martinis first. You want one?"

"I'll try it. I've never had one. It's Dr. Grant's favorite cocktail."

"Brace yourself. It packs a wallop. But it's the best drink ever."

I'd been re-reading, maybe for the fifth time, the reader's report on my essay, complimented by the praise and especially by the close attention Professor Marshall had paid my work. He recommended changes, always respectfully, and explained why, and offered suggestions for revision. It looked like an ideal model I might imitate on my own students' papers.

"I got good news," I said, following Kaiden into the kitchen. "The journal wants to publish my essay...if I revise it. I got positive readers' reports."

He set down the Gilbey's. "Really, Troy? Hey, that's great! That's a big deal, idn' it, getting an essay published? Wow! A job offer's bound to be next!" He gave me a quick hug and a peck on the cheek. "I'm proud of you, guy!"

"They want a lot of work," I said, waving the Marshall pages. "But I think I can do it. And the suggestions are good. I see that. They'll make it better. What's that you're putting in now?"

"One teaspoon of vermouth, the rest gin. And this," he said, lifting a bottle of green olives, "this is the perfecting touch: two drops of olive juice. It's called a dirty martini. Add the ice, and stir. Never shake. Stir. And, straining off the ice like this, serve, one whole olive, on a pick, in each. Like so. The glasses should be chilled and frosty. We'll put these in the freezer when we're done, for next time. To us," he said, lifting his glass. "Be careful. Sip."

"To us," I said, wondering what it meant. "Whoa! That's...strong. Good...but strong."

"Let's take them in the living room. Okay if I warm up the gumbo for tonight's meal? It won't be good much longer. I'll start the rice after we've sipped."

He poked at the fire I'd made, and we took separate chairs.

"This is really good, Kaiden," I said. "I could get used to this."

"Slowly. Did you get Monte off okay?"

"I guess. We said goodbye in the car. He was afraid he might cry at the gate."

"He's very nice, Troy. I can see why you like him."

"Why is that?"

He started. "Oh, I meant... I can see you like him."

"He says he loves me."

"Well, that makes two of us. And counting Jack...!"

"Stop. Don't."

"Don't you think we should talk, though, about the visit?"

"What about it?"

"Well, how it all went. The way you wanted it to? Did yawl have a good time?"

"I think we did. It ran a little long. He said he didn't want to leave."

"Did he say anything about me?"

"Oh, he liked you! He liked you just fine. And he loved your cooking! You made a big hit with that. And he was very grateful for your hospitality."

"Did yawl get done everything you wanted to? I mean, was it a satisfying visit for you?"

"What're you really asking, Kaiden?

"I think you know."

"Do you really want an answer?"

"Do you want to give me one?"

"No, but I figure I owe you one. Do you want it now."

"I don't think you owe me anything. But for the sake of our relationship, you'd better tell me, yes or no."

"Yes."

"I thought so. There. That's better."

We were quiet for a bit.

"It had to happen, Kaiden. It had to. It brewed and bubbled all through Jubilee, through his earlier visit, it was right there waiting to happen through our plans for this one. So it did. We had sex. I think we both enjoyed it. I don't regret it. I don't know what it meant. And I'm very sorry, deeply sorry if we've...if I've...hurt you. I'd truly hate to hurt you."

"Thank you for telling me. I think I'm kind of glad it happened. I figured it might. I guess I agree it had to. If I'd been in your shoes, it would've happened. I'm even a little glad you enjoyed it. Maybe you'll teach me new tricks. But yes, we'll need to figure out what it meant, what it means. What I don't want is for it to change anything...between us. Let's live with the knowing for a while and see how we feel. Could we agree on that? Just carry on as usual?"

"May I ask you something? What did you mean the other night when you said that about Monte running off with an airline steward? You said it was a joke. It sounded nasty."

"It came out all wrong. I've thought about it, and I think I know what happened. And I'm really really sorry. It was raw, naked jealousy. I'm ashamed of it. I'd worked so hard, really hard, not to be jealous of Monte…during his visit. But that was jealousy talking. Maybe a little about the steward but the steward was a stand-in for what I was so afraid might be happening. I was so afraid of losing you to Monte and his…uniform, his glamorous plane! I was even conscious of that fear, but I lost control of my tongue. I'm sorry I hurt his feelings. Did I hurt his feelings?"

"He's not holding a grudge. He liked you, Kaiden. He respects you."

"May I refresh your drink? I'll put the gumbo on to warm…and heat water for the rice. Come with me."

"So are we okay?" he asked, bustling about the kitchen.

"Let me tell you one thing I told Monte…about us. He wanted more from me than I can give him. And I told him that. It isn't that what he wants already belongs to you. I told him that whatever he and I did doesn't — won't — change my feeling for you. I don't know how it works but I don't *feel* like there's any competition among us here. What he and I have doesn't impact what you and I have. That's how I feel about it. Is that clear?"

He laughed. "No, sweetheart, it's kind of garbled. But I'll take it. We're copacetic, aren't we? We're all right about Monte? How about we drink to Monte?"

And we did, from fresh glasses.

\* \* \*

Jack's phone call awakened me the next morning. "Roll out," he said; "Kyle's been arrested. It's in today's *Picayune.*"

The Upstairs Lounge, a queer bar on Chartres in the Quarter, had been the scene of a brawl the night before, and police were summoned. Fighting ensued between customers and cops, Jack said the paper said, insults flew, blood flowed, and arrests followed, among them Kyle's, and his name and address appeared in the paper, with a sentence or two about his and his family's standing in the city (his father was a councilman). "He'll buy his way out, of course," Jack said, "but there'll prob'ly be repercussions. You might want to take note in light of your invitation."

I hadn't yet told Kaiden about it but now did. "We're invited. And now this!"

"Shouldn't we go?" he asked. "As a sign of support?"

"Will they even have it now? How do I reply to the invitation now?"

"Don't you want to go?"

"No. I didn't want to even before. That's why I didn't mention it to you yet. No, I don't want to attend. Do you?"

"Well, if they still host it, as a sort of defiance of the publicity, in the teeth of it, it might be great fun, doncha think?"

"No, but how do I decline the invitation now? I can't write. They might be checking his mail."

"Oh don't be absurd. The paper didn't say he'd been charged with anything, did it? Didn't Jack say?"

"No. But he's arrested, so he must have been charged. He did tell me those guys have Tulane yearbooks in their apartment. What if the cops search the place?"

"You're thinking they might have circled your photograph and sprinkled stars around it, with your address and phone number and all?!"

"Don't make fun. This could get serious."

"You're exaggerating. There may be buzz for a week or so, but long term this won't amount to a thing. This is New Orleans. Nobody'll care for long. I think we should go. Accept the invitation."

"No. I can't go. The best thing is to toss the invitation. Ignore it. And hope there's no record. Ignoring it will send the right message: no thanks; don't write back. Will you be disappointed?"

"Yes."

"Write then. Accept. Jack says he'll go with you!"

But I tossed the invitation with the address.

\* \* \*

By Sunday noon, I'd set to work on my revision and by nightfall had a plan. As Jack had pointed out and I'd ignored, my treatment of the "organic nature" imagistic pattern in *Cain* was lame compared to my reading of the other three motifs, but I right away spotted the weakness and saw a way to strengthen it: the ironic version of positive nature appears in the negation figured by Eve's apple, and I'd stupidly omitted mention of that crucial image. Professor Marshall also thought, like Dr. Grant, that I needed to anchor myself more firmly in previous scholarship: nothing I'd found duplicated my thesis, but Marshall said I should prove I'd done my homework. This would require additional research and some doctoring of footnotes, but shouldn't take long. Otherwise, Marshall only wanted some minor stylistic polishing, and he identified lapses and exampled improvements. Meanwhile, I had three term papers to finish: I've already told you about the results of my essay on Yeats's "Second Coming" for Dr. Grant, but in real time it remained to be written. I'd about decided to unpack "Et tu, Brute" for Wally Gibson's Shakespeare essay, bringing out *all* the implications of Julius's seemingly simple question, which actually evokes his entire relationship with Brutus. And for Professor Schwartz's paper, I planned to discuss Milton's departures from the Biblical text in telling us Samson's great story, and why he omitted or changed details, looking particularly at the curious ending of the play. Not very exciting, that one, but I figured I was pretty well situated to take on a biblical text and a favorite tale of my youth. And I wouldn't have to plow through the "Paradises" several more times.

Plus, a stack of student themes awaited my grading, and another set was due in three weeks. For the current assignment, students might choose one of three assigned lyric poems for analysis in a four- to five-page typewritten essay, composed under my usual directive: "Please tell me *how* the poem means what you think it means. And try not to kill the poem in the process!" I give full credit for the "how" part to John Ciardi and his inspiring textbook introducing poetry to freshmen. The "kill" part is manifestly hypocritical, for my students will almost certainly have learned their slaughtering skills from my own instruction.

On the far horizon lay the dreaded preliminary examinations, four five-hour exams on consecutive Wednesday afternoons in late October and early November covering the whole of English and American literature from *Beowulf* to Virginia Woolf, as we learned to name the span: (1) Old English and Anglo-Saxon English literature through the Renaissance; (2) late seventeenth and eighteenth century English literature (including Milton); (3) nineteenth century English and American literature; (4) contemporary British and American Literature. The go-to sourcebook for prep since 1959 was the massive *A Literary History of England* by A. C. Baugh, far too weighty and expensive for grad student ownership; but the Library owned two copies, the Department another, and one already worn copy had been bequeathed by a former graduate student to his successors and could be checked out from the Department secretary for two-week stretches. Reservations of these latter copies were already booked through July. The graduate faculty did not provide reading-lists for these exams; when asked what material we were responsible for, professors always smiled and said, "Everything!" Exam sheets had to be returned with our filled bluebooks, but some of our generous and thoughtful predecessors had scrawled out, after each exam, what they could recall of the questions, and these, unedited by professors and staff, survived in a Department file and could be checked out for short periods. Naturally, copies were made and circulated, and proved helpful in our preparations. Seven of us signed up for the tests, four others besides Jack, Bailey, and me. I proposed to Jack that we study together at least one evening a week, evenly dividing up the material according to our areas of special training and interest: he was better at dates and events and titles, I at plots and themes, terms and devices. Together, we imagined questions and composed answers. He invited me to return to our former room for these sessions, and I quite liked being back there. It pleased him to tease and flirt, sometimes, and me good-naturedly to decline. Kaiden was fine with it.

President John F. Kennedy visited New Orleans on May 4th that year, a Friday, and I dismissed my class so we could all watch the cavalcade of visitors pass down St. Charles Avenue en route from the airport to City Hall, where he delivered an address to a vast crowd, perhaps mostly Roman Catholic, the very feature of his resume that set distance between my family and me on his qualifications for the presidency. I'd been thoroughly taken with him from the moment of his announcement of candidacy: his extraordinary good looks, his hair, his killer smile, his accent, his elegance and eloquence, his wit and charm, his brother Bobby, and of course his liberal politics. I'd become interested in politics back in 1952 when Estes Kefauver ran for the Democratic nomination for President, and I sat by our radio, with my own accounting pad, jotting down numbers as convention delegates loudly and dramatically cast their votes for nominees over the raucous disorder of the floor. I repeated this little bookkeeping scene in '56 and '60 too, and was thrilled by Kennedy's unexpected success in '60. The St. Charles trolley had been paused for the parade, and we were allowed to stand along the tracks as the President's limo convertible sped past toward downtown, he tanned and smiling and waving from the rear seat, his hair tossing in the breeze, within ten feet of ourselves.

Father moved later that month, having bought new living room, bedroom, and office furniture, and set up housekeeping in the Lake Charles parsonage, where his and Mother's requested renovations had been completed. The church loaned him a used Plymouth for pastoral calls and for the occasional trip back to Madison for a night or two with his wife. Mark, though, had failed pre-calculus math — almost certainly because of heavy involvement in the successful spring baseball season where his team, captained by himself, had won the district championship —and would have to re-take the course in summer school, and pass it, to keep his standing on the team. I half-wondered whether he'd rigged his own math failure in order to avoid a summer helping Father settle in Lake Charles.

Then in June, Kaiden learned that his father planned to sell the Magazine Street house in which we lived, our Garden District palace, where we were so agreeably ensconced for, I thought, the remainder of my Tulane career. But it wasn't to be. Father Carlisle also decided it was time that Kaiden, now gainfully employed, assumed more financial responsibility for his upkeep, and slashed Kaiden's allowance by a third. We had two months to make other housing arrangements. Whether our parents had been communicating, I doubt, but the timing of my own could not have been more inconvenient, for instead of increasing my own monthly cut of the presumably higher salary, as I'd hoped and thought fair, it too was reduced by 25%, on the disciplining assumption that Kaiden's luxury had taught me extravagance. Jack invited me to return to the room we'd shared, but I suspected even he doubted the wisdom of that idea. Kaiden almost panicked, and sort of froze in place for several days, uncertain where and how to begin seeking alternate accommodations. I went directly to the Gradate Student Housing Office and discovered that the newly completed dormitory on the campus, Robert Sharp Hall, would reserve the top floor of one wing for single male graduate students, and, moreover, that one resident would be designated an "advisor" for the floor and live there at no cost, with no responsibilities except to be available in case of need. Might I be interested in applying for the job? I completed the application form in about a minute flat.

The return to dorm room life wasn't appealing but the financial benefit more than made up for the allowance deficit, and the prospect of living so conveniently on campus was an attraction. How Kaiden and I would manage and adjust was uncertain: I didn't want rid of him, no indeed, and our living arrangement was congenial and comfortable and retained its exciting, even thrilling occasions, and of course his cooking was a huge bonus. But the weight of the pending exams pressed hard on me; I was mildly frightened, and I resented time lost on books to sustain relationship. I didn't greatly begrudge the opportunity for a change.

In July, Kaiden was promoted to junior assistant chef at Broussard's and offered a new schedule: one week as luncheon chef, the next as evening chef, so to learn and practice the entire menu (and, it looked like, prepare for another promotion down the line). And he would give up the street-peddling, which Kaiden was more than ready to do. At about the same time, a restaurant colleague, recently promoted from senior busboy to apprentice waiter, lost his roommate and offered the opening to Kaiden. It was a furnished two bedroom unit in a three-story building, Kaiden told me, in the Quarter within walking distance of the restaurant, with a small kitchen and a sitting room, and a large interior patio shared with other units. "He's straight and has a girlfriend," Kaiden said; "and when they share a bed, it's hers." My advisor's quarters didn't qualify as a suite, merely a dorm room, with two pull-out single beds. "We'll figure it out," Kaiden assured me. Broussard's bought Kaiden's cart and packed it into a storehouse of relics behind the kitchen. He in turn purchased a barely used Schwinn Jaguar Mark IV 3-speed that Ben knew of and put him onto. Luckily, I got the dorm adviser's job…and my *Cain* paper was accepted for publication.

Ben began read-throughs of "Cat" with the other actors and crew in late June, against an opening scheduled for mid-August. He showed up at my dorm room days after I'd moved in — in my circumstances they allowed me in before the fall students arrived — to present me with a copy of his "Christmas Gift" lyric, now printed in *The Appalachian Review*, a small regional journal "of no repute at all," he said; but I could see he was proud of his poem, as was I for him. He wanted Mark's address to send him a copy, and I happily handed it over.

I asked him: "Do you have to tailor your Big Daddy to the actor's interpretation — the guy who's playing him? — or can you be your own original BD?"

"So long as mine isn't so eccentric and deviant it throws the other actors off," he said, "I can be me. Before we open, we'll do a few rehearsals with me in the role. No, you can't; they're closed. But there's an alternative. Since Le Petit is dark on Mondays, a week from next Monday, at 2 in the afternoon, we're doing the show with us understudies in the major roles. Guests by invitation only. They wanted to give us an opportunity to play before a live audience, and we may not get to, since everybody's healthy and looks good for the full run. So our stand-by Brick and Maggie and Big Daddy and Big Mama and Mae, we five, will perform that afternoon, and the regular cast will take their roles in our support. Here're two tickets for you...and Kaiden or Jack. Stick around for a party in the lobby afterward. Should be good fun!"

"Sounds like it! Thanks, Ben! Kaiden'll be working but Jack'll probably want to come. Wow! You as Big Daddy! Terrific!

"But, Ben, I have a burning question about 'Cat.' If you can answer it, I'll come see you in the play. If you can't, you shouldn't be in it! What's the 'click'? The click Brick keeps waiting for in his head. The click he's drinking to make go off? What is that, and what does it mean?"

"I don't know. It's just a click. Why does it have to mean something?"

"It's in a Tennessee Williams play. Everything means something. Do you mean to say yawl haven't talked about this click in cast meetings? Your director hasn't *said* what it means?"

"Not that I remember. Brick says it'll give him peace, doesn't he?"

"He does. And it apparently does. When he says, near the end, 'There!' Like it's just...clicked. I want to know *what* clicks?"

"I can ask my director. But I don't know. Will you still come?"

"Of course! Maybe a little light bulb chain will click in *my* head during the play and I'll learn."

"You sound obsessed."

"I prob'ly am."

"So am I." He grinned. "Take a look out the window and see why."

"What're you talking about. Out the window?"

"Down in the quad."

His motorcycle was parked down below, and on its main seat sat a rather hefty girl with very long, very yellow hair, strands of it lifting lightly into the air. She wore black capri pants and bright yellow sneakers to match the hair.

"Marianne Merriweather. How's that for a musical name?"

"She's yours?" I asked.

"Working on it," he said, grinning.

"Congrats, Ben. She's an actor?"

"She's working on it," he laughed. "Aren't we all? Better scoot. I've left Marianne down there too long. By the way, give Monte my best! I really liked that guy! And that cool plane of his! Good to see you, Troy!"

Monte had written from time to time over this long stretch, always sweetly, always lovingly, often remembering details of our visit, nearly always signing off by reminding me that we both carried traces of each other somewhere inside ourselves. He frequently repeated his invitation to Houston for the Christmas holidays, and said his parents joined him in encouraging my visit. It began to sound like a good way to celebrate success on my exams, and to avoid a holiday in Lake Charles, but I didn't want to jinx anything by assuming a passing mark and making plans. He may have welcomed my move to the dorm and out of Kaiden's reach, but he wrote little of it, and rarely mentioned Kaiden or alluded to his relocation. After all the talk about his phallic jet, I'm reluctant to say he loves the plane, but clearly he remains enthralled by the thrills it affords him and delights in the new training required of him.

Jack and I agreed to take three days off from exam preparation to work up calendars and syllabi for our fall freshmen courses, both of them the standard "introductions to literature," his in the short story, mine in poetry. It was our second go at both, and although I'd been satisfied with my first effort and had received encouraging evaluations, I wanted to scratch poems that had bombed in class and find new ones less demanding of me. My paper topics had also been bland and open-ended and less inspiring of creativity than I knew I could make them with a little effort. And since with a semester's practice I'd gained some confidence as an instructor, I wanted to move away from my lecturing posture and open up the class for give and take: preparation and distribution of study questions on each assigned poem (our text should have provided them) might help bring about discussion.

As the exam dates approached ever more swiftly, Jack and I found ourselves drifting into sympathetic companionship with the other aspirants (except Bailey) as we crossed paths in the library and the Department hallways. The sense of our miserably isolated competitive victimhood and persecution began to lift and shift into one of shared struggle in an achievable endeavor, where cooperation might prove mutually beneficial. My studying once a week with Jack had partly relieved that sense but it almost dissolved now in casual exchanges with fellow grads about where we were in the chronology of authors, the endless succession of texts, the complicated histories of critical methodologies, the petty, nit-picking quarrels over interpretive cruxes and niceties that marked our research and study. Rather than wilting under the numberless sub-plots of Trollope and Eliot and Dickens and Thackeray, we learned to laugh at our own bewilderments, to write mocking limericks and parodies of critical theories and even of revered poetic art ("The Idiot Boy," "Stopping by Woods…"), to swear reckless oaths ("I'll never get my doctorate if I have to read more than the first canto of "The Faerie Queen"!), and even to desecrate the margins of honored theoretical treatises with derisive cartoons. There was something slightly hysterical in all of this, but our irreverence partly relieved the anxiety and made us feel marginally less inferior in the unremittingly weighty presence and pressure of our literary gods.

Teaching freshmen also relieved. Not even the dimmest of our charges thought us gods but we were duly recognized as their leaders and awarded a modicum of authority and respect, so long as they were respected in return. And there were always redemptive moments, exciting occasions of discovery and revelation and reward, on both sides of the lectern. Here's a memorable one:

Our text for the class was Wordsworth's Petrarchan sonnet, "Composed Upon Westminster Bridge, September 3, 1802," a mild, lovely meditation upon the tranquil London cityscape as it appeared to the poet early one fall morning upon his departure for Dover:

> Earth has not anything to show more fair:
> Dull would he be of soul who could pass by
> A sight so touching in its majesty:
> This City now doth, like a garment, wear
> The beauty of the morning; silent, bare,

Ships, towers, domes, theaters, and temples lie
Open unto the fields, and to the sky;
All bright and glittering in the smokeless air.
Never did sun more beautifully steep
In his first splendor, valley, rock, or hill;
Ne'er saw I, never felt, a calm so deep!
The river glideth at his own sweet will:
Dear God! the very houses seem asleep;
And all that mighty heart is lying still.

We reminded ourselves of the structure and rhyme scheme; we identified the sites enumerated by the poet, named the poetic devices (simile, metaphor, personification, alliteration, internal rhyme); I remarked upon the "absolutism" of his declarations ("not anything," "Never did," "Ne'er," "I never felt," "all..."). And then I asked, "What *quality* of the scene forcefully impresses the poet? What pervasive feature of the cityscape does the speaker repeatedly emphasize?"

"Its beauty," said Malcolm Clark, "its natural beauty," probably thinking of Wordsworth's reputation as a nature poet.

"Yes, he mentions nature," I said, "but natural beauty may not be what most interests our speaker in this sonnet. Yes, Joel?"

Joel Norton is a small, quiet, gentle boy, sweet-tempered, not so much shy as reserved, patient, thoughtful, and exceptionally bright. "It's the calm," he said. "It's the tranquility that strikes him. He finally exclaims about it in the penultimate line. He almost swears about it, he's so dumbfounded."

"And why should he be surprised by tranquility?" I asked.

"Because cities aren't."

"Can you elaborate, Joel?"

"Well, cities…bustle. Cities are noisy. They're never calm. London is, in this sonnet's picture of it. What gets to the poet is this city's difference. Or how his view of it is different."

Joel had the class's attention, and mine. "And is he comparing it, implicitly comparing it, with something else?" I said.

"Maybe, like Malcolm said," Joel went on, "with natural beauty, or the beauty of the nature he's forever extolling. This city he's looking at is more like a natural scene than it's like the city it actually is?"

"Very good, Joel. I think that's right. You're saying his imagination is re-making a cityscape into a natural phenomenon he can then regard as beautiful?"

"Yes, sir," Joel said, "but it's more…it's more sinister than that, isn't it? In the final line, he says the 'mighty heart' of the city is 'lying still.' Sir, a still heart is a dead heart. Isn't he killing the city as it is in order to make it into something beautiful he can admire? A silent, inert vista? And when he does that, the 'mighty heart' is not only still in death; it's also *telling* an untruth: it's lying, about itself. It's misrepresenting what it *is*. Isn't it, sir?"

I was stunned. So was the class. They turned their eyes alternately on him, on me, on the text. I also quickly re-read lines I knew by heart. Two consecutive, resonant puns in the final line, and I'd never seen them! There was nothing to do but acknowledge the keenness of Joel's insight.

"This is what we sometimes call a 'teachable moment,' class," I said humbly, "and Joel is our teacher. It's an astute interpretation, Joel, and spot on. Insofar as I know, it's completely original. And convincing. For the benefit of the class, I should add that it runs against the conventional view of this sonnet. But it's a plausible and ingenious reading. We thank you, Joel. I salute you!" The smiling class applauded him. He blushed becomingly.

"And sir," he added: "You said he's leaving the city... for Dover. Does his physical departure from London signify an attitude toward the scene he's describing? How he feels about this re-imagined vista? I mean, he's giving it up."

"That might be an over-reach," I said. "It would raise problems. And the poem doesn't mention a departure. The bridge of the title may point to transition, or even connection, but I don't think that supports your reading."

"Why," Dwight Markham asked, "why is the river the only thing that moves in the poem?"

"Maybe it's resisting arrest," Trent Jarvis said, and half the class giggled.

"I suspect the line is there only for the end rhyme," I offered. "It's the weakest line in the sonnet, and discontinuous with the whole."

"Or maybe," Joel's hand went up, "maybe by its rebellious contrast, the moving river — the active *will* of the river — points to the stasis everywhere else? Highlights it?"

"So this one natural resource," I ventured, having been mildly chastened, "resists even the transforming imagination of the poet?"

You see what I mean, though:  Moments like that — with discerning insights — rare as they are, uplift the spirit, heal the sore spots, ease anxiety, and help redeem all the shit. I could hardly wait to tell Jack.

\* \* \*

Ben showed himself a phenomenal Big Daddy in the role! He owned the stage when he was on it, and even when shouting at it from the balcony outside. Less raucous and turbulent than Burl Ives, he was subtler and thus nastier; his snarls chilled. But he came across as genuinely loving toward son Brick, and forgiving, and even understanding of Brick's grief and the loss that spawned it. A compassionate heart showed through the anger and fear and disappointment and hurt. The bitter rage toward Big Mama was hard to watch, but her own exasperating aggravation probably earned it. Our friendly audience displayed generous appreciation, and the afterparty overflowed with good will and encouragement all around. I didn't learn another meaning for 'click,' but possibly I set aside obsession with it.

# PART THREE

---

## ONWARD

# 30

October 16, 1962
Nellis

Dear Troy,

This is strictly confidential. I've been reassigned.
I can't say to what mission. But some risk may
be involved. I'll try to stay in touch with you
but I may not be able to. I'd like to believe that
you'll pray for me and for all of us. Please don't
show this letter to anyone or say anything about
it. That could get me in trouble. I miss you and
love you.  Monte.

Needless to say, this was both mystifying and alarming.
That he sounded frightened frightened me. I don't think

he'd ever said the word "pray" to me, not even during all those religion-soaked weeks at Jubilee.

Two days later came another note: "Dear Troy: I may be flying over New Orleans soon. I'll try to send you a message. Monte."

What these communiques may have been about was clarified four days later when President Kennedy announced in a nationally broadcast television address that Russians were installing medium- and intermediate-range ballistic nuclear missile sites in Cuba. He ordered a naval quarantine of the island effective immediately, and informed Secretary and Chairman Khrushchev that the U.S. would not tolerate the introduction of offensive weapons into Cuba. I did not own a television set but saw this address, as did most of my dorm mates, in our crowded fourth-floor lounge.

"Cuba's only a thousand miles from here," someone said.

"The mainland's only ninety," someone else observed. "Have your draft cards ready!"

Back in the room, my phone rang.

"It's Ben," he said. "Does Monte know anything about this?"

"I don't know," I truthfully said.

"Well, let me know if he does." And he hung up.

Jack rang. "Did you see that?" he said. "Holy shit, what's going on? Do you want to come over?"

And then Kaiden: "Can I see you after work? Around ten?"

"That's too late, Kaiden. I'm sorry, but no, better not tonight. Let's meet tomorrow, if you've time?"

"Ten in the morning, then? Your room?"

It occurred to me briefly to wonder whether it took an international crisis to bring my friends into contact. Should I schedule a meeting?! On the other hand, I too worried. I remembered a decade earlier when a lot of folks got exercised over the possibility of nuclear war, and several good books and excellent movies cashed in on those fears, and for a while people dug bomb shelters in their back yards, but the craze had faded, and insofar as I knew no shelters pocked our neighborhood.

I figured it was unrealistic and evasive, possibly gutless, not to allow at least ten minutes of class time for student reflection and comment on this rapidly developing story. But they seemed more excited than worried. Of course: they were young and thought themselves safe and immortal. It didn't occur to me that they might ask what I thought.

"What would you do, sir," Caleb Wright asked, "if the air-raid sirens went off?"

"I'm not sure, Caleb. Find my slingshot? Do you have a plan?"

"I'd head right up to our dorm roof," Peter Green boasted, "and watch the missiles fly in!"

And shit your pants when they did, I uncharitably thought.

We went through the usual motions, the regular routines, but everybody acted on edge, fretful, preoccupied. Mothers stocked up on baby food, groceries, water. Men gathered in clumps on street corners with newspapers and frowns, biting on pipe stems and sucking cigarettes. Neighbors assembled on porches and in front yards and shared bulletins from the televisions that blared from dawn to midnight. And then on Sunday the twenty-eighth the crisis suddenly ended when Khrushchev agreed to remove all Russian missiles from Cuba on the U. S. promise not to invade the island. An almost audible national sigh of relief accompanied our view on Monday of a massive Russian ship inscribing a wide white semicircular wake to the left on a very blue Atlantic sea as it reversed course and headed back east to its home. With a degree of equanimity and celerity nearly matching the frenzy and hysteria that met the crisis, people seemed apathetically to settle back into routines largely indifferent to the brush with catastrophe. I urged Ben to write a poem about that.

Monte's next message, dated October twenty-fourth, arrived on the twenty-ninth as a wrinkled, soiled telegram, and read: "Over New Orleans. Hey there T. Love M." How he managed to send it, if indeed from his speeding jet overhead, I cannot imagine, and doubt that he could tell me. It must have been unlawful. But I loved his daring, the sheer hutzpah of the dispatch, and his thought of me. I assume he was flying reconnaissance over Cuba from Nellis, or circling with other jets near its air space in case of a combat emergency, but it does seem a long distance for him to shuttle every day. I'm sure he's unable to tell me.

Kaiden did not keep his morning appointment with me but we made a date for him to visit on his next night off, which would be Monday, two days before our first prelim exam on Wednesday from noon to five. I'd asked him to bring roast beef sandwiches and root beer from Maple Street. He arrived about six, stepped in, locked the door, leaned against it.

"C'mere," he said.

"We can't, Kaiden," I said. "I have to study."

"I have to hold you," he said, "and feel you hold me."

So we did, tightly, and kissed hard.

"That's enough," I said. "Let's eat. Unlock the door, please."

"IknowIknowIknow. You have to study. But we have to talk. This is not working out. I miss you too much."

"Really, Kaiden, this isn't a great time. Can we just have supper...and not get into...?"

"Do you actually *like* living here? Don't you even have a second set of sheets?"

"No. I had to buy these at a thrift shop. I get by."

"I have to move, Troy. We're too crowded, and it's too much, being with George at home and at work. I'm cross and depressed all the time."

"Well, I'm kind of stressed right now, K, and I can't think about moving again. This suits me. It's convenient. Maybe after the first of the year.... Or over semester break. Except, no, wait, I have a job here. I can't leave. See how rattled I am! I don't even know...."

"Well, we have to figure something out. I don't think I can live without you around. I need you around,

Troy. I really miss, you know, sleeping with you. I need to love you."

"Don't, Kaiden. You're making it harder…so to speak! Look, I miss you too. But I can'I. I've got these damnable exams, and I really have to put them first now, and until they're over, I can't get distracted and distressed by…by…our…well, our domestic situation. I'm sorry, but I can't deal with this stuff right now."

"Well, fuck, Troy," he said, flushing, "I'd rather not be 'stuff' to you, if that's what you think this is. I'm hurting, and I need you to help me. Don't you dare turn me away!"

"Four weeks, Kaiden. That's all I need. Four short weeks, and we'll be forevermore done with school exams. And we'll figure out housing. But I can't right now."

"You don't want me to stay the night? I could."

"That would be wonderful," I said; "but no. I've got a whole notebook to get through tonight. Starting now. In forty-eight hours I have to…."

"Yeah, take an exam. You said that. Really, you know," he said snuffling a little, "I do understand, and I'm sorry to make things worse for you, but being away from you, being without you, is really hurting me. I can't hardly stand it," his tears leaking now.

"Kaiden, you have to stop; you've got to get control of yourself and go. I miss you too, terribly, but we can't be together for a while. That's just how it is. I'll be in touch by phone, let you know how things are. But we'd better stay away from each other for now. We'll make up for it later. There will be a later, you know. There'll be heaven after this hell. Look ahead to the bliss, all right? Please?"

"It's not somebody else, is it, Troy?"

"Damn it, Kaiden! Just stop. No. It's nobody else. It's work. Don't you understand that my future employment is riding on my success in these exams? I have to pass. And right now you're getting in the way. Get ahold of yourself. This isn't like you at all. Finish your sandwich and go. I'll call. Here, kiss my lips and go!"

"Well," he said quietly, "good luck."

\* \* \*

The six of us staggered out into the hallway after the first exam — Bailey had finished ten minutes earlier and left — and huddled, Jack and Keith and I lighting up, though we'd been allowed to smoke during the exam, and had.

"Not too bad," Jack said; "the Old English/Anglo Saxon part was a snap, didn't you think? But the non-Shakespeare Renaissance? A killer. Renaissance *prose*? Didn't they all write iambic pentameter?! Who reads that crap?!"

"I hadn't," Keith said. "And I didn't quite finish the *Beowulf* translation. Troy?"

"I didn't stop writing," I said, "but I prob'ly bluffed a lot. Some of those I.D.'s were really obscure. I might have cleared a C-."

"They don't grade them," Neville said. "Not letter-grade. You pass or fail. And they don't tell us till we've finished all four tests, and even then not which tests we passed or failed. If we bomb one, we have to retake the set."

"Don't remind us," Chris said. "Did yawl get the one about *sapienthia and fortitudo* in *Beowulf*?"

"Yeah," Ryan said. "Dr. Morehouse filched that one from a brilliant article by Robert Kaske. I happened to read it during the course and remembered enough to make do." I'd also read it but kept quiet.

"You have a favorite hardest question, Troy?"

"Oh yeah: 'Discuss the beginnings of literary criticism in sixteenth century England.' Who besides Sidney, and maybe Campion and Daniel, would that be?"

"That's more than I remembered," Neville said. "Anybody else want a beer?"

"Just one," I said.

"He said, joking," Chris said.

**31**

The call came around suppertime on the day before our third exam. The male voice identified itself as belonging to a Herbert Stockton. "I taught Monte in Sunday school and am longtime friends with his parents," he said. "They asked me to call you and gave me numbers. You are Troy Tyler, correct? I'm afraid I have tragic news."

He said it was a routine training mission out of Nellis. He said Monte began losing altitude at 3000 feet. He said the commanding officer told Monte to eject, but Monte spotted a grade school in his flight-path and stayed with the aircraft to steer it away from the school, thus sparing the lives of four hundred children, although taking those of five civilians in a housing development, and losing his own, in the explosive crash. Arrangements were pending, he said.

The news was all over the networks, and in the headlines of the evening and morning papers. Ben was the first to arrive at my dorm room when I returned to it, numb, from the tv lounge.

"Oh God!" he sobbed, folding me into a hug. "Oh God, Troy, I'm so sorry, so God-awful sorry!"

Then Jack was there, damp-eyed and discomposed and disheveled from his desk, then Kaiden, also weeping, still in his apron. "Thanks for coming, guys," I said. "It's hard to believe, idn it? I don't think I do believe it."

"How can we help?" Kaiden asked.

"I don't know. I don't know what I'm doing, what to do. Just stay with me for a while. Talk to me. I'd like to throw that chair through the window."

"I'll help," Jack said. "You want me to get some beer?"

"No, not really. They're saying he's a hero. For missing that school."

"How could he even think to do that?" Kaiden asked, "with the plane crashing?"

"A hero would," Ben said.

"I should send something," I said. "Flowers?"

"Flowers and a card, maybe a letter," Kaiden offered.

"I can't write. Not yet. What would I say?"

"You won't attend the funeral?" Jack asked.

"How can I? We've got these tests, two more tests. But I *should* go. I should be there. But I don't know that I want to be there. No, I don't want to. Would you, Ben?"

"I can't make that call for you," Ben said.

"That means you'd go. But I don't know if I can… or even want to. There'd be bus fare and a hotel. And I have two jobs. I can't just leave."

"And the tests, one tomorrow," Jack reminded us.

"And I wouldn't' know anybody. His Air Force mates will be there, all in uniform. I'd stand out. And how would we explain who I am? I might be an embarrassment…to his memory."

"Wouldn't his parents want you there? As his best friend?" Ben asked. "Wouldn't *he*?"

"What if his Mom put me in his room? Gave me his bed? I don't think I could bear that…but I couldn't bear to turn her down, either."

"Flowers and a card, then," Kaiden repeated. "With a note."

"You could visit them after the exams," Ben said.

"Would you like us to leave?" Jack asked.

"I guess so. No. Oh, I don't know. I may need to be alone. I should study. This test is supposed to cover my best period. I should go over my notes."

Kaiden covered his face with his hands and shook his head but said nothing.

"Couldn't you at ask for a postponement?" Ben said. "Surely, in the circumstances, the Department would sympathize?"

"No, I don't want to postpone. I'm primed. And it'll be a distraction. For twenty-four hours I could use some distraction. I can get back to all this on Thursday. Maybe the shock'll be over by then."

"Haven't you even cried?" Kaiden asked. "You don't look like you've cried."

"No," I said, a little surprised myself. "I don't think I have. Maybe I'd have to believe it to cry. I don't think of him…I don't think of Monte…as…gone."

The other six knew when we gathered for the nineteenth-century exam the next day. And they all, including Bailey, spoke consoling words. I hadn't slept much and still felt numb, but I also felt kind of eager to get started on what should be my best showing. Dr. Grant called me outside before distributing the exam sheets and offered condolences and a gentle pat on my shoulder. And expressed satisfaction that I'd showed up.

The others had waited in the hallway afterward.

"You feel like a beer, Troy?" Neville asked.

"Thanks, Neville, but I guess not. I think I'll walk. Jack?"

"Let's head over to the Park," I said to him outside. "It won't be dark for a while yet. Do you mind not having a beer?"

"No, it's fine. You feel okay about the exam?"

"I won't get honors but I think I passed. How'd you do?"

"So-so. Not my best. I think we're all a little bummed…."

"I guess I'd like to think about Monte now, Jack. May we?"

"Of course," he said, reaching out to touch my arm.

And before we could even start, I broke down, as though the very mention of his name opened the floodgates. Jack led me to a bench and we sat, his arm around my shoulder while I let go, without words for a while, just sobs, still with disbelief now mixed with horror too at what he must have suffered in those final seconds before impact, wondering whether he regretted his decision against ejection, whether he prayed, whether his whole short life flashed before his eyes, whether he knew now, wherever he was, that he was being honored as heroic, whether he'd said goodbye to me.

"I can't tell him goodbye, Jack," I said. "I want him back."

"So do I," he said. "This is all just so wrong. So senseless. He didn't have to die."

"But he did. He did have to. In that circumstance, Monte had to die. He couldn't have lived if he hadn't… hadn't stayed with the plane, and diverted it. No, he knew what had to be done, and did it."

"You should say that in an elegy. You know all about elegies, Troy, and you should write one about Monte."

"No, no. It's all too raw. I couldn't write. I don't even know how to write his folks."

"You will. Did you send the flowers?"

"Not yet. Maybe we could do that now. There's that place over on Broadway, might still be open. Would you do that with me now?"

We did. A tasteful, dark green wreath with red and white carnations. Signed, "With sorrow and love, Troy Tyler (Jubilee)." Jack helped me pay the balance.

"You want to sign it too?" I offered.

"No," he said. I learned later that he and Ben and Kaiden had pooled resources to wire white lilies.

National press coverage continued through the funeral. Ben found copies of the *Houston Press* at a downtown newsstand and brought one to me along with the *New York Times*. Monte's remains were such that the casket stayed closed. His parents combined a religious service at their Baptist church with a military ceremony at the gravesite, with flags and rifles and taps. Crowds gathered at both sites amid torrents of flowers, many mourners in uniforms. A reception at the family's home followed the interment where the city mayor and several decorated Air Force officers from Nellis spoke. I was gratified to have this information but it confirmed my decision not to attend the obsequies. I could not have endured the closed casket or the taps.

Within eight months, the Congressional Medal of Honor for Bravery, affirming Monte Trevalyn's official status as hero, was conferred upon shoulders I'd held in my arms.

I composed and typed a three-page letter to Monte's parents, finding that once started I didn't want to stop. I had much to say, and I believe Monte helped me say it well. I revealed nothing he wouldn't have wanted them to know, but I told them much they probably didn't know about how splendid a man he was and how kind and thoughtful and generous he was to me, and how crucially important in my life. And what an exemplary Christian man he was. I remembered funny stories about him from Jubilee, and moments safe to tell from his visit to New Orleans. I cried over the letter, felt better for finishing it, but the grief lingered and smoldered and became enduring heartache.

Around Thanksgiving, I received from his mother a small, gift-wrapped package containing a handsome, glittering diamond and a handwritten note: "Monte bought this for you, Troy, so you should have it. He told me it was for you. He said he wanted to give it to you but was afraid you might misunderstand."

Oh my boy, oh my dear boy, how joyfully I would have misunderstood!

In its gold setting, I wear it to this day.

The nightmares began shortly after the funeral. Night after night, I replayed the crash in my head, what I imagined the moments just before it to have been, and awoke screaming, and sometimes vomited. A passing thought could bring tears; once I had to step away from class to recover. And then later came the resurrection dreams, when I brought him back, into remembered scenes and into situations purely imaginative where we were happy together. I moved from bright moods to dark ones, unpredictably. Just about anything could make me weep, or want to. The instability soothed as much as annoyed me: I reasoned it was part of a natural grieving process and yet resented its disturbance. I often raged over trifles.

And then one afternoon came an unexpected impulse to visit church. I'd not been in a church for months and months, perhaps not since I was last at home. Across the street from the Newcomb campus on Broadway was the Episcopal Chapel of the Holy Spirit, an attractive, inviting A-frame structure with large panels of colored glass up and down the front and yellow-tinted windows along the sides. I didn't think about going there, or why I wanted to; I just went, found it open and empty, and took a seat in the consoling quiet. I knew that Episcopalians usually knelt and prayed before liturgies began, and although I didn't feel observed by persons living or dead, I went to my knees. In my tradition, prayer, modeled on The Lord's, always included asking, but I couldn't think of a single thing to ask for, even though I was nearly all the time prostrate with mysterious need. Next up in the paradigm text was "hallowing" the name. I'd dis-hallowed it in my impatience with Kaiden, but that was a slip. "Kingdom come...will be done..."? That didn't speak to me, or for me. And I had plenty of "daily bread." So what was I doing on my knees? Should I beg forgiveness? For what sins?

And then a dark and ugly thought crept into my mind. I tried shrugging it off, but it stuck. It wanted attention. I tried formulating it: What if everything that happened was God's punishment? A penalty for abomination?

We had sinned, there could be no doubt of that. Or maybe there *was* doubt of that. We'd harmed no one, least of all ourselves. We'd loved. I did not see how our love merited the catastrophic discipline of Monte's abrupt elimination from the planet, for loving. Yes, yes, I knew all the tiresome old arguments against our kind of loving, but we were enlightened and long over and past all of that, weren't we? And yet…and yet…wasn't there a possible explanation *in* all of that for what had happened? If we were wrong, if sinful, punishment was just. God had once wiped out an entire city for loving as we'd loved. Monte had wanted me to attend seminary with him — not for entirely pure reasons — and I'd declined: was I now supposed to pick up his mantle and apply? Was he being punished for my failure to respond to a call I'd never heard, or was our love the provoking sin here? I didn't know what message, if any, the calamity carried. Reason whispered that I'd tilted into craziness, but my heart, maybe my soul, felt uncertain. It seemed entirely possible that Monte and I had strayed together into a love that had pissed off God, and were paying for it, he radically, with everything, and I with wildly unfair and comparatively minimal misery.

I called Ben in, told him.

"You're not serious," he said, not unkindly.

"I am. It's not impossible…that we invited this. That this is just. Except that the penalties are all awry."

"You're saying God killed Monte because you and Monte slept together?"

"He didn't save him. It comes to the same thing. I'm saying God left me alone to suffer."

"You can't mean you want Monte to suffer instead of yourself," Ben said.

"No. But look: God punishes disobedience. It starts with Eden, and continues all the way through the Bible. God gets ticked off and punishes. It's at the heart of the Christian faith: Jesus died so *we don't* get punished."

"Oh for heaven's sake, Troy: the Bible's not history; it's mythology. It's a great story, but it isn't factually true. You know this. What's happened to you?"

"Monte died…is what happened to me. You're not hearing me, Ben."

"I'm trying to, Troy. I am. I wonder if you hear what you're saying. More to the point: in loving Monte, in loving Kaiden, you recognized and accepted authentic desires you'd forbidden yourself to have, natural desires you were born with. Why would God punish that? Would Monte really want you to become a stranger to yourself because he died in a plane crash?"

"Monte died for a reason. I'm trying to figure out what it is. Maybe I have."

"Maybe you haven't. And can't. Monte did not die so you can suffer. No, there's no reason to it. Accidents aren't reasonable. That's why they're accidents."

"They have causes. Something causes accidents. Why couldn't God have caused Monte's plane to crash to punish...what we did?"

"Troy," Ben said after a pause, "why did you and Monte do what you did?"

"Because we loved each other. We wanted each other."

"And how did that happen?"

"What do you mean? We were drawn to each other...we desired...."

"Biologically. Where'd you get that particular biological desire?"

"I don't know what...."

"You didn't manufacture that desire. You're not responsible for that desire. It came with you. It's your *nature* to desire other guys."

"But God said it's wrong. God says it's a sin."

"No, He didn't. God never said a word against it. Neither did Jesus. Not one word. And Jesus loved everyone, told us to, and pretty tightly bonded for years, in love, with his little band of friends. The apostle Paul had a little trouble with men cohabiting, and fundie evangelists ran with that, and the whole thing got codified in stone by an intolerant culture disposed to distrust difference. The culture disapproved, Troy, and the culture punished, aided by the church. You need to remember you didn't *choose* your sexual identity."

"But I did, Ben. I did choose. Kaiden told me the foolproof test was to ask who you thought about when you masturbated. And my answer came up male. And then I *chose* a guy to have sex with."

"You recognized the truth of what your gut revealed. You assented to it. You did *not* choose your orientation. You accepted, sensibly accepted, a truth about your created being, revealed by your unconscious mind, and affirmed it with action. You had nothing whatever to do with originating it."

"I dunno, Ben. It just feels wrong. It didn't before, and now it does. Why is that?"

"You're desperate for an explanation of Monte's death. Eventually we'll get a mechanical one. There's not another one. It was an accident. Putting God into the works gums them up. And feeling guilty yourself is sort of self-empowering, as though something you did made Monte die. Your understandable grief, your painful and necessary grief has sent you off the rails here, Troy. You figured out guilt back at Jubilee: you told me, and Kaiden told me, about that, but it's come back to steal your reason here. You can't change who you are because you've taken a temporary dislike to it. And you're not responsible for *being* who you are. You *are* responsible for making the best of it. And you're not making the best of it by feeling sorry for yourself for causing Monte's death by loving him. Surely you get the absurdity of that. You ought to be celebrating his heroism."

"I do. He was so...courageous. Unbelievably brave...."

"Believe it. Imitate it. It's going to take some courage for you to get past this illusion of your responsibility because you're just a little bit proud of it. And it may take even more courage to feel good again about loving guys. But the legitimacy of you loving guys is not at issue here. That issue got settled a while back. You carry the gene. Denying it or neglecting it would warp who you quintessentially are. Embracing it will be courageous, even heroic. You and Monte can be brothers in bravery."

"You know, Ben," I said, "we're just circling around here…wandering around and around what death means to the living, for the living. Maybe wandering around is all we can do. But it doesn't feel like enough, does it?"

# 32

All of us passed the prelims, Bailey with High Honors, Jack and I with Honors. The announcement inspired elation, of course, among the whole English graduate constituency, encouraged hope, and we seven enjoyed minor celebrity for several days. Dr. Grant offered smiles and waves as we met in the halls, and once gave me what I took as a heartening wink that I imagined might reference Monte's passing. My class even brought in iced doughnuts to hand around. I still had the Milton paper to finish, and semester finals to sit, and freshmen themes to mark and their exam to write, but generally the load began to feel lighter, systematically arranged, and manageable.

Kaiden gave me a week after the last prelim exam before showing up on his afternoon off.

"Just wanted to check on you, Troy, be sure you're okay. Yes? You look good."

"Yes, relieved, still busy. You?"

"Okay. Not real happy with my housing but a solution may be at hand."

"Yeah? Like what?"

"My roommate George and his girl just got engaged. I don't believe a fetus is involved but he wants to move in with her, I guess thinking he's entitled to more frequent nookie than he's getting now. Anyhow, he's nice enough to give me time to find a replacement roommate before he leaves, so I'm not stuck with the full rent. Of course, he's looking too. For some reason or other, I thought of you!"

"Kaiden, I've told you: I have this job. I'm settled in here. I don't mind it. I kind of like the convenience to everything on campus. I'm not looking to move again."

"I'm offering the Quarter. I'm offering me. I know how we can fix up my place, cheaply, and take serious advantage of the patio. And also: I've found out back an old empty tool shed with light and heat that looks to me like it's just waiting to become a writing studio for you! Under my creative, re-decorating hands! A desk, a chair, a cot for naps, a shelf for the coffeepot. It might've once been used as an overflow guest room for renters but it's empty now, and I'd love to ask management if we could have it for minimal rent if I cleaned it and fixed it up as a writing studio for you. Whyn't you come take a look at it?"

"I told you. I have this job. I can't just up and leave it."

"Sure you can. How many grad students do you figure are already lined up at the Housing Office to get it? Free rent? They'd fill the vacancy before the ink dried on your resignation. Besides, you're not really a grad student anymore and shouldn't be living in a dorm. You're a candidate for the Ph.D. You've graduated to new status. A dorm room is beneath you."

This was hogwash, of course, but it registered. I had sort of moved up. And the notion of my own studio had definite appeal.

"You think we — you and I — could just pick up… where we left off…as roommates, I mean?"

"Why couldn't we?" he said. "It hasn't been that long. The place's almost as nice, and the kitchen's adequate, and there're two baths but only one shower, and plenty of space for two, and nobody ever uses that really nice patio. Or the studio."

"How much is the rent?"

"About what you were paying before. And I'll bring home free food from the restaurant all the time."

"You can do that?"

"Now that I'm on a reduced income, I do. It's always good, too."

"Maybe I'll come for a look, if it's okay."

"Now?" he asked.

I had to think this through. It felt hasty and maybe reckless, too soon after Monte, too soon to be reasonably happy again. It felt vaguely unsuitable. And I wasn't sure living with Kaiden again would restore my contentment. What did that entail? We still both wore the bracelets but with what meaning to each of us wasn't clear. Would we share a bed again? I didn't want to cheapen K's enthusiasm but with Ben's advice in my head the idea of resuming had its appeal. Whether I had more privacy here than Kaiden offered seemed unlikely, for my grad student charges were forever popping in with questions and complaints and tattles. And maybe I could strip down Kaiden's cart to its former identity as bike and use it for transportation and exercise. No, the central question, I saw, was Kaiden himself. And Monte was somehow or other tied up with that. I couldn't keep Monte out of the calculus.

I wrote his parents a long seasonal greeting, thinking how terribly sad the holiday was certain to be for them and hoping the voice of his friend might lift their spirits (I also wanted to ask what plans they had for Monte's sweet little MG but knew it would be improper to ask), and then left for Christmas at home in Lake Charles. Mother and Mark were there for two weeks before returning to Madison for his final half-year of high school, where he was indeed president of his senior class and captain of the baseball team which expected a second district championship. He'd turned into a handsome, strapping kid, with our father's shoulders and a cheerful, confident disposition. He brought the lovely Caroline his girlfriend (not the Roman Cajun child) down for two nights to meet us and to show off her pianistic skills (which were considerable and interested me a good deal, though hymns weren't included in her performance repertoire). Mark also took me aside with the *Appalachian Review* for an explanation of several lines in Ben's poem.

"It's very good, isn't it?" he said; "I'm just not so great with poetry." But he was obviously very pleased to have been remembered in the verse.

"It is," I assured him. "And there'll be more of it. Keep an eye out. He's very fond of you, Mark; he asks about you. You should keep in touch with him. He's going to be famous."

As usual Mother kept busy in her new kitchen, preparing my favorites including the snowball desserts and honoring our tradition of feasting on beignets on Christmas morning. "We're very happy, Troy," she said, "about you passing all the tests and getting so far along toward the doctorate degree," kissing me on the forehead and patting my cheek. "I'm really so proud of you, son, and so is your father. You know, he never had the chance to try for a higher degree. A Th.D. You can do this for him. We keep wondering whether you're going to bring a nice young lady home with you soon? To meet us. Mark's already getting ahead of you on that front!"

"I yield," I said, a little sourly.

Father was cordial. "We're both pleased by your success on the exams, Troy," he said, almost warmly, "and I look forward to learning what you intend to write your thesis on."

"Dissertation," I said. "I haven't finally decided, but we're working on it, Dr. Grant and I. He's my adviser and Department Chair."

"And we were sorry to hear about your friend. Charles, was it? He's famous now. It was in the papers and on TV."

"Charles Montgomery Trevalyn. Monte. Yes, I've been pretty broken up about it."

"You were especially close?"

David-and-Jonathan close, I wanted to say. "He was my best friend…at Jubilee. And after. He planned to apply to seminary, maybe become an Air Force chaplain."

"A commendable calling. He was at Baylor, right? Mark is probably going to LCC. Right, Mark?"

"I haven't decided yet."

"Are you happy to be here, Father?" I asked. "You like your new church?"

"We're very well-matched. God brought us together. I believe we're going to create an…an inspiring ministry. Your mother thinks so too."

"Well, I'm glad for you. Are you happy enough to give me back my whole allowance? Things are a little tight right now."

"They're not exactly lax here. We're trying to maintain two households, you see. You're not having to borrow, are you?"

"Once in a while. I pay it right back, though, from my next month's pay."

"I don't want you borrowing. Before you go back, tell me how much you need and I'll see what we can do."

"Thank you, sir. That's very generous."

"Don't count on generous. I said we'd do what we can. By the way, did you hear anything more from that lawyer…Hollister, was it?"

"Isn't he a member, sir? Don't you know him?"

"We have a lot of members. I know who he is. Have you heard…?"

"No sir. Nothing more."

"Do you see Ben? I liked that boy. He played a thoughtful chess game. Good strategist."

"Yes sir. He's a very good friend. We see each other."

"And the other one?"

"Yes. Kaiden. Corky. The one who rode horses with us. He works for a really fine restaurant in the…in the… um, Quarter."

Father looked at me over his glasses. Nodded. "Is there a young lady in your picture yet?"

"No sir. Not just yet. I'm so busy…with school, you know…and the two jobs."

"Well, don't put it off too long. Time's fleeing chariot and all. Who said that? I never can remember."

"Marvell, sir. Andrew. And it's 'winged' chariot. But 'fleeing's' good too."

"I knew I could count on you to know."

\* \* \*

I owed Kaiden a response to his invitation but upon my return to New Orleans from Lake Charles I was immediately distracted by a note from Ben slipped under my dorm door: "Call me as soon as you're back. —B."

"Look at your calendar," he said, "for Saturday the twelfth of January, and reserve noon to two. Plan to meet me at Jack's shortly before noon. He's going to drive us somewhere. I can't tell you where, but you should dress in a jacket and tie and look smart. I have a surprise, and I guarantee you're going to like it!"

Whatever was he up to? Ben rarely got visibly excited, but he sounded pumped and eager. "What?" I asked. "I'm not getting dressed in the middle of Saturday unless I know why. What's going on?"

"Honestly, I can't say, Troy. I swore I wouldn't, but it's nothing bad. You'll love it."

"Does Jack know?"

"Only what you do. I can't tell anyone. But Jack's agreed to drive us. Not far."

"If it's not far, why can't we just walk?"

"We should arrive by car. Don't ask me anything else."

"Do I need to prepare something? Bring anything?"

"Maybe great expectations! Twelve noon on the twelfth." And he hung up.

I rang Jack. "Can I come over? *May* I come over? To visit?"

"Sure. What's up?"

"I'm coming to find out!"

He met me at the Audubon Place gate and ushered me down the avenue to the residence. "I'm really glad to see you, Troy," he said. "You look great! Have a good holiday?"

"I went home…to my folks' new home in Lake Charles. You?"

"Me too. Back to Ruston. For some stress-free relaxation and free food. How're you dealing with the grief?"

"Learning to. It's not easy. But the nightmares have about stopped, and I don't cry so much. I'm getting back to stable."

We trooped up the stairs to our former room. "It looks good in here," I said, mildly surprised at the neatness and warmed by the familiarity. "You're housekeeping now?"

"As you say, learning to. Have a seat. It's nice to…to have you in here. You want to smoke?"

"Yeah, thanks." We lit up. "So what's going on with Ben? You've talked with him?"

"Yes, but damned if I know what he's got cooking. He won't give me a clue. But it's got him excited. You're coming?"

"I guess. He's pretty insistent. You know he's got a new girlfriend. You reckon he's going to announce his engagement?"

"Why would he want us there?"

"Maybe as bridesmaids!"

"Or he might have a book contract…for a poetry collection? That would account for the excitement."

"But not for the dress-up," I said. "Why would we dress?"

"Will he? I've never seen Ben in a coat and tie, have you?"

"No. I guess we'll have to wait. He said you'd drive us."

"Yeah, but not where. He's having a lot of fun with the tease so it must be a pretty good surprise. How's Kaiden doing?" He looked down at my wrist.

"We haven't seen a lot of each other…since I moved to the dorm. He has a roomie in the Quarter, but the guy's moving in with his fiancé, so Kaiden's on the hunt…so to speak."

He waited, looking at me. Then he asked, "You're a candidate?"

"I don't know, Jack. He's asked me. I'm not unhappy in the dorm. It's convenient. I like the free rent. You're nearby. But the truth is…the truth is, I'm kind of lonely, you know? I don't know if it's specifically lonely for Kaiden or…or just for somebody. It's prob'ly worse since Monte died."

"You're keeping busy, though."

"Lord, yes. The new term's starting. What'd you sign up for?"

"Grant's seminar; contemp drama with those two guys; and Griffin's Satire. And I'll officially audit Advanced Creative Writing, though I might switch to regular credit since I have to do all the writing assignments anyway. It's kind of a lab class, with everybody reading everybody's writing, and I'd have to fully participate. To participate fully."

"A whole semester of satire?!"

"He starts with background in eighteenth-century poetry, skips the nineteenth, where there's no satire, and bears down on 20th century, where there's a lot. That's the part I'm mostly interested in."

"Hmmm. The nineteenth century has Byron, some Shelley; Uncle Oscar Wilde; Lewis Carroll; Twain; Dickens and Thackeray. Eliot. Even Austen. Didn't you just pass pre-lims?"

"Show-off! I was thinking of satiric poetry. But I'll give you Byron."

"We'll share two classes: Grant's seminar and the drama. That should be fun."

"Yeah, I'm thinking I might learn something about short-story writing from Hawthorne and Melville."

"Have you read Melville's *Billy Budd*?" I asked.

"Love it. Have you?"

"Is Billy queer?"

"No. Claggart is."

"Are you regularly seeing someone, Jack?"

"Well, I'm not regularly seeing you, Troy. Why is that?"

"It might be Monte," I blurted, without thinking, startled by his question.

"Meaning?" he asked.

"I'm not sure. It…it feels like seeing someone would be…I dunno, like a betrayal maybe, disloyalty? I know it's silly…."

"It's ridiculous, Troy. It's probably a distortion bred by your grief, but you can't go around brooding the rest of your days and denying yourself your own life because Monte lost his. He wouldn't want that of you. Your friends don't either."

"I can't get him out of my head, Jack. He's always there. I feel as though I'm somehow accountable to him. Like he knows what I'm doing and thinking."

"He's dead, Troy. Monte's dead. Say it."

"I can't. I mean, I know it but I can't say it, like that."

"And there's something else: You're dragging around like you're the only one hurting over this. Like it's your own special private grief. It's not. He was our friend too. Especially Kaiden's, who knew him as long as you did. And you know I liked him too. It might help everybody if you showed a little concern for how the rest of us are handling his loss."

This stung — I heard the choke in his voice — but I knew he was right.

"Thank you for saying that, Jack. I know it's true. I've been selfish…and uncaring of you guys. When you've been so generous and kind to me. I'm sorry. I'm sure yawl miss him too."

"No, let's have no more crying. We've cried enough. Just be *aware*, Troy, that *we're* aware too. It's prob'ly our first real experience of mortality, and it's…well…it's ugly and painful…and scary. But we know that because we're alive. We can't go around numb and blind to life, or we might as well be dead too."

"You don't…well…feel his presence?"

"I miss him, but, no, I don't feel haunted. There's empty space where he was. That's the present absence you feel as presence. It's not Monte…watching you, judging you. Holding you back from moving on. It's not him holding you. It's you holding Monte. Let him go,

Troy. You can, you know. That's allowed. He's not here to mind."

He stood and stepped to me. "Hold me instead," he said.

\* \* \*

The first week of the new term swept in with its usual whirlwind of fresh faces, new routines and syllabi and assignments and texts and transfers and adjustments, and memos and meetings and conferences and negotiations, and resolutions to reform and correct and improve and develop, and never, ever to ask for another extended deadline or grant one, and we were again launched, I into my final term of course work for the Ph.D. Resolutions notwithstanding, I had not yet begun writing my dissertation prospectus and already felt behind, though there were no deadlines except my own repeated ones. I *had* apologized with feeling too Kaiden for neglecting his own grief while I massaged mine, and with difficulty and doubt asked him to look elsewhere for a new roommate. I would remain in the dorm for the time being.

On that Saturday, I'd walked over from the campus to Mrs. Burkhart's home where Jack met me on the sidewalk to await Ben. I'd never seen him look so sleek and handsome: dark navy suit, his standard white shirt now ornamented with gold links, a subtly striped red-and-blue tie, a four-pointed white pocket square, polished black shoes, his thin hair parted and carefully combed over in a professional business style. I wore my gray suit, blue shirt and pink-and-blue bow, a daring lavender fluffed pocket square matching a lavender wool scarf casually flung around my neck against the mild chill, black tie-up banker's dress shoes, and the gold bracelet. Ben roared up on his bike in a black suit, white dress shirt and a sober, narrow, solid gray tie and black boots. A stylist must have trimmed his normally bushy black beard and mustache back to an extremely close scrim ghosting the cheeks and lip, and clipped the rowdy hair into a neat, executive contour.

"Cary Grant!" Jack quipped. "Where's Ben?"

"You need a limo," I said; "the bike's all wrong."

"I'm trying to look like you," Ben said. "You'll soon see why. The car ready, Jack?"

We piled in, me in the back, and headed up St. Charles. "Just make for the Quarter," Ben directed; "anywhere around St. Peter's."

"Ah ha!" Jack said. "Hurricanes at Pat O'Brien's, right, Ben?"

"Not even close," he laughed.

"You need to tell us, " I said; "prepare us! All this mystery is giving me the fantods!"

"Open the glove compartment, Ben, and hand him the smelling salts!"

The Quarter's narrow streets already filled and milled with tourists, some unusually clad in bright winter wear, some already nursing cans of beer, slowing our progress into the depths of the Vieux Carre.

"Pull into one of those reserved spaces to the left, in front of Le Petit," Ben said.

"I know!" Jack said, obeying. "You've got a new role! You're going to announce your debut in the professional acting world! Right, Ben?"

"Or," I said, "you've won an acting award! For Big Daddy! You've invited us to celebrate your Best Actor trophy!"

"Nope!" Ben whooped, booming with laughter and pleasure. "Both wrong. But we are going in there. Straighten up," adjusting his own jacket and tie.

He led us around the side of the building to a door and knocked. An elderly, uniformed cleaning lady with a mop opened it and gasped. "Is that you, Ben? Lord a'mercy, you don't look yourself...but you do look... pretty! Come in, come in, boys. They're waiting for you, Ben."

We followed him down a long, narrow, well-lit hallway lined with posters and photographs of dramatic scenes and framed theater programs to another door where he knocked again. It opened from the inside, framing a suited, portly, balding gentleman wearing a gold chain across his vest, rimless glasses, and a broad, gracious smile. "Good afternoon, gentlemen, and welcome to Le Petit du Theatre Vieux Carre."

His French was melodious. A seated lady and two gentlemen, all fashionably dressed, smiled at us across a long conference table. A third man, in a sweatshirt and corduroys and a butcher-boy cap, hadn't stood when we entered. The youngest man, the second one standing, looked faintly familiar.

"I'm Jeremiah Hancock," our host said, "President of Le Petit's Board of Governors. This is Mrs. Jessica Fitzgerald...and these two are Whitworth Vaughn and Kyle Mason, also Board members, and seated is Derrick Tribune, one of our directors. We are a sub-committee of the Board's Executive Committee. Ben, would you do the honors, please?"

Good God! It *was* Kyle Mason! From Dixie's! Who'd invited me and Kaiden for cocktails! What the hell?!

"Good to see you again, Troy," Kyle said when Ben finished; "and you, Jack. "Why don't we all sit down, with Jessica? Mrs. Fitzgerald. And Derrick."

Nobody except Ben seemed surprised that Kyle recognized and spoke to us. I swallowed hard, took a breath, and tried to quiet my quaking heart.

"Thank you for coming, gentlemen, and you, Ben, for coordinating this meeting. I apologize for the mystery, and I'm grateful for your willingness to come without knowing why. For the time being, this meeting must remain confidential. It's all entirely legal; nothing nefarious is going on. You're perfectly safe. But this is serious theater business, and leaks might imperil the plan we're proposing. We're trusting you to keep our conversation confidential. Are we clear?"

We looked at each other and nodded.

"All right. Here's some background. The play scheduled here for August has been withdrawn. Its author, Patrick Sullivan, you've probably heard of him, died after a long and debilitating illness around Thanksgiving, and his widow, a French lady of some distinction, decided to move back to Europe and take with her our permission to stage his last play. She objected to it all along, arguing that it didn't represent her husband's best efforts and reflected his deteriorating mind. We didn't contest her decision. But we're left with a gap in our schedule. Now, you may not know that Le Petit has a long tradition of featuring, from time to time, local talent. We don't advertise it, but in this town word gets around the artistic community and we hear about playwrights and plays and sometimes we help to produce new ones... here. Why don't you pick up the story there, Patricia, since you were involved?"

"Thank you, Jerry," she said. "It's a pleasure to meet you gentlemen, and to see you Ben, in your elegant new bearing! So: a while back, our Ben here mentioned to Chuck Nolan, our long-term senior stage manager, always on the lookout for new material, that he knew of a collaboratively written play by friends of his about Thomas Chatterton, the English poet, and Chuck casually mentioned it to me. Now as it happens, I wrote my senior history honors thesis at Sophie Newcomb on literary frauds and hoaxes, and in the course of researching it I read a good deal about Thomas Chatterton. The idea of a play about him interested me, and I invited Ben to tell me more. He kindly offered me a copy of the play. I thought it good enough to take the liberty of sharing it with others. All of us here have now read it, admired it, and, with your permission, we'd like to give it a future in the theater."

"That is," Mr. Hancock said into the silence, "we're wondering if you'd have any interest in working with us to produce your play at Le Petit."

We stared, gobsmacked. Blinked. Looked at each other, speechless.

"Which of you is spokesperson?" Mr. Hancock asked. "Ben?"

"No sir," Ben said. "I believe that would be Troy. Mr. Tyler."

I coughed, cleared my throat. "I'm sorry, ma'am, excuse me, but you've sort of taken my breath away. Yes, of course we'd be interested in discussing…in talking with you about that, if you're actually serious. I don't mean to doubt you…."

"What he means is 'yes,'" Ben said. "He's very complimented, aren't you, Troy, and you too Jack, we're all hugely complimented by your interest, just as I told you we would be. And we'd love to talk with you about working together on the play."

"Splendid!" Mr. Hancock said, rubbing his hands together. "Excellent. Now, who owns the copyright to the play?"

"I'm sorry, sir," I said, "I don't believe it's copyrighted."

"Well, if it's finished," he said, "it's automatically copyrighted. If the author says it's finished, it's copyrighted. But it may not be fully protected till you register the copyright with the Library of Congress. Who owns the play?"

"I guess we do," I said. "We wrote it, co-wrote it."

"No," Ben said; "Troy and Jack wrote it. I may have advised a little here and there, from the sidelines, but they wrote it. It's theirs."

"Is that right?" Kyle asked. "Troy and Jack co-own the manuscript?"

"I guess so," I said; "I'm not sure how that works. Legally, I mean. I guess we do, Jack and I. Jack?"

"Well," Jack said, "I don't know who else would. Other than us. We. Us."

"Look," Kyle said; "I can take care of this part right away, as a favor, at no charge. You do need to get the play officially copyrighted and registered. Do you both want to be registered as co-authors?"

"Could we please hold on for a second here?" I asked, unsurely feeling my way along. "May I smoke? Would anybody care to join me?"

"I will," Mrs. Fitzgerald said, bringing up her leather purse and reaching out a pack of Camels and a silver cigarette holder. Jack, too, lit up, as did the man who hadn't stood when we entered, the director, Mr. Tribune. When he bent for his bag, I saw that he sat in a wheel chair. Kyle stepped to a side table and brought ashtrays to ours.

"This is all pretty wonderful, people," I said, benefitting from the brief pause, "but kind of...well... mind-blowing too. And it's moving pretty fast for us... us amateurs. Before we get much farther into it, could you say what other matters we'll need to discuss and settle, you know, before we...um...legally commit...to anything?"

"He's right," Mr. Vaughn said. "We need to gear down and back up and be sure our new friends here know what they're getting into…what we're getting them into. We don't want to take advantage, even inadvertently."

"No," Mr. Hancock agreed. "We surely don't. Well, Kyle's going to take care of the copyright. What else, Jessica?"

"The script isn't perfect, Troy," she said; "we think it's a little rough in places. Le Petit has a whole stable of staff writers we can call on as needed. We might want your permission to employ them to revise your script… working with you of course. We would negotiate with you and Jack on any recommended changes before implementing them: you would have to authorize any changes in the original script. But good, dependable, professional help is available to us."

"We've also wondered," Kyle said, "what you and Jack might think about setting your play to music? Making it into a musical. That party at the end of Act Two would make a dynamite showstopper scene in a musical. And how's this for a lyric line: 'Chatterton, Chatterton, Chat…Chat…Chatterton…?' Like that beat?"

"What about casting?" Jack said. "Would we have any control…any say about the cast?"

"That's normally the director's call," Mrs. Fitzgerald said, "but if you feel strongly about his or her choices, we could probably negotiate. Isn't that right, Derrick?"

"I don't anticipate any problems in that direction," director Derrick said, exhaling.

"But that," Mr. Vaughn said, "that's exactly the sort of question we all need to understand is in play. There must be dozens of them. We should've put together a list before this meeting. I suggest that we do so — we as a committee and you co-authors and your adviser too: and meet again to review the lists and answer questions. We need on the table all the essential groundwork rules and understandings we have to agree on, or agree to defer to others, before we get any farther into planning."

"It's a fine idea," Mr. Hancock said. "Do you agree, gentlemen? A list of everything you want clarified before we decide to move ahead, every question you want answered?"

"Could we have a week?" I asked, thinking we might need two.

"We might be a bit pressed for time," Mr. Hancock said. "For an August run of, say, four weeks, we have about six months to get it ready. But yes, you may have a week to think and consult and prepare your questions. We're confident we can get a production ready by August without compromising our standards or the quality of your work...if we get started right away and waste no time. Now, today I'd like you to sign your agreement on a right of first refusal for Le Petit. All it means is, if some other company offers to produce your work, you must let us know before you accept it so we can counter. It doesn't mean you're permanently committed to us as your producer. Either party can withdraw before production begins...on a date we'll specify. It only means you can't sell the production rights to anybody else without informing us. Let's see, how would $500 be to secure that agreement."

"We pay you or you pay us?" I asked.

"No, we pay you for the rights to produce your play."

"I know all about a bird in the hand, sir, but I'd still like longer to think about all this before we sign anything. We need to think and talk it over. You know we're complete novices, sir. God knows we're not looking for a better deal. We're thrilled by your interest and excited by the prospect of working with you. But we need to understand as completely as possible what we're signing on to do and *how* we'll work together with you. Would you be willing to hold that document unsigned until we next meet…assuming you want to meet again. We can talk then about everything we've thought about meantime, and probably then sign?"

Mr. Vaughn was smiling. "I admire the caution, guys. We needn't sign anything yet. Let's keep talking. One week? Look at our calendar, Jessica?"

"We're clear for Saturday the 19th, at this hour," she said. "Here again?"

"Troy," Kyle said, "I'll need the authors' legal names and addresses and a title for the play for the copyright and registration. Please call me with them at the number on this card. For the title, we were thinking of 'Tommy' or 'Tommy-Boy.'"

We were quiet until piling back into the car and then bedlam broke, with everybody blasting at once.

"Can you fucking *believe* this?!" Jack yelled. "Damnation, Ben, you brought this off! How the hell...?"

"I just mentioned to a coupla guys backstage that I knew about this play...and the next thing I knew Mrs. Fitzgerald asked me for a copy. I only had the one — don't get worried, Troy; I made only one copy — and copied it for her, and like she said, she must have shared it with other Board members. Some of them. The ones back there."

"Well, if what Mr. Hancock said is true, we're already covered since it's a finished play. And it'll soon be registered as copyrighted."

"Mr. Mason looks awfully young to be a Board member," Ben said. "How does he know you and Jack, Troy?"

"Tulane connections," I said, poking Jack in the back as a reminder to keep mum on this subject. "He's older than he looks. The family's rich...and important."

We kept talking — fast, over lunch, and beyond — with me jotting a list of questions and concerns around casting, production costs and whose, pay, costumes, sound and lights and printing and photography and advertising, whether to include Park (unanimously, no), whether to include music and dancing, how to find a puppy and train it, what to title our play, and a lot about contractual protections and liabilities, as though any of us knew zilch about those legal subjects except that we'd better find out.

What I knew no contract would protect me from was Kyle and my father, my silent worries over neither of whom could go on any list of concerns. Had Kyle put himself on the subcommittee because I happened to write a partly queer play he might co-produce and so guarantee necessary contact with me over many days and nights? Did he actually admire our play or simply desire me? I saw the smarmy ego in the question and felt embarrassed by it but couldn't dismiss the doubt. He hadn't yet noticed — to me, anyhow — my rude refusal to acknowledge his invitation to cocktails but he must be aware of it, and might connect it with the newspaper notice of his arrest. I had no solid grounds for determining how to relate to him in this new context, nor did I firmly know whether I wanted to despite the obvious attractions of his status, his looks, his affluence, his apparent interest in me. I decided to stand back and allow him to initiate commerce, if commerce was to be.

Surely secure in his new position, my father wouldn't feel threatened by my association with Le Petit Theatre, should he learn of it, though he would take no pleasure or pride in my joint authorship of a doubtful and probably in his view obscene script, should he allow himself to see or hear of it. Publicity of it would embarrass him and my mother and almost certainly advance an estrangement already begun. Withdrawal of the trifling bonus in my allowance Father had recently granted wouldn't much affect my standard of living, especially if funds from the sale of our play, or permission to produce it, should materialize; but I wouldn't welcome permanent alienation from my family wrought, or perceived to be wrought, by presumably indecent, smutty writing disrespectful of its manifest moral value. And how Mark would respond to our play, and how it would impact his high school reputation, and conceivably his college applications, especially at LCC, were not the least of my worries. But I couldn't see backing-out now, and with what excuse? My father might accept a true, written explanation of what had happened — after all, I hadn't *sought* publication or production — or even if he didn't, one would give him time to prepare his own response and to wash his hands of me.

**33**

Ever since writing my *Cain* essay, I'd been randomly dipping into Byron's canon, and systematically reading the recent three-volume biography of his Lordship by Leslie Marchand, already recognized as the definitive life, on the lookout for a dissertation topic, and had been so fascinated by the poet's 1816 lyric, "Fare Thee Well" — a haunting, melancholy, uncertain poem written to his alienated spouse — that I returned to it repeatedly for inquiry and reflection. Thus had an idea taken root and now sprouted: for Byron's verse throngs with what I came to call "valedictory moments," instances of separation and fragmentation, between and among persons and entities, always vexed by his stubborn ambivalence on which one he favors, relationship or division. HIs two long works, *Childe Harold's Pilgrimage* and *Don Juan*, feature itinerant protagonists forever leaving people and sites, and re-engaging with others; countless lyrics picture coupled hearts and broken ones; and most frequently of all are Byron's introductory poetic bondings with his readers and his even more elaborate and extended concluding departures from them. His early life was often scarred by deaths of relatives, including the father, of beloved schoolmates at Harrow and Cambridge, ultimately of his great friend Shelley, and of his cherished Newfoundland dog Boatswain, many of these, including the last, honored in elegies from Byron's hand. Famously, Byron abandoned as many women as he bedded (or was bedded by: the jury's still out), and made great literature of their alliances and ruptures. In due course, I began cataloguing such instances, sensing a pattern, certainly an obsession with the dissociative moment, and took my collection to Dr. Grant.

"It's impressive, Troy," he said. "And interesting. Do you imagine you're focused on valediction because of your recent loss?"

"It's possible, sir."

"May I ask how you're handling that?"

"I'm still sad, sir…but…mending. Thank you for asking."

"If you need to talk, don't hesitate to come by."

"Yes sir, thank you, sir."

"So…you intend to discuss Byron's farewells in relation to…?"

"I don't yet know what they mean, sir, but I suspect that collectively the recurrence will tell us something about Byron and relationship, in relationship…."

"And how is that of literary interest?"

"Well, it's also psychological, sir; but maybe study will also reveal something about Byron in relation to... with his audience: his need, his desire for and dependence upon readers, and also his dislike of the dependence even as he courts it. It's his equivocation, sir, his ambivalence and...um...hedging; his reconsiderations in and about relationships that interest me, and the... um...the squirrelly language he uses to render them. I don't know what I'll find sir, but I believe the pattern, the changing dynamics of the pattern, are pretty darn interesting. Literarily speaking, sir. I'll analyze the variations in the representations of the pattern."

"'Squirrelly,' Troy?"

"Well...um...indecisive, sir. Slippery. Equivocal."

I knew I'd garbled it, but, really, I was just beginning to investigate, just compiling my materials.

"When you're a little farther along, write it up as a prospectus and we'll circulate it. Do you have preferences for your committee membership?"

"Are you agreeing to direct me, sir? I'd like for you to."

"Thank you, Troy. I'm happy to have the job, conditional upon our approval of the prospectus, and look forward to working with you. We should include Professor Livingston, don't you think? And Professor Meyer from Newcomb."

"Yes, sir; I'm taking Professor Livingston this term."

"No, you're taking her course. I believe the professor is already taken!"

We laughed. "I'll find a couple of others," he said; "maybe from the eighteenth-century."

"Or specialists in it, sir?"

"Touché!"

"Not Professor Schwarz, if you please, sir."

"Okay," he grinned. "Now, Troy, sit back. I have one more thing." He paused to light up, offered. I joined him. He exhaled and continued: "You should know that I've been invited to teach in Harvard's summer school, and I think Katherine — you know my wife? — and I will accept the offer. As you may know, I do not drive. Katherine doesn't want to drive all that way without help. So we wondered whether you'd like to drive us up to Cambridge in our car and spend the summer there working on your dissertation? Forgive me for saying so, but I believe you'd stand a much better chance of getting ahead with that job up there than down here. And you'll want to have made a substantial start on it well before the MLA convention and job interviews after Christmas. Would that have any appeal for you?"

"Of course it would, sir. I'd be thrilled. But I'm sure I can't afford it, sir. I can prob'ly keep my rent-free job in the dorm through the summer, and my folks don't…. can't, really…. But no, sir; thank you very much. I'm so sorry, but I don't think I can accept your…your amazing offer, sir."

"Well, why don't you pop around to our home and talk to Katherine? It's time you two met. I'm happy to lend you a thousand dollars to help with your summer expenses. You can pay me back over time or however is

convenient for you. I believe this is in your best interest, Troy, and I hope you'll seriously consider helping
us out."

Well, why not? Suddenly it looked affordable. Why
not explore it? Be persuadable. I rang his home from the
department office and with Mrs. Grant's permission
popped around to it, right then.

She turned out to be rather plain of face and figure
with graying hair pulled back into a bun and clear plastic
eyeglass frames, looking rather like a slim maiden aunt
or a librarian; but they had two children, both girls, the
elder slightly younger than I, the other in her late teens
and still living at home. Welcoming me into the rather
modest but cozy and comfortable-looking living room,
my hostess gestured to a cushioned chair and offered me
a gin and tonic.

"I'll join you," she said encouragingly. So I agreed,
although it was only mid-afternoon.

She reappeared shortly with the drinks, settled onto
the sofa, and crossed her stockinged and — I couldn't
help but notice — shapely legs, adjusting the folds of
the dress over her knees. "As we're going to be companions for the summer, you may call me Katherine, Troy,"
she said easily, lightning a Marlboro with a match, for
I'd been stupidly retarded in fumbling out my lighter.
"Would you care for one? I rather like the smell of a
struck match, don't you?"

"Thank you, ma'am," I said, "I have my Kents."
"Yes, ma'am. It's a pleasing aroma." I lit up in the pause,
and sipped my drink. "That's very good. I like the lime."

"Leo takes his gin with vermouth," she said, smiling. "Every evening at 5. You'll find that we have to stop around that time on the road. For cocktails. When we're traveling, Leo mixes his martinis beforehand and takes them along in a thermos. He doesn't trust anybody else to get them right."

"No ma'am," I said, uncertain how to follow up. "Ma'am, I'm not sure…," I began; "I told Dr. Grant… I'm not sure I can accept…." And then I blurted: "But I've had my driver's license since my sixteenth birthday, ma'am, and I've never had an accident or a traffic ticket. I obey speed limits. I never drink and drive."

"Good," she said, and "Yes," sipping. "That's good to know. Leo says you're entirely trustworthy." She paused, took a drag, exhaled. "I understand this is sudden, Troy, that we've sprung this thing — this opportunity! — on you, and you may want some time to think it over. But we'd sure love to have your help, and your company, in Cambridge. How about you and I plan a little experiment, a little warm-up exercise in the car, just driving around town to get you familiar with it and to give me a chance to see you drive?"

"Yes'm. That would be fine. May I ask what make it is?"

"A Chevy Impala. Fairly new. I find it easy to handle. Can you drive a stick shift?"

"Yes'm. I learned on one. I prefer stick shift. I can also drive an automatic."

"What about parallel parking?" she grinned. "I'm kidding," she giggled. "But on the streets of Cambridge, you need to know how."

"Yes'm. I'm pretty good at it, at home."

"Have you ever driven in a city, Troy? There's not only Boston but other large cities on the way, not all with bypasses around them. Would you be comfortable…?"

"I think so, ma'am. But no, I've never really driven in a large city. I've ridden plenty around here, though, in New Orleans, with friends."

"Maybe we'll practice a little here then," she said, kindly.

She'd charmed me right away with her pretty smile and dimples and tinkling laugh and light, relaxed manner: her cordiality and warmth. Not the dour librarian at all.

"Tell me a little about yourself, Troy," she said, tapping her cigarette. "Where's your home?"

"I don't have one…except here, at school. I mean, my parents…my father lives…mostly lives…in Lake Charles; he and my mother…well…they…temporarily…live apart, for my brother's sake. I'm sorry, it's kind of complicated. I grew up with both parents in Madison, not far from Alexandria. They live apart now while my brother finishes high school up there. You see, my father got a new job…that required him to move. Temporarily. Well, no, not temporarily. Mother will join him in Lake Charles when Mark graduates this spring."

"I'm sorry if I embarrassed you, Troy. I think I understand. So have you ever traveled? North?"

"Nome. I've never been north of Mason-Dixon. I'm just a country farm boy. This would be my first time to cross the line. That line. I'm very excited about the opportunity. You and Dr. Grant are very generous and kind. Thank you, ma'am."

"You're helping us out. We're glad you can. I expect you're a good deal more than just a country farm boy. Leo certainly thinks you are."

"He does…ma'am? Oh, well, thank you again."

"You have other interests…than English literature?"

"Oh yes. Piano…I play the piano. I write. I love the theater. I acted a lot in high school."

"And you also drive!" she laughed. "You chauffeur! Can you change a tire, Troy, on the highway? It doesn't matter if you can't; I'm just curious."

"What, ma'am? Oh, sorry. Um, excuse me. Tires? Oh, I guess in a pinch, I guess I could fix a flat. I never have, though."

"Nor have we," she giggled again. "We'll just have to look out for nails."

"The best I can make out," she went on, after a moment, "it's about fifteen hundred miles from New Orleans to Boston. Leo doesn't like us to drive more than six hours a day, so we might spend two nights on the road. Of course we'll take care of your motel room and board. You'll want a motel with a pool, I expect."

"That would be great, ma'am. But…ma'am…."

"We'll have room for one large suitcase and a duffle. Not a really big one, though."

"Yes'm. That's all the space I'd need. Excuse me, Mrs. Grant, I'm so sorry…and embarrassed. But I need to leave now. I have to go…to take care of something right away. I'm sorry…but I really must excuse myself."

"Are you all right, Troy? What is it? Can I help?"

"No, ma'am. Thank you. And thank you for your hospitality. The gin and all. And the information. Thank you so much."

"But are you sure you don't want to talk now? You seem…alarmed."

"No ma'am. I'll be okay. I'm sorry…I just really have to…go…please."

I headed straight for Jack's, where the front door was ajar, and headed up the stairs.

"What the fuck!" he exclaimed, opening the bedroom door. "You look like shit! What happened?" I knew I'd pulled at my hair on the way over and tried to smooth it back. I knew I was flushed and sweaty and breathless; I saw my shirttail hanging out.

"I am *such* a fucking *IDIOT*," I yelled, hurling myself inside and striding about, beating my fist into my palm. "I've lost my fucking mind, Jack! I've just ruined everything!"

"Here," he said, "sit. Sit right there….and breathe. I'll be right back."

[*Chalandritsonos*, I whispered to myself while he was away: *Loukas Chalandritsonos!*]

He returned momentarily with a wet, warm washcloth and gently wiped my face and ears and neck, massaged my shoulders. "Easy," he kept saying, "easy there, boy."

"I'm not a horse, Jack," I said. "But I sure as hell am an idiot jerk!"

"All right," he said. "Now tell me, slowly, what's happened."

I did, slowly, through my hands on my face, almost blubbering, breathing hard.

"How could I forget what we'd just agreed to… for the summer?! I was so thrilled by what Dr. Grant offered…and so full of crapola about my own dissertation, I didn't think about anything else, least of all about our stupid play, until right there in the middle of Mrs. Grant's living room…I did think of it…and panicked. They'll never speak to me again. He won't direct me. This is so fucked up!"

Jack let me rant for a while longer and then put a stop to it: "Now listen, Troy: Nothing is ruinously fucked up. It's just a little confused. We can fix it. Dr. Grant offered to take you to Harvard with him this summer, to let you drive him, and you agreed, not remembering we'd made play plans for the summer, is all that right? So now you have a hard decision to make, between two equally (?) attractive opportunities. Obviously, you can't do both. D'you want to talk through your options now, with me, and see which makes better sense for you? Or which you want more? Or do you already know? As I figure you do. And you're crying like a brat because you can't have both. You ought to be rejoicing you've got the choice. I'm sorry to be brutal, Troy, but this isn't a decision you need to brood about. You're one damn lucky bastard to *have* a choice. We can kick around diplomatic ways to get out of the commitment you can't honor, if you'd like to do that. But I may not be especially nice about it. Because of course I'm jealous."

"Well, you stand to gain, don't you, if I step away from the play?"

"I could get real mad about that remark if I thought about it. But no, I'm not taking full credit for writing the play. You did most of it, we both know that, and you'll still be down as co-author. And we all lose if you're not part of the production."

"You think I should withdraw then...from the play?"

"I can't address 'should.' I'll tell you what I think I *would* do in your shoes. It's not what I want you to do. I *want* you here for the summer, nearby, with me, both of us scratching away at our dissertations and talking about them with each other, both of us working on the play production, both of us together watching our play get staged in August. But you'd be a colossal fool to refuse Grant's offer of a summer of concentrated work on your dissertation under his practically daily supervision on a campus with maybe the richest research resources in the country. You know, don't you, that the Houghton Library is also there, which is a goldmine of Romantic materials? You might even finish your diss, and then defend it back here in the fall, which would clear the decks for you to focus on a job search and get primed for the big MLA Convention and slave market right after Christmas. And you wouldn't have to give a single thought all summer to our piddling little play. So what I'd do is pick up the conversation with Mrs. Grant and finish it. And — though this is also against my own interests — I'd call Kyle on that number he gave you and arrange to tell him personally about your conflict, and your preference — your professional preference — and let him inform the Board, and maybe the Board could figure out a way to keep you minimally involved in plans, if you wanted to be, from a distance. They might be a little disappointed but I'll guarantee that every one of them would completely understand that fulfillment of your professional obligations trumps any satisfaction you might get from messing about amateurishly all summer with a play that could get canceled at any point. I'll be disappointed too."

I called Ben and asked him to meet me that evening.

"Jack's right," he said; "the opportunity's golden. I don't know anything about the research advantages but to have the director of your work virtually *sponsoring* it — *underwriting* it — shows extraordinary belief in its potential and goes a long way toward guaranteeing its success. And to tell the truth, once we work out all the agreements with the Board about permissions and casting and editing and such, they might be just as happy to have one author out of the way during production work and rehearsals. I'd be glad to help Jack out with revisions, if we're asked. But I don't remember other authors at Le Petit being much involved, once rehearsals begin. Some of them like to attend, and we can't keep them out; but they're probably not essential at that point."

"You're saying I won't be missed?" I asked.

"No, Troy. You can stop the pathetic act now. We'll all miss you. I'm saying we'll have your input through the early stages, and beyond a certain point in development, your presence might not be required. It's mostly all the director's call, then."

"I noticed that the director — was it Derrick? — didn't say much at our meeting, and didn't seem real happy to be there."

"It wasn't yet his scene. That was yours and Jack's."

It occurred to me later that Ben might not have been unhappy to find a way opened for him into more active participation in planning the production. Hadn't we, way back, talked about him playing Ginsberg? And now he had acting experience at the theater. I might say something about that, to the right people, before leaving.

\* \* \*

Still not having a better title than "Tommy" to present to Kyle, I rang the number he'd given me anyway and asked whether he could confer with me to discuss a problem. He invited me to lunch at his office.

The brown-and-gold sign in front of the large, two-story home on Prytania Street read "Mason, Mason, Potter, and Caldwell." Inside, natural light from the tall windows lining the front and a softer glow from three large chandeliers flooded the lobby; soothing classical music wafted throughout, paintings hung the walls, potted green plants flanked sofas and chairs. A yielding gray-and-blue floral rug spanned the central space.

A young, suited, smiling secretary sat at a reception desk bearing a typewriter, pads, accessories.

"Mr. Tyler?" she asked brightly. "Mr. Mason is on the second floor. He's expecting you. The stairway's just there."

"The main office is on Canal," Kyle said, rounding the dark desk and extending his hand. "This is our Garden District branch, with four more offices. Those are my father's and uncle's names on the sign, with the other partners, but they're all downtown. Those of us housed here aren't yet partners. Please sit down." He gestured, and eased into the large red leather executive chair behind his desk, leaned forward.

"It's good to see you, Troy. I'm glad you called. I've ordered lunch. It'll be along soon. If you'd like to smoke, please do." He scooted a desk ashtray in my direction, went quiet. I lit a Kent.

"Thank you for seeing me, sir," I said. "I hope it's okay if I brought a little problem to you. Not exactly a legal problem, sir. It's more personal. I'm here because you're on the committee...the Le Petit Board."

"Don't concern yourself about fees. Just tell me your personal problem. I can probably help."

He listened attentively, his fingers — one sporting a heavy Tulane ring — interlaced on the desk, his very blue eyes on my face, his full lips not quite smiling but looking ready to. The black, neatly-parted hair curved above the fair forehead and lay smoothly back over the ear. The navy suit-jacket draped his shoulders smartly, cut to define his runner's shape, its lapels framing a perfectly knotted burgundy knit tie over a white starched shirt and a fluffed burgundy pocket square above cuffs sporting silver links. Tanned, poised, still, he looked proudly youthful yet utterly professional, and as handsome as a god.

"I see," he said when I'd finished, but still sat forward, unmoving, looking intently at me. After several beats, he extended his left hand, palm up, and quietly asked, "May I see your bracelet?"

I blinked, extended my arm. He took my hand in his, held it, then brought his right hand over ours and touched the bracelet, lifted the band to look at the reverse, settled it back into place.

"It's very beautiful," he said. "A gift from Kaiden?"

"Yes sir, it is. He has an identical one. I mean, with his name."

"Sweet," he said, and sat back, moved the chair away from the desk, and crossed his legs, one atop the other.

"Your personal problem," he said: "it isn't insurmountable, and hardly inconvenient. I can deal with it, make it okay with the Committee and the Board. Once we're contracted — once you and Jack and Ben have all your questions answered and everything's arranged the way yawl want it — you'll just need to be available if *we* run into trouble with the production. And if we do, you'll be reachable by phone, won't you? I wouldn't anticipate the need, but so long as we retain the presence and cooperation of Ben and Jack, and one or both of them is/are authorized to speak for you, and we have your permission to proceed in your absence, and have contact numbers for you — you could give them to me — I don't see a problem, personal or professional."

"It's as easy as that, sir? To fix things, I mean?"

"I'll take care of it. About when would you need to leave for Yankee-land?"

"I'm not sure, sir; prob'ly around the first of June."

"So we've got approximately four months to get everything laid out to your satisfaction, and then minimally two months for the staging. It's doable. I'll inform the Committee, of course, but insofar as I'm concerned, you're free to plan your summer in Cambridge...at Harvard!" He smiled broadly. "Only," he added, the smile fading, "Personally, I'd rather you spent it here."

A knock on the door announced the lobby secretary with a trolley and two trays.

"Pork wonton soup with veggie spring rolls," Kyle said, "from Commerce, just down the way. And iced tea heavily sugared. All okay with you?"

"Oh, yes sir. It smells wonderful, sir, thank you."

We spread large cloth napkins on our laps and faced each other across the desk over the aromatic soups. He crossed himself.

"You're Catholic?" I asked, in some surprise.

"You're not?" he said, laughing. "Yes, it's the family tradition. Not yours?"

"Oh no. My family's Baptist. I don't belong anymore."

"Ah, a renegade! I know a lot of Baptists, and they're all renegades!"

"What does that mean, though? What you just did there?"

"I made the sign of the Cross. It's a habit. I hardly remember from the catechism what it means. I think I mean I'm grateful for my food, and I hope it, well, blesses my body. That sounds funny to say, doesn't it, 'blesses my body'?"

"Kind of. Baptists don't think the body is blessed."

"Well, I do." He looked the obvious follow-up question at me but I ignored it.

"You were at Tulane for seven years? Law school too?" I asked.

"A full quarter of my life! And loved every second of it. Are you happy there?"

"Pretty much, now that most of my exams are done. You're twenty-eight?"

"I'm under thirty," he said, grinning. "How old are you, Troy?"

"Almost twenty-five. I hope to stay here awhile."

We laughed, and went quiet.

"Speaking of staying," he picked up: "as I said before, personally I'd prefer you stayed here for the summer. We should get to know each other." He held the spoon halfway to his mouth; the blue eyes looked intently at me again.

"Well, sure. That would be good."

"You missed a pretty good cocktail party."

"I'm sorry…we couldn't make it. A conflict."

"Really? I figured it was that damned newspaper story. Surely you saw it."

"We did. I felt bad for you."

"Not bad enough, though, to offer condolences and encouragement at the party. But I can't say I blame you. It was a bad rap, and the paper apologized a coupla days later. I guess you didn't see that. I wasn't arrested. I've never been arrested. And I wasn't part of the brawl that night. We were there. We were guilty by association. I don't have a record."

"I'm glad," I said. "I think the story kind of spooked us. We didn't know you, and were so surprised you knew me…we didn't know what to think about the invitation. What it might mean…or, you know, involve. But I'm sorry I was rude."

"Only a little harm done. The bruise has healed." He smiled.

"But what about your folks? Wasn't there fallout? Embarrassment?"

"My folks have known about me since I have… at age twelve. They're cool. Most of the people on the Council with Dad probably also know. And you know New Orleans. Almost nobody cares. We're trying to get permission to organize a Queer Krewe for the Mardi Gras parade, and then maybe in a couple of years there'll be a Queer Ball. It's only a few churches, the Baptists among them, who care anymore. Queer's almost fashionable in New Orleans."

"Really? I'm not out there enough to know."

"So are you? Out, I mean? That's kind of a coming expression for, you know, not hiding you're queer. Being open about it."

"Well, no, I still…hide it…maybe a little even from myself. My folks don't know. Or I don't think they know. Not from me, anyhow. You should know that my Father is a Baptist minister."

"What? Wow! No kidding! Oh, that's hard. How're you handling that?"

"Carefully. I don't want them, or my younger brother, to know."

"Understood. But what do you mean, hiding it from yourself? You're living with a guy. You have a male lover. I've seen you together…at Dixie's!"

"Actually, not any more. His father sold our house out from under us. I'm living in a Tulane dorm now. Kaiden's…temporarily living in the Quarter, with a co-worker."

"You miss him?"

"Of course."

"I didn't think to order dessert. You want me to?"

"Oh no. That was very good. Thank you."

"So, Troy," he said, patting his mouth with the napkin and pushing back, "how about we catch a movie on the weekend? Which night is best for you? I'll drive my Corvette."

"Wait, sir. I don't know if I…."

"What? You've never heard of quid pro quo?"

"Well, yes sir. But sir: I have a boyfriend. Don't you?"

"I have many friends, Troy, most of them boys. C'mon. How about Saturday?"

"I can't, sir. Thank you, but I can't. It wouldn't be right."

The blue eyes narrowed. "You're actually turning me down?"

"Respectfully, sir. Yes. I must."

"Rubbish. You surprise me, Troy. I thought you and I…. But all right. Never mind. I'll call you. Now: have yawl decided on a title for your little play? Remember, I need one for the copyright."

"I'm thinking about *Prodigy*, sir."

Red flags fluttered throughout this encounter. First, he was older, not by much, but older; I'd never been with an older guy, and felt a little intimidated by the idea, by the experience and power and maybe knowledge it implied. Second, he was rich, and showed it. Kaiden came from money, too, of course, but never talked about it, wasn't ostentatious about it, shared it. And Kyle was Catholic: I know there's nothing inherently wrong with that, but I'd been taught from the cradle that Romans were pagan and poisonous; I'd had a bias planted in me, and however unreasonable it was, here it fueled the suspicion and distrust I already entertained toward this man. And he was comfortable with his queerness, probably proud of it, while I was still hiding. He might have lied about the arrest: how did Jack, who read Mrs. Burkhart's *Picayune* every day, not see the second, apologetic article? Moreover, the ease of his fix with the theater, however much I welcomed it, looked suspicious. His "blessed body" remark felt forward and distasteful. He'd sort of forgiven our party absence only after being snide about it. To his claim that queer was "fashionable," I wanted to say, "Not where I live." The adjective in "little play" insulted it. And worst of all, he'd played the quid pro quo card. I *owed* him for arranging things with the theater Board?! Huh-uh. In fact, the more I thought about all this — meaning Kyle and the play — the better I began to feel about putting some distance between it and me for the summer. But I still liked my title for the play.

I made it all up with Katherine Grant a day or so later over freshly-baked chocolate cookies and sweet milk before we drove around the South Carrolton neighborhood and through the Garden District in the long black Impala with the stick transmission, all the windows down and her pretty gray hair trailing out the passenger's. She understood completely about my forgetfulness and forgave it, and then asked a lot about our play and congratulated me on Le Petit's decision to produce it. "It's a pity we'll have to miss seeing it," she said, and I didn't disagree but secretly felt relief that she and the good Doctor G. would be spared the raw parts of a doubtfully tasteful script. She remained sweet and cheerful and light-hearted and attentive but not overbearingly directive throughout the test-drive and the parallel parking exercise, all of which went supremely well. "That's a high pass" she said, as we pulled into their drive. "Just remember next time to adjust both rear-view mirrors before you start."

34

Since moving into the dorm, I'd earned a bit of a reputation as a fast, reliable typist from my grad student
charges needing help getting their seminar papers neatly
formatted and printed to professors' instructions; and
since I hated copying poor grammar and sloppy phras-
ing, I also became known as an editor worth paying to
clean up flawed punctuation and clunky style. So far no
one had complained about my editing; I probably flattered myself that they'd even noticed it. But the number of papers left at my door with early deadlines for
return multiplied by the day, my Smith-Carona clacked
late into the night, my pockets plumped...and my dissertation prospectus languished. The last thing I wanted
was to end this unexpected and very welcome flow of
income, but I needed to regulate my workload or leave
campus. Regulation would fail as long as I remained

visible and vulnerable to pleading, and I couldn't abandon my advising responsibilities for any length of time. But the thought of my own private studio away from campus began to assume an inviting, not to say compelling, aspect. Besides, it was long past time for me to get back to Kaiden on his earlier offer, and, if it were still open, possibly rethink it. I called him.

"I'll be home by 6:30 tonight," he said, "with dinner. You've got my directions?"

The gated entrance buzzed, rattled open, and I stepped onto the dark red tile flooring of a rectangular patio open to the moonless sky. Ahead of me, centered, stood a trickling fountain guarded by four large urns spilling wilted begonias from their lips. Three stories of apartments overlooked the space, the lowest level facade framing arched doorways leading to dimly-lit stairwells. A slatted swing hung crookedly by ropes from a wooden frame against one wall. Potted bamboo stalks and leafy ferns and stubby palms and prickly cacti and sprawling palmetto plants and tall, exotic grasses crouched among wrought-iron chairs and tables and cushioned lounges. One corner sheltered a grille, another a trellis wrought with ivy; damp leaves slicked spots on the tile. A string of colored bulbs trailed loosely across the tops of the archways. The still air, heavily humid, bore a faint scent of green, like old, wet moss. Probably once chic, the courtyard had begun to slide toward the New Orleans version of comfortably shabby genteel, and maybe was already in line for the newly fashionable gentrification.

I heard his step just before he hugged me from behind, nestling his head against my shoulders, his hands pressed to my chest.

"My Troy," he said softly.

"Kaiden," I said, turning into him, holding him.

He held my face in both hands for a second or two, staring into my eyes, smiling, then stepped back. "It's wonderful to see you, Troy. Thank you for calling. Please come on up."

And up the dim stairs we climbed to the second floor and his surprisingly neat sitting room with two small sofas and plump chairs and big, fat, colorful pillows and shapely end tables with complementary glass and ceramic shaded lamps, and several large paintings from the house we'd shared, and a glass-top coffee table holding art museum books and under it a checkered gray area rug from the blue bedroom where Monte had slept. A large mirror on one wall caught the lamplight and pleasantly lit the room; on another hung a large television screen. Classical piano purled from a radio.

"It's very pretty in here," I said, "and...oh, I dunno, cozy...restful. Did you decorate?"

"Well, the pictures, of course, and a little bit more. George's taste is pretty good, but he's already taken a lot of his stuff to his fiancée's. You want a drink?"

"Not especially. But if you're having...."

"I've mixed martinis," he said, grinning; "the dirty breed."

He wore a navy sweatshirt, the sleeves pushed up to his elbows exposing the muscular, veiny forearms and the bracelet, and snug, light gray chinos and gray sneakers without socks.

"Just take a seat and I'll get them. I didn't have time to whip up some Cajun Creamy Crab, but I brought a sample of Broussard's crawfish dip, which is almost as good. The first time we had the crab we were in our flesh-phase phase, remember?"

He brought in a loaded sliver platter (elegant, frosted martini glasses, a glass pitcher three-quarters full, a crock of ice cubes, a jar of pimento green olives, a plate of crackers, and a bowl of yellow dip flecked with red), and rested the tray gently on the cocktail table.

"There," he said, stepping back and looking down at it proudly, a folded white towel on his arm. "Look good?"

"Looks ravishing!" I gushed. "And yes, I well remember our flesh phases. We were so…cautious."

"We were so scared!" he corrected, carefully dropping the cubes into the pitcher; "and so sweet. And we're still sweet, aren't we?"

"I hope so. And still a little scared?"

"I expect so. Sometimes," he added, stirring. "Oh blast, I forgot a fork for the olives. Do you mind if I finger them out?"

"Not at all."

He lifted out one at a time, with one finger, not dripping a single drop, deposited each in a glass, and then held the wet finger to my lip.

"Salty," I said. "Did you plan that?"

"I didn't, truly," he said, giggling. "I just forgot the cocktail fork."

"You said you were sometimes scared. Are you scared now?"

He handed me the full glass, raised his own. "Here's to cowardice! Has anybody in the entire world history of cocktail drinking ever toasted cowardice?!"

We snickered and sipped.

"Are you serious, Troy, or are you just monkeying with me?"

"I'm kind of serious…because I'm kind of scared. Some stuff has happened."

"Well, you're kind of scaring me now. I wasn't scared — or not much — till you asked."

"Do you know what's scaring you…now?"

"I think I'm a little scared of why you called. Of what we might be doing here now?"

"Me too. I'm not sure. But I need us to talk. I have to tell you something."

When I finished telling him, he asked: "For the whole summer? You're going north for the entire summer?"

"That's the plan. Three months of solid work on the dissertation. It's a priceless opportunity, Kaiden. I can't turn it down, not without messing up things with my director."

"And you're walking out on Ben and Jack and the play…just when it's found producers?"

"Not exactly, no. I'm sort of suspending my participation…or participating remotely, if they ask me to. We'll keep in phone contact. This might be a good thing. I'm beginning to lose interest in that project. Kyle's a part of that."

I told him about my lunch with Kyle.

"Nasty," he said. "You really think he lied about the arrest?"

"I think he might lie about anything...to get something he wants."

"And he wants you?"

"He asked me out. Can you believe he played the quid pro quo card?"

"Super crude. And you're giving up your adviser's job at the dorm?"

"I'll have to take a summer's leave, if they'll give me one. I might want the job back in the fall."

We both went quiet. I lit up. He held out his hand for one, used my lighter.

"Is this where I repeat my offer, Troy?"

"Is it, Kaiden? I don't know. If it is, and if you're going to repeat it, there's prob'ly something you should know before you do: there may be a problem."

"Do you want to tell me?"

"Not really, no. But I have to. It's Monte."

"Monte?! What?"

"He's in my head, Kaiden. It's like he's locked in here, and I can't shut him off, or out. Not all the time... but...but whenever I think about sex: he's in there watching me. I haven't had sex with anybody — except myself — since Monte died, and even that feels kind of like I'm betraying Monte. I know it's crazy. But if I move back in with you...."

"Well, you're welcome to...."

"Wait. You might expect.... Look: there's nothing I'd love better than to take you to bed this very second, you look so damned gorgeous and sexy, but I don't know whether I could, you know...well...perform, like, satisfactorily. It's not physical. I don't have that problem. I'm already half-erect just talking about it. But whether I could...you know...get into it...make you happy and satisfied, with Monte in there watching: he doesn't exactly object, only sometimes frowns or almost shakes his head: he's just *there*. I think I'm the one disapproving, but I don't know why. I don't think I'm still grieving, or not a lot. I don't cry much. I do think I still love Monte, or his memory, prob'ly more than I ever did when he was alive, and I think I always will love him...the memory of him. But not in place of loving you...instead of loving you and Jack and Ben and other people very dear to me. And I'm really scared of misleading you into expecting we'll just pick up where we left off a while back. I can't... mustn't...hurt you. But I've no confidence that I won't, by disappointing you. Can you understand any of this?"

"I think I understand most of it; and I thank you for telling me. I actually love you for telling me. I know it wasn't easy to. But I think you're still grieving Monte, and I like it that you loved him enough to grieve him so deeply and so long. But Monte's not the disapproving agent here. You are. You disapprove of your love of Monte, and you blame yourself for his death. Oh not consciously, no: but deep down you're scared to death that your loving Monte cost him his life. Ben and Jack and I have talked about this, and that's our consensus. You can't forgive yourself for loving Monte. And that unforgiveness is stopping you from loving at all, in the same way, again."

"Wait. You and Jack and Ben have talked about this?"

"Of course. Why wouldn't we? You've talked to us. We care about you. We all want you…back."

"And yawl really think that…about me?"

"Well, I do. And we all agree that you need to leave the isolation of that dorm room for some kind of social life. Some kind of relationship except with a fantasy Monte. You're eating yourself alive, Troy…and I seriously wonder if it's going to get worse in Cambridge, where you'll know nobody. Working with the theater and that big group at the church might have gotten you out of your own head, but now that's gone. Moving in here with me might be a step in a new direction, so the offer stands, on a condition: not in September when you get back. Now. Before you leave. You're kind of critical right now, and you need a change. I can't live with you and not want you, but I can hold off and give you a little time if that's what you need. But I'm going to expect a relationship: you know, rapport. Contact. You want to inspect the digs now?"

"You sure you want to try this, Kaiden?"

"You need to be too, Troy. You have to promise to try. For your own sake as much as for mine, all right?"

It was larger than it looked, this apartment, with two baths, a better kitchen than he'd let on, and a second bedroom bigger than my dorm room with a desk below two windows overlooking the patio, and more closet space. The bed was a double, with side tables and lamps, and three-shelved bookcases lined two walls. A stuffed chair piled with George's clothes sat across from the desk under a pole lamp, and a straight-backed wooden one tucked into the desk. "I'm across the hall," he said; "we have central heat. You see the thermostat just there. And the shed — where I might fix you up an office — is down these back stairs and maybe six steps along a brick sidewalk to the door. D'you want me to get the key?"

"Just a second," I said, looking around again. "This is good space, Kaiden. That desk's larger than what I had at Jack's. And those shelves are terrific. Look, you're still working different shifts — early and late — alternate weeks, right? So you're here in the apartment until mid-afternoon one week, and then the next you work until 6 or so daily and come home? Is that about right?"

"About. It's not exact, but that's the rough pattern."

"So I'd have a good stretch of time alone in the house every day, just different hours. And we could have meals together here or out on different days. I'm thinking that with the little seniority I've got now in the Department, I might could arrange a two-day teaching schedule for Tuesday and Thursday, and have all of MWF here for writing. Why would I need a studio? This bedroom is more space than I had at Jack's, and have now."

"You don't want to even see the shed?"

"No point. Didn't you say you'd have to fix it up to be usable? Why bother?"

"Of course I'll have to talk to George, but I'm pretty sure he's eager to move the rest of his stuff in with Frances."

"And I'll have to talk to the Housing Office. You're really ready for this to happen…soon?" I said.

"What's Monte say?" he asked.

"Monte's mute…so far. I may not be listening."

"Don't, then. We can think about it overnight. You can call me tomorrow."

"Is it really this easy, Kaiden? We must be forgetting something."

"We're forgetting dinner. Aren't you famished? We also forgot to refill the glasses."

He'd brought cold chicken and mashed potatoes and English peas with basil and mushrooms from the restaurant, and set everything on the stovetop to warm.

"Not our fanciest food, but not bad as leftovers. Not from patrons' plates; left over in the kitchen. It would've been tossed. But it's fresh and good, and oughtn't to be wasted. I don't want any more booze, do you?"

"No, but there's one more thing: can that old bike of yours, the one with the cart? Can it be rehabilitated as a bike…for me to ride back and forth to campus…and save a little trolley fare? I could ask Ben to look it over?"

"Sure. It's just sitting over at Broussard's. And Troy: I thought of something else too: you know, some folks get their sexual jollies watching other folks have sex. You reckon Monte's one of them?!"

I actually laughed with him.

\* \* \*

Yes, the Tulane Housing Office already had a list of graduate candidates for a dorm advisory position; I moved, with Jack's help and car, the day after resigning, and before George had cleaned out the last of his things. Jack didn't utter a word of disappointment and wished me well, I thought a trifle doubtfully. And then told me he'd just submitted a draft of his dissertation prospectus to his director, and awaited approval. This raised some prickly sweat in my pits. A sweet word to the Department secretary who assigned freshman sections landed me a Tuesday/Thursday teaching schedule, at 9 and 11, ninety minutes each, of Introduction to Poetry to classes of 22 boys; but this didn't turn out as conveniently as I'd imagined: in my hurry, I forgot that, along with teaching, I was also taking my last three courses, two on MWF, with the seminar also on W, so I was on campus five days a week.

The Le Petit Board made no trouble over my proposed "leave," and Mrs. Fitzgerald even wrote a note congratulating me on the opportunity to study and write at Harvard. I thought it best to excuse myself from the second Board meeting with the authors and adviser but I heard all about it from Jack. He didn't exactly say that Derrick the Director (now officially appointed to the job) seemed happy to be rid of me, but I got the impression he was. They accepted my *Prodigy* for the title, which I thought a little pedestrian and flat against my second suggestion, *Wunderkind*, but Ben called it clarifying and Jack didn't weigh in. He did, though, against adding music. And that question remained unresolved, for Kyle and others, including Mr. Hancock, wanted the splash and color of a musical. The extent of my vicarious participation also remained somewhat murky, I assumed to be later determined strictly on the basis of need, which might be minimal. Derrick asked Ben to audition for the Ginsberg role, and urged him to re-grow the beard.

I facetiously titled the fourth and maybe final draft of my prospectus "Breaking Up Is Hard To Do" after Neil Sedaka's hit last year of the same name. Of course the loftier subtitle would follow: "Lord Byron and the Poetics of Valediction." Byron himself would probably hoot at the pretension of "poetics," but since Aristotle in his treatise gave the word prestige, I reckoned I might get away with using it once.

My parents received the news of my summer plans with equanimity, asking only that I spend several days with them around Mark's graduation in late May, which for his sake I was pleased to do. He'd made a tremendous success of his senior year as class president and baseball star, and was already accepted on an athletic scholarship at LCC, which, with the automatic tuition break, should make my father even prouder. I'd said nothing in that quarter about *Prodigy*: after all, the project might fold before reaching the stage. I not exactly hoped it would, but I might not greatly mind if it did. On the other hand, I thought a lot about it through the dark night watches, and sent along tweaks of the script fairly often to Jack.

I'd stashed Dr. Grant's check in a savings account I couldn't touch until June, and continued to type/edit papers for my needy grad student buddies. Katherine reached out occasionally to be sure I was still aboard for the driving, and recently offered — if it's all the same to me — to pass all the driving to me and co-pilot with maps and directions through the tricky urban bypasses. Dr. Grant, she said, always rode in the back seat, even when she drove, with a book in his lap. We'd leave at 6 on the first day, with sandwiches she'd made for lunch, and the good doctor's thermos of cocktails.

Kaiden and I've probably got on better than either one of us thought we might. A couple of weeks before Valentine's Day, he began to talk about preparing a formal "sweetheart dinner" on the evening of the day itself for the two of us right there in the apartment, and his enthusiasm caught me up and together we planned the menu and the wine and the paper decorations and the hi-fi music to accompany the meal, and went together to the formal shop to rent me a true tuxedo, as he of course had his own. He also ordered flowers for the living room and the "table" — my desk covered with a white sheet and moved to the center of the bedroom — and set with such meager "china" and glassware and cutlery as we had: and more than half the fun was how improvised and makeshift and even tacky everything was except ourselves and the meal, of course, which was a fantastic rare tenderloin after an amazing Caesar with the raw egg and anchovies, and crisp asparagus and cheesed creamed potatoes and a sweet bread pudding he'd made himself with luscious butter sauce. I guess I knew all along it was a set-up of sorts but after the long period of fasting and restraint, I was randy for relief, so when he moved from his chair to my lap after the dessert, I hesitated not an instant to give passion rein. Happy Valentine's Day!

# 35

The drive north could be called uneventful only if you omitted everything that passed before my wide and startled eyes after we crossed the Tennessee state line east of Bristol. All was new, and I felt awe before it. Both Grants were geographically experienced, of course; but Katherine had also done some homework, refreshed herself on history, and proved an exceptional guide and commentator on the country we traveled: who'd settled it, farmed it, what they grew, their politics, their prejudices, their cultures, and so on. Dr. Grant chimed in sometimes from the back, usually about their literatures, but also, and surprisingly to me, about their faiths, their churches, and how their literary achievements reflected their religious beliefs and those beliefs shaped their literatures. He remarked upon the small country churches that dotted the landscape everywhere through the southland but even north of the line, too, and on how often their architecture betrayed their denominational affiliation, so that he could guess the latter before an identifying name on the building became legible. Apart from a moment when I nearly killed us all on a Baltimore bypass by cutting across two lanes to catch an exit we'd missed a notice of, I did all right at the wheel, but the near miss — and we all screamed! — slowed me into a more cautious mode, and they were generously forgiving, after catching their breaths. Dr. Grant did begin to fidget around 4 p.m. on the first day, Katherine nodded to me, and we soon spied a motel they liked the looks of, and stopped for the night. I took a bracing swim, cleaned up, and at their invitation came to their room, where Dr. G. refined Kaiden's recipe for a gin martini: only three drops of vermouth, he advised, two of olive juice, olive optional (remember Auntie Mame's caution, he said, that olives take up too much room in the glass!). Repeat once. I staggered off to the cafe with them, jabber-mouthing, thrilled to my very core to be doing this whole thing.

But my giddiness sobered at the table where the Grants both crossed themselves, bowed their heads, and the professor murmured a few words over the food. Respectfully, I bowed my own.

"I'm sorry," I said, "I didn't know...you were Catholics."

"Anglicans," he said. "High-church Episcopalians. Katherine's father is an Anglican priest. We met at Hamilton College, which has, or had then, a strong

Christian community. You were raised in the church, weren't you, Troy?"

"Yes sir. By a minister father. Of a different faith. But I'm always pleased to meet another preacher's kid... Katherine! May I ask why you do that, cross yourselves?"

"Make the sign of the Cross?" he said. "It's an affirmation of our faith. Acknowledges our Christianity. Expresses gratitude for salvation. Something like that."

As surprising as all this was — stunning, really! — I also, I have to admit, found it vaguely reassuring, mildly comforting. We shared a turf here. We spoke this other language, in similar accents, though we never had before, to each other. We might could now, if we wanted to.

The next day, heading north under a brilliant blue sky, Katherine asked about our play. I'd prepared for this one and so rattled off kind of dismissively some sanitized basics of the plot, but then Dr. G. pulled himself up from the back seat against the front one and said, "You know, I used to teach Chatterton, as a pre-Romantic. You've probably noticed, Troy, that our Romantics text gives him pages at the beginning. He's a fascinating fellow, and not properly valued. All that scandal got in the way of appreciation. How'd you get interested?"

So I told them about Park and how we started, which amused them both, and then Dr. G. held forth for a while with views of Chatterton's verse and stories of the scandals I'd never heard, and which that night I called Jack to repeat to, in case he wanted to use them in our script. Stupidly, it had never occurred to me that Grant might be a resource for our play. His and Katherine's expressed interests in it made me feel slightly better about the project while stirring up jitters they might see it.

Late in the afternoon, about the time the good doctor was due to get antsy, we topped a ridge and looked down upon the vast unrolling expanse of the Hudson valley with the grand, majestic river itself coursing north to south under the amazing Tappan Zee cantilever bridge with seven traffic lanes! I think I gasped at the vista. I know I said: "My God! It's bigger than the Mississippi!" — a line that aroused hilarity in the car and got repeated countless times over the summer to Yankee acquaintances of theirs.

Katherine kindly offered to drive us through the myriad small towns neighboring Boston and the city itself over to Cambridge so I could absorb the sights. It was by far the largest metropolitan area I'd ever encountered, and I would have been intimidated, even frightened, had not the Grants' running commentary proved so informative and engaging. Cambridge streets and neighborhoods, monuments and churches and statues and shops and crowds of students immediately drew me in, and Harvard Square and glimpses of the Yard and institutional buildings beyond the gates already surpassed in grandeur and glory the splendor my imagination had cast upon these sites.

#29 Dunster Street was a large brown boardinghouse about six blocks off the Square in a dowdy neighborhood. Through the Summer School Housing Office, I'd booked a single room on the second floor for three months. The Grants dropped me and my bags off on the sidewalk out front, said they'd be in touch, and drove off to the house arranged for them on the other side of the Square. And just like that I was at Harvard, alone, to write.

The large desk with a fluorescent lamp and swivel chair and a black telephone faced two windows overlooking the tarred roof of a garage below and toward another brown rooming-house next door. I'd have to get the telephone connected. On top of the chest of drawers rested a medium-sized hot-plate, a small stew-pan and skillet, two glasses, a dinner plate, a paring knife, and two sets of cutlery; a small, humming refrigerator sat next to the chest. To the right of the desk, a narrow single bed tucked against the wall; to the left sat a wooden armchair with an orange cushion. An iron bar with legs and hangers and a bath towel and washcloth stood to the left of the door. A trash can and a box of liners hid behind the door when it was open. A note from Housing to me at Tulane had located the door key under the bed pillow, the bathroom to the right down the hall, and shops two blocks out the front door to the left. The place looked fairly clean, smelled okay, but felt warm, and no window unit a/c was in sight. I used the toilet — happy to note it had a shower — and unpacked, resting to the right of the lamp the silver-framed photo of himself Kaiden had slipped into my suitcase, and arranged my typewriter and books and pencils and pads on the desk. I found the key, and headed out for food, soap, Kents, and an ashtray. Peanut butter and cigs turned out to be my staples for the summer.

The next morning I made my anxious way to the famous Harry Elkins Widener Memorial Library on the Harvard campus, with its endless stacks, and presented at the portals the letter from Dr. Grant testifying to my status as a legitimate graduate student in need of the research facilities of this institution, and requesting permission for me to enter the stacks and to check out items from its incalculably wealthy collections. Check-out permission was denied to non-resident students but I was given a card allowing me to request items from the stacks and to use them anywhere in the reading rooms of the building. I staked out a seat at the end of a table in the giant main reading room, next to the towering windows, and, always arriving as soon as the Library opened, reclaimed it almost daily for the remainder of the summer. As a Visiting Professor of English, Dr. Grant was assigned a carrel inside the stacks, and twice gave me a tour of them. He used the carrel nearly every day, and about twice a week stopped at the arched doorway of my reading room on his way in and glanced my way, with a smile and a tiny wave, I thought to make sure I was there and working. I didn't at all mind, and felt looked after.

They invited me to dine with them at their temporary home every now and then, and some memorably splendid meals and conversation we enjoyed there. Once, Dr. Grant also invited the distinguished Harvard professor Dr. Howard Mumford Jones to join us. I've forgotten how they met, but it was clear to me that Dr.

Grant revered this renowned scholar, so of course I practically quaked in his presence too. In a year — the manuscript must have been in press when we met — he would publish his *O Strange New World*, which would win the Pulitzer in the next. At some point during the evening, at a break in the dialogue with his host, Professor Jones asked me the subject of my dissertation. I gave him the austere title and a brief word about my approach. "No, no, no," he said emphatically, putting down his fork; "you can't write about Byron like that. You must find another subject, another method!" He frowned — scowled, it felt like — at me and at my director.

Shattered, I excused myself early, fled home, and hurled myself onto the bed [*Chalandritsonos. Chalandritsonos!*], hurting in my depths. But the next morning, habituated, I returned to the reading room and sat dumbly, numbly, wondering what to do. Then Dr. Grant waved at me from the door, crooked his finger.

He draped an arm around my shoulder — he'd never before touched me — and walked me slowly down the hall. "Now Troy," he said gently, "you must try to forgive Professor Jones for that remark, and then forget about it. It's ill-informed and mistaken. He's old now, and angry and disgruntled about a lot of things, and he doesn't understand what you're doing. You have a thoroughly respectable topic and you're doing good work on it. Carry on. I'm sorry I didn't defend you last night but it would have done no good, and would have prolonged your pain. So let's shake it off and get back to work. All right?"

"Thank you, sir, for saying all of that. And for the encouragement. But what did he mean, 'you can't write about Byron like that'? Like what?"

"I'm not certain, Troy; but Howard has a beef with the new critics. He's an historian. He hates the now fashionable formalism that ignores what he values. That, of course, is what you've been taught, what you're teaching, and it's basically the methodology you're using. It's what nearly everybody is using now and will use until the next fashion dethrones it. It's completely legitimate and authorized. You don't need to be experimenting with a different one. My advice is to hunker down and get on with your writing. You've had an unfortunate encounter with one of the great minds of the century, and you're wisely going to defy his counsel! That's a conquest! Congratulations! Now. Our daughter Kathy is visiting us next weekend and we're thinking of driving to Concord for the day on Saturday. Wouldn't you like to join us for the outing?"

It was cleansing, healing, that advice. And I returned to work with a lightened heart and firm resolve. I'd show 'im.

And Saturday was a joy...except for the misty, ghostly fog that shrouded everything we wanted to see. Kathy, slightly younger than I, with her mother's height and skinny frame and flat, plain face, seemed as indifferent to my gender as I to hers, so whatever ambitions in that direction, if any, Dr. G. may have entertained found no traction. She'd recently graduated from Smith and would enter grad school at the University of Michigan in September in history, going for the doctorate. She appeared to know everything about Concord history, and shared her knowledge liberally with us on the trip. We began at the site of the Old North Bridge and "the shot heard round the world," and moved on to the former homes and attached museums of Emerson and Thoreau and Hawthorne and Louisa Mae Alcott and her large family, and the Old Manse and Wayside, and Walden Pond — the size of which startled me, along with its availability to swimmers — and the very interesting replica of Thoreau's cabin where I poked about, and finally to the Sleepy Hollow Cemetery and its Author's Ridge where so many literary and other notables are buried. Our group then disbanded so that we could individually revisit any sites we wanted to linger in, agreeing to gather back at the car in an hour. I returned to one of the two Hawthorne homes and then to the Pond, and at a shop there purchased a little glass vial of what was said to be Pond-water as a memento of our visit. Everybody but Dr. Grant was huddled against the chill back at the car. After ten minutes of waiting I began to feel some concern, but Katherine said she imagined he was meditating at someone's grave and had lost track of the time: "Why don't you climb back up to Authors' Ridge, Troy, and see if you meet him on the way?" I found him standing silently at Hawthorne's grave, staring down at it, water beading on his head and face. He looked up at me, his eyes moist. "Hawthorne is buried here," he said, solemnly, gesturing down at the ground, his palm open, as though reaching.

\* \* \*

Kaiden wrote postcards at least once a week — gossipy morsels from the restaurant, joke lines from TV, a phrase or two of a favorite song lyric, reminders of his love — and Jack brief letters as often with news of the play's continuing development in production. Kaiden rang every Saturday night at 6 if he wasn't working, and Jack and/or Ben on most Sundays around the same time with items too complicated to write about but of little moment to me. Still, it was good to be kept informed, and I welcomed the company, as I had no other. The Board finally relinquished the idea of a musical, deferring to the authors' preferences, but had given Ginsberg — the role now owned by Ben Moore! — a flute both to soothe Chatterton's anxious moods and to encourage dancing at the big party scene at the end of Act Two. And of course we now had Bud and his recorder too. There'd been difficulty finding a suitable dog to play Noodle, but the three of us insisted on keeping a pup in, and at last a performer rejected after her audition offered her three-year-old red long-haired dachshund to the cast if allowed at least a bit part in the show. Everybody fell in love with the pet and tolerated the actor in crowd scenes. A program cover-design was in the works by an artist on contract with Le Petit; the co-authors' names would of course appear prominently on the cover, and Ben's as "Advisor to the Production," over a printed contemporaneous sketch of Chatterton's face, head, and russet, shoulder-length hair. The Board had agreed to pay a total of $600 for the permissions, with $250 going to each author and $100 to the advisor, and 15% of each night's box office take to each author. Two actors rehearsed the role of Chatterton, both equally fine, Jack said: Le Petit thought it might star both boys on alternate nights. Neither one was Jack, for in the end Jack, after observing the auditions of the ultimate winners, grew faint of heart and decided not to try-out. Back in March, Ben had repaired Kaiden's old bike for me, but since then he'd overhauled it, and Kaiden said the machine hummed along now like a dream, and was eager for its new owner, me, to return.

Of certain interest to Kaiden was my discovery of Pier 4 out at the Boston harbor. I'd never tasted lobster until the Grants took me to this popular restaurant actually built on a pier, and after that meal I didn't much want to taste anything else. My oh my what sweet, soft, supple flesh, cracked free of hard red shell — those succulent nuggets dripping butter, with stubby little fresh buttered corn cobs to accompany! Through the summer, I'd limit myself to peanut butter and canned soup and Kents for a couple of weeks of hard labor at the desk and then grab a subway and a bus all the way out to the Pier for an evening of indulgence on a platter of steamed lobster with beer and feel like a very lucky boy, although a lonely one. Walking home from the subway late one night, I got jumped by a carful of hoods and treated to a blackened eye, a battered cheek, a bloodied nose, and a hoarse chorus of "Faggot!" and "Queer!" and "Pervert!" but, earlier warned to carry cash in my front jeans pocket and not a wallet, I lost nothing but a little dignity and composure. Katherine didn't allow me to walk home from their place after that.

At the Widener, I looked up "Anglican churches in Boston/Cambridge" and found Trinity Church in the city, and as kind of a lark took a subway over the next Sunday and found that I quite liked the "liturgy," as they named it — the "service," in my former tradition: I mean, I *really* liked the formality, the ceremony, the pomp, I guess, although it was pretty heavily flavored with crossings and genuflections and kneeling on the prayer benches at every pew. And the music plumb knocked me out. The "nave," they called it, housed the largest pipe organ I'd ever seen or heard, and the fifty-voiced choir — I counted heads — in gorgeous red robes with white stoles blended with spine-tingling precision and balance. The sermon, or "homily," was kind of so-so, but then the chief priest's administration, with assistance, of the Holy Eucharist ("Lord's Supper"), even if you didn't understand every word and gesture, was an absolute showpiece of gracefully designed choreography and poetic narration. I even enjoyed the incense, although I wondered whether you're supposed to. Most of the congregation was older than I, and folks seemed a tad frosty; but at the "Passing of the Peace," they shook my hand and nodded amiably enough. The church lived a far piece from Dunster, but — still charmed by the subways and thrilled by their speed — I didn't much mind the long ride.

I also located Christ Church Cambridge, on Harvard Square. Nothing about it — I walked by and peeked inside and picked up a leaflet — suggested Anglican to me (as though I knew what would!), but it was pretty clearly at least Episcopal, and I'd bet it attracted students and others more nearly my age. One phrase in the pamphlet sort of obliquely welcomed "difference," perhaps foreseeing a development I came greatly to admire in the Episcopal church.

Dr. Grant reported that my Committee unanimously approved my prospectus. I've tried to give him at least thirty pages of analysis every fortnight, and so far he'd returned them, marked, within three days. And so far, he'd offered few substantive comments, merely editorial corrections and suggestions and marginal question marks to indicate doubts. Oh, he said I over-reached in my reading of "Fare Thee Well" but proposed I finish the entire project before rewriting the introduction to anticipate and accommodate what followed it. And he wrote that my analysis of Byron's great address to the Ocean concluding Canto 4 of *Childe Harold's Pilgrimage* was "the most sophisticated, professional and persuasive writing" I'd given him so far, "thoroughly validating the hypothesis and the argument advanced in your prospectus."

Sometimes, though, in the dark night watches, I wondered what I was doing way up here, far off from where I really belonged and felt at home, in this foreign country where I knew nobody, banging away at an essay nobody but my committee would ever read, if they did only because they had to, and which might or might not land me a job teaching how to read poetry to a bunch of rich and indifferent kids who'd never read anything again but their fat bank books, while I tried to figure out how to avoid disgracing my parents by publishing a dirty play about a bogus poet, and also how in the world to love back dearly and sincerely the sweetest boy ever to walk the planet who certainly loved me and wanted me as his own forever. It got tough, you know?

\* \* \*

Dr. Grant again beckoned me out of the Widener Reading Room.

"I wanted to be sure you've discovered The Houghton Library," he said; "right next door. I know you're working on Byron, but as a Romanticist…! Collect your papers and come with me now, and I'll show you around."

The Houghton, it turns out, is the repository of the largest collection of John Keats material in the world, thanks largely to Amy Lowell's magnificent gift early in this century. The collection includes, Dr. Grant informed me, the first draft of Keats's romance, "The Eve of St. Agnes," and manuscript versions of the "Chapman's Homer" sonnet and the ode "To Autumn," and many papers and letters and books and drawings and paintings related to Keats and other Romantic luminaries, although regrettably little about Byron ("Yale," Dr. Grant said, "boasts of owning a curl of Byron's hair sealed in a locket!"). Of course, showing me around didn't give us even scholarly access to any of these priceless and extremely fragile materials, but with his clout and Southern grace Dr. Grant persuaded the head librarian, whose name I recognized as a notable Shelley scholar, to show us *something*; and he brought out a copy of Oliver Goldsmith's *History of Greece* owned by Benjamin Robert Haydon and given to Keats, with the inscription, "To John Keats, from his ardent friend, B. R. Haydon, 1817." So we got to touch a surface also touched by the hand that penned "Ode To a Nightingale." After such an introduction to this Holy of Holies, I felt permitted and privileged to return several more times to browse the protected cases and shelves with their countless treasures from "my" period, and left nothing less than awed after every visit.

"I also wanted to ask," Dr. Grant said as we walked back to the Widener, "whether you know what the MLA is and whether you're a member?"

"The Modern Language Association, sir? And no, I'm not a member."

"Well, sign up," he said. "I think the grad student fee is only $5. You can drop your membership if you like after this year, but you have to belong now in order to attend the Chicago convention for three days or so right after Christmas for job interviews. A New Orleans train goes practically to the front door of the Palmer House Hotel, where you'll want to stay. Go ahead now and enroll, so to receive all the Convention material in good time, including the job listings."

He really is taking care of me, I thought gratefully. But news of job interviews, while exciting in prospect, opened up a whole new avenue of opportunities for anxiety and stress. Was this *life*? When did we get to relax? [*Loukas Chalandritsonos* whispered his name to remind me to.]

*Prodigy* was down to open at Le Petit next weekend, and Jack, from his hectic manner on the phone and brief, scrambled notes, was rattled. The series of little glitches he mentioned seemed to me trifling snags easily resolved — I even helped to unravel some of them — but now one of the Chattertons had come down with shingles, and had probably exposed other cast members to it. They were checking to see who'd had chicken pox and who hadn't — the other Chatterton hadn't — so the whole production, Jack feared, might be in jeopardy. I recommended doubling the rehearsals with Jack in the lead role at half of them, just as I'd imagined him that day at Mrs. Harrison's. I don't *think* I hoped the whole thing would crash around the illness, but I might've.

So I put it to Jack, flat out: "Are you comfortable taking the Chatterton role? Does your gut want to?"

"If you think I can pull it off."

"Well, I sure saw you as Chatterton…in my little vision. You pulled that off. Okay, look: schedule an extra rehearsal with you in the part. Then canvass the cast, confidentially; see what they want to do, after seeing you. Listen to Ben. You and Ben then decide. Whatever yawl decide's fine with me."

"I wish you were here, Troy."

"Buck up!" I said. "Now go!"

We were sitting in the Grant's kitchen, the three of us, sipping tea, reflecting back over the summer, planning to pack up and head home. I prattled on about the Houghton and the diss and Concord and lobster and my freshmen — "Dr. Grant" this and "Dr. Grant" that — until Katherine piped up: "Troy, why after all this time don't you just call him Leo?"

Leo? Whoa! He was my professor! My director. He was Dr. Grant.

"Oh. Well," I said, stalling, "if he asks me to call him…Leo…I guess I would."

"All right, Troy," he said. "Call me 'Leo.'"

"Okay, Dr. Grant," I said, not even hearing myself until they cracked up.

\* \* \*

After our Valentine's Day re-acquaintance, you might call it, Kaiden and I had resumed irregular intimacies, and in my reckoning their satisfaction helped to effect a decline in the frequency of my nightmares about Monte's crash. So did their subsequent transformation into resurrection dreams of our long and mostly happy friendship without any of the admonishments or cautions in my earlier recollections and fantasized reconstructions of him. He didn't vacate my mind; I still felt the ache of his absence. But his presence lost its monitory aspect and became genial and benign. I missed him; in my Cambridge loneliness, I might've even longed for him; but I didn't pine. I didn't fantasize about having him back. That Monte and Kaiden were nothing alike

enabled me, imaginatively, to engage them simultaneously but not competitively, to entertain each without
slighting or shunning one. This isn't to say that the effects of their presences matched: Monte's was always
more potent, weightier, freighted more pressure. Kaiden's
carried less impact. But their co-habitation in my mind
felt cordial and comforting, absent the stress of rivalry.
Kaiden's remained the more vivid because reflecting the
steady gaze of the image watching me twenty-four/seven
from the silver frame on my desk.

He picked up right away, laughing, surprised to hear
from me. "Hey, hey, my man Troy! It won't be long now!
When do yawl leave for me?"

"Several days. Listen, what d'you hear from the
guys…Jack and Ben?"

"Well, they're real busy…with the play. Why?"

"There's a little problem. The lead's sick. The whole
thing may be falling apart. I'm kind of scared…."

"Of what? Wait. These are competent people…pro-
fessionals…running that theater. Jack and Ben…they're
on it. What're you scared about?"

"Failure, I guess. Or exposure. Success? Success
brings exposure. I dunno, Kaiden. I just feel scared…
it's all going down the tubes…and my parents, you
know, if my parents get wind…if it comes out…you
know…everything…? I'm just really unsure about everything right now…. Can you help me with this…get
me through this?"

"Yes I can. You just hush up now, Troy, and listen
to me. How old *are* you?! Not the age you're sounding

like. Pay attention here, buddy boy: we're two days from opening, and this thing's rolling right along on its own steam: it's got energy and momentum, and you need to get ahold of yourself and enjoy the rush! You can't do a damn thing from up there now except maybe call Ben and Jack with encouraging words. I'll order flowers for the cast in your name and send a telegram on opening night. You've come down with a bad case of nerves, fella, so get your lame ass to a bar and drink enough to cry for a while and then jerk off and get some sleep! We all *believe* in this thing you've achieved here, Troy, and we're all fucking excited it's about to *happen*! You're about to be *revealed* as the author you so want to be! So cut this wimpy number and show me the guts you showed the world when we split Jubilee! That there is the Troy I love. Say you love me, and that you're gonna be fine!"

\* \* \*

Here's how things were shaping up: This was Wednesday. The play opens Friday night and continues Saturday night. No Saturday matinee. Reviews might appear Saturday morning, surely by Sunday. Dr. Grant's last class is Tuesday morning, his final exam Wednesday at 9. He'll turn in his grades on Thursday, and we'll leave around noon. That would probably put us home on Sunday afternoon, a week and two days after the play opens. The theater is dark on Sunday and Monday. Should the play run through the second Tuesday — that is, eight shows — I could see it, if I was still living and dared to.

Determined to finish the draft of my "Beppo" chapter before we left Harvard, I plugged in at 8 on Thursday morning and worked until 6, and again in the evening at home, and then kept the same hours on Friday, having arranged to call Kaiden at home at 11 p.m. for a report on opening night. I didn't want to think about work between 6 Friday evening and Sunday noon, to give myself plenty of time to absorb and overcome whatever news of our opening would come to me during those hours. So, with nothing but the final stanza of "Beppo" remaining to wrap up, I left the Widener at 6 on Friday and headed for The Coop, the Harvard version of a "cooperative" store and home of everything Harvardian and for sale at a discount to everyone — mostly Harvard and MIT students and faculty — who'd bought a membership for a nominal fee. As always crowded and lively and loud, it offered just the diversion and distraction I craved, and I gave myself into its tide, and shopped: a black Harvard baseball cap for Ben; matching crimson and white Harvard sweat shirts for Kaiden and me; a mug with the Harvard seal for Jack; a Harvard apron for Kaiden, and a set of handsome Harvard scenes placemats for the house. Harvard key rings for all of us. Routine, predictable gifts, I guess, but as Harvard items classy, and a good use for some of the permissions money I'd been paid. This took me to about 7:30, a half hour before the *Prodigy* curtain. I ducked into Gio's crowded pizza parlor on the Square, and took out my latest leisure-reading choice, Christopher Isherwood's new *A Single Man*, familiarly sad in more ways than one. To round out the evening on a lighter note, I bought a ticket at the Harvard Square Loews for the late screening of "The Pink Panther," which kept my attention playfully diverted for a couple of hours. Inspector Clouseau's closing response to questions about how he'd gotten where he was put me in mind of my own situation: "Well, you know," he says, "it wasn't easy."

* * *

"It…was…a…*SENSATION*!" Kaiden burbled, before I could even ask. "Absolutely sensational! Everybody starred! People sobbed during Ben's Epilogue, and then gave the cast a standing ovation…maybe for five minutes! A full house, too: they were wild for it! I'm so proud of you I'm still crying. Oh, God, Troy, it was *fantastic*! Even the doggie: somebody gave Noodle a bone during the curtain call! I mean, out in the lobby during intermission I heard nothing but praise. They said Jack gets his turn tomorrow night but tonight's Chatterton was terrific…and still looks healthy…except when he died on stage. It doesn't matter what the reviews say, this thing's a hit with the crowd. They laughed and oohed and ahhed and cried and clapped and stomped and hooted. Ben *was* Ginsberg! I'm pretty sure he actually smoked weed on stage, 'cause the smell of grass was all over the place inside. Man oh man, what a show!"

"Are you shitting me, Kaiden?" I finally got to ask. "Don't shit me on this."

"No shit, Troy. Everybody loved it. Your Chatterton may be a rock star! I mean, people were actually asking in the lobby, 'Who was he? Was he real?' And you know what? One scene, he kissed his boyfriend on the lips, while with his other hand he pulled back the covers on the bed!"

"I didn't write that, but I love it! Oh yeah! What about the girlfriend?"

"Oh, he took her right into the bed, both of them *under* the covers! And the sets, Troy! Wait'll you see what they did with The City Lights Bookstore! And Chatterton's little cubbyhole at the back of it. There's a blowup poster of his garret bedroom, too — the one in the painting — in the lobby, and the stage set of it is a perfect duplicate, with the big church showing through the window."

"Are they having a party to wait for the reviews?"

"If they are, I wasn't invited. But I didn't go backstage. I hurried back here for your call. I'm going to see the show again, but I'm working tomorrow night. When're you getting home?"

"Prob'ly a week from Sunday afternoon. We can't leave till Thursday. D'you think the show'll last that long?"

"Till Thursday next year, maybe! I dunno why it wouldn't, the enthusiasm in the lobby tonight! Oh, I forgot to say, the costumes are terrific too: the hippie — the 'beat' — dress is so, well, *right*...and realistic, for everybody! I mean, it all looks so believable and true."

"Okay, Kaiden," I said. "Thanks for all this! It's really wonderful news. You're good to let me know. I'll expect to hear from Jack and Ben about any reviews.

And maybe even the Board. Tell everybody hey for me. Good night, Kaiden."

"I miss you, Troy," he said. "Night. And oh: congratulations…you fucking *playwright*!"

Late as was the hour, I couldn't help myself and rang Ben and Jack, but nobody answered. Sleepless, I wrote them both warm letters of congratulations and gratitude based on Kaiden's account. I even teared up a little over how affecting and fervent I felt and sounded.

Ben wasn't quite as euphoric on Saturday noon as Kaiden had been but nonetheless came across positive: "No reviews yet except mine here: I thought Lloyd McCready as Tommy a little too delicate but overall convincing and sympathetic, even appealing, and the audience seemed to love him. Jack'll be stronger: a sturdier image of The Poet. We were a little slow to start but by the middle of Act I we found our rhythm and kept the pace lively after that. Lots of laughs at the right places and none when a couple of girls tripped over lines. I did my best and loved playing Allen. You were right about that. And, Troy: I was actually impressed, I mean truly, by hearing the script performed as a live play: I dunno what it was exactly, but maybe having an audience out there kicked us up a notch, and I realized how fine the writing is when delivered well. You and Jack nailed that script! You should be very proud."

This meant something. "Thanks, Ben," I said, a tremble in my voice. "Yawl keep it up and I might get to see you. We'll be back in a little over a week."

"I *think* they scheduled a two-week run, but I'm also pretty sure that the next play isn't supposed to open till mid-September, so there might be room for stretching it. Let's see whether we get crowds. Last night we were packed."

"No, didn't they say a month run at that Board meeting? Two weeks would be pretty good, though, I guess."

Jack rang early on Sunday morning. "Here it is," he said, "in the *Times-Picayune*, page 37, Entertainment Section, with a photo of the party scene, nobody in it named. You want to hear it?"

"Do I? Do you want to read it to me?"

"Here's the headline: 'Le Petit Features Local Talent in New Play.' The article sort of 'features' that facet of Le Petit's history — its occasional promotion of New Orleans dramatists and actors in original work. And it gives the theater a lot of credit for that. It goes on to say nice things about our production…and some not so nice things…but not many."

"What's not so nice?"

"Organization. This reporter — one Madeline Twitchell — says it's loose, needs tightening. Says it's too 'talky.' But then she also compliments the dialogue as 'authentic' and 'believable,' and says we get the San Francisco 'beat' culture accurately and 'with fetching charm.' But she finds us 'static': she wants more action, less chatter, 'when nothing happens and the plot doesn't seem to be going anywhere.'"

"She's prob'ly right about the over-talking part. But it's a play. Characters have to talk. What else didn't she like?"

"Not much. What she did like — listen to this! — is 'the consistently impressive literary quality of the script. The writing, even when excessive, meets an exceptionally high standard, and promises continued outstanding achievement for the co-authors.'"

"Oh, wow, *that* feels good!"

"She singles out Marcia Kimbrough — Tommy's mother — for the 'pathos conveyed and aroused by her sorrow over the ailing son.' And also Ben, for 'capturing both the Ginsberg bravado and diffidence as I've experienced it in the man.' I guess she knows him. But she thought Tommy 'soft' and sometimes 'pathetic' and 'lacking in person the heft and forcefulness of his verse.' She admires the costumes — Gladiola Peytonberry gets a line, and so does Mrs. Harrison — and the sets, especially the bookstore. Plus, she thought the big party 'unusually well-staged,' though 'more dancing' would have 'enhanced its verisimilitude.' And at the end she compliments the Epilogue as 'exactly the poignant, touching conclusion the play and its poet require....' Here's the best part of that : 'Bud's sweet recorder complement with Schubert airs solaces not only the desolate, despairing Chatterton, but inspires deep sympathy for him." Future audiences, she adds, 'should prepare to fall in love with Noodle the dachshund pup, blessed with a rich coat the color of his master's hair.'"

So I guess we passed.

\* \* \*

For Tuesday night, the night before his final exam, the Grants invited me to their home for one martini before we left for a second one and the lobsters at Pier 4 to mark the end of our summer adventure. I took along everything I'd written and revised of the dissertation — all 290 pages of it, including the finished "Beppo" chapter — and handed it to him along with a business envelope containing $50 in cash, the first installment in my payback of his loan. "The rest'll probably come in $25 increments," I said apologetically, "over many months…but eventually…. I can never thank you enough, sir, you and Katherine, for making possible this great summer of work and fun…and learning. I am eternally grateful, and I hope I have adequately repaid…and will continue to repay…your enormous generosity, and your faith in me, with acceptable scholarship."

"You're welcome, Troy," he said; "it was our joy." And, weighing the box: "It feels substantial!"

"That leaves only the Juan-Julia episode of *Don Juan*," I said, "and the last lyric, the ultimate farewell verse, but the *DJ* will probably be the longest chapter, and the most important."

"Can you call him 'Leo' now, Troy?" Katherine said slyly.

"Nome, not yet. Maybe when I've paid up."

"Would you like to mix our martinis this evening, Troy?" he asked. "You know the drill."

I filled them in, over drinks and dinner, on what I'd learned about the play's early reception, and, with some quailing, invited them to be my guests at a performance if it was still running when we got back. They politely said they'd love to see it (but in the event, didn't). I mused that the fittingest farewell I'd ever experienced was this fine feast of shellfish flesh!

The only possibly consequential subject I can remember we talked about on the drive home was their church affiliation. I told them I'd looked up "Anglican" and visited Boston's Trinity and poked around Christ Church Cambridge, and wondered about the differences between Anglican and Episcopal, and what church they belonged to in New Orleans.

Dr. Grant said the differences depended on the parish — meaning the geographical area served by a particular church — but that basically the Anglican liturgy was a little "stiffer" and more formal and ritualistic and, well, ceremonially British than the Episcopal one; theologically, though, the two congregations pretty much read from the same book, he said, only the Anglicans might use an older version of it. They were members of St. George's on St. Charles, although they preferred a "higher" liturgy but didn't know where in the city to find one. If I were serious about exploring the faith, he said, I might prefer The Chapel of the Holy Spirit, which he thought catered mainly to students and was on Broadway across from the Newcomb campus, probably the chapel I'd strayed into that afternoon. If I ever wanted to talk about the church, he said I should let him know and come by.

# 36

My first clue that something major developed at home was the scaffolding around our building in the Quarter: all around it, extending above it, planked walkways inside it and poking out from it. The courtyard had been swept and neatened, the plants trimmed and watered, the fountain scrubbed of green slime and the spout of fountain water strong and sparkling. And then the envelope with my name tightly taped to the banister in our stairwell: "Troy: Come to 301 up this staircase! ~K."

He opened to my knock and wrapped me in hugs from all limbs. "At last, at last," he kept saying, "at last you're finally home!"

"This is home? What the hell, Kaiden? What's happened? What's going on here?"

It took a while to tell and to clarify, but here's a short version: A day or so after I left for Cambridge, his father paid a visit to his son on the second floor and was, in Kaiden's word, "appalled" at the apartment, and almost immediately declared, "You can't go on living here! I won't have it," apparently forgetting his own responsibility for our relocation. He looked up the management company, Kaiden explained, then the owner, and, intending to file a formal complaint about the condition of the property, learned that the new owner was planning the very "gentrification" I'd earlier imagined might be in line for the neighborhood, and this ever alert developer Mr. Holt Carlisle discerned an opportunity.

"The new owner," Kaiden went on, "was already over his head, so Dad offered to buy a portion of the property and to help with the total renovation if he could rebuild an 'Owner's Suite' on the top floor as an apartment/office for himself and his local connections to use as necessary for business, or to rent out. I don't know what all was involved but it developed very fast and the first thing I knew the scaffolding was up and the construction guys were swarming all over the place. And Dad was talking to architects and designers, and pretty soon tenants were moving or negotiating to stay, and Dad was saying you and I could move into the Owner's space as soon as it was livable if we wanted to for the same rent we were paying over on St. Charles, at least for a while, *if* we would keep an eye on the building until they hired a resident manager and had an apartment ready for him. That is, we'd need to keep the patio neat and pretty, and the stairwells picked up so prospective renters would like what they saw. It didn't seem like too much to ask, and I said we would. I thought you'd go for it...and I wanted to surprise you!"

"You thought you'd surprise me by moving me out of our apartment?!"

But I was laughing...because from where I sat what I saw was pretty wonderful:  the room was huge, with tall windows at the far end looking across rooftops toward Canal Street, the space between there and here big enough to accommodate a dining table and chairs plus ample living room furniture. The floors were planks of knotted wood dark to light brown to almost blonde, and polished to a gloss. The walls weren't yet painted but the doorframes — five of them! — were wide and Ivory-soap white and the crown moulding around the ceilings wide and artfully curved.

"Three bedrooms," Kaiden continued, "the master almost as big as here, and large enough for a king-sized bed which Dad has already ordered; and the third one'll be an office...your office if you'd like. Most of our stuff is still downstairs, and we'll go back down there as soon as you've toured...but I did want you to see this space first thing! You like it?"

"Of course I like it, Kaiden. Who wouldn't? But are you sure about this? There has to be a catch. What is it?"

"Well, I guess there is, sort of. Dad will save on a resident manager if we share the responsibilities for a while. First, we keep the courtyard presentable and the staircases tidy. Second, we be available to show apartments to prospective tenants. We let them in and hang around while they look and answer what questions we can and refer the others to Dad's business associates. On days when I work late, I could escort in the mornings. If you had a two-day teaching schedule, you could escort two or maybe three afternoons a week. We could limit and announce the days and times for escorting. That's just until the reno work is finished and Dad hires the resident guy. He'll furnish if new tenants want that… at more rent. It'll all be very handsome and contemporary. And we might have the use of the big suite till you graduate. We can ask for that. We might have to isolate in our bedrooms for a few business hours and meetings now and then if Dad's people need to meet here, but he'd let us know in advance. You want to look at the rest of it now?"

That it was mostly empty made it look spacious, but it was definitely large, even rather grand. There was central air and heat. The plumbing and electricity were already hooked up. The kitchen appliances — all black and white — were new. A dark blue steel tanker desk sat in the office with an armed, swivel executive chair on rollers facing two big windows overlooking gardens. Both baths had tiled showers and lighted mirrors. The hallways were wide, the closets deep.

"You've planned the next phase of my life, Kaiden," I said as we returned to the great room and took seats in the straight-backed wooden chairs, "and I'm grateful for your thoughtfulness…and the work you've already done. But have you signed anything committing us to this new arrangement…giving up the other apartment downstairs?"

"No, I haven't. I have an informal agreement with Dad only to offer this rental space to us through next August. For roughly what you paid at the house. Plus the chores. If we don't take it, he'll prob'ly make it available full time to his people or hold it for visiting guests of his companies. Of course he expects to fill up the building with other tenants. I haven't given notice on the down-stairs apartment."

"Okay. Good. We have some time to think? How long?"

"I'll ask him. But you think…you think you might like it up here?"

"I just need to get used to the idea a little. You have to admit it's kind of a shock."

"But a happy one? Okay. Let's move downstairs. Let me lock up."

Downstairs, fresh flowers and greenery bloomed from three large vases in the living room.

"What now?" I asked, almost ready to be annoyed.

"We're partying tonight…a homecoming party and a play party. Ben and Jack are coming for dinner! They can't wait to see you." He took me in his arms and kissed me hard. "Now go get ready!"

The boys were boisterous and bumptious, full of themselves, cocky in the afterglow of their theatrical suc-cesses, eager to talk of them and glean more praise. Jack presented me with a matted, framed copy of Madeline's column with the photo, and systematically dismantled the review's reservations and objections. After several drinks, Ben, who'd regrown his beard, reprised for us a couple of small, hilarious scenes with Jack on all-fours and barking as Noodle! They jostled to report anecdotes from rehearsals and performances, gaffes and slip-ups, and highlights of audience reactions, positive and not so much. They aired ideas for revisions, for tweaks of lines and gestures, adjustments to costumes, and retailed bawdy jokes about lustful romps among the cast. They remembered Kyle's two visits to rehearsals and mocked his too-apparent ignorance of theatrical affairs. They parodied Derrick Director's nagging peevishness, and his favoritism toward certain cast members, young and female. They fantasized about future developments: extended runs, stagings at other sites, contracts, next roles. They did get around to asking me about Cambridge after I'd handed out their Harvard gifts, but just about everything not *Prodigy*-related got played down and side-tracked. Of course Kaiden strutted with the meal — his Cajun creamy crab dip with drinks, and crawfish étouffée with spicy green beans, which we ate from platters balanced on our laps while sipping a crisp Sauvignon Blanc. Although tired from the drive, I may have relaxed and thoroughly unwound for the first time in three months, and downright luxuriated in the camaraderie of my pals, who seemed to relish showing-off to me: performing for me. At the end, Ben lumbered out with a rose clamped in his teeth, snickering. "See you Tuesday night!" I said at the door. Jack pecked me on the cheek; "I'll be Tommy," he added, grinning. Kaiden and I viewed the wreckage, shrugged, and made for his bed, I with an abundantly grateful heart.

* * *

Excited — arguably inspired — on Tuesday night, my boys and their mates went at it full steam ahead/all ahead full, performing flawlessly, at the tip top of their game, and made me prouder of them than I had any right to be. They flowed easily, naturally, as though born to their roles and familiar with the streets, at home in San Fran and comfy with each other, mingling colorfully through the City Lights aisles and (pace Madeline) dancing up a very storm in the party scene. Made-up, Jack, who'd let his hair grow longer to resemble the pageboy Chatterton sported, appeared handsome, strong, sturdy, with none of the delicacy Madeline complained of in the other Chatterton, determinedly ambitious and committed as poet and downright endearing as lover, tender with sweethearts and the pup. Even when pitching his bogus verse (yes, we sometimes got honest about that), Jack charmed with a killer smile and a wink that almost invited the target's doubt. Ben dominated the stage when on it, by turns rambunctious and subtle, now noisy, now harmonious when pretending with the flute, and especially affecting in his elegiac tribute to Chatterton at the end, when sniffles could be heard. They both took a few harmless liberties that improved my sometimes overreaching rhetoric. Three times they finished each other's sentences, once with Ginsberg furnishing the rhyme-word the boy couldn't find for his tetrametric line, which I thought a clever gimmick for dramatizing the synchrony of their Romantic minds. Neither of them upstaged anybody, least of all each other, but mixed and blended and shared and supported with ease and grace. No hints of Big Daddy in Ben's Ginsberg. They both spoke clearly, cleanly, and Jack's crooning of two short Chatterton lyrics both surprised and touched me nearly. Ben's triumph, I thought, was in revealing just enough affection for Chatterton to render persuasive his generous paternalism without suggesting sexual attraction. For his part, Jack showed a frank boldness of homosexual interest without camp or compromise of his ardor for artistic success. That he could so starkly capture on his hollowed and forsaken face the exhaustion of Chatterton's corrosive illness and the intensity of his continuing labors at the desk despite it stirred me as a searing, even transporting theatrical moment, and his finest acting feat. The standing ovation at the curtain from the crowded house thundered affectionately at length. After all of that, it sounds flat — banal, even — to conclude with this, however heartfelt, commendation: Ben and Jack were both convincing in their roles. For the time they had my attention, I believed them.

And yet…and yet…something lacked. I could identify nothing as exactly wrong, but something desirable was absent. Throughout, I felt myself increasingly and uncharitably impatient, somehow wanting something not there but unable to call its name. Was there an aura of amateurism? Not damaging, but qualifying, palliating: lessening. Intangible, even as to location, but unmistakable in affect everywhere I looked? Inarguably, we were not professional. Maybe we got close but fell short, and I felt the dissatisfaction of the near miss. It wasn't that we lacked energy; it was more that our energy lacked refinement, was vaguely clumsy and tripped over itself. Was there something fundamentally tentative in our work? Did we hold back…or did we lack the where-withal *to* hold back?

Or — and this thought, once registered, stuck —: perhaps the problem was mine, or me. I had moved on. I had in effect finished with this project back in March, when setting my eyes upon Cambridge, and in fact, not merely in effect, left *Prodigy* behind, for another kind of writing, another occupation. I don't want to say I was above it, but maybe I'd moved beyond it, away from what I could do for it and it for me? It did feel slightly dated: not old, exactly; no, on the contrary, it felt youth-ful. Youthful *and* old, for me, as in prior. I had done my best with this project, and it had served my interests ably. It had worth. But I'd grown past it now. And satisfaction dwelt in these thoughts. The timing was brilliantly apt for leaving. We'd made a success. We *are* amateurs, after all; and we'd made an amateur success. Let it be.

The play closed on the Saturday after my atten-dance, at the Board's direction. It hosted a cast party in the Garden District branch office lobby of Mason and Mason which broke up when somebody yelled "Cops!" and we all saw the flashing red lights and dived for doors and windows, Kaiden and I huddling in a neighbor's back yard until the danger passed. There was no denying the smell of weed in the house and even outside it, but probably because of where we were and who owned the property, the cops settled for a warning and went home. I thought the way we ended a fitting one and wondered whether Kyle had staged it. Jack and I earned some royalties as authors, he and Ben some fees for acting; what we'd learned, I postponed thinking about.

\* \* \*

I'd informed my folks, by letter, of the summer plans back in March when they were firm, and then wrote them three times from Cambridge to prove my whereabouts with the postmarks. Mother had worried about my going off "on my own" into foreign parts, and Father had acknowledged that it might be "an opportunity" but wondered how I could afford it (without offering to help). I did not admit the loan since he disapproved of borrowing. I now dropped them a note saying I'd returned with an almost finished dissertation. Here is Father's reply:

September 2, 1963. The Parsonage.

Troy: With a heavy heart I acknowledge your recent note. We are pleased that you made good academic use of your summer up north but disappointed and dismayed by your apparent embroilment in the production of an opprobrious play at a disreputable theater in New Orleans, allegedly as its co-author. I remind you that you have apologized for and repented of an earlier entanglement with the subject of this drama (I refer particularly to your blasphemous inclusion of narratives from Holy Scripture in your script!). Your shameless re-engagement with the subject is categorically unacceptable to us; and in the absence of any reasonable explanation for this deeply indecent display of hurtful disrespect toward ourselves — this contemptuous betrayal of your faith by dishonorable participation in the distribution of profane and obscene material for public performance — we regretfully inform you that you are no longer welcome in our home. My position is such that I cannot be seen to countenance what you have done by offering you hospitality. Nor do we wish to. Your behavior is unconscionable; we believe you know it to be so, and knowingly persist in it. To me, that is as close to unforgivable conduct as one can get. We will pray for you.

Sincerely,
The Reverend Ernest Ethan Tyler
Pastor

"You okay, Troy?" Kaiden asked, handing the sheet back to me. "You look pale."

"I'm okay." [But I'd whispered *Chalandritsonos* several times.]. "Pretty blistering, idn' it?"

"Well, they're praying for you."

"I wonder. That line is basic preacher code. From him, maybe more threat than promise."

"Will you respond?"

"Why? He sounds done with me."

"Maybe not in the long run. It wouldn't hurt to apologize."

"I can't, Kaiden. I don't feel sorry. Or rather, I only feel sorry they can't or won't understand."

"Maybe you could write your mom? Or call her?"

"He says she's with him on this. I figure she is."

"But he says there might be an explanation. Like maybe he's expecting one?"

"No, it would be a weaselly cop-out. He'd want a repudiation. He'd want an unqualified disavowal. I can't give him that."

"Or won't?"

"Well, I won't, either. It's not possible. I can't *feel* that it's right to repudiate my work. That work has value."

"Will he cut you off? I mean, your allowance?"

"Probably. He wouldn't let me starve, I don't think. But he's not going to support me. I'll just have to take in more typing work."

"How do you reckon they found out?"

"It's in the papers, Kaiden. They were bound to find out. I knew they would. If I hadn't been such a chickenshit about owning up to them, I might've avoided all this. It's my fault. I should've told them. He might've given me a little credit for telling them."

"Why not tell them now? That you regret not telling them…before?"

September 7, 1963

Dear Father,

Thank you for your recent letter. I'm so sorry to have neglected to inform you and Mother that the play was about to premiere. I meant to, but in the rush to finish my Cambridge work and head home, I simply forgot. Please forgive me.

I'm afraid that you have over-reacted to my participation in the production of *Prodigy*, the play I co-wrote for Le Petit Theater. I do not believe you could entertain such opinions of it as you wrote of, had you actually read or seen the play. It re-imagines the life and career of an eighteenth-century British poet, Thomas Chatterton, who did in fact in his admirable ambition to become a recognized artist forge a few documents but also composed under his own name and imprimatur a considerable body of thoroughly respectable and praiseworthy poetry considered estimable by such important figures as Dr. Samuel Johnson of *Dictionary* fame, and later scholars of our own day. We updated the (tragically short) life story and set it in San Francisco where Chatterton's works currently enjoy some renown among members of The Beat Generation, themselves founders and practitioners of a new literary fashion now

being studied in American and European colleges. Life in eighteenth-century England was
rougher, coarser than we're used to over here
now, and our play realistically but never lewdly
or obscenely reflects harmless habits of behavior
accepted and practiced by respectable citizens
of the time. That we might be mildly put off
by such conduct only witnesses the advances in
propriety of our own civilization and customs. I
regret your misunderstanding of our intentions
and accomplishments in the play, and I hope
you will reconsider them in light of the literary values we believe we not only enshrine in
the drama but honorably practice in our art. We
would be pleased to offer complimentary tickets
to you and Mother for excellent seats at a future
performance of *Prodigy*, should the theater re-
stage it.

Yours sincerely,
Troy Tyler

P.S. It may interest you to know that I've become curious about the Anglican/Episcopal
Church, and am looking into it.

**37**

In late November the air just blew out of everything. Everything wilted, withered, turned limp and soggy and as a gray as the new President's face. We wept and mourned and despaired. I trudged over to the Chapel that afternoon and cried and puzzled and cried some more in the quiet, and on the way back met Professor Meyer walking alone, with wet eyes, behind Newcomb Hall. "Twice in one lifetime is too much," he said softly, I suppose remembering Roosevelt's passing. "You know," he went on, "the only elegy I then found comforting — and I re-read them all! — was Whitman's. You might know it." I could practically quote it but I didn't find it comforting. I didn't find comfort. The whole wretched catastrophe was such a mindless, heart-wrenching and crushing waste of youth and beauty and promise and hope. I felt emptied, and not just from throwing-up.

Broussard's had closed for the evening, so Kaiden and I sat at home holding hands and listening over and over to Schubert's "Adagio" from the string quintet on the hi-fi, a plaintive air that grows disturbed and dissonant before resolving quietly back to the major key. I canceled my classes and thought everybody should. It was a ghastly, bleak, horridly dark time for every sanguine heart.

# 38

Although alone and depressed over the holidays while Kaiden visited his folks in Vicksburg (he'd invited me, but I pled work), I finished my term papers on time and with such distinction (all A's, with professorial recommendations that I revise and submit for publication my essays on Hardy and Melville), I felt eligible to finagle a two-day teaching schedule allowing me to teach Tuesday and Thursday mornings and keep office hours till 4 but avoid coming to campus, most weeks, on MWF; thus I could play real estate escort and maintenance man at the apartment house on those days when I wasn't writing about *Juan* or typing other students' essays. Progress on *Juan* moved faster than general renovation on the property; but the Owner's Suite was nearing completion, and Mr. Carlisle had deputized Kaiden to shop for furnishings, which task he embraced with relish, so we were

hoping to move in before Thanksgiving. Bad weather
had delayed outdoor work on the structure, and sup-
plies ran short, as a consequence of which tenant calls
and visits were few and demanded little of our time. I'd
posted notices of my availability for typing and editing,
and as term paper due dates approached, business picked
up. Within a few weeks of finishing a complete draft of
the dissertation, and at Dr. Grant's suggestion, I began
considering topics for papers I could prepare for reading
("auditions") on campuses to which I might be invited
for job interviews.

Meanwhile, information on the Chicago convention arrived in my box: I reserved a Palmer House room,
bought the train ticket, and pored over the 1963 MLA
Job List. Inasmuch as I thought I wanted to remain in
the South after grad school, I looked first for advertised
vacancies at institutions I'd heard of and knew something about. These were halcyon days for the humanities: college literary majors were on the rise, institutions
competed for freshly minted Ph.D.'s in language and literature and the fine arts; and it wasn't unusual for candidates like Jack and me to score ten or more interviews
at the Convention. Four of mine were with colleges,
back-up schools since I expected to prefer institutions
with graduate programs, if given the choice. UVA said it
might call during the Convention, so I counted it among
my ten. I figured, when applying, that Duke and Penn,
my one Ivy, were out of my league, so not getting interviews with either didn't break my heart.

Jack bagged six, three where we'd compete, though not for the same job, as he was an Americanist. He'd actually submitted his finished dissertation draft to his Committee, and might even defend it before Christmas, which might put him a step ahead of me in the hiring line. But Jack had no publications yet, although he did have editorial decisions "pending" at three journals. He'd wanted us to share a room at the Palmer House but I thought that a really bad idea, and let him down as gently as I could. We rode up and back on the train together.

Kaiden was also interviewing! Now a junior chef in Brossard's kitchen, he'd become a little restless there and begun discreetly looking into other possibilities and said he'd had one interview, he couldn't say where. On the other hand, he was filling up our old living room with design magazines, maybe only for ideas of furniture for the new digs but possibly in support of longer range notions: a couple of times he'd mentioned the new School of Design out at the University of New Orleans...but Corky giving up cooking seemed like a long shot to me.

Nobody at Tulane tutored us in Convention protocol. Rumors floated around about how interviews were set up and what happened at them, and what conferences and lectures and panels to attend, and which institutional and publishers' cocktail parties were essential to be seen at, or even where and when to lunch and dine and with whom and how to get there and what to wear; but it didn't seem to occur to professors that new attendees might benefit from the experience of oldsters, and grad students who had some had left campus for the jobs theirs had gotten them. Nobody handed out a map to what looked from here like a hectic hive of hustle.

Our Christmas present to each other, Kaiden's and mine, was the move upstairs, although what I "gave," other than effort and elbow grease, wasn't obvious. Kaiden and his father had not skimped on accouterments, for the Owner's Suite was to be the model unit for showcasing the decorative potential of all the other unfurnished apartments available as rentals, and for demonstrating the owner's expectations of his tenants' own beautifying budgets, unless they depended upon him to furnish. As an office/residence, our place expressed a semi-official tone, with lots of leather and metal and glass and linear shapes and crackling abstract art in the living/dining room, and dark wood and metal again in the office. Kaiden's bedroom was downright spacious with the king-sized bed and a chest at the foot and an eight-drawer dresser and a free-standing full-length mirror, one club chair and an incongruous but cozy rocker possibly in honor of JFK, and a set of brilliantly colored prints of koi ponds with the fish at the head of the bed. A plush gray carpet covered the floor, and navy blue curtains draped the two windows. Skinny metal floor and table lamps proliferated. A black and white tiled bathroom linked his bedroom with mine, and a white and pale green one ended the hallway. My bedroom had a double-bed, a gorgeous antique roll-top desk with cubbyholes and a new Olympia typewriter, a swivel chair, a club chair matching the one in Kaiden's room, and a dresser with mirror. Both bedrooms and the office housed quite large closets. A braided area rug accented my floor, and soft, dove-gray curtains dressed my windows. Kaiden had of course over-furnished the very modern, brightly lit kitchen with white appliances and natural wood cabinets, and a butcher-block round breakfast table with black metal drug-store chairs. The stove-top had six burners. A long set of low bookshelves lined one wall of the hallway. Mr. Carlisle encouraged us to fill the shelves, and to decorate the hall with colorful modern art. "Not hotel 'art,'" he added, the quotation marks palpable. Kaiden and I initiated the king bed and its fabulous sheets the night before I left.

\* \* \*

My first impression of Chicago? Extreme cold and high wind and heavy snow. It was bad enough to have to pack up and leave Christmas the day after celebrating it, but for as many seasons as anyone remembered, the MLA Convention had always alternated between New York and Chicago at the very time of year when both cities usually wallowed and skewed belly-deep in snow, so that it habitually began with delays and catch-ups and re-schedulings, which made everybody cross and edgy when we were all already nervous about the high-stakes games played there. The professors didn't have to worry about interviews (although a lot of them spent many hours examining ourselves in smoky hotel rooms also smelling of stale coffee and dirty socks), but a *lot* of them were on the programs to present papers at maybe

PAUL ELLEDGE

a hundred or more variously (and often narrowly) specialized sessions. MLA was of course *the* site for showing off one's latest scholarship, and competition for the lecterns was fierce. I tried to book my interviews around sessions likely to attract teachers and scholars of British Romanticism, in hopes of meeting some and making connections, but I quickly realized that these gatherings were mostly old-boy reunions where few heeded the delivered papers and all ignored newbies like myself who were useless to them. I recognized a few of the names on the badges, and gawked, but lacked the guts to introduce myself.

Most of the larger represented English departments — certainly all of the Ivies — hosted parties in their suites for friends and former doctoral students, now prestigiously situated and enjoying themselves as slick advertisements for their degree programs; but these festivities were by invitation only. The publishers' parties, on the other hand, opened their doors to everyone, and the free liquor flowed. Their purpose of course was to sell textbooks, and the reps scrapped like dogs for contracts, flogging their latest editions and trashing their competitors'. These raucous parties packed in the guests, who then spilled back out into the hallways where grown men pressed drinks upon (the few) young female grad students and (the fewer) older women faculty, and may even have offered and accepted jobs...of one form or another. Steamy stuff appeared to be in the offing, or already happening, and nobody seemed to think a thing about it. I sipped little and stayed low, with interviews the next morning every day.

On the first night, I showered and bedded around 9, and was almost asleep when the phone rang.

"This is Frederick Bullock," the gruff voice said, "English Chair at UVA. Is that Troy? What're you doing, young man?"

"Not much, sir," I said, startled but instantly alert.

"And why're you at home? You're hunting a job, aren't you? Why aren't you out there stalking?"

"I have early interviews, sir. Tomorrow."

"Glad to hear it. But if you're not otherwise engaged at the moment, come on up for a chat. I'm in 1108."

And just like that, my first interview. I scrambled back into my dark suit and tie, combed, brushed, dabbed, and headed up, clueless about what to expect or how to prepare in the minutes I had.

A large man, fiftyish, tall and heavy, bald but for a lightening fringe around the back, with a florid face, big ears and hands, and dark, piercing eyes under quizzical brows, in a brown suit with a burgundy and yellow striped bowtie, he smiled, extended his hand, wrapped mine.

"Scotch?" he asked. "I'm having some."

I didn't much like scotch but I knew it was fashionable among a certain class of males and some academics, and figured I'd best accept. "Just a little, sir. With water. As I said, I have interviews tomorrow morning."

"You did, yes. But this is the MLA, Troy. We drink here! I'll make it light. Your first MLA, is it?"

"Yes sir."

"'And how's it going so far?'"

"It's kind of overwhelming, sir."

"To me too," he said, kindly, dropping the bonhomie. "It's gotten too big, too powerful. Too political and self-important. Lost its way and purpose."

"Really, sir? But everybody seems to have come."

"That's one of the problems. Everybody. But never mind. Are you all set…to make the most of being here? Of the opportunities?"

"Well, sir, to be honest: I don't really know how. I have interviews and all, and I have the program, of course, but I don't really know how best to…um…'to make the most of…of the opportunities.'"

"Then I'm your man," he grinned. "Look, Troy: I want to be straight with you: let's call this the job interview I'm not authorized to have. My dean has to approve our interviews, and he hasn't authorized the job I'd hoped to offer you, if we liked each other. We don't have an opening for a new British Romanticist. But fresh Ph.D.'s with two respectable publications are pretty rare specimens these days, and your record is sterling and your recs among the strongest I've read, and your application materials are of all things original and even interesting! Notice I didn't just reveal anything about your file! So if things go well here — as they've started: I see that you listen! — I'm prepared to go home and argue with his honor the dean for another position. I might not get it; so you mustn't count on my success. But I may ask you not to accept another offer before calling me. Do you understand what I'm saying?"

"I think so, sir. Thank you, sir. I'm…honored."

"And you're willing to be interviewed under that condition?"

"Of course, sir, if you wish to interview me."

"And he's *polite*!" he guffawed. "And respectful! All right. We'll get to the interview part in a while, but for now maybe I can put up some guideposts to help you find a way through this…this crazy jungle of a Convention, if you'd like me to. More scotch?"

I guess it was obvious how pathetically needy I was. He might have figured it out from my paperwork, or possibly he just got off on being a big smart daddy-type for helpless weenies like me, but anyhow he started at A for Always Show Up Early and worked his way down to Y for Yell If You're Stuck on the Lift (but not in that infantile way!), and by the time he finished I figured I might could make it to Thursday without losing the hotel or my foolish, rattled mind. I mean, this stranger *gave* me the orientation tutorial I craved from my Tulane professors, when he wasn't even my teacher. He proved especially helpful about the interviews, instructing me in what questions to ask and which ones not to, and which to avoid answering and how. I could smoke if my interviewer did but not otherwise (I was already not smoking here 'cause he didn't). Don't offer him or her a fag. Never accept coffee or a drink: you might spill them, and then where would you be? Don't ask about your competition for the job or the salary. It's okay to ask about course loads if you call them something else, like "hours per week in the classroom." Don't ask about committee assignments; everybody has them. Don't ask anything that makes it appear you'd avoid or try to avoid work. Don't brag about your publications: we have your resume. Never ask when you'll hear from us, or how many students your classes have. And so on. He also told me about protocols at the sessions: Never correct from the floor anything a speaker says in his paper, even if you know it to be mistaken. Bad form, he said. Never willingly embarrass a speaker to gain points. Never quarrel with another questioner. Never publicly ask a question of more than thirty words. Never try to talk privately to presenters about *your* latest ideas for an essay; only compliment their papers, briefly. He taught me tricks for getting around the hotel, for avoiding long lines at the elevators (use the service lifts); how to snag a good table in a crowded restaurant without over-tipping, and which hotel restaurants were fastest, which bars the best sites for meeting distinguished guests, at which doors to find taxis, where they stashed the umbrellas, where to replace lost badges, and where the loos were. Routinely check your fly! Never leave your outer wear in the hallways outside the interview room, he said, if you expect to get it back. Always thank the committees — once — for their time in interviewing you, but don't expect to correspond with them from home. And never, *ever*, interrupt their questions or over-talk your answers. Answer only what you're asked, as briefly as possible.

"Oh yes, and the exhibits: hang around in the Exhibition Hall. Leave your name and address with any publisher who'll accept it: you might get advance copies of new texts to consider adopting. But don't waste time talking to these flunkies about ideas for your own next book. Write the editors. And while I'm thinking about it: you're likely to get asked, in a year or two, after you've published your first book — you'll get asked to review new books of scholarship in your area. Refuse every one, until you're an established professional. It's a minefield: nobody ever really likes his or her reviews, although everybody thinks he wants all he can get. Enemies lie that way (pun intended). Reviews take huge chunks of time, and they earn you *no* credit with your Chair or Dean. They're not legit 'publications,' and don't count. No, write your articles instead…just as you're doing. Maybe some of all this will be helpful outside that door? Any questions? Or would you now like to tell me more than you wrote about your dissertation and how close you are to finishing it? We expect new colleagues to arrive with the degree in hand."

My other interviews, all but one, sort of blurred together: after the fifth, I could almost predict the questions, pretty much in the order they arrived, although now and again came the odd-ball, outlier queries, either to trip me up or to relieve the boredom of the routine ones: "What other topic might you have taken up if not Byron?" "What poet should be dropped from the standard Romantic syllabus?" (Did they know I knew about Chatterton? I ran with it!). "Do we really *need* that prefatory note to 'Kubla Khan'?" And once, from a youngish wag heedless of his joke's age: "I've always wondered: What *are* Keats, anyway?"

"Well, they're not Burns," I said, but nobody got it.

The Vanderbilt interview, though, turned out memorable. When he finally opened his door, Professor Woodrow Clifford — Chaucerian, 19th-century specialist, and Acting Chair of English for the ailing Randall Stewart — looked drowsy, puffy, as though I'd awakened him, and was vigorously blowing his nose into a spotty white handkerchief. With disorderly white hair and jowls, geezer-ish, in a proper suit but house slippers, he turned away to finish the job, leaving me half in, half out of the doorway.

"Excuse me!" he said, laughing, his back to me. "You caught me! Come in, come in, you must be Mr. Tyler. It's only me, no committee. [Did I hear Jack's correction?] Let me have your overcoat."

He took it into the bedroom, returned, the handkerchief gone, he still wearing the slippers. "Please make yourself comfortable in that chair at the table," he said, pointing to a furniture grouping against large windows overlooking, from the 28th floor, a snow-coated downtown Chicago. "Lovely, isn't it?" he said.

"If you like snow," I said.

"You don't?" he asked, sounding surprised. "Well, we don't get a lot of it in Nashville, so it's nice to see some drifts once in a while. You've been to Nashville?"

"Yes sir. Many times. But I've never seen the campus."

"Why would you come to Nashville and not see the Vanderbilt campus?"

"Our mistake, sir. I hope to see it soon."

"I've seen a lot of it, 'late and soon,' as the poet said, and everywhere in between. Which poet, by the way, would that be, do you happen to know?"

"Yes sir. Wordsworth, sir, in a sonnet."

"Yes, we've seen most of it, in our time, Betty Jean and I. She taught at Ward Belmont, you know. We've been in Nashville for most of our lives, and now that she's gone, I wouldn't know where else to go. Besides, I love Vanderbilt; I guess it's my home now. But I might retire soon. They'd like me to, you see. But I'm the obvious choice to fill in for Randall, since I chaired before he came and I know the ropes. Though I guess there aren't really any ropes to speak of. I wonder where that expression comes from? Would you know?"

"It must be nautical, sir, wouldn't you suppose?"

"I suppose so. Come to think of it, Chaucer may use it in 'The Shipman's Tale.' But you don't like snow, you say."

"I probably don't have enough experience to know," I said. "But I like the ice cream. Snow-cream, I mean. Made from snow."

"Why, yes!" he said, smiling. "Yes, indeed-y. Snow cream! D'you suppose we could order up some here?"

We laughed. Without thinking I reached into my jacket pocket, remembered, pulled back my empty hand.

"If you were reaching for a cigarette there," he said, "I wonder if I might prevail upon the goodness of your heart to lend me one? People have been smoking in here all day, and I'm not supposed to, but I just know I'd feel better if I took a drag or two....?"

"Of course, sir," I said, and brought out the Kents and the lighter, shook two out for us, lit his first.

"Ah, that's better," he sighed, with a long exhale. Then he reached awkwardly behind his back with his left hand, onto the window sill, lifted the rather large, glass, rectangular, overfull ashtray between thumb and little finger, brought it around toward the table between us, lost his grip...and fumbled the lot out onto the carpet, ashes and butts and used matches and gum wrappers and discarded gum and balled tinfoil and burned pipe tobacco and gunky cleaners and toothpicks and clipped nails and wadded tissues scattering everywhere. I leapt up and stooped to clean while Dr. Clifford let fly with a huge, bellowing belly-laugh, took another drag from his Kent, and dropped to his knees, the air around us sifting with soot.

"Oh I am such a doddering old oaf, I am, I am," he cried, "and what my dearly departed Betty Jean would say, if she could see me now, heaven forbid! It's no less than I deserve for trying to sneak a smoke!" He righted the ash tray and began replacing the butts into it, one at a time, still laughing. "You must try to overlook my clumsiness, Mr...Mr...Tyler, was it? I am so sorry. By the way, I'm Woodrow Clifford," brushing his hands of ashes and extending the right one. And there we were — Vanderbilt Department Chair and fuddled prentice — on our knees, eye to eye, pawing at garbage like alley rats.

\* \* \*

On the southbound train, Jack and I reviewed. He'd liked the Rice committee, and felt more at home with it than I did, talking about how we'd teach literature to mostly science and engineering freshmen. We both thought the LSU team the least professional though for me the easiest to chat with, and the Chapel Hill crew the most attractive of the three committees we both saw. We both hoped to hear back from UNC, but whether they'd follow through with two prospects from the same southern school seemed doubtful. Emory remained at the top of my own list, and I thought I'd acquitted myself pretty well with its committee of five — two women, two men, plus a chairman, two of them Romanticists. Davidson moved up to my second choice for its excellence of self-representation, but it still had no graduate school; and yet it came across, especially in its salary and its teaching expectations of me, as compelling enough to urge reconsideration of my preference for institutions with advanced programs. So did Southwestern's. Sewanee disappointed: it showed itself snooty, privileged, and pretentiously British. (The profs teach in black gowns!) And Birmingham Southern went to the opposite extreme, toward folksy, laid-back informality but warm and affable for all that, but without graduate programs. The ashtray accident seemed to have shaken Dr. Clifford awake — or maybe the fag cleared his head — and back into the present, and sharpened his wits, for we settled into a pleasant and enlightening and often exciting conversation about Vanderbilt and its under-graduate mission and the English Department's ambi-tious vision under Dr. Stewart and its expanding grad school and opportunities for overseas teaching and, if deserved, early consideration for promotion to tenured rank. Pretty impressive and inviting. I kept UVA high on my list in the unlikely event that Bullock came through for me. I'd accept Rice if only Rice offered; but I might choose Davidson or even Southwestern over it. Jack and I both thought we might come out with some attractive options. But we'd also both seen a mighty lot of other hungry young hopefuls hoofing around the Palmer House halls.

With Dr. Grant's permission, I decided to cut Byron's final lyric from my analysis: "On This Day I Complete My Thirty-Sixth Year" didn't really qualify as farewell verse, except to love and loving, in preference for a soldier's career and honorable death in battle. But it's also sometimes said to be, paradoxically, a declaration of love for Byron's Greek page Loukas Chalandritsanos, which notion I'd like to investigate and still might someday, but that inquiry would take me somewhat off my current track. (You remember I sometimes whisper the name when angst takes me over; I know it's child-ish and silly, but the syllables somehow soothe and sta-bilize.) Moreover, my present conclusion, on Juan and Julia's affair and parting, which portion of the epic ev-ery Romanticist knows, was pretty strong — two inter-viewers had asked me to elaborate — while the last lyric isn't as famous. So essentially I'd finished a draft of the dissertation and now awaited Dr. Grant's feedback, and, with it in hand, my Committee's decision on its acceptability. Committees rarely overturned a director's approval, but dissenting or doubtful members could make for an uncomfortable defense: you wanted to address in the text any misgivings you knew of before heading into the defense, at the successful end of which all members signed off on the title page. The new Olympia machine would produce my final copy.

I'd end my Tulane teaching career in the spring with two more sections of the freshman Intro to Poetry in a revised edition to take account of a few complaints on the student evaluation forms: I still got high marks overall but a few students objected to "obscure" quotations to identify on exams, and regarded my corrections of their prose as "picky," and two others (no doubt collaborating) said I sometimes, in leading class discussions, played "Guess what I'm thinking." I could keep such objections in mind. At all events, it looked like I had pretty clear sailing ahead, with ample time for finishing all requirements and for preparing campus presentations if I should be invited anywhere...and of course for getting all of my clients' essays typed. Where I perched sort of felt like the catbird seat!

# 39

Bailey was the first to report success. She'd last summer married an advanced Tulane med school student now applying for residencies in the Chicago area, and had herself landed a teaching position in Shakespeare at Northwestern where, she rather brashly announced, the spouse might also find appointment. Hers was, unmistakably, a dazzling coup for Tulane English, and we were all expected to show pride. Some of us did.

Dr. Bullock of UVA wrote my first reply, regretting to inform me that his Dean wouldn't authorize an additional English slot; but he'd "enjoyed" meeting me and felt confident I could look forward to a "distinguished career," which he would watch with interest. I replied with a sincere thank-you note for his generous kindness to me.

Then, following hard upon one another, came declinations of further interest from Davidson, Sewanee, LSU, and Rice, and then actual offers from Southwestern at Memphis, Birmingham Southern, and Vanderbilt. UNC and Emory invited me to campus for additional interviews and presentations of a paper to the department faculties. Vanderbilt apologized for *not* offering a visit, but its Chair, Dr. Stewart, had died in early January and the Department, Professor Clifford said on the phone, just wasn't up to entertaining a guest right then. I rang Ben.

"Birmingham and Southwestern offered $5500 but four classes per term, twelve hours, and six probationary years before consideration for tenure. Probability of summer teaching if I wanted it and few others did. Both have summer programs in England."

"Between Birmingham and Memphis," Ben said, "I'd pick Memphis, but both are kind of provincial, aren't they?"

"Well, so's Nashville, wouldn't you think? Vandy offers $6000 now, and $6500 if I have the degree in hand on arrival, with nine hours of teaching per term. UNC also pays $6K, for twelve hours, but Emory $7000, with a nine-hour teaching assignment per term. But at Emory I'd have to beat out four other candidates; they've invited five of us to campus. I don't like the odds. And I'd dread the inspection and the audition. UNC's interviewing two others on campus. Whadaya think?"

"What's the Vanderbilt downside?"

"Well, none that I see, unless that Nashville is the Southern Baptist capitol of the galaxy, which would probably please my folks…not that they're speaking to me. And all I have to do is say yes?"

"And Birmingham Southern and Southwestern are both colleges. How's that feel?"

"Kind of scary. I might get stuck…and never be able to move up to a university."

"What does Kaiden say?"

"Kaiden? What does Kaiden…? Oh. I don't know. We haven't yet talked. I just got these letters and calls…."

"And Jack? What's Jack heard?"

I stopped by his room. "I've got one offer," he said, "from Kent University. Rice wants me to come to campus, present a paper. UNC says no thanks. Haven't heard from Notre Dame or Kenyon. Wash U wants me to send an essay and — oddly — a sample American lit syllabus. Sounds like more oversight than I'd like. Congratulations on your UNC invite."

"Where's Kent? You never told me you applied there."

"Sleepy little nowhere Ohio town. Kent State. Back-up school. Just your standard Midwestern liberal arts place, but I have an aunt and uncle living there, and Kent advertised an opening for an Americanist, and they're paying $7000 for three classes per, one of them an upper-level class — that is, for majors — my first term. I might go to Rice for the experience of presenting if Kent'll wait for an answer. I dunno. I might be more…

comfortable in Kent than in Houston. But it gets cold up there."

Dr. Grant said: "Vanderbilt. It's on the move. It has money and a future. Unfortunately, they've recently lost Randall Stewart, who as your friend Jack Latimer surely knows was an eminent Hawthorne scholar, so the Chair might be unoccupied and contested for a while. UNC's English Department is distinguished but crowded. Promotion will be competitive. You might be happier in a smaller environment…like Vanderbilt's…or Emory's. Between the two, Emory has the marginally better reputation in English right now, and it has more money even than Vanderbilt, Coke money, and its students edge out Vandy's in the national rankings…and it has Atlanta, if you want a city. On the charts, it's kind of a toss-up, Troy. You won't go wrong either way. It might benefit you to visit both campuses. Get the feel of each."

"Could I ask Vanderbilt to pay for a trip? They didn't offer."

"It might be tricky. You don't know whether they have a back-up candidate, should you decline. But they probably do, and they might choose him or her if you take too long to decide. And of course you'd need to present if you visit, and undergo more interviews and meals."

"And risk elimination. What would you do, sir?"

"I'd probably tell Vanderbilt the truth. Tell them you're invited to visit another school and are considering it. See what Vandy says, but understand you're taking a chance if you ask to wait. They're not likely to withdraw their offer on the spot, but they'll probably give you a deadline for responding. On the other hand, Vanderbilt might be moved by the competition to sweeten its offer. I hear it hates to lose to Emory. In any case, you could accept Emory's invitation, keeping in mind the competition there."

Dr. Clifford at Vandy said they were hiring a second person, probably another new Ph.D., this one in Restoration and Eighteenth Century British, and the Dean wasn't likely to approve two campus visits. "It wouldn't be fair to bring you and not h...the other candidate. I'm sorry."

"How long do I have to respond, sir?"

"Would ten days be sufficient? Ten days from today?"

"Could I have two weeks, sir? I may need to make... I may need them, sir."

"Ah, I see. Campus visits in the offing, eh? Well, congratulations on your popularity! We figured you'd have other opportunities. All right. Two weeks. Earlier if you can."

\* \* \*

"How could LSU reject you?" Kaiden asked. "Not very neighborly." I'd just run through my early results with my roommate.

He stood in my bedroom doorway, still in his PJs and robe though it was past 10, a coffee cup in hand.

"Maybe because they're neighbors. Maybe too much the same southern vogue? So whad'ya think otherwise?"

"I finally get a say?" he asked.

"What does that mean?"

"Well, you haven't exactly asked me up to now. Oh, you've dropped a few college names but we've never really talked…about where you might move to…and what happens then."

He moved toward me, placed the cup on the desk, took hold of my shoulders.

"I'm sorry, Kaiden; I didn't realize…. I mean, I didn't think…."

"I reckon not," he said, digging into my neck and shoulders. "But I understand. No matter where you go, you're leaving. You're leaving me. You've made up your mind to go. I guess where you go isn't really my business, is it? You seemed to think I shouldn't care where you're headed?"

"Ouch!" I exclaimed. "That hurts! You're pinching. We should have talked about it, though. I'm sorry I left you out. We still can…talk. You want to?"

"Not really. What difference could it make?"

"Stop it, Kaiden. That really hurts."

"You'll decide where you want to go: my opinion wouldn't enter into it. You'll make the best choice… for you. Besides, I don't know anything about any of it. For right now…." He paused, slapped my neck on both sides. "For right now, I propose another choice…: a way for you to make it up to me!"

"That stung, Kaiden. What're you doing?"

"Propositioning! Proposing a choice for repairing the damage!"

He turned my head so to glare down into my face, his own stern, his eyes dark.

"What?" I asked.

From behind my chair, he reached over my shoulders to grab the ribbed elastic band around the bottom of my Harvard sweatshirt, and jerked it upward, then the T, and raked his fingers across my naked pecs. "How about some sex, big boy? We haven't had any sex since the night you got home from...from that place on the shirt."

"I'm working, Kaiden. I need to work."

"Well I need some sex. That's your choice here, to make it up to me." He moved around sharply and sat on my lap, kissed me, his tongue plowing into my throat. "Now," he said; "on your bed."

It took a while, and felt rough and tearing — callous: slightly bruising; not quite hurtful but coarser, more rugged than he'd ever been with me, and on his part strangely troubled and angry. We ended panting and sweaty.

"What was that?" I asked, hoarsely.

"Homosex," he said, "in case you've forgotten."

"Are you mad at me, Kaiden? You sound angry."

"I dunno, Troy. Maybe. You've been...away...from me. I don't mean the trips. You've been away from me even when you're here. I don't know where you are anymore?"

"I've just been busy, Kaiden. I'm sorry if I've neglected you. But I had all this work...."

"I respect your work and always have. I even made this office for you to work in. But I'm not sure you're respecting me…in this relationship. My needs. We never go anywhere anymore. We don't have people in. We don't even talk much. We rarely have sex. We're a coupla regular, ordinary, humdrum queers in a very queer ghetto in the queerest city in America outside of San Fran, and we hardly ever have queer sex, only twice since that night after the cast party when we were stoned…and you hate actual, legit, bonafide fucking anyway, with your aversion to anal. It's what queers do, you know, have sex! Except us. What's wrong with us, that we don't?"

"No, Kaiden; that's not true, none of what you said. We're *not* 'ordinary, humdrum queers.' Why would you even think that? What we have is special. It's different. It's always been different. And that's what's made it special, ever since Jubilee. Don't trash it. Don't make it like what all those other queers out on Bourbon have. They're not us. We're sure as hell not them."

"We are exactly them. And they're us. We need to know that, own that, mix with them, learn them. Accept them as…brothers. Kin. This fantasy that we're somehow…different…in the sense of special and better… more 'refined' or 'purer' or something…: it's just your pretty, frilly little fantasy, Troy, and it's totally false. You need to scrap it."

"Monte would never ever say that about us. He knew we — he and I — were different and special."

"Monte! Monte? Shoot, Troy, what does Monte matter now? And here? Monte's been gone for months. Why are you even thinking about Monte when we're talk-ing…trying to talk…about us?"

"Because we loved each other. And the way we loved each other was very, very special. I hate your saying it wasn't. That it's special is what made it okay. And it made us different…from every queer beyond the gate out there. I know in my bones this is true, and I…I love the truth of it. You and I have something special too. You know it: you confirmed it with these bracelets. You cel-ebrate it every time you give me something, every time we have sex. And you've given me and given me, oh, ever so much, all the time! All of that makes us different and special…in what we feel for each other. Don't…don't… foul that by saying it's like what those creeps out there do and pretend to feel."

"I can believe you loved Monte, Troy — that's what you're saying, you know. What I can't believe is how you're letting — or *making* — what you think is your everlasting love of Monte keep you from loving anybody else. God knows, I've tried every way I know to encour-age your love of me, from Jubilee on, and maybe you almost did once or twice; but you don't really, not deeply or long-term. Blessings on you for never telling me you did. But, Troy, I'm getting tired of waiting for you to say the words, since I know you won't, or can't, mean them even if you do. No, you and I've gotten to some kind of an impasse: much as I hate to admit it and give up, I think with you leaving and all — leaving me and all — maybe the time is right to quit pretending and hoping that true, bone-deep…and, well, enduring love's going to happen between us. I don't know that I can or want to keep on trying to make it happen. It's too…too painful and disappointing…every time and all the time. And it's wearing me out."

"Are you breaking up with me, Kaiden? Are we not going to be boyfriends anymore?"

"I guess I'm thinking we might loosen the ties a little, for a little while, and see how things go. Mardi Gras's coming up on the 11th. And Kyle Mason — you remember Kyle? — Kyle's giving a cocktail party on the Monday night before Fat Tuesday. Would you like to go, with me, socialize, have a few drinks, eat some King Cake, make some new friends…?"

"How'd you hear about this party?"

"Kyle invited me. And also you. You're also invited."

"Kyle Mason called you with an invitation?"

"He's been to the restaurant a few times. He'd really like for us to come."

"I seriously doubt he'd want me there. You know how I feel about Kyle. I don't like him. Or trust him. And I don't think you should either."

"Troy: I kind of do like him. He's actually asked me out. I said no, but I might want to say yes, sometime, if he asks again."

"You want to trade me in for Kyle Mason?"

"Please don't do this, Troy. Don't be like that. I'm just floating out an idea…about going to a Mardi Gras party."

"Well, no. I don't want to. And that's not all you're doing. I won't go. But I'm not going to stand in your way…if you want to. Hell yes, go on and tell him you'll come, that fucker, for all I care. I have plenty of work to do."

"You'll always have plenty of work, Troy."

\* \* \*

"I'm taking Kent State," Jack said, between big bites of a Burger King cheeseburger dripping mayo and catsup and strings of wilted lettuce. "They upped the offer to $7500 if I'd accept it now and skip the campus visit to Rice. And — get this! — they don't require a book for tenure! At least for now. Articles will do it for the current chair and dean, possibly even fiction, if I publish enough of it to teach the subject. They do require 'excellence' in teaching. But they don't mind if I dress casually for it!"

"And you're happy with all that, Jack?"

"I'm happy to be through messing with it. I'm happy it's settled. They're flying me up in the spring to meet folks and look around. Yeah, I'm excited!"

"I can tell. I'm happy for you, Jack. Really happy! Congratulations! You know you're really *wanted* up there!"

"Well, at least somebody wants me!" He paused, maybe to be sure I'd heard him. "And where are you in this business?"

"I prob'ly said," snagging a couple of his fries, "Emory wants me to compete on campus against four other candidates; and I think I'm chickening out of do-ing it. It feels like a stacked deck. What if the others are all Ivy-trained, and I'm the token outlier? I looked up the catalogue, and they've got Ivy grads already on board. If they'd watch me teach a class, I might chance it, but I'm nervous about presenting a half-baked essay and getting quizzed on it after. I'm not real comfortable extempore."

"What about UNC? You going over there?"

"Grant says the Department's 'crowded.' That competition for promotion will be keen."

"If the colleges are out, that leaves Vanderbilt, right?" Jack asked. "The Commodores are shit in football and every other sport but basketball, once in a blue moon; but I know a couple of Vandy grads who loved being there, and aren't even country music fans. What's holding you back?"

"Emory, I guess. But I honestly don't know, Jack. A part of me says I should be thrilled to death with a Vanderbilt offer; and I've now heard they're hiring another newbie, so I wouldn't be the only rookie; and they talk a great game about their undergraduate mission, where Emory's bigger on their graduate school. Atlanta's prob'ly too big for me, but Nashville might be about right...though I don't care a fig for country music...."

"Oh, Troy, Troy," he said, grinning: "you're just delaying the orgasm while enjoying the stroke! You've decided on Vanderbilt. Call 'em and accept. You've made up your mind...haven't you?"

"Make it $6750 for the degree in hand," I said to Dr. Clifford, my voice shaking, "and I'll cancel campus visits and commit to Vanderbilt now."

"Wonderful!" he said. "I'll check with our Dean and ring you back."

He did.

"Done!" he said. "Welcome!"

"It's Vanderbilt," I said to Kaiden in our sparkling living room, now hung with paintings from our former Magazine Street house. "The Humming Bird train connects New Orleans to Nashville."

"Did you get everything you wanted?" he asked, dropping his backpack and sprawling on a sofa.

"Just about. And I don't have to make any more trips. Everything's settled. I wanted to let you know."

"Thank you. 'Vanderbilt.' It's such a distinguished, elegant name. Have you seen the mansion?"

"That's Asheville. Or near Asheville,"

"I know. I've been there. I asked whether you have."

"Yes, several times. When we used to go to the eastern version of Jubilee, in North Carolina. We always went through Asheville, and sometimes stopped for a tour of the mansion and its gardens. Magnificent! You reckon Vanderbilt faculty get free admission?!"

"Add it to your contract!"

"Did you accept Kyle's invitation to the party?"

"Yes, and he said I could still bring you."

I wasn't especially keen on getting dumped by Kaiden so he could take up with Kyle, but the more I thought about it, the more I saw a sort of sense in it. They both came from money. Both had powerful businessmen — operators — for fathers. Both families were prominent in their communities. Both of them were ambitious professionals with excellent starts on productive careers. Both were active social creatures comfortable at parties with drinks in their hands and friends in their faces. One was Baptist and one Roman but neither seemed seriously religious or likely to proselytize the other. Both apparently thrived on sex — homosex — and made no apology for it. That was a main thing: their appetites for sex and avid appreciation of its joys, and their absolute incapacity for finding anything shameful in it. Both respected etiquette, displayed exquisite taste, honored decorum. Kyle might play a little fast and loose with the very law he practiced, and he mightn't skirt guile when it offered advantage, but perhaps Kaiden could train him out of the temptation, or by his own immaculate example discourage it. Kyle owned a powerful personality, but as Kaiden proved when the spirit and the occasion so aroused him, he could be a force. They shared layers upon layers of compatibility. Kaiden could do a lot worse, and may — I recognized! — already have. I would miss his sweetness, his effervescence, his almost unfailing good will and kindness, not to mention his generosity. But I clearly saw in his litany of complaints that he was right: I had signally failed him, selfishly failed the relationship, in part because we were imperfectly matched, partly because I'd been a heel.

I avoided Mardi Gras like the plague I felt it to be but Kaiden, though he worked extra-long hours during Carnival, also appeared to indulge in its follies without harm to his system. We both ignored Valentine's Day. No, wait: I did; and he wasn't here that night so...they prob'ly didn't. I'd asked him not to bring Kyle in for overnights, and so far he'd obliged. Spring Break came

and went with both of us working, I finishing dissertation revisions — not extensive; my Committee had been
kind — and keeping my typing clients happy while also
banging out my own final copy. Classes moved along
smoothly. I began correspondence with a rental agency
in Nashville and liked the looks of a brand new 12-sto-
ry apartment house near campus opening in the fall.
It would probably be at least a year before I owned a
car, so I needed a place within easy walking distance of
the campus, and this Oxford House — whose name I
nearly revered — fit the bill; I reserved a two-bedroom
unit on the top floor, having no idea I'd have to shift
to a second-floor efficiency for financial reasons before
the first term ended. Well, $6750 looked a lot bigger
in the contractual letter than it turned out to be in my
budget. Jack passed his defense With High Honors. I
should add, though, that nearly every defender received
High Honors because that designation qualified you for
entrance into The Gladys Baker Connolly Prize competition for the Best Dissertation presented in each division of the College of Arts and Sciences: Humanities,
Science, and Social Science. So every department handed out High Honors to get their candidates entered. My
own defense was scheduled for Monday, April 20th, 4
p.m. Graduation for Saturday, May 30th, 9 a.m.

# 40

March 10, 1964

Dear Mother and Father,

I write to let you know that I've accepted the offer of a three-year assistant professorship at Vanderbilt University in Nashville, Tennessee, beginning in late August, at a salary of $6750 for the first year. Tulane graduation, where my doctoral degree will be bestowed, is scheduled for 9 a.m. on Saturday, May 30th. I will be honored if you and Mark attend the ceremonies, and be my guests at lunch afterward.

I've reserved an apartment in a new building near the Vanderbilt campus. How I'll transport my clothes and books and records and few household goods to my new place is as yet unclear, but I'm working on a plan. I have the place from August 1st, so I hope to move in late July.

Please know how vastly grateful I am to you both for all of your loving support and assistance — emotional, financial, and otherwise — your encouragement and counsel and sacrifice and prayers, over the last eight years of my education. I know I have not always appropriately received and appreciated it, and I ask your forgiveness for my shortcomings in that respect, and for any disappointments that may have hurt you. You have been remarkably steadfast in your devotion, and wondrously caring in your benevolence. From my overflowing heart, I most sincerely thank you. Troy

\* \* \*

I rang Jack after lunch on Friday.

"Busy? How about meeting me at the Audubon gate in half an hour for a walk in the Park? It's a really beautiful day!"

Kaiden and I had satisfactorily arranged our domestic assignments to share them about equally: I actually enjoyed the outdoor chores — tidying the courtyard, tending the potted plants, cleaning the fountain, trimming the ivy, scrubbing the grille — and he turned the tours into lively social occasions that sounded like parties from what I overheard of them. Half of the units were now spoken for, a few already occupied, and the rest undergoing basic renovation before listing. Mr. Carlisle came by occasionally, seemed pleased with his investment and the progress on its development, and always made a point of being nice to us, once in a while treating us to lunch if we were both around for it.

Were I typing — which I usually was — I didn't hear the construction people; and my version of conducting the escorts didn't take long: no appointments messed up this afternoon.

Jack and I headed across the trolley tracks and into the Park where I locked the bike to a rack.

"Well, Jack," I said; "we've just about made it! Did you think we ever would?"

"Never doubted it!" he laughed, and took out his cigarettes, offered.

"We're going to have to quit, you know," I said, taking one. "The Surgeon-General says they're ruining our health."

"My parents have been saying it for fifty years," he said, "while smoking two packs a day."

"You heard about Bailey?"

"You mean her marriage or her honors?"

"Both. So you have."

"I've wondered whether she'll compete in the Humanities or the Social Science divisions," Jack said. "I think she wrote about Shakespeare's history plays and himself as historian."

"Oh, humanities. English nominated her."

"Is yours submitted?"

"Final text, yes. I defend on the twentieth of April. Any tips?"

"Maybe. Your director'll start by asking you to describe your project, your argument, what you think you proved. Write that out in a paragraph, memorize it, recite it. As long as you keep talking, nobody can ask questions. No, I'm kidding: don't over-talk. The description should be as short and to the point as you can make it. If they start interrupting or yawning, you've overdone it. It's better if you can relax going in, Troy; it's actually sort of social, just a conversation more than a test. Remember: you're the smartest person in the room on the subject. They know that, and they respect that. They know it's your time to shine. And they want to help you do it."

"That's actually helpful, Jack. I hadn't thought of it like that."

"You're welcome. Any other questions about that?"

"No, but I've got another one. Let's take a bench. What's your status with your draft board?"

Of course most of us had enjoyed "student deferments," annually renewed, all through college and grad school. But what might happen now, with Viet Nam heating up by the hour, routinely haunted our minds and shadowed our planning.

"I think my deferment expires on my next birthday, this summer," he said; "but I'll check with my board before leaving for Kent."

"But what then? Are they still giving deferments for 'essential employees'? You know, for work necessary to keep the country running?"

"Ryan says he'll ask his new employer to write his board arguing for that, or something like that. Teachers have been deferred in the past."

"What if you're drafted, Jack? Would you go?"

"Well, I won't want to, of course; but I don't know. I might not. Would you?"

"I can't see myself soldiering. Fighting. I just can't imagine it. I've thought about leaving the country. For Canada. Or I might file for C.O. status. I do have objections — moral objections — to this damnable war."

"I've thought about enlisting in the Coast Guard. That looks sort of safe. Safer."

"And I've even considered telling them…you know: at the physical exam."

"Well, yeah. That's an option. Could you actually do it? I think I could. How would they make you prove it?"

We laughed. "I don't know if I could actually say it," I said, "right there naked in front of everybody also naked, and the sergeant in my face. I prob'ly wouldn't… and then go over the fence that night."

Yes, we laughed. But we both recognized the gravity of the topic. There was a very real chance, even a good chance, that without radical measures we could both be drafted and posted to that stinking swamp on the other side of nowhere, and never be heard from again. It could easily happen, in the twinkling….

"I'll ask Vanderbilt right away what options I have for deferment," I said. "There must be a campus office for counseling about that. My birthday's not till October."

We went quiet for a moment. Then Jack said:

"Do you know yet when you're leaving town? For Nashville?"

"No; I thought maybe late July. I've rented a place beginning the first of August."

"You don't have a car yet, do you?"

"No; my new place is walking distance to work. I prob'ly won't have a car till next summer."

"So how're you getting to Nashville? Train? The Hummingbird?"

"Haven't thought about it. I prob'ly should."

"It's about eight hours driving."

"Yeah. So?"

"It's sixteen hours to Kent. Nashville's halfway to Kent, and pretty much on the way."

I looked at him. "So...?"

"Well...I thought...if we want to leave about the same time, and you don't have a lot of heavy furniture, I could drive you to Nashville, help move you in, spend the night...maybe finally teach you to whiffle-shuffle cards...and head north the next day?"

I felt the tears welling, swallowed. "Oh, Jack. That's the...that's the nicest offer. Really? You'd do that?"

"The question is, would you?"

"I'd like that very much, Jack. I would."

"Understand, though: I'd want to make love to you…that night. Once more."

I didn't need to think about it. "Yes," I said. "I understand. I'd…I'd like that too." I touched his arm.

"Well then…let's count on it. How much luggage will you have?"

"Clothes. Books. Sheets and blankets, a few towels. Coupla pillows. Records. My only furniture's the hi-fi. And the old Smith-Corona. Household goods all belong to Kaiden. That's about it."

"You might want to think about switching to a component stereo; they're the new thing in sound. And a lot more compact than the boxy old hi-fis. But we could prob'ly squeeze it into the trunk. The legs come off, right? And we've got the whole back seat. I own about the same amount of stuff."

"Hang on. The apartment's not furnished, Jack. There won't be a bed. Or dishes or anything."

"We could split the cost of a motel room. That'd be more comfortable anyway. Move you in the next morning."

"You really think this will work, Jack? It's…it's awesomely generous and kind."

"And fun! 'Road Trip!' And just think what's at the end of it! Jobs! Professing! Let's hit the road, Troy!"

"I pay half the gas bill, right?"

\* \* \*

March 24, 1964  The Parsonage

Troy:

Thank you for the invitation to Tulane's 1964 Graduation Exercises. After considering it and praying for guidance, your mother and I have decided it would be unwise in the circumstances for us to accept it, as I have significant responsibilities here on the following day. But because we believe the family should be represented at so momentous an occasion, we would like to send Mark, if you would arrange for our friend Ben Moore to escort and chaperone him for the day. They could observe the ceremony, and join you for lunch following it. Mark will bring a camera to record the event for our album. We will expect you to conduct yourself responsibly throughout the day, mindful of your brother and the standards of behavior to which he is accustomed and trained to revere. Please acknowledge your acceptance of these conditions. We will provide a car for Mark's trip. You will need to advise me on how and where he should find you. He may determine it advisable to drive over on the previous afternoon. If so, we will arrange accommodations.

We wish you a good visit with Mark. Please convey our warm regards and our thanks to Mr. Moore for this favor.

Thank you.
The Reverend Ernest Ethan Tyler

"That's what they want," I said to Ben on the phone. "I know it's a big favor but I was going to ask you to come anyway, and join Jack and me for lunch afterward."

"It's a compliment," he said. "And of course I'd be pleased to 'escort' Mark. But he must be, what, twenty by now? Does he really need chaperoning?"

"He'd say not…but since it's you, he'll be tickled. He's crazy about you. I think it'll be fun to have him here."

"Have you made reservations for lunch? You know the city'll be crawling with crowds."

"No; I'll get right on it. Where should Mark meet you? And when? The ceremony starts at nine. Everybody meets on the field for speeches and such, and then the colleges peel off for degree conferrals. Yawl would go with the grad school crowd."

"It'll be a circus, Troy, the crowds and all. We'd never find each other. Look: what if we invite Mark to spend the night before here? I'll take my sofa, give him clean sheets on the bed. Actually, don't I owe him a bed for taking his that Christmas? Payback time! We could dine somewhere and get breakfast early the next morning and go to the campus together. Wouldn't that be easier than trying to meet? And he'd have to leave Lake

Charles awfully early to get here and to the right place on the campus by nine. It would be a huge hassle."

I figured it best to get Mark on board before asking the parents, so I rang him at LCC and found him thrilled at the prospect of seeing Ben and at last visiting New Orleans, if maybe a little less so over watching me graduate. As I'd need to explain fully before Father interrupted with a veto, I wrote the details in a letter to him including Ben's contact info so they could deal directly. He'd have a harder time denying Ben than me.

\* \* \*

With the defense still a couple of weeks away, my own classes running almost on automatic, and end-of-semester paper due dates for clients not yet imminent, I found myself feeling feckless, adrift.

The gym was ever near, of course, but my bike provided plenty of exercise, and I didn't like to work out alone. Kaiden and I were still trying to find an even keel, Jack reworked essays for publication, and Ben continued to grind away at the two motorcycle repair shops. Presumably, Neville, Keith, Chris, and Ryan sweated against the dissertation submission deadline. I thought of calling on Dr. Grant, but we had no current business and he had a Department to run, and Katherine probably wouldn't welcome a drop-in at their home. But thinking of the Grants reminded me of their faith and of the Doctor's invitation to talk with him about the church if I wished. But *what* about it?

To find out, I borrowed from the Library a copy of the 1928 *Book of Common Prayer*, which every pew-rack at the Chapel held multiple copies of, and for part of three days found myself absorbed by its pages. I knew that the *Book* shaped, possibly dictated, the Church's liturgies, but not a scrap more about the directions themselves or the various materials accompanying them. What grabbed me, though, what arrested and riveted me about everything I read, was the transcendentally artful *language* of the volume. Thomas Cranmer, I learned, was its principal author, and in my immediate conclusion, a master poet, a perfect genius of a writer. I must have heard some of it during my one morning at Trinity, but reading it proved a whole new and infinitely richer experience. The prose was not merely eloquent and elegant; it was radiantly beautiful: majestic, lyrical, passionate and rhapsodic, both serene and sedate, with balanced parallelisms and sonorous imperatives and reverent declaratives and fervent pleas. I kept pausing to copy out striking phrases: "he hath scattered the proud in the imagination of their hearts"; "the rich he hath sent empty away"; "we, being ordered by thy governance"; "Fulfill now…the desires and petitions of our hearts as may be best for us…"; "by his one oblation of himself once offered…a full, perfect, and sufficient sacrifice, oblation, and satisfaction…"; "comfort and succor…." Two nearly synonymous ones in particular stirred my blood: "thine inestimable love" and "your immeasurable love…." Imagine that: "immeasurable love"! And then this one: "…in returning and rest we shall be saved, in quietness and confidence shall be our strength." One does hope so: that sentiment recurred as I soaked in the mellow, magical modalities of this book. Theology aside, I might find a place for myself amid such liturgical resplendence. Might it tell me what I want, what I'm hardly aware of missing? Allegedly, Nashville was a city of churches. I could check them out.

\* \* \*

My examiners gathered on Monday, April 20, at 4, in the first-floor seminar room of Gibson Hall: Professor Grant, Professor Patricia Livingston, Professor Meyer, Professor Karen Schrader (Fine Arts), and Professor Thomas Venable (History) (two members from related departments were mandatory), my director in the Chair at the opposite end of the table from me. Clean ash trays sat at every place. Each professor had bound copies of my work at hand, as did I, and a yellow pad.

"As you know," Dr. Grant growled in his signature voice, "this is Mr. Troy Tyler's defense of his dissertation, 'Parting Shots: Lord Byron and the Poetics of Valediction.' Do you know everyone here, Troy?"

"Yes, sir," I nodded and gave them my best smile. Everybody had dressed up, including me.

As Jack had predicted, Dr. Grant asked me briefly to summarize the argument of my thesis, which I did, from my memorized text.

"We're in no hurry here, Troy," Dr. Grant grinned when I'd finished; "you might want to slow down a little...so we don't miss anything. Now: would you tell us how you arrived at this subject and why you deemed it important."

I began with the lyric, "Fare Thee Well," and went on to review my discovery of numerous "farewell occasions" in Byron's canon, and to suggest how his variations in poetic representations of them helped to define a discomfort around them probably rooted in traumatic losses of loved ones during his boyhood and early manhood; I argued that Byron's richly ambivalent relationships with his readers often appeared in the openings and conclusions of his poems, and that the anxiety of "leaving" his audience at the completion of a work sometimes reached traumatic proportions, manifest in hesitations, reversals, contradictions, and repetitions, with artistic, psychological, and canonical consequences. I chose the parting of Don Juan and Donna Julia to illustrate, and related its date, June 6 in an unspecified year, to Byron's Harrow Speech-Day farewell of June 6, 1804.

"It's an interesting theory," Professor Livingston said, first out, I imagined, to impress Dr. Grant, for this was, I knew, her first dissertation defense since her arrival last year. "But I'm wondering why you dropped the thirty-sixth year birthday poem from your discussion, after promising in your prospectus to conclude, conclusively, with it."

And we were off! It was lively and entertaining, even jolly at times; and although I can't claim to having completely relaxed, I didn't work up a sweat either. I wasn't certain that Professor Schrader had actually read my essay, but Professor Venable certainly had, and portions of *Don Juan* too, and offered interesting suggestions for interpreting the "war cantos" with my theory in mind. Professor Meyer wanted me to discuss the episodic nature of *Don Quixote,* and wondered whether its structural stuttering also reflected problematic author-audience relations. It embarrassed me to admit that I'd only "read around in" Cervantes's epic, and couldn't meaningfully address his question. Dr. Grant asked me to compare Byron's "romantic" and "satiric" works as *vehicles* for the expression of his "dissociative impulses": which was the better genre for "resolving" the predicaments they wrought? I said that satire afforded more opportunities for wise-cracking about them, and that got me off the hook and elicited a laugh. Dr. Livingston pressed me on Byron's final lyric: "I believe you should have concluded with it," she said. "It's the ultimate valedictory verse! It concludes not just his artistic career; it ends the *life.* It bids adieu to the foundational operative emotion that *defined* Byron's life and career. It strikes me as a staggering renunciation. And for what? For a soldier's uniform! I'm not critiquing your dissertation, Troy; I'm questioning your choice...your choosing to omit analysis of a poem that almost seems designed — foreordained! — to conclude your study! And I don't believe your very compelling argument up to that point can find a satisfactory conclusion without some consideration of it."

'I understand," I replied, shrinking a little, though, under what might, if I let it, feel like an assault. "Perhaps I should have considered it. And this is to say nothing yet of Loukas Chanlandritsonos's role in or behind the poem. But let me suggest that the whole ruse is Byron up to his old ironic tricks again, saying one thing while meaning its opposite, or anyhow a different thing. What if the poem is a mock farewell to love masking its profession of love for the boy, as I suspect it is. What better way to cover or disguise such a revelation than under a soldier's fatigues?"

"Well, that would be worth saying, wouldn't it?" Dr. Meyer asked.

"Yes sir," I said, "except that it's rather far from my point."

"Ah," he added: "but that's what a dissertation is for! To make *everything* relevant to its point!"

We sort of trailed off after that, before Dr. Grant, checking his watch, invited me to finish by quoting the Guiccioli limerick, with my ending.

"In front of the ladies?" I asked.

"Yes!" they both responded, laughing.

Once guests had departed following a small reception in their home, the Grants presented me with a first edition copy (1821) of Lord Byron's *Cain: A Mystery*, and a black, leather-bound copy of *The Book of Common Prayer*, with my name inscribed in gold on the front, which combination of volumes inspired wisecracks about the sagacity of its fitness for me! Leo said the committee had unanimously voted me an Honors pass, in mild reluctance to go higher because I hadn't mastered Cervantes and in one view hadn't quite finished my argument. Fine with me: I wouldn't want to compete against Jack, or even Bailey, for the big prize of Best

Dissertation overall. Then off we three went for prime rib at the Royal Orleans in the Quarter.

\* \* \*

No one could have ordered a more glorious morning for our Graduation Day. The massive lawn fronting Gibson Hall to Freret Street had been trimmed to a golf-green gloss; the giant oaks and magnolias had leafed out to offer shade against a sun already warming the humid air and likely to scorch by early afternoon. Extravagantly colorful, beaming crowds pressed and milled, staked out seats among the folding wooden chairs precisely stationed across the grass, aisles like emerald rills. From a distance, the amplified University Band alternated among lively classical favorites and popular show tunes, with occasional military rhythms hinting at the pompous march to come. The printed program stated that a woman from the A & S Economics Department had won the Dissertation Prize. On the steps of the University Theater to the left clustered dignitaries in vivid, flamboyantly hued gowns, among them Robert McNamara, U. S. Secretary of Defense, Tulane's guest commencement speaker (and a controversial choice to many of us), and University officials of various stripes. Security personnel with walkie-talkies smoked nearby. Large, satin, emblemed banners, elevated on staffs, representing each of Tulane's colleges, restlessly bobbed along Freret Street, prepared to lead graduates simultaneously down six different aisles toward the distant stage where undergrads would later receive their diplomas.

Ben and my brother Mark had found their way to each other last evening — I'd called to check — dined at the Camellia Grille, breakfasted this morning on take-away Danish and coffee, and linked with me in the long, long column of students backed up behind the "Graduates" signs on the quad. I'd parked Kaiden in a folding chair as near to the stage as we could get, and retreated to find Jack, alphabetically ahead of me in the line, where we hugged and shook and admired our black gowns with velvet strips down the front and three black bars on each sleeve.

"But how can I smooth my trousers in this silly gown?" Jack asked, giggling.

Mark looked exceptionally smart and studly in a dark suit and bright tie: the boyish grin persisted, and the dark hair hung and swayed longer than the parents probably approved of, but he seemed more solid some-how, more assured and self-possessed, and every bit the commanding star athlete he'd become according to LCC reports. He took charge of our little group and arranged us for photographs, and then roamed off for atmospheric shots of the festivities.

"Save some film for later," I cautioned, "when Kaiden joins us."

"How's that going?" Ben asked me in an aside. He looked immaculate — no grease visible anywhere — the big beard combed, the hair slicked back, handsomely decked out in a navy blazer over a tie-less blue shirt tucked neatly into light jeans themselves tucked into the polished black boots.

"We're okay," I said. "He'll be happy to see you."

President Longenecker welcomed us, the University chaplain pronounced an invocation, and the choral master and his choir led us in the alma mater, at the end of which Pres introduced Secretary McNamara, whereupon a rustle stirred in several sections when maybe a hundred students total stood, now wearing black armbands, assembled in the center aisle, and walked silently toward Freret. I looked briefly for Jack, thinking that if I spotted him among the protestors I'd join them; but then I saw him, in his seat several rows in front of me, craning his own Inchabod neck to watch them. I'd heard nothing about any planned demonstration and neither had Jack, he told me later; evidently few had: the audience around me fidgeted and murmured and then settled back down. Mr. McNamara had droned on through it all, his signature lenses flashing like fire in the sun. He finished with the expected bromides in about twenty minutes to respectful applause but no ovation. Another chaplain, this one Roman, prayed a shorter benediction, and President Longenecker dismissed all of us except Arts and Science grads to our separate degree-awarding ceremonies on other parts of the campus. We found Kaiden after a bit of hunting and proceeded to our lucky venue, McAlister Auditorium, directly in front of my former dorm and across from the UC. On the way in, we came upon Dr. Grant. Cordial introductions followed, Dr. Grant told Jack and me what to do when our time came, Mark primed his camera and flashgun, and we two graduates found our reserved adjoining seats toward the front. Dr. Grant — no way was I thinking of him as Leo in this grave and austere moment of solemn investiture! — proved gracefully adept in draping my hood and gently adjusting the little triangle of soft silk at my throat, and heartily shook my hand, smiling broadly, his eyes sparkling.

"Dr. Latimer," I said to Jack as soon as our assembly was dismissed: "Be the first to call me by my new name!"

"Dr. Tyler," he grinned, and took me warmly in his arms.

"Do you believe it?" I asked quietly.

"Not quite," he replied, gently stroking his stole.

Dr. Grant excused himself. I took Kaiden aside.

"I'm really glad you came, Kaiden," I said, my arm around his shoulder. "It means a lot to me to have you here for this moment."

"I wanted to be," he said. "I'm very proud of you, Troy. I prob'ly know better than anybody how hard you worked to reach this point. I hope you're happy today. You look happy, and that makes me glad."

I pulled back the sleeve of my gown to show the bracelet. "May I keep this?"

He pushed back his own sleeve to reveal the gold-wreathed wrist. "I'm wearing mine, you see."

"Yes," I said. "Doesn't Kyle mind?"

"He doesn't get a say."

"We had a good run, didn't we?"

"Damn straight! Well, I guess it wasn't always exactly 'straight.' But it was damn fine!"

And then, after a pause, he added: "Do you remember, Troy, that this is how we started? By you leaving me back there at the train station, that first day in New Orleans?"

"It doesn't get easier, does it?"

"No."

"I'll miss you, Kaiden. I expect I'll always miss you."

"May I say I hope you will? I miss you too."

"Will you hug me now?"

We did, and briefly clung. I swallowed hard, tucked my diploma under an arm so to clasp his extended hand in both of mine, to hold it. And hold it. And stroke the bracelet with a finger.

"Did you get that shot, Mark?" I called to him, laughing. "Be sure to show it to Father!"

"Got it!" he grinned.

"You ready, Ben?"

We headed straight over to the tents on the UC quad for strawberries and champagne.

"Walk with me, Mark," I said, steering away from the others. "You know you can't drink any champagne."

"Sure I can. I can handle it."

"No. I promised Father…to look after you. You're driving. You mustn't drink. I'll find you a Pepsi."

"I'm twenty, Troy. You don't need to look after me. One glass of champagne. I've never had any. I'd like to taste it."

"Not today. Not on my watch. Ben wouldn't approve either."

"Ben and I drank beer last night."

"Then you've had enough. Let it go, Mark."

He reached into his inside jacket pocket. "Mother sent you this," he said, handing me a pink envelope with floral decoration.

"What? Cash?!"

"$200. For stuff you need in the new apartment."

"Wow! Really? She didn't need to do that! Does Father know?"

"I don't know. I doubt it. I think she felt bad about not being here."

"How're things going back there…for you, I mean?"

"Oh, LCC had a winning baseball season, and I'm staying behind to help coach a Madison little league team this summer. I declared a poli sci major and I'm thinking about law school later. My new girlfriend's Lorelei Paxton, from Aleck, also a sophomore."

"Pretty name!"

"Pretty girl!"

"You and the folks getting along all right?"

"Oh, sure."

"Do they say anything about me?"

"Not much. They're happy you're graduating. They sent congratulations."

"Father?"

"Mother. Troy, I know about *Prodigy*. I think it's pretty cool you did that, but I'm sorry it's messed you up with Father."

"Well, me too. How d'you know about it?"

"Some lawyer in Father's church found out. Father told me, thought I should know, he said, in case word got around."

"So everybody knows?"

"I don't think so. I'm not there, but I haven't heard any talk. Father's job's not affected."

"And we're okay, you and me?"

"Of course. I'm really proud of you…in this!" He fingered my hood, patted my shoulder.

"What's happening here?" Ben said, strolling up with a half-filled glass in one hand, a napkin with berries in the other. "My third," he said, lifting the glass. "What're you and my man Mark up to over here all private and secret-like?"

"I'll find a Pepsi," Mark said.

"Just catching up," I said.

"Well, Troy," he said, slightly slurry: "This is really something, idn' it? Doctor Tyler! But I'm making it 'Doctor Troy!' Nice ring to it! How's it feel?"

"Good. It feels over! Thanks for coming, Ben. And for taking care of Mark."

"Call it my little graduation gift…*one* of my little graduation gifts. Mark's a great guy. But then he's got a great brother! I was gonna surprise you with this but… but…I got a little bit behind. I admire you, Troy; I've always thought you were really something…very special: so smart and creative…and, well, so persevering… with such stamina…and resilience. You went through some kinda hell but you never gave up. You did…you finished…this very…big…thing, this amazing thing!

And what I'm saying is…what I'm doing is: I'm writing a poem about you, to celebrate all that. It's an ode…about effort and success; about conquest and triumph. About you…about you comin' through! I hope it's worthy of you. 'Cause I love you, man; I *esteem* you! And I'm gonna miss you *real bad*! How 'bout a hug?"

He threw his big arms around my shoulders, squishing berries against my neck.

\* \* \*

In the vestibule of our apartment complex when I returned home that evening I found the overhead bulb dark; I groped for the chain and clicked it on. In my postbox lay a white business envelope with the return address of the Vanderbilt University Department of English. Inside, a brief note from Dr. Clifford, and a clipping from the *Vanderbilt Hustler*, the campus newspaper. The clipping, with photographs, reported the recent hiring of two assistant professors of English, one, a British Romanticist, from Tulane, the second one, from Stanford, Loukas Laskankaris, a specialist in Restoration and eighteenth-century British literature and a third-generation Greek, both aged twenty-six, both single men.

*Wait! What? Loukas? Loukas!*
*Seriously? Loukas?*
*And Greek!*
*Good God!*
I laughed out loud.
*Loukas: in the photo, captivating; magnetic.*
*Suspiciously glamorous.*

*With Monte's onyx eyes and stormy curls!*

*Preposterous! Inestimably unlikely! Immeasurably inconceivable!*

Yet there he was. Name of Loukas. His photo grinning at mine.

Loukas. *Loukas!*

*Imagine!*

I laughed and laughed. Thunderstruck.

Awed: with brimming eyes and banging heart.

Wordless with wonder.

# ACKNOWLEDGMENTS

*Of all the authors, artists, scholars, doctors, and students — including writers Peter Ackroyd, Louise Kaplan, Linda Kelly, John C. Nevill, and E. W. H. Meyerstein and other creative inquirers — who have in manifold ways so industriously and generously enriched our understanding of Thomas Chatterton over the years;*

*Of my cherished friend Jack Murrah, with deepest gratitude, for patient, steadfast support and sustaining encouragement;*

*Of Dr. Kenny K. Collins, my brilliant friend and comrade, and the most vigilant, creative editor on the planet;*

*And of Douglas and Ray, early beloved, ever dear.*

Printed in the USA
CPSIA information can be obtained
at www.ICGtesting.com
JSHW012035130823
46472JS00005B/15